CW00666457

The
SELLAMILLION

The
SELLAMILLION

A. R. R. R. ROBERTS

GOLLANCZ
LONDON

The right of Adam Roberts to be identified as the
author of this work has been asserted by him in accordance
with the Copyright, Designs and Patents Act 1988.

First published in Great Britain in 2004 by
Gollancz
An imprint of the Orion Publishing Group
Orion House, 5 Upper St Martin's Lane,
London WC2H 9EA

A CIP catalogue record for this book is
available from the British Library

ISBN 0 575 07611 9

Typeset at The Spartan Press Ltd,
Lymington, Hants

Printed in Great Britain by
Clays Ltd, St Ives plc

www.orionbooks.co.uk

CONTENTS

Ainusoul: the Music of the Ainu

A. R. R. R. Roberts

The Sellamillion: The History of the Sellāmi

The History of the War of the Thing™

Appendices

The Sellamillion

An Introduction, by B C D 'Pierrre' Roberts

My grand-uncle A. R. R. Roberts has achieved a
globally world-wide famousness the world over for
his celebrated Heroic Fighting Fantasy masterpieces:
The Soddit, *Lowered off the Rings* and *Farmer Giles of
Yokel-Caricature*. Now sadly deceased or 'passed on'
as he himself put it, it falls to me to collect together
his uncollected Fantasy writings and offer to the
public these valuable sketches, designs, memoirs
and other writings under the general title *The Sellamillion*.

1. Life

My grand-uncle's full name was 'Adam Robinson?
Robertson? Robins? ah, Roberts I See Do Excuse
Me I'm Dreadfully Sorry I Left My Spectacles In
The Vestry', which is how the Rev. Roland Adorno
baptised him, reading from a chit given him by the
organist. It was this full version of his name that was,
for legal reasons, entered on the birth certificate.
Accordingly, and although my grand-uncle was

known to his myriad fans by the abbreviated form of his name, the full surname was required for all official arenae.[1]

His career at the University of Oxford, where he sat in the Ikea Chair of Dead and Terminally Ill Languages, was lengthy and successful. He distinguished himself as a scholar and also as a member of the group known as 'the oinklings', the celebrated pork-themed writers' group, who met Thursdays throughout term to discuss their various literary productions over bacon and chops.

2. Two Robertses's?

It is sometimes said, with some justification, that there were actually two A. R. R. R. Robertses: A. R. R. R. Roberts, the noted and bestselling fantasy author, and Professor Roberts I See Do Excuse Me I'm Dreadfully Sorry I Left My Spectacles In The Vestry, the Oxford scholar. Indeed, my grand-uncle himself declared that he was 'split' or 'divided'

---

1 This I take to be the plural of *arena*. Although, actually, when I look at it written down like that, it may be that 'arena' is *already* the plural of 'arenum.' Is that right? If it is, then that would make 'arenae' the plural plural of arenum. I don't mind admitting I'm nervous – it's no easy thing writing an introduction to a collection of writings by a world-class philologist and grammatologist. I could so easily make a fool of myself. I'm anxious to get the grammar and such just so.

after this fashion. 'There are two of me,' he told the *Oxford Times* in an interview late in his career. 'The writer and the academic. Both, luckily, are called Roberts, and at the moment both live in the same town. It has not always been arranged so neatly. Two years ago the two were Geoff Kapitza, a Shrewsbury-based supplier of industrial ceramics, and Susan Eley, the author with David Blackbourn of *The Peculiarities of German History*. That was a rather awkward set-up, I don't mind telling you.'

As one illustration of the sort of life my grand-uncle lived in the ivied halls and hallowed ives[2] of Ballsiol College, Oxford, I append this record of a conversation he had with his distinguished colleague Professor Sir Algernon Islwyn De Vere Hedgecock Twistleton Faineant Mainwaring Featherstonehaugh Jones. In common with many of the Fellows of Ballsiol, Professor Jones frequently congratulated my grand-uncle on what he considered a properly and unashamedly-hyphenated Traditional English surname. [The following excerpt is from *Porter! A Porter's Life*, by Henry Porter, Porter of Saint Peter Hall, Oxford]

---

2   This should be 'eaves'.

I was sitting [writes Porter] in the Porter's box at Saint Peter's, drinking some Port and reading a local historical account of Portsmouth, when Professor A. R. R. R. Roberts entered the college, visiting a friend. In the course of his ingress he happened to bump into Professor Jones, who was exiting. 'Well,' cried Professor Jones, warmly, 'if it isn't my good friend Professor Roberts I See Do Excuse Me I'm Dreadfully Sorry I Left My Spectacles In The Vestry. A very good evening, *anima dimidia mea.*'

'My dear Professor Sir Algernon Islwyn De Vere Hedgecock Twistleton Faineant Mainwaring Featherstonehaugh Jones,' replied Professor Roberts, genially, 'how wonderful to see you.'

Professor Jones's face fell.

'My dear Professor Roberts I See Do Excuse Me I'm Dreadfully Sorry I Left My Spectacles In The Vestry,' he expostulated. 'I fear I must correct you – it is pronounced "fanshaw".'

Professor Roberts naturally looked abashed. 'I am sorry, my friend. I thought I had pronounced it "fanshaw".'

'You did indeed pronounce the penultimate element of my surname "fanshaw" and most correctly. But you mispronounced the earlier element – it is pronounced "fanshaw", and not "hedge-cock" as *you* said.'

'I cannot apologise enough,' declared Professor
Roberts. 'Allow me to address you again, my dear
Professor Sir Algernon Islwyn De Vere Hedgecock
Twistleton Faineant Mainwaring Featherstonehaugh
Jones, in the hope of correcting my grievous error.'

Professor Jones shook his head. 'No, no,' he said.
'This time you got the first "fanshaw" right but
monkeyed up the second one.'

'I did? I said "fanshaw", didn't I?'

'You said "farnshow"; quite, quite wrong.'

'Professor Sir Algernon Islwyn De Vere Hedgecock Twistleton Faineant—'

'No, no,' interrupted Professor Jones, becoming
heated. 'Faineant isn't "fayno", as you say it, it is
pronounced *"fanshaw"*. Must I write it down in pho-
netic script?'

'There is no need to be offensive,' retorted Professor Roberts, bridling.

'I'll be offensive if I choose,' returned Professor
Jones, hotly.

'A figo,' said Professor Roberts.

'A figo for *you*, sir.'

The two professors were forever falling out with one
another in this fashion.

3. The Soddit

My grand-uncle first wrote his children's classic *The Soddit* on the back (and later, when he ran out of space, on the front in thick black felt-tip) of certain student examination papers he was supposed to be marking. After its publication and unexpected success, his publishers pressed him for a sequel. As he wrote to his dear friend C John Lewis:

> My publishers pressed me for a sequel again yesterday. I do wish they'd stop doing that. Always pressing, poking, can't keep their hands to themselves. 'We'll keep on doing this,' Stanley Nonwin told me, pressing a tender spot near my spleen, 'until you deliver the sequel, you little jerk.' Or at least that's what I think he said. His editorial assistant, Hefty Jill, was sitting on my head and had my arms in a three-quarter nelson at the time. I fear I shall have to oblige them.

His three-volume gymnasium-set fantasy, *Lowered Off the Rings*, was written during the war, and published to great acclaim on both sides of the Atlantic. The acclaim was, as it happens, for a different book: *Brass Rubbing* by Juliana Nederlandia. But as Nonwin told my grand-uncle 'That's not the important thing – the important thing is that there is acclaim sloshing about. It creates the right sort of atmosphere into which to release a new book – means that people are favourably disposed towards books in general, you see.'

Nonwin's optimism was duly rewarded when *Lowered Off the Rings* became a Hot Hundred Bestseller-List-Chaser Likely-to-Sell title in the *Midlands Advertiser* 'What's Up in Books?' supplement. With great sales came great fame. 'I find,' my grand-uncle wrote to his friend Lewis, 'that I am famous. It is not fanciful to say so. The fanfaronade of fandom treats me with frightening familiarity.'

4. The Sellamillion

The world created by A. R. R. Roberts was no mere fantasy flimflam or flapdoodle, believe you me. It was fully rounded, no, wait a mo, that doesn't roll off the tongue right, not the fully rounded, that's fine, the bit before. 'Believe you me'. I'm not sure that that sounds right. Hmm, hm, um, how about, 'You believe me'? Maybe that's better. Or, even, 'Believe me, you!' Yes, that's the best one. Vocative case. I say, Miriam, when you transcribe this bit into your word processor, could you please cut out my dithering and so on? Just cut straight to the – yes, right. Thanks.

So, hem, yes, Upper Middle Earth, no flapdoodle, on the contrary, where was I, yes – it was a lifetime's work; a detailed land of many nations and languages. The present volume assembles the background myths and stories to the *Soddit* and to *Lowered Off the Rings* as well as much alternate material, early drafts, and the like. By the way Miriam, that's a lovely chemise. No, really, a very nice purple.

The volume includes material relating to the 'singing' of the cosmos into being by the Ainu, the 'souls' or divine subordinates of the Creator, as well as the History of the Sellāmi, a magical artefact stolen from the Undying Lands. Certain elements relating to the War of the Thing™ that also formed the basis of the *Lowered Off the Rings* trilogy.

Well, enough of my yakking! No, on second thoughts, Miriam, don't put that, put something conventional like 'I will not weary the reader with lengthy preliminaries, et cetera et cetera'. Oh, and we'd better say that we're using some of the letters that C John Lewis exchanged with grand-uncle as a sort of preface to the volume. In addition to this preface. A postpreface preface. Post-preface, but pre the, um, face of the main text.

I'd like to thank my three research assistants, who

have worked tirelessly helping me assemble this collection of disparate material: Gabriel Kay, Guy Bedevere and Adrian Ladyofthelake.

Some letters between A. R. R. R. Roberts and C John Lewis
The Genesis of the Sellamillion

Cedric John Lewis was perhaps the most famous of my grand-uncle's many friends. He has, of course, subsequently gained worldwide celebrity as the author of a Fantasy sequence of his own – the 'Nerdia' books: a series of children's fantasy adventures about two boys and two girls who clamber, with some difficulty, through a magic sock-drawer in an interdimensional wardrobe, thence into the magic kingdom of Nerdia where they meet the gentle though dispute-prone Lion Aslef and the Wicked Queen Feminist, who is evil, wrong, misguided and I-want-my-supper-on-t'table-when-I-get-in. Not all admirers of these books realise (so cunningly and cleverly did the author conceal his spiritual aim) that Lewis wrote them as allegories to express and proselytise his own religious faith, with Aslef representing The Christ. The books in the sequence are: Volume 1, *The Passion Of The Lion, The Wicked Jews Who Murdered Him, and The Wardrobe*; Volume 2, *The Boy*

And His Horse And The Unspeakable Immorality They Got Up To Together Because They Did Not Attend Properly To The Commands of Leviticus; Volume 3, *The Voyage Of The Duty To Tread down Upon Heretics*; Volume 4, *HIV Is God's Plague On The Immoral* and the final volume, *Worship My God Ye Infidels Or You Will All Burn Forever*. He, and the other members of the 'oinklings', corresponded extensively with my grand-uncle during the composition of his Fantasy writings; and from this extensive correspondence I have selected a few letters that cast, I think, an interesting light on the production of the *Sellamillion* itself.

My dear AR

I'd be very grateful if you'd let me know your opinion of the following, which I found in the Library's Casanova MSS archive yesterday. I hope to include it in my forthcoming *Venetian Jokes*:[3]

> —*I say I say I say, my Doge has no nose.*
> —*No nose? How does he smell?*
> —*Lacking a nose he cannot smell at all, which is if anything a boon when we consider the notoriously unpleasant odour associated with the Venetian canals.*

By the way, how's your Fantasy epic proceeding?
Best wishes,
C

Dear C John

Thank you for the joke. Very droll.

I'm glad you ask about the Fantasy epic. I confess I'm having a spot of bother with Nonwin about the

---

3   Lewis's *Venetian Jokes* was eventually published by the Oxford Open Press Syndicate in four volumes under the title *Parlo Parlo Parlo: the Jokes of Venice*. Unfortunately, Lewis's policy of translating not only the jokes but also the surnames of the original creators of the jokes led to difficulties when an over-zealous copyeditor overapplied the system. Lewis wanted the name of the celebrated lover 'Giacomo Casanova' rendered as 'Jack Newhouse'; but in the first edition it was instead rendered throughout as 'Fuckall Barrethome'. The entire print run had to be pulped.

follow-up to the *Soddit* and *Lowered Off the Rings*. He wants another of the same stamp, and won't take no for an answer. Worse than that, he won't take 'yes, in a year or two' for an answer either. I tried explaining to him that the conventions of academic publishing permit an author a dozen years to assemble material and another seven to write it up, but he spoke scornful words in reply.

Apparently the marketing department has a slot with the *Fantasy Book Club – Not So Much A Club, More Thor's Hammer!!* (I give you the exact title of this organisation, down to the last exclamation mark) for February, and the sequel must be ready by then. What am I to do? My imagination is utterly mined out and exhausted. What shall I do?

Warmest regards, A

Dear AR

I advise prayer. In fact, I've just published the enclosed little book, *The Joy of Grace and the Gracefulness of Joy*, with Christian Publishing Inc. I make so bold as to send you a copy in the hope that it is of some devotional use. In particular, I'd like to direct your attention to Chapter 5 *Those Who Say 'Christ' instead of 'The Christ' Will Go To Hell For Evermore* and Chapter 11 *God Was A Carpenter, which means that All Articles of Woodwork and/or Furniture Are Sacred, Therefore Anybody Defacing, Denting Or Mistreating Woodwork Will Go To Hell For Evermore*. I hope it is of some use in your dealings with your publisher.

   Best Wishes,
   CJL

Dear Lewis

Thank you for the book, which I shall read at my earliest opportunity. I note with particular pleasure the topic of Chapter 14, *God Created Man in His Image, but Some Men Look* Exactly *Like Monkeys For Crying Out Loud, Hairy Knuckle-Dragging Weirdos That They Are: a Paradox in the Conflict Between Christianity and Darwinism Addressed*. It is about time somebody got to the bottom of that particular theological conundrum.

   Here's news: I've just had the strangest conversation, on the High Street. To be honest I'm not sure what to make of it. I was walking along on my way to college this morning when I was stopped by a tall, handsome blonde-haired chap wearing plenty of velvet and a monocle. He said 'excuse me,' and was most polite throughout; but he insisted that he had read my published Fantasy books and they were 'often wrong'. He added that I had done very

The Sellamillion

well, by and large; but that there were certain crucial
errors in the text.

I demurred, obviously; and suggested that I might
be permitted a little leeway with my own fictional
inventions – hoping to imply that, as author of these
fantasies, *I* can hardly be 'wrong'. At this he gave me a
very strange look, and thrust into my hand a sheaf of
unbound manuscript. 'You'll perhaps find the
following notes I have made on the genuine
mythology of interest,' he said. I thanked him and
tried to decline the gift, but he wouldn't take the
papers back. When I asked to whom I owed thanks
for this unusual gift, he replied that his name was
Terry (I think), and that 'no thanks were necessary'
beyond the correction of certain misapprehensions
about the nature of Upper Middle Earth. Then he said
goodbye, linked arms with a beautiful but vacant-
looking young woman, and walked away.

And do you know the strangest thing of all? The
beautiful young woman with whom he departed had
only one hand. Is that not strange?

Better go and look at this manuscript. Best wishes,
A

xxvii

Part 1

Ainusoul: the Music of the Ainu

[*Editor's Note*: the 'Ainusoul' was the earliest element in my grand-uncle's personal mythology, dealing as it does with the creation of Upper Middle Earth, the coming of Evil into that world, the creation of elves and various other things. It is, strictly, a separate thing from the 'Sellamillion' proper, which concerns that magic artefact known as the Sellāmi. I print the 'Ainusoul' here in six sections, beginning with the first. Obviously. It exists in a remarkably finished form, perhaps the result of many separate processes of revision and polishing; the contrast with the later material in the 'Sellamillion' is very noticeable. Well, I noticed it anyway. And you will notice it too. I mean, if you want to. I'm not instructing you to notice it or anything. Only if you feel like it. Really, it's up to you.]

The Creation

In the beginning, 'twas *Emu*, or *Ainu*, the one, that in Asdar is called *Rhodhulsarm*, and verily he 'twas, was rather, for he was without form and escheweth the vacancy *of* Chaos. Yea, verily, even *unto* the vacancy thereof. And He *did* call in veritude with Furious Wrath and a Mighty Wind, which did *Blow Mightily*, and He did Summon with Wormwood *and* Gall the *Cornet, Flute, Harp, Sackbut, Psaltery, Dulcimer* and a really pretty quite impressive variety of brazen instrumentation, actually. Then sayeth *Emu*, 'Behold! I shall Spew Ye From My Belly *and* Devour you thereof, and cry in a big voice.' And the Holy Spirits that are called Valūpac, gathered about Emu and their names are Gion, Poll, Gorge, Thingo, and Moregothic. And the Creations of Emu, the holy souls called Valūpac, sayeth, 'What Shall ye Cry?' And He replieth *to them*, 'He that diggeth a pit shall fall into the darkness thereof. A bundle of Myrrh is he who smiteth me, with the gnashing of teeth and the wailing of flutes from the bowels of wailing and the chins of gnashing. For how agree the kettle and the earthen pot together? Yea, verily, *even* unto the agreeing thereof.'

And his Creations said to Emu, 'Do what?'

And Emu said, 'Didn't I just explain it?'

And the Holy Spirits did reply, 'Yeah, great, great, what was the, er, middle bit again?'

And Emu said, 'Just sing. I'm going to sing the cosmos into being and your job is to sing backing vocals. OK?'

And the Holy Spirits replied 'Ahh' in tones of dawning comprehension.

And so they sang.

But one Spirit among the Backing Singers of Emu was not pleased with the harmony, and this was Moregothic. He said, 'What's all this then? Are we just going to be singing all through eternity, is it? Can't we have a breather, maybe a drink?'

And Emu said, 'Just get on with the baritone line, for crying out loud, you're spoiling the close harmony.'

And Moregothic said, 'My throat is hurting.'

And Emu said, 'Well that's your own fault, now, isn't it? I told you, sing from the chest, from the chest, *laaa*! like that, not the throat, you'll be giving yourself polyps if you're not careful. And if you do, don't say I didn't warn you, don't come crying to me, or croaking, don't come croaking to me if that's what happens.'

And Moregothic said, 'So, just out of curiosity, really, I'm wondering why an all-seeing, omniscient and all-powerful God of Goodness would allow something like oesophageal polyps to develop in the first place?'

And Emu, colouring a little, said, 'That's just part of my ineffability, isn't it?'

And Moregothic said, 'You what?'

And Emu repeated, in a tight voice, 'My ineffability.'

And Moregothic, though he seemed to be nodding in agreement with this Divine pronouncement of the ultimate mysterious and transcendental unknowability of God's Will, yet he said under his breath, 'No effing ability, more like.'

And Emu said, 'I heard that! I heard that, that's no way to talk to your Supreme Being and, I might add, Creator, though I've got no thanks off any of you for that. Just a couple of words, thank you never hurt anyone, gave you the best years of my omnipotence and this is how I'm repaid.'

And Moregothic said, 'Well if you're going to be like that, I'm off.'

And Emu said, 'Well, go off then, see if I care.'

And Moregothic said, 'I will.'

And Emu said, 'Go ahead then.'

And Moregothic said, 'I will.'

And Emu said, 'I'm all-powerful, I could create a million more Backing Singers for my song if I wanted to.'

And Moregothic said, 'If you're so all-powerful, how could it be that you've mistaken me for somebody who gives a toss?'

And so it was that the great cleavage occurred between the Almighty Emu and the Dark Lord Moregothic.

Of the Coming of the Elves and the First Wars of Good Against Evil

So it was that Moregothic fled the realm of Asdar and came to Upper Middle Earth. And Upper Middle Earth had been sung into existence by Emu and his subsidiary spirits, the Valūpac, and accordingly it wasn't terribly well defined – very beautiful, I'm not denying that, lovely in a sort of haunting way, but not very *precise*, if you see what I mean. Lots of mist, a bit of sky, but when you tried to pick out specifics it all sort of blended in. A bit melty ice-creamy, if you know what I mean. A little bit too much late Monet. Cotton-woolly. Candy-flossy. You get the picture.

And Moregothic said, 'Blimey, this is something of a bodge job, isn't it?'

And he realised he was talking to himself.

So Moregothic made for himself followers. He took the earth of Upper Middle Earth (the earth after which the land was, I suppose, named); and because it was only song and without words, it could be

impressed with a great many different interpretations; and so Moregothic did create creations
with it. Creatures, I suppose you could call them,
which is, I suppose, where that word comes from.
That had never really occurred to me before.

First he created four dragons. First, he made the
Dragon of the East, who was a league from snout to
tail, with blazing golden scales and scarlet eyes. And
he made the Dragon of the West, whose skin was
blemishless and blue-purple, and whose eyes were
bright with the silver of the evening star. And he
made the Dragon of the North, who was ice-white,
with breath that chilled and claws that shattered the
strongest metal. And at the last he made the Dragon
of the South, who was wine-coloured with olive-
coloured eyes, and wings as wide as stormclouds;
and his nostrils shed lightning upon the sky that fell
in thorn-shapes through the darkening air. And
these four mighty dragons reared from the dust in
glory.

And Moregothic had brought over from Asdar one
of the junior Valūpac, who had elected to rebel
against Emu, and to share in the labours and share
in the triumph of Moregothic. And this being was
called *Sharon*, for nobody seemed to realise that this

was a girl's name. And Moregothic made him his lieutenant.[4]

And then he blew his breath into a fistful of earth, or something along those lines, and created a mighty army of evil creatures, that he called Orks. He intended fully to call them Awe-Inspiring Warriors of Darkness, but breathing in to speak this terrible name a fragment of dust flew up his nose, causing him to half-cough, half-snort, and so they were ever after known by that noise.

Now, the four great dragons were the mightiest of Moregothic's creations; and their being contained the greatest proportion of the earth of Upper Middle Earth and the smallest proportion of the breath of Moregothic; and ever after they were the least bound to his will, the most ornery and independent. And the Orks were the least part fragments and motes of dust from the original matter of Emu's song, and were the largest part breath and spittle of Moregothic, and they were the most bound to his will and the evilest.

The Dragons took wing and flew. But they found

---

4 You, dear reader, must decide whether you intend to pronounce this word in the manner of the forces of Good and Light and Reason and Decency, as Emu does himself, 'luptenant'; *or* you can pronounce it in the evil, deformed, Forces-of-Darkness manner of Moregothic, 'lootenant'. The choice is yours.

the air through which they passed a bit neither-this-nor-that, a bit to-be-frank-with-you-vague; and they conversed amongst themselves saying, 'This is the problem with creating a world with nothing but music, very pretty but not specific enough. What's needed here are some words – give the song some shape, meaning and so on.'

And so, as they flew through the air, the Dragons spoke. And they spoke forth the sun, to burn light and heat upon the world. And they spoke forth the high air, which is blue fire and blue smoke; and they spoke the lower air, which is clear; and they spoke the mountains, and the restless oceans that chafe against the girdle of the land. And they spoke glaciers, and towering waterfalls, and deserts of sand and deserts of hard rock.

And Moregothic saw all this and, though he was surprised, yet he said, *'That's* more like it, some structure – that makes it all much clearer, yes. Words are much better at doing that than just music by itself, as it turns out.'

Now Emu in Asdar had his sleeve tugged by his Holy Ones, and they said, 'Er, Mighty One, have you seen what Moregothic is doing over in Upper Middle Earth?'

And Emu, looking round, said, 'Good *grief*. No, this won't do at all.'

And he dispatched the Spirits of the Valūpac to Upper Middle Earth. There they found a land carved from the rugged beauty of the poetry of dragons: they found mountains like massy clouds brought down to the horizon and condensed into granite. They found wildernesses of pebbles, and deserts of red grit. They found a coastline where the sea was mad in its rage and headbutted the land over and over. And they found mighty waterfalls hurling themselves over the raw cliff in two thousand white twining lines from the black pool above, like the tentacles of a great albino sea creature.

And, seeing this, the Valūpac spoke words of their own. For though they could not undo the speech of the Dragons yet nevertheless what they spoke chimed contrapuntally with the Dragonwords.

They spoke woods, and rolling grasslands, and the mild beasts of earth and forest. They spoke rivers that rolled as vowels down the flanks of clover-covered hills; they spoke fish that darted as consonants within those waters. They spoke birds that jewelled through the air, and butterflies which wave greeting at the world as they fly; and these birds and these butterflies are words that seem brief yet

11

contained great wonders. And at last they spoke people to live in these beautiful places, whom they called *elves*, which, in the primary speech of creation, meant *words*.[5]

And the Valūpac departed and returned to Asdar.

The first Elves were made in the new land between the mountains Ered Loonpants and the Capital Sea. These were the Tree Elves, and they were a beautiful people, tall, with large eyes and large ears, with wide smiles and dark hair. And the first king of these Elves was called Tuoni Bleary, the King of the First Elves. And the land was called Blearyland; and in the mornings and the evenings, in memory of the original wordless song of Emu, the land was spread with cloth of mist and haze that spilled the sunlight in gold and honey, in topaz and blood. And when the sun had risen, or had gone quite behind the horizon, the land acquired the harder-edged loveliness that the Dragons had given it. And because the elven peoples thought the most beautiful views happened during the fuzzy, bleary, unfocused dawn and dusk, they did praise it in an imprecise song:

---

5 [Author's note] Compare the Latin *elevate*, from *levis* 'light', meaning to illuminate, to raise up to comprehension, to provide meaning; which is to say, 'word'.

Look: I *believe, very much, you know, in beauty*
And I think it's important to recognise
The very important role played by, you know,
the beauty community. Indeed.

And the Elves built a great city amongst the trees of
Hipinonsens, north of the great forest of Taur-ea-dorpants, and this city they called Tonjon, though the other
races of Upper Middle Earth tended to call it Elftonjon,
which means 'spangly top on taur-ea-dorpants'.

And King Bleary said, 'Like, you know, this is a
terribly encouraging development, which represents
a year-on-year increase in city-ness *in* the Blearyland
area in real terms.'

And Robin 'Goodfellow' Cük, Prince of Elves said,
'Indeed, hmm, huarr, gnarr, ashahahaha,' and did
make a strange high-pitched keening sort of noise.

And King Bleary promised his people a golden
age. He decreed there would be a social structure
that treated all elves fairly, to be called the Elf-fair
State; and he decreed a National Elf Service for the
treatment of sickness, and free elfucation provision.[6]

---

6   For did not King Bleary himself say his priorities were 'elfucation,
elfucation, elfucation'? And did not the publishers of this volume also say
'we would like to apologise in the abjectest terms imaginable for the barrel-
bottom nature of the jokes contained in this particular paragraph of the
Sellamillion, which exceeds EU maxima for groans-per-phrase by 300%'?

And the people believed King Bleary, and there was much rejoicing throughout the whole of Blearyland.

Now Moregothic watched this latest development from his fastness in the north, which he called Cumabund, which means 'calling this place a fastness is, frankly, to speak ironically, since its dominant characteristic is on the contrary how *slow* everything is here; ice-bound wilderness, huge cyclopean blocks of granite, massive architecture but nothing much to do all day except plot evil plots and stare at the snow-covered landscape.' For it is sometimes the case that a single short word can only be rendered into another language with a hugely lengthy paraphrase. That's just the way it is with translation, can't be helped.

And Moregothic gathered together his horde of Orks, and said unto them: 'Righto, chaps, I'm sure word has reached you of the increasing populations of Elves to the lands south of here. Now, some of you may be asking yourself, "Why did the Dark Lord himself decide to build his fastness Cumabund up here amongst the frozen wastes and black granite peaks, where nothing grows and even the crows perish as they fly through the air?"'

And with one voice, the five hundred thousand

Ork warriors cried, 'Oo no, my lord, the thought never crossed our minds, honestly.'

'No, no,' said Moregothic, indulgently, 'the rumours *have* reached my ears, and it's perfectly understandable. I'm not going to have anybody flayed alive for saying such a thing – I'm not a monster, after all. Well, to be exact, I *am* a monster, strictly speaking, but, well, you know what I mean. Allow me to explain.'

And the mighty horde of Orks cried, 'My lord, you're spoiling us, really you are.'

And Moregothic said, 'No, couldn't quite catch that, the legion on my left hand was slightly out of synch with the mass to my right. It came to my ears as a sort of raging confusion of noise. Something about boiling, was it?'

And the mighty horde of Orks cried, more slowly and with distinct pauses in between the words, 'My lord, you're spoiling us, really you are.'

And Moregothic said, 'Ah, yes, got it that time. Well, you're my Orks and you deserve the best. The truth is, this is a slightly rubbish location for a fastness – but what you need to understand is that when we came here, and the Dragons added words to Emu's music, thereby creating a much more structured and rational cosmos to live in, it was all much of a muchness. But now that Emu has sent his Valūpac over here, they've smartened things up *no end* down south. When I was last down there it was all barren rock and hailstones, but now I hear it's pleasant woodland, parks, rivers full of fish, all manner of interesting wildlife. Anyway, anyhow, anyhew, to cut a long story short, I've decided we should invade. There's plenty of space for all, and as a special bonus we get not only to slay, but also to smash, crush, drive before us, listen to the lamentations of the severely wounded – which is to say, all your favourite hobbies.'

And the Orks did cheer; and raised their hook-ended sabres over their heads and did brandish them in the cold air.

And Sharon did say, 'Good idea, my lord.'

And so it was that a great Army of Darkness came raging out of the frozen north, and fell upon the elven populations of the more temperate south as a wolf falls upon a flock of sheep, or a hawk upon a flock of doves, although, now I come to think of it, it's rather confusing to have the same word to describe collective gatherings of sheep and birds. I mean, are there two more different sorts of creatures than, say, sheep and birds? Sorry, I don't mean to go off on one, it's just a particular bugbear of mine.[7]

So, running out of time, barely have time to tell you about the mighty battle between the Elves and the hordes of evil. Ten years of solid fighting. The forces of Darkness had it all their own way at first, but then, just when all seemed lost, you know the drill, a single heroic self-sacrifice turned the tide, I'm not sure of all the details, but that doesn't matter particularly. Anyway, finally Moregothic was over-thrown and chained up, using a really big chain. And I mean *really* big.

And the mighty Elvish lords who led their differ-ent tribes in this great fight were called Tuoni Bleary, and Nodihold, and Manwëewer Lukithatime. And from their respective peoples descended the three great tribes of the Elves; the Bleary, the Nodiholdor and the Man-Wëers.

But although Moregothic was chained with the really big chains, the Elves had not captured Sharon,

---

7 Which reminds me, I meant to include the 'Bugbear' amongst the hideous progeny Moregothic created: it being, as you surely know, a gigantic half-insect, half-polar-bear hybrid, with eight albino hairy arms, mandibles instead of a mouth, big muscles, and a special iron exoskeleton that it has to keep oiled with seal-oil from fresh-caught seals. Nasty piece of work, I can tell you.

nor had they extinguished the existence of many of the Orks.[8] And they scattered into the wild wildernesses and 'wa!' wastes (so called because people often let out a cry of babyish terror on first seeing them), and lived for many generations in those places. And Nodihold did say to King Bleary, 'Should we not pursue these agents of wickedness even unto the furthest reaches of the Earth and put an end to them, for fear that they will regather, regroup, and come back to attack us another time?'

And King Bleary did say, 'What? No, clearly there is no need for the public expense of such an expedition. I mean, look: it's pretty cold up there, and *I* believe that they'll all get chills and sneeze themselves to death, or something. Intelligence reports from the Central Inelfigence Agency suggest that no further threat exists to the elven way of life.'

And Nodihold did scratch his massy elven sideburns, like unsightly growths of moss on the sides of his otherwise smooth and golden face, and did say, 'Are you sure? I mean, it seems like leaving it rather to chance. Couldn't we just send one squad of soldiers into the wilderness to make certain?'

---

8   Damn, forgot them again. This should read '. . . Orks, *and Bugbears.*'

18

And King Bleary said, 'I will institute a far-reaching consultative process, the Big Conelversation, to open up the process of regal governance to the Elvish people.' Which, as Nodihold knew, was King Bleary's way of saying 'no'.

And afterwards Manwëe came up to Nodihold and said, 'So? Are we going to finish what we started, or what?'

And Nodihold shook his head mournfully, and replied, 'Manwëe, we're all crazeee now.'

And Manwëe asked, 'All what?'

'Crazy,' said Nodihold, 'sorry, I had a sort of hiccough when I said that and it did something strange with the final syllable. But is it not crazy to leave our future to chance in this manner?'

And Manwëe said, 'Excuse me for a mo, I need to take a comfort break.'

And so the Elves lived in safety for a little space.

Of The Unchaining of Moregothic

The unchaining of Moregothic is told in the Lay of Ladylay.[9] Now the Evil Lord had been chained up with these *really* big chains for ages.

And Moregothic did say to the Elves who guarded him, in the dungeons of Cumabund, 'Look, this chain is really rather uncomfortable.'

And the great Elven lord Ladylay, who was charged with guarding him, did reply, 'Hmm, well, you should have thought of that *before* you led a flesh-eating horde of Orks from the howling north to wage war upon Elfkind, shouldn't you? Eh?'

And Moregothic did reply, 'Fair point, fair point, only there's this link digging into the small of my back, very uncomfortable. Could you just slip the chain off for a mo, so I can readjust it? It'd take thirty seconds, and I promise I won't bother you any more after that.'

And Ladylay did say, 'I don't know.' And he

---

9   Also known by some authorities as 'the Lay of Crosmybigbrasbed'.

turned to his deputy Crosmybigbrasbed, and said, 'What do you reckon?'

And Crosmybigbrasbed shrugged.

'Alright,' said Ladylay. 'One minute. Only you have to promise not to try any funny business when the chain is off.'

'Funny business?' said Moregothic, as if the very thought was absurd and even offensive to him. 'Guys! Come on, guys – it's me!'

'Say "I promise".'

'I promise.'

But Ladylay was not to be fooled so easily, and he said: 'Say "I promise", followed by what it is that you promise.'

'I promise not to try any funny business when the chain is off.'

And they took off the mighty chain, and Moregothic did leg it, and Ladylay did stand holding the chain, looking like a bit of a twit really.

And Moregothic fled to the far north, and there assembled around himself his followers again. And he said to his army of Orks, 'Well it's pretty clear the one mistake *I* made was to put all my eggs in one basket, ork-wise.'

And his Orks said, 'Eggs?'

'What I need,' said Moregothic, 'is a bigger and a better army, with a fully diverse and ethnically integrated range of evil creatures.' And so he created new, bigger Orks; and also Giant Ants of Death, War-Ouliphants; and he created monstrous smooth-headed cave monsters, the Baldtrogs; and he created Goblins and hordes of terrible flesh-eating monsters. And then he said, 'That ought to do it, really.'

And word reached the Elves in the south that a mighty muster was mustering in the frozen north. And they were sore afraid. Indeed, sores were the least of the things they were afraid of. They were more afraid of being torn to blood-scattering pieces of quivering flesh, speared, devoured, and utterly killed.

Of The Coming Of Men into Blearyland

It was during this era that a new race came to Blearyland, travelling from the east over the mountains. These were *Men*, who are mortal and proud yet had the capacity to become portly and cowed. They arrived in the elvish forest Taur-ea-dorpants, a ragged band of men and women and children. And the Elves did accost them, saying 'Hey! What are you lot doing in our forest?'

And Riturnov, who was King of these new peoples, did reply 'Is this Southlands Bec?'

And Fingorbuffet the Nibblesome, a prince of the Elves, did reply, 'No, no, you're miles off, mate – *miles* away, you should have taken the left turn at the waterfall by Ered Loonpants.'

And Riturnov did reply, 'I *knew* it, I told Harrison we was on the wrong road. Ah well, ah well, we're here now, too late to start off again today. You got anything to eat?'

At first the Elves were wary of the newcomers, who ate and drank like gannets, frankly, and who had hair growing out of every part of their bodies

23

save only a small space around their eyes, and a second hairless patch between eyebrows and hairline, I mean yuck or *what*. For no Elf has such extensive body hair, excepting only the slight hairiness of Nodihold, and the much more extensive hirsuitery of Wiurdi the Beardy, the elf with a pelt.

Now, when Men first came to Blearyland they were fleeing an unspeakable horror in the east, and when the Elves asked Men from what it was that they fled they replied, 'Which part of "unspeakable" don't you understand? – The basic concept resides in a thing not being speakable about, alright?' After which they went '*tch*'. And the Elves were sore ashamed.

But after many months, and much drink shared, the Elves came to form an alliance with the sons of Man, and with their daughters, though not with their brothers, who were, frankly, a little standoffish.

And so King Bleary agreed a treaty with the Men of Numenorwhat? that they did take up arms together to fight the evil of Moregothic. And they told Men of Numenorwhat? lengthy epic tales of the evil of Moregothic, and of his bitter lieutenant Sharon, of his chaining up, and the unfortunate unchaining incident that happened subsequently, which was just plain unlucky, not anybody's fault actually, just one of those things.

'So the upshot, with regard to this wicked More-gothic, is that he's loose again, is he?' asked the Men. 'Just run it past us one more time, how he got free from the giant chain?'

And the Elves did hmm and ha, and did look at their shoes for a bit. Then they did say, 'But anyway – anyway – the *important* thing is that together we shall fight the forces of evil! Together we pledge our courage and our blood to defeat this terrible enemy who blights Upper Middle Earth.'

And after much ale, the Men did cry, 'Yes! Yes! Let us band together in a great alliance, and fight shoulder to shoulder against evil and tyranny!'

And the Elves did say, 'We will spill our blood gloriously, as brothers!'

And the Men did agree. 'And we shall be daunt-less,' said the Men. 'No daunting for us. We shall fight without daunt of any kind.'

'Hurrah!' cried Men and Elves together.

And when they had sobered up a bit the following day, Men returned to the elven halls and said, 'Look, *great* news about the alliance and all that, *really great* news, we're simply chuffed, we really are, it's just that, well, we were talking to these wood-hewers and they sort of, well to put it frankly, they told us that – well, let me, let me put it this way. You know this evil lord chap, and his evil lieutenant that we have pledged to fight to the last drop of blood in our veins?'

And the Elves did say, 'Yes? What about them?'

And the Men did enquire, 'Well, we were just curious, it's more, you know, curiosity than anything else. But who else is on *their* side?'

And the Elves did say, 'An army of half a million terrible Orks, Giant Ants of Death, War-Ouliphants, fifth-column ouliphants who try to infiltrate our cities and blend into the crowd to subvert our defences from within, although to be honest they're not terribly successful; Baldtrogs; Goblins; Trolls and many terrible flesh-eating monsters.'

And the Men did ask for clarification, saying, 'How many of those last lot?'

And the Elves did say, 'Hordes.'

And the Men did say 'Oh' in a small voice, and did assume a doleful countenance, which the Elves did assume was a reflection of a certain hangover, which sometimes did afflict the children of Men after the consumption of certain quantities of beer.

But the alliance was binding, and Men and Elves stood shoulder to shoulder.

Of The Coming Of Dwarfs into Blearyland

It was round about this time that Elves and Men first noticed that Dwarfs had come into Blearyland. And when they taxed them with their coming, and asked from whence they came, and for why they had left that place, the Dwarfs did say, 'Been here ages bach, you just didn't notice us. Simply ages – longer'n you, I daresay, look you. Under the ground, see. Underneath, out of sight, out of mind, see.'

And the Elves did say, 'Pull the other one.'

And the Dwarfs did say, 'No, no, honestly.'

And it being impossible to prove or disprove it, one way or another, Elves and Dwarfs left it there for the time being.

And the dwarf-kingdoms of Blearyland were carved from the very living rock, but also from the dead rock, which was easier to carve actually, since it wasn't given to moaning and trembling and crying hot lava when you cut into it with a pickaxe. And the great dwarfish cities were named Khāzi, Khazhak-stān, Khizzikhizzi, Khāztofthousands and the dark dwarrow-dwelling of Khāz-by-Garinewman.

And the Elves did say, 'Look, I'm really sorry about this, but you just can't stay. We're just not a big enough country to accommodate whole new populations. It's not as if you're genuine asylum seekers, you're more economic migrants.'

And the Dwarfs did say, 'echo-gnomic migrants' and did laugh proudly and mightily, as if they had said something funny, and some amongst the Dwarfs did go 'Hi-ho! hi-ho!', with the second part spoken in a smaller voice as if it were an echo of the first, and this in turn did provoke the Dwarfs to further hilarity, such that they fell to the floor laughing, although they did not hurt themselves so doing, the floor not being very far for a Dwarf to fall as it happens.

And the Elves more or less gave up at this point, and left the Dwarfs to their own devices.

Of The Coming Of Munchkins
into Blearyland

Shortly thereafter a great army of Munchkins did arrive in Blearyland, singing mighty songs and bringing with them buildings and road design of a surprisingly advanced design, bearing in mind that the Munchkins themselves were not only just two foot tall or so but also markedly infantile and pliable. But the Elves said, 'For goodness' sake, this is just too much, I mean, I'm as much in favour of ethnic diversity as the next man, but enough's enough. Go on, you lot, away with you.' And with kicks, cuffs and general ya!-ing, they did chase the Munchkins to the borders of Blearyland and nudged them over the edge.

And the Elves did say, 'And stay out,' and did brush their hands together with alternating up-down strokes.

Of the Great Destruction wrought by Moregothic, and of the Attempts Made by the Elves and Men to wreak Destruction upon Moregothic, and of the wreakage of Destruction upon Moregothic, which was eventually wranged, or possibly wrekted

So Moregothic wrought great destruction upon the lands of Blearyland. And the Elves and Men formed a mighty alliance and made war upon Moregothic in an attempt to destroy him, which attempt was ultimately successful. And Moregothic was burnt to crispy embers.

A More Detailed Account of the Great Destruction Wrought by Moregothic, and of the Attempts Made by the Elves and Men to wreak Destruction upon Moregothic, and of the eventual Destruction of Moregothic

It has been brought to my attention that some people, I mention no names, they know who they are – that some people were, shall we say, *under*-satisfied with the previous account of the great destruction wrought by Moregothic, and the attempts made by the Elves and Men to wreak destruction upon Moregothic, and of the Destruction of Moregothic. Well, I *thought* I got straight to the pith of the matter in my previous account. But I suppose there are people for whom pith is not enough. If you want a pith-free, husk-heavy account, who am I to disagree? Your wish, my command, and so on, and so on, et cetera.

Very well then. Pay attention. I'm not going through this more than once.

Moregothic had fled even further to the north, and he built himself a new fastness which he called Winter-underland.[10] And as he constructed it, his mighty army did sing a spine-chilling song about Moregothic's new kingdom.[11]

And Moregothic planned his terrible revenge upon all of Upper Middle Earth, making sure this time to cross the 't's and dot the 'i's, the lower-case 'j's and any umlauted 'u's that needed it. 'I shall leave nothing to chance,' he told his lieutenant, Sharon. 'I have assembled an army ten times as large as my previous army, and recruited monstrous and flesh-rending shock-troops instead of a measly rabble of Orks.'

And Sharon did say, 'Good *idea*, my lord' with great enthusiasm.

And Moregothic did say, 'Isn't it, though? And I tell you what, I've had *another* good idea as well. I shall seal my invulnerability with – guess what?'

And Sharon did ponder, going, 'Hmm, hmm; oh, now, now – could it be magic?'

---

10   Because it was mostly constructed under the land. And because so far north it was always winter. To be frank, I reckon you could have worked that out for yourselves, if you'd put the effort in. But *oh* no, not you.

11   Mind you, any song can be described as spine-chilling if the spine gets chilled; and any spine will be chilled if the ambient temperature is low enough. That's common sense, that is.

'Magic, yes,' said Moregothic, and he did nod smugly. 'I shall summon the four Dragons of this world, for they are the beings in which magic is most potent. And they shall lay upon me a spell of protection so strong that not the Elves, not the Valūpac, not Emu himself could break it. I shall fashion the spell such that no chain will ever bind me again, because I don't mind telling you I didn't like that chain-up business one little bit. I shall weave the spell so cunningly that no creature shall be able to lay hand on me, or weapon, that nothing fashioned by elvish hands will be able to destroy me. I shall be invulnerable, and immortal, and shall ride to flaming victory.'

'Excellent, master!'

'Isn't it, though?'

And Sharon said, 'Could I have a similar spell made for me, master?'

'Certainly not,' said Moregothic, gruffly.

'Not even,' said Sharon, in a small voice, 'a little one?'

'Be off with you,' snapped Moregothic. 'I've no time to be worrying about underlings.'

Now the fastness of Moregothic was a huge network of tunnels and groined chambers, of corridors and deep dungeons; but one portion of it projected

above the frost-hard ground, and this was a tower a
thousand feet tall, seemingly slender as a white stalk
of wheat against the huge backdrop of mountains,
yet forty yards wide and builded of blocks of white
granite interlocked more cunningly than a cun.[12]
And Moregothic did climb to the very summit of
this tower where the air was clear, and sword-sharp
with cold. And he spoke a spell of summoning for the
Dragons. And the four Dragons answered his call,
and flew in the air around the tower, such that, from
a distance, it seemed as though a whirlwind and
snowstorm possessed the tower.

'I command you!' Moregothic cried.

But the Dragons had grown in spirit and power
since their creation, and were wilful, and independent of mind; and though they hearkened to Moregothic's call yet they did hold back. For he had
created them, and much of his power had passed
into them; and now they were balanced between
obeying him and wishing his destruction. But the
voice of command compelled them.

'I command a spell from you,' cried Moregothic,
throwing the words from his throat into the chill and
windy air. 'I must be invulnerable to harm. There

---

12 Latin *cuneus* 'wedge'; hence 'any wedge-shaped object'. No, really.

must be no chink in my protection, no gap in the strength of magic that wraps me around.'

And the Dragon of the North sang:

> *Though only fire may kill ye*
> *Yet no flame can harm ye*
> *Yet no spark can wound ye*
> *Yet no heat can hurt ye*

And Moregothic said: 'Excellent! Yet, why do you say that fire may kill me? Can you not cast the spell such that fire has no purchase upon my body at all?' But as he asked the question he knew, in his heart, that to cast such a spell would be to quench the fire that ran in his own veins, to destroy the fire of his heart and his spirit, and that this would annihilate him. And so he contented himself with the magic that told him no flame, or spark, or heat could hurt him.

And the Dragon of the South sang:

> *Though only elf may slay ye*
> *No elf hand may touch ye*
> *No elf weapon affront ye*
> *No elf word discomfort ye*

And Moregothic made plaint, saying, 'This also is

good! Yet why should it be that even elf might slay me? Can you not cast the spell such that no creature of *any* kind has power upon me?' But as he asked the question he knew that his captivity in the dungeon of the Elves had given to them a special power over his fate that could not be undone without undoing his fate altogether, and that would annihilate him. And so he contented himself with the magic that told him no elf hand, weapon or word could hurt him.

The spell was complete. And Moregothic felt the power of the magic bind itself to his body and he cried, 'Good, good, yet must I have stronger assurance still. If I am struck with sword, arrow or spear, will that kill me?'

And the Dragons cried '*No!*'

'If I am drowned in the sea or smothered under the earth, will that kill me?'

And the Dragons cried '*No!*'

'Might man, dwarf or beast kill me?'

And the Dragons cried '*No!*'

'You say only an elf may kill me, yet no elf may kill me?'

And the Dragons cried '*So!*' And their voices were loud in the snow-thronged air.

And Moregothic said, 'That seems to tie that up.'

And he called aloud again: 'You say only fire may hurt me, yet no flame can touch me?'

And the Dragons cried '*So!*' through the mournful hissing of sleet.

And Moregothic was content, for the magic was very strong. But when such a charm is cast upon a magical being, a price is paid; and in return for this charm Moregothic surrendered part of his divinity, which passed to the Dragons. And he thought to himself, 'It matters little, for it is but a tiny splinter of my divine power, I retained the most part – and in return for this small loss I have rendered myself invulnerable. The price is worth it.' What he did not realise was that in the matter of divinity, which is infinite, a tiny portion is yet the whole, and the whole is but a splinter. But this thought did not trouble Moregothic until later.

And the Dragons departed; for they had laid their eggs in the stone of the earth, and fled away to the barrenness beyond the north where no creature save them can pass.

Now Moregothic was confident, and he led his army south, and laid waste to the west, and the fires of his army did eat up the east, and he brought flood and drouth to the south. And the Elves despaired of being able to stand against him: for his army was powerful and merciless. And the Elves cried aloud 'Woe! woe!' by which they meant to allude to their own sorrow or sadness, rather than to say 'Hey dude, slow down' or anything of that nature. And word reached them of the spells which kept Moregothic safe, which lowered morale in the elf camp even further.

The woods were burned, and the pastures defiled; elf homes and the hearths of men were trampled and destroyed, and ork and monster roamed at will. And Riturnov the King, first king of Men, was slain in a fray near a haywain, as he was lying in pain with his main troop of Men slain around him. His son Reriturnov was but a child, and the kingdom of Men was ruled by the regent, Strete.

At last the great elf-general Fimble and the War-lord of Men, Rokett, mustered the last remnant of the army of the Elves and of Men. 'Come,' he cried, 'we must drive this army of evil back whence it came.'

And the Elves mounted horses for the first time, to ride alongside the cavalry of Men; and they rode down the downs to collide with the Ork footsoldiers in the foothills; quite an impressive sight, actually, that cavalry charge. And the Army of Darkness broke in confusion.

But within three days it had remustered, and it drove hard against the Elves at the Battle of the Difficult Summe. And the Elves, counterattacking, suffered heavy casualties. For they were hampered by an overdemanding high command which ordered advancing troops to calculate the cube root of any four-digit prime in base 7 whilst walking slowly towards enemy arrow-fire.

And Fimble fled from the slaughter with only four dozen soldiers alive, the last survivors of the great army of Elves. And Rokett rode with him, with only three score of men left alive, the rump of the army of Men. They rode hard to the east, but their way was blocked by monstrous warrior-ants of prodigious size whose snippy-mandibles could sever a person in two with the merest snicky-snack, and Moregothic mocked them from his saddle on the thorax of the largest of the war ants, saying 'Elves! Don't you mess with my ants. You cut off their heads, they come *looking* for you.' And many Elves and many Men died in that place.

So the remnant of the elvish and mannish armies rode west, but ran against the edge of the land, where the ocean chafed and chewed at the strand. And so they rode north, wearing out their horses in their flight. And Moregothic's terrible army pursued by day and by night, for the taste of flesh was in their mouths, and lust-for-death was in their hearts.

As the Men and Elves rode further north, the land became more barren and cold; and snow lay in the hollows of the ground though the sun was up; and frost made mud stone. And still the Army of Darkness pursued them, so that even though their horses died the Elves were compelled to hurry further on foot. And they passed to the frozen lands where snow lay over all the ground in every season of the year like white topsoil, and sunshine reflected from the whiteness to dazzle the eyes in daytime, and starlight made the land glitter in the cloudless nights. Their breath came now as wraiths to leave their bodies like souls departing, and a great weariness was upon them. And after much suffering, which wore down the resistance of some of their number even unto death, they reached the frozen peaks of the Mountains of Byk.

The land here is broken and jagged, just as the Dragons created it at the beginning of days, with frozen waterfalls, boulders yet unsmoothed by wind or erosion, and harsh spires of ice reaching up to the sky in defiance. And Fimble said, 'We have come to the most terrible place in Upper Middle Earth. Here we shall make a stand. For we cannot flee forever.'

And Rokett spoke, saying, 'No, I suppose not.'

Here the last of the warrior elves and the last of the warrior men climbed the lower peaks of Mount Ezumasrevenge, and prepared to make their last stand, side by side. 'Perhaps,' said Rokett, 'we may yet slay Moregothic.' But they remembered the words of the Dragons' Spell, and knew that their swords and arrows were useless against him. 'At least,' said Fimble, 'we shall die gloriously.' And the other Elves said, 'Er, great, yeah, that's certainly a consolation,' and they added sotto voce 'as we contemplate our imminent and bloody deaths.'

Moregothic arrayed his horde around the base of Mount Ezumasrevenge, cutting off all possible escape, and then he made camp for three days and three nights. And as the last dozen elven warriors and the last score of Men shivered on their crag, the army of Moregothic feasted and danced beside giant fires; and the sound of singing, and the smell of cooked food wafted through the night.

The sun rose on the last day; and elf and man prepared themselves each of them to fight and each of them to die, for there was no hope. And at Moregothic's order, Orks and Baldtrogs swarmed up the lower slopes. Battle was short, sharp and shocking; many Orks and several Baldtrogs fell slain, but also slain were six of the twelve Elves and half the small force of Men.

And Moregothic pressed the attack with his monsters, ants, wargs, trolls and other nasties; and though they fought bravely the last warriors could not withstand, and withdrew further up the mountain.

And Moregothic called after them, 'Fools! Whither do you fly? Can you take wing like the birds of the air and soar to safety?' And he laughed, saying, 'You are already dead.'

And he marched himself into battle, for he had no fear of elf or man, protected as he was by the most powerful spell the new world had ever seen.

Seeing him approach, Fimble ran forward, carving a path through the bodies of furious Orks with his sword and his right arm. And Fimble struck at Moregothic with his sword, but the Dark Lord was proof against the weapon and it shattered like glass blade striking stone. Fimble's heart despaired at this, for he knew that the Dragon magic protected Moregothic against any assault he might make. And yet even in his despair did his courage flare up; for despair can feed rage as straw a fire, to burn bright though briefly.

And, weaponless, Fimble leapt upon the armour of

Moregothic, and struggled upwards like a mountain-
eer, and placed his hands around Moregothic's neck
to throttle him. But no elf hand might hurt the Dark
Lord, and where his hands touched Moregothic's
flesh his hands burned within like acid, and dissolved away to reeking smoke. And Fimble lifted
away the stumps of his arms in agony.

Moregothic laughed to see this. 'And is this the
greatest warrior the Elves can send against me?' he
mocked. 'A handless cripple and his band of stragglers? Though it be said only Elves might slay me,
yet is it also decreed in Dragon magic that no elf
hand might hurt me, no elf weapon assail me.'

And Fimble, howling in rage, threw himself forward with his last strength; and he bit with his mouth
at the Dark Lord's very face, and bit again, and bit
a third time. Handless as he was, armed with no
weapon and speaking no word, yet Fimble struck at
Moregothic.

And the Dark Lord cried in surprise and pain, and
smote at Fimble with his black-bladed sword; but
Fimble clung on, even as the blade cut his flesh. And
Moregothic staggered in pain, and his foot stumbled
on the edge of the crag, and so he fell.

His fall was mighty, and he fell hard upon the
broken ground, where the stalagmite spires of ice

rose up needle-sharp. And one mighty blade of ice pierced Moregothic's breast as he fell upon it and it thrust through. And he lay in pain on the frozen ground, impaled upon this terrible shaft.

And at this moment Moregothic knew that the Dragons had deceived him. For the ice pierced his chest, and its terrible cold burned his heart, and chill seared his flesh; and so he died. And with his death a great terror fell upon his soldiers; and they fled wailing and crying to the furthest reaches of the frozen wastes; and many fell into crevasses, or starved amongst the forbidding peaks. And Sharon found his way to Moregothic's Winter-underland, and there he hid himself in the deepest dungeons and nursed the terror in his heart at the death of his master and his maker.

And the last six Elves gathered the body of Fimble from the dead face of Moregothic, and burnt him in honour on a warrior's pyre. And the last of the Men took the body of Moregothic and cut it to pieces with their swords; for, being dead, he was beyond harm, and so the spell was broken and their swords could cut. And Elves and Men took a brand from Fimble's funeral pyre, and set fire to a bonfire on which they burnt the remains of Moregothic to cinder and ash; for, being dead, he was beyond harm, and so the flames could now consume him. And so Moregothic was overthrown.

And the last Elves made their way back to the warm south, and rejoined their women and their children; and over many years they rebuilt their nation. And the Men returned as heroes, and were cheered in the streets. Although after a solid ten months of them relating their war stories, the general population did get a bit bored with hearing them over and over, and tended to adopt slightly fixed, pixilated expressions when they heard the opening sentences of one of the stories, and put their minds elsewhere.

Part 2
The Sellamillion:
The History of the Sellāmi

The Theft of the Giant Sellāmi

Now in Asdar did Emu reside, and he was happy, mostly, although the afternoons did sometimes seem perhaps a trifle on the long side, and time sometimes hung a *little* heavy on his hands. But by and large it was pleasant enough, and Emu did occasionally cast a glimpse over the waters to Upper Middle Earth, and have a long look, and then turn back to Asdar. And only once did he travel to Upper Middle Earth, and that for a brief time as it can be told below; and never again did he come to that land.

In Upper Middle Earth the days were marked by the sun rising and setting, and in the night-time the stars wheeled around the hub star in the northern sky. But the sun and the stars are material things, and they cast no light in Asdar, which is no material realm. Instead Emu had constructed a gigantic pole of gold, and at the top he placed a giant Sellāmi, crafted by his own hands. This strange and beautiful thing Emu imbued with great magical power, by processing the bounty of Asdar into a single mysterious artefact, something like a jewel: long, and slender, with gorgeous facets of pinky-red and dazzling white. And in this object Emu captured the light of illumination, and a certain flavour of brilliance; and he fixed it atop the tall pole. And it cast a great light over Asdar, and the inhabitants of that blessed realm said 'Ooh, isn't that pretty, that's *much* better, being able to *see* and everything, no more banging inadvertently into things and not knowing who you were talking to and so on, and indeed carrying on talking, thinking you were talking to somebody even though they'd actually moved away.'

And for a long age the beings in Asdar were content under the light of the Sellāmi.

But in Upper Middle Earth, the evil Sharon roused himself in the lightless dungeons of Winter-underland. And with the destruction of his Master Moregothic his power had diminished greatly. But though weak in evil he was still cunning; and he said to himself, 'If I steal the Sellāmi of Emu, then its potency will restore me.' And Sharon then said to his highest-ranking Orks 'I shall create a monster to terrify the world!'

And his Orks said, 'Yes! yes, my lord, bring terror to the world with your evil creation.'

'A dog,' I think, said Sharon, thoughtful.

To which his Orks replied, 'Um, OK, a dog, alright, I suppose so.'

'I mean,' said Sharon, hurriedly, 'a really *big* dog. No laptop pooch. A man-in-a-suit size dog. *Really* big teeth. A scary dog.'

'Scary, yes,' said his Orks, warming to the notion. And they added, 'Yes, why not. A dog – a hound, yes.'

And so Sharon created a monstrous dog; a huge beast with eyes like glowing coals and a hideous slaver. And he said to his Orks, 'Actually I was thinking of giving him something truly terrifying – put down that tankard of blood-wine, Yrkh. I don't want you to spill it on my leather carpet in terror when I say this – that's right – I was thinking of giving my monstrous dog—'

'Yes, my lord?'

'What, my lord?'

'—giving it – luminous fur!' And the evil Lord Sharon looked about his followers with eager eyes. 'What do you think, eh? Eh? *Pret*-ty *terr*-if-fying I should say. Don't you think? Don't you think that's the most terrifying thing you ever heard of? Eh? What? Eh?'

And the Orks looked frankly nonplussed, giving one another eyebrow-shrugging looks in what they hoped was a surreptitious manner, said, 'Er, very good my lord.'

'*Isn't* it?' said Sharon, earnestly. 'Isn't it, though? Puts the willies up *me*, I don't mind telling you, just thinking about it. The fur is *luminous* you see.'

'Right,' said Yrkh. 'Yes. I, er, see.'

'Yes, my Lord,' said another Ork, whose name has not been recorded by history. 'Willies, yes.'

'Ooo,' said Sharon, shuddering. 'Just the *thought* of it. It's like regular fur, only . . . it *glows in the dusk*! Ugh!'

And the teeth of this monstrous hound were long and pointy, but worse than their pointyness was their colour, a sort of yellowy-cream colour with little brown flecks. Most horrible was the pong that emanated from them. And the name of this hound was The Hound of the Bark-Evil, this being the most intimidating name Sharon could think of. 'Because,' he said, 'he is a hound of darkness and his very bark will be a bark of evil.'

'Excellent idea,' said the Orks, looking over their shoulders as if somebody they absolutely had to talk to right now had just walked into the room, even though no such person had in fact come in. 'Terribly scary. No, really.'

And Sharon sensed that his underlings were not as

scared by the whole luminous dog thing as he was, and said in a brisk tone, 'Yes, well, there we go, hideous hound. But I've also, actually, been thinking – maybe we need a *second* hideous creature to aid our evil schemes. I mean, in addition to the dog.'

And he mustered his army of Orks, and corralled the warrior ants together in the lowest of the low dungeons. And with monstrous science, and with the eye-gore harvested from hideously tortured victims, and a mutant assistant called Igor, he produced a hideous monstrosity, a vast warrior ant, thirty feet high, with huge protuberant compound eyes and alarmingly snickersnack mouthparts. And this creature Sharon called Ughganggooligooligooligooliwojda-ant, or Ughgooglyant for short.

And Sharon led his army to the coast, and built a mighty port, which he called 'Starboard' just to be awkward. And here he ordered that, for miles around, the trees be felled, and the timber be cutted; and his Orks did ask, 'You mean, oh Dark Lord, the trees should be *fallen*, and the timber *cut*?' 'Yes,' said Sharon. 'That.'

And the Orks built a great fleet of boats, shaped like ducks, with tall carved prows shaped like duckheads, and broad bases like ducks' undersides, and a little sticky-outy platform at the back. And these ships were dedicated to Wickedness; and Sharon called these ships Duck-W for that reason. W for Wicked, you see? And he sailed through the cold waters of the Capital C[13], and through the swell where the sea was green as turf and the hills of water shifted sluggishly, raising the ships up and dropping them down. And Emu, seeing this fleet approach the shores of Asdar, sent a great storm to sink the fleet; but the Duck-Ws were built robustly, and though the waters turned white, and waves thrashed and roiled, and the sea went all epileptic, yet still did they not sink.

'How are they doing that?' said Emu. 'I deliberately put a bleeding great ocean between Upper Middle Earth and Asdar to prevent things like this. How are they managing to avoid drowning?'

'They have built,' said the Valūpac in subdued voices, 'craft from wood, O Creator.'

And Emu said, 'You mean to tell me that that wood stuff *floats*? Well split my liver with a brass harpoon, I had *no* idea.'

And the Valūpac said, somewhat sheepishly, 'Um, didn't we, er, tell you about the floatiness when we created the trees, oh Lord? I thought we did. I mean,

---

13 Capital *Sea*. Sorry.

we certainly meant to tell you. Perhaps it got crowded out by all the other things we had to tell you.'

And Emu did look very severely at them. And he did mutter to himself crossly, 'Bloody great things, don't *look* like they should float, honestly, incompetence, it really is.'

And so it was that Sharon led an army of Orks, together with a giant luminous dog and a monstrous giant ant, into the fabled paradise of Asdar. And battle was joined.

The Valūpac did flash through the sky like lightning, and they felled Orks with great strokes of fire from the clouds; but Sharon mounted upon the neck of his gigantic ant, or 'gigantiant' for short.[14] And he galloped away over the hills of Asdar, with the great hound barking at its heels. Or, now that I come to think of it, perhaps not 'heels'. I think I'm in the right when I say that ants don't actually have, you know, *heels*; their legs probably go straight down to, I don't know, hooves, is it? But you know what I mean; the monstrous ant – well, I was going to say 'scuttling', since I suppose that's what ants do; but let's be honest, 'scuttling' just isn't a big enough word to describe the great lolloping strides of its twenty-foot legs.

---

14   Or 'gigant' for even shorter.

And on the beach the Valūpac put terror in the hearts of the army of Orks, and destroyed their ships utterly, and chased them into the sea. But Sharon was not amongst the slain.

And soon Sharon and his gigant and his dog arrived in that part of Asdar called Isle of Langahans, where the great pole, not a lamp-post, honestly, more just a pole that happened to have a light-emitting object at the top of it, was situated.

And the hideous hound of Sharon did sniff monstrously at the base of this great pole, and then, again monstrously, did relieve itself by raising one of its monstrous legs. And the Valūpac went, 'Urh, that's *foul*.'

At which Sharon did laugh aloud, for he rejoiced in the epithet 'foul'.

And Ughgooglyant did cut at the base of this pole with his terrible chitinous mouthparts, and did sever it through, such that it fell over with a mighty crash. And Sharon did wrap the fallen Sellāmi in grease-proof paper and tuck it inside his Evil Jacket. And, casting through his mind for the right thing to say at such a momentous moment, he called aloud, 'Aha! Ahahahah!'

And the Hound of the Bark-Evil did bark in

an evil way, and did snap at anybody who came close.

And Emu said, 'This is plain rubbing me up the wrong way and no mistake.' And he did lay a trail of gigantic luminous sausages over the pastures of Asdar in a sort of meaty dotted line. And the hideous hound of Sharon gobbled up the sausages one after the other, and was thereby led away from his Master, and over a hill, where Emu was waiting with a frying-pan of monstrous size. And he did smite the great dog on the head with this pan, and lay him low.

'Sharon,' he called, 'your Orks have been pushed into the sea by my Valūpac, and your dog has been felled!'

'Fallen,' Sharon called back. 'And I don't care.'

'Give way!' called Emu. 'Your blasphemous assault upon my paradise has been rebuffed. Your evil has broken over the rock of Asdar and fallen away like the fleeting ocean wave.'

But the laughter of Sharon was raucous and jibeish. 'The Sellāmi is mine,' he called. 'I shall carry it back to the fastness of the Winter-underland, where a great cleaver is waiting to cut it into many slivers – and with these fragments I shall grow strong. The power of your magic will sustain me for eons.'

A. R. R. R. *Roberts*

'There's no escape,' called Emu. 'You are surrounded. Your ships have been destroyed, your
army vanquished. Surrender!'

And Sharon called back, 'You'll never take me
alive, Creator!'

'Don't be a fool, Sharon,' called Emu.

And Sharon fired out half a dozen bolts of foul
magic, and Emu and the Valūpac ducked their
heads behind the hills of Asdar. And then Sharon
spoke to his ant, saying, 'I hereby promote you to
queen.'

And Ughgooglyant sprouted great grey-silver
wings, and launched into the air, carrying Sharon
away from Asdar, and back over the wide waters of
the Capital S[15], to Upper Middle Earth.

The blessed beings in Asdar did watch him fly off
with heavy hearts; and, since he was taking the
Sellāmi with him, darkness fell over the land of
Westersupanesse. And Emu, Creator of all things,
Supreme Being, did say: 'Oh.' And then did add:
'botheration.'

The great ant Ughgooglyant landed in the mountains
of Byk, in Upper Middle Earth, and Sharon did

15 Sorry. This should be C, obviously.

58

rejoice. 'Yea, now I possess the sacred Sellāmi, and it shall make me strong.'

As for Ughgooglyant, he, or perhaps I should say she as it turns out, tucked her wings back against her carapace and crawled into a deep cave in the mountainside, where he, she, it, whatever, laid many eggs, spawning hideous progeny that, although much smaller than their terrible parent, yet troubled the lives of Men and Elves for eons to come, spoiling their picnics, crawling in lines round the edges of their kitchens, and so on.

Emu was not pleased by this development. But, since the land of Asdar was cast into darkness by the loss of the Sellāmi, his Valūpac could not see the expression on his face, and decided to be hopeful about things.

'Well,' said Emu. 'First, I am *seriously* considering going over to Upper Middle Earth to have a word with that Sharon chap.' And the Valūpac were astonished, for Emu had never before travelled to Upper Middle Earth, and the rumour had gone round that he didn't like to travel actually.

'But most pressing on my to-do list,' said Emu, 'I'm going to reroute this ocean so that it doesn't lead directly to Asdar for any invading army that feels like floating here on those tree things that you made in Upper Middle Earth – and they looked so massive and heavy, too. Never crossed my *mind* that they'd be able to float in water.'

The Valūpac coughed, and mumbled something in reply here that was neither particularly audible nor supposed to be.

And Rhengo spoke up, saying, 'If you reroute the ocean such that it no longer leads here, where *will* it lead?'

'Oh,' said Emu, airily. 'I'll link it through an inter-dimensional gateway, and it'll turn up somewhere or other.'

Of The Great Battle of Taur-en-Ferno and the Disembodifying of Sharon

For many generations, Elf and Man had lived in peace in Upper Middle Earth. But now Sharon the Evil rose from the ashes of Moregothic's fall. With the great power of the Sellāmi of Emu, he was restored in evil; and he was able to use the immense power of the artefact to create for himself an army of wicked creatures: Baldtrogs, Giants, Scalyticks, I-Spiders with Maia-lidlaiders, Lurkers, Shirkers, Berks, Urks, Orks and Southwogs. And he led this army out from the frozen north to attack the south, and so avenge the death of Moregothic in the blood of Men and Elves.

This great force cut a swathe of destruction up through Illbhavior, and then cut a second swathe back down through Lothlomondwisky. Then they cut half a swathe, well a little over half if I'm being honest, let's say three-fifths, although it wasn't precisely that fraction, a shade under, alright if you want the exact number twenty-nine fiftieths of a swathe of destruction up into Blearyland. And they mustered at Taur-en-Ferno.

And Lord Sharon triumphed, ordering his men to sing 'We Are The Evil Champions' in mockery of Creator Emu's well-known predilection for sing-songs and all that. But, try as he might, he could not coordinate the voices of half a million evil creatures, such that the song which should have gone

We Are The Evil Champions, My Friend
And We'll Try our Hardest to Offend

instead sounded like a non-specific *waah-wooh* ocean of roaring that lurched upwards two tones and a semitone for 'hardest' but otherwise bore no relation to any tune known to man or elf. 'Alright, alright,' Lord Sharon ordered his horde, 'that's enough singing, blimey, what a racket.' And there was silence for a little space, with a little muttering, but then you'd expect a bit of muttering with a horde of half a million.

And against this fearful foe was assembled the great Army of Light. I mean light in the sense of *illumination* of course, sunlight and goodness and such, not light as in 'not heavy'. Some of these soldiers of the Light were very heavy indeed, let me assure you. I don't, by the way, mean 'fat', when I say that. I was going for more a sort of spiritual gravitas, combined with some big swords and, you know, shields and things.

Anyway, not to go off the point.

Emu, Lord of Light, Creator of the Cosmos, arrived at Taur-en-Ferno three hours late, saying, 'Sorry, sorry, something popped up at the last minute, what's going on here then?'

Now the Valūpac, Lords of Light, Lieutenants of Emu, were Gion, Poll, Gorge and Thingo; and they had assembled together a great army of the Good: Elves, Men, Dwarfs and some others whose names and addresses have been withheld at their own request. And this army occupied the higher ground at Taur-en-Ferno, arrayed in great ranks of gleaming golden armour and silver spears. And their helms shone in the light, and the sunlight glistened off their helmets, which as I'm sure I don't need to tell you are different things to helms, common mistake that, people always getting them confused. And their greaves were bronze. On their . . . um, legs, I think it is, that's where greaves go. Shins, I think. Or perhaps they're more sort of a codpiece. Anyway, anyway, that's not the important thing: the important thing is that their armour was all very neat and lovely, shiny in the sunshine, and there was *lots* and *lots* of it, armour, I mean, because there were just *loads* of soldiers – thousands and thousands, all properly arranged in neat ranks. As opposed to Sharon's army of evil beings, which was more like a rabble, people milling around, talking amongst themselves whilst their officers addressed them, and otherwise being disorderly. Really, behaving shockingly. Speaking with their mouths full. Scratching themselves. I'm sure you get the picture.

And Lord Poll, the Valūpac, knelt before Emu, Creator of the Cosmos, and said, 'Sire, we were awaiting your coming to lead our mighty army against the forces of Darkness, here arrayed before us, that ye may smite them utterly from Upper Middle Earth.'

And Emu did say, 'Right, lead the mighty army, I see. Well, that's all very fine and dandy and, you know, excellent, but the thing is I'm more involved in the *music* line of things. Less army ordering-about, and more, you know, singing and such.'

And Lord Poll said, 'But sire, your loyal men await your omnipotence to vanquish evil utterly and trample it before you.'

And Emu said, 'I *could* do that, yes, could do that, of course. But, the thing is, well, to put it at its simplest, I'm a lover, not a fighter. And, besides,

you're doing such a good job here that I think I'll just
– just—' And mighty Emu did smile weakly, and
look over his own ineffable shoulder at the lands of
Westersupanesse from whence he had come as if he
had just remembered something he had left there
that he really needed to pop back for, right this
minute.

And Lord Poll said, 'But Lord, the army assembled by Evil Sharon is great, and mighty in its
malignancy, and moreover has something of a hooli-
gan look about it, like it's all about to kick off.'

And Emu said, 'Tell you what, tell you what, I'll
have a quick – you know, do a quick – parley
thingumy, with Sharon. OK?'

And Emu, Master of Creation, did fly through the air
over the host, taking the form of a hippogriff, and did
reveal himself as Lord of Light on a patch of turf
where Sharon happened to be standing.

And Sharon mocked the Lord of All. 'Ha!' he
called, 'look who it isn't.' And his crack-o-doom
troops, the personal bodyguard of fang-toothed
Wargs, echoed, 'Har-har-har!', which as you know
I'm sure is the more withering and dismissive form
of the more conventional 'ha-ha-ha'. And Sharon
mocked and jibed, saying 'Well *upon* my soul if it

isn't the Lord of Creation. How *nice* of you to pop by.
How *well* you're looking. Did you lose weight?' and
other words of a similarly insincere and ironical
nature.

And the fang-toothed Wargs said, 'Har-har, good
one, my Lord.'

And Emu, Prince of Creation, did say, 'I'm warning you, your army is going to get a *pret*-ty *blood*-y
nose if you insist on, you know, all the fighting and
such.'

And Sharon said, 'You're warning me, are you?
Some nerve, that is. We shall micturate from an
elevated position upon your boys, that's what we'll
do.' And he laughed at his own circumlocutionary
mode of speaking, whereby a vulgar slang expression
is rephrased in a more pompous and elevated idiom
for comic effect. For such things amused him, and
he liked to say *extracting the michael* and *go forth and
multiply* and *Robert is your mother's brother* and things
along those lines.

And Emu said, 'Well, all I'm saying is, wouldn't it
be better for your lot to disband, not that I'm reading
the riot act or anything.'

And Sharon said, 'You don't frighten me.'

And Emu said, 'Oh, *don't* I.'

And Sharon said, 'No.'

And Emu said, 'Oh, *don't* I.' And he waved his hand, and Sharon lost all corporeal form, and his armour clattered to the turf in a great pile.

And Sharon said, 'Oi!' in surprise and alarm.

And Emu, looking round about with an innocent expression said, 'Sorry, what?'

And Sharon said, 'You pack that in, you've magicked away my corporeality, you cheater. Just you undo that spell, undo it *right now*, oo, I feel most queer, lacking all material bodily existence all of a sudden.'

And Emu said, 'Who, me?' with wide eyes.

And Sharon said, 'Don't act all innocent with me, Buster.'

And there was a great sucking in of breath by the fang-toothed Wargs, for Sharon in his pride had dared so daringly as to call the creator of all things Buster.

And Emu said, 'I don't know what you're talking about.'

And Sharon said, 'Yeah, right, like anybody else around here is liable to deprive a person of their corporeal form with a wave of their finger. Just give me back my body, and then we can get on with the, you know, fighting and warring and such.'

And Emu said, 'What's it got to do with me?'

And Sharon said, 'Now, come along, play fair. You are supposed to be the fair one, after all.'

And Emu said, 'Oh, give you back bodily form, is it?'

And Sharon said, 'If you don't mind.' And he spoke with a certain primness.

And Emu said, 'Well.'

And he waved his other hand, and Sharon resumed bodily form, but not the form he had had before. For where before he had been a towering shape of blackness, with mighty limbs and mightier thews, assuming thews come in the plural, as I think they do, not *entirely* sure what thews are, but pretty sure that Sharon's previous form had included them and that they were mighty – anyway.

—now he was a gigantic eyeball. He lay now upon the sward, three feet across, globular, and filled with vitreous humour. And he was squashy, lacking any internal skeleton or form; and bits of grass and grit did adhere to his moist, adhesive outer layer, causing him thereby some considerable discomfort, I don't mind telling you. Yet being one of the Valūpac, albeit a fallen one, Sharon could still speak. And he said, 'Stop mucking about, this is no good, I've not even got limbs.'

And Emu said, 'Corporeal form, didn't you say?'

And Sharon said, 'How am I supposed to pick up me sword? Couldn't you at least give me a tentacle or something? A tentacle, that is, with a, you know, opposable thumb, so that I can wield a sword? Or something?'

And Emu said, 'Is that the time? Look, I'd love to chat, I really would, but I have to fly.'

And Sharon said, 'What, not even an eyelid? Come on, one single eyelid, that can't be too much to ask. I'll get retinal burn-out without it.'

And Emu, Lord of Creation, transformed ineffably into a gigantic moth, and flew off, becoming a little distracted by a nearby campfire but soon sorting himself out and returning to Westersupanesse, never again to travel to the lands of Upper Middle Earth.

And Sharon's personal bodyguard picked up the Lord of Darkness, and wrapped him in the softest blanket they could find, although it wasn't especially soft, the quartermasters of Evil having earlier received strict instructions not to make their blankets too easy on the skin for fear of mollycoddling the troops of Darkness. And they laid him in a tent, where he complained bitterly about the twigs stuck round the back of his eyeball.

And the battle of Taur-en-Ferno was joined, and great was the slaying, the slayage, the slay-total, slayen, um, great was the number of the slain, and fires burnt the massive trees of the forest, causing the squirrels and birds to be trapped in the upper branches, until brave fire-squirrels fought their way up in little red outfits and rescued as many of the trapped as they could.

And after the battle was finished the Army of Darkness was in retreat over the lands of South Blearyland, although the Army of Light was also pretty pooped, and had been reduced to one-twelfth of its original size, what with casualties and so on.

And Sharon retreated to the grimly named land of Moider![16] And he ordered his Warg bodyguard to carry him to the very top of the tall tower of Cirith Connoli, where they positioned him under a sort of makeshift umbrella. And Sharon was even sourer in mood than before, and plotted a terrible revenge upon the world.

---

16 [*Author's note*] It is unclear whether this exclamation mark represents a glottal stop, or the mortal remains of an unfortunate parchment weevil who got under the elbow of one of the scribes. Gruf the Dwarf was the first of the free peoples to see this land with his own eyes; he returned in dismay, calling aloud 'It's Moider!, I tell ya!'

Of the New Way of King Bleary and the Effect This Had Upon the Elves of Upper Middle Earth

King Bleary the Elf called a great moot, or meet, one of the two, I'm not sure, could have been either one to tell you the truth, I had a sort of bunged-up condition afflicting my orifices when this story was related to me and to my wax-packed ears the two words sound exactly alike. But the important thing is that they met at the moot.

Or mot at the meet.

I fear I'm straying from the point.

'Elves,' said King Bleary, 'first of all, well done on defeating evil. But. Look: we need to improve our casualty reduction target-achievement-rates. And we need to reprioritise our strategic realignments. I've decided to take *personal* charge of the "Ultimate Evil: Just Say No" campaign.'

And, at his side, Robin 'Goodfellow' Cük, Prince of Elves said, 'Wearhllll *eek*! hmm grmm mnmm personcharsayno,' and concluded with a strange high-pitched whinnying.

And the King roused the moot with a great speech. 'We need a better tomorrow for Elves. And a better tomorrow after that tomorrow, and a better tomorrow after that tomorrow the day after tomorrow. This is not the end. It is not the beginning of the end. It is not the end of the beginning, nor the end of the end, nor the middle ending of the beginning's end – no! We have not reached. The end of our endeavour, nor. The ending of the endeavour's proper end. Indeed, it is quite hard to pinpoint exactly where we are on the line between beginning and end, except to say that we *are* on that line, and this I say to you without fear or favour. Let us therefore. Brace ourselves to do our duty. And move into the broad sunlit elflands of a brighter tomorrow, a cleaner, healthier, fairer, better, elfier tomorrow. Yet, if we work together. We can put behind us the hindmost, move beyond the hindsight, hinder the hinds. What is our aim? Victory, victory at all costs, victory never mind the price, costless victory, pricelessness, however victorious the victory may be.'

And the Elves were most impressed by this, and cheered their king loudly. And then the King said:

'After extensive negotiations with Lord Sharon I am pleased to say that we, the Elven people, are

The Sellamillion

able now to extend the hand of friendship to the
Orkadian peoples. With the best qualities of Lord
Sharon's belief-system matched with the core values
of our own, the future is bright. Thank you, Emu
bless you, and Emu bless Elflandia!'

Now Nodihold did say, 'Er, what was that last bit,
sire?'

'Emu bless Elflandia.'

'No, sire, the bit before the Emu bless bit?'

And King Bleary smiled. 'For too long,' he said,
'our land has been riven by the tired old ideologies of
"good" and "evil". It is time for us to wake up to the
truth of the modern world, that so-called "goodness"
does not work – however noble its aims it ignores the
reality of human nature, it cannot generate wealth or
provide the social cohesion necessary for a modern
elvish state. These tired and exploded dreams have
dogged us for too long! I say to you, the road to the
future is neither "good" nor "evil", but a third way, a
Bleary new ideology. Lord Sharon and I have had a
number of very fruitful and productive meetings on
this matter. I'm pleased to report that he is the sort of
Being of Evil I can do business with.'

'But – sire,' said the Elves assembled there, 'have
we not dedicated ourselves to fighting Sharon and all
that he stands for?'

'Which,' said Bleary, 'is *exactly* the point I am making. It's so last-generation, this knee-jerk denigration of Sharon's achievements. True, I have not always been in agreement with his personal style. But it is foolish to deny his many achievements, in slimming down the Upper Middle Earth economy—'

'—killing and laying waste—' cried Nodihold.

'—which are,' said Bleary, speaking more loudly and fixing his face in a more resolute expression as if to say *hecklers will not intimidate me, I speak out fearlessly*, 'which are both very effective ways in slimming down an economy, or indeed a country, cutting out the surplus fat and making Upper Middle Earth competitive on the global and interdimensional stages. My Blearyist way forward combines Sharonite vigour and energy with the best of the traditional "goodness" which has always been a proud part of elven politics.'

And the Elves were confused, and did say, 'Um, I don't know, sounds plausible I suppose . . .' whilst others did say, 'It's a betrayal of all that elfishness means', and so the debate continued, and King Bleary remained king for a little space.

But eventually the Elves realised that their king was a shyster of shocking depravity, and cast him from the throne, and exiled him from elflands forever. And he was compelled to go seek succour with Lord Sharon; and the former Prince Robin Goodfellow was renamed Robin Badchap, and sent away with his master, though he complained the whole time that he had been misunderstood, and that everything he said had been to contradict what Bleary had argued, yet could nobody understand his complaint, any more than they had been able to understand his original comments, and so his doom was sealed. And the Elves raised up a new king, called Gondor 'the Brownie'.

Of the Rage of Sharon

Now did Sharon concentrate and magnify his rage and despite.[17] And his vassals grew more afraid of him than before, since although he was only a gigantic eyeball nevertheless he was powerful, his will was strong, and few could stand beneath his stare without themselves blinking or looking away. And his Ork captains called him 'Stare-Master' and were themselves often starestuck in his presence.

But Sharon did complain mightily, saying 'It's *extremely* uncomfortable, I don't mind telling you, being a giant eye with no eyelid. I've got this permanent spot of blankness *right in the middle* of my field of vision. I didn't realise until this moment just how constricted the focusing power of the eye is – only a small percentage of the retina focuses a sharp image; most of the rods and cones relate movement, shade and colour in rather vague terms. And without eyelids the cells in that central portion of my

---

17   This sentence is either incomplete, or else it isn't. On balance I think I'll plump for the latter.

retina are frankly overstimulated, and are burning out.'

And Lord Sharon's retinal fatigue did make him vastly grouchy. And accordingly he planned a huge war against Elves and Men to take his mind off it, as far as that was possible.

And though he possessed mastery over his follow-ers, yet he possessed none of the motor anatomy or eyeball-musculature that moves the eyes in other creatures; and so to look upon something new he perforce must order one of his underlings to pick him up and physically relocate him.

At the beginning this process was uncertain, and Orks would lift his great spherical bulk with their faces averted, and expressions indicative of con-siderable distaste, for the skin of Sharon was slimy and unpleasantly pliant, and he did not smell good.

And on one occasion, Sharon, at the top of his tall tower in Moider!, ordered members of his personal Orkish bodyguard to re-orient him by lifting him and swivelling him through twenty degrees the better to view happenings on the Plains of Polcadot many leagues distant and far below his vantage point. But the Orks charged with this great deed did fumble, and jabbing Sharon in the tender part of the eyeball with an armoured knuckle, did make him call out 'Oi, watch it, clumsy', which inspired them with such terror that they dropped the great eyeball of Sharon.

And the eyeball of evil did fall from its special podium, and roll across the tower's topmost platform. And Sharon did call out 'He-e-ey! O-o-oh!'

And as the Orks scrambled to retrieve the eyeball they did collide with one another in their haste and terror, and one of them was in such fear that he ran hard into the side of the podium, breaking his nose.

And Sharon's eyeball rolled perilously close to the top of the spiral staircase, which staircase ran the whole length of the height and depth of the tall tower. And Sharon wavered on the top step. 'Quickly,' he called, 'catch me – use your foot if you have to – before I aaaaaiiiii!' And it was too late.

And Sharon did bump down the many stone steps of the spiral staircase, saying 'Ow! Ow! Ow!' all the way down. And at the bottom he did bounce surprisingly high, saying as he travelled through the air 'Oh noo-oo-*ooo*'. And an Ork soldier at the bottom made a flying leap to try and grab the Dark Lord in the air, but only succeeded in knocking him with an outstretched hand, such that he flew in a great arc through the main gate of the Tower of Cirith Connoli, and rolled away down the parched grassy bank outside. And the Lord of all Darkness finally came to rest in a ditch, pupil-downwards, and as his quivering Orks retrieved him from this undignified position he did say, in a worryingly calm-sounding voice, 'I am *far* from happy about this, I can tell you all *that* right now.'

And after Lord Sharon had been carried back up all the steps and reinstalled on his special podium, underneath the umbrella, he did order a severe punishment of the Orks who had handled him so clumsily.

And after this came Bleary the fallen elf to Cirith Connoli, abashed and cast out by his own people, and Robin Badfellow with him. And Bleary did say to Sharon. 'Look, I know that politics, ruling people, involves some tough choices. Some hard choices. Toughness and hardness. And I say, you know, *I'm* the man to make those tough choices and hard choices. There are those who say, Tuoni, *be* soft and weak, but I say, I'm sorry, that's just not the sort of elf I am. So I say *to* you, Sharon, look: you're a leader. On the world stage. And I'm a leader. On the world stage. You're a person who spans the generations, and who has been a source of inspiration, of one sort or another, to practically everyone. And so am I. So, *let* us put our differences behind us, and. Agree an alliance between our two great peoples.'

And Sharon did reply, 'My spies tell me you've been ignominiously kicked out of Elfland as a traitor.'

'Look,' said Bleary, 'a lot of things have been said by a lot of people. But let. Me just say this. We'll respond to those charges. At the proper time. And not before. We'll respond *after* the official enquiry has concluded its work. It would be quite wrong for me to prejudge the outcome of that enquiry.'

'You come to me as a worm crawls on its belly,' said Sharon, 'and as a worm you shall serve me, the lowliest of my lieutenants.'

And Bleary did reply, 'That's *luptenants*, O Evil One.'

And Sharon did say, 'Shut up.'

And Bleary did say, 'Certainly, O Dark Lord.'

Of the Death of King Gondor in Battle

Guided by the inside knowledge of Bleary, Sharon
was able to slip his troops past the defences of Elves,
if not those of Men. And one night, when the moon
was one-dimensional rather than two- and the stars
seemed more distant than usual, a troop of Orks
came silently out of the hills and attacked the elvish
city of Twinned-with-Elfton.

King Gondor was asleep, and yet he roused himself quickly and prudently and strapped on his
armour. And though many Elves were slain in their
sleep, yet many Elves did pull swords from under
their pillows or from specially constructed sword-
stands beside their beds, and battle the insurgents.

For Elves are fierce fighters, and do not easily lose
heart; and though the assault had the benefit of
surprise yet did it falter as the Elves rallied themselves. They pushed the Orks back and to the outskirts of the city, and as dawn began to smooth away
the darkness from the sky they had formed phalanxes and the Orks were in disarray.

Seeing, from his high place, that the battle was

going badly, Sharon summoned a hideous Baldtrog from his cave; and this great lumbering creature lumbered into the elven city, reducing many of the wooden houses to mere lumber with his great lumbering club. And the sunlight reflected from his hideous bald head did affright many Elves, and frighten them too. And seeing the confusion of their enemies the Orks did re-muster and assault again.

And King Gondor did cry, 'Let us not be down-hearted! Let us attack, but prudently!' And he led the charge, although with a fitting caution, and when the conditions of battle were right, and drove the Baldtrog back to the Stream Inkcold. And finally the Orks fled through the cold waters, and the Baldtrog, getting water on his bald head, did start to cry, and it seemed that victory would belong to the Elves. But at the last moment of the fight, an arrow pierced Gondor's body, and though the wound was not fatal the poison upon the arrowhead was.

The last moments of Gondor the Brave are recorded in the 'Ballad of The Last Moments of Gondor the Brave', still sung amongst the Elves to this day, unless they can think of something better to sing.

The Sellamillion

That day did Gondor, called 'The Brave'
   Get swatted by an arrow
Which stuck him in an early grave
   By sticking in his marrow.

At first he said, 'We must attack
   We must attack right now!'
But later he did say 'Alack'
   And also 'Urgh' and 'Ow'.

He led the elves in battle's press
   With awe-inspiring bellow
But now, as good as we can guess
   His bones have gone all yellow.

Laid low by his arch-enemy
   It's a coffin he's interred in;
His skin has gone all parchmenty
   And 'RIP''s his wording.

Poor Gondor! For Gondor, once 'the Bold'
Is now 'Gondor the Covered-in-mould'.
Gondor! Our once delicious king,
Is now a deliquescing thing.

Oh Gondor's lost his majesty,
And Gondor's lost his honour,
And Gondor's lost his middle d
For Gondor is a goner.

> *Oh no!*
> *An orkish arrow thwacks a tush.*
>   *Alas!*
> *'Tis Gondor's gluteus maximus.*
>   *Beware!*
> *An orkish warrior hacks him as*
> *He staggers from the strife.*
>   *Bewail!*
> *Just as French bread lacks houmous*
> *So Gondor lacks all life.*
>
> *He lies upon the grass*
> *With an arrow in his*
> *Body.*

The Orks were scattered to the hills, and hunting parties hunted them down. Party, here, is not supposed to suggest any kind of dancing, drinking or letting down of hair; these were very grim hunting parties indeed.

Gondor the Brownie was burnt upon a pyre; and his people mourned him for three days and three nights. And a new monarch was crowned, Queen Eve the Elven, daughter of Gondor and inheritor of the tainted line of King Bleary.

But because the Elves had fought the Orks alone,

an estrangement grew between the Elves and the Men. The Elves did say, 'Where were you lot, eh? Fine bloody alliance this turned out to be. Here it was, all kicking off, and you decided to have a bloody lie-in.' And the Men did reply, 'They attacked in the middle of the night! It was a surprise attack! How were we supposed to know?' And the Elves did say, 'You didn't exactly *fall over yourselves* rushing to help us when you did hear about it, did you?' And Men did say, 'Well, if you feel that way about it, maybe we'd be better off without an alliance.' And the Elves did say, 'Suits us.' And Men did say, 'Fine.' And Elves did say, 'Fine.'

So it was that the great alliance of Men and Elves fell into desuetude. And Queen Eve Attim, of the line of Arthur-Brick,[18] did vow: 'Nevermore shall my line have dealing with mortal Men.' And this vow caused great trouble in after times.

---

18 This noble elvish line of princes and princesses were so called because they combined the wisdom and courage of the fabled King Arthur with the strength and buildability of a brick. Apparently. And – before you say anything – yes, there *was* a mythological figure called Arthur in the traditions of Upper Middle Earth, just as there was in our world. Just one of those strange coincidences of names, that's all.

Of Belend and Lüthwoman

The First Part of the
Tale of Belend and Lüthwoman

At this time the kings of Men were drawn from the royal house of Prorn. King Prorn the Mighty ruled seventy years and he ruled wisely and well; but he was slain eventually in the Battle of Nirhastings, pierced by many orkish arrows.

His son, King Prorn II, inherited the throne, and he also ruled wisely for many years, but died at last, as is the fate of all Men. Historians disagree about how he met his end: some say that he died battling a monstrous Baldtrog; some that he was slain by an Ork raiding party; some that he led an assault against Sharon and was burnt up by lava on the slopes of Mount Dumb; and some that he died at home, straining at stool. He was succeeded in his turn by King Prorn III, known as the Grrreat.

Now the sons of Prorn III were Stronginthearm, who grew to manhood strong in the arm; and

Braveface, who grew to manhood with the bravest face in all of the realms of Men. No terror could frighten his face, no debilitating or demoralising emotion could cause his lip to crumple or his eyes to moisten up. And the third son of King Prorn was Belend, who grew to manhood with a certain impressive attribute, into which we shall not, at the present time and in the present company, go.

Belend was a solitary soul, who spent much of his time in the woods and amongst wild animals, although not in a, you know, *funny* way; nothing odd, just a healthy, manly enjoyment of the outdoors, fresh air, a good hike, the company of big hairy bears, and so on. And he grew to full manhood, and an extremely full manhood it was too, if you know what I mean. And one day he was walking in early autumn amongst the trees of Taur-en-Ferno, with their flame-red leaves and pollen blowing off the heads of oaks like smoke.

Now, Queen Eve Arthur-Brick Attim III had one child, and this was the beautiful Lüthwoman. And one day she went wandering in the woods singing songs, swimming naked in the pools, and doing all that kind of woodland thing.

And Lüthwoman was fairer than all the fair, well-formed, elegant, light-footed and fair, or did I say that already. Anyway, she was a princess of the Elvish race of outstanding natural beauty. And Belend, seeing her, fell in love with her immediately and without delay; and approached her chivalrously and got into conversation with her. And the two of them wandered amongst the trees, talking and getting to know one another; and the longer they talked the more Lüthwoman found herself drawn to Belend. For he was handsome and courteous, and as he told her tales of his many adventures, fighting Orks, travelling in the woods of the north, and befriending the wild animals she was favourably impressed.

She said, 'Belend, you are the throngetht and bravetht of the thonth of Men.'

To which Belend replied, after a short pause, 'You what?'

'Oh Belend,' gasped Lüthwoman, flinging herself upon him, 'My paththion for you ith a thrange and overwhelming thing! Though you be mortal and I a printheth of the elvith rathe, yet mutht I embrathe you! Take me in your throng armth and kith me. Kith me! Kith me!'

And Belend replied, 'No, didn't catch any of that.' But, being no fool, he did not spurn the physical advances of so beautiful a woman, and he kithed her long and hard.

❄

The love between Belend and Lüthwoman was a mighty love, a passionate and majestic love; and after a twenty-minute rest it was a passionate and majestic love a second time. And they resolved, she and he, that they must be married.

But there had never been a marriage between an Elvish woman and a Mannish boy; no, nor between an Elvish lad and a Mannish lady.[19] No, nay, never, nonaynever not once had elf mated with aught else but elf and mortal with aught else but mortal,[20] and that had always been the way it was. But the love between Belend and Lüthwoman broke through these barriers. It was Romeo and Juliet, it was Starsky and Hutch, it was Scooby Doo and Shaggy; it was a love that shattered preconceptions and flew in the face of society's prejudices, yea, veritably flew in society's-prejudice's face like a moth flapping and making society's-prejudice flap its hands around its face and go 'Urgh! Get off!'

---

19 I don't mean a lady with, you know, a moustache or anything like that. I mean a human woman. But you had already worked that out, hadn't you?

20 Nor ork with aught but ork, nor ort with aught but ort, but that's a different matter.

And Belend came to the Elven Queen Eve, of the Eleven Elves of the Evening; and did say, 'Um, ah, don't mean to butt in, um, sorry to,' for he was rather embarrassed and, not being in the habit of talking with royalty, he didn't know what to say. So he cleared his throat, and thought to himself 'Here goes' and said: 'I wonder if I might have an audience, ma'am.' But instead of saying 'ma'am' as he intended, he was so nervous that he sort of coughed or barked halfway through the word, saying 'ma-akh!-akh!'

And Queen Eve the Elven was not impressed.

She was sitting on her silver throne, at the head of her great hall, and the benches to the left and right were filled with the noblest and handsomest of the Elvish princes and princesses, who revered her as the inheritor of the line of Bleary and Gondor.

'What is it, mortal?' she asked. 'For never in many long years has one of the sons of Men dared to enter the halls of the Elven Queen. Know ye not that our onetime alliance has fallen to desuetude?'

'To what?' asked Belend.

'Desuetude.'

'Ah,' said Belend, nodding and going for an 'of course I understand what that word means' expression on his face. 'Anyway, I really fancy your daughter.'

And Queen Eve was astonished and astonied, as well as being astied and a'ed.

'Silence!' she cried. 'Insolent mortal!'

'Sorry,' said Belend, reddening, and standing awkwardly with one foot resting upon the other. 'It's just—'

'For know this,' cried Eve, lifting her arms for a more properly melodramatic effect, 'I am Queen of the Elves. I have taken a vow that neither I nor any of my line shall have anything to do with the sons of Men!'

'Right,' said Belend. 'Well that's a bit awkward, you see, because I was rather hoping that Lüth-woman and I could get married.'

'Marry her!' cried Queen Eve, in amazement and scorn.

'She and I are in love.'

At this Queen Eve laughed. 'Men know nothing of love! Only Elves have the capacity for love: in Men it is merely lust, sentiment, habit and self-delusion. For how could it be otherwise? For Elves endure, and so their love endures; but Men wither and fade, die and pass into nothingness, and so their love is fickle.'

'Nevertheless,' said Belend growing more confident, 'I love her, and she loves me; and we wish to marry.'

'Impossible! I shall never permit it.'

And Belend did shuffle about a bit on the smooth marble flags of the elven hall, and look about him at the rows of hostile faces. And he did say, 'Oh go on.'

And Queen Eve laughed loud and contemptuously; and her nobles, and princes, and princesses laughed, following the lead of their monarch. And Belend did blush redder still, faced with the derision of these haughty elven lords and ladies.

'I say,' he said. 'This isn't very courteous of you.'

'Never in my reign,' said Queen Eve, with a curl to her lips, 'has any mortal Man dared such boldness.'

'I love her, and she loves me,' said Belend a second time. 'I ask your blessing upon our union.'

'Blessing! Rather a curse. I say you shall not marry my daughter.'

'Be careful,' said Belend, growing bolder. 'Not lightly are the curses of Elves uttered, and easily do they go astray in the wide world. I say I will marry your daughter Lüthwoman, and so says she. Shall my word come into conflict with your word? Say again.'

'I am Queen of the Elves of Upper Middle Earth, ageless and deathless; you are mortal Man,' said Eve. 'Should your word and mine come into conflict, yours would shatter as glass and mine prove adamantine.

92

My own life will wither and die before my word is broken. But do you speak truly when you say my daughter has chosen you over a noble Elvish prince?'

'She has.'

Eve shook her head. 'It cannot be.'

'Why not? I am worthy,' said Belend, growing bolder still.

'Can you prove such worth?' asked the Queen. 'I say you cannot – it is beyond the power of any Man.'

'Not beyond *my* power, lady,' Belend boasted.

'Very well, Belend son of Prorn,' said Eve, laughing again though not kindly. 'So be it. I lay a task upon you. Fetch me the Sellāmi that Sharon hoards in his fastness in the dead land of Moider! – Bring me that treasure of Emu, which has fallen into the grasp of evil to our cost, and you shall have the hand of my daughter in marriage.'

And the lordlings and ladylings of Elfland did laugh at this task, for it seemed to them impossible to achieve such a quest. But Belend gathered himself up to his full height, five foot ten and three-quarters, and did say, as gravely as he could, 'I shall do this thing, my lady, and after it is done I shall claim what you have promised me.'

And Belend left the Halls of the Elves, to travel, as

all thought, to his certain death. And none who saw him leave expected to see him alive again.

The Second Part of the
Tale of Belend and Lüthwoman

And when Lüthwoman heard what task had been set upon her beloved Belend she wept, and he comforted her in his special way, which stopped her weeping but not her cries. And after this the two of them resolved to embark on this perilous quest together. 'For,' said Belend, 'Two heads, like two breasts, are better than one.'

And Lüthwoman did say, 'Cheeky!' and make as if to slap him, but did not really slap him, it being a feint, comical play-acting of a pretend outrage rather than an actual assault.

And they did kiss once more, and caress, and make cooing noises, and call one another 'snooglums' and 'wiggly-pig' and 'jonny-tommy' and such like. And any persons that overheard them in this exchange did desire to throw up, frankly.

So it was that, one bright morning, Belend and Lüthwoman rode out together from the yellow-green spring leaves of Taur-Ea-Dorpants, and along the bridle path that they hoped would lead to a bridal path, and thence to an unbridled passion, and similar puns upon the word 'bridle' too numerous and too groany to list here.

'But,' said Lüthwoman, 'how thall we protheed? For Moidor! ith many leagueth from here, and there are hordeth of Orkth and other uglieth between uth and the throne of Tharon, Lord of Evil, Lidleth Eye that ever watcheth our advanthe. And the Thellāmi of Emu ith his motht preciouth pothethion, the object from which hith magical power largely deriveth – and none knowth in which guarded room or locked thafekeep he holdth it.'

To which Belend replied, 'Right, insofar as I understood any of that, I *think* you're asking about how we're actually going to go about grabbing this Sellāmi thing, yeah?'

And Lüthwoman nodded.

'Oh,' Belend said airily. 'I'm sure something'll come up.'

And they travelled for many days, south and east and slept at night under the far off stars, lying in one another's arms for warmth. On the third day they came to the mighty River Raver.

Now, the River Raver is the widest and wildest of

all the rivers of Upper Middle Earth. It gallops through its sharp-cut banks faster than the fleetest horses; and it is deep and cold, for its waters flow straight and hard from the frozen peaks of the Blue-joke Mountains, the Ered Loonpants. It is a league wide at its narrowest, and no bridge crosses it; and along its length are many waterfalls and stone-jagged tumbles. And no swimmer, mortal or elf, had ever gone into these waters and reached the far side.

Here Belend and Lüthwoman stopped for a day and a night, for they could not see how to cross the foaming torrent. Belend constructed a boat from leaves, which he stitched together with strands of grass. It was just about large enough for two, and it took the shape of a hollowed-out avocado skin. But when Lüthwoman looked at it she said, 'If you think I'm getting into *that* to croth the mighty river, you're very much mithtaken.'

And Belend did reply, 'Hey I understood all of that! I'm definitely getting better at understanding you.'

And looking again at his leaf/grass construction, he had to agree with her that it was pretty flimsy-looking, actually. So they did not attempt to cross the river that day, and slept on its banks that night.

The following morning the song of dawn birds rose

like flute music over the drone of rushing waters, and the sun was young and bright in a pale sky. Belend and Lüthwoman departed from their path. They made their way along the northern bank of the River Raver. After a day's trek their ears became weary of the incessant roar of the river, which grew almost as a great weight upon them, heavier with each hour. And Belend craved silence, and the peace of a forest glade; and Lüthwoman craved warmth, and air dry with midday sunshine, for her clothes and hair were wet with the spray that swirled from the water like smoke at its many rapids, waterfalls and hollows. The very air was damp and cold.

Their hearts misgave.

And Belend did say, although he had to yell for his voice to be heard above the shout of the river, 'Shall we return to Taur-ea-dorpants? Shall I take you back to Elftonjon and face the scorn of your mother? For I fear we shall never cross this great river.'

And Lüthwoman did reply, speaking shrilly in her attempt to raise the volume of her words above that of the flowing water, 'Thith eth*peth*ial thummit of thircumthtanthes ith thuch that thlinking back to the foreth ith thtrark impothible, or tho it theemth to me.'

Belend looked puzzled momentarily, and then he did grin exaggeratedly, and nod, and say, 'Yes, yes, quite right', as if he understood any of this.

They slept another night beside the titanic growl of the river, and the sound of it insinuated into their dreams and made them uneasy; and Belend dreamt that he stood before a great crowd who jeered and yelled; and Lüthwoman dreamt that she moved amongst innumerable lowing cattle of gigantic size.

In the morning Belend tried to catch fish with a line from one overhanging crag of the riverbank; but the fish of the River Raver are swift-moving and their thoughts are cold as the water, and few are attracted by a fisherman's lure. And so the two went hungry and walked east, always hoping that as they moved upriver it might grow less fierce, or flow more navigably, or that they might come to shallows or a bridge. But they did not.

And in the evening, sore and weary, and hungry, they came to a glade of conifers. And within this wood they chanced upon a house, little more than a hovel, made of whole timbers and roofed with a thatch of fir-sprigs. And they hallooed at this door, and said 'Anybody home?' and 'Hello?', which word is more usually a greeting than a question although they used it in the form of a question on this occasion.

Now, inside this dwelling lived a being of great age and great wisdom; and she had many names: she was called Witch?, or Dot, or to those who were fond of her, Auntie Dot: although, in the original language of the making of the world, her name had been at first *Punctus*. And she came out of her hut as a crone, very aged although her eyes were bright: it was as a crone that she had been first made, for she stood at the end of things. She smiled at her visitors.

'My lady,' said Lüthwoman, 'can you give uth your aid?'

'We have travelled far and are hungry,' said Belend. 'We are sorry to trouble you.'

'Young lovers,' said Witch?, 'you are welcome. I know you, Belend, and you also Lüthwoman, most beautiful of the daughters of Elves. And I know all about your quest.'

Belend and Lüthwoman were amazed; and Belend asked: 'Are you a witch?'

'I am Witch?'

'That's what I asked.'

'No,' said Witch? 'That is my name. Witch? – with a question mark at the end like that.'

'What – Witch??'

'Witch?'

'That's what I was asking you.'

'I was confirming what you said.'

'Dame Witch?' said Belend. 'I am confused. I have never before heard that names might have question marks at the end of them.'

And Witch? cackled at this.[21] 'Punctuation is my being, children. For in the beginning of things, the world was made as a beautiful though formless thing, because it derived from the affecting but insufficiently descriptive song of Emu. And the four great Dragons of Making did fly through the unformed world and did *speak* the world we see into existence – the sky and sea, the mountains and the rivers; and later Emu's angels came and spoke other words, speaking the fields and birds, the forests and animals into being. The world around us is a sentence, named into being. But a sentence must end with a punctuation point, or it will unravel; and so I was spoken into being: and so it is that I am the oldest of this world's created beings. And my function is crucial, for without me the sentence as a whole would not make sense.'

Belend was amazed to hear this. 'And so,' he asked, 'great mother, what manner of punctuation point are you?'

---

21 She wasn't laughing. This was a sort of cough that afflicted her, 'cak! cak! cak!'.

And Witch? did smile. 'To know that,' she said, mysteriously, 'is to understand the nature of existence. Such knowledge comes only with great effort, my children, and cannot be simply given away to all who pass and think to frame the question.'

'Well,' said Belend, pondering for a moment. 'It's either going to be a full stop, or a question mark, isn't it?'

'Or a colon?' essayed Lüthwoman.

'Well, a colon doesn't really end a sentence, does it?' countered Belend. 'No, I think it has to be a question mark or a full stop. Or perhaps an exclamation mark. Unless the sentence of the world ends with a dash like an experimental poem – and I don't think that sounds right.'

'You are wiser than first impressions might suggest,' said Witch?.

'Does the fact that you are known as Witch? mean that your nature is that of a question mark?' Belend asked the old woman.

'Not necessarily,' she replied. 'For I am also known as Aunt Dot, to some.'

Belend thought about it. 'It seems to me, great mother, that you are a question mark for all that; because I would prefer to believe that the world finishes in an open-ended manner, and that when it does end it will be answered in some way. If it ends only with a full point, then it is a closed thing and a limited thing; and I would prefer to believe that it is open.'

'Sir Belend,' said Witch?, 'you speak well, and what you say may be true or it may be not. Although there is a danger for anyone in shaping your understanding of the world around your preferences – for the world is not necessarily what you wish it to be. But I will say this: because of who and what I am, I live at the end of things, looking back. And so it is I know many things: I know your natures and your hopes, and I know the powers that oppose you – and they are mighty and terrible.'

'Can you help uth?' asked Lüthwoman, in a quavery voice, which is to say, crisply.

In reply Witch? smiled, and invited them inside her house for some tea.

Inside was dark, close and smoky; and yet a bright fire burnt in a flagstone grate, and there were tree-stump stools and a low table. And Aunt Dot the Witch? fed her guests with honeyed bread and fresh-brewed tea.

'So, my children,' she said, when they had supped their fill. 'You are hoping to cross the great river?'

'We must make our way to Moider! to confront the evil Sharon and regain the Sellāmi of Emu which was stolen. For only by doing so can we marry.'

'And it is marriage you wish?'

'It is.'

'Sharon is very old and powerful, and full of evil,' said Aunt Dot, gazing into her turf fire. 'His magic is a strong magic. But I am older, and my magic is stronger still.'

'Will you help us, great mother?' asked Belend in an agony of hope.

'Sir Belend,' said the crone, smiling. And the ridges and grooves of her aged face glistened in the firelight. 'All things are written into the great sentence of the world, all things for good or evil. I can change neither the letters nor their order.'

'It mutht,' said Lüthwoman, 'be a pretty long and complicated thententhe, all in all.'

'Oh, it is, Princess Lüthwoman,' said the crone. 'And few understand it. Even Sharon does not – at least not entirely, although he *thinks* he does.'

'But you understand it?' asked Belend.

To this Dame Dot only smiled.

'Great mother,' said Belend, humbly. 'I do not understand. Since you are so great and so powerful, why do you not claim this world as your own, and rule it in great majesty and state? – instead of living here as you do, in this small hut of wood thatched with fir-sprigs?'

'Don't you like my house?' asked Dame Dot.

'Oh no-no-no,' said Belend, hastily, for he had enough wit to know that it does not do to offend a witch. 'It's lovely, really lovely. Very nice. Rustic. Very rustic. Compact and bijou. It has,' he added, searching hurriedly for the right words 'um, tremendous charm and simplicity.'

'I actually *prefer* the dark, window-free look, mythelf,' said Lüthwoman, nodding along energetically with what her lover was saying.

Dame Dot seemed amused at this, and poked the fire with a charred lump of wood. 'To answer your question, Sir Belend,' she said. 'There are those who have wisdom, and there are those who have power. And then there are those who have power *and* wisdom, and having both means being wise enough to know that power is a poisoned sweetmeat. You ask me if I will help you reach Sharon and recover the Sellāmi. I can help you. But only if you know the magic charm that will compel my help.'

She looked inscrutably at them, and then inscrutably at the fire. And the fire looked back inscrutably at her, although Belend and Lüthwoman looked not inscrutable but alive with hope and anxiety.

And Belend did rack his brains for all the magic words and charms he had ever heard, and all the stories of witches his wetnurse had ever told him, to try and think what form of words might compel so magical a creature to help them. And the longer he thought the more confused his thoughts became, for he had no magic in him, and was not wise in magic lore.

But Lüthwoman spoke. 'Aunt Dot will you help uth,' she said, '*pleathe*?'

And this was indeed the magic word. 'Yeah, alright,' said the witch.

The crone got to her feet and shuffled across her rush-strewn floor to a rude wooden box in the corner of her hovel. This she opened, whereupon its rusty hinges made a rude noise, for it was a rude box. She took out something wrapped in cloth, and brought it over to Belend and Lüthwoman.

'You have many perils before you, and even if you achieve your end your perils will not be over,' she said. 'Take this,' and she handed Belend a small square of stiff parchment. And upon the parchment was written: '*Get ye Gone fro Gaol*'.

'What does this do?' Belend asked.

'I'd have thought it was obvious,' returned the crone, a little crossly, as if Belend's slowness of mind annoyed her. 'Just you stick that in your pocket or pouch for now. And you, my lady, take these.'

And from the cloth she took three small things, each no larger than a knucklebone. These she gave to Lüthwoman. And looking closely at them, Lüthwoman thought them the dried husks of insect bodies, or the fossilised cocoons of some locust or cricket-type thing.

'These,' said Witch?, 'before you start nagging me with questions, are Bugs of Truth. Very useful creatures. They are inert in the presence of truth, wrapped into their shells as you see; but they feed upon *untruths* – and in the presence of an untruth, they will come to life and flight, and devour the lie as it flies. But pay attention: each will only eat one untruth – after that they fly away, burrow into the ground, digest the lie, and produce an egg, a process which takes twelve years. So it is that they are precious, and rare, and I'd recommend you not to waste them. Carry them with you – but I warn you, if either of you utters a lie, they will burst to fluttering life in your pockets and you will lose them.'

'What happens when they devour the lie?' asked

Belend, who was far from clear on the point of these strange beasts.

'The speaker's words are turned from untruth to truth of course!' snapped the witch. 'You're not very with it, are you? Now, off you go, off you go, get on with your quest thingie and leave an old woman to her bingo and Battenberg.'

Belend and Lüthwoman thanked the crone long and sincerely. 'But,' said Belend, tentatively, for he was aware of the risk of outstaying their welcome, 'we cannot cross the mighty River Raver, so how can we come to Moider!?'

The crone went '*tch!*' and shook her head, but she spoke kindly. 'Alright, alright. Come outside.'

And they came out of the hovel into the glade, and the roaring of the river was loud in their ears again, and gnats swirled in the air like pollen, and the air smelt of pine and turf and woodsmoke. Behind the hut was a woodpile upon which were two leather saddles; they were slim saddles, without stirrups, but they were beautiful, for they were decorated with elegant swirled patterns. 'Take these,' said the crone, and even though she spoke quietly Belend and Lüthwoman could understand her perfectly despite the roar of the river.

'What shall we do with them?'

'Take them to the river's edge,' said the crone, turning away from them to go back inside her hut. 'Saddle the horses you find there, and you will be able to ride across the river.'

They thanked the crone with all their hearts, and left her glade carrying the gifts she had given them, and made their way down to the riverside.

The Third Part of the Tale of Belend and Lüthwoman

So Belend and Lüthwoman returned to the River Raver. But at the river's edge they found no horses, and though Belend searched all the fields and copses about they found none, nor any trace that horse ever came so far south.

And they thought they would return to the crone's hut and ask her advice; but although they retraced their steps through the dewy grass, and though they found the glade again, yet they could find within it no trace of the crone's hut, or the crone herself. And by searching fruitlessly they wasted many hours, until finally Belend said: 'I think she is only to be found when she chooses to be found; for she is a creature of great and tricksy magic. We will not find her hut, howsoever long we look, unless she herself wishes it.'

So they went back down to the river's margin, and sat there. It began to rain, gently at first, and then with more force. Belend and Lüthwoman huddled together under a riverside tree, even though it gave them but poor shelter; and they watched the rain making stubble on the river's rapid surface, and they listened to the grass hissing under the rain.

Away to the west were the dragon-sculpted peaks of the Ered Loonpants, enormous, overstriding the horizon. The two lovers stared at the distant mountains through the drizzly air, and could see that a mighty storm was playing amid the purple-white peaks. Clouds black as night-sky were snagged on the summits like billowing robes in the strong wind. They blurred the mountains with torrents of rain, and stitched peak to peak with threads of lightning.

'If that storm moves from the mountains west,' said Belend, speaking the thought that was in both their hearts, 'then we will be drenched.'

'Or worthe,' said Lüthwoman, looking at the spate; for the river was swollen with rain and rode high against its banks. 'If it floodth . . .'

And Belend and Lüthwoman held one another more tightly, and wondered what to do.

❋

The storm seemed to grow less, and after a little while the rain lifted and sunshine fell instead of water. Belend and Lüthwoman stood and looked about them, feeling their hearts lighter. And in the tree above them a bird chirruped over and over, like a squeaky wheel.

Belend shielded his eyes with his hands and looked to the mountains on the horizon; and his heart grew heavy again. For the storm was still playing hugely about the peaks of the Ered Loonpants. Grape-coloured clouds were piling higher and higher upon them, throwing strands of lightning at the mountains, and washing them with heavy rains. And as Belend looked, he saw avalanches; and though they were so distant they looked like shards falling from chalk, yet he knew they were truly vast quantities of snow tumbling down the mountain, to fall into the cold lakes at the base of the mounts from which the River Raver flowed.

And as he watched, he saw a bulge of water move, seemingly slowly in the great distance, down the higher reaches of the river. And he knew the mighty river was breaking its banks in a vast spate. 'Lüthwoman,' he said, taking hold of her. 'The river is flooding, as you feared. The floodwaters will reach us in a short while; and the time is too short for us to escape. Even if we were to climb this tree, it would be swallowed by the angry waters, torn roots and all from the ground and broken in the fury of the flood.'

'Mutht we, then, die?' asked Lüthwoman.

'If we must,' said Belend, 'then I am glad to die with you. For in death we shall not be divided, and my dearest wish is to remain with you, unsundered, forever. For your mother swore that she could never consent to our marriage; and I swore regardless that we would always be together. And now it seems to me that Fate has found a way for our two oaths to hold, neither being broken, and neither conflicting with the other. For although no ceremony has joined us, yet death will join us; and although your mother has still not consented to our marriage yet shall we always be together.'

And he wept, and Lüthwoman drew him closer to her. They could both hear, above the noise of the rushing waters, a deeper thrum, as the front of the spate drew closer to them.

'We must clutch one another tightly,' said Belend, 'so that even when we drown our bodies are joined.'

'And mutht we then drown?' asked Lüthwoman in fear.

Belend replied: 'We cannot escape.'

But as he spoke the words a Bug of Truth came to life in Lüthwoman's pocket, and struggled against the cloth. It flew out into the air and devoured Belend's words as he spoke them, such that – as much to his surprise as to hers – he found himself saying 'We shall never drown, you and I, for such is not our fate.'

And the Bug flew into the high air and was carried on the winds to the west.

'I don't underthtand,' said Lüthwoman. 'You thaid the flood was inethcapable. Tho why do you now thay that it ith not our fate to drown?'

Belend looked at her with a wild surmise, his eyes bright. 'I thought to say that we must drown,' he said. 'But a Bug of Truth took my words from the air! I must, inadvertently, have spoken an untruth when I said we must drown. Can it be that we will survive? But how?'

And at that moment, with a roar that shook the trees, the floodwaters raced round the river's bend. Belend saw the foaming whitecaps at the wave front, and he suddenly understood. 'Quick!' he cried. 'Take up the witch's saddles – for there,' he pointed, 'are the horses we must ride across the river!'

Lüthwoman's hands had only just grasped her

saddle, holding it before her, when the wall of water struck. She cried in fear, and Belend did so too: but the flood flung them high in the air, clear of the water, and as they came down their saddles fastened to the surging backbones of foam of the river. Lüth-woman, agile and elven, pulled herself round and settled gracefully into her saddle even as it twisted and shook on the river's back; and although Belend was clumsier and tumbled back into the water, yet his arms were strong and he did not let go of the magic leather. And he was able to haul himself upwards and pull himself onto the saddle, such that he too was sitting astride the river's spate. And in this fashion they clung to the pommels, and rode the bucking waters.

The Fourth Part of the Tale of Belend and Lüthwoman

And so Belend and Lüthwoman rode the flooding River Raver, flying gloriously past the landscapes of lower Blearyland. And sunlight smashed a thousand rainbows from the foaming spray all around them; and joy lifted their hearts.

For some time they rode the river west; and

Belend began to worry that they would be swept out to sea before the flood abated. But shortly the river widened, and turned to the south, and here the flood burst its banks completely, and Belend and Lüthwoman were carried swiftly over the fields of the South.

And fast as eagles they came to the low hills that mark the beginnings of Moider! Here there was a bend in the hills upon which Sharon had encamped a great army of Orks, and it was called 'Ork-knee' because it somewhat resembled a knee, and because Orks lived there. These Orks were placed there by Sharon to guard the northern approaches of his kingdom.

When they saw the approaching floodwaters they abandoned their posts and fled; but the fastest legs cannot match the speed of floodwater, and they were caught and drowned, trampled (as it seemed to Belend and Lüthwoman) under the very hooves of their watery steeds.

It was against these hills that the floodwaters spent themselves, ebbing and dissipating into numerous pools and marshy land. And Belend and Lüthwoman were lowered to the ground, until they had been deposited on the splashy turf. They found each other and embraced, and then sploshed through the knee-high water until they had moved upland and into a drier area.

'We have saved ourselves many days' walking,' said Belend, 'and we have slipped past Sharon's guards. These hills grow into the mountains of Moider!, ahead; and if we press on we shall arrive at the very lair of Sharon himself, the Evil One.'

'We are near to the end of our quetht,' said Lüth-woman. 'But how thall we prevail upon Tharon when we come to him? How thall we compel him to give up the Thellāmi?'

And Belend had no answer to this question.

They made their way up into the higher ground, and the Unpleasant Mountains rose starkly before them. These mountains, bare of vegetation and black with volcanic sand, surrounded the terrible land of Moider! which Sharon had claimed as his own.

Belend and Lüthwoman thought they had seen enough water, and been drenched and chilled enough, for a lifetime; yet that night, as they huddled together in a hollow of black sand, they were thirsty, and wished for moisture.

'If we are thucthethul in our quetht . . .' Lüth-woman began.

'Thuck-what?' interrupted Belend.

'Don't be cheeky,' she said, slapping him lightly on his manly chest. 'All I'm thaying ith – if we return to Blearyland with the Thellāmi – thall we marry?'

'Of course, my darling.'

'And live together?'

'Yes; for I could no more be parted from you than parted with my own heart.'

'Where thall we live?'

'I shall build us a great house in the forest, equidistant between your home and mine. It shall be a mighty timber structure, three stories tall, with many chambers; and it shall be beside a forest lake, fringed with poplar and elm.'

The thought of this pleased Lüthwoman. 'And how will the interior be decorated?'

'The what?'

'The interior.'

'Well,' said Belend. 'I really hadn't given it much thought, to be honest. Some open pine, I suppose. Antlers over the fireplace. That sort of thing.'

'I wath thinking,' said Lüthwoman, 'cuthionth.'

'Cushions?'

'Yeth. And three piethe thuites. With throwth.'

'Srows?' said Belend, growing confused.

'No – *throw*th. And a floral pattern on the wallth. A bit of chrome in the kitchen, perhapth.'

'You'd like that?' said Belend, a little aghast.

'Oo yeth, I like a bit of chrome in my kitchen. Flowerth everywhere. And bowlth of dried bloththom. Do you like the thought of that, my darling?'

To this Belend replied, 'Yes, my love – anything that makes you happy.' And his words provoked a flutter in Lüthwoman's dress; and in the moonlight one of the Bugs of Truth flew out. It caught Belend's words in the air, and gobbled them down, such that Belend heard himself saying instead 'It sounds so appalling that it makes me want to gouge my scalp with daggers or squeeze cacti under my armpits, anything to take my mind off the thought of it.'

And Lüthwoman leapt to her feet in outrage and hurt, crying 'Belend! How could you be tho unfeeling!'

And Belend leapt likewise, and said, 'Never mind that now! We've lost another of the Bugs of Truth – that's two down, and only one to go. Catch it, quickly – they're too precious to lose!'

But leap and grab as they might, the Bug of Truth escaped them, and flew high in the air to flutter away eastwards.

'That leaves only one Bug of Truth,' said Belend. 'We'd both better be careful not to utter anything untruthful, or we'll have none of the critters left at all.'

But Lüthwoman was still in a huff about Belend's hurtful comment; and she insisted she sleep alone in the hollow of black sand, and that Belend sleep 'over there' on top of the mound of sand, and added that 'if he thought he wath getting any tonight' then he had 'another thing coming'.

In the morning they were reduced to licking the dew from the bald rocks of the Unpleasant Mountains. And they trekked on, and made their way towards a gap between two peaks. 'On the far side of that,' Belend said, 'is Cirith Connoli, the tower in which the evil Sharon resides.'

They walked all day, trudging through the dark sand, and they walked on into the cool evening; and by midnight they had passed over the shoulder of land. And on the far side they slept. And in the first light of dawn they saw before them the mighty tower of Cirith Connoli, tall and slender, like a great black stick of celery reaching into the sky. I mean, ridged and stiff like celery; not moist or sprouting little green leaves like celery. Obviously. But I just thought I'd make that absolutely clear. Wouldn't want there to be any misunderstanding.

'Perhaps,' said Belend, his throat parched and stomach empty. 'Perhaps we should have brought a sack, or something, filled with provisions, some food, a canteen of water.'

And Lüthwoman nodded. 'Well,' she said, resignedly, 'we'll know for nectht time.'

And they picked their way down the side of the Unpleasant Mountains, and approached the base of the tower.

The tower was guarded by Sharon's personal bodyguard of Orks; and a cohort was stationed at the main entrance.[22] Belend and Lüthwoman snuck up behind a great boulder and peered round the edge of this to spy out the area. 'How can we creep past those guards?' Belend asked. And after asking this question he looked around, and said, 'Lüthwoman? What do you – Lüthwoman? Where are you?'

And he looked forward and saw Lüthwoman walking in plain sight up to the guards. And he did say, 'Oh crikey,' and hurry from behind the boulder to catch her up, calling 'Lüthwoman! Wait for me!'

---

22 The Ork army operated on the following structural principle: the basic soldier was the individual Ork; above that was the pairing of ork soldiers, the 'co-ork'; above that the band of one or two dozens Orks, the 'cohort'; and finally the mass, or 'cohorde'. Occasionally Orks were sent into battle without the backup of a cohorde, which is to say 'cohordless'.

And Lüthwoman, Princess of Elves, stood proud before the gate, and said 'I am Lüthwoman of the Elveth of Taur-ea-dorpantth! Thith ith Belend of the Landth of Men. We have come to thpeak with your mathter, Tharon! Take uth to him!'

And the Orks were greatly surprised and clustered around the pair, prodding them with spears and growling in their own dialect, Orkockney. 'Wos your game? Nah! Yuravinalarf, intcha? Leave it aht!' and so on.

And they hustled Lüthwoman and Belend into the tower and dunked them in a dank dungeon. In addition to being dank this dungeon was also dark. And dinky. Here they clung to one another, and Belend asked his love 'Why did you walk up in plain sight like that?' And she replied, 'I thought it would be a good idea. Anyway, we're inthide now, aren't we?' And he did say, 'Inside a dungeon.'

Sharon kept Belend and Lüthwoman in the dungeon for three days and three nights; and he fed them only spoiled meat; and they drank only what they could scrape from the cold stone of the walls. But after a time he became curious as to why they had come, unarmed and alone save for one another, to his tower. So he had them taken from the dungeon and brought before him.

And so it was that Belend and Lüthwoman beheld the giant eyeball of Sharon; and it was a little shrunken from its glory days, but still it was a giant globe of evil. Although the white portion was rather scuffed, and bloodshot like a child's red-crayon drawing of winter trees, and dented. And he had been placed by his underlings upon a special dais.

The great Lidless Eye of Evil did laugh and say 'Whom have we here? An Elf woman and a mannish, um, Man? What brings you to my lair?'

'An age ago,' said Lüthwoman, 'you thtole the Thellámi of Emu. We have come to retrieve it from you.'

At this Sharon laughed again, heartily. Or eyebally, I suppose, if you want to be strictly literal about it. 'Indeed I did steal the Sellámi!' he crowed. 'And I have no wish to return it. Why should I? It is mine, and I relish the power it gives me. Do you see this?'

And around his spherical body Sharon wore a chain of black gold.[23] And pendent on his chain was a slice of the sacred Sellámi itself, cut from the whole Sellámi, and with a circle hollowed out from its

---

23 Which is to say, a chain made from a special form of metallic gold that looks black – not a chain made from *oil*. That would be a pretty ridiculous object. You wouldn't be able to hang anything on it, for one thing.

centre so that it could be threaded onto a chain. Lüthwoman and Belend gasped with horror when they saw it – for only a creature of the lowest evil would desecrate so sacred object as the Sellāmi by slicing a sliver from it, and then hollowing out the middle, such that it became a mere hardened circle of rind. Yet did this 'Thing' possess some of the power of the sacred Sellāmi.

'You have mutilated the Sellāmi!' cried Belend.

'Ach,' said Sharon, dismissively. 'It's only a sliver. The rest of the Sellāmi is intact; I am keeping it for my future purposes. You see, the magic of the entire Sellāmi is too *potent*, even for a being such as I – it being created by the Creator himself. Trying to use the entire Sellāmi for my magic ends was like trying to paint a three-foot-by-three-foot picture using an entire fir tree as a brush. But *this* way I wield the power of the whole artefact *in miniature*. Much more manageable. I can produce mini-artefacts chipped from the whole, fitted to this world in which we live – Upper Middle Earth is of course a lesser creation than Asdar. This slice that I wear now contains enough magic to serve my purpose; and when that magic is exhausted, I shall cut another sliver from the whole. I call this magic Thing a "Tiny Morsel", or "TM" for short.'

And Sharon laughed again with great gusto.

And Lüthwoman did shudder at the evil of Sharon; and Belend moved to comfort her, but was prevented by the milling Orks shoving him back with their weapons.

'Where ith the retht of the Thellāmi?' demanded Lüthwoman.

'Why should I tell you?' said Sharon. 'My wish now is that you be executed horribly and painfully by my Orks. What good, therefore, will the knowledge of the Sellāmi's whereabouts do you?'

'Where ith it?' pressed Lüthwoman.

'It is in a safe place,' mocked Sharon. 'In a room in my domain. This is a room with two entrances, or exits, yet not a room you would ever want to enter – for, even if you knew its location, the key to the door is your own flesh, and you would leave the room quite changed from how you entered it.'

And Belend and Lüthwoman puzzled over this riddle.

'Yet,' said Lüthwoman, 'if it ith a room in thith tower, we may yet find it.'

At this Sharon only laughed.

'Take us there!' demanded Belend. 'Take us to the Sellāmi!'

And Sharon laughed loud and long at this

presumption. 'Your bravery is matched only by your foolishness!' he declared. 'Take you to the Sellāmi? Never – you shall *never* know where it is, for the Sellāmi will be mine for ever!'

And as the Evil Lord spoke these words, the final Bug of Truth stirred in Lüthwoman's pocket, and came to life. It crawled out and flipped into the air, catching Sharon's words as they were spoken: a great lie from a great liar, yet the Bug of Truth gobbled them in flight, and Sharon instead said:

'The Sellāmi is in the belly of the Pig of Doom, which terrible creature I keep in a great pit behind the tower. I feed this beast on my enemies, and upon any Orks that displease me – they are thrown, alive and screaming, into the deep pit, and the Pig of Doom devours them with great chompings; and in the belly of this terrible creature I keep the incorruptible Sellāmi beyond the reach of my enemies.'

And the Orks were astonished that Sharon had revealed this secret, for not even his closest lieutenants had been privy to the true location of the Sellāmi. And Sharon, paranoid in his fear and possessiveness, had thought no room in his castle safe enough from theft, and so had fed the remainder of the Sellāmi to his monstrous Pig. But he was horrified at what he had said, for it had not been his intention.

'Why did I say that?' Sharon cried. 'What came over me? Curses! – but *look!* Look! A Bug of Truth! Kill it, smash it, crush it—'

And the Orks ran in circles, and flailed in the air with their weapons, hoping to slay the Bug of Truth and so please their master; but the bug was agile, and flapped out of reach; and it flew high through an open casement and flew to the north. And there, eventually, it found a pleasant field, and burrowed into the soil; for it had devoured an unusually large lie, and had within itself food for a long time.

But Sharon's rage was kindled now.

'You worms!' he cried. 'How *dare* you trick me into revealing the true location of the Sellāmi! How dare you! I had planned to kill you quickly and cleanly, here: but now instead I shall fulfil your request – I shall take you to the Sellāmi, and instead of a quick death you shall meet a terrible and painful demise at the jaws of the Pig of Doom!'

And at this news Belend did tremble, and Lüth-woman moan. Because, after all, nobody looks forward cheerily to the prospect of being eaten by a giant pig. Nobody I know, anyway.

✳

When Sharon had put the sacred Sellāmi inside the Pig of Doom he knew that the magical artefact could not be corrupted or digested inside the pig's gut: for the Sellāmi, being not of this world, cannot be consumed by it. On the contrary, he knew the Pig would hold the Sellāmi in a safe and hidden place, and that when the pig died he could cut open the pig's belly and retrieve the artefact. But he had not planned on revealing this secret place to anybody, and now he was bitter and angry.

He ordered his Orks to seize Belend and Lüthwoman, and decreed that they be cast into the great pit to be devoured by the hideous pig. And to them he said, 'Your end is fitting, for you came seeking the Sellāmi, and you shall be taken to it. Let you not, therefore, complain.'

And Belend did stand as proudly as he could, bearing in mind that he had Orks hanging off him and poking him in the small of the back with spears and so on, and replied: 'I do not complain, Lord of Darkness, for I am content to die by the side of my love.'

And Lüthwoman looked over to him and said, 'Aah, that'th thoo thweet.'

And Belend did blush a little, and look at the floor, and say, 'Well, it's true.'

126

And Lüthwoman said, 'I love you too, my nea-tumth-thweetumth.'

And Belend said, 'Love you, gurgly-tum.'

And Lüthwoman said, 'My little love-monkey.'

And Belend said, 'My tweaky little—'

But at this point Sharon intervened, shouting, 'Oh for heaven's *sake* throw them to the pig. Jeesh, it's enough to make even an eyeball vomit.'

So Belend and Lüthwoman were dragged down the stairs and out of the Cirith Connoli; and in the wasted land behind the tower was a great and deep pit, and at the bottom of this a monstrous pig, large as a whale, well, maybe one of the smaller breeds of whale anyway, a dolphin whale or a small killer whale or something like that. And it snuffled and grunted, and picked over the bones at the bottom of its pit, and eagerly awaited its next meal.

The Fifth Part of the Tale of Belend and Lüthwoman

There is no Fifth Part of the Tale of Belend and Lüthwoman. There is, however, a sixth, should you still be interested.

The Sixth Part of the Tale of Belend and Lüthwoman

And so it was that Belend and Lüthwoman were hurled into the pit of the Pig of Doom. They fell far, for the pit was deep, but their landing was cushioned by the layer of muck at the bottom of the pit, the precise nature of which was something into which they, neither of them, had any desire to enquire too closely.

Orks lined the rim of the pit, looking down, jeering and yelling; and Sharon himself stared down upon them from the top of his tall tower.

The Pig of Doom, scenting new food, came trotting over towards the newcomers; but Belend got proudly to his feet and held forth his hand in a 'halt!' posture.

'Stop!' he called. 'Pig! Before you devour us, listen to my words. For I am Belend, of the royal line of Prorn, and I have spent my life wandering the forests of my native land, befriending bears, deer and pigs wherever I have found – ow!'

And he did say 'Ow' with great force and sincerity, because the Pig of Doom had bitten off his hand and swallowed it, as a morsel.

Lüthwoman screamed, or to be precise thcreamed, to see this; and Belend fell to his knees, and clutched at his stump. And he said: 'What do you think you're *doing*? For crying out *loud*, there's plenty of time to eat us, there's really no need to be so impatient, ow, ow, *owww*.'

And the Pig of Doom heard the words. In all his long years in the deep pit, nobody had ever spoken to him as if he were a rational creature. But, as it happens, he was such a creature, very intelligent animals, pigs, actually. And he heard the words, and felt a bit sheepish, rather than his usual piggish. And he held back from devouring the rest of Belend for a little space.

'Hell's *bells*, that stings,' said Belend, trying to staunch the flow of blood from his stump by wrapping his shirt around the wound in a sort of ball of cloth. 'Ouch, ow, ow, ow, *ow*,' he added.

'Sorry,' snorted the Pig.

'Couldn't you even let me finish my *sentence*? I mean, what's the bleeding *hurry*?'

'Got a bit carried away,' said the Pig. 'Sorry. Only they usually feed me Orks, and Orks taste yucky, frankly, between you and me. I got a bit overexcited, to be honest. You look just so much tastier than my usual fare. People think I'll eat anything, and actually

I will, pretty much, but that doesn't mean I lack all sense of culinary pleasure. Quite the reverse. Actually, do you know what I really fancy?'

'What?' asked Belend, although his tone of voice implied somebody not happy with the cosmos and he spoke snappishly.

'Truffles. Oo I'd *love* a truffle right now. You got any truffles on you?'

'No,' said Belend and he looked at his partner. 'Have you got any truffles on you, dear?'

'Thorry,' said Lüthwoman. 'No.'

'Ah well,' said the Pig.

'Ith it true,' asked Lüthwoman in wonder, 'that you carry the thacred Thellāmi in your belly?'

The Pig's face assumed a pained expression. 'Yes, that's perfectly true. It's not at all comfortable, I don't mind telling you. Sharon chucked it down here a while ago, and I gobbled it down without thinking twice. But I can't seem to digest it. I can feel it as a sort of jagged lump, about here.' And he tapped one of his flanks with his left back trotter.

'Think,' said Belend, his voice faint, 'think I've got the exsanguination under control.'

'Look,' said the Pig. 'I really am sorry about the, you know, eating your hand and everything. It's just that . . .'

130

'Will you listen to me, Pig?' asked Belend, getting to his feet. 'Will you hear me out?' And he was much paler than he had been before.

And the Pig replied, 'Alright, I suppose that's only fair. But, just so's you know, after that I *will* have to eat you. They won't give me any more food until I do, and, well. You know. Pig's gotta eat, after all.'

'Listen to me, Pig,' said Belend, looking woozy, as if he were about to pass out. 'I possess the power to free you from this pit, and carry you far away from Moider!, into the wide forests of the north.'

'You do?'

'Yes,' said Belend. 'Forests absolutely stuffed with truffles, just lying there under the topsoil, waiting for your snout to uncover them.'

'Oo!' went the Pig, going all dreamy-faced. If you've never seen a pig's face go all dreamy then you have missed something remarkable, believe me.

'But you have to promise not to eat us,' said Belend. 'And you have to agree to come with us to the Court of Queen Eve before you get the free run of the forest. Deal?'

'Deal!' said the Pig. 'Abso-pigging-lutely. Get out of here? Truffles for life? No *question*.'

So, with Lüthwoman's help, Belend climbed up onto the hog's back. And Lüthwoman climbed up to

sit in a position in front of him, and she clutched onto
the Pig's ears; and Belend hooked his stumpy arm
around Lüthwoman's waist. And with his good arm
he brought out, from his pocket, the small rectangle
of parchment, upon which was written *'Get ye Gone
fro Gaol'*.

'Here,' he called. 'I play this card!' And he cast it
on the floor.

And they were released from their prison; the Pig
of Doom rising into the air before the astonished
and angry Orks, and floating past the tall tower of
Sharon like something from a nineteen-seventies
album cover. And Sharon's rage was immense and
terrible, but impotent; for there was nothing he could
do. The Pig of Doom flew north, carrying its two
passengers with it.

And the Pig said, 'Wheeeeeeh!' But not in a
shrieking terrified piglet sort of way, more in a
delighted, isn't-this-fun manner.

They flew over the wasted lands of the south, where
floodwaters still lay in great stretches; and over the
swollen torrent of the River Raver; and they flew
over the southern boundaries of the great wood
Taur-ea-dorpants, until they came to Elftonjon.

And the Elves were astonished to see this Pig

flying through the air, and more astonished to see it coming down to land on a stretch of turf before the margin of the forest, on the outskirts of Elfton. And they were even more astonished than this to see Lüthwoman, their princess, clamber down from the Pig's back, helping the injured Belend after her.

Messengers ran to fetch the Queen, and she was carried forth on a silver litter, and placed before the Pig; and the nobles of Elfton gathered around these ragged and wounded travellers. Yet, despite their disdain, the fabled hospitality of the Elves was not abandoned; and the new arrivals were refreshed with elf-bread, elf-honey and elf-tea. Finally the Queen spoke.

'I sent you, Belend of the tribes of Men, on a quest to retrieve the Sellāmi, and I see you took my only daughter with you into this hideous peril. Is this your love for her, that you would risk her life?'

'My love for her,' said Belend, somewhat refreshed by the elf-tea, but still weak and pale, 'is such that I cannot be parted from her.'

'Have you brought the Sellāmi? I do not see it.'

'Indeed I have brought the Sellāmi, your majesty. It is inside the belly of this Pig of Doom.'

Gasps ran through the crowd; for they were amazed and disbelieving. But the Pig, sensing that his moment had come, spoke up. 'It's true. Sharon had me imprisoned in a pit, and fed me the Sellāmi, to keep it – as he thought – safe and hidden. But this Elf and this Man discovered his secret, and freed me.'

'I asked you to bring me the Sellāmi,' said the Queen, angrily. 'And instead you have brought me a talking pig?'

'Not *instead of*, your majesty,' said Belend, proudly. '*In addition to*. You did not specify that I was to bring you only the Sellāmi and nothing else. And so I have brought you the Sellāmi *and* a pig.'

'But how am I supposed to get it *out* of the pig?'

'With respect, your majesty,' said Belend, 'that also was not something specified in your instructions when you sent me on the quest. I have fulfilled my part of the bargain, and I ask that you now fulfil yours.' And Lüthwoman did embrace him happily, and the two of them beamed smiles at the assembled Elves.

But Queen Eve was not pleased, and glowered. 'It is true,' she said, speaking slowly, 'that I said to you "bring me the Sellāmi, that treasure of Emu and you shall have the hand of my daughter in marriage". And I must be true to my word. But I also swore that you would never marry my daughter – for, you are not one jot or tittle less obnoxious to me now than you were before you went away. The thought of you and my daughter together, of you living in the same house, of you starting a family – this cannot be endured.'

And she pondered for a while; for the oath of a monarch is not lightly to be cast aside. And finally she spoke.

'I have decided: I shall keep both my oaths. Do you come to me to palter with me over the terms and conditions of the quest on which I sent you, Belend, son of Prorn? Then hearken.' And her face grew dark as a stormcloud. 'Belend the Onehanded, you yourself teach me the way I must go to preserve my oaths. You shall have the hand of my daughter in marriage, but the rest of her shall stay in Elfton with her own people.' And she called for an axeman.

And tall elf guards tore the screaming Lüthwoman away from Belend; and he was too weakened by exertion and loss of blood to fight them away. And he collapsed to the ground, sobbing in frustration and agony.

So it was that Queen Eve ordered the cutting off of the hand of her own daughter. The axeman severed her left hand with a single blow of his silver axe, and elf healers hurried to bind the wound and staunch its hurt. And Lüthwoman fell into a swoon, and was lifted aboard the Queen's litter and carried inside the town; and the crowd dispersed. And soon Belend was alone and weeping in the dirt.

And the Pig of Doom coughed discreetly, and after a while said, 'So, am I done here? Only, I thought I might wander into the – you know, the forest and have a look for truffles.' And he received no reply from Belend save his sobs, and so he departed into the depths of Taur-ea-dorpants.

And after a short space a messenger came from Queen Eve, and stood before the prone son of Prorn. 'Belend,' he said. 'I carry two things from the Queen. One is this object.'

And he threw the severed hand of Lüthwoman upon the dirt before Belend.

'The other,' he continued, 'is this speech. The Queen says she has fulfilled her obligations to you, and kept her oath. She orders you to leave this land, and never to return. You are a proscribed person. If any Elf sees you within these lands, they are to kill you on the spot. If you are still found here tomorrow at dawn the soldiers of the Queen will hunt you down and carry your severed head to the Queen. Begone – you are banished.'

Belend quietened his own tears, for he did not

wish to cry before the insolent messenger of the Queen. And he picked up the hand of his beloved, rose to his feet, and departed from those lands.

The Seventh and Final Part of the Tale of Belend and Lüthwoman

Belend made his melancholy way north, eating mushrooms from the forest floor, and honey from beehives; and though the bees stung him in their miniature, multiple fury, yet he was heedless of that. He carried Lüthwoman's severed hand with him at all times, tucked into his shirt.

He did not return to Manly town, for his grief was too great. Instead he made his way to the great amber lake of Lothlomondwisky, and dwelt in the land of Pebles for a certain time, living with himself and with his sorrow only. And when men came to fish in the lake, Belend did not make himself known to them, but instead crossed the River Optik where it empties into the lake and crossed the stony land of Pebbles beyond. For he could not bear the company of others.

Winter came; and the wind became peevish and cold, and found the holes in Belend's clothes. And a small, chill rain fell upon him. He clad himself in the skins of rabbits he trapped, working the pelts with flints and curing them in the waters of the Loth. And he ate the flesh raw, for he could start no fire in the constant drizzle. And at all times he kept the hand of his loved woman about him: and this, being elf-flesh, did not degrade or decay, but stayed pure and white, as if carved from ivory.

And one day, when winter had lasted so long that he had almost forgotten what it was to be warm, or see flowers bloom, Belend had wandered so far as to chance upon the Standing Stones that are truly called the Dragon's Claws. For these monoliths, though they appear to sight and touch nothing more than great stones arranged in a circle, are in fact something else. The Dragon of the North, so the legend has it, carved the great Mount Ezumas-revenge with his own claws; and so mighty is this mountain that it broke the fingernails of even so vast a creature as the dragon. And the Dragon of the North shed his claws, and grew a new set; and the claws fell from on high and embedded themselves in the turf far north of Taur-en-Ferno.

Belend came to this place, and sat inside the circle. And he could sense the powerful magic of the place, for Dragons distil the greatest creative magic of any living beings. They made much of the world, and then they seeded the rocks and the mountains with life (and life that followed a complex pattern of developmental metamorphosis, I might add).

And in this place it occurred to Belend to bury the hand of Lüthwoman in the exact centre of the circle. And that night he slept over the burial site, and wept at having lost his love.

But in the morning he awoke to something strange and wondrous; for from the planted hand had grown a new Lüthwoman, whole. She was lying naked on top of the grass, with her hand tucked into the ground. And when Belend pulled her hand free of the dirt it was cold and dead as ever it had been; but the rest of this new-grown Lüthwoman was warm and quick with life.

His joy was so great it threatened to snap his own grip on life, making his heart stumble in its frantic beating, and a red mist passed before his eyes; and he embraced and embraced her, and wept, and howled his happiness to the winter sky.

It was not long, however, before he understood that although this creature possessed the physical form of his love, yet her mind was blank and her head empty: she had no speech, and made no sign of understanding. And Belend's heart fell again. It seemed to him a mockery of the fates that his Lüth-woman should be taken from him, and this empty shell given in her place.

Still he took her with him, and dressed her in rabbit skins; and she ate hungrily as a child when he gave her food, but otherwise she sat silent and pliant, or walked when he pushed her, or stopped when he stopped. And they made their way south down the western edges of Taur-en-Ferno. Hope remained in Belend's heart that this wraith might grow slowly to awareness, but many months passed and she was as blank as she had been at the beginning.

And on the west coast of Upper Middle Earth, Belend tarried. For he had decided what to do, but was uncertain whether he would be able to maintain the resolve to do what must be done. And he sat for long hours staring at the sea, with the mute simula-crum of Lüthwoman by his side. And he watched the sun setting, casting a sheen over the calm waters like a dew; and as the sun's rim kissed the edge of the horizon, and red spilt over the rippled surface of the ocean, he was resolved.

He trapped deer in the sparse woodlands of the west with snares made of creepers and the boughs of trees; and for a rude iron blade he traded the carcasses of these with fishermen who lived on the coast. This blade he sharpened on the flat stones of a coastal stream, all the time with the simulacrum of Lüthwoman watching him non-comprehending.

Then he sat beside her, and spoke to her long, explaining what he must do, and saying how sorry he was, and how he would be as kind in his cruelty as he could; but she understood nothing. And then he took his blade, and took her left arm, and cut the hand from the arm.

She cried with pain and fought him, but he held her and dressed the wound with mosses and skins. And very soon the fit passed from her, and she seemed to have forgotten the pain utterly, for she became as blank and pliable as before.

Now Belend made his way east. And his time in the wilderness, trapping animals and avoiding company, had made him cunning in the ways of the wood, expert at disguise, skilled at moving undetected. And so he led the simulacrum of Lüthwoman through the trees of Taur-ea-dorpants; and one night he crept into Elftonjon. Although discovery would have been death, yet he evaded detection, and crept about the town with the silent copy of Lüthwoman beside him.

And he made his way to the royal palace, at the heart of the town. Here, in the shadow of an eave, he left the simulacrum of Lüthwoman sitting. And he climbed the flank of the royal palace, and slipped through a casement, and stealthily returned to the side gate, opening it from the inside. And he drew the simulacrum of Lüthwoman in through the gate and brought her upstairs.

This night there was a feast in the central hall, and although servants came and went, to fetch and carry, yet were the corridors and rooms of the palace mostly empty; and Belend was able to mount the stairs unobserved, and finally he came to the door of Lüthwoman's chamber.

Here he put his hand in at the lock and opened it, and crept inside. Lüthwoman was asleep on her bed, but woke to hear his tread, and almost called out.

'Hush,' he said. 'It is I.'

And she wept to see him, and they embraced. 'But,' she said, 'it ith madneth for you to come here, for you will be killed on thight. And,' she added, fingering his shirt, 'what'th thith? Rabbit? That'th *tho* lath theathon.'

'I have come to take you with me,' said Belend.

'I have dethired nothing elthe for long monthth,' wept Lüthwoman. 'But it cannot be! My mother would never retht until I wath returned to her. It would mean war between Elveth and Men, and an army of elvith warriorth would comb the landth of Upper Middle Earth until I wath retrieved – and you would thurely die in the protheth.'

'Got that pretty much all,' said Belend, nodding, 'except for the last word. But it doesn't matter. I have a plan.'

And he went out of the room and returned with the simulacrum of Lüthwoman. And the real Lüthwoman was amazed, and examined her double in great detail.

And Belend stood looking admiringly at the two versions of the beautiful Lüthwoman standing close to one another; and he meditated on the various possibilities it presented him. But there was no time to be lost with such idle fancies; they could be discovered at any time; and so he led the simulacrum of Lüthwoman to the bed, and made her lie down; and soon she was asleep.

And Belend and Lüthwoman crept out of the palace, and out of Elfton, and fled through the woods, and never again returned to that place.

Later that night the Queen sent a messenger to summon her daughter down to the feast. And the simulacrum of Lüthwoman was brought downstairs and sat at table and ate heartily; but she would answer no question, and make no comment. And the Queen, knowing something was wrong, ended the feast in confusion, dismissing her guests, and called the finest elf doctors to the palace. They examined the simulacrum of Lüthwoman, but they did not comprehend that it was but a simulacrum, and took it for the real individual. And so they told the Queen that her daughter had lost her mind, most likely with grief at losing her lover. 'It may be, your Majesty,' they said, 'that she has lost all powers of speech, or of rational thought.'

And the Queen was greatly grieved, but try as she might she could not restore her daughter to her faculties. Over the months that followed, she tried herbs, and magic charms; she tried imploring her daughter, and hypnotising her after the manner of the Elves, but Lüthwoman remained as blank as ever. And the Queen said, 'The glory has departed from the house of Bleary, a cursed house, for now my only daughter has lost her mind in the madness of love for a mere mortal.'

Of the real Lüthwoman, one-handed, with her one-handed lover Belend, this story does not tell much more. They fled together to the north, to the pleasant meadows and copses of the land south of the River

Optik; and here Belend did build a house, and Lüth-woman did decorate it after her heart's desire. And they traded occasionally with the Men of that area, and became known to them, although not by their birth-names. And they were married, and some say they had children, but others say not.

But Queen Eve had sworn that Belend would never marry Lüthwoman, and had said also that her own life would wither and die before her word was broken. And, though unbeknownst to her, yet Belend and Lüthwoman married after all; and she did sicken and grow thin. Though an Elf and not fated for death, yet did she grow closer and closer to death.

And eventually she died: a rare fate for an Elf, to die otherwise than in battle. And she was mourned by the Elves, for she was the inheritor of the line of Bleary. But amongst the Men she was not mourned, for her story had spread through the land, and mortals called her 'Eve the Cruel' for the manner in which she had upheld her oaths.

Some amongst the Elves did say 'We should crown her daughter Queen, for she is the only remaining inheritor of the line of Bleary'. But others did say, 'Her mind has gone, and her soul lost utterly; she can never rule the Elves.' And so the

Elves fell into division and confusion, and one party separated from another party.

So ends the tale of Belend and Lüthwoman.

Of Sharon's Dream

Now Sharon was piqued to have lost the Sellāmi. I mean, really, very, very annoyed indeed. You can understand his position, I'm sure, losing the most powerful magical artefact in creation and everything; it's bound to tick you off. He raged hard. He raged himself ragged. He railed at his Orks, slaying many. Then he raged again, or re-raged. And, having worn himself out with so much raging, and feeling weak, he reined in his rage, or de-reraged, and then he slept, for he had exhausted himself. And he slept for twenty months long, because the loss of the Sellāmi had worn him out so utterly.

As he slept he dreamt, and he saw a great shape filling the whole sky, black and purple and swirling like a stormcloud. And as he looked more closely he saw that it was a Sky Boa, a serpent of untold length and girthed with black muscles, tight to crush and destroy, and it writhed through the air like an ever-twisting band of darkness.

Now Sharon had never dreamt before, and he was terrified by the apparition. But after a little time he realised that the wraith could not harm him, and he grew bolder. 'Creature!' he called. But even though his was the voice of a Valūpac, yet it was barely a squeak in the howling gale of his dream.

'Sharon,' called the beast, and its voice was the shattering of worlds and the growl of icebergs chewing at the land. And Sharon quailed, and thought to himself, 'It is the spirit of Moregothic, slain in this world and refused entrance to the next, and so it inhabits the space between the earth and the sky in sorrow and rage.'

'Master?' said Sharon; and this was a word he had not framed in speech for an age and an age.

'Sharon,' called the apparition. And now it seemed to have a head, and its head was like a black bull except that its mouth contained sharp viper teeth of bright red; and below its neck were two strong arms, like the arms of a man, except that they ended in great talons instead of fingers; and its body tapered away over many leagues into a long tail like a huge eel. And as Sharon looked, the beast's claws were clasping its own tail, and feeding it into its own maw, and it was devouring itself. And with each bite of its colossal mouth, lightning sparked and branched away with a brightness that seared the eyes. But as Sharon gazed, this sudden brightness did not illuminate the dark, which grew more involved, minute by minute.

'Master,' called Sharon, in his dream. 'Why do you visit me in this form?'

'To warn you,' said the serpent, 'beware the promises of Dragons.'

'The promises of Dragons were your undoing, Master,' cried Sharon, full of sorrow.

'The Dragons give, but they also take. They always give as they always take. You must be ready. You must be clear before you treat with them what their price is, and you must be prepared to pay it.'

'Death was the price *you* paid,' cried Sharon.

'Ensure that the charm they weave you is watertight,' howled the serpent. 'Leave no chink in the magic. Leave no gap through which destructive fate may assail you!'

'Master!' called Sharon, in an agony of sorrow and despair and fear. And he awoke.

Never before had Sharon's servants seen his eyeball coated in the clear salty liquid in which he found himself on awakening. Nor could anybody say whence these gallons of tears had come, for though he was an eyeball, yet Sharon lacked the ducts through which tears wash the eye in other beings.

Nor could any say how he had dreamt, for he had never experienced a dream before, and the Valūpac do not dream.

Sharon contemplated the dream for a long time, and resolved to follow the advice he decided was contained within it. He could summon the Dragons, and make a binding deal with them; and he bent his cunning to the task of forming a charm that allowed no loopholes. But there was also the matter of the price to be paid, and he pondered this for a long time.

Twelve years passed after the Sellāmi was stolen from his realm; and all that time Sharon mustered a new army, vast and hideous, and armed them, and prepared his way. And, from time to time, Sharon would hear stories of a monstrous pig living in the forest of Taur-ea-dorpants in the middle of Upper Middle Earth; and he said to himself, 'That's where the Pig went.' So he resolved to steal back the Sellāmi to himself, or at the least to discover its location, for here, he thought, was a price that would purchase the Dragons' magic.

And so he marshalled a small band of his troops, and sent them north into Blearyland. His most trusted lieutenants he sent too, Bleary and Cük too.

They built ships, for they were skilled in the crafts of boatbuilding, and crossed the flooded lands of the River Raver, and so they came to the north. They did not engage in open battle with Men or Elves, for that was not their instruction; but when they came upon small groups or travellers they slew them and word spread to all the towns of the north of their doing.

And they captured Men and Elves, and tortured them, and so learned the story of Queen Eve, and how her daughter was driven to madness and blankness of mind by her love for a mortal, for so the story went. And they learnt that a monstrous Pig of Doom haunted the Forest of Taur-ea-Dorpants, and so they made their way into the forest.

And on the seventh day of searching through the trees they found the Pig, rooting at the turf to uncover truffles.

And Bleary said to his second-in-command, 'Look, there he is. You go and get him.'

And the Ork looked at the giant pig, and at his flesh-shredding teeth, and the strongly efficient action of his masticating jaws, and at the sheer *size* of the bugger, and did reply, 'Fat chance.'

'Look,' said Bleary. 'I'm giving you a *direct* order.'

'And I'm giving you a *direct* not on your nelly.'

'Do you want Sharon to be peeved?' said Bleary.

'Because, believe me, he will be peeved. He'll be very peeved indeed.'

'You want the pig,' said the Ork, in effect resigning his commission with these words, 'you go get him.' And this Ork was not sorry to leave the Orkish armies, and he travelled far, eventually setting up a smallholding, farming lemmings and selling the pelts on the outskirts of Ill-bhavior. But his subsequent life is not the concern of the present tale.

Bleary ordered the rest of his men to charge the Pig, but they were swiftly disposed of by the monster, who bit some of them in half, and batted others away with powerful sideswipes of his head, and scared others away by snorting and grunting very loudly. And the Ork raiding party withdrew in disarray.

Bleary travelled south again with the survivors, and reported what he knew to Sharon. And, as Bleary had prophesied, Sharon was peeved; and vented his anger on a couple of Orks who happened to be digging a latrine trench not far from his tower, which was bad luck for them. But after that he calmed down, and thought to himself, 'At least I know where the Pig of Doom has gone.'

Of Sharon's Decision to End Things
Once and for All and for All

After meditating on the situation for a long time, Sharon the Evil called Tuoni Bleary to his side, and he said to him: 'Tuoni, I have been fighting this war against so-called Goodness for ages and ages. Moreover, where most people use that phrase to mean "for forty-five minutes" or "for three months", I use it in a strictly literal sense: first age, upper second age, lower second age, third age – I've stuck it out. It's enough to try the patience of an evil saint. Well, I've decided that enough is enough.'

'Your tautologies are indeed glorious, O Evil One,' said Bleary.

'I've decided,' said Sharon, 'to end this war once and for all.'

And Bleary said, 'Good idea, O Lord. So, when you say for *once and for all*, what do you mean by "all"? – Do you mean "for all people"?'

'Yes,' said Sharon. 'End it for once and for all people. And, come to think of it, for all time.'

'So you're planning to end it once and for all and for all?'

'Exactly,' said Sharon. 'Once and for all and for all. If one is, for instance, doing a crossword, then a temporary or partial solution is simply no good. The only solution that's any use is a *final* one. Surely we can agree on that.'

And Bleary squirmed and smiled and said, 'And how will you do this thing, O Darkling? I listen.'

'To end it once and for all and for all,' said Sharon, 'I shall defeat all the forces of so-called Goodness in a mighty battle, slay their commanders and make prisoners of their followers. And I shall bind the world of Upper Middle Earth with a charm of such potency, a charm of such power-to-create, that it will hold the realm in my grasp for ever.'

'How will you frame such a spell?' asked Bleary, afraid.

'The Dragons will do it,' said Sharon.

It was spring again, and the long winter had passed, and the peoples of Upper Middle Earth felt their hearts expand with hope as the season changed. The wheat grew green in the north, and red windflowers were dotted amongst the stalks of wheat. On the meadows and downs the grass was feathery, and young figs grew white and woolly on the trees. All the green land seemed refreshed under the blue sky, washed with hurrying bright showers, and sparkling after each with sunshine anew. Men forgot for a while that there was such a thing as evil in the world, and though Elves do not forget, yet even they delighted in the warmth in the air, and sang songs beneath the chalk moon and purple sky.

And it was at this time that Sharon had himself carried to the very top of the tower of Cirith Connoli, and placed there alone on his podium. It was sunset, the sky red-gold, with olive-coloured clouds lying in layers over the western horizon. And he had about him the Thing™, in which still inhered much of the power of the Sellámi.

Using the power of the Thing™, Sharon summoned the Dragon of the South.

And the Dragon answered his call, drawn by the Thing™. He rode the air, and pressed down upon it with wings broad as clouds; yet he brought no tempest with him as he flew, but rather he poured fluidly through the air. His eyes were green as cypress leaves, and his skin glowed dark as wine.

He circled the tower at Cirith Connoli with immense slowness. And even Sharon was afraid, but he overcame his fear.

'Dragon!' he called. 'You are the oldest and the most powerful of magic creatures in Upper Middle Earth. And yet there is an artefact older and more powerful than you – the Sellāmi, for it was created by Emu.'

And the Dragon circled the tower in the air, slowly, slowly, and said, 'I know it.'

'You shall make me a spell,' said Sharon, 'and I shall tell you where you may find the Sellāmi. None but you are mighty enough to take it from its present hiding place, and yet you do not know where it is hidden.'

And the Dragon circled the tower again in the air, and said, 'I shall do it.'

'So!' cried Sharon. 'But listen to me, Dragon. I know how you and your kind betrayed my master of old, Moregothic: for you gave him a charm of seeming strength yet at the last it betrayed him to death and extinction. This shall not be my fate. Do you hear?'

The Dragon said, 'I hear.'

'I must be lord over *all* Elves and Men, for as long as Elves and Men exist.'

The Dragon said, 'It shall be.'

'I must be invulnerable to harm.'

The Dragon said, 'It shall be.'

'I must be immortal.'

The Dragon said, 'It shall be.'

'I must be victorious in any battle.'

The Dragon said, 'It shall be.'

And Sharon demanded these four things, for he knew there were four Dragons. And he thought that there was no loophole, or ambiguity, or weakness in this charm.

The Dragon of the South said, 'These things shall come to pass when we have the Sellāmi.'

And Sharon replied: 'Agreed – all save this sliver, which I wear about me now. This I shall retain, and you will agree that my retention will not affect the spell.' The Dragon of the South reared in the air, and spread his wings so wide that they blotted out the light from the setting sun. But Sharon was not afraid: 'You shall not trick me,' he called, 'as you tricked Moregothic! Accept my terms, or get you gone.'

And the Dragon folded its wings, and flew slowly once around the tower.

'It shall be,' he said.

The land was silent, as dumb as death; no insect stirred and no wind moved. The skies were silently changing form, with the clouds forecasting nightstorm; a great cloud gathered in the west, breeding thunder and lightning in its body. For this was the mightiest spell that had yet been cast in Upper Middle Earth. The hollow hills trembled, and Orks fled whimpering to their bunkers and holes.

And Sharon gloried as the tempest broke around his tower, and the lightning revealed itself in a thousand burning shards, and blue rain fell through the dusk. Far away, Men and Elves saw the conflagration on the southern horizon and wondered at such sudden and malevolent weather.

The four Dragons flew together to the middle of the world, and the wood of Taur-ea-Dorpants. They had not been to this place, singly or together, since the creation of things; but they flew there now.

And within the glades of this forest was the Pig of Doom. Tall as a house, keenly aware of its surroundings by scent and eye, this beast feared no hunter, acknowledged no predator. No forest lion or bear could dent its thick skin; no hunter's spear could harm it. It roamed where it wished, and drank from forest streams, and grubbed truffles and tubers with its shovel-like snout.

Its life was good.

But the Dragons came. Though they were vast, yet they were nimble in the air, and they swirled low over the treetops. The shade cast by their wings made the bark of the trees blue and darkened the leaves. The Pig of Doom looked up.

Now, being alone in the woodland, there was nobody with whom to speak, yet nevertheless it spoke, and said: 'Uh-oh.'

And the Dragons did gather in the sky above the Pig of Doom. And the Pig did take to its trotters in no uncertain manner, and, well, I was going to say scuttled away, but I'm not sure, on reflection, that it would be proper to describe a creature as large as a house running as fast as it can as *scuttling*. Galloping, I suppose, although that makes you think of horses, doesn't it, rather than seventy tons of mobile pig. Well, it was moving rapidly, anyway, that's what I mean to convey. Because the Pig of Doom knew that in the centre of the wide forest of Taur-ea-Dorpants was an outcrop of rock, overgrown with trees; and an opening in this led down to a deep cavern, for the world, breathed into being by the words of the Dragons, is hollow. And the Pig thought to itself, I'll lie low, in a literal sense, 'til these Dragons buzz off. Sooner I get there, he thought, the better.

And the Dragons flew through the air over the trees following him.

The Pig of Doom looked up again and saw the

shapes of the Dragons sweeping through the sky above the highest branches, and he quickened his stride. He, shall we say, *lumbered* through the trees I suppose, except that 'lumbering' implies a lumpish, ungainly, slow gait, and this pig moved with excessive rapidity. I'm beginning to think that there just isn't a word in the language to describe the extremely rapid movement of a seventy-ton pig through a forest; a state of affairs which is, I'm sure you'll agree with me, a shame. Anyway.

The Pig, casting nervous looks into the air to check on the progress of the Dragons, ran head first into a massive elm. The tree shattered into many fragments, and the Pig of Doom hurtled rump over snout, crashing into further trees in the process until it lay, stunned, in a motionless heap.

The Dragons brought themselves together in the air above the supine pig.

'Wait,' called the Pig, in a woozy voice. 'Ur, ooh, wait.'

'Pig,' called the Dragon of the South. 'We must claim the Sellāmi that is in your belly.'

'Belly!' said the Pig, struggling to get to its feet. Or to its trotters, rather. 'Belly, pah. People are so rude to pigs. If I were an Elf, or a Man, you'd say *intestine*, or *innards*, or something.'

160

'Nevertheless,' called the Dragons. 'The Sellāmi must be ours.'

'To be honest,' said the Pig of Doom, 'I'll not be sorry to be shot of the thing. Terrible indigestion it has caused me. Terrible – sticks into my flesh something shocking.'

'The Sellāmi is too powerful for flesh to touch,' said the Dragon of the West, 'even flesh as tough as yours, O Pig. It has corroded your innards, melted itself into your very bones.'

'Well,' said the Pig of Doom, 'that would explain the indigestion. And it would explain why I can't seem to vomit the horrid thing up. Ah well,' it said, resigning itself to its fate. 'I've had a good run, for a pig. Ate one too many Orks, perhaps, but I've certainly enjoyed the last few years, with the truffles and all.'

And he presented himself to the Dragons; and they paid tribute to his bravery, and called him, 'Some Pig'.

Then the Dragons reared in the sky and blew down with fire from all four mouths; and the Pig of Doom met his own Doom in the fiercest of conflagrations, blinded by the heat and light and breathed from existence in an instant.

The fire burnt through the Pig's flesh, and it

peeled back as a book peels its pages away in smoke
when thrown onto a hearth fire. And the trees
around burst to flame as brands, and a great tower
of smoke rose to the air, and was bent by the wind
and dispersed over the land of the east.

The Dragons stopped their fire; and below them
was a great circle of black earth, smouldering and
glowing in many places; and the edge of the circle
was formed of flaming trees; and in the very centre of
the circle was the Sellāmi, unharmed by heat and
unsullied by ash.

The Dragon of the North took it in its talons, and
the four Dragons flew away.

Stormclouds followed their tails, and spring rain
fell on Taur-ea-dorpants, extinguishing the fires. And
soon grasses grew in the scorched circle at the very
heart of the forest, and out of the fertile ash came
poppies and orange windflowers; but no trees ever
grew in that space again.

The spell was completed; and Sharon, in his tower of
Cirith Connoli, felt a great surge of strength flow
through his being. And he exulted.

'The charm is complete!' he called. 'I am armed
with total power, for the Dragons have promised me
that I shall be lord over *all* Elves and Men, for as

long as Elves and Men exist; and I am invulnerable to harm; and I am immortal; and I shall be victorious in any battle. This magic has no chink or loophole, but by the force of inevitability I shall dominate the whole of Upper Middle Earth. None shall escape.'

And he gathered together his army, and prepared to march north over the River Raver and to subdue all the peoples of Upper Middle Earth.

Of the Sense of Foreboding Experienced by Men and Elves

Men and Elves watched with foreboding as the season curdled, and spring seemed to retreat. As the power passed from the Dragons to Sharon, so the sky grew bone pale, and a bleak wind came searching from the north, withering the green wheat and turning the white blossom to ice on the trees.

And King Prorn III, Lord of Men, called his advisers about him. 'Tell me why it is,' he asked them, 'that the season reverses? The land has become inhospitable; winter succeeds spring; bears and wolves prowl the woodlands, and only yesterday I slipped on some ice on my bathroom floor and barked my shin, very painful, that.'

And the royal advisers could not explain it, except that it boded ill for the lands of Men. 'Surely,' they said, 'Sharon is mustering forces, and war is coming.'

'Then,' said Prorn, 'let it come. Though the land grows cold, yet the furnaces of our armourers will stay hot enough.'

'Sire,' said the King's adviser, 'let us send a

messenger to the Elves of Taur-ea-dorpants; for if war comes, there should be alliance between our two peoples.'

But the King grew angry at this counsel. 'Elves? Never! I have sworn a great oath never again to have dealings with the Elves. Did not an elvish witch steal away my youngest son? Did not Queen Eve herself treat him as a criminal, threaten him with death, and cast him into the wilderness – where he wandered crippled in body and struck down by grief in his mind, even unto his lonely death?' For Prorn, not knowing the true fate of his son, believed this to be the truth of things. 'It was a black day for Men when Belend fell in love with that elvish sorceress, and it is better if Elf and Man keep themselves well apart.'

'But if war comes . . .'

'If Sharon invades,' roared Prorn, 'we shall meet him in battle and defeat him! We have fought him many times before, and always we have prevailed. The blood that my heart pumps is the blood of a noble line, for I am descended directly from Rokett the Man, who fought Moregothic himself in the wastelands of the north! And if the Elves trouble us, then we shall fight them too.'

And Prorn ordered granaries stocked with all available food, and instituted rations for all his

people. And he also decreed that all Men with the
skill to work metal should aid the armourers; and the
noise of hammer chiming on anvil rang out like bells
across Mannish lands. Swords were crafted, and also
spears; shields were fashioned from oak and covered
with tanned leather. Parchment was painted with
various public messages, including *Careless Ork-Talk
Costs Lives* and *Dig (in the Chest of your Enemy with a
Spear) For Victory*. The land was busy with pre-
paration for war.

In the elvish kingdoms of central Upper Middle
Earth, however, the poisoning of the seasons was
met with less incomprehension. For Elves, wise in
the ways of nature and skilled at interpreting the
flight of birds, knew that Sharon had upset the
natural balance with some great spell. And they
were filled with terrible foreboding.

Worse, the elvish kingdom was afflicted by the
wasting away of Queen Eve. Never before had an
Elf fallen sick in this manner, and Elves had pre-
viously believed that such illness was the curse only
of the mortal. Yet did she sicken, and her coughing
shook her like a bough troubled by the winds, and
with every cough there came blood into her mouth.
Eleven years she sickened. Some said that this was a

punishment for having mutilated her own daughter; and some said that it was part of the malign magic that Sharon worked to turn the season back from spring to winter, but none knew how to cure her.

And after long suffering, Queen Eve died, the first Elf to die of anything other than wounds in battle. And though many thought her cruel, yet the Elves were stricken with grief.

None knew how to go on; for elfkind had always been ruled by the line of Bleary, but now the only descendant of that line of royal rank was the simulacrum of Lüthwoman. And some said, 'We must crown her Queen, for all that her head has been emptied by grief and madness'; and others said, 'She can never be queen, for she lacks all will, thought or word, and is nothing but an eidolon; and how could she reign?'

And meanwhile the two other great tribes of Elves, the Nodiholdor and the Man-Wëers, disputed amongst themselves what to do. Elsqare was one of the Nodiholdor, and he said: 'Can you not read the signs in the natural world? War is coming, and we must meet war head on. Now is not a time for internal fighting between elf and elf; but we must unite and defeat the common enemy.'

The leading Elf of the Man-Wëers was Túrin

Againdikwittingdn, and his counsel was otherwise. 'I say the Queen must be crowned, for Fate has provided us with her at this time. And if her reign is a silent one, and if she does not command us into battle, then this too is fated. Therefore, if Sharon comes, we should retreat, and let the Men confront him; go north, go west, and cede the land to him.'

'Coward!' called Elsqare in rage.

'Rather caution, which you call cowardice,' said Túrin, raging too after his fashion, 'than the reckless wildness of the Nodiholdorim, which would bring destruction upon all elfkind.'

And so a great division opened up in the heart of the elvish people. And Túrin declared that the eidolon of Lüthwoman was Queen, and readied his followers to leave that land; and Elsqare commanded his followers to prepare for war, and polish their very attractively designed armour, and make sure to clear all the dirt and grime from the lines of swirly engraving on the swords, and so on.

Of the Breaking of the Storm

Sharon bred new Orks from the mud of Moider!, and fashioned a greater army than any had yet seen. And he pondered long how to over-ruin the whole of Upper Middle Earth, and finally he was ready.

In form he was a gigantic eyeball, so ungainly that it was quite a palaver moving him, actually; for this form was weighed down with the curse of Emu that had put him in this form. Yet he knew the Dragons' magic guaranteed him victory in battle only if he himself were present. And so he planned and pre-pared for twelve months: and this period was the first winter year, for all through its length the season remained unchanged, and frost was in the ground.

At the end of this year he used the Thing™, and his newfound Dragon power, to spawn a brood of eyeballicules. At the back of his eyeball-body was a spot to which would have been attached, had this been a regular eyeball in a regular body, the optic nerve; and with magic Sharon opened this as an orifice, and from it emerged a great stream of balls, some large as footballs, some small as insect eggs, and all sizes in between. A thousand flew out, and a thousand more, and every one was an eyeball of Sharon, through which he could see the world and influence its course. And these balls rolled about the floor in all directions, piled high. And Ork guards, running around in terror as they often did, did slip upon them, for they were roll-y under their feet as myriad marbles; and they did fall hard upon their snouts with cries of 'U-hurg!' and a clattering sound.

And the eyeball-spawn of Sharon spilled from the casements, and ran down the staircase, and many of them rolled clean away from the tower and were carried away by streams or picked up by birds. But birds that ate them could not digest them, for the Dragons' magic made Sharon invulnerable to harm, and they died and their bodies rotted where they fell.

So it was that Sharon's eyes were disseminated throughout Upper Middle Earth, and many of them remain unaccounted for even today. Many ended up being mistaken for marbles by eager marble-collecting children – a terrible mistake to make, for though they somewhat resembled marbles, and grew glassier and harder over the ages, nevertheless they were distillations of Evil; and anyone who played marbles with them would be sure to lose. Lose, I say!

With the terrible shame and despair that attends the loss of a game of marbles! Evil! Woe! Beware!

And I say to marbles-players: *you have been warned*.

This magical feat exhausted Sharon, and he slept for another twelve months. But he awoke, when eventually he did, to a new sense of the world around him, and a new power.

Sharon made his final preparations for war and conquest. Because no living horse could bear to carry Sharon, he ordered his Orks to slay ten stallions, and after death they stitched them together, and reanimated them to create a single hideous frankenstallion. And this was the terrible steed of Sharon, the big-mouthed horse of Pan-tomby – for upon this dark large-toothed steed he desired to make tombs for all, and furthermore all his constituent parts had come from the tomb, so therefore did Pan-tomby become the name of his steed. And terrible was the gnashing and chewing and swallowing that attended this steed. And if you think ordinary horse flatulence is an unpleasant thing, you should have had a whiff of what came out of this undead quadruped. And, obviously, when I say 'you should have had a whiff' I mean 'you should count yourself lucky that you never *had* a whiff'. Two words: *desolate odours*. Enough said.

Sharon took one of his eyeball-sized eyeballs, which is to say a conventional-sized eyeball, and he clothed it in a cloak, and charmed a mailed glove to hold the rein. And above his non-existent head he crowned himself with the golden crown of Supper's Ready, for he planned to devour the whole world. And he wore the Thing™ around his non-existent neck.

So Sharon the Evil rode from the tower of Cirith Connoli at the head of a mighty Army of Evil, to claim possession of all of Upper Middle Earth.

The first people of Blearyland to know of the coming of Sharon were the fishermen who dwelt on the western coast. For they fished, winter or summer, and where crops failed and fruit did not grow, Men and Elves both had traded with the fishermen. So they were doing alright, financially, thanks for asking. They got by. They were comfortable, I suppose you'd say. Actually, it's not very polite to probe into their fiscal affairs, so perhaps we'll leave that for now, if you don't mind.

One day a certain fisherman, called Wetman, was fishing in the dark mid-sea, alone in his coiled hull, when a huge-headed sea serpent rose from the waters.

'Heed me!' called this beast, and his breath came over the small ship as a stench of rotting fish, and Wetman saw the glistening roof of the monster's mouth, and its baleen teeth. He trembled, fearing that his death was come.

'Heed me!' said the serpent. 'I am Urd, and I dwell in the deeps of the ocean with my many sinuous kin. But I know this much about the dry land: the dead Men and the dead Elves of the dry land are buried in the earth, and their bodies sink slowly through the sightless ground as clods sink through water, only more slowly. And they pass eventually into underground rivers that though unseen still run, as all rivers do, to the sea. There I and my brood devour the bodies of the dead, for this is our food. Heed me! I bring fell news to the land of Men – I tell you that the age of Men and of Elves is drawing to a close. The Evil Lord has made a deal with the Dragons, and now no Elf or Man can resist him, for he is invulnerable and immortal and cannot be defeated in battle. Many will be slain in the days to come, and I say to you, and to all men, bury your dead, do not burn them in heaps. Because unless they are buried they cannot feed my brood, and if I am not fed then I shall be forced to leave the ocean and to slither across the lands in search of a meal. Heed me!'

And Wetman, shuddering with fear and cold replied, 'That's very interesting, only, um, why are you telling me this?'

And Urd said, 'Aren't you a mighty king amongst mortal Men?'

And Wetman said, 'No, I'm just a fisherman.'

And Urd said, brightly, 'Sorry! My mistake – crossed wires somewhere, I'm sure. Sorry to have bothered you.' And he sank beneath the waves.

When Wetman returned to his harbour home, dazed by this encounter and wondering how to relate it to his fellows, he discovered that the entire town was otherwise occupied. For a monstrous crowd of ocean salamanders, seawolves, marine warlocks and other horrors of the deep had come crowding out of the sea and were attacking the town. They came wet from the sea surge, and their hook-ended swords glistened, but they were strong with slimy muscle and they killed many.

The survivors fled, and made their way to the court of King Prorn, bringing their terrible tidings with them.

They were met by Men of the south, who brought terrible tidings of their own. 'Sire,' they said. 'We have dwelt for generations past on the northern bank of the mighty River Raver, and so great is its flood

that none might cross it; for the river is too wide to
span with a bridge, and its turbulent waters make
swimming impossible, and it is treacherous for boats.
And for an age Orks have sometimes crossed in little
boats, and we have sometimes fought with them, but
only a few at a time can cross by this route. But now
a dire fate has befallen us.'

And the King did ask, 'What?'

'The River has frozen solid as far west as the Bend
of E,' said the Men of the south. 'For we have had
nothing but winter for twenty-four months, without
spring or summer to thaw the chill. And now a mighty
host of Orks has crossed the ice, and has driven all
Men and Elves from the southlands. None have been
able to stand against them.'

At this terrible news, the cry of 'Sorrow!' was
taken up in the streets of Mantown, and people left
their houses and came into the open. 'Should we
fly?' they said. 'Gather our belongings and move
north?'

'No!' said the King, standing in his stirrups to
address the crowd in the main square, 'we must not
flee, or we will be forever on the run. We shall meet
this army of Orks and defeat it in battle!' And some
of his people slipped away to the north with their
most precious things in sacks on their backs, for a

dread was in their hearts; and others ignored their despair and strapped on their armour.

News of the advancing army of Orks reached Elfton as well; where the Coward Elves, as they were called, had long been making their preparations for departure. 'The time has come,' they said. 'Why die in pointless battle? By flight we remain immortal.'

And Elsqare and his elves replied, 'Take your blank Queen and leave if you will. But is there anywhere to flee? It seems to me that you do nothing but postpone the inevitable end of all things.'

And Túrin replied, 'Must you *always* be so gloomy? Would it *kill* you to think positively just once?'

To which Elsqare said, 'I'm only saying . . .'

And Túrin continued, 'You're a real mug-of-mead-half-empty sort of elf, aren't you?'

And Elsqare, rather wounded in his feelings, said stiffly, 'I like to think of myself as a realist.'

'Pessimist, rather,' said Túrin.

'At least I'm not a coward,' snapped Elsqare.

'Oh, you're *wild*,' said Túrin, perhaps speaking ironically, it's not obvious, but certainly not meaning anything praiseworthy by the word. And Túrin left with his followers and they made their way west. But they encountered a marauding band of sea-monsters and Orks, and doubled back on themselves, trekking across the northern grassplains to Lothlomondwisky.

The last army of Men, and the last army of Elves, marched out to meet the horde of Orks on the Plain of Crossed Swords. And there they arrayed themselves, on separate sides of the battlefield. And neither army would so much as talk with the other, because each side blamed the other for the whole Belend and Lüthwoman thing. The Men viewed Lüthwoman as 'no better than she ought to be', which phrase the Elves did not quite understand but which they assumed was meant to be insulting. On their side, however, the Elves viewed Belend as a gigolo, a lounger, a chancer, and a seducer who had had his wicked way with the pure daughter of Queen Eve.

The Men did say 'Your elvish seductress brought about tragedy and the death of the King's son.'

The Elves did say 'Well if it comes to that – your priapic young man brought about the madness of the Queen's daughter *and* the death of the Queen *and* the ending of the royal line Bleary which stretched to the beginning of time, which trumps your distress I think. Besides, though the King's son died – well, he was a mortal Man and doomed to die sooner or later.

But Queen Eve was an immortal Elf, and did not deserve her fate.'

The Men did consider this argument, and after much thought did reply, 'Yah!'. And some of them did display their naked hindquarters to the elvish soldiers, who looked away with expressions of haughty disgust.

And so there was no prospect of alliance between the armies, even though they faced the same enemy.

And so it was that the army of Sharon swarmed over the horizon. It was the largest gathering of Orks ever seen under the skies of Upper Middle Earth. It stretched the whole of the horizon from east to west, and its troops poured on and on as if fed by a ceaseless source. Some Orks were albino-white and foul to see, and some were green-skinned and icky, and they had noses, some more than one. But many had only one functioning eye, having torn out the other in honour of Sharon their leader whom they honoured as a god, even though this resulted in them having greatly lessened depth-perception capacities. And they were armoured with heavy iron breast-plates, and wore Le Creuset helmets of great weight and solidity.

Soon they covered the whole ground with their

number, and they chanted in terrible unison 'Blood! Blood! Blood!' and stamped their iron-shod feet in time, and the tremors travelled through the ground to the armies of Elves and Men.

And then they fell silent, for they sensed the arrival of their Lord and Leader was near. And the silence was more terrible to the Men and Elves than the chanting.

Prorn the King called across the space to the Elvish army, saying 'You're always ready with a wise-crack, Elsqare, say something to lighten the mood.'

Elsqare looked out at the thick crush of orkish bodies, and said only, 'Actually, nothing very comical occurs to me.'

So Prorn turned to his own men and called out, 'Be ready to fight, and be not afraid to die, if die you must. But fight!' And his men cheered, although it sounded but a weakly hurrah in the cold air.

And Elsqare turned to his men, and said in a clear bell-like voice: 'Unaccustomed as I am to pre-battle speeches, I would just like to take a moment to thank you all for turning up, many of you at terribly short notice. Believe me it's *very* much appreciated. And I'd like to thank the caterers for supplying the salted meats – it may be two years old, but it tastes no more than fourteen months.'

And a smattering of applause rippled through the elvish army.

As one the Orks began calling 'Doom! Doom!', and this created a deep rumbling wash of sound. For Sharon was approaching on his horse Pan-tomby. A path cleared through the horizon-spanning tangled thicket of orkish warriors, and Sharon rode forward.

And at the sight of him all hope left the hearts of the Men and the Elves; for the Dragons' charm made Sharon their master, and their wills were not enough to fight the potency of this magic. The irony of the spell was that the truest warriors, whose loyalty was strongest, were least able to fight – because their hearts told them that Sharon was their true and liege lord; whilst at the same time the most fickle of the soldiers, whose sense of loyalty was weakest, were best motivated to defend themselves, for they barely recognised any master but themselves in the first place.

Many threw their weapons and themselves on the ground in despair; and Prorn himself wavered. 'Blearyland,' he called to the high heavens. 'A cursed land, named for a cursed king. And so the curse works itself out in blood and death.'

And the Orks laughed and jeered, and some coughed and cheered, and some others acted daft and weird, and others otherwise expressed their delight in their imminent and total victory.

Sharon pulled up his terrible frankenstallion at the head of his army, and rose up in his stirrups. And, with the power of the Thing™ he cast his voice into the sky so that every elvish and every mannish soldier could hear it.

'Hearken!' he called. And because his voice was projected at a point close to the Thing™ itself, there was a shrieky feedbacky sort of noise that made Orks, Men and Elves alike duck their heads down and clutch their ears and wince markedly. So Sharon made certain adjustments.

'Sorry about that,' he said. 'That's better. So – hearken! Listen to me, you the last army of Elves, and you the last army of Men. Know this, that the Dragons of Making have granted me a fourfold charm: and that by their magic I am lord over all Men and all Elves forever – and that I am invulnerable, and immortal, and invincible in battle. Purge your hearts of hope! Your doom is to die, or else live on as my slaves.'

And Sharon laughed, and his laughter was thunder in the mountains, and the rattling of the wings of innumerable crows ascending in winter skies, and the grumbling of icebergs. He went: 'Ha ha ha ha ha!

Ah-*ha* ha ha! Ah-ho ho ho! Ah-ha-ha ha! Ah-ha-ha
ha!' And, furthermore he went: 'Ha! Ha! Ha! Ha!
Ha! Ha! Ha! Ha! Ha! Ha! Ha! Ha! Ha! Ha! Ha!
Ha! Ha! Ha! Ha! Ha! Ha! Ha! Ha! Ha! Ha! Ha!
Ha! Ha! Ha! HA! HA! HA! HA! HA! HA! HA!
HA! HA! HA! HA! HA! HA! HA! HA! **HA!**
HA! HA! HA! HA! HA! HA! HA! HA! HA!
HA! HA! HA! HA! HA! HA!' And he laughed so
hard he made himself wheezy, and had to sit back
down in the saddle, saying 'Oh, dear, oh dear, oh.
Dear.'

And the Orks cheered.

But the last hope perished in the breasts of Men
and Elves, for they knew in their hearts that what
Sharon said was true: every Elf and every Man was
drawn to Sharon as lord. Some fled, deserting their
comrades in this darkest hour; some ran towards the
orkish army with their arms up; and only a very few
remained about their leaders.

And Sharon called, 'Charge!'

And so his myriad Orks bellowed and howled
with blood lust, and surged forward, like floodwaters
made flesh and armed with steel. They cut down
those few Men and Elves who had run forward to
declare their allegiance to Sharon, for they were
careless of whom they killed.

The two armies of Men and Elves that remained were nothing but rumps; yet, through sheer blind habit, or else through some twist of character that resisted the Dragons' charms, they readied themselves for the fight. Prorn himself raised his sword and screamed, a scream such as a wind-spirit[24] might make in the height of the tempest; and in this sound he found release from the agony of conflicted loyalties the appearance of Sharon had produced in his breast. And he stepped forward as the front rank of slathering Orks crashed upon him; and he swung his sword from left to right, cutting down three enemy warriors, and he swung his sword from right to left and cut down two more, and then the crush overwhelmed him. And his body was slashed by many hatchets and trampled under many iron-shod feet, and the life was cut and crushed from his frame. And so ended the life of King Prorn III, known as the Grrreat.

His bodyguard fought as well as they could, though hopelessly outnumbered. And for a little while the very size of the Ork army prevented them from making their victory an immediate thing, for

---

24   A zephyr, or Spirit of the Howling Gale; not a clockwork spirit of the sort that keeps your wristwatch wound over a period of several years.

the Men stood in a circle with their weapons out, and only a certain number of Orks could present themselves at any one assault. So the Men fought on, cutting and hacking, until a wall of ork corpses grew before them; yet Orks still clambered over the top of this and rained down blows and axe-ended spears upon them. One by one the guard of Men perished. Prince Stronginthearm, Prorn's strong-armed firstborn, died of a gash that cut his head in twain.[25] Prince Braveface, Prorn's second-born, died under a savage barrage of hook-ended swords.

Nor did the Elves do better. They fought with elegant coordination, sweeping their long gold-decorated steel lances to and fro and clearing great swathes from the mass of advancing Orks. But there were always more Orks to come clambering over the bodies of their fallen, and soon even the strength of the Elves was exhausted, and their formation was overrun. Some Elves died there and then; some were carried off to be mutilated or torn to pieces by howling bands of Orks; and some few were captured by Sharon's personal bodyguard – who alone of the horde possessed a modicum of self-restraint amongst all the blood lust and berserker fury and such.

---

25 Which is to say, into twelve pieces.

And so Sharon had brought before him a dozen Elves and fewer Men, clad about with cruel iron-thorned chains, their hands bound at their backs. And they were forced to kneel before the Evil One and his terrible steed on the blood-sodden ground.

'Yield,' he called, 'and swear allegiance to me as your Lord, and I shall not kill you quite yet. For I have need of slaves, and my torments may yet spare you for years yet.'

With the Dragons' magic pressing upon their heart neither elf nor man could resist. Elsqare the Elf, the last Nodiholdor of noble blood still alive, swore allegiance to Sharon the Dark Lord. And so did all the Elves, and all the Men.

So ended the last battle, with evil victorious. The Orks of Sharon's horde spent their fury, making the land around the battlefield a wasteland in their ber-serker rage, until the rage passed off them and they had a berserker hangover. Which only made them grumpier. And there really wasn't enough berserker-seltzer in the stores of the medical orderlies to go round, and some people got very snappish and unhappy, let me tell you.

And Sharon rode to Elfton, with his captives in chains behind him, and made it his new capital. Thus came to an end the history of Men and Elves; for neither lived happily ever after – the Men, because they were mortal and could not live ever after, regardless of their mood; and the Elves, because although they *could* live ever after, it was very hard for them to be happy under the new regime.

Sharon rode about his new kingdom, and in every place he came he commanded automatic fealty, because the Dragons' magic was strong. And even if elf or man had been able to stand against him, they would have faced the fundamental problem of his invulnerability, immortality and invincibility. Which is, I hope you agree, something of a poser.

Of the Tyranny of Sharon, or the 'Sharonny' as it was called

Sharon exulted in his victory. He established a capital for his new empire on the site of Elfton. 'Pull down this elf town,' he ordered the Elves of Taur-ea-dorpants. 'You shall build me a new capital.' And the inhabitants of Elfton were compelled by their malign allegiance to tear apart their own homes and temples, and scatter the debris.

And Sharon set ork overseers over gangs of Men and Elves, to quarry and drag great stones, to cut timber with giant scythes and fashion it, and to build up a vast new building. He commanded men to sieve the lakes of Blearyland for gems to decorate his throne; and to lay down hundreds of fleeces to pan gold from the flowing streams; and ordered Elves to labour twenty hours in the day to raise up the great blocks of stone.

And so, over twelve months of the hardest labour, and many deaths, a great and stark palace uprose. And largely it was composed of rectangles and blocks, and these were built in an uparching lopsided dome, tall as a mountain. And inside was a huge green-black hall, and here Sharon's great lidless eye sat in state upon a vast eggcup of gold, for this, he had discovered, was the best shape for his throne. And all the leaders of Men and Elves left alive trooped into this hall, before the sneering and mockery of phalanxes of Orks, and paid homage to Sharon.

His new capital he called The Sharonage, and over the gateway he placed a sign that read: *Dunberserkin*.

Sharon sent out Tuoni Bleary and Robin Badfellow to scout the land for twenty strong, tall individuals, ten elvish and ten mannish, and these were brought bound to the Sharonage, although they were not tortured or broken. For Sharon required their bodies to be strong.

And they were bound to metal frames in one of the dungeons of the new fortress, and ork surgeons clustered around them, grunting and chuckling; and into the chambers rolled and bounced two score of Sharon's brood of eyeballs, swarming over the black flagstones like hideous insects, rolling and squeaking.

And each of these Men and each of the Elves had their own eyes pulled out with bill-ended tongs; and into the oozing sockets the ork servants pushed two of Sharon's eyeball offspring. Yuk. I mean, I'm sorry to have to relate that last bit, which is pretty repulsive I know, but, you know. The story requires it. So if you've stopped shuddering, we can proceed.

And when this foul surgery was completed the Men and Elves were released from their frames to fall to the floor in despair. And some of them burned in their hearts to end their lives at that time, and some burned to seize metal pokers or blades and kill as many as they could. But all were bound by the Dragons' curse, that Sharon be lord over all Elves and Men, for as long as Elves and Men exist. And Sharon commanded them to take horse and ride about Blearyland making his will known to Elves and Men, and to give him – as he sat in the Sharonage – views of the land he now ruled.

These twenty individuals were called the Eyes of Sharon, although they were known to Men and Elves as the Scary Score of Scanners: and their tragedy was that they served Sharon's evil through no fault of their own, for they were noble spirits, but of a fell necessity. And though they were compelled to do as Sharon commanded them, yet did all Men and Elves shun the Scary Score. They fed them, and gave them shelter, and surrendered their horses to them, because they must; but they loathed them all the same.

And Sharon set his most trusty subalterns as lords over the various shires and provinces of Blearyland, and laid a heavy tax upon them but gave them free rein to treat their underlings as they wished. And for those of the Orks who craved manflesh or elf-flesh to eat, they were permitted to purchase this food for a certain price. And for those who yearned to command troops of mannish slaves, or to force Elves to labour in the fields, they were permitted to do this.

Many copses were burnt; and many creatures killed; for winter continued to prevail in the land, and the myriad Orks were hungry. So many trees were burnt to heat the soil, and many forest animals were slain and eaten.

And yet did Sharon grow uneasy even in his triumph, for he thought again and again of the Dragons' magic. And whilst he could see no weakness in the promise of invulnerability, immortality or invincibility, yet he pondered the fact that he had been granted dominion over only Elves and Men. He thought of the creatures of Upper Middle Earth that were neither elvish nor mannish, and worried over the harm they might do him.

So he sent some of his Eyes to treat with the Dwarfs; but they were uninterested in the happenings in the lands of Men and Elves, being mostly concerned with their own subterranean affairs. 'Leave us alone, bach,' they said, 'and we'll leave you alone. Common sense, that.'

Yet still Sharon fretted. So he sent a command through the whole kingdom, that any person who knew of any danger to his might from a being outside the realm of Men and Elves, should declare it. And none could resist this command.

One day a man approached the gateway of the Sharonage. The fir-needles were tooth-white with frost, and the crust of ice on the snow cracked under his feet leaving deep pitted footprints, and the sky was blue with perfect cold.

And he begged entrance, to approach Sharon himself. 'Why?' demanded the gate-guard in scorn. 'In answer to his command,' replied the man, with great grief in his voice.

He was led to the throne-hall, and Sharon's great lidless eyeball did stare down upon him. 'Why have you come?' he asked.

'In answer to your command, O Lord,' said the man.

'Speak!' said Sharon eagerly. 'Tell me!'

And the man said, 'I was a fisherman, and one day at sea I encountered a sea creature called Urd, who told me that he and his brood in the deep waters feed upon the bodies of dead Men and Elves, buried in the earth, that wash out eventually to the ocean. He warned me that should we stop burying our dead in the earth, then he and his brood would go hungry, and would leave the ocean and swarm over the land to eat.'

Sharon was glad to learn of this, for Urd was such a creature as was not covered in the Dragons' charm; and though he knew himself still invulnerable, immortal and invincible, yet he had no wish to encounter this sea serpent.

As he told his tale, the fisherman wept. And Sharon asked, 'Why do you weep?'

And the fisherman was compelled by the charm to answer him truly. 'I weep to have revealed this to you, my lord. For although I and my kind are all prevented from rebelling against you, yet I yearned to see this realm of yours wasted by these sea beasts, for my heart is dead with bitterness at your dominion.'

Sharon laughed at this. 'Truly!' he said. 'Well, fisherman, *my* desire is to increase your woe. So we must appease these Sea Beasts. You shall ride out with these half dozen of my Eyes, to the lands of the west that abut the sea. And there you yourself shall choose fifty people from each village and a hundred from each town; and they shall be slain by my Orks and buried in the ground, as offerings to Urd. I command you to do this thing, and then to return here to me to see what other tasks I may have for you.'

The fisherman wept at this, and yet had no choice but to obey. And in this barbarous manner was the threat of Urd abated by Sharon.

And Sharon sent his Eyes throughout the land, and ordered all Elves and Men to swear an oath that they would never plot against him, seek to overthrow him, or rise up. And with tears and despair, all swore this oath. For they could not do otherwise.

Of Eärwiggi

Once there was a boy called Eärwiggi, which in
Elvish means 'ceremonial earmuff made of horsehair';
and in after times he was sometimes called Eärwiggi
of the Mighty Fib, for his destiny was bound up with
a fib that could bring down evil empires and change
the very fabric of the world. It is a strange and
instructive story, and its moral is: always tell the
truth – unless telling a *small* fib can bring down evil
empires and change the very fabric of the world.

Now Eärwiggi was born in a small home on the
banks of the River Optik, and he grew up there with
his mother and father. He grew strong and tall, and
learnt how to fish from the river, and how to take the
honey from bees without being stung by them; and
he learnt which forest fruit and mushroom are good
to eat, and which not.

He had neither brother nor sister, and there were
no neighbours nearby; but from time to time visitors
would come by, to trade with his parents, or travelling to some other place and hoping for refreshment;
and some of these visitors were elven, and some were

Men, but never Elves and Men at the same time. And when he asked his parents about this they said: 'Once in this land Elves and Men were friends; but there has been a falling out recently, and now no Elf and no Man will greet the other in friendship.'

'What sort of falling out?' asked Eärwiggi, for he was always curious.

But his parents were reticent. 'Oh,' they said. 'Grown-up stuff.' And they taught him the stories and traditions of both Men and Elves.

And then one year there came dire news from the outside world. It was said that the land languished under winter when it should be spring. But although the rest of Blearyland was laid over by winter, yet the field and hollow by Eärwiggi's home, and the bank of the river there, were not afflicted. Visitors were amazed to discover this; the only place in the world not afflicted by the curse of ice.

'Something terrible is abroad,' said one broad-bearded man who had come to trade metal for smoked fish, and fabrics woven by Eärwiggi's mother. The trade had been made, and now he sat in their hearth drinking ale. 'Some say that Sharon has made a pact with the Dragons of Making, a terrible spell. They say that he will cast the world in an endless winter.'

Eärwiggi was sitting under the table, holding its leg, as he sometimes did. And he could see his parents exchange a mysterious look between them.

The trader noticed it too, by the firelight. 'Yet you are free of the curse here,' he said. 'The land outside your walls is fresh with late spring, when the rest of Blearyland is frozen and dead. How can this be?'

'We do not know,' said Eärwiggi's father.

The trader stared hard at both of them. When he spoke eventually, it was with a grim tone: 'Some say that you are enchanters. Is it so?'

Eärwiggi's father shook his head sorrowfully in the firelight.

But the trader would not stay. Though it was dark outside, and bitterly cold beyond the borders of this house, yet he gathered his things and left. After that very few traders came, and soon Eärwiggi was left with none but his parents for company.

Eärwiggi reached the age of eleven, which is an important age of transition to the elvish people, the age they say when a boy ceases to be a child. And on this day Eärwiggi's father took him to the copse by the river to teach him the arts of boat-building. And they worked at this in the day, although it was no labour for Eärwiggi delighted in it and accounted it play. And they worked again the following day, and the day after.

As they worked together, Eärwiggi said to his father: 'Father, I am worried.'

'Worried about what, my son?'

'It seems to me that I am akin to the travellers who come here, and not akin to you and mother.'

'Aching?' asked his father.

'Akin,' clarified Eärwiggi.

His father laughed aloud at such a strange statement by his son, and said, 'Why would you say so?'

'The travellers who come here have two hands, as do I. Yet you and mother have each but one hand. Are you a different race to the Elves and the Men of whom you have told me?'

His father shook his head, and wiped sweat from his beard with the crook of his arm. 'No, son,' he said. 'I lost my hand to a wild beast, and your mother lost hers to – an accident. Together they are only a pair of accidental injuries. But you are our son, created by the two of us together.' And he drew his son to him and hugged him.

That afternoon, after the boat-building was done, Eärwiggi knew his last purely happy day. And in later years he thought back to this day, and thought that there must be such a moment in all lives; a transition point from the carelessness of childhood to the anxieties of the fully grown. Such a moment can only be known afterwards, when time has already swallowed it; but it remains sweet for all that.

The moment was by the river. The landscape in the distance was austere; the mountains in the east cold and tall, and even the hills to the south were capped with snow. Yet the land around Eärwiggi's home was green. He stood knee-deep in the grass watching the river flow smoothly past; and the surface of the river was touched by motes like stars in a moving sky as water boatmen stood upon the water. Fruit trees that grew behind the house were feathery with blossom. A cicada hidden somewhere in the grass tried its voice by fits, as if practising upon a long unused instrument.

He heard shouting from the front of the house, and the moment broke.

Running round to the front he found his father and mother standing in their doorway, and a band of men on horseback in the road before them. The leader was the spade-bearded trader who had sometimes visited. 'Sharon has walked an army across the frozen River Raver into Blearyland,' he called, and his face was red with choler. 'The King has ordered all Men to join the army, for we must fight the last great battle now.'

Eärwiggi's father said nothing, but it was clear from his face that he did not intend to go with these people.

'Are you not a Man?' bellowed the trader, leaning down and shaking a sword in his wrath. 'Can you deny it?'

This puzzled Eärwiggi, for he had thought his father elven, and had assumed that he himself was elven also. But his father did not deny that he was a Man, only folded his arms across his chest.

'Why would you not fight?' growled the trader, 'a man with a family in the face of such a threat? Are you a coward? Or – are you in truth a sorcerer? Have you made some deal with Sharon?'

'No!' said Eärwiggi's father, fiercely.

And the horses of the band of Men started and shuffled their hooves. And the trader leant back in his saddle; until one of the other Men said, 'Kevin, he's crippled, a one-handed man – maybe that's why he's loath to fight.'

And the trader glowered, and said nothing. And then the Men wheeled their horses and rode away, except for one man whose horse farted as he spurred it, and danced up on its hind legs tossing him to the floor.

And it was peaceful in Eärwiggi's home once more.

Week followed week, and Eärwiggi heard no further tidings of the world outside. Yet he wondered about the great battle being fought to the south; and he tried to imagine the clash of weapons, the stern charges of soldiery, the bravery and the dying. But one morning Eärwiggi got up from his bed to find his parents sitting downstairs simply staring at one another.

'What's wrong?' he asked.

'Eärwiggi,' said his father. 'A dark hand has touched our hearts. Some dreadful thing has happened in this land, and it has touched our spirits. We fear the worst. If anything should happen to us, you must travel far from here: to the north and the west, on the northern bank of the river, and far away. Do you understand?'

Eärwiggi said he understood, although his heart was unready.

The weeks continued to pass, and Eärwiggi and his parents went about their usual business, but something had changed. His father and mother were spirit-broken, oppressed by some heaviness within their hearts that saddened Eärwiggi even though he could not understand it. And though they had no tidings, yet they knew that the battle had gone badly for Mankind.

And one day a band of Orks appeared and at their head a strange shrunken figure, with something of an elvish cast to his features and yet without the dignity or beauty of an elf. His large lips wriggled like slippery ropes, alternately revealing and concealing a set of teeth that a good-sized goat would have been proud to own. Inverted J eyebrows of exaggerated size gave a supercilious cast to his protuberantly gobstopper eyes. He was wearing motley like a jester, but motley full of holes and covered in many splattery stains. It was, in fact, mottled and mothy motley.

'I am Bleary,' he announced, 'and I am your new King, or more strictly your sub-king, a sort of junior king or kingling, serving the community here under the overlordship of Sharon. Who is Big King. I heard in the town upriver that a patch of ground here is still in spring, when the rest of Sharonia is in winter, and I see that it is true. Can you explain it?'

'We cannot,' said Eärwiggi's father.

'Hmm,' said Bleary. 'Hum. Most odd. Ah well, I

like it here. I shall make this my official country
residence. You,' (he pointed at Eärwiggi's father)
'and you' (he pointed at Eärwiggi's mother) 'are
commanded by Sharon himself to make your way to
the place formerly known as Elfton, to help with
municipal construction.'

Eärwiggi's father stepped forward at this command, and Eärwiggi clutched his leg, saying 'Father,
do not obey this command!'

And his father replied, in a low voice. 'I cannot
help myself. Run, son. Flee this place. Do not go
south, for that way will lead you to Sharon and your
doom. Go north, and west, and find if there be any
free place left in Blearyland.'

And he walked through the door, and his wife
walked with him, helpless against the command;
and they walked without resting until they reached
Elfton, and a dark fate.

But Bleary, looking over his new property, and
shooing away Orks who were chasing chickens
across the yard, came upon Eärwiggi sitting underneath the table in the hearth room. 'What's this?' he
said. 'Sprog, is it? Thinking back, I did specify the
man and the woman with my command. This damn
Dragon magic – you've got to be so careful to phrase
these things precisely, or objects fall through the net.

Alright, you little tyke. I am *ordering* you, on behalf of Sharon the mighty, to follow your parents – walk south, do not stop until you reach Elfton, and join in the construction work. Off you go.'

So confident was Bleary of the power of the command that the Dragons' magic gave him, in the name of Sharon, that he paid no more attention to the boy; and his Orks were gorging themselves on the homestead's livestock in the barn, and he hurried out to remonstrate with them. So Eärwiggi hurried from the house.

But he did not walk south. Instead he crept down to the river, and the boat that he had built with his father, and he pushed this into the water and climbed in, lying down in the bottom of it, and allowing the waters to carry him west.

Eärwiggi's boat took him down the long stretches of the River Optik and into the broad amber waters of the Lothlomondwisky. He paddled the boat to the northern shore, and pulled it into the sand. Using a fallen bough he levered it over to make a roof, and burrowed under the sand at the stern to make an entrance. With thread and hook, and a twist of his hair as lure, he caught a salmon in the stream, and cooked it on a driftwood fire.

But the land here was barren with snow, and Eärwiggi underneath his boat-roof slept poorly because of the cold. He was still tired when the morning came, and he rubbed his eyes and pondered his fate as he walked beside the lake. The shore of the lake was sandy, with pebbles set in the sand. And when he looked more closely at the sand he saw that it was composed of tiny fragments of thin shells, broken by waves into patterns of miniature crescents and stars and other shapes, shells frail as paper. He thought to himself: did shrimp and watersnails think their shells would keep them safe in such a world?

Now, the winter was severe across Blearyland, but more severe still further north; and the wolves of the far north had been driven south by weather extreme even for them. They flocked from the Wa!-Wastes into Illbhavior, and roamed the northern shores of the River Optik. And as Eärwiggi wandered lone and lorn, a pack of wolves scented him. And they came in a tight pack, loping across the sand.

Eärwiggi saw them approach, and thought quickly. He looked to the frost-furred trees at the top of the beach, and looked to the swiftly approaching pack of wolves. And he ran, fast as his eleven-year-old legs could run: but not to the trees. Instead he ran straight into the amber waters of the lake, and swam out. The water was cold as death is cold, and Eärwiggi gasped; but still he swam.

The wolves gathered on the water's margin, but did not come any closer. They turned and turned in tight circles, with their long shaggy muzzles and yellow eyes always pointing at Eärwiggi, waiting for the time when he was too tired and was forced to come ashore. For a while Eärwiggi trod water, and wondered what to do.

But then he heard somebody speaking a language he did not understand; and the words of this language were as follows: 'Bach! glub! glub! over*yeer*! Look you!'

And looking around Eärwiggi saw a figure floundering in the water, a little way from where he was. So he swam over to the figure, crying aloud with the cold as he pushed his arms through the water.

'Hello,' said the figure. His broad head was just visible above the water, but Eärwiggi was aware of the furious action of his limbs underneath the surface.

'Hello,' said Eärwiggi.

'Bit of bother, look you,' said the figure. 'A little help would be very special.'

'Alright,' said Eärwiggi. 'What's the problem?'

'The problem is that my beard, like, is tied to a boulder under the water. On the lake bed, do you see, blub-glub.'

'How did that happen?'

'Oh, it's a long story, actually. But, you see, what with the beard tying me here I've been treading water. For quite a long time in fact. We Dwarfs we're strong, and good on endurance, but there's a limit, and I'm not far off that limit now, I'd say.'

'Oh dear.'

'If you'd be so good as to swim down – you can feel your way down the beard like a hairy anchor chain. Unsnag it, and I'll be forever in your debt.'

So Eärwiggi took a deep breath, and dived under the water. It was many yards to the lakebed, and he pulled himself down the dwarf's beard through the peat-red waters. He could see his way as he swam, but he felt down to a slimy smooth boulder, around which the dwarf's beard had been wrapped and tied. Though the water was cold enough to chill his heartbeat, and though he worked blind, yet Eärwiggi had nimble fingers and he was soon able to unpick the knot.

He struggled to the surface, and took as deep a breath as his frozen lungs allowed him. 'I can't thank you enough,' said the Dwarf. 'I was on the verge of going under the water then, I don't mind telling you. Let's get over to the shore.'

'There are,' Eärwiggi panted, 'wolves . . .'

'Bah,' said the Dwarf. 'Wolves? Neither year nor there.'

'Year?' said Eärwiggi, who was confused and weary with the great cold.

'Come on,' said the Dwarf. He splashed over to the beach with strokes of his little arms. And the wolves saw him coming, and gathered in a pack. The Dwarf reached the shore as the wolves prepared to lunge for him, each animal competing with its fellow for first bite. But the Dwarf plucked heavy pebbles from the sand under the shallow water, and hurled them with his muscular arms. A first pebble struck the lead wolf between its eyes and split its skull; a second caught another wolf in the same spot, with the same result. The Dwarf drew back his arm for a third throw, and the remaining wolves turned their tails and ran for the treeline.

The Dwarf collapsed face down in the water. As Eärwiggi dragged him up the beach, with no small effort, and many fallings-over, he murmured, 'Glad that second stone sent the rest away. I wouldn't have had the strength for a third throw, look you. That's what three days and three nights treading water will do for your muscles, la.'

Eärwiggi dragged the Dwarf to the upturned boat, and left him under cover there. Then he caught more fish from the stream, and lit a fire, and dried himself and his clothes, and did the same for the Dwarf's clothes. And after sleeping for many hours, and eating his fill of fish, and wringing out his beard and plaiting it and tying it several times around his waist, the Dwarf became more much conversational.

'My name,' he said, 'is Nobbi. And I am in your debt, young fellow.'

'My name is Eärwiggi. And I am in yours. Debt I mean. For you drove off the wolves.'

'Driving off wolves? That's sport, that is. Don't mention it.'

'Sir Nobbi,' said Eärwiggi, 'where are you from? For I notice that you say *thass* instead of that's, and *year* instead of here.'

'Dwarfish accent, that,' said Nobbi. 'Mel. Oh. Dios. *I* think so, any rate.'

'And how did you come to be tied to the rock at the bed of the lake?'

'Ah,' said the Dwarf. 'Long story.'

'We have time.'

'Not for this story. No, when I say long, I mean long. *Long*. Last all winter in the telling.'

'They say the winter will never end.'

'Well,' said the Dwarf. 'Quite. What about you?'

'My parents have been made into slaves by the Evil One, Sharon. He has overrun the whole of Blearyland, and made all the people into slaves; for a Dragon's spell has given him dominion over all Men and Elves for as long as there are men and elves.'

'Hmm,' grunted Nobbi, in assent. 'Politics, is it?'

'Politics?'

'Always *some* politics going on with Men and Elves and Orks. Good one season, evil the next. The way I see it, good, evil, whichever: the government always gets in.'

'I don't understand,' said Eärwiggi.

'If I was you, boy,' the Dwarf continued, 'I'd take a dwarfish perspective on things. I mean, if fighting the ultimate battle of good against evil actually *changed* anything, they'd make it illegal. Don't you think?'

Eärwiggi pondered this. 'You do sound a little disillusioned with the whole political system, Sir Nobbi.'

'Disillusioned?' said the Dwarf. 'Perhaps I am a

little jaded, la, with the two-party system. Why does it have to be *either* good *or* evil, see? Why can't we have a ethical system that truly represents the rainbow of moral positions real people adopt in the real world, see?'

But this conversation was only puzzling to Eärwiggi's head. 'Surely I should be good – shouldn't I? Strive at all times to tell the truth, for instance?'

'Truth,' said Nobbi, knowingly.

'Isn't the truth better than lies?'

'Sometimes,' said the Dwarf, tapping his prodigious nose.

'At any rate,' said Eärwiggi, 'I still hope for the final victory of good over evil.'

'You think?' said the Dwarf. 'Why?'

'Well,' said Eärwiggi. 'My parents told me many stories as I grew up about the history of Upper Middle Earth, and in all of them it seemed that good was defeated, that catastrophe was inevitable, that evil was about to prevail for all time – until at the *very last minute*, with the last glimmer of hope, good triumphed.'

'Stories,' said Nobbi, sucking the last flesh from the bones of the salmon Eärwiggi had caught. 'You think because it's been like that in history so far, that it'll be like that in the future? Why should it?' He flourished his hand in the air with a turning motion, and said, 'Good triumphs at the last against the odds one time. Good triumphs at the last against the odds a second time. Good triumphs at the last against the odds a third time, la. Does it seem likely to you that it's going to go on and on like that?'

'Um,' said Eärwiggi. He could feel the last ember of hope dying in his heart, and it was an uncomfortable feeling, a bit like indigestion but more spiritual.

'Pooh,' said Nobbi, by which he meant to express dismissive scorn. 'If you toss a coin and it comes up 'eads six times in a row, do you say to yourself "well this *proves* that no matter how many times I toss this coin, it'll always turns up 'eads?" Is *that* your logic?'

'So you're saying . . .'

'Law of averages, isn't it,' said the Dwarf. 'Sooner or later evil is bound to triumph. *That's* politics, see.'

'So Sharon is now Lord of Upper Middle Earth for ever?'

'Could be.'

'And has evil finally triumphed after all? It is a grim thought.'

'What was it you said the Dragon magic said? For as long as there are Elves and Men? Best get used to it.'

'But if I fall into the hands of the Orks, they'll

211

make me a slave and work me to death – or eat me – or otherwise crush my spirit and destroy me.'

'Master Eärwiggi, you saved me from drowning, and you've fed me, and I'll repay you by keeping you out of the 'ands of the Orks. Where are you travelling?'

'West,' said Eärwiggi, remembering his parents' words. 'And north.'

'Cold up north,' said Nobbi. 'But I've always wanted to go west. So west we'll go.'

And the first thing Nobbi did was to draw forth a myth-army knife from his belt, and with it to skin the two wolf carcasses.

'You mean,' said Eärwiggi, 'that you had that knife all along? Why didn't you just cut your beard with it and swim free?'

'Cut my beard, bach?' said Nobbi, horrified. 'Do you *hear* what you're saying? Cut my own beard? That's sacrilege, that is.'

And he scraped the skins and dried them in the wind; and he cooked the meat and salted it at a salt-lick nearby; and when the skins were ready he wrapped himself in one and Eärwiggi in the other.

In this fashion, protected against the winter and with a small store of food, the Dwarf and the boy travelled together, moving west along the northern shoreline of the Loth. And they had many adventures, too many to relate here, frankly.

They passed through a desolate landscape, white as summer clouds but chill as death; and the northern wind was a malicious thing, that insinuated itself in at the crevices and rents in their garments and seemed to cut their skin with its very chill.

At last they reached the western seaboard.

They found a camp of two dozen Elves, who were sitting on the strand in a state of considerable dejection. The shell of a boat, half-built, was abandoned on the shore behind them. The Elves sat before their tents, staring at the sea with eyes full of misery.

When Eärwiggi and Nobbi came upon them they were, at first, full of terror thinking them Orks come to kill; and when they saw that the newcomers were not Orks, they fell to tears and wailing. Eärwiggi had never seen Elves crying before.

But this was not the most amazing thing to Eärwiggi; for as he looked around the group he thought he saw his mother, sitting on a rock and looking out at the ocean with a blank face. He approached her and cried out 'Mother!' And though she looked at his face, there was no recognition in her expression.

'Wait,' said the Elves, running over, 'what are you doing?'

'This is my mother,' said Eärwiggi, his eyes full of tears, 'although she pretends not to recognise me.'

'Your mother?' cried the elves. 'Never! This is our Queen, and she has never taken to herself a husband, or borne children. For, as we think, the evil of Sharon has stolen her wits, and left her mind smooth and blank as a new fall of snow over the fields. She cannot be your mother.'

Yet, through his tear-blurred eyes, it seemed to Eärwiggi that the elven Queen was his mother for all that; for she was fair of face, and she had only one hand. And he clasped her one hand and kissed it, and kissed her face; and his tears fell upon her face, and she looked amazed. Her features formed themselves into a questioning expression, and she spoke one word: 'Eä', which is Elvish for 'in or at or to this place or position'.

The Elves stood back in wonder; and Queen Lüthwoman herself seemed to register emotion for the first time, for she looked around her with an expression approaching amazement.

'Child,' said one Elf. 'My name is Túrin Againdik-wittingdn, and I lead this band – for as you have heard, our Queen lies under some curse. Yet never has she spoken any word since her madness fell upon her, and now you have lifted Sharon's curse. Who are you?'

'My name is Eärwiggi,' said Eärwiggi. 'And in this woman you call your Queen I recognise my mother, who was married to my father, and who raised me beside the River Optik far to the east of this desolate place. But my parents were commanded by the authority of Sharon into servitude in Blearyland, and they could not resist. How this woman comes to be here I do not know.'

'It is a mystery,' said Túrin. 'For we left Blearyland and came to this shore before Sharon came to this land and victory. We planned to build a boat and sail the Capital Sea, to try and make our way to Westersupanesse, where we hoped to find a land beyond Sharon's malignancy.'

'We can see the boat,' said Nobbi. 'But it looks to me only half finished.'

'Alas!' cried Túrin.

'Alas!' answered the Elves, and they cast their hoods over their heads.

'Alas?' repeated the Dwarf, in disbelief. 'Come now. Who *says* that? Pull those hoods back, boyos, and stop mincing about. Tell us what happened.'

'We had built half the boat, and looked forward

with hope. But then came a troop of Sharon's soldiers, Orks and beasts, led by a man who bore Sharon's eye in his head. He declared himself the Eye of Sharon, and we could not resist him. His command was a law to our heart, for such is the Dragons' curse. So he ordered us to stop working on the ship, and since then we have been unable to so much as lift a timber to the structure. And he ordered us to prostrate ourselves on the sand, and laughed at us. "Escaping?" he said. "No, you shall not complete your boat, for I order it, and you must obey. And neither do I give you leave to travel any more in Blearyland. But look!" And he laughed again. "There is seaweed to eat, and snow to drink, so you may yet be happy." And so he left, and since he had forbidden us to travel in Blearyland we are stuck here. From time to time he, or one of his kind, stops by as they pass, to laugh at us more.'

'I shall finish your boat,' said Eärwiggi. 'For Sharon's command does not move my heart.'

They were much amazed at this; and yet it proved true. For over the following twelve days, Eärwiggi worked on the boat; and Nobbi helped him. And as the days passed, the land by this portion of seafront thawed, and snowdrops grew, and grass was revealed as the shift of snow withdrew a little. And again the Elves marvelled.

'Truly,' they said, 'the curse of Sharon does not compass you, young Eärwiggi. You are slight in years, but great in power.'

And each night Eärwiggi embraced the elven Queen, and kissed her good night. And every morning she spoke another word.

The first day she said 'Eä!' a second time.

The second day she said 'Eä!' a third time, and Eärwiggi began to fear that it would be her only word, and that her wits were almost as blank as before.

The third day she said 'Se!' And the Elves greatly wondered to hear this, for in Elvish this words means 'utter specified words in a speaking voice'. 'She is amazed at her ability to speak,' declared Túrin. 'As we are! Thus she says this word.'

The fourth day she said 'La!' And the Elves were puzzled, because this meant nothing in Elvish. But Nobbi declared it a word of dwarfish provenance, and suggested that she might be turning into a dwarf; which discomforted the Elves greatly. And they sang mournful songs of bearded queens. But privately Eärwiggi thought it sounded very unlikely.

The fifth day she said, 'Meal!', which means food. And they fed her.

The sixth day she said, 'No!' and looked crossly

upon them. And they were afraid and ashamed, for it is a dire thing when one's monarch looks crossly upon one.

The seventh day she said, 'You!' And they were amazed. 'Me, your majesty?' said Túrin. 'What? What do you want?' But she said nothing more that day.

The eighth day, she said 'Twits!'

The ninth day, she said, 'List!' And Túrin looked sorrowfully, for it seemed to him that his Queen was now simply saying random words.

The tenth day, she said 'En!' and Túrin said, 'What, the letter "n"? That doesn't really make sense.'

The eleventh day, she said, 'To!'

The twelfth day, she said 'Me!' and she pointed at the rocky hills, not far from the beach, which were the westernmost low peaks that grew, moving east, into the Mountain of Byk. But the Elves remained mystified.

And finally the boat was completed, and the Elves thanked Eärwiggi heartily. 'And now we shall leave this land, burdened with the cursed name Blearyland. For although we cannot disobey Sharon, yet his Eye commanded us only to desist from building the boat, and not to travel upon the land, and neither of these things have we done. So we shall hope to reach Westersupanesse, and be free at last from the curse. We say to you: come with us, for your help has been invaluable, really it has.'

But Eärwiggi looked at Nobbi, and said, 'Thanks but no thanks.'

'You sure?' pressed Túrin. 'The land here is cursed. Evil has triumphed. There is nothing to be done but turn our backs on it as a bad job and look for something better.'

'Perhaps,' said Eärwiggi. 'But I still feel I should remain.'

'Then farewell,' said Túrin. 'You have served us well, young Eärwiggi, and one day perhaps we can repay you. Until that time, I urge you to keep your face clean, and always to tell the truth, for these are the badges of Goodness.'

And Eärwiggi smiled, but took this advice with a pinch of salt.

So the Elves made their farewells, and gave Eärwiggi and Nobbi such gifts as they could, and then they pushed the boat from the shore and sailed west, over the horizon. And the last figure Eärwiggi saw was Lüthwoman, Queen of Elves, standing in the prow, or stern – I always get those two mixed up, don't even get me started on port/starboard – anyway, standing at the back of the boat, and waving.

And the thaw had freed a small portion of her mind, such that she recognised Eärwiggi, and smiled at him as she went off. She waved to him with her stump, and then looked at it as if confused for a little space; and then she waved to him with her hand, which was a much better waving device.

And soon they were gone, and the sun followed them over the horizon as if it too were leaving Upper Middle Earth forever.

But the next day came, as next days always do, with a watery sunrise in the skies to the east. And though the whole land laboured under evil tyranny, yet it got on with the business of stirring under the sunshine, to the best of its ability.

And as Nobbi dug tubers from the soil just above the beach, Eärwiggi sat on a stone, and he saw a worrying thing: for a rider on a black horse looked down upon them from a distant hill. He could surely see the green land, like a bite from the otherwise covering snow; and he could see the empty beach, with only a boy and a dwarf by the sea.

And when Eärwiggi looked again, the rider was gone.

Nobbi returned, and the two of them cooked the tubers, and ate them for breakfast. 'Thank heavens,' said the Dwarf, 'them Elves has finally gone. Thought they'd be here forever with their farewells and singing.'

'So,' said Eärwiggi. 'You understood what the Queen was saying, over those twelve days?'

'You'd have to be a moron,' said Nobbi, 'not to understand.'

'Or an Elf,' agreed Eärwiggi. 'Yet I wonder at her words. Can the great Sellāmi truly be here, on this shore, at the very western limit of the mountain chain?'

'Difficult to say really,' said the Dwarf. 'But it's easily checked out, look you.'

So they put on their wolfskins, and made their way over the surface of the deep snow, where it glittered with frozen dew. In an hour of hard walking, sinking their tread into the snow and hauling out each leg to take the next step, they reached the westernmost foothills of the mountain chain, where stark rock dipped down from the spine of peaks eastwards as if a great stone head were reaching to the sea to drink.

The stone presented a blank face to most approaches, yet there was a cave mouth, or so it seemed, where the rock swirled and curled over a black space. So Eärwiggi and Nobbi investigated; and the air inside the cave was cold and sulphurous, and they did not venture inside.

'Here,' called Nobbi. 'Here. Here.' And he pressed himself against the left-hand archway of this cave mouth.

'Where?'

'Inside this rock, look you.'

'*Inside*? How can you tell?'

'Dwarf-knowledge,' said Nobbi.

'I do wish you'd explain it to me.'

'Well,' said Nobbi, feeling his way over the expanse of rock. 'We Dwarfs come into being inside rock, you see. Born there, like. That's what I was doing at the lakeside – I had been quickened, laid if you like, in the rock at the lakeside. Only the lake level must have risen during the time I lay insensate in the stone; and when I broke out, my beard got snagged.'

'That's the story?' said Eärwiggi. 'You told me it was a long story.'

'It is,' said Nobbi. 'Quite. Don't you think?'

'Not really, no.'

'I gave you the shortened version.'

'So you're a newborn? Effectively?'

'Oh we're different to Elves or Men. We're born

with the wisdom of our people already inside us. Anyway, bach, la, look you, never-mind-that-now, what it *means* is that I have a certain *feeling* for stone. It means, for instance, that I know exactly where to smite it—' and he punched the rock hard with his fist, in a sudden motion '—to open it up.' And where Nobbi had punched, the rock split, and inside was the fabled Sellāmi.

They clustered round the opening. 'Oo!' said Eärwiggi.

'Oo,' agreed Nobbi.

'Pick it up,' suggested Eärwiggi.

'*You* pick it up,' said Nobbi. 'It'd have a deleterious effect on me, bach.'

'Deleterious?'

'Trust me.'

So Eärwiggi plucked the Sellāmi from the living rock, and carried it back across the snow field to the beach, by the stream. It felt hot in his hand, and he tucked it inside his wolfskin to keep it safe.

For a while Dwarf and boy sat on the beach beside the stream and debated what to do. But in the midst of their conversation, they heard a yell.

On the far side of the stream was a troop of ork soldiers, together with two – not one, but *two* –

separate Eyes of Sharon, each one mounted on a
black horse.

On hearing that a portion of the north-west was
free of winter, and that strange things were going on,
he had thought to himself: two eyes are better than
one eye, and so I shall send my two most potent
emissaries to see what is going on.

'You!' called the first Eye of Sharon. 'You!'

And Eärwiggi looked as innocent as he could, and
looked over his shoulder, and then tapped himself in
the chest as if surprised, and said, 'Me?'

'Yes! What are you doing here?'

'Nothing.'

'You are under the command of Sharon!' called
the Second Eye. 'I command you to tell the truth.'
But Eärwiggi did not feel this command in his heart,
and thought to himself, 'Not likely.'

At this Nobbi stood up and took out his knife.
'Leave him be!' he called. 'He's my friend and I'll not
stand by to see him bullied.'

'We have no quarrel with you or your kind,
Dwarf,' said the first Eye. 'But we have dominion
over all Elves and all Men. Boy! What have you
been doing here – speak truthfully.'

And to this command, any Elf or Man would have
said: *we have uncovered the fabled Sellāmi from the rocks*

over there, and here it is. And the Eye of Sharon would have said, 'Give it me.' And any Elf or Man would have done so. But Eärwiggi did not say this. Instead he scuffed the sand with his foot, and looked sideways, and said, 'Nothing,' in a sulky voice.

'You are our slave,' said the second Eye. 'We will send you to the work-gangs in the south, where you will die of exhaustion, or perhaps survive if you are strong and ruthless, I care not which. But first you will explain to us how you came here.'

At this Nobbi grabbed Eärwiggi in a protective hug. 'If you want him!' he called aloud in the clear air, '*Come* and claim him! If you think you're *hard* enough!' He continued taunting across the little stream. 'Come on then, claim him! Go on. Call that claiming? That's *rubbish*, that is. My *granny* could claim better than that, look you! Yah! You couldn't claim candy from a baby, you lot. He's my mate, bach, and you'll not have him.'

So the Eyes of Sharon splashed over the stream on their fierce black steeds, and the ork warriors trotted after them on foot. They surrounded Nobbi and Eärwiggi the two of them, and the Dwarf was forced to concede, 'Alright, you've come over the stream nice and prompt-like, I suppose that counts as claiming.'

Now the fate of the world hung in the balance.
For it occurred to the Eye of Sharon to kill the boy
there and then, just because he was in a bad mood.
And had he done this, then Blearyland would have
languished under the Sharonny until the ending of
time. But he did not kill him; he stayed his hand,
although not from mercy; but the death toll in Upper
Middle Earth had been rather high lately, and it
was getting harder to find slaves to make up the
numbers of the work gangs. And so Eärwiggi was
spared.

And the Eyes of Sharon did not bother to bind
Eärwiggi's arms, for they were confident of the power
of the Dragons' magic to hold him to his will. Instead
the first Eye addressed the Dwarf. 'Sir Dwarf, our
quarrel is not with you. Go, and leave us to our
business with our slave here.'

'Well,' said Nobbi, rubbing his beard. 'I don't
think so.'

'Look over there!' called the second Eye. 'The
boat has gone!' And he spurred his horse and rode
over the beach, to the place where the elvish boat
had been constructed. Its keelprint was still in the
sand, and spare timber and tools were piled by the
grasses at the head of the beach.

The second Eye galloped back along the beach to

the place where Eärwiggi stood. 'Do you know any-thing of this? Answer me truly.'

'No,' said Eärwiggi, grinning.

'There is strange work here,' said the second Eye. 'There were Elves here, and they had been forbidden either to complete their boat, or to travel anywhere in the land. So where are they?'

'Perhaps,' said the first Eye, 'they pulled their incomplete boat into the water in despair and drowned themselves?' He said this with an almost hopeful inflection of voice.

'Possibly,' said the first Eye. 'Although I have never heard of Elves committing suicide before.'

Nobbi cleared his throat loudly. It was a tremend-ous, rumbling, thrumming throat-clearing, such as only Dwarfs can properly manage. It sounded like scree falling down a great slope. 'Right, boyos,' he said, pulling himself to his full height, which by coincidence was exactly the same height as Eärwiggi. 'Now, you two – I've a question, and I want to address it to Sharon himself.'

'Speak to me,' said the first Eye. 'Verily I *am* Sharon, wearing this mannish body as a tool.'

'No,' said the second Eye, crossly. 'Speak to *me*. I am the true Sharon.'

'I was here first,' said the first Eye.

'And *I* was created Eye of Sharon before you,' said the second Eye. 'Talk to me, Sir Dwarf, and Sharon will answer your question.'

'No, Sir Dwarf,' said the first Eye. 'Ignore this man – he is a merely secondary, subsidiary Eye. I'm the one you should address.'

'Me!' yelled the second Eye.

'*He* said,' said Eärwiggi, pointing to the first Eye. And at that moment, as in the dead eye of a storm, everything fell silent, so that his words could be heard by all: the Orks ceased their mutterings; the sea surf seemed to hush to silence; the wind dropped away; and the two bickering Eyes were speechless with their respective rages. And so Eärwiggi spoke, and rarely have any words spoken by a child been so significant. The words of Túrin returned to him: *always tell the truth and something about the face*, because actually Eärwiggi couldn't remember the second part. And he thought of the Sellāmi tucked into his clothes. And he spoke.

'*He* said,' said Eärwiggi, pointing to the first Eye, 'that he was going to kill you. I overheard him.'

There was a moment of silence. The fate of the world turned on its pivot.

'Oh you *did*, did you?' roared the second Eye.

'No!' called the first Eye in outrage. 'What? Hey –
no.'

'Do you know that doesn't surprise me at *all*,' said
the second Eye.

'What are you talking about?'

'I always thought you were a murderous swine,'
said the second Eye. 'And I don't mean that in a good
way.'

'You take that back!' said the first Eye, livid. 'You
just apologise and take that back right now!'

'You're *plotting to kill me*,' said the second Eye.

'No I'm not,' snarled the first Eye. 'Though heaven
knows you deserve it.'

'The boy has a command upon him to tell the
truth!' cried the second Eye with furious emphasis.
'Can you deny it? – It is the Dragons' magic.' He
turned to Eärwiggi. 'Boy, speak again, and speak
only the truth. Did this creature say he was going to
slay me?'

'Oh yes,' said Eärwiggi. 'When you rode over the
beach a moment ago. He said "When I come back.
I'm going to stick him with my long black sword."
And he called you a rude name.'

'Oo, I never!' yelled the first Eye. 'He's lying!'

'He has the *Dragons' spell* upon him,' shrieked
the second Eye. 'He *cannot* lie! You, however, are

composed of *nothing but* lies and treachery. Since being appointed one of the Eyes of Sharon you have spent the entire time plotting to rise up against your own Master.'

'How could I plot like that?' howled the first Eye, in an ecstasy of rage and fury. 'I am not Sharon's servant, but part of Sharon himself. You talk gibberish. Your brain must have rotted away – are your wits truly so maggot-eaten that you would think . . .'

In a trice, the second Eye whipped out his black-bladed sword and sheathed it again in the first Eye's chest. The victim's eyes opened even wider and looked even more furious, which Eärwiggi would hardly have believed possible, although there it was, for all to see. His speech broke off in mid word with a gurgle, and he fell straight out of his saddle to the damp sand.

The Orks sucked in a collective 'Ha!' of horror, and all took a step back.

The second Eye looked with surprise at the sword in his hand. Vapours curled off the blade, and a dribble of blood ran from the point. 'Er,' he said.

At exactly that moment the ground shook violently.

❈

Eärwiggi was thrown off his feet by the tremor; and even the stocky, sturdy Dwarf had a job not falling over. The Orks squealed in terror, and fled away, some south, some east. The body of the slain Eye of Sharon twitched on the sand as if going through a second death spasm.

The second Eye's horse reared up, and sloughed him off backwards, before cantering whinnyingly away over the dune grass and onto the snow. And the second Eye lay screaming.

The ground shook a second time.

The sea seemed to boil, and throw up exaggerated waves, twice or three times as tall as they had been only a moment before. For a third time the ground shook.

Eärwiggi got on all fours and looked north. The cave where they had found the Sellāmi had collapsed. The rocks above were shaking, trembling, rearing in great spasms, as if the mountains themselves were feverish.

Getting to his feet, the second Eye looked around him with fear and horror on his face. His eyes were black and sightless, and he stumbled. 'Something is very wrong here . . .' he said.

And with the mightiest tremor yet the mountains burst to life, and upreared into the air. The second Eye screamed and fell on his face.

'It is the ending of all things!' said Eärwiggi.

'Now let's not *leap* to conclusions,' said Nobbi, before his voice was drowned out by a tempestuous rushing of wind. The sea's edge sucked back and ran away from them, withdrawing half a league to reveal wet mud and seaweeds and gasping fish dancing in plain air.

A shadow passed over them; and the Dragon of the North, awake again, was circling very slowly through the air over their heads.

The Dragon of the North spoke: 'What is your name?' And his voice boomed and rumbled, as the earth shivered its last trembles and settled itself.

To begin with, Eärwiggi thought he must be speaking to somebody else. He prodded Nobbi's shoulder, and nodded at him, raising his eyebrows, as if to say 'Go on then.' But the Dwarf said, 'He's speaking to *you*, bach.'

So Eärwiggi said, 'Eärwiggi.'

'You have the Sellāmi?'

Eärwiggi thought about telling another lie; but then he thought to himself 'If I lie all the time, then people will know the truth simply by inverting what I say. So I shall tell the truth on this occasion.' He looked up at the huge beast. It hung in the sky above the beach, filling the view; although at the edges of his great rock-like frame Eärwiggi could see the sky behind. It looked darker, and clouds were hurrying over it at a great rate as if keen to get away.

'Yes,' he replied. 'Do you want it?'

'No,' said the Dragon. 'It was in my claw, but it froze me to the margin of Upper Middle Earth – as you saw. I cannot carry it, as I hoped.'

'Carry it?'

'Away.' And he swum through the air in a circle, nodding his great head at the west. 'It should not be here. It disturbs the balance of this world. We are ready to pay the price to be rid of it.'

'We?' asked Eärwiggi.

'My brother dragons,' said the Dragon of the North. 'The time has come.'

'I don't understand.'

'Sharon hoped to form an unbreakable spell. He took much of our power from us to fashion the spell, and its words are our words, and they are words of making. He commanded that he be lord over all Elves and Men; and that he be invulnerable to harm; and that he be immortal; and that he be victorious in any battle. And with these words he has enslaved Upper Middle Earth, for they are powerful words.'

'But,' said Nobbi, with a great smile on his face, 'You, laddo, have resisted his magic!'

'Your mother was an elf, and your father a man,' boomed the Dragon. 'And you are both elvish and mannish, and yet neither. As neither man nor elf, Sharon could not command you.'

'Even the winter thawed around you,' said Nobbi.

'The problem with a being such as Sharon,' said the Dragon, 'is that he can only see the one thing or the other. He must inhabit the centre, and margins make him uncomfortable. If looked at in terms of *one thing* or *the other thing* his charm was firm. But here, at the margins of the world, it frays.'

'Frays?'

'The Eye of Sharon is both Sharon and not-Sharon, for he is a Man possessed by Sharon. Sharon cannot be harmed, or killed, or defeated in battle; and so the second Eye was victorious, and alive, and unharmed. But *Men* can be harmed, or killed, or defeated in battle; and so the first Eye lies dead. And the first Eye was Sharon, also, and so the spell is broken.'

'Is it so simple?' asked Eärwiggi.

'No,' boomed the Dragon, mournfully.

'Sharon fought Sharon!' chortled the dwarf. 'Both must be victorious by the terms of the spell, and yet both *cannot* be victorious – for to be victorious means to defeat the other. The spell circled back on itself, a serpent devouring its own tail! It *fused* itself.'

'Is the spell broken?' Eärwiggi asked again. 'Just like that?'

'No,' boomed the Dragon, 'and yes, for this is the way of all answers to the really complicated questions.'

'How do you mean?'

'The spell is made of our magic, and of our words; and the world itself is made of our magic and of our words. The spell is broken, and not broken. It is broken, in that Sharon no longer commands the hearts of Men or Elves, and he can be harmed and slain and defeated in battle. But it is not broken, so long as the world is unbroken; and some part of Sharon remains immortal, imperishable, invincible. So mighty a spell cannot simply disappear in a puff of smoke. Its unmaking will unmake the land that we made; and it will unmake us also, for we are the speech that spoke the land, just as we are the speech that spoke the spell.'

'Well, this is most alarming news,' said Eärwiggi. 'It sounds, after all, like the end of the world.'

'End,' said the Dragon, 'and beginning. The tremors are starting now, in the heart of Blearyland;

and they will soon reach us here at the edge of things. Already Sharon's tower has fallen in rubble, and his Thing™ has fallen from him and been washed away in the flood, to fall from sight and mind. Already his Orks flee in terror or fall into chasms in the earth. Soon the land will be broken, hills will tumble into valleys, fields will rear up as new mountains, and everything will become new. Yet Men and Elves will survive, and the new world will continue.'

'Dear me,' said Eärwiggi. 'What a to-do.'

'It is indeed,' boomed the Dragon, lifting his head to the hurtling clouds and the wine-dark sky, 'a To-Do! We shall soon perish, broken to fragments by the upheavals of this land we made.'

'Oh. I'm sorry to hear that.'

'Don't worry. We have laid our eggs in the rocks of this world, and a new generation of Dragons will arise eventually, smaller than we but more removed from the evil of Moregothic who created us, and wiser in their way. We accept our fate. Will you now accept yours?'

'My fate?'

'You must carry the Sellāmi over the western ocean, and return it to Emu who made it.'

'But there isn't time to build a boat!' said

Eärwiggi. And truly it seemed so, for the hills on the horizon were shuddering like jellies, and trees and rocks were bouncing into the air; and the air was bruised with the distant sound of apocalypse.

'Climb onto my tail,' said the Dragon, whisking his huge rocky tail through the air and laying it along the beach. 'Quick now.'

As Eärwiggi clambered up he asked, 'Will you carry me through the air?'

'Not I,' boomed the Dragon. 'I cannot leave this land I created, and the Sellāmi is too heavy a thing for my power. But you can take it in your hand. By cutting off the end of it, Sharon opened its magic potency; for it is full of light and power. Hold it tight, with the severed end towards the ground.'

'Alright,' said Eärwiggi, doing so. 'Then what?'

'You'll see,' said the Dragon. And he lifted his tail into the air again.

'Goodbye!' Eärwiggi called down to Nobbi on the ground. 'It was nice knowing you.'

'Glad to know you too,' said the Dwarf. But Eärwiggi was already high in the air, and the world beneath had shrunk away.

From here he could see the great spread of lands to the east, and the stippled deserts of ocean water to the west. And it was a vantage point from which the spreading wave of earthquake destruction was clearly visible, shaking the whole landscape; as if the fields and hills and mountains were made not of solid substance, but of a sluggish fluid, and a great wave was passing through them, undoing and remaking.

The Dragon whipped his tail round; and with a tumbling sense of falling in his belly, Eärwiggi dropped hundreds of yards; yet still he clutched onto the Sellāmi.

And with sudden and devastating force, the Dragon of the North whipped his tail round again and hurled Eärwiggi westward into the air. He screamed. He couldn't help it. He was flying free like a chucked pebble, with the seas wrinkling far below him.

And with a great shudder, the Sellāmi came to life in his hands. Light gushed from its severed end: light of all colours, streaking behind him as he flew: a comet's tail of red and gold, of spring green and sky blue.

He flew so fast that the wind tugged at his face, pulling his mouth open and squeezing his eyes shut; and he could no longer hear himself call. But ducking his head down and forcing his eyes open, he saw the path of many colours he was marking across the sky. And even in his fear he was amazed.

And from the ground those Elves and Men who survived the upheavals of their world looked up in amazement also. Never before had such a thing been seen in Upper Middle Earth. And at first it was called 'Eärwiggi-in-the-sky'; but afterwards, when people thought back and decided this was a pretty silly name for it they called it instead 'rainbow'.

Eärwiggi flew, and the force and noise of the air pressed him close about, but still he cut his way through the sky.

Behind him the Dragon of the North broke into ten thousand fragments of stone, some great boulders, some small shards, and scattered across the landscape; and Nobbi did call out 'Crikey o'bikey' and hide his head; and by great good fortune, or perhaps by good fate, none of the ten thousand fragments fell upon him.

And in like fashion did each of the four great dragons perish with the breaking up of this, their greatest spell.

Eärwiggi passed through the highest point of the sky, where the blue aether was close enough almost for him to touch; and below him the sea was ever more distant, and the curve of the world was clearly visible. The sun's light and heat was strong upon this place, and one thought crossed his mind; that he was the most alone and free of any Upper Middle Earthly individual.

And then he began to fall in a great arc. But although the fall curved down and down, yet as he clutched the Sellāmi it seemed to Eärwiggi that his speed was slowing, and that he was less falling and more floating, until he caught a glimpse of a fresh green landscape, and the crisp frill of white breakers on a golden beach, and then he plopped onto the turf of Asdar.

'Wow. *That*,' he said to nobody in particular, 'was quite a ride.'

So it was that the Sellāmi was returned to Asdar. Of Eärwiggi little more is known; some tales say he lived in happiness in Asdar forever; other tales say he returned to Upper Middle Earth, to find a changed landscape and new adventures. But of Sharon all the tales agree: he was cast down in the ruin of his orgulous castle, and his spirit fled whimpering to the high sky where it was lost to memory. And his Thing™, the last remnant of the Sellāmi in Upper Middle Earth, fell into floodwater and was washed away, whither none knew.

And Men and Elves rebuilt their cities from the

ruins of the land. And the name of Blearyland was wiped from official records, for all agreed it had brought nothing but bad luck; and instead the land was called Elfriardor. Or Manland, according to some. Or Dwarfswereherefirstshire according to others.

So ends the tale of Eärwiggi.[26]

_____

26   Whose name, clearly, is not derived from the Elvish for 'ear covering' after all, but from the Old Mannish meaning 'air-way' or 'air-path', on account of his fantastic journey through the sky.

The Voyage of the Darned Traitor

During that time when the whole of Upper Middle Earth was overrun by darkness and Sharon was Master of All Things, certain Elves, called for obvious reasons the Coward Elves, fled to the far north and west of Blearyland. And there they built themselves a boat, called by them *The Spirit of Exploration*, but called by everybody who remained behind and lived under the terrible yoke of Sharon *The Spirit of the Darned Traitor*.

As Sharon laid waste to Blearyland, Túrin Againdikwittingdn took his people, and escorted the vacant-headed Queen Lüthwoman to the uttermost western shore of Upper Middle Earth. There they began building a boat, but the construction fell under the malign influence of one of the Eyes of Sharon, who came upon them. And they fell at his feet as he ordered them to cease building the boat, and ordered them also not to roam the land but to waste the rest of their days sitting on the cold beach. And they were powerless to resist his command, and languished on the beach for many months.

But to their aid came Eärwiggi of the Mighty Fib; and being half-elven and half-mannish he was un-affected by Sharon's magic, and he completed the boat on their behalf. And they thanked him and bade him farewell, and sailed away to the west.

The voyage lasted many weeks, through storms and over calm seas, under glassy skies and under cloud that drooped low enough to envelop them. Beneath the keel of their boat the unsatisfied surge sucked with importunate lip, and threatened several times to swallow them whole; but they stayed true of heart, and steered the *Darned Traitor* west, always west. 'And at the end,' said Túrin Againdikwittingdn, 'we shall arrive at the coast of Westersupanesse, the paradise of Asdar.'

But he was unaware that Emu, annoyed by pre-vious evil incursions, had rerouted the route that led over the surface of the sea through an inter-dimensional gate to another place.

And after long voyaging, the mariners thought they saw the end of the ocean; and the horizon of the sea glimmered with a strange light, green and pink. And the sky greyed, and storm clouds collided above them with great crumpling crashing noises. Lightning twigged flickeringly across the darkness. Rain filled the air all around with plummeting water;

and everything was soaked; and the waves began to tip and heave. And as Túrin called his crew to the deck a twisting tunnel of black wind engulfed the ship.

They were wrenched, as it seemed, full out of the sea and thrown high in the air; and yet, at the same time, they felt motionless and the wind and rain fell away. A strange quiet was all around them. Túrin, gasping, his wet clothes steaming in the newly dry air and his hair standing strangely on end, stood on the deck and looked at what had become of the world around them. It seemed as though they were in a long tunnel formed by the twisting arcing lines of a whirlwind; yet it was perfectly still and perfectly quiet. So close did the walls of this tunnel seem to be that Túrin thought he could reach out and touch them; but when he did they crackled and snarled with shards of light, and he felt a jarring jolt up his arm that left his limb numb for many minutes.

But then the tunnel fell away from them on all sides, and the *Darned Traitor* found itself floating again in water; and on either side were green fields; and soon they drifted underneath a stone bridge. And they found themselves in a populous city, with houses and shops of stone, and many people crowding the stone-set paths, and curious carts that moved without horses.

And they docked, and wandered the strange city. 'Are we in Westersupanesse?' asked the Coward Elves.

'We must be,' said Túrin. 'This must be paradise.'

And they were surprised, frankly, that paradise had quite so many bicycles. To say nothing of the buses. But it doesn't do to query the inscrutable designs of providence, or risk the wrath of Emu, so the Coward Elves wandered around for a while. And when they returned to their ship it had been impounded by the municipal authorities for non-payment of moorage charges.

And over many years in paradise the Coward Elves eventually settled down and Túrin Againdik-wittingdn opened a small tobacconist's just off Saint Giles, and lived there with Queen Lüthwoman; and the other Coward Elves lived in various places, some in the university, some in other towns. And of their various lives, nothing more is told in this tale.

Part 3
The History of the War of the Thing™

[*Editor's note*. My grand-uncle's notes towards *Lowered Off the Rings*, his gymnasium-set allegory for the great War of the Thing™, indicate the extent to which his publisher and himself were keen to introduce the mythology of Upper Middle Earth to as many people as possible, or as George-Ann Allen Nonwin put it, 'to milk every last purple cent outta this baby.' He and my grand-uncle experimented with recasting the material in various forms, and various media; some of which are illustrated below.]

Letters between A. R. R. R. Roberts and George-Ann Allen Nonwin. **Lowered Off the Rings** *takes shape.*

My grand-uncle had been working on tales set in his Fantasy world for many decades without ever interesting a publisher. He regularly sent out portions of the MS to all the publishers he could think of, and regularly received rejection letters, usually by return of post. Indeed, his breakfast was ruined unless he had one or two really good rejection letters to ponder over his Sultana Bran. 'I find a rejection letter to be better than the best commercially produced laxative available on the market,' he once told me.

But all that changed when my father met the publisher George-Ann Allen Nonwin. 'A curious fellow,' A R R R R wrote to a friend shortly after he first met the publisher for lunch. 'It seems that his parents had been unable to reconcile a certain argument over whether "George" or "Ann" was the better name for a child.' Nonwin accepted the manuscript of *The Soddit* for publication, and commissioned

Dunglewis Carroll to illustrate it. The book was, of course, enormously successful, and spent no fewer than two weeks in the 'Hardback Illustrated Fiction for Children Published by a London Publisher in Red Covers Top Ten Bestselling Books' Bestseller List, at No 9 and No 10 respectively.

Nonwin, naturally, wanted my grand-uncle to pen a sequel to this successful book, and suggested an adventure narrative concerning the Ultimate Battle of Good Versus Evil, with the Awful Sharon battling the forces of Men and Elves. With some soddits in it. But my grand-uncle, used to the specialised demands of academic scholarship, found it hard to adjust to the requirements of commercial publishing. In the early stages he was compelled to ask George-Ann for assistance. If this galled his sense of pride to a certain extent, then matters were not helped by Nonwin's sometimes brusque tone.

George-Ann Allen Nonwin Publishers,
Tuesday 19th. Morning. About eleven o'clock. Well, eleven-oh-four if you want me to be – eleven-oh-five, it just flipped over as I was writing that last bit.

Dear A R R R R,

Re: the Big Fantasy Sequel. You tell me you are having some trouble with the conceptual framework of this. Come, my dear fellow, it's child's play.

It must be a thousand-page epic spanning a whole continent with a *dramatis personae* including many scores of characters. The narrative must concern the very biggest topics, the battle of Good against ultimate Evil, the importance of free will, the seductive power of wickedness and so on. Naturally, in framing such a story, you will need to consider *not only* individual items of personal jewellery but personal accessories and adornment in general. I advise you to build the story around a single magic item of gold frippery.

    Sincerely,

    George-Ann

Dear George-Ann

    Thank you for your very helpful suggestions.

    A R R R R

My grand-uncle followed his publisher's advice, and attempted to recast his mythic material around some fictional component. After several weeks racking his brains he lighted on the conception of a magic ring that renders its owner invisible. Nonwin, however, queried the logic of this conception.

My dear A, Of course (it is, after all, self-evident) any thousand-page heroic Fighting Fantasy trilogy dramatising the bloodsoaked ultimate battle of Good against Evil, must be constructed around an item of jewellery. So far so good. But why, old boy, have you lighted upon a *ring* that renders its wearer *invisible to others*? I'm afraid I just don't see the logic. Why should a *finger-ring* render you invisible? A magic golden monocle, maybe – The Monocle of Sorrow, perhaps? Spectacles at a pinch.

    G

In the event, A R R R R worked on the monocle idea for seven anguished months, before finally and reluctantly abandoning it. It crops up in many early drafts of the first volume; but after much labour he decided that it was artistically unsustainable.

Dear G-A-A,

    I confess I've had, finally, to abandon The Monocle of Sorrow. And, of course, it would be absurd to revert to the 'Magic Finger-ring of Invisibility'. Might I prevail upon you for an opinion as to which of the following looks most promising?

    The Earrings of Doom!
    The Bellybutton Stud of Evil!

The Wristwatch of Terror!
The Brooch of Disaster!
The Tiny Gold Dolphin On An Eighteen-Carat
    Chain of Misery!
The Medallion of Ultimate Evil!

I have also been rethinking the choice of titles for the
three constituent books. I feel that, to be in keeping
with our democratic age, I should downplay the
heroic kingliness of the original titles, and choose
something with which citizens of a modern democracy
will identify. Please notify the printers to reset all
proofs with the following titles:

1. The Fellowship of the Single Transferable Vote
2. The Two Funding Authorities
3. The Return of the Democratically Elected Upper
    Chamber

The overall title should be *Lord of Bling*.
Best wishes for Easter, A

Nonwin pressed for the Brooch of Disaster, but
A R R R R found that the notion of a single evil
earring had seized his imagination. He rewrote
chapter seven 'Eighteen Carats of Catastrophe' with
a brooch, but didn't like the result. As he explained
himself to Nonwin:

After much consideration I've had to abandon the brooch. I have to say I feel that my Earrings of Inaudibility are a *much* stronger artistic conceit. Let me pick, for example, one moment from many from my thousands of pages of manuscript, to illustrate how dramatic and exciting this piece of personal adornment could be.

The Fell Walkers of Fell Darkness were upon them, their great black coats and black boots crunching upon the dead pine needles. Freudo stumbled backwards, and before he knew what he was doing he had slipped the Earrings of Doom upon his earlobes. With horror he saw the King of the Fell Walkers stride close and closer to Sham's sleeping form. 'Sham!' he cried, 'Sham! Look out! Rouse yourself, Sham, and flee! Fly! Flee!' But, of course, the Earrings had rendered him wholly inaudible.

You see? To rewrite that scene with a brooch would be to lose all dramatic excitement. I do hope you agree.

    Sincerely,
    A R R R R

A week later my grand-uncle wrote the following note, which demonstrates how strained relations with his publisher had become.

George-Ann,

I called your office several times yesterday by
telephone, only to be told that you were 'out at lunch'.
Do you really expect me to believe that a publisher
could be out at lunch *from eleven-twenty in the morning
until nearly three in the afternoon*? Pah – pah I say. No
conceivable lunch, in any profession, could take so
long. Clearly you were avoiding me. I will confess that
I am hurt and distressed by your evasion.

A.

PS: I hear on the grapevine that the Baroness Orczy
is presently working on a three thousand page Heroic
Fantasy based on a magical Naked-Lady-Tattoo of
Power, drawn in the biceps of the central character. If
she can get away with that notion, I really don't see
how my Earrings of Doom can be denied me.

As late as March, A R R R R was still battling
Nonwin over the precise shape his central Decorative Golden Adornment of Catastrophe should take.
A series of letters from June of the same year illustrate how passionate each man was on the subject.

The 'Snug', Covent Garden,
Thursday afternoon

My dear R,

Go for the brooch. Earring is plain silly.

With very warmest and best wishes,

George-Ann

Suburbia, Friday

Dear G-A,

No it isn't.

Sincerest wishes,

A R R R Roberts

George-Ann Allen Nonwin Publishers,
Tuesday

Dear R,

Thank you for your communication of the 17th inst. Yes it is.

Sincerely,

George-Ann

Suburbia,
Thursday

Dear George,

No, it isn't.

With warmest regards, and best wishes for yourself and your family,

ARRRR

George-Ann Allen Nonwin Publishers,
Monday

Dear R,
 Yes it *is*.
 Sincerely,
 George-Ann

Suburbia,
Thursday 30th

Dear George,
 No, it isn't.
 best, A

George-Ann Allen Nonwin Publishers,
Friday 31st

Dear R,
 Yes it is, and before you reply, let me add: yes it is.
You're a stubborn, brick-headed idiotic twit of a man.
You smell. I find myself compelled to utter impolite
speculations concerning your mother. You kissed a
dog once. You enjoyed it. You've never kissed a girl.
You're stupid and you smell. You run like a midget.
You bite your nails.
 With heartfelt regards,
 George-Ann Allen Nonwin

A. R. R. R. Roberts

Suburbia,
Wednesday 3rd

Dear George,
Listen to me: No, It Isn't.
best, A

George-Ann Allen Nonwin Publishers,
Saturday morning

Dear R,
I'm sorry to say that I was unable to read your last communication, because after opening the letter I was forced to put my hands over my eyes and go *wa!-wa!-wa!-wa!-wa!* at the top of my voice. I must therefore conclude, without evidence to the contrary, that you concur in my judgment that, yes, it is.
George-A

Suburbia,
Monday 8th

Dear George,
You're a child.
sincerely, A

George-Ann Allen Nonwin Publishers,
Tuesday 9th

Dear R,
You are, you mean.
George-Ann

258

Suburbia,
Wednesday 10th

Dear George,

   I know *you* are, but what am I?

   sincerely, A

George-Ann Allen Nonwin Publishers,
Thursday 11th

Dear Sir,

   George-Ann Nonwin is out of the office today, and will deal with your enquiry on his return.

   Sincerely,

   Jill Philips, pp. G-A Nonwin

A postal strike terminated the correspondence at this point.

Farmer Greenegs of Ham

[*Editor's note*: this manuscript, an early draft of my grand-uncle's *Lowered Off the Rings* work, has recently been discovered in the Ballsiol archives. Instructed to provide a sequel for his children's book *The Soddit*, A. R. R. Roberts initially pitched his sequel at an even younger demographic. The manuscript is illustrated with preliminary sketches by Dr Douglas Zeus]

p.1   'I do not like this Magic Ring
       I do not like it, Sam-old-thing.'

p.2   'Would you like it in the Shire?'

       'I would not, could not in the Shire,
       I do not like its words of fire.
       I do not like this Magic Ring,
       I do not *like* it, Sam-old-thing.'

p.3   'Say—
              In the dark?
       Here in the dark?
       Would you, could you, in the dark?'

The Sellamillion

'Sam, I'll tell you this in actual fact—
I hate this magic artefact;
I do not like it in the dark
I will not treat it as a lark
Not in a field, not in a barrow
Not in a mountain pass that's narrow
Not in a broader mountain pass
I'd sooner kiss your hairy

p.4   Toes
I *do not like* this Magic Ring
I *do not like* it, Sam-old-thing.'

p.5   'Here
At Mount Doom?
Here, up Old Doom?
Will you be wearing it any time soon?'

'I do not like this ring of power
I do not like it *any* hour.
I do not like it here, or there,
It is not something I will wear.'

p.6   'Here in the third volume?
Now! In the third volume—
Could you, would you? Can it be
That you'll give way in volume 3?'

261

'I *did not like* it in volume one.
Nor in the volume that's just gone.
I do not like it in *this* volume.
Any more than being chased by Golume.
Not with Departure nor Return of King
I do not *like* this Magic Ring.'

p.7 'You say it's what you can't abide.
Try it – try it – *then* decide.
Try, before committing ringicide.'

p.8 'Say!'

p.9 'I *like* this Evil Ring.
I do! I like the awful thing!

And I *will* wear it on my finger!
And I *will* be apocalypse-bringer!
And I *will* drive my allies mad!
It is *so good*, to be so very bad!
I'll use it to bring blight and woe
From wizard's peak to dwarfish toe.
To shift from seen into unseen,
To turn bread blue and hens-eggs green,
And generally make mortals glum.
Thank you!
Thank you!
Sam-old-chum.'

[Later that year, Nonwin persuaded my grand-uncle to write up some of his personal mythology in more populist form. The first fruit of this new resolution was the script of a situation comedy, which Roberts hoped to sell to the BBC. Filming was not completed on the pilot episode, and only this portion remains.]

Ent's Army

Theme:
Who do you think you are kidding, Mister Sauron
If you think Old Forest's done —
We are the trees that'll hoomm hooooooooommm hmm.
Hmmm.
We are hmmmmmmmmm.
[pause: 7 minutes]

Mr Elm goes off to the Haradvale on
The 821-
year old drover's path —
But he comes home each evening
And he's ready with his gum (exuded-from-a-small-incision-in-his-bark)

So
Who do you think you are kidding, Mister Sauron
If you think Old Forest's —
Hmmmmmmmmm.
Hom, hoom, hmmm.

Scene: *The Old Forest. Many trees. Enter* CAPTAIN MAINBEARDING, SERGEANT WISDEN, CORPORAL JUNIPER, PRIVATE POPLAR.

CAPTAIN MAINBEARDING: Pay attention trees. I'm afraid the Orks are – hooom, hoooomm, hoommmmmm. [*dozes for twenty minutes*] Ah! Yes, the Orks are – hmmm – presently setting fire to my lower branches.

CORPORAL JUNIPER: [*speaking very slowly in a deep bass-baritone*] Do-oo-ooo-o-o-oo-oo — o — oo — on't . . . pa — aa — a-aaa —

PRIVATE POPLAR: Mr Mainbearding! [*pause: 3 minutes*] Mr Mainbearding! [*pause: 7 minutes*]

CORPORAL JUNIPER: — aa — a-aaa — a-a-a — a —

PRIVATE POPLAR: Mr Mainbearding! An ork paratrooper has fallen – hoom – into my branches – hmmm hmmm – and is now dangling from them.

Dangling, he is. What – hmm – what shall I do, Mr Mainbearding?

CAPTAIN MAINBEARDING: [*shaking his head slowly*] You stupid sapling.

CORPORAL JUNIPER: —aa-a-nn—nic! Do—oo-oo-o —o-o-oo—oo . . . [*His roots settle into the soft loam and he goes to sleep*]

SERGEANT WISDEN: [*observing* JUNIPER] Ah, the sweet rainwater-sodden earth, the life-giving water of the ground. He does like it up him.

The Adventures of Tommy Bythewho

[*Editor's Note*: Very little remains of my grand-uncle's abortive attempt to recast the material of *Lowered Off the Rings* as a rock opera, tentatively entitled *Ring, Ring, Why Don't You Give Me A Greatly-Lengthened-Though-Horribly-Attenuated-Life-of-Gnawing-Anxiety-and-Maniacal-Possessiveness*.[27] Of the original forty songs, only a dozen or so were ever recorded; the Earls Court Spectacular, performed with full band and backing orchestra on ice, closed after only three months, and the soundtrack album only reached number six in the album charts, selling a pitiful 600,000 copies]

Song: *Tis balls, Wizard*

Ever since I was a young lad I've been Aryan blonde
   and tall
From Mirkjaggawood down to Fanguverymuchhorn,
   I'm the prettiest elf of all,

---

27   Later retitled *Bing Sings 'Rings'*.

But I've not seen anything like him in any elven hall,
That Tommy Bythewho-oh
He hardly fits this tale at all—

   Duh-∂uh, ∂uhh, ∂uhh, ∂-∂uhh,
   Duh-∂uh, ∂uhh, ∂uhh, ∂-∂uhh.[28]

He stands like a hippy, he'll smoke almost anything,
Hardly ever speaks in prose, he much prefers to sing,
Doesn't care for money, unmoved by its kerching,
That Tom Bonglemmehaveago
Sure isn't affected by the Evil Ring—

   Duh-∂uh, ∂uhh, ∂uhh, ∂-∂uhh,
   Duh-∂uh, ∂uhh, ∂uhh, ∂-∂uhh.[29]

He's an authorial symbol,
He isn't like the rest
      of the characters
He's a strange anachronism
And he wears a velvet vest.

He lives in an oddly stylised version of the nineteen-
   sixties even though this tale is supposed to be

---

28   Elvish. Translation: 'Yes, yes, oh very much so, yes, indeed,/Yes, yes, oh very much so, yes indeed; *oh* yes.'

29   Elvish. Translation: 'No, No he's not, certainly no, no,/nope, not in the slightest, oh no, what on earth gave you that idea, certainly not, no.'

timeless and was in fact written between the
    nineteen-teens and 1950s,
Apparently very important to the author, although
    few readers complain if these Scenes are cut clean
    out from the movie on account of the narratively
    thrifty s-
        elections of the director,
That Tommy Bythewho-oh,
He don't hardly fit this tale at all.

He's a transparent allegory,
Of a rural English idyll
But in terms of characterisation
He's a load of twaffling piddle.

Other songs composed by my grand-uncle for this
Musical Interlude included:

* *Tom Bythewho Prelude: Wap-dang-a-dingle-doh-a-derry-down-the-dongle-dung*
* *'I'm Free! And Freedom Tastes of Not Having To Spend Seven Years Filming in New Zealand'*
* *'See Me, Hear Me, Feel Me (Not in the Movie Version You Won't)'*
* *'I'm your Wicked Uncle Ernie, Interfering with Young Children, and I'll Make You Very Uncomfortable Indeed When, in Twenty*

Years' Time, the Composer is Arrested for Internet Child Porn Offences and You Look Back on This Song And Think, Blimey, That Puts Things In An Unpleasant New Light, Doesn't It?'
- *'Talking 'Bout My Sellamillion'*
- *'Boromir, Boroyur (ah-haa)'*
- *'Moria – I've Just Seen a Mine Called Moria'*
- *'Gimli, Gimli, Gimli, A Dwarf After Midnight'*
- *'(She Told Me To) Ork This Way'*
- *Tom Bythewho Rousing Conclusive Chorus: Wap-dang-a-dingle-doh-derry-down-the-dongle-dung (reprise)*

Soundtrack available on 'His Evil Master's Voice'/ Nonwin-recordings.

Under Mirk Wood: a Play for Voices
By Bob Dylan Thomas Boombadillo

First Dwarf: To begin at the beginning: a small wood, under the starlight, look you, bach, though they go mad they shall go into that good night, dumb, and fuse the green under apple boughs, bach, la, dew.

Second Dwarf (Molly): [*falsetto*] That giant spider kissed me!

Third Dwarf (Gomer): [*baritone*] Kissed you?

Molly: [*falsetto*] Underneath the branches.

Gomer: [*baritone*] Underneath the branches?

Molly: [*falsetto*] He was trying to fill my veins with poison, wrap me up and lay eggs in me, and all for the sake of love.

Gomer: [*baritone*] All bite and no bark, some spiders. All bark and no bite, some trees.

Molly: [*falsetto*] O love! Spider love.

Gomer: [*falsetto*] Nothing sweeter.

Molly: [*baritone*] Afterwards back to his for flies and, er, more flies. One kiss for me, one kiss for him, and one for the teapot.

Gomer: [*falsetto*] Now you listen to me young Dwarf Molly –

Molly: [*baritone*] Hang on a minute . . . shouldn't I be doing the falsetto?

Gomer: [*falsetto*] What do you mean . . . oh wait up, you're right . . . [*clears throat*]

Molly: [*falsetto*] Chasing the giggling spider children down to spider farm . . .

Gomer: [*baritone*] Look you, la, bach, boyo, see, dew, bach, look you, leeks, Rugby football, sheep, curry, beer, male voice choirs, *look* you.

Ork Sonnets

I.

Shall I compare thee to an ugh! ugh! ugh!
Thou art more ugh!ular and more *urrh! arrrh! urh!*
Gnaargh! shall *Urghh!* gnash-gnash-gnash—
MANFLESH!! uh! uh! uh!
Arrrgghhhh!
Aaaaaaarrrrghh!
Ugh!! UGH! hath all too short a UGH!
RAAAAAGGH! WAAAAAARRGH!
Thank you. Gestetnered copies of my selected poems
Are available in the lobby, price three groats.

II.

You've
got
to
Fight the power!
Fight the powers of Man!
You've got to *hack* the helmet,
Disem*bowel* the man-warriors—

272

You've
> Got
>> To

Feed your belly

Feed your belly on the carcasses of your enemies.

You've got to *apply* an emollient, perhaps a *fat*-based product like lard to the back of your head to stop your helmet chafing, also very important, that.

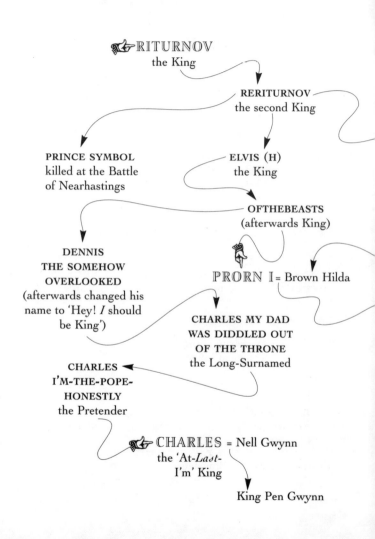

RITURNOV
the King

RERITURNOV
the second King

PRINCE SYMBOL
killed at the Battle
of Nearhastings

ELVIS (H)
the King

OFTHEBEASTS
(afterwards King)

**DENNIS
THE SOMEHOW
OVERLOOKED**
(afterwards changed his
name to 'Hey! *I* should
be King')

PRORN I = Brown Hilda

**CHARLES MY DAD
WAS DIDDLED OUT
OF THE THRONE**
the Long-Surnamed

**CHARLES
I'M-THE-POPE-
HONESTLY**
the Pretender

CHARLES = Nell Gwynn
the 'At-*Last*-
I'm' King

King Pen Gwynn

The Royal Line of Mannish Monarchs
(MOSTLY MEN)

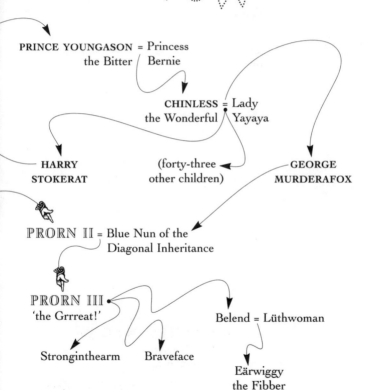

PRINCE YOUNGASON = Princess
the Bitter / Bernie

CHINLESS = Lady
the Wonderful / Yayaya

HARRY STOKERAT

(forty-three other children)

GEORGE MURDERAFOX

PRORN II = Blue Nun of the
Diagonal Inheritance

PRORN III
'the Grrreat!'

Stronginthearm   Braveface

Belend = Lüthwoman

Eärwiggy
the Fibber

Appendices

Note on Pronunciation

The following note is a guide only, not a comprehensive account of pronunciation in the works of A. R. R. R. Roberts, or any other writer or document, except this document, obviously.

CONSONANTS

C   always has the value *sea* (as in 'seabiscuit'), except when its value is *kay* (as in 'kayleigh'), unless it is being pronounced *as part of a word*, in which case it is pronounced 'c' (as in 'crunching celery' or 'haecceity').

CH   pronounced as 'c' only with an 'h' after it, *except* when the 'h' part is sort of included in the 'c' part that precedes it, as if instead of two letters there *is* actually only one letter, that happens to have been written down as two letters, perhaps to use up space (as in 'Why is it *always* me who has to write them a postcard? I've nothing to say to them! They're your family after all. Jeesh, I suppose I can just talk about the weather but write in really large letters').

DH   pronounced however you like. No, really.
Whatever takes your fancy. Pronounce it 'q' or 'x' if
you want. No skin off my nose. What do I care how
you sound in the privacy of your own home?

TH   has it ever struck you how *odd* it is that the river
Thames is spelt the way it is? I mean, I'm not a
world expert on word-spell-ology or anything, but
if a word is pronounced Temz, then shouldn't we
write it that way? Or would that make our capital's
river look too much like an Eastern European
bottled lager? These are the sorts of things that
batter into my head as I lie in my bed at night, you
know. The phrase 'keeps me awake at night' is no
mere expression in my case. It's an actual state of
affairs. You ask my wife.

VOWELS

IE   is always pronounced 'eye-before-ee' *except* when it
is pronounced '*except*' after *sea*' (see 'c').

AI   has the value of somebody shot in the stomach
anywhere east of Sri Lanka or west of the
International Date Line.

ERG   has the value of somebody retrieving something
that has rolled under a table, perhaps a bread roll
or some coins, shuffling out backwards on all fours,

not quite gauging the distance properly, and trying to stand up with their head still largely underneath the table.

OU   has the value of somebody with a mouthful of soft-crumb pastry who has inhaled a small crumb of the soft-crumb pastry inadvertently, but can't quite cough properly because their mouth is packed with a sodden mix of flour, butter and saliva.

UW   has the value of somebody caught with a swift backhander that makes their face flip sharply to the left, and propels a tiny stream of dribble horizontally from the corner of their lip.

ACCENTS

`   means that the letter (but not the whole word) should be pronounced with a German accent.

¨   means that the letter (but not the whole word) should be pronounced with a generic 'Asia Minor' or 'Middle Eastern' accent.

~   means that the whole sentence should be spoke in cod-Spanish, and 'olé' added at the end.

ώ   looks a bit testicular, don't you think? Honestly, sometimes I think the people who invent typefaces just get a bit bored from time to time and slip a few in to see if we notice.

ψ   candelabra
Ø   man with bowler hat on at rakish angle
Þ   pregnant lampstand

Nonwin Press are proud to announce

**An exciting new development in Fantasy fiction
The upgrading of a Fantasy classic**

Do you love A. R. R. R. Roberts's *Lowered Off the Rings*?

Yeah? You do?

So do we.

But there's one problem – isn't there? *You* know what we're talking about.

At a mere 1200 pages and three volumes it is simply too short. How can any true Fantasy fan enjoy a book that's over as soon as it begins?

For this reason Nonwin Press has commissioned Fantasy author Roberts Jordan to recast this classic book, to bring it into line with the demands of modern fans of Fantasy fiction.

Roberts Jordan's
The Lord of the Wheels of Time

A 144-volume rewriting of *Lowered Off the Rings*. Each volume guaranteed *at least* 1000 pages long, with *at least* three maps per volume, lists of characters, glossaries, and a full-colour hyperrealist painted cover art.

283

The Soddit

NOT!
The first few minutes of prologue in
A MAJOR NINE-HOUR MOTION PICTURE EPIC!!!

When he's not being A. R. R. R. Roberts,
A. R. R. R. Roberts writes proper books under the
pseudonym Adam Roberts. Ones we publish are:

Salt

On

Stone

Polystom

The Soddit

or,

LET'S CASH IN AGAIN

or,

There, and Back Again, dammit, where did I put it, where is it, I don't believe it, I must have left it There, over Again to There, oh for heaven's sake, it's not here either, Back Yet Again, fuming, oh there it is, it was by the front door all along.

A. R. R. Roberts

GOLLANCZ
LONDON

First published in Great Britain in 2003 by

Gollancz
An imprint of the Orion Publishing Group
Orion House, 5 Upper St Martin's Lane, London WC2H 9EA

Fourth impression 2004

A CIP catalogue record for this book is available
from the British Library

ISBN 0 575 07554 6

Typeset at The Spartan Press Ltd,
Lymington, Hants

Printed in Great Britain by
Clays Ltd, St Ives plc

Bingo

Chapter One

THE UNEXPECTED PART

❦

In a hole, in a highly desirable and sought-after portion of the ground (the hole two doors along went for three hundred thou last month, near enough, although admittedly it was double-fronted and had a newly turfed roof) lived a soddit, the hero of our story. His name was Bingo 'Sac' Grabbings. Not a name he chose for himself, of course, but one decided on by his mother. Easy for her to say, of course; she didn't have to live with it all through school and adult life. Parents, eh?

Where was I? Oh, yes.

In a hole, then, lived Bingo. It was a fair-to-middling soddit hole, with a circular blue-painted door, fine blue tiles in the bathroom with a cheesy blue mould growing on them, blue beetles, silverfish, silvery worms, all manner of moistness and a kitchen area from which it was next to impossible to clear out cooking smells. Nevertheless in soddit terms it was a reasonably desirable residence. Bingo's aunt, the severe Vita 'Sac' Vile-Vest, had designs upon this very sod-hole, although

Bingo was in no mood to give way to pressure from that branch of the family. He was a soddit of forty, which in soddit years was next to nothing, a mere bagatelle, less than a bagatelle in fact; well, technically about four fifths of a bagatelle, but still young, that's my point.

Soddits are a race of little people who live *in the earth*, which is where their name comes from (you'll learn a lot about names and where they come from if you pay attention as you read, believe me). Scholars and philologists have established the derivation of the name, evidenced by an ancient rhyme:

> *Cleave the sod with your trusty spade*
> *Dig out a house that's quite like a grave*
> *And should your neighbour not return your wave*
> *Cleave the sod with your trusty spade*

Now it is an interesting thing that soddits don't tend to call themselves 'soddits', for reasons I'll come to in a minute. But 'soddit' is the generally accepted term. Once upon a time a traveller from the country of the bigger people roamed far and wide through the country of the littler folk, through the County of the Hunchkins, Shrimpville, Littleputia, the Land of the Lepercorns[1],

---

[1] A brave little folk afflicted with the most repulsive and contagious foot diseases. Foot diseases are, it must be said, something of a common theme for the Counties of the Little.

Jockeyton, and into Hobbld-Ahoy!, the home town of
Bingo, the hero of our tale. On his return to the human
town of Brie this big 'un traveller found his way to a
tavern, and sat meditating on his adventures, and his
fellow big 'uns gathered around him curious as to what
he had seen. 'What did you discover?' they pressed him.
'Who did you encounter?' 'I met a—' he started to reply,
and drew a great shuddering sigh into his body, before
concluding in a lowered tone, 'soddit,' and reaching for
his tankard of ale. The name of the particular soddit he
encountered has not been recorded, but it was clearly a
meeting that had a profound impact upon the big man,
for he stayed inside the Dragon-Queen Inn at Brie for
two days and two nights drinking all the time and
speaking to nobody, and soon afterwards left the area
never to return.

Soddits build the accommodation portion of their
houses under the ground, and they build their coal-
cellars, wine rooms and sometimes large rooms with
ping-pong tables in them above the ground. They insist
that this is the most logical manner of arranging living
space, and indeed Hobbld-Ahoy! planning regulations
have made any other form of domestic building illegal,
although this does tend to result in living quarters
prone to damp, to worms, to mould, to associated
asthma and bronchitis for the inhabitants, whilst coal,
wine and ping-pong bats are the most burgled items in

this burglary-prone town. But a tradition, after all, is a tradition.

Soddits, as I say, don't call themselves soddits. In their own tongue, which is queer and old and full of syntactical-grammatical inconsistencies, they call themselves *hobblds*. Now, there's a reason why they refer to themselves in this manner, and not by the name of soddit like everybody else in the world, and the reason is found in their feet. Shocking feet, they have. Just shocking. Whatever the reason – and soddits down the ages have blamed the gods, or an ancient wizard's curse, or inadequate orthopaedic practice, or congenital disease, or a dozen other factors – whatever the reason, soddits are almost all of them afflicted with appalling arthritis of the feet. Their feet are swollen and gnarled, many three or four times their normal size, with toes like coconuts and ankles like condoms stuffed with pebbles. This arthritis is extremely painful, and is indeed no laughing matter, although queerly it is a condition that does not spread to any other part of their body. But it gives their feet a strangely deadened, different colour from the rest of their bodies. Moreover, it makes it impossible for the adult soddit to wear shoes, for the pressure of leather against the inflated flesh of the feet is too, too ghastly. This means that the diminutive folk walk only with difficulty and excessive slowness; and accordingly adult soddits spend much of their time searching for the cushion of perfect softness, making little grunts as they collapse into their sofas and using their hands physically to lift their feet on to their footstools.

And now you know everything that you need to know about soddits, or hobblds, excepting only one or two minor details, such as the fact that they are food-loving and drink-loving and enjoy conviviality. And that they like to wear waistcoats and corduroy. Oh, yes, and that they smoke pipeweed a great deal and that accordingly they die younger than they otherwise would of cancers of the mouth, tongue and throat as well as of heart disease. What else? That they are conservative, rural, bourgeois, middle class. That they speak with a slight Birmingham accent, oddly. And, also, that despite their manifest disadvantages – their diminutive stature, their crippled elephantiasitic feet, their small-mindedness, their disinclination to listen to strangers or change old ways, their addiction to tobacco and alcohol, their stagnant class-ridden 'respectability' – despite all this, they have developed the most modern semi-industrial culture in the whole world, with water-mills, steam-foundries, comfortable housing, pipes, pop-guns, spectacles, velvet clothes, charming little flintstone churches, books and fireworks, whilst the rest of Upper Middle Earth is languishing in the dark ages of swords, horses, and burying their dead under enormous mounds of earth. Funny that. But, you see, the ways of the world are strange and sometimes inexplicable.

Bingo was sitting on his most comfortable sofa one morning, with his poor swollen arthritic feet resting on a green velvet cushion on the footstool in front of him. He was staring at the knuckled toe joints of these feet, the place where the individual toes meet the body of the foot, and these joints were staring back at him, like ten radishes. He was feeling the full weight of the misery of existence, poor old Bingo.

There was a series of bangs on the door, loud and startling, the sort of noise that might be made by a naughty soddit child stuffing a firecracker in the key-hole, lighting it, running away, hearing the dis-appointingly soggy pop, coming back vexed and kicking the door off its hinges with his as-yet unspoiled, bovver-booted feet. Young people today, eh? What can you do? Tch.

Bingo sighed. 'Go away,' he called. After a pause he added, 'Go away.'

The banging continued on the front door.

There was nothing for it. Bingo got slowly to his feet, and made his way to the door, flinching with each step and uttering all his usual expressions of pain, including 'ah!', 'ouch' and, half under his breath, 'ow-ow-ow'.[2]

Bingo did not like having a round front door. Who would? Geometry dictates that such a door be held in place by only one hinge, and that this hinge cannot be placed in the most effective load-bearing position, so that the doorway is draughty and the door unwieldy to open, and able easily to be kicked completely in by any soddit still young enough to be wearing boots. But tradition is tradition is tradition, and this was a tradition which Hobbld-Ahoy! planning regulators enforced with particular zeal. Bingo pulled open his door.

Outside, standing in the sunshine, was a wizard. Bingo had never seen a wizard before, but the 'W' on the front of his poncho could only mean he was one of that magic brotherhood. Either that, or he was a Munchkin of unusually developed stature and had put his poncho on upside down.

The knocking noise was continuing, louder than before.

---

[2] Which is to say, the noises somebody makes not when they are in actual pain, but when they wish to communicate to the world at large that they are experiencing a sensation of slight discomfort. Nobody suffering *actual* pain – let us say, a broken leg, or having their shoulder pierced all the way through with a Wharg-rider's arrow – would ever say 'ouch'. If somebody in such a situation *were* to say 'ouch' we would think not that they were in pain, but that they were taking the piss.

Bingo looked up at the wizard.

'Yes, well,' said the wizard in a booming voice. 'I'm sorry about that.'

'Sorry?' Bingo repeated, uncomprehending. He looked at his still-knocking door.

'The knocking spell I put on your door. It's a common enough wizardly spell, you know,' he bellowed, as if talking into a gale. 'I'm too fragile at my time of life to go banging at doors. Banging at doors! I'm too old and fragile for that. So I've put the knocking spell on, do you see?'

Bingo looked at the door. 'Can you turn it off, please?'

The wizard seemed not to hear. 'Thank you!' he said, in his stentorian voice. 'But, really, you're *too* kind. It's a small spell, but potent. Potent!'

'How long does it last?'

'Yes, yes,' boomed the wizard indulgently. 'But can I turn it *off*? That's the question. And the answer? The answer is "can I buggery". Hard to do, do you see? Easy to turn it on, that spell, but fiercely difficult to turn it off.'

'How long does the spell last?' said Bingo, leaving a space between each word and moving his facial muscles in a more marked manner as he spoke.

'Grabbings?' shrieked the wizard, his shaggy eyebrows rising and his eyes staring intensely. 'Grab-

bings?' He stepped forward, filling the doorway, bent
down and stepped into the hallway of Grab End.

Bingo spun around as the huge figure of the wizard,
bent nearly double, moved rapidly along the hall and
into the main sitting room, shouting Bingo's surname at
the top of his voice. All the while the front door carried
on making its deafening racket, like a heavy item of
wooden furniture clattering down an endless flight of
stairs. Bingo stumbled after the wizard, calling out
'hey!' and 'ow-my-feet!', and came through to the
sitting room to find the old wizard parked there in
Bingo's own sofa (which though large for a soddit was
chair-sized for the man), beaming toothlessly at him.
'So you are *Grabbings*, are you?' he shouted.

'Yes, yes I am,' replied Bingo. 'But, look, I'm sorry
but I'm afraid I'm going to have to ask you – I'm sorry –
to leave. You can't come in. You can't sit there.'

'It said "Grabbings" over the door, you see,' said the
wizard.

'I'm going to have to ask you to *leave*,' said Bingo, in a
louder voice.

'Grabbings,' said the wizard, putting his finger to his
cheek to mime contemplation. 'A burglar's name, is
that?'

'I'm a gentlehobbld of independent means,' said
Bingo, wincing as a sudden pain arrowed up his leg
from his left foot, 'and I'm asking *you* to *go, now*.'

'I thought so,' said the wizard, smiling knowingly. 'I thought so.'

'*Leave! Please!*' screeched Bingo.

'Too kind,' said the wizard, taking off his hat and placing it on his lap. 'Two sugars, for me. My name is Gandef and I am a wizard, yes indeed. The famous Gandef. Don't be scared. I promise,' he said, chuckling to himself, 'I do – I promise – although I *am* a wizard, I promise not to turn you,' he went on, his chuckling bubbling up until his shoulders and his whole head were shaking with the hilarity of what he was saying, 'not to turn you into a *toad* – arch-CHHTTGH QOOF-QOOF-QOOF,' he added, coughing so abruptly, so prodigiously and body-spasmingly that it looked, for a moment, as if he were going to shake himself out of his seat and on to the floor. 'AWARGH – SCHW-SCHWO'AH KOH-KOH,' he coughed. 'K'OAH K'OAH K'OAH K'OAH K'OAH K'OAH K'OAH.'

Bingo, alarmed, sat down in the second-best chair.

'K'OAH, K'OAH K'OAH K'OAH K'OAH,' the wizard continued.

'Are you all—' Bingo started to say.

'K'OAH K'OAH K'OAH K'OAH K'OAH,' the wizard concluded, and let his head flop backwards. His colour had drained away, and little dregs of spittle were visible on the grey of his beard just below his mouth. 'Blimey,' he said in a strangulated voice. 'Oh dear, oh dear.' His right hand fumbled in the pocket of his gown and brought out a pipe, his left hand brought out a wallet of pokeweed, and with trembling fingers he filled the bowl. 'I'll be better in a moment,' he croaked, muttering a small spell to bring a yellow flame from his right thumbnail so that he could light the pipe. For long minutes the wizard simply sucked noisily at the stem of his pipe, making orgasmic little moans between breaths, and swiftly filling Bingo's front room with a smoke so acrid and dark it made the little soddit's eyes smart. 'Oh that's better,' Gandef murmured, sucking in another lungful of heated tobacco particles and air, 'so much better.'

'Are you all right?' Bingo asked, a little nervously.

'Eh?' Gandef shouted. 'What? You'll have to speak up. My hearing's not what it used to be.'

Away in the hall, behind him, Bingo could hear the door still knocking away to itself. 'I—' he started to say, but realised that he didn't know how to finish the sentence.

'Oh, *once* upon a time,' said Gandef, 'my hearing was better than an eagle, and my eyesight better than a – well, a goodly eyed animal. I don't know. Something with a very good and acute sense of sight. An eagle. Yes. But age takes its toll, you know.' The wizard hawked, and so enormous a noise of wrenching phlegm emanated from his chest that Bingo shrank back. 'I tried a most potent Noise Amplification Spell once upon a time,' Gandef was saying, his voice meditative, though still loud. 'Marvellous spell. I could hear the birds speaking to one another in trees over the horizon, I could hear the rustlings as the clouds rubbed against one another in the sky. I could hear the sound a rainbow makes as it arches its back over the world. Then a dog barked behind me and I burst my left eardrum. Won't try *that* again in a hurry. I actually wet myself – imagine it! A wizard! Wetting himself in terror! Wouldn't do for that piece of news to get around, the forces of evil and all that, important to keep up appearances of, you know, magic and potency. I'm not actually a man, you see – I'm a sort of angel.'[3]

---

[3] This is true, actually. The best theological thinking today suggests that when you die and go up to heaven you'll find God surrounded not by people in white with wings, but instead by a large crowd of crotchety, beardy men in big hats with nicotine-stained fingers and swords. As the Philosopher once said: The world is not only stranger than we imagine, but stranger than we *can* imagine, and more imaginative than we can imagine too, which is something of a contradiction, don't you think, where was I? Hold on, bear with me for a minute, angels, old men, ah yes, ahm, ahem, stranger than we imagine, stranger than we *can* imagine, stranger than we *will* imagine, stranger than we *shall* imagine, stranger than we *can't* imagine, stranger than we *shouldn't* imagine, stranger than we *wouldn't* imagine *if we could*, stranger than you can imagine *but not me*, and so on. Anyway, I think we can both agree I've made my point.

He chuckled to himself. 'Covers a multitude of sins, that. Sharp's the word!'

'I don't quite follow,' said Bingo.

'They'll be here in a moment, Our Friends from the Dwarf. From, uh, the dwarfland. They're the salt of the earth. Which is to say, they've dug up and sold the salt of the earth. And also that they've ploughed salt *into* the earth of people they didn't like. But we'll stay on their good side. Oh yes. We'll draw up a contract, I'll get the map out, and we can head off tomorrow. Be on our way.' He cleared his throat, or to put it more precisely, he moved half a stone of snot from one internal location to another, and then drew a deep breath through his pipe.

'Come again?' said Bingo.

But Gandef had fallen asleep, his head lolling, his still lit pipe rolling from his fingers and tipping smouldering tobacco over the matting that served for a carpet in Bingo's soddit hole.

The first four dwarfs[4] arrived half an hour later, hammering on the door so violently that it jolted off its latch and collapsed inwards. 'My door!' squealed Bingo, scurrying as fast as his deformed feet could take him out into the hallway.

---

[4] This, by the way, *is* the correct plural form of 'dwarf'. Look it up if you don't believe me – really.

'Apologies,' said the first dwarf, treading on the wreck of the door as he stepped inside. 'We were knocking for a while, look you, but seeing how the door was knocking anyway by itself I don't think we were being heard. I got a mate who does doors.'

'Does doors lovely,' said the second dwarf.

'Oh, he'll do you a *lovely* door,' said the first dwarf, with a flush of agreement. 'Lovely big *hefty* door. Soon as he pops along, he'll quote you, lovely boy, la, bach.'

'There's been a misunderstanding,' Bingo gabbled at them. 'I'm sorry that you've been inconvenienced, but you've got the wrong hole. Nobody here called Grabbings. No wizard, there's no wizard here. You'll have to go away.'

From behind him, in the sitting room, came a series of axe-like chopping noises such as can only be produced by a man who has scoured the walls of his lungs red and smooth over many years of dedicated smoke inhalation.

'That's the boyo,' said the first dwarf, stepping past Bingo. 'Failin,' he said. 'I'm a dwarf, la, boy, see, yow, bach, dew,' he added. 'This is my cousin Qwalin.' The second dwarf bowed. 'And behind him are Sili and Frili, also cousins, see?'

'I haven't the victuals—' Bingo began, in desperation. But the four dwarfs were already in the sitting room, singing tunelessly but loudly, one of them bouncing lustily on the wizard's chest to wake the fellow up. Bingo turned about, cursed the gnawing pain in his left toes, and turned again as four more dwarves[5] stepped boldly into his house.

'Mori,' said the first dwarf, who was holding a clipboard. He was a strong-nosed dwarf in green, with a waterfall of beard and eyebrows thick as caterpillars. Or as actual pillars. 'Allow me to introduce my cousins, Tori, Orni and On. Oh *my*,' he added, stepping towards Bingo. 'Haven't *you* the smoothest of chins!'

The four dwarfs kicked their beards out from under their feet and clustered around Bingo, treading on his toes as they did so. 'Oo,' they said, running callused fingers over his chin. 'Oo.'

'Get off,' Bingo said, flapping his hands before his face like little wings.

'You'll have to excuse us, see,' said Mori, leaning his clipboard against the wall and taking off his dwarf hat. 'It's a rare sight for us, a bare chin – a sight of rare beauty. Wouldn't I love a bare chin!'

'Wouldn't *I*!' said Orni.

'You'll say, shave,' said Mori, clapping Bingo in a manly clasp, his arm around the back, his powerful hand crushing Bingo's shoulder. 'You *will*, you'll tell me, shave.'

---

[5] Sorry, that one must have slipped through the proofs.

'I won't,' said Bingo.

'Can't,' said Mori, as if in correction. 'Psoriasis. Terrible. Allergy to bauxite. Couldn't shave if my life depended on it. Stuck with this ap-*surd* hippy beard.[6] I hate it.'

'We *all* hate it,' said Orni. 'All hate our beards.'

'All of us in the same boat. Smells, la,' said Mori confidentially. 'Food gets stuck in it. I found a chicken bone in mine yesterday. Anyway, anyhow, anyhew.' He released Bingo. 'Is the King boy here yet?'

'King boy?' said Bingo.

'Thorri, our King, heavens bless him. No? There you go. I can hear merry being made, though, look you, begorrah, la, bach, boyo, see, dew, bach, look you, so we'll go on through.'

Bingo stumbled to the larder, and brought out a selection of the food he possessed. The dwarfs devoured it all in quarter of an hour. In dismay he tried telling the group that he had no more, but they wouldn't take no for an answer, explored his hobbld hole thoroughly and completely ransacked it. They rolled out his one and only barrel of Soddit ale, and tapped and drank it. They sang all the while, whilst

[6] Which is to say, a beard that reaches down to one's hips. Why? What else did you think this might mean?

Gandef sat in the corner tapping his foot not in time to the music and smoking. They sang:

> *When you walk with a dwarf keep your head down low*
> *So as not to draw attention to his height,*
> *For a dwarf's hold on his temper is only so-so*
> *And a dwarf has no fear of a fight.*
> *Walk on, walk on, crouching all the time*
> *Though your hips are racked with pain –*
> *Walk on, walk on, with a bend in your spine*
> *Or you'll ne-ver walk again,*
> *You'll NE-ver walk again.*

After which they sang, or rather they howled:

> AND! WE! WERE! *SI-I-INGING!*
> SONGS AND ARIAS –
> DWARFS IN THE LARDER –
> OH ME, OH MY.

After which they insisted that Bingo join in with the quaffing, despite his protestations that he was normally a very moderate drinker. They drank toasts to his smooth chin, and his smooth upper lip, and they sang more songs: raucous songs, caucus songs, ribald songs, dribbled songs, hymns, whims, theramins, chim-chim-cherees, songs that were hard, songs by bards, songs that left you scarred (emotionally speaking), drinking anthems, looting anthems, puking anthems, footy anthems, beauty-pageant anthems, and 'Bess You Is My Woman Now'. They sang a-capella, a-patella[7] and *any umber-ella-any-umber-ella*. At some point in the proceedings the remaining dwarfs came in, Ston, Pilfur, Gofur, and Wombl; and finally there entered a diminutive little creature, small even for a dwarf and barely an inch taller than Bingo, who introduced himself as 'Thorri, King you know', but who seemed to be accorded remarkably little respect from the other dwarfs. But by this stage Bingo was well drunk, tanked-up, reeling and rocking, and soon enough he was falling over and getting up with a silly expression on his face. He was as unsteady on his feet as a newborn colt that had been force fed half a bottle of whisky. Then Gandef began singing a song, and got halfway through the first stanza before he started coughing with shocking vehemence, making a series of noises like a roof-load of snow collapsing twenty feet to the ground. Forty-five seconds of this and the wizard was too weak to stand, and collapsed back on to the sofa gasping and fumbling with his tobacco pouch.

'My new friends,' said Bingo, with tears in his eye

---

[7] The sort of song you sing when somebody has just kicked you in the kneecap.

and alcohol compounds in his bloodstream. 'My new
friends! How sweet it is to have friends – to make new
friends!'

'Strictly a business arrangement, Mr Grabbings,' said
Mori. 'We have a quest to undertake, and we need your
help, that's all.'

'You need my help!' repeated Bingo joyously, his
cheeks wet. 'My friends!'

'Yes, yes,' said Mori, pushing the over-affectionate
soddit away. 'Let's not lose proportion, look you, bach,
la. There's a dragon, see, and he's got, eh, well shall we
say . . . treasure. Let's call it *treasure*.'

'Gold?' asked Bingo, his eyes circular.

'What's that?' said Qwalin, 'Yeah – yeah, that's it.
Gold. That's a good one.'

'Gold,' said Mori, looking significantly at his fellow
dwarfs. 'All right? We all clear? Mr Grabbings here is
to help us nick us some *gold*. Yes, that's it, we're on our
way to steal the dragon's gold. See?'

The dwarfs made various noises of dawning comprehension.

'So,' said Mori, turning to Bingo, 'we figured – and
this is only a rough plan, see – that we'd go over there
and distract the dragon boyo with some close-harmony
baritone singing whilst you steal the, eh, *gold*, you being
a thieving little tinker, or so we've been led to believe –
no offence.'

Bingo's heart was flush with new comradeship and love. He sobbed like a child, trying to hug Mori and unburden his heart, to say how he'd always felt, somehow, distanced from the other soddits, as if there was something that held him back from them, and held them back from *him* – it wasn't easy to say what exactly, but on occasion he'd stand at his door with a glass of dry hobbld martini in his hand and watch the evening traffic making its way up Hobbld-Ahoy! high-street and over the bridge into the thickening gloom and feel, somehow, a great emptiness inside himself, a sense of purposelessness of it all – the way the narrow respectability of his world felt sometimes like a suffocating velvet cloak – and all along the thing he'd been missing was right here, this sense of purpose, belonging to this band of brothers, united in a common aim. Sadly the ale, which provoked this chain of thought in Bingo's mind, also prevented the articulate expression of it, and the best he could manage was a 'such-a-lovely-buncho-blokes-lovely-feller-love-you' and a further series of throaty syllables like the noise a dog makes just before it throws up.

'Now,' Mori continued in a louder voice, backing against the wall, 'are you OK with our plan, boyo, look you? Remember, the only problem to this quest thing is that the – eh – the *treasure* is in the possession *of a dragon*. Right?'

'Dragons!' said Bingo. 'They don't frighten me. Insectivores, aren't they?'

'No,' said Mori. 'I wouldn't describe them as insecti-vores.'

'Well,' said Bingo, waving his hand dismissively and wobbling on his feet. 'Does it matter?' He'd long since reached the level of alcoholic uncoordination where it becomes difficult to place the right thumb upon the end of the left little finger, and indeed had gone somewhat beyond it, to the state where it is difficult to get one's upper and lower lips to connect.

'Smug the Dragon,' said Gandef, erupting apparently from sleep. 'A fearsome, terrible sight, he is, the mighty wyrm in his desolation.'

'Terrible, terrible,' said the dwarfs in unison.

The ale swirled in Bingo heart. 'I'm not afeared!' he squealed, trying to clamber on the table.

'Smug the Dragon!' Gandef bellowed, rather carried away with himself. 'Terrible Smug! Marvellous great dragon! Bah!' He coughed once, twice, and then thrummed a long, enduring note on the taut surface of the mass of phlegm held in his chest.

The dwarfs brought out their own pipes, and soon the smoke was so thick in Bingo's sod hole that you couldn't see the smokers for the smoke.[8] Moreover, the

---

[8] I've got a PhD you know, from Cambridge University. I just thought you might be interested in that fact. I'm not some bloke making this up from thin air, I'm a proper scholar, I studied Anglo Saxon and everything.

smoke that came out of the dwarfish pipes had a strange savour to it, a slightly herbal, fruity, pleasant, drowsy, hey-man edge to it, a whiff of 'Rings, eh? They're, like, all hard round the outside and all, like, nothing at all in the middle, isn't that weird? The way they can be both really *really* hard on the edge and *really* soft in the middle, d'you ever think of that?' and a slight odour of 'Hey I'm really really hungry, you got any, like, scones or something?' The excitement and passion drained out of Bingo wholly, and he lay on the floor with his feet in the grate, humming along as the dwarfs sang another song.

> *Smug the Magic Dragon*
> *Are we afraid of he?*
> *In his Magic Dragon-grotto-place,*
> *No-o-ot like-a-lee –*
> *We'll travel over earth,*
> *And we travel over sea,*
> *To beard that dragon in his den, look you now*
> *Most assuredly.*
>
> *Oh yes we will, I tell you now,*
> *You better believe we'll do it*
> *We will, oh yes we will, oh*
> *Yes we will, we're going to it,*
> *I'm telling you we will*

It's practically good as done,
We're going that way right now,
That dragon's, well, let's just say, I wouldn't want to be in his
    shoes.

Gandef was shouting something at this point and had
to be calmed. Then, under the illusion that he was
whispering discreetly into Mori's ear, he boomed, 'I
was thinking, why don't we tell the young soddit that
we're off after some *gold*? Eh? Wouldn't that be sly?'
Mori's voice, much lower, came murmuring indistinctly
through the fug. 'You see,' Gandef bellowed, louder
still, 'if the soddit *thinks* we're after some *gold* then he
won't ask after the *real* reason for our quest – do you
see?' Again, Mori's voice, now more urgent but still
indistinct, muttered in the dark. Bingo, from where he
was lying, could just about see the pyramidical shape of
the wizard's hat, and the hunched silhouette of Mori
trying to communicate with the old man. 'I can't hear
you if you *mutter* like that,' bellowed Gandef petulantly.
'All I'm saying is that this would be a *good cover story* as
far as the soddit is concerned. That way we don't have
to tell him what we're *really* going for yrkh, yrkh,
mmbbmmmdd.'
    It seemed to Bingo's eyes, in the smoke-obscured
candlelight, as if Gandef's hat had been dragged

sharply down to cover his whole face. But the young soddit's eyelids were slipping down in irresistible sleep, and he couldn't focus any more.

Trollps

Chapter Two

ROAST MUTT

ᏫᎷᎦ

Bingo was woken by the smell of Gandef's pipe, the smoke of which caused a stinging sensation in the mucus membranes of his sinus and gave him a mixed impression of singed hair, burning bark and smoking rubber. The young soddit, coughing, pulled himself into a sitting position to find Gandef reclining lazily on the sofa.

'Good morning, young master Grabbings,' the wizard said genially, and sucked at the stem of his pipe so hard that his eyeballs shrank back in his skull.

'What time is it?' Bingo squeaked. But as he asked the question his eye lighted on the half-hunter squatting on the mantelpiece. The hour lacked some minutes of nine. He rubbed his eyes, and *some minutes* came into more precise focus as *fifty minutes*. 'Ten past eight?' he gasped. 'Ten past eight *in the morning*?' (Soddits, as I'm sure you know, like to sleep until noon – a habit so entrenched in their culture that the idea of a clockface having the dual function of 'a.m.'

and 'p.m.' is for most of them only a notional and theoretical hypothesis.)

Gandef nodded intelligently. 'Bright and early,' he said. 'Ah! The first pipe of the day. The first is always the sweetest.' He took another drag.

'Dwarfs!' said Bingo, getting unsteadily to his feet. 'Drink! Potweed! Hallucinations!' His head felt like it had been turned inside out, had tent pegs hammered into it, and then folded back in on itself again.

'Yes, yes,' said Gandef indulgently. 'It is late, I know. But Thorri didn't have it in his heart to wake you. You looked so peaceful. But you'd better get a move on. Did you read the letter?'

'What letter?'

'Good. I'm glad that at least you read the letter.'

Bingo found the letter after a ten-minute search through the desolation and chaos that had once been his front room. Written upon the finest dwarfish parchment, a form of scraped and treated stone, it read as follows:

Honourable sir,

On the offchance that you have forgotten our arrangement, we beg to remind you that should you fail to present yourself at the Putting Dragon Inn at Byjingo by nine a.m. we would be obliged to consider you an enemy of all dwarfkind and would thereafter hunt you down and slay you like the vermin you are. At nine sharp, mind for we depart on our great quest eastward to confront the evil and condescending dragon Smug in his lair.

Yours dwarfully,
Thorri (King) and Company.

P.S. Mori begs to remind you that the purpose of our quest is *gold*, honestly, *gold*, lots of gold, and nothing else, certainly not anything non-gold.

'Hunt me down and slay me like the vermin I am?' said Bingo, a catch in his voice.

'Lovely illumination on the "H" don't you think?' said Gandef, looking over the soddit's shoulder. 'That's a little rugby ball flying through the top portion, and Barijon standing to the left of it. A great dwarfish hero, he.'

'Will they really kill me if I don't turn up?'

'Oh no, of course not,' said Gandef, shaking his head forcefully and chuckling a little. 'No, no, nothing like that. On the other hand,' he added, tamping some more tobacco into his pipe bowl, 'they certainly will kill you if you don't turn up. It's a sort of dwarfish tradition, you see. Punctuality. That,' he added, mysteriously, 'and sheep.'

In a blind panic Bingo fled from his front room, stepping over the wreckage of his still-knocking door, and scurried along the main street of Hobbld-Ahoy! as fast as his sore feet would permit in the general direction of Byjingo.[1] He arrived at the Putting Dragon Inn with one minute to spare, panting and clutching at his agonised feet. The dwarfs were waiting for him, standing underneath the painted inn sign (which represented a trouser-clad dragon attempting to hole a tricky twenty-foot putt whilst a salamander stood in the background).[2]

'Just in time, lad, la, boyo,' said Mori, as the Byjingo town clock chimed the hour, or rather thudded once, which is what it did every hour of the day, ever since a bored soddit youth had stolen the bell to wear as a hat. And with that the dwarfs shouldered their packs and started away on their great quest, Bingo limping complainingly along behind them.

[1] The Jingo, upon which Byjingo is located, is a clear, fast-flowing stream that joins the Great River Flem a score of miles south-east of Hobbld-Ahoy!. Legend has it that the stream is named for its resemblance to an alcoholic drink of clear purity and great strength popular amongst the soddits. Flowing from the ice-capped northern mountains, through the fruit orchards of the County of the Hunchkins (to the north of Soddlesex), the Jingo often carries chunks of pure mountain ice, and bobbing whole lemons in its stream.

[2] Golf is a popular Soddlesex game. Its origins are to be found in ancient Soddit religion, a faith which involved worship of a deified potato, and to which attached a ritualised contest to plant next year's crop by striking the potatoes one by one with a magic staff so that they flew into predug holes. This, it hardly needs adding, was a highly inefficient way of planting potatoes, and the potato crop was always very poor, something the soddits blamed on the anger of their god Spahd rather than their own incompetence.

❁

They stopped in Cremone to buy a beast of burden, a pack-animal called Bony – which name was (the salesman, 'Honest Anthony', insisted) a wittily ironic reference to his fat girth and good health, 'like calling a really large feller called John Little John, you see,' he said. Neither Bingo nor the dwarfs saw, but didn't want to reveal their ignorance. None of them had much experience with ponies, and believed the salesman's explanation that the protruding rib-like spars running round this creature's torso were a form of protection against predation, somewhat after the manner of an armadillo. 'Ain't Mother Nature a wonderful thing?' he added, as he pocketed their money.

Having loaded their supplies on to this one sorrowful beast the party made its way east, through gently rolling hills, gently downing downs, gently platting plateaus (platting in the sense that river, road and crops appeared to weave and unweave, drawing together and pulling apart as they crossed the land). By noon on the third day they had entered the Tiger Woods, where dangerous wild animals lurked in every sand trap, and where the potato game was originally invented. After many adventures, which I don't have time to go into, they got out the other side of this dangerous and exclusive place. They travelled over the river Tim's, named for one of the most famous legendary heroes of the Little Counties (Tim the Tiny,

River-Namer), and into Ply Wood. Here the going got slower. Bingo had to sit down every thirty or forty yards to rest his feet, and the dwarfs became crotchety with the delay. Pilfur and Gofur finally picked him up between them and carried him, but he complained at the bumpiness of the ride and they dropped him.

By sunset of the following day[3] the party had reached the Wood of Wooden Trees, and all were exhausted. The dwarfs had taken it in turns to carry the soddit, and had reached the end of their tether. In fact, they had tied a second tether to this end, and had reached the end of that too, which gives some indication of just how far they had gone. Really quite far, tether-wise, as I'm sure you will agree. Sadly their packhorse, Bony the tiny Pony, the only pony for sale in all of Cremone (sold them by phoney Tony the only pony-owner in Cremone) had

---

[3] I'd just like to say that the publishers have cut out *pages* and *pages* of my best stuff from here . . . I originally had the group enjoying all sorts of adventures in the Counties of the Little, fending off an attack of the Not Nice Mice, hurrying through the infestation of Piccadilly Flea Circus and the like. My favourite episode, which I begged and begged to keep in, but they didn't listen to me, was all about the land of the Tellurite Tubbles – those hard, metallic tub-shaped creatures, cyborg beings of terrifying inhumanity with computer screens inlaid in their torsos and weird shaped antenna coming out of their Upper Processing Units. Their ear-piercing cries of 'Annihilate! Annihilate!', 'You! Will Be! Annihilated!' and 'Tubble-tora-tora-tora-die-die-aaaiiee!' have charmed and delighted young children for many years.

fallen into the River Flem and drowned, carrying away nearly all their supplies. They were left only with a cauldron (that Tori was wearing as a helmet).

Dark fell as they made camp. It was a fell dark. Everybody in the company was hungry.

'You,' said Mori, prodding Bingo with the blunt end of his axe pole. 'Go and find us something to eat.'

'You're joking?' asked Bingo, rubbing a dock leaf on the soles of his aching feet. 'That's, you know, exactly like a joke, right?'

'There's firelight through the wooden trees,' said Gofur, pointing at a glowing splodge of orange light in the distance. 'Go and see who it is, and pinch some of their food, grabber, that's what you're here for, look you, a, yes, oo, bach, la, very.'

The other dwarfs made various noises of agreement. Amongst these noises were grunts, growls, two 'I agrees', one 'yes, off you go boyo', one 'I should say *so*' and one 'Mavis!', but this last was from a dwarf already asleep and was probably unrelated to the matter in hand.

Bingo was too tired to argue the case. He crept, biting his lower lip to stifle his grunts of pain, through the wooden trees of the wood of trees, moving always towards the gleam of the firelight. Soon, with a minimum of snapping twig sounds, rustlings, hootings of disturbed ground-nesting birds, sotto voce 'ouches' and 'ows' and the like, he got to the edge of a small clearing, and had a clear view of who was warming themselves by the fire within it.

Trollps! Four, great, whopping, stony trollps. Enough to give even the bravest soddit the collywobbles. They were sitting in a circle, roasting three dogs over the open fire. 'Ah,' said the nearest of them, licking his lips with his massive, stony tongue, 'roast mutt again.'

'Yer likes yer roast mutt, don't you Burt?' said a second trollp.

'That I do, Gerd,' agreed Burt, pulling one of the carcasses from the fire, dripping and sizzling on a stick, and taking a great squelching bite from its flank.[4]

Trollps, as you know, are fearsome creatures. It is

---

[4] The publishers have asked me to make it clear that they in no way endorse the cooking and eating of dogs, particularly not bassets, ladies, tramps, dogs that can say 'sausages' if you stick a thumb against their soft palate, the dog from the Famous Five or any other household-pet-style animal. Dogs are for Christmas, and for leaving on the side of the A308 in the new year, *not* for eating. *Cows* are the ones for eating, not dogs. They're big enough to look out for themselves, after all, whereas a brown-eyed whimpering Jack Russell is not. Remember the slogan of the 'Dogs Are People Too' organisation: 'Dogs Are People Too!' (The 'Cows Are People Too' organisation slogan is far more equivocal: 'Cows Are People Too, Though Not Very Bright People, And We Got To Admit It People With Extremely Tasty Flesh When Roasted Or, Better, Grilled, And Served With A Mustard And Dill Sauce, Some Chips, String Beans, A Nice Glass Of Red Wine, Oooh, Go On Then It Won't Matter If We Have Just The One, There Are Millions Of Them In Big Sheds Up North').

now many years since they left their traditional sub-pontoon habitat, and their traditional diet of goats, to roam far and wide in search of a fuller sense of self-expression and some quick cash. They are of course gigantic in stature, five foot eleven is not uncommon and some are as tall as six foot one and a half, and their proportions are similarly huge, bellies like boulders, arms like the roots of great oak trees, a head that looks from a distance as if it's wearing a steel helmet until you get closer and realise that that's just the shape of the head. Trollps, being creatures of nature, grow a straggly moss on their chests, arms and legs; they grow a stubble of little thorns from their chins, but the tops of their heads are smooth as water-polished stone. Their eyes are red as garnets, and their brows are beetling – not in the sense of having independent legs and a tendency to scurry away, but rather in the sense of jutting or overhanging in a threatening manner.

These four hefty trollps had come down from the mountains hoping for some business from the north-western cart salesman and middle-farm-management population. They were dressed in the traditional costume of their race: lacy underwear, garter belts, stockings (made of the same wire mesh used by some to construct fences), little fluttery red silk skirts which tended to ride suggestively upwards in the slightest breeze – and which, if the breeze were anything more than slight, tended to become cummerbunds – and a saucy little French Trollection low-halter button-up top, also in red. Burt had personalised his outfit with a natty little silk-ribbon neck bow, very continental, and Bill – the tallest of the four – wore flats rather than the brick-heeled Ralph Lauren trolletto shoes of the others. Gerd wore elbow-length gloves that had been a bridal white once upon a time, although they had now gone a rather muddy pink colour in the wash on account of being put in the laundry with man-blood still on them one too many times. Old Gil, the fourth member of the group, was the master make-upper of the four. His slab-like lips were carefully outlined in fifteen pounds of lipstick, very fetching. His tiny glowing eyes were surrounded by four thick, tangled rows of eyelashes, giving him the appearance of having large and grotesquely overfed Venus fly traps fitted to the front of his face. Which, indeed, may have been how he achieved the effect.

Bingo had not enjoyed a hot meal since the day before, and his mouth started watering at the smell of the roasting dog. He peered from behind a tree trunk, and slipped soundlessly to another tree trunk to get a better view, pressing himself close against this for cover and taking another cautious look. Sadly for him this last tree trunk was not a tree trunk at all, but Gerd's leg. He was suspended in midair, squealing and kicking his legs, before he knew what was happening.

'Hey! Crikey, blimey, love a duck and apples'n'-pears,' said Gerd, displaying his catch to the rest of them. 'Look what I've found!' He pronounced this last word 'fanned', but Bingo assumed that he meant 'discovered by chance', 'obtained' rather than 'cooled by agitating the air with a fan'.

The trollps clustered round, and gave a few exploratory pokes of Bingo in the ribs with their massive fingers.

'A snack!' said Gil. 'Bags he's mine!'

'There's bare enough in 'im for a mouf-ful,' said Bill.

'Lumme, cor, 'Ackney and Bermondsey,' said Gerd, 'a mouf-ful is all I want.'

'But ooze?' challenged Burt. 'Ooze to get the mouf-ful?'

'I caught 'im,' said Gerd.

'I bags'd him fust,' said Gil.

'I say we draws lots,' said Bill.

'Lots of wot?' said Burt.

'Are there any *more* of you mouf-fuls round about?' asked Gil, bringing his great stone face close up to Bingo's. The stench of Amour de Troll washed up the soddit's nose.

'No!' Bingo squeaked.

'Gah,' said Bill, grimacing. 'Bound to be,' said Gil, nodding.

With nary another word Bill, Gil and Burt lumbered

off into the woods. Bingo, gasping, dangling in midair, consoled himself by thinking that the three trollps were making such a loud noise that the dwarfs would surely be warned of their approach. Then he thought that the dwarfs were fierce and hardy warriors and would quickly defeat the trollps, and his captors would soon be nothing but rubble. Sadly, he was wrong in both these thoughts. No more than ten minutes later the three trollps returned, each with a brace of dwarfs. All the members of Thorri's band had been tied with their own beards, a humiliating circumstance that did not so much add insult to injury as multiply insult plus injury by shame to the power of agony. When they were all deposited, like giant hairy pupae, in a pile by the fire Bingo was trussed with an old trollp garter belt, and placed on top of the heap.

'That's more like it,' said Gil, sitting down on the broad boulder he'd been using as a stool and rubbing his great stony hands together at the fire, sending stone chips skittering into the air. 'That's a feast, that is.'

'Dwarfs,' said Burt, smacking his lips, or to be more precise, clacking them together. 'Tasty! Pukka!'

'I got nettles in my garter,' complained Bill, fumbling under his fine silks. 'Bloody forest.'

'Hark at 'er,' said Gerd. He affected an effeminate voice, or as close to one as his enormous stone vocal cords permitted him, to add: '*Got ne'els in my gar'er*'.

Then he sniggered, a sound like a row of gravestones falling over domino fashion. 'Ponce,' he concluded.

'Nance,' snapped Bill.

'Dunce,' said Gerd.

'Berk,' said Bill.

'Jerk,' said Gerd.

'Merck,' said Bill.

'Oi!' said Burt. 'Cut it out.' Actually he said 'Cu ih ah', but the other two trollps understood what he meant well enough. They glowered at one another. Bill smoothed out the creases of his red silk skirt against his enormous thighs. Gerd looked haughtily away into the forest.

'All we got to do now,' said Old Gil, 'is work out the best way to cook 'em.'

'The best fing wiv dwarfs,' said Bill, 'is to soffen 'em up, with a meat tenderiser, or a shovel maybe, and then chop 'em up.'

'Nah, nah, nah!' said Burt with scorn in his voice. 'You dahn't *cut* dwarfs, you *rip* 'em. And then you put 'em in a pot wiv onions, peppers, dozen cloves o' garlic, some cardamom, *green* chillies not red ones, and a lemon. Forty-five minutes, take the pot off the 'eat, *then* add the basil, bay leaf, touch of mint, frow in four dozen carrots, put them on the 'eat again, only *don't scorch* 'em, two hours, layer over with cream and brandy, Demerara, stir some more, 'nother lemon, fish out their 'ats and boots (keeping 'em for stock) and serve the whole fing up with six hunnert-weight of spuds. Cushtie, that. Lovely. Pukka.'

'Or we could just sit on 'em,' said Bill.

'All right,' said Burt.

The trollps regarded the pile. 'Tell you what, Gerd,' said Bill. '*You* sit on 'em.'

'Me?' said Gerd, outraged. 'Why me?'

'You got the biggest bum.'

'Bugger *off* have I!' said Gerd, standing up in his fury. 'Gil's is twice my size.'

'Yer lie!' roared Old Gil, standing up also.

'Remember that leather skirt you bought in that Dongor boo-teak?' taunted Gerd. 'Oh we laughed at that, all right. Made your bum look like two cows fighting in a leather tent, that did.'

'Laugh at me behind my back!' Gil yelled, and put his fist into Gerd's face. The ground shook with the terrible force of the blow, but Gerd did not so much as flinch, nor did his expression change. He pushed out with his right arm, aiming a devastating hook and catching Gil, smack in *his* face. The blow made a noise like a thunderclap. Cups containing water that happened to be standing on the ground nearby jiggled little bullseye patterns of ripples in their surfaces. But Gil didn't flinch either. The huge trollp made no sound. To be honest with you, there's little point in trollps fight-

ing, since it's almost impossible for them to injure one
another and they don't really feel pain. But they sometimes go through the motions, just for the form of it.
After a few more punches on either side Gerd and Gil
sat down.

'Please kind sirs,' squealed Bingo, who had been
summoning his courage and trying to think of what to
say. 'Don't eat us! We'll give you gold!'

'Gold,' mused Burt. 'I ate some of that once. A corn
factor in Bardbury gave me a gold bracelet, had it
engraved 'n all – "to my darlin' in memory of the
happiest weekend of my life, your snugly-puggly J.
Harrow Whettlestone Jr, Corn Factor and Mercer,
Seasonal Rates".' Burt sniffed as if moved by the
memory. 'I ate it, o' course, but it did somefink shocking down below . . . you know what I mean.'

The other three trollps grumbled their agreement.

'It ain't specially digestible,' said Bill. 'Gold.'

'Wait a minute,' said Gil. 'Corn factor in Bardbury?
You got a arrangement wiv a corn factor in Bardbury?
What we doing skulking in these woods if you got a
comfy berf in Bardbury?'

'Well,' said Burt shiftily. 'Trufe is, he's a special little
feller of mine.'

'Share and share alike,' insisted Gil.

'And I would,' said Burt. 'Only I et him last spring.
He used to take me on special trips, it was lovely, the

best hostels, fine clothes, as much dog as I could eat, but then one morning I woke up and looked at him and thought, "You're a pretty tasty gent," so I et him, and there it was.'

'Enough natter,' said Bill. '*I'm* going to squash me a dwarf. Better do somefing or we'll be ere all night.'

He stood up and picked a wriggling dwarf from the pile. But whilst he was up, Gerd pulled another dwarf from the bottom of the pile, and quickly slipped it on to Bill's boulder. As the unwitting trollp sat down there was a sound of revolting flatulent squelchiness. He looked startled, and his three friends began their rolling, ponderous, stony laughs. 'Oho,' said Bill, with a stern face. 'Oh that's very funny, that is,' he said sarcastically. 'Oh, I'll split me sides laughing at that.'

'Should have seen your face, Bill,' said Burt.

' 'Ere,' said Bill. 'You 'av this one.' He tossed his dwarf to Gil, and got gingerly to his feet trying to unstick the object that was now adhering limply to his hindquarters. Meanwhile, the three other trollps took their own dwarfs, placed them carefully on whichever slab or boulder they were sitting on, and sat back down. The whoopee-cushion noises sounded wetly round the ring. For several minutes there were no further sounds in the clearing save the gnash and gulp of four trollps eating.

Things were looking grim for the company.

'This one,' said Gil shortly, 'tastes a bit of chicking.'

'Everyfing tastes of chicking to me,' said Bill. ' 'Cept gold,' he added.

'Are you supposed to take the shell off of 'em before you eat 'em?' asked Burt, picking a mangled chunk of chain mail out of his great teeth with a fingernail like a paving slab.

'You smell,' came a rather quavery but fairly deep voice, the sort of voice an adolescent boy might inadvertently employ when he is on the cusp of slipping into manhood. 'You smell and, ah, nobody likes you.'

'Oo said that?' snapped Gerd.

'It was Bill,' said the quavery voice.

'No it wasn't,' said Bill.

'It came from over there,' said Gill, standing up and pointing towards the trees.

'No it didn't,' said the quavery voice. 'It was Bill. He said you all smell really unpleasantly and, uh, that you, oh I don't know, that you're a disgrace to the name of trollp.'

'Oo *is* that?' said Gerd.

The voice cleared its throat in a moist fashion, and seemed to slip down a semitone: 'Don't you speak to me like that, young Bill, you're the one who's a disgrace. I happen to know that the other two agree with me when I say that you've let down the honour of trollps everywhere.' There was a momentary pause. 'That was Gerd.'

Gerd was standing. 'I don't sound anyfink *like* that,' he declared, reasonably enough.

'No, no,' said the voice, 'that was definitely Gerd. I'd say that he's trying to pick a fight. Are you going to stand for that, Bill? Are you aHurgh Hurgh! Hurgh! Hurgh! Hurgh! Hurgh!' The voice was suddenly coughing so hard it was making the leaves nearby shudder. 'Hurgh! Hurgh! Hurgh! Hurgh! Hurgh!' it said.

Gil reached into the trees with his enormous hand, and brought out a wriggling figure dressed in a grey poncho and sporting a conical hat.

'Hurgh! Hurgh! Hurgh! Hurgh!' said the figure.

'A wizard!' said Gerd. 'Now don't that just cap everyfink?'

'I've never et a wizard before,' said Bill with glee in his voice.

'He's a bit scrawny, like,' said Gil, examining him. 'But 'e'll do.'

'Hurgh!' said the figure, the coughing subsiding. 'Hurgh!'

'Gandef!' squealed Bingo. 'Save us.'

Gandef, suspended in midair by the stone grip of a trollp's fist around his neck, managed to twist his head enough to look down upon Bingo. The look on his strained face seemed to say, *What do you think I'm trying to do, you twit?* It seemed to add, *And now look at the situation I'm in. What are we going to do now? It's all very well for you, but I'm a man of advanced years, I can hardly tackle four fully grown adult trollps by myself, bearing in mind my chronic lumbar pain and everything, not that I'm one to complain, I'm only saying.* A twist of a wizardly eyebrow seemed to ask, *Can't you reach one of the dwarf's swords, cut your bonds, free the rest of Thorri's company, dig a large pit, lure the trollps into it and quickly cover it with several hundred tons of earth?* As the despair on Bingo's face implied a negative answer, the look concluded, *You're a waste of space, useless, the lot of you.*

All in all, it was an exceptionally eloquent look.

'Now,' Gandef rasped, addressing the trollps. 'Gentlemen. I advise you not to be hasty. I should warn you that I'm a wizard.'

'So?' said Old Gil.

'Well, I could be trouble for you. In fact,' he wheezed, trying to loosen Gil's fingers with both his hands, and kicking his legs pitifully, 'in fact – isn't that the first ray of sunshine, dawn creeping up on you unawares, ha-ha?'

Burt looked over his shoulder. 'So it is.'

There was a pause.

'Well,' said Gandef, his face growing increasingly purple and his voice increasingly gasping, 'shouldn't you make a dash for your trollp cave?'

'Why would we want to do that?'

'Well – you know. The dawn, the sunshine will, you know. Kill you.'

'No it won't,' said Gerd. 'Wot a odd notion.'

'Oh,' gasped Gandef. He seemed to be casting around for something else to say. 'You sure?'

'Quite sure,' said Gerd.

'I went on holiday to the Souflands last year,' said Bill. 'Lovely sunshine there. Got a nice tan. I say tan, it was more a sort of process of oxidisation.'

'If you could just—' Gandef hissed, the purple of his face deepening almost to black. 'Be so kind as to – just put me down—'

'Wot's he saying?' said Burt. 'Put him down for a mo. Gil.'

The wizard dropped to the ground. For a while he lay panting, whilst the trollps discussed amongst themselves the best way of adding him to the meal.

'That's it,' said Gandef, pulling himself shakily to his feet. 'You've made me really quite tetchy now.'

The four trollps stopped talking, and looked down at the wizard.

'As a gentleman,' Gandef went on, 'I'm prepared to give you fair warning. Untie my companions here, apologise to them properly, and I'll let you be on your way. But I warn you, if you persist in this boorish behaviour, I won't be answerable for the consequences.'

'Wot consequences?' said Bill.

'Terrible consequences,' said Gandef, shaking his fist, or, possibly, simply holding his fist out such that it manifested his tremulous old-man wobble.

'Don't believe yer,' said Burt. 'Terrible conscience-quenches for *oo*? That's what I wants to know.'

'Terrible for *'im*, I'd say,' agreed Gerd.

'Shall I stamp on 'im right away?' offered Gil.

'I *am* a wizard,' Gandef observed, with a tone in his voice that might have been hurt pride. 'After all.'

'And?'

'I'll put a spell on you. I've got some pretty un-comfortable spells, you know.'

'Har har har,' said Burt, speaking the laughter rather than laughing it in order to convey a sense of con-descending and sarcastic dismissal.[5]

'I do so know some spells!' said Gandef. 'Terrible spells, some of them.'

'Bad, are they?' said Bill.

'Oo, yes,' said Gandef.

'What's your *worst* spell?' asked Bill.

'I could,' said Gandef, with dignity, 'turn you all to stone. Easily.'

---

[5] Why does this only work with laughter? If somebody tells you a bad joke and you say 'ha ha' you express a withering contempt for the feebleness of their sense of humour. But if they throw poor quality pepper in your face and you say 'sneeze sneeze' instead of actually sneezing, it doesn't have the same effect at all.

'But we're already stone,' Gerd pointed out. 'Why should that frighten us?'

It seemed to Bingo that Gerd had a point. 'Hmm,' said Gandef, as if considering this.

'Turn us to stone!' said Burt. 'That's a good 'un!'

'Go on,' said Gil, 'do your worst.'

It wasn't easy to see in the dimness, for the shadows of the trees threw an obscurity over everything in spite of the growing light of dawn, but to Bingo's terrified eyes it seemed that the towering figure of the trollp froze for a moment, and then drained away to nothing. The other three turned to their comrade with puzzlement on their faces, and a moment later each of them also shrank away to nothing, losing the substantiality of stone and dribbling away downwards. They vanished completely. For a while the soddit could not believe his eyes.

Gandef settled himself on a bounder not stained with dwarf blood and lit his pipe, puffing meditatively for a while. Then, as if remembering something trivial that had slipped his mind, he got up, shuffled over to Bingo and undid his bindings. The two of them freed the remaining dwarfs, and in five minutes everybody was huddled round the fire, rubbing their stiff limbs and eyeing the still-singeing dog carcasses with hungry, if disgusted, eyes.

'Gandef?' Bingo asked in a small voice. 'You can hear me properly now?'

'Oh yes,' the wizard said, sucking on his pipe. 'You all seemed to be in a sticky situation, so I ratcheted my hearing spell up a notch or two. I don't like to leave it on all the time,' he added. 'It runs my magic strength down.'

'What did you do,' Bingo pressed, 'to the trollps?'

'Turned them to stone, just as I threatened.'

'You turned them,' said Mori, who was kicking his feet through the remnants of the creatures, 'to sand.'

'I didn't say what *kind* of stone I was going to turn them into,' said Gandef. 'It only goes to show, never cheek a wizard. I'd suggest you scatter that sand through the forest in all directions. It's still alive, you see, and it'd be better for us if we stop it from, well, *accumulating* again. Then we ought to be off.'

Coward(ly) Elf & Wild(e) Elf

Chapter Three

A 'SH'

◖◍◗

'Sh', said Gandef.

They had been travelling for three days, sorrowfully at first in memory of the four fallen comrades, then wearily, and finally in a crotchety fashion. They did not tell tales, or sing songs. Neither did they sing tales or tell songs. The mountains grew on the horizon, but grew very slowly.

'Is that *the* mountain?' asked Bingo. 'The one to which our quest is directed?'

'I wish,' said Mori dismissively.

'Phumf,' said Tori, a sort of nasal equivalent of the same sentiment. 'Look you,' he added, with his mouth rather than his nostrils.

They walked on for a while.

'I'm terribly sorry,' Bingo hazarded, 'for the loss of your – um, comrades. Comrades? Brothers?'

Tori looked grumpy. Bingo felt dopey for having asked.

'We dwarfs,' said Mori, 'do not like to parade our

grief, look you. We're a secretive folk, a tough, stout, thrawn people.'

'Right,' said Bingo. 'I understand. What's "thrawn" mean?'

'Thrawn,' repeated Mori. 'Well it's sort of . . . it's a word that refers to the dwarfish, to the dwarfish, um. Well. Hmm. Wombl,' he called. 'Boyo, what's "thrawn" mean?'

Wombl was trudging along on the far side of the group. 'Thrawn,' he grumbled. 'Is that, you see, a word for slave?'

'No,' interjected Frili. 'You're thinking of "thrall".'

'Oh, so I am, so I am.'

'Is it that, kind of, sea creature?' piped Gofur. 'Looks a little like an insect. Lives on the ocean floor.'

'No, no,' said Mori. 'It's a *dwarf* word, isn't it? It's got something to do with dwarfs, see.'

It was at this point that Gandef said, 'Sh!'

Everybody stopped.

'Elves!' said the wizard. 'See them, in the trees?'

The party stopped at the edge of a great forest, glorious in silver birch, golden-green leaves like sequins, fragrant and expansive. Gandef pointed, and Bingo could just make out thin, sharp, clever-looking faces looking back at them from boughs in the wood.

'Elves!' he gasped.

'Elves,' grumbled the dwarfs.[1]

'Do we have to go through this damn elf-infested forest?' demanded Mori. 'Wizard? Can't we go round?'

'Well,' said the wizard, apparently in reply to some completely different question. 'There are two different races of elf, you see. I'll tell you. There are the Star Elves – or the "In The Gutter Looking At The Star Elves" as they are more properly known – and there are the Tree Elves, the *Herbertbeerbohmtree* Elves. I won't attempt to translate the elvish epithet. Of these two great people, the former likes the plants of the world, particularly the carnations, and especially the purple carnations, which they like to pluck from the places of greatest danger and to set in the front of their clothing to display to all the world. This delight in the dangers of carnation-plucking has led to them being called the Wild Elves – but do not call them so to their face, for

---

[1] As is well known, there is no love lost between elves and dwarfs. By *no love lost* I mean that they do not love one another. Now that I come to think of it, I suppose the phrase *no love lost* might be taken to mean that the two peoples loved one another so completely and with such zealous stewardship of their love that all of it was directed at the loved party, and none of it went astray, none of it was wasted on ants or milkmaids or fine clothes or things like that. But that wasn't the sense I intended to convey. I meant the other sense. Perhaps I should have said something like *dwarfs and elves hated one another*. That would have been less ambiguous. But it's too late now. Oh dear. Too late! Too late!

the phrase was not meant kindly. The Tree Elves, however, avoid all such danger. Elves are immortal provided no external force kills them, and the Tree Elves take the understandable view that they should do all they can to avoid being killed by some external circumstance. The Wild Elves despise them for this reason, and call them the Coward Elves – but do not use the name yourself, or call them so to their face, for the phrase was not meant kindly. And it is true to this day that the Wild Elves are often truly Wild. I have known a Wild Elf wear bright purple breeches with a lime-green and orange-checked tunic. No Coward Elf would have the courage for such attire. Tweed is about as courageous as they can be.'

Mori smiled warmly at the old wizard. 'The fact that you can't comprehend a single word I'm saying,' he said, clasping the wizard's old hand in his, 'encourages me to call you, to your face, the most tedious old codger in all of Upper Middle Earth.'

'Thank you, my dear dwarf friend,' said Gandef, his eyes moist with emotion. 'Thank you indeed.'

'So,' said Bingo, who had actually been quite interested by Gandef's little exposition. 'So – these elves in the Last Homo House; are they Wild Elves or are they Coward Elves?'

'I've no cladding idea,' said Mori, utilising a mild dwarfish stone-based expletive.

'The answer to your question,' said Gandef boom-ingly, 'is no. On the other hand, you're probably wondering whether these elves of Bluewaterdel are *Wild* Elves or *Coward* Elves. It's a complex matter, but I think I can explain it.'

Mori sighed.

'Elsqare himself is a Wild Elf. But he took as his partner a Coward Elf, the beautiful Olthfunov, and accordingly groups of both races cohabit here. But their time is not our time. The days pass differently for them, as a fleeting flicker; they do not rise until noon, and they often nap. Alas!' he cried suddenly, 'For the tragedy of this forest is that the two races do not cohabit contentedly.'

They were walking between the trees of the beautiful forest now, and an elf sauntered from the shade to stand in the path before them. He was tall and elegant and his garb was of green velvet and silk, and he stood leaning his torso at a slight angle to the vertical, supporting it by placing a hand upon his own hip. His eyes glittered; or one of them did, for in front of it he wore a circle of purest glass.

'Gandef the wizard,' he said languidly. 'And com-panions. I *do* declare.'

'Ah!' said Gandef. 'Sunblest, the Elf of the Morning, is it?'

'*I* am Elstree the Tree Elf,' said the elf in a hurt voice.

'Surprised I am, O wizard, that you did not recognise me. Did we not once share a small lakeside cottage for a fortnight of relaxation and occasional swimming? Nevertheless, I greet you, and shall take you and your companions to Lord Elsqare himself.'

'Oh, well, I suppose that's a fair question,' said Gandef, beaming. 'I'd say the answer was bread, except in the winter months when it's probably a meal of chaff.'

Elstree's eye shield of glass twinkled in the sunlight. His head leaned five degrees to the left. The wind moved in the trees behind him.

There was silence for the space of several minutes.

Eventually, Elstree beckoned to them all to follow him through the woodland.

Lord Elsqare himself was seated in a throne made of boughs and carved branches, high in a tree. He was an elf of indeterminate age, dressed in purple and blue, and he wore the carnation and the polished crystal eyepiece of the Wild Elves. Mori whispered to Bingo that all the elves lived in trees, odd though that seemed to the rest of the world. And, truly, Elsqare was surrounded by elves in amongst the leaves, all of them peering haughtily down at the travellers.

'Gandef the wizard,' said Elsqare. 'How good it is to see you again. Fares your quest well?'

'About half past four, I'd say,' returned Gandef. 'Hard to tell precisely,' he added, 'without a watch.'

'And *you* are Thorri, King of the Dwarfs, or I am mistaken,' continued Elsqare, unfazed.

Thorri bowed so low his beard inched along the ground before him like a caterpillar. 'I am honoured to be in thith thelebrated palath of elvithneth,' he said.

'I'm sorry?' asked Elsqare. 'Didn't quite catch . . .'

'Our noble King,' struck in Mori, 'declares himself at your service, Lord Elsqare.'

'Thorri,' said Thorri, in a miniature voice, casting his face to the ground.

'We have suffered on our travels,' Mori continued. 'We have lost some of our company – brothers, comrades, glorious in death.'

'Really?' said Elsqare, perking up. 'How so?'

'Trollps,' said Mori severely. 'They took four of our comrades before we were able to destroy them. Qwalin, Orni, Ston and Pilfur, may their names be writ in glory.'

'Dear me,' said Elsqare. 'To lose one dwarf might be regarded a misfortune. To lose four looks like carelessness.'

The elves twittered their twittery laughter.

'What did you say, look you?' said Mori, his face reddening.

'To lose one dwarf,' Elsqare repeated, 'might be regarded a misfortune. To lose four looks like carelessness. It's a witticism.'

'A joke?'

'A witticism.'

'You mean,' said Mori, 'that you regard the death of four individuals as the occasion for humour? In what way is it *careless* to have you friends killed? Where's the carelessness in that? Surely that's tragic, not funny.'

Elsqare looked marginally perturbed. 'The good end happily,' he said, 'the bad unhappily, that is what dwarfishness means.'

'Wait a minute,' said Mori. 'Have you ever had four friends die on you all at once? How would you like it if somebody accused you of carelessness, when—'

'I think,' said Elstree the Tree Elf stepping forward, 'that there has been a misunderstanding. Let us not, elf and dwarf, become enemies.'

'Indeed not,' said Elsqare languidly. 'After all a man cannot be too careful in the choice of his enemies.'

A few elves in the tree behind him tittered and chattered at this.

'The choice of your enemies?' said Bingo. 'How do you mean? People don't *choose* their enemies. That's not how it goes. Your statement doesn't really mean anything.'

Nobody spoke.

Gandef broke the silence with a single percussive cough. But then he too fell silent.

Bingo became conscious of the fact that everybody was looking at him. He cast around for a topic of non-contentious conversation. 'Must be hard living in a tree,' he said eventually. 'Couldn't you dig a nice, modern little ditch and live under the soil as God intended? If it's good enough for dead people, surely its good enough for you? There's quite a lot of soil over there, for instance.'

'We're with the soddit on this one,' said Mori. 'Living in trees? I ask you.' He looked around. 'I don't *actually* ask you, bach, you see, look you, it's only a figure of speech, isn't it?'

'Tis true, life is hard,' stated Elsqare. 'There is only one thing worse than being an elf, and that is *not* being an elf.'

A dozen elves laughed, twittering like swallows. The laughter died away.

'I don't get it,' said Bingo. He became uncomfortably aware of dozens of elvish eyes, each pair focusing a cut-glass look down upon him.

'You don't *get it*?' said Elsqare, sounding, for the first time, peeved. 'What d'ye mean?' He fitted his cunningly worked elvish monocle back into his eye.

'Well, I only mean to say,' said Bingo cautiously, 'that I don't quite . . . I mean, when you say that. Don't you *like* being an elf?'

' 'Course I do,' snapped Elsqare. 'Absurd question!'

'Well,' said Bingo. 'It's just that if you say "there's only one thing worse than being an elf", you're implying that being an elf is a miserable thing, and that only "being anything else" is *more* miserable. In effect,' he went on, warming to his theme, 'you're saying that *any* existence is appalling, and that the only salient characteristic of an elvish existence is that it is marginally *less* appalling than any other existence. I suppose I can understand somebody expressing a position of such nihilistic absolutism, but it's difficult to construe it as a . . . as a joke, do you see? I don't see why that's funny. I mean, if existing is *so* terrible, wouldn't tears and lamentations be more appropriate?'

There was silence amongst the trees for the portion of several minutes. Finally Elsqare spoke. 'Anyway, you'd better come up and have some tea.'

They clambered into the trees up elegantly carved wooden ladders, and after much bouncing of boughs and unsteady steps, they were all arranged in a semi-circle about Elsqare's throne. Tea was brought. Everybody sipped, and nibbled at the scone-like Elvish weybread. Gandef smoked. Elsqare's face assumed a pinched, rather pained expression as if he expected more from his guests. At one point he announced, 'I have always felt that work is the curse of the tea-drinking classes,' and smirked. But although a few of his followers hiccoughed briefly with laughter, the line was greeted with non-comprehension by the dwarfs and he fell silent again.

The tea was finished. The last crumbs of Elvish weybread consumed.

The silence grew longer, taller, and more oppressive.

'At last,' Elsqare said. 'Here comes my partner, Olthfunov the Fair. He'll liven proceedings up. Olthfunov! Coo-ee! Up here.'

A stouter elf in green, with a high forehead and a somewhat lumpish nose, was coming up the ladder. 'Guests?' he said. 'How delightful. How wonderful. Is that Gandef I see, snoozing against the trunk back there? And dwarfs, how marvellous. We must have a party.'

Introductions were made.

'So you're a soddit, are you?' Olthfunov enquired of Bingo. 'Where are you from, little man?'

'Soddlesex,' said Bingo. 'Do you know it?'

'Indeed,' the elf replied. 'Very flat, Soddlesex.'

'Oh,' said Bingo. 'Well, quite flat, I suppose. There are several hills, though, and—'

'You're off to the Minty Mountains?'

'In that direction, yes.'

'Very,' said Olthfunov, with a catch of suppressed glee in his voice, '*uppy-downy*, the mountains. Don't you think?'

Bingo could hear tittering behind him. 'I suppose so,' he said.

'Ol,' said Elsqare. 'I'm sorry to say that our friends have lost four of their companions.'

'Dear me,' said Olthfunov, sipping his tea. 'How so?'

'Eaten by trollps, it seems.'

'Ghastly creatures, trollps,' murmured Olthfunov.

'Indeed. And,' Elsqare added, in an aside, 'they're somewhat touchy on the topic, so have a care.'

'A care,' said the Coward Elf. 'Naturally. Sensitive area, I'm sure. But,' he added, bursting into song, or – to be strictly accurate – if not quite bursting, then certainly sidling into a sort of half-song, half-recital:

> *Oh, don't let's be beastly to the trollps*
> *When our Victory is finally won,*
> *And when peace inevitably followps*
> *We can give them a sugar-topped bun.*

He concluded with a rapidly murmured, 'Thank you, thank you, too kind,' and sat back.

The wind shuffled through the higher leaves of the trees. Away below them a fox barked.

'Lovely,' said Elsqare acidly.

'Followps?' queried Bingo.

'Obviously,' announced Mori, 'we'd love to stay, love to stay, look you, but we've a long journey ahead of us.'

The dwarfs stirred, as if rousing themselves to leave.

'Of course,' said Elsqare. 'Off you go. Bon voyage. Please allow us to help you on your way with some supplies – salted goods and such. Where is it you're off to?'

'Over the mountains,' said Mori. 'Through the great forest.'

'I say,' Elsqare burbled. 'How exciting.'

'To the Only Mountain.'

'Really? Isn't that the estate of Smug the Dragon?'

The dwarfs nodded, looking grim.[2]

'Well, best of luck, best of luck. Do call in again on your way home, if you're passing.'

'Oh!' said Gandef, who was helping himself to a fifth scone as he noticed that everybody else was on their feet and climbing down from the trees. 'Are we off then?'

---

[2] Mind you, it's easy to look grim with a great big beard. The tricky thing, with a great big beard, is *not* to look grim.

Sollum

Chapter Four

RIDDLES IN THE DA-DOO-DOO-DOO, DA-DAH-DAH-DAH IDIOM

ᏮᎿᏬ

The following morning was a midsummer's morning as bright and beautiful as could be imagined. The sun danced on the water.[1] Gandef, Bingo and the dwarfs walked towards the Minty Mountains. They reared from the horizon.

'Is that our destination?' asked Bingo as he limped alongside Mori. He asked the question more in hope than in expectation of a positive answer.

'No,' said Mori. He added, in a singsong, 'No no no no no no no no', running down the notes of the musical scale. 'No, boy, no, boyo, no. We've somehow to get *past* those Minty Mountains, and then cross the mighty

[1] Not literally, obviously. This sentence is meant metaphorically – which is to say that sunlight waltzed and pogoed from wavelet to wavelet like little parcels of photons on amphetamines. Dear me, imagine if the sun were *literally* dancing on the waters! My! That would mean the agonising and fiery death not only of our heroes, but of the whole world, a global apocalypse and ultimate disaster! Dear me!

River Misissiisiisisiissississsippisipisipipsofactoisisipi-sipi,[2] then find our way through the scary and inhospitable Mykyurwood. Only then, my laddo, only then will we approach the Only Mountain.'

'Only Mountain?'

'Well – not the only mountain, of course. *Strictly* speaking, look you, there are plenty of other mountains. But it's the Only Mountain Worth Mentioning if you're a dwarf, see, la. It's many days' march from here. And thrice as many days' stumble.'

Bingo limped on in silence for a while. Then he spoke.

'Mori,' he said. 'I can't quite shake the sense that the purpose of our quest—'

'Gold,' said Mori at once, without looking at him.

'Sure, yes. Right. Gold. Yes. But I can't quite shake the sense that our quest – although ostensibly undertaken for gold—'

'—gold—' agreed Mori.

'—gold, yes, it not *actually* being undertaken for gold at all.'

The two marched on for several minutes.

'So?' Bingo prompted.

'Eh?' replied Mori.

---

[2] For convenience sake this river in future will be referred to as the River M.

'Am I right?'

'Right?'

'About our quest?'

'Gold,' said Mori in a loud voice. 'That's what it's about. Now if you'll excuse me I have to go talk to— to one of the others, you know.'

He scurried away.

The whole party slept under a large gooseberry bush that evening, and by noon the following day they had reached the feet of the Minty Mountains. This great chain of mighty snow-skullcapped peaks stretching from the frozen eminence of Mount Gungadin in the north all the long leagues down to the Gap of Next in the south. The steep sides of the myriad denticular mountains that made up this chain were, all of them, sparkling with clean, bright ice: gleaming and white with snow. To stand at the foot of this gigantic and impenetrable wall of towering rock is to be awed by the sublimity of the natural world; the mountain's slumberous voice echoes through your very being. In the mountains you feel free; there you can read all through the night, if you fancy it, and go south in the winter. The air of the mountains is clean, fresh, sharp, inspiring.

'Buggeration,' said Bingo, as he collapsed on a boulder and started rubbing his sore toes. 'We got to go over those, now, have we?'

'Mountains,' said Mori, with a tear in his eye and a finger twisted into his beard. 'Beautiful beautiful mountains, look you. Beautiful beautiful beautiful beautiful beautiful beautiful beautiful beautiful beautiful beautiful beautiful beautiful beautiful beautiful beautiful mountains.'

'Dwarfs like mountains, then, do they?' asked Bingo.

'Well, not really, look you,' said Mori. 'We prefer the underneath of mountains. But just look at those lovely things! Look how smooth the sides are – how hairless and smooth and perfect! That mountain there, for instance, lovely, lovely, smooth as a baby mountain.'

'And we need to get to the other side of them.'

'Ah yes,' said the dwarfs in unison.

Bingo looked at his swollen, ruddy, throbbing feet. 'Do we have mountaineering equipment? Ropes, thick socks, that sort of thing?'

'Ah no,' said the dwarfs in unison.

'Well I really don't think we should go over those mountains. I don't think my feet would stand it. They're not good in snow. Gandef?' Bingo appealed to the elderly wizard, although he had to raise his voice. 'Gandef? Do you intend that we climb over those mountains?'

The question was repeated only eight or nine times before Gandef finally understood. He had been silently counting the mountain tops, pointing to each of them in turn and munching his lips as if fixing the number in his mind: a curious exercise, but something – Bingo assumed – wizardly. Perhaps the number of peaks visible had a mystic aspect. Perhaps Gandef couldn't count anything without silently moving his lips and pointing.

When Bingo's question was finally beaten into his skull, he snorted with derision. 'Climb them?' he snarled. 'Do I *look* to you like a counting mimer?'

'You what?'

Miro placed his right hand behind his right ear in dumb-show of *say again*.

'Are you deaf?' snapped Gandef. 'I *said*, do I *look* like a mountain climber? No, no, no. We'll not attempt to climb – we'd never make it. Luckily we can go *under* the mountains.'

'Through the Coal Gate?' asked Tori, in awe and terror.

'Through the cavernous and echoey spaces under the mountain?' added Fili.

'And out via the Cavity through which plunges the icy River Floss?' said Sili.

'No, don't be ridiculous,' said Gandef in annoyance. 'I mean go *through* the Coal Gate – and *out again* through the cavemouth Cavity on the other side. It's the only sensible way.'

'But the Coal Gate is enchanted, Gandef,' Sili pointed out.

'Ah,' said Gandef, settling himself down on a tree stump and getting out his pipe. 'I'm glad you asked me that, young dwarf. Yes, that's a good point. But I've carefully counted the mountain peaks, and there really don't seem to be any more here than there were the last time I came.'

Dwarf looked to dwarf looked to soddit, but none had any idea what the wizard was talking about.

'So I don't think we need to worry about *that*,' said Gandef with satisfaction. 'On the other hand, the door of the Coal Gate is enchanted – I don't know if any of you were aware of that. I'll have to rack my brains to try and come up with the magic word. I'll use some of my most powerful opening spells.'

After the wizard had finished smoking his pipe, and after the ten-minute phlegm-hawking episode that followed, the party made their way through the stumpy valleys and past an evil-looking pool to the Western Coal Gate. It was mid-afternoon. Shadows were lengthening. A roseate light lay like a red film over the land to the west: the fields, copses and forests, hay-stacks, the occasional cottage. Bingo stood looking at the land he was leaving behind, a tear in his eye. Behind lay everything he knew. Before him lay only darkness and mystery.

Gandef was having a spot of trouble with the Coal Gate. Carved from one gigantic piece of anthracite, forty foot tall and forty foot wide, this mighty entrance was sealed by a Great and Terrible Spell cast by Yale of Yore. Gandef sat smoking for a while, muttering. 'There are two portions to the spell,' he explained. 'First we need to see where the door is exactly. No good me firing Opening Spells at a blank piece of coal!'

'And how can we see where the door is?' asked Bingo quaveringly, looking in awe at the perfectly sheer, black face that faced him. As faces, I suppose, are wont to do.

'Oh no,' said Gandef. 'Whatever gave you that idea? First we need to find out where the door actually *is*. But the edges of it are only visible by moonlight. And tonight is a new moon, so no moonlight. And tomorrow I doubt if there'll be enough moonlight to show it up. And it looks like cloud. All in all,' he said, sucking his pipe between the sentences, 'we could be here a fortnight at least. Perhaps we should give up?'

Bingo expected the dwarfs to complain noisily at this wizardly suggestion, but in fact they were lying on the floor in a state of some dejection. Perhaps, he thought to himself, the loss of their comrades had affected their morale.

'Moonlight,' said Bingo, 'is only the light of the sun reflected *off* the moon, after all. Can't we shine reflected sunlight on the door? How would the door know the difference?

Gandef acted as though he hadn't heard the little soddit, as perhaps – indeed, as probably – he had not. But Mori was heartened by the idea. He roused himself from his despondency, and with Bingo's help they unwrapped one of Thorri's shields, leaning it against the rocks in such a way that sunlight bounced off the silvery inner surface and fell on the black cliff before them. At once the outline of a great door became visible, together with several lines of elegantly carved elvish.

'What do the silvery letters say, Gandef?' an awed Bingo whispered to the wizard.

'Wassit?' Gandef replied.

'The elvish writing on the door,' he said more loudly, pointing. 'What does it say?'

'What?'

'What does the *ELVISH* mean in *COMMON SPEECH*?' yelled Bingo, directly into the wizard's ear. 'There! There!'

'What?' said the wizard, following the line of Bingo's arm. 'Ah! Look at that! Some elvish characters! Will you look at that!'

'What,' three dwarfs hollered in unison, 'do they mean?'

'What's that? What do they mean?' said the wizard.

He examined the writing for long minutes. 'Squiggle, squiggle, squiggle,' he concluded. 'I don't know. That one there looks a little like a *p*,' he offered. '*Poqqop*? That mean anything to anybody?'

The dwarfs, standing in a line, did not look impressed. 'You mean you don't know?' asked Mori in disgust. Gandef could read the dwarfish expressions even if he didn't hear Mori's rebuke.

'And how should *I* know?' he asked, sulky. 'I'm not an elf, I'm a wizard. You should watch out. Have more respect for wizards. Miserable dwarfs.'

'Never mind interpreting the writing,' said Mori, his beard twitching with annoyance. 'Can you just open the door?'

'I just told you,' said the querulous wizard. 'I *can't* interpret the writing. But I'll tell you what: why don't I just open the door with a spell?'

The dwarfs nodded, an action – given the shortness of their necks, and indeed of their whole bodies – more evident in the waggling of their beards than in any other respect.

Gandef settled himself before the door and lit his pipe. 'You watch this,' he told nobody in particular. 'It's the most powerful opening spell I know.' He breathed out, breathed in deeply, and intoned in a booming voice: '*Quandog quandoggli.*'

Nothing happened.

'*Quandog quandoggli*,' Gandef repeated.

Nothing happened.

Gandef sucked his pipe for a while. 'Try a different opening spell,' Bingo offered. The wizard looked at him, nodded his sage head sagely, and cleared his throat.

'*Quandog quandoggli*,' he said.

'I'm not sure that spell is working terribly well,' Bingo suggested.

'*Quandog quandoggli, quandog quandoggli, quandog quandoggli*,' Gandef said, with tremendous rapidity.

'I don't think—'

'*QuanDOG*,' Gandef tried. '*QUANDoggli.*'

'I'm almost certain that neither of those words is the magic word,' Bingo said, in as loud a voice as he could manage. The sunlight was starting to fade. Once it had gone, and with a moonless night in the offing, they would have to camp there until the morning: and Bingo didn't like the look of the evil-looking pool. It looked evil. 'Perhaps—'

'*Qua-aa-andoggli*,' said Gandef, putting the word through a strange musical contortion, starting warbling and high and dropping to a baritone for the final syllable.

'Perhaps if you tried some other magic words—'

'QUANDOG!' shouted Gandef. 'QUANDOG-GLI! QUAN-AGH! ACH! A-KOOFKAH-KOOFKAH!'

It was the worst coughing fit to seize the wizard that Bingo had yet seen.

Gandef went, 'UH-KHOO! UH-KHOO! UH-KHOO! UH-KHOO!' He went, 'KLAK! KLAK! KLAK!' He drew enormous amounts of breath into his lungs prior to going 'HOOOGH! HU-HOOOGH!' and shaking his hat off as he swung his head back and forth. He went, 'WHO-WHO! WHO-WHO!' as if he were asking a question. He went, 'K'OAH K'OAH K'OAH K'OAH K'OAH K'OAH K'OAH.' He went, 'oooohh god' in a low and miserable voice and then immediately added, 'Hurgh! Hurgh! Hurgh! Hurgh! Hurgh!' with great emphasis.

When he had finally finished, he slumped slowly to the ground moaning, gasping 'I'll be all right in a minute,' and scrabbling ineffectually in one of the pockets of his poncho for his tobacco.

'Look!' said Bingo.

It was impossible to say which of the many noises inadvertently produced by the wizard had been the one to open the door, but there it stood, open as wide as you like. It seemed he had chanced upon the magic word in extremis without even realising it. The dwarfs cheered weakly. It seemed that at last their luck was changing.

They picked up the whimpering, ash-faced wizard and carried him inside. As they stepped over the threshold, the door started to groan, heaving shut behind them.

They lit torches, and explored the space within. It was a towering lobby, carved, it seemed, from the very living rock, with numerous stairways going up and down away from the space. 'Let us camp here,' said Mori. 'After a rest we can choose a path and make our way under the mountain.'

All were in agreement.

They lit a fire under the portable cauldron and stewed up some salt beef, with some salt potatoes and salt garlic for taste, and salt-preserved beer to wash the meal down. It was belly-filling, thirst-creating stuff. After about forty minutes, Gandef seemed to have recovered sufficiently from his cough-ing spasms, and helped himself to a hunk of beef ('I'll just have a hunk of this,' as he put it), a chunk of potato ('. . . just a chunk . . .'), and got a little drunk on the beer. For a while he amused himself by repeat-ing 'hunk-chunk-drunk' sixteen or seventeen times. Then he grew sombre. 'Dark in here,' he observed, several times.

He lit his pipe, and smoked in silence for a while.

'It's an amazing place,' said Bingo to Mori, who was sitting next to him polishing his cleaver.

'Ay,' said the dwarf laconically.

'And this enormous hallway was carved from the massy living rock by dwarfs?'

'This,' said Mori, 'and caverns a hundred times as huge! A thousand yards tall, leagues and leagues long, supported on carefully fashioned pillars of intricate design and towering height, enormous staircases carved from pure marble, great groined spaces the length and breadth of the whole Minty Mountains! You are seeing with your own unworthy eyes the Great Dwarf Halls of Dwarfhall, the Mines of Black Maria, the great achievement of our race!'

'Blimey,' said Bingo.

They sat in silence for a while.

'And all this,' Bingo said, the question occurring to him as he asked it, 'carved out with – what? Hand axes?'

'Trowels,' said the dwarf. He seemed to be looking, studiedly, in another direction.

'Trowels? All of it? Gracious. And are there – if you'll excuse the question – many dwarfs in the world?'

'We don't,' said Mori, 'like to talk of our personal affairs.'

'But, let's say,' said Bingo, becoming interested, 'that there are – I don't know – ten thousand dwarfs in the world. How much stone can one dwarf clear in a year with a trowel?'

'These be the great mysteries of the dwarf miners,' mumbled Mori, still looking away.

'Let's say half a ton. That's five thousand tons a year,

five hundred thousand tons over a century assuming every dwarf in the world worked at the project without break. That would barely empty even this lobby.'

Mori mumbled something else, of which only 'maybe' and 'difficult to judge' were audible.

'To carve out halls running the whole length of the mountain range,' Bingo carried on. 'That must have been the work of hundreds of thousands – no, of *millions* of years. How long have dwarfs existed? To say nothing of the enormous number of trowels you must have gone through . . .'

'All right,' said Mori hotly, putting his face close to Bingo's. 'All right, don't go bleating and blurting, look you. Have you *tried* chopping into solid rock with a little bronze trowel? It's no easy matter. But don't give the game away, boyo. Some of the others still believe the legends.'

'Legends?'

'Yes, yes, yes. That dwarfs are great miners, so speaks the legend. There *were* mines once, or so we believe, yes, certainly, look you. But it's been a long time since any dwarf worked in one. They were all closed down long ago.'

'Oh,' said Bingo. 'What do dwarfs work at now?'

'In shops, mostly. Markets. Sometimes in the entertainment industry. Singing dwarfs have a certain appeal to certain bookers. Perhaps you've heard of Qyli the Singing Dwarf? No? Lovely singer. Big teeth. But our legends are important to us, do you see. Don't take them away.'

'Does this,' said Bingo, with renewed interest, 'have something to do with our quest? Does the real reason for—'

'Gold,' said Mori firmly and finally.

Bingo didn't think it worth pursuing that line.

'But I don't understand,' he said. 'If you didn't build these great under-mountain halls, who did?'

It was hard to say in the ruddy half-light of the dying fire, but it seemed to Bingo and Mori shrugged. 'Nature,' he said.

'Nature?'

'They're hollow. All the mountains. In fact, although you may not realise it, everything's hollow here, even the trees. The hills have got chambers and rooms inside them – nothing's solid all the way through.'

'What a bizarre notion,' said Bingo.

'I know, bach, but the world's stranger than most people realise.'[3]

'But how can it be? The mountains hollow?'

'According to one myth of creation,' said Mori, 'the world was blown up like a big soap bubble by the Great God at the beginning of things. The smoky breath of

[3] See? I told you so. Oh, but nobody listens to *me*, I know.

life puffed up the thin crust of the Primordial Flatness into the bumps and peaks and curves of the world we see today. 'Course, that's only a myth.'

Their conversation was interrupted by a distant thudding noise. Suddenly the party were gathered in the centre of the lobby clutching each other in fear and apprehension, all except Gandef who hadn't heard the thudding and was caught up in the scrum.

They prevailed upon the wizard with much shouting and repetition, to place upon himself a hearing spell. Grumbling and complaining Gandef did so. 'Ah,' he said, when the spell was successfully achieved. 'What's that noise?'

He stood with his head cocked, listening.

'Drums,' he said finally.

'But whose?'

'Gobblins, of course,' said the wizard. 'Who else?'

'Gobblins?' said the dwarfs, shrinking back.

'They're bad, then, are they?' asked Bingo. 'Gobblins?'

'Terrible,' said Gandef. 'Servants of the Dark Lord who must not be named . . .'

'You mean the Great and Evil Sharon,' said Tori.

'The Dark Lord must not be named!' snapped Gandef. 'Yes, Gobblins. Terrible, bad. Dear me, they must have taken up residence down here, the evil creatures. Perhaps I should have thought of that before

I brought us here. It slipped my mind. But actually, now you come to mention it, there's no doubt that these mountains are absolutely swarming with Gobblins. Dear me, yes.'

'What are they?' asked Bingo, who didn't like the sound of this at all.

'What? Gobblins?' said Gandef. 'Long ago the Evil Lord took races of harmless, virtuous turkeys and chickens from the fields and yards of Upper Middle Earth, tortured them hideously and transmuted them into a warped, monstrous and easily suggestible species to fill the ranks of the mighty armies of Darkness and to do the Evil One's bidding. You'll know one when you see one, my young soddit: you'll recognise the turkey provenance of their ghastly and monstrous appearance: the wattles of flesh at their neck, the small heads, the alarmed expression in the eyes, the tendency to scurry around in circles shrieking and so on.'

Gandef puffed at his pipe.

'Perhaps,' he concluded, 'it might be better if we retreated out through the door and climbed *over* the mountains, after all.'

No sooner had the dwarfs expressed their complete agreement with this proposition, than there was a mighty crack, a bang, and Gobblins swarmed into the hallway.

Enormous Gobblins! There were four to each dwarf,

and two even for Bingo.[4] They were over the group before anybody knew what was happening, and legs were shackled, arms pinioned, beards yanked and the great swarm was carrying the prisoners away, clucking and ducking their heads in triumph, in an instant.

Things looked black for the company; both in the sense of 'their prospects looked unpromising' and in the more literal sense that 'they couldn't see anything because of the dark' – since they were carried down unlit corridors, through unlit hallways, and on on. 'Take 'em to the Gobblin King!' the Gobblins sang. 'Take 'em to the hall of the Gobblin King!' Then they sang their terrible song.

> *I feel like ∂wa-arf tonight!*
> *Like ∂wa-arf tonight!*
>
> *I feel like ∂wa-arf tonight!*
> *Like ∂wa-arf tonight!*

[4] Obviously, when I say 'enormous' here I don't mean it in an absolute sense. Given that we've already established that Bingo the soddit is a fellow of diminutive size, it would be pretty stupid to suggest that a creature half his size is 'enormous' in any objective sense of the word. 'Minuscule' would be the better word, if I were framing this in objective terms. But I meant 'enormous' in comparison with other Gobblins. That, and the fact that 'tiny, miniature, hardly-there-at-all Gobblins swarmed into the hall . . .' lacked the necessary smack of the alarming. Or so it seemed to me.

Then they flapped their hideous arms up and down, and sang another of their songs in their own brutish language which went like this:

> *Ga-ARG ga-ARG*
> *Guggle-guggle-guggle*
> *Gugg-ARG guggle-guggle*
> *Guggle-guggle-guggle*
> *Guggle-guggle-guggle*

It went on and on.

'Gandef,' hissed Mori. 'Do something!'

'My head hurts,' called the wizard. 'The noise of that explosion in the lobby was amplified by the hearing spell. It's most annoying. My ears are full of this infernal ringing noise. Hang on – hang on.'

There was a dazzling, silent flash of blue-white light. For an instant Bingo could see everything in the broad corridor down which they were being carried: the curving upward arches of the tunnel walls; the hideous seething mass of Gobblins carrying their helpless cargo. Then his face smacked against the rock floor, and he rolled to the wall. Gandef's spell seemed to have snapped the iron chain that held his hands, and he tried dizzily to pick himself up. More than a little dazed by his fall, he saw Gandef standing tall in the middle of the Gobblins, wielding a great shining sword, slicing it back and forth. His face was grimmer and more determined than Bingo had ever seen it before. 'Take that, you Gobblins!' he was yelling, and his sword went snicker-snack and snacker-snick. 'Cleaver and Carver!' the Gobblins cried in terror, running hither and thither in their confusion. 'Chopper and Decapitator!' And, truly, Gandef's sword was making short work of the long Gobblin necks, cutting off head after head. The newly beheaded Gobblins ran hither and thither with, if anything, more eagerness than the ones with heads. Sili the dwarf, freed from his bonds by Gandef's spell, rose to his feet amongst a crowd of swarming, panicking Gobblins. The glowing sword, scything backwards and forwards, swept towards the hapless dwarf and in a moment his head, still in its tight-fitting helmet, was bouncing and rolling down the corridor. 'Sorry!' Gandef sang, as he continued chopping.

Then, from behind, came a terrible war cry, and by the light of Gandef's shining sword Bingo could see an enormous mass of Gobblins filling the corridor, all with hatchets and beak-shaped axe heads, and all charging towards them.

He got to his feet and ran as fast as his soddit legs could carry him. For long minutes he ran, his chest pumping, until a stray rock tripped him, and he fell down a side-staircase towards a smack on the head and oblivion.

When he came round it was dark. Very dark. Very dark indeed. Imagine the darkest you can image. No, really, go on. Have you got a good mental picture of darkness in your head now? Right – this was *darker* than that. That's how dark it was. Bingo crawled around in the dark, and knocked his head against the wall. He tried to stand up but he found it hard, in the dark, to distinguish up from down and he ended up falling over. After this he crawled on.

Then something happened. Something of the utmost significance, something that was to change his life for ever – and the lives of everybody in Upper Middle Earth, everything. Nothing was ever the same again afterwards. The most significant thing to happen in Bingo's life, although *he* didn't realise it at the time. But just because he didn't recognise the significance of the moment, and just because it isn't, actually, now I come to think of it, actually *alluded* to at any place in this book – just because of that, I wouldn't want you to miss this moment. It's terribly *terribly* important. Do you see? I can't tell you why, exactly, not at this stage. Indeed, it may not become apparent even by the end of the book. But take my word for it.

What happened, terribly important as it was, was

this: Bingo stumbled upon a Thing.[5] It was a small Thing®, and was lying in the corridor out of the way. It did not seem to Bingo to be a terribly important Thing® either (although, as I have said, he was wrong in this, and it was indeed terribly important). But he put it in his pocket, and continued crawling.[6]

Almost immediately he heard a voice. The voice said: 'Hello.'

Bingo had crawled, he saw, into a cave. He stood up. The cave was very, very dimly lit – by a sort of phosphorescent lichen that grew on the roof of the cave, although Bingo didn't know that. In the cave was a pond, and in the middle of the pond was an island, and on the island lived a creature called Sollum. Now, Sollum was a mournful and solitary soul. He lacked the gregarious playfulness that endears people to their fellow creatures. He lacked the ability to pretend interest in stupid or repetitive things. His interests were philosophy, metaphysics, ontology and psychology (especially the schizophrenic condition). Month by month he had been alienated from his original community, until, ultimately, he was driven down deep into the mountain's depths, to live in a solitary hut by a

[5] The Thing® Bingo found is a Registered Trade Mark and may not be used, invoked or quoted without permission of the Estate.
[6] That's it. There's nothing else to say about it at the moment. But it is, believe me, a really really imortant development.

chilly pond eating raw fish and occasionally killing passers-by – an existence too common to our academics and university lecturers. Hearing somebody coming down his corridor, Sollum had splashed through the water to meet the newcomer.

'Hello,' said Bingo.

Sollum sighed. The sigh started as a hiss, and ended with a reflex closure of the soft palate that closed the noise off with a labially approximately sound. From this noise, if you can believe it, had he derived his name: for his sighs were the most notable thing about him.[7]

Bingo looked around. He could just make out the smooth surface of the pool and the nearer walls of rock that surrounded it. He peered at Sollum, and noted the knobulous bald head, the large thoughtful eyes, the doleful cast of the mouth.

'How do you do,' Bingo said, remembering his manners. 'I seem to have lost my way.'

[7] His original name was Seagul, although it was a name he had not heard for many years. Now, if he ever thought of it, it only brought to his mournful mind the memory of mockery and jibes, of his neighbours and relations pouring scorn upon his dedication to philosophy with cries of 'Jonathin Leadenstone Seagul! We shall chase you from our community with mockery and jibes, for we are happy to be blind to your wisdom and relish our own idiocy, oh yes.' Such speeches had left Sollum no choice but to flee far, far underground.

'Indeed,' said Sollum, imbuing the word with tragic overtones.

'I'm Bingo Grabbings,' said the soddit. 'I'm a soddit, you know.'

'Ah,' said Sollum, on a dying fall. He thought to himself that his own origins were not far removed from soddit life, and that he had cousins who had married soddits, and it all brought miserable and depressing memories into his head. It was an unfortunate turn-up. He had been pursuing a train of solipsistic philosophy for seven years, and had been uninterrupted save for the occasional gormless Gobblin getting lost and ending up roasted on Sollum's Sunday lunch table. Nothing is better suited to the prosecution of a truly solipsistic philosophical line of thought than absolute solitude. And now he had been interrupted.

'What's your name?' Bingo pressed.

'Sollum,' said Sollum.

'Splendid name. I say – can you help me?'

Sollum sighed. 'Help you?' he said eventually.

'Yes. I seem to have lost my way. Banged my head, too.'

'Your head,' repeated Sollum slowly. Then, as if he were reciting the lines with a certain distaste, he added, 'Tasty head, a choice feast, a tasty morsel it'd make me.' Then he sighed again.

Bingo, not really following this but feeling more than a little uneasy, said, 'Right,' in a nervous voice. 'Can you help me?'

'Well,' said Sollum unwillingly. 'Perhaps the question is, whether there is such in the cosmos as an action willed unconditionally, which is to say, freely, or whether all creatures are determined by the doctrine of Necessary Causes.'

'Quite,' said Bingo, after a pause.

'On the other hand,' said Sollum, 'if you were to claim rights of victory – if you were to defeat me in some contest or other, such that my compliance was compelled . . .' He trailed off.

Bingo stood and waited.

'Riddles?' offered Sollum.

'Yes,' said Bingo.

'Very well. I'll riddle me you, and you can riddle you me,' said Sollum, his immovable face looking simultaneously haughty and sorrowful, as if he were examining Bingo's pathetic little life from on high and was underimpressed by what he saw.

'Riddles,' said Bingo. 'All right. You ask first.'

'Very well,' said Sollum. He swallowed noisily, making a sound like a rubber ball bouncing on a springy mattress. 'I shall go first. This, we have agreed. Then you will go. The first to be unable to answer a riddle loses the contest.'

'All right,' said Bingo, sitting on the floor and crossing his legs.

So Sollum asked:

Given that the ontological necessity of existence must be defined as essential to Being itself, how can such grounding of the epistemological function be articulated without assuming an a priori and unwarranted existential premise?

It was silent in the cave for a long time. Somewhere, far out in the pool, a fish brushed against the underside of the water's surface, disturbing it for a moment before sinking back into the depths. It made a noise like this: *plop*.[8] Bingo took a deep breath into his lungs and then exhaled slowly.

'So you want an answer?' he said.

'Yes,' said Sollum.

'An answer to your riddle?'

---

[8] Indeed, the fish in quesiton was called Plop by his friends for this reason. His proper name was Smeagoldfish, but the other fish tended to call him Plop as it was easier to pronounce. On formal occasions he might be addressed as Smeagoldfish-Plop, but for most occasions it was just Plop. But I'm getting off the point. The fish isn't important to the onward movement of the story. Not at all, in fact. You won't encounter the fish again. Stop reading this note right now, and go back to the main body of the text. Do as I say! No argument – or you can go straight to bed, and I won't finish writing the book for you.

'Yes.'

'The riddle that you just asked me?'

'Yes.'

'Right. Well, I'd say that the answer to that one is,' said the young soddit, pulling at his left ear lobe with his right hand. 'Is,' he repeated, drawing the syllable out, 'I-i-i-i-i-is'. He sniffed, rubbed his eyes. Then he said, 'The answer to that one,' very slowly, lingering over each word. Then he said, 'I-i-i-i-is' again. Then he sat in silence for two minutes.

Eventually Sollum prompted him. 'Yes?'

'Yes what?'

'Your answer?'

'I thought I'd finished,' said Bingo.

'Oh,' said Sollum lugubriously. He pondered for a while. Then he said: 'I don't understand.'

Bingo, with only a momentary hesitation, lighted on the opportunity. 'Oh you don't *understand*?' he said, with a sarcastic inflection to his words. 'My answer too complex for you? I *am* sorry. I *do* apologise. It's a shame I didn't put it in simpler terms. Would you like me to try and phrase my answer in simpler terms for you?'

'No, no,' said Sollum hurriedly. 'I wasn't saying that. Your answer is, um, *is*. Is that right?'

'You're the one who says so,' retorted Bingo.

'No, no,' said Sollum again. 'I think I see. The present participle of the verb to be, is that what you mean?'

'Ah,' said Bingo knowingly. '*Is* it, though?'

'You're right, I suppose,' said Sollum in a small voice. 'Any act of questioning can only take place within a semantic framework that assumes one or other tense, one or other relationship to the contextual temporal configuration. Perhaps by foregrounding the is-ness of is, the continual process of existing that is necessarily embodied in the process of time itself, you do answer my riddle.'

'Well,' said Bingo, trying to colour his voice with suggestions of mysteriousness and veiled wisdom. 'If you say so, *I* shan't contradict. *I* shan't,' he added, as if he couldn't rule out the possibility that somebody else in the vicinity might.

A fish twanged at the surface of the still pond from beneath, and sank again. This was a different fish from the one before mentioned.

Bingo, who was inwardly congratulating himself for getting out of that tricky position, was startled by Sollum's moist and mournful hand on his knee.

'Your turn,' said the creature.

'You what who's-it, what?' returned Bingo.

'You can ask your riddle now,' Sollum explained with quiet and doleful patience, 'and if I can't answer it then you win.'

'I win,' Bingo repeated. 'Very well. My riddle.'

So Bingo asked his riddle:

The Soddit

When is a door not a door when it's ajar?

Sollum contemplated for a while, and then sighed softly. 'I wonder,' he said gravely, 'whether you have inadvertently included the solution to your riddle in the question?'

'Aha!' said Bingo. 'But do you *know* the answer?'

'I was only suggesting,' Sollum repeated, 'that perhaps you meant to ask only the first part of your question, and perhaps intended to retain the second portion *as* the answer?'

'Don't try and weasel out of it.'

'You could ask another one if you liked . . .'

'Answer!'

'But you've already—'

'Answer!' chanted Bingo. 'Answer! Answer! Answer!'

'When,' said Sollum, through tight teeth. 'It's. A. Jar.'

Bingo rubbed his chin. 'So you knew that one, did you?'

'It's my turn,' said Sollum. 'It's my riddle. And if you can't answer this one, then I win.'

'Sure,' said Bingo jauntily. He felt he had done rather well with the previous riddle, and his confidence was building.

Sollum asked:

What happens when an irresistible force meets an immovable object?

'Goes around it I'd say,' replied Bingo quickly. 'Like the wind and a fencepost. My turn! Now then, let me see, let me see. Riddle-riddle-riddle.'

'Wait a moment,' said Sollum. 'I'm not sure your answer addresses the point of the riddle . . .'

' 'Course it does.'

'I don't think so.'

'Does.'

'No,' said Sollum. 'It doesn't.'

'Does.' Contradiction was a game much more in the soddit's taste than this abstruse riddling business. Bingo was getting his contradiction to Sollum's denial more and more rapidly.

'Does not.'

'—Does!'

'No, Mr Soddit, it really—'

'—Does!'

'But if the force alters in some way, then it is surely a resistible force, and that's denied by the terms of the riddle—'

'Isn't,' said Bingo.

'It is,' said Sollum.

'Isn't,' said Bingo.

'It *is*,' said Sollum.

'Isn't,' said Bingo.

'*It is,*' said Sollum.

'My turn! My riddle now! Don't be sour-grapes. You have to answer my riddle or I'll win.'

Red lorry, yellow lorry, red lorry, yellow lorry, rellery yellery, red yellory?

'Now,' said Sollum, his serious manner starting to fray at the edges a little, 'that's not *actually* a riddle at all, is it? Be honest with me, little soddit. That's a *tongue-twister*, isn't it, and not, in fact, a riddle at all? I mean – isn't it?'

'Definitely not,' said Bingo, looking to one side. 'Where I come from that's quite a famous riddle. Down my way. That's definitely a riddle. You could ask any of my people and they'd all say, oh yes, riddle, that's a riddle. So, yes, now the question is, can you answer it?'

'Answer it? You haven't *phrased it* in the form of a question,' said Sollum, his voice starting to warp with hints of frustration and annoyance. 'Be honest, play fair, and admit that it's a tongue-twister.'

'It sounded like a question to me,' said Bingo piously.

'Naturally, since you inflected the line with a rising tone at the end to mimic a questioning delivery. But that's not actually phrasing a riddle in the form of a question. That's just putting a question mark at the end of it. You could put a question mark at the end of any sentence whatsoever, but that wouldn't necessarily make the sentence a question.'

Bingo whistled a tune he had just invented, which consisted of four randomly chosen musical notes. Then he said, 'Is that the answer you're giving me? Because I have to say you're *not even close* with that answer. Not even close.'

'No of *course*,' snapped Sollum, 'that's not my answer. That was me pointing out that the *so-called riddle* you *pretended* to ask me was no such thing.'

'So is *that* your answer?'

'No, no, no,' said Sollum, becoming quite agitated. By the faint blue light of the phosphorescent lichen, Bingo could just about see Sollum's dark froggish hands flapping in front of him. 'Why aren't you listening to me?'

'I'm going to have to press you for an answer,' said Bingo.

'But you haven't asked me a proper riddle!'

'Time's running out – you need to give me an answer now.'

'Don't be ridiculous!'

'Red lorry?' said Bingo, leaning forward. 'Yellow lorry? Your choice!'

'I insist—'

'Ga-ah,' said Bingo in a warning tone. 'Answer!'

'But —'

'An*s*wer! Come on, come on!'

'I just —'

'Time's running out, seconds ticking away.'

'Red lorry!' shrieked Sollum.

'Ha-hah!' crowed Bingo. 'Wrong! Wrong! The answer was *yellow lorry*. It's obvious when it's pointed out to you, isn't it? I win! Hurrah for me!'

'That doesn't make any kind of sense at all,' steam-whistled Sollum. His earlier serious and grave manner seemed to have been evaporated by his annoyance. 'You picked one at random.'

'Now don't be a bad loser. Nobody likes a bad loser.'

'If I'd have said "yellow lorry" you'd simply have told me that the answer was red lorry.'

'Oh really?' said Bingo in a reasonable tone. 'That wouldn't work at all, now, would it? Red lorry – that wouldn't fit.'

'*You*,' said Sollum, his voice dropping almost an octave and acquiring a gravelly undertone. But he didn't finish the sentence.[9]

'So,' said Bingo, hopping to his feet and hugging himself in the near darkness in glee at his victory. 'I win. Incidentally, what do I win?'

---

[9] My guess, for what it's worth, is that Sollum was either going to say, '*You* are right, you're the winner fair and square,' or else '*You* want to share a fish and gluten fondue?' But I could be wrong.

Sollum sulked for a minute. 'You get to eat me,' he said shortly.

'To eat you?' repeated Bingo.

'That's what we were playing for. If I'd have won, I'd have certainly eaten you. Since you won you have to eat me. To tell you the truth,' the creature added, his tone becoming self-pitying, 'I'm almost glad. I'm more than sick of living down here in the dark. Go on, eat me. Start with my legs.'

'I don't want to eat you,' said Bingo, alarmed at the thought.

'Oh,' said Sollum. 'You must. It is a function of inevitability, the doctrine of necessity. And besides, you won.'

'Can't I just get you to show me the way out of here?'

'Ooh,' said the creature. 'No, that wouldn't be right.'

'We could have another riddling contest,' suggested Bingo. 'If I win, then you have to show me the way out of here. And if *you* win, than *I* have to show you the way out of here.'

'But I don't want to be shown the way out of here,' said Sollum.

'And I don't want to have to eat you,' snapped Bingo. 'Come along now. Be fair. I did win the riddling contest, after all.'

'Are you,' asked Sollum morosely, 'surrendering your

rights to me qua meal, and freely giving up the opportunity to eat me?'

'Yep,' said Bingo.

Sollum sighed. It was a deeply sorrowful noise. Had Sollum's pool been a pool of tears he had himself cried at the inherent sorrow of things, his sigh could not have been more sorrowful.

'You wound my honour, sir,' he said. 'And my honour is the only value I have remaining in my life. My life must end, sir, or I must dedicate myself – carefully, cunningly, inexorably – to wreaking my revenge upon *you*. In fact, apart from my honour, I have only one Thing® in the world of any value. It is a Thing® of great antiquity, a Thing® of great value and many uses. With it I find the only consolation my miserable life affords me.'

'Now there's a turn up for the books,' said Bingo. 'Wouldn't you know it, but I found a Thing® in the tunnel as I was coming down here. It's in my pocket now.'

There was silence. In the dim blue light Sollum opened his mouth, a downward-crescent scowl. His teeth, Bingo noticed, were sharpened to points, like golf tees.

'Really?' he said, his voice a little strained.

'I daresay it's the one you were just talking about,' Bingo continued. 'Finders keepers of course, but isn't that a wonderful coincidence? First I win the riddling business fair and square, then it turns out I've got your Thing®! Funny old world.'

'Perhaps you'd care to return it to me?' asked Sollum. His whole manner bespoke a pessimistic anticipation of an answer in the negative. Bingo, accordingly, provided one.

'No,' he said. 'I say, could you show me the way to—'

His soddit instincts saved him. Sollum, incapable of simply abandoning himself to his rage, was advancing upon Bingo with a steady, determined, serious gait, fully intending to tear out his throat and feed on his quivering corpse in a steadily determined and serious manner. He made a clawing sweep at Bingo's head, and only a sort of half-duck, half trip saved the soddit's life. After that Bingo was running, as fast as his little soddit feet could bear him, upwards this time, away from the silent pool and the enraged philosopher.

'Give me back my Thing®!' howled Sollum, a little way behind.

'Not likely,' Bingo whispered under his breath. His hand went to his pocket and there his fingers apprehended the Thing®. Its myriad magical properties, amongst which were included a form of compass-orientation device, a means of seeing in the darkness, and a means of adding speed to running heels, propelled Bingo at tremendous speed along the corridors underneath the mountain. He ran up, along ledges, mounted spiral stone stairways, ran through cavernous hallways, and at last – panting severely – emerged blinking at a precipice high in the sunshine.

He had reached the easternmost extent of the mountains. To his right a mighty and ice-cold river – the Great Floss – tumbled and gushed out of this cavemouth in the eastern flank of the Minty Mountains. The sunlight glassed his eyes momentarily, but, blinking, he could see that he was almost free. Only a forty-foot drop into the bubbling icy whirlpool that the Floss made as it tumbled out of the mountain was between himself and escape.

'Good grief,' somebody below yelled. The voice was only barely audible above the grinding chomping clatter of the waterfall.

Bingo squinted. Below him, a long way below, a group of eight dwarfs and a stooping old wizard stood next to the water's edge. One of the dwarfs, Bingo couldn't see which from this distance, was pointing up at him.

'It's Bingo,' he heard. 'He's not dead after all!'

Behind him, Bingo heard a hiss. He glanced back, and saw Sollum slinking up the ledge towards him, keeping his left hand on the rockwall at his side, and making menacing shaking and swiping gestures with the right. 'First,' the philosopher said in a bitter tone, 'you refused to eat me. Then you stole my Thing®. A painful death is too good for you. On the other hand, since it is the most I can inflict, it'll have to do.'

Several of the dwarfs below were now waving and shouting. Bingo looked at the rapidly approaching figure of Sollum. He looked at the mighty flowing torrent to his right, as solid-looking as stone though it foamed and flexed in its fall. He looked at the drop beneath him. There was nothing for it. He clasped the Thing® in his pocket, hoping devoutly that one of its magical properties was to enable a person to fly, or at least float, and he jumped.

For a moment it seemed as if his prayers had been answered. The world seemed to freeze, and he had a wonderfully clear view of foothills leading down to open pasture and the fertile fields surrounding the Great River M. But then, with a stabbing sense of panic, he realised in the pit of his stomach that he was falling. The view slid upwards, and with a sensation of sharp pain tangible on every single inch of the outside of his body he was immersed in the churning outflow of the Floss.

His world was now white, bubbling, rotating, and utterly disorienting. There was no breath in his lungs. Had a firm dwarfish hand not grabbed his ankle as it snorkelled its way momentarily above the surface and hauled Bingo out he would certainly have drowned.

But there he was, gasping and shivering on the grass under the clear blue sky of morning. Away in the sky, seemingly very far, he heard a wavery voice cry out in its frustration and malice: 'Grabbings! You have incurred the wrath of a philosopher! And a philosopher, once he hates somebody, hates for ever! *For ever!*'

Biorn the Bare Man

Chapter Five

QUEER LODGE

❧

'I know this land well,' declared Gandef. 'Two days' march down the side of the Floss and we come to the famous Mill. There we may replenish our supplies – needful, since *some* of us,' – he glowered round at the dwarfs – 'left our baggage behind when Gobblins attacked.'

'And *some* of us,' Mori retorted, 'were too prissy to be carrying any baggage in the first place, you idle great wizard.'

'Well said, Master Dwarf!' Gandef replied, laughing and clapping him on his back. 'Well said! I like a fellow who's big enough to admit his own failings! And I like a chap with the sense not to cheek a wizard – *very* important that, sharp's the word. But we needn't worry. When we come to the famous Mill we'll replenish.' He clearly like the sound of this word (Bingo wondered how he could hear his own speech when he was so deaf to other people's), and repeated it over and again as they walked. 'Replenish. Replenish. Replenish. Replenish.'

'I may have left the bags behind,' Mori muttered, 'but 'twas not I who chopped off Sili's head by mistake.' He scowled.

'Replenish. Replenish. Replenish. Replenish,' said Gandef, in time to his strides.

And in this fashion the company marched for the rest of the day, the dwarfs complaining of their grumbling bellies and sore feet, the soddit going 'ouch' and 'ow-ow-*wah*' intermittently.

They spent a chilly night camped under a riverside tree; but it was not their fate to get an uninterrupted night of sleep. They had just settled down to rest, the dwarfs wrapping their beards duvet-like about their bodies and Bingo shivering in his corduroy, when wolves sprang upon them. It was as if the darkness took shaggy shape: the night sky transformed into muscle and pelt, the stars jagging into the form of white teeth, the low red moon being swallowed by a lolloping tongue.

'Wolves!' shrieked one of the dwarfs.

Bingo smelt the hot, sharp stink of wolf, and heard a growl by his ear. He leapt awake.

In two minutes everybody had scrambled up the tree, Bingo levering himself up in the midst of a knot of beards and stocky limbs. By the dim starlight Bingo clutched his branch as tightly as a gonk clutches the end of his pencil.[1] 'Gandef!' he called down. 'Gandef!'

But the wizard was still asleep on the ground, as the wolves milled around him. 'Gandef!' called Mori. 'Oh savannah! This is terrible. Somebody wake him up!'

The wolves did not pounce on the snoring wizard immediately, suspicious perhaps of his lack of movement. 'Gandef!' the dwarfs called. 'Wake up!'

It was useless.

The lead wolf, grey and lean, moved his muzzle slowly towards the wizard's face. His jaws clicked apart. His white fangs glinted in the starlight. 'Gandef! Gandef!' shrieked the crowd of dwarfs in the tree above. 'Wolf!' they cried.

The wolf angled his head through ninety degrees, all the better to be able to vice the wizard's neck between the two rows of his terrible teeth. Bingo leaned as far

---

[1] A gonk, as of course you know, is a small marsupial from the land of Gonkor, far to the south. They are intelligent creatures though small – the smallest of all the peoples of Upper Middle Earth, which is saying something – and they admire learning above all things. But their own books, written with their own tiny pencils on *teeny-tiny* pieces of paper (ahhh!) are too small for other scholars to read. More adventurous gonks have tried writing with man-sized pencils, a process that resembles, for them, nothing so much as tossing the caber, and although they have written little more than fragmented wavy lines by this method they persevere. Plucky little fellers. Ahhh-hhh! Swee-eeet.

down from his branch as he dared. 'Wizard! Beware! Be wakeful! Be watching out for your throat!'

And then the soddit saw something startling. A wisp of smoke crept up from Gandef's mouth, though his pipe was cold and in the pocket of his poncho. Further puffs followed. Tentacles of smoke drifted upwards. The wizard yawned in his sleep. And then, quick as a lightning flash, fire jabbed out of his open mouth and caught on the dry fur of the wolf.

The beast reared back, yelping, but the flames were already wriggling on the top of its head and spreading down across its neck. As the wolf writhed, butting into its fellows, it spread the fire. In an instant the whole pack was whinnying like horses and dancing a macabre dance as their fur caught aflame. Gandef was on his feet, shouting, 'What? What? What?' at the top of his voice, waving his arms and staring wild-eyed about him – the better, Bingo assumed, to nurture the panic in the wolf pack. And if this was indeed the wizard's plan, it was working. The wolves howled, scattering over the hilltops. Some raced as flaming torches. Some, unlit, skeetered away from their fellows' whimpering, and stretched their long legs in flight. In moments the landscape was empty of wolves.

The stars twinkled, as if in silent silvery applause.

'Gandef!' the soddit called down in glee. 'A brilliant spell! That put paid to them!'

With remarkable rapidity, Gandef scaled the trunk and positioned himself on a branch next to Bingo.

'What?' he asked. 'What?' Bingo had never seen the wizard's eyes quite so wide.

'You lured the beast on!' Bingo enthused. 'You enticed it to come close, and then you put out a fire spell and burnt it up!'

'Where the *bloody hell*,' asked Gandef, 'did those *wolves* come from?'

'You put them to flight, Gandef!' said Bingo.

'They're dangerous, are wolves,' said the wizard, blinking and looking about him. 'Who was on watch duty? Why weren't we warned?'[2]

The dwarfs were reaching down from branches higher up to clap him on the shoulder, laughing at the plight of the wolves. 'They eat people, do wolves,' Gandef said.

It was at this juncture that somebody noticed Wombl was missing. They called his name a few times, in a desultory fashion, and then explored the ground under the tree, but it was clear enough what had happened to him.

---

[2] Advertently or inadvertently, Gandef is here quoting from a famous Upper Middle English poem, the *Hex of Fish*:

> *Wild weather woke us worryingly* *Why weren't we warned?*
> *Hurricane hurled from the heavens* *Old oaks uprooted sevenfold*
> *Whose fault but the weathermen?* *Typical TV types.*

They spent the rest of the night in the tree.

The following day Gandef led the company along the banks of the river. 'Don't be downhearted,' he announced. 'Soon we'll arrive at the famous Mill, and then we'll feast and replenish.'

They reached the Mill by noon, but it was nought but a fire-blackened ruin, timbers poking from the ground like shards of coal, the land all about laid waste. The trees had burnt to the ground, leaving only charcoaled twigs and tar-black stumps. Gandef stood, puffing on his pipe, and surveyed the desolation. 'Gobblins,' he said at length.

'I'm hungry,' said Bingo.

'This is a sorry pass,' said Gandef.

'I'm hungry,' said Bingo.

'Wizard?' said Mori. 'What shall we do? Is there none other who can give us shelter in this dangerous, open land? What if the wolves should return? What if a huge army of Gobblins, in their rage, should flock out of the Minty Mountains to track us? What if we should die of exhaustion and hunger and our bones be picked clean by eagles?'

'Your optimism does you credit, Master Dwarf,' said Gandef. 'But no matter what you say, I'm afraid this *is* a sorry pass we find ourselves in. There is no help for it, we must go visit Biorn.'

'Biorn?' the dwarfs echoed.

'I'm hungry,' said Bingo.

'Biorn,' said Gandef, shaking his head.

'Do you mean Biorn the Bear-man, who is a man by day and a bear by night?' asked Failin, a quaver in his voice.

'No,' replied Gandef crisply. 'I didn't catch a word of that.'

'What's it?' said Bingo. 'Bear-man?'

'Biorn,' said Mori, picking a burnt twiglet from the ground and examining it. 'The legends that surround him are dire. Bestial, is he.'

'There's nothing for it,' said Gandef. 'He's a moody man, so we'll have to be on best behaviour. But his house is very neat and tidy. Don't do anything to enrage him, though, or he'll like as not rip your arms and legs from your torso and then jam the red soggy ends of the arms into the sockets where the legs should go, and vice versa with the legs in the arm sockets, afterwards making you dance upside down on your leggy-arms for his amusement.'

Nobody knew what to say to this. Gloom settled on the company.

They carried on alongside the river, Gandef regaling the company with several anecdotes of Biorn's reputation as bear-man, all of which involved the words 'wrenching', 'ripping' and 'agonising', and two of which ended with the same phrase: 'to join the heap of still-quivering flesh'. He seemed to find these stories rather heartening, and laughed several times, or to put it more precisely produced on several occasions a sort of hybrid laugh-cough. But the dwarfs became more and more sombre as he went on.

Soon enough they cut away from the river and made their way through fields of honey-smelling clover tall as a dwarf's chest. 'Come!' called Gandef, marching through the meadows up a gently sloping hill and leaving behind him a wake in the grass like a boat in the water. The sun was hot above them. 'I'll need to cast a hearing spell on myself in Biorn's house,' Gandef announced to the party. 'So, please, no sudden noises.' He summoned his magic spell, and it appeared in his hand in the general area of his right ear.

Finally, as they crossed the brow of a broad hill, they came across a great log-built hall standing in the midst of the open land. As they came closer, through a perfectly planed wooden gateway into a neatly tended market garden, Bingo could see how precisely and elegantly the timbers of the house had been put together.

There, in a yard before the house, stood a towering, broad-muscled blond man. He was holding a chicken by its legs and eyeing it. 'Teasing me!' he chided the bird. 'There's that look in your eye. But I can't take a chance on a chick like you.' He shook his head and put the bird back in the pen. 'It's something I couldn't do,' he added, to nobody in particular. His voice though carefully enunciated, had a strange flattened and pursed accent to it, a manner of speech the like of which Bingo had not before heard.

'See those hands!' whispered Gandef, with the booming-echoey whisper in which the wizard specialised. 'How huge and muscled! He could tear a fat book of spells in half with those hands! He'd make short work of you lot, that's for sure.'

The owner of the hands looked up at his visitors.

'Biorn,' called Gandef, with a forced heartiness. 'Hello!'

The big man stared impassively at the approaching company. 'Wizard!' he boomed. 'And Gobblins? No – no – dwarfs. Dwarfs are better than Gobblins. You are all welcome.'

'Thank you kindly, Master Biorn,' said Mori, bowing low. 'And may I compliment you on the extraordinary and beautiful smoothness of your chin?'

'My chin,' said Biorn. The expression on his chiselled features did not change at all as he spoke, but he seemed to Bingo more courteous than Gandef's description had suggested. 'Yes, yes, I have a smooth chin. My brother has a blond beard, and a great musical talent on the fjord-horn and the stringed linchirping. But my chin is smooth.'

'Biorn!' said Gandef. 'It is many moons since last we met. You may indeed have forgotten, it is so long ago. Hmm. But now I visit you again, with a company of dwarfs and a soddit, in the middle of a great journey to the east. We have suffered in our travels, and many of our fellows have – by their own idiot negligence it is true, but nevertheless – got themselves killed. We were hoping for some of you fabled hospitality.'

'For sure,' Biorn replied. 'Come inside.'

They stepped through the wide doorway into a huge timber hall, with planed and polished wood beams, square-cut columns of darker wood, and everywhere a pleasant piney, honey-sweet smell. Many items of attractive wooden furniture were neatly arranged about the place. The dwarfs lined up with Bingo at one end, nodding politely and pointing out the more attractive furnishings to one another. Gandef sat himself in one of Biorn's chairs. He seemed, to Bingo, a very nervous wizard.

'And do you like my house?' asked Biorn, with his odd, up-and-down reverse-camber intonation.

'Very nice,' said the dwarfs, more or less in unison.

'Nice,' agreed Bingo, 'is precisely the word.' It did not seem to him to be the house of an arm-ripping, leg-pulling-off maniac. But then again, the man's torso was unfeasibly crammed with muscle, and his neck was thicker than his head.

'This chair,' said Biorn, grasping a chair with his enormous, tanned, blond-downy hand. 'It is tinted clear lacquered solid beech with Wharg skin green-woven seat.' He held it so that everybody could see. 'I have many chairs.'

'So you do,' said Mori.

There was a pause.

The blank expression on Biorn's face did not change. 'I call my chairs my four-legged friends,' he said. Then, after a two-second pause, he laughed a series of precise laughs, *Hü hü hü hü*.

Everybody joined in, their eyelids more widely separated than was usually the case when they laughed. 'Ha! Aha! Yes, very good. Ha-ha. Excellent.'

Biorn put the chair down.

'And over here,' he added, stepping to one corner of the interior space, 'is what I call Biorn Central. I mean by, of course, that, the kitchen. It all happens here: meals, playtime, a bit of wolf-skinning work brought home. Family life revolves around here, and so I have designed it practical and also with durability, but with adult taste into the bargain.' His blond eyebrows, like strips of yellow felt, sagged a fraction. 'Although, as I have no family, it is only I who occupy the Biorn Central.'

'No family?' asked Bingo.

'No. I am Biorn, the bear-man. I am man in day, and bear in night. I have yet to find woman who will *bear* with me.' He waited two seconds, and then laughed at his own joke: *Hü hü hü hü.*

'Excellent,' everybody said, squeezing grins out of their faces with all the vigour they could manage. 'Aha! *Awfully* good. Ha-ha. Ah.'

'I use the word "bear",' Biorn said doggedly, 'in the two-way sense of large shaggy-pelted wood-dwelling animal, and also endure. This is punning. Sometimes a woman comes, sits and eats with me at my Lokka dining table, which is solid oiled beech, with one extension leaf stored underneath the table surface. Maybe we eat, she and I, meat, bread, or drink a honey beer. But then the sun will be sinking, and I will be turning into a great roaring bear, and she will not usually be staying longer than it requires to exit through the main door – Markör antique-style sap-stained solid spruce, handles included.'

Biorn's face seemed blandly untouched by the poignancy of his own tale.

'Perhaps,' said Bingo in a slightly squeaky voice, 'you might find a bear-woman . . . ?'

'Bear-woman, for sure,' said Biorn, nodding. 'Of course, this is my dream. But I need not only bear-woman, but – since I cannot join my life with hirsute female – a bear-woman who will be contented to depilate. She may use the bees' wax, or she may use my specially sharpened dining knife, with wooden handle and flower pattern twenty-seven – I do not mind.' He looked from face to face. 'I have many bees here,' he added. 'I am the Wolf of Bees.'

'Right,' said Bingo, dwelling on the *i*.

'It is woman that I am waiting for, for sure,' said Biorn. 'Sometimes I feel I would be doing all right, if it wasn't for the nights.'

'Nights,' agreed Mori, 'can be a bugger.' He laughed nervously.

Biorn stepped over to the far wall. 'This shelf,' he said, 'in bi-ply laminate with silver brackets, I was putting it up yesterday. I was doing this putting-up the day before you came.'

'It's,' said Bingo, 'very good. Very, uh, shelvy.' His hunger got the better of his fear. 'You got any, you know, food?'

'Ya, for sure,' said Biorn. He stepped over to a free-standing larder unit, and gestured towards it with his open palm.

Biorn brought out some honey, or as he put it, 'honey, honey'. He brought out honied loaves. He served a dish of tripe, and the dwarfs tucked in with an appetite that seemed to wane within seconds. 'Biorn,' asked Mori.

'Er – don't misunderstand me, but – er, this is *super* tripe, er – but does it have *honey* in it?'

'For sure,' said Biorn.

'Gracious,' said Mori in a low tone.

At first Bingo was so grateful to have something to eat that he was oblivious to the physical proximity of Biorn, his enormous flesh-shredding muscles, his tediously monotonous voice. But as sunset darkened the skies outside, and Biorn lit a log in his Arås stone-block fireplace, Bingo started to feel the dreary weight of the bear-man's presence press down upon him again.

'I have known your wizard,' Biorn was saying, pronouncing the word 'wheezer', which Bingo thought rather appropriate, 'for many years.' He put a musical kink into 'years', such that the '*y*' started on a low E, the *ears* slipped up to an A#.

'Have you really?' replied Mori. 'How interesting.' The dwarf, although he wore an unnaturally wide grin on his face, looked rather uncomfortable on his chair, leaning forward stiffly and pressing his legs together tightly like a man desperate to go to the toilet for several simultaneous and pressing reasons. 'How interesting.'

'Ah yes, he is friend of animal, he is famous Raddledghastly the Ragged, for sure, and all animals – such as I am myself an animal, as I have been saying – know him as friendly.'

Gandef, smiling manically, leant towards Mori. 'He

thinks I'm Raddledghastly,' he hissed through set teeth. 'Play along with it! Don't let him know the truth! We mustn't upset him, or he could flip into his bear state. That would be a disaster.'

He stopped, and turned his head to see Biorn staring at him.

'You are whispering,' observed Biorn placidly.

Everybody was silent.

'I,' said Gandef, looking around him, sweat appearing on his forehead like diamond studs, 'was,' he concluded lamely.

'Please to share,' said Biorn, sing-song.

'I was – ah, telling Mori how, ah, lovely your roof beams are.'

Biorn looked steadily at Gandef. He tipped his massy blond head backwards through ninety degrees and looked up at the ceiling. Then he levelled his gaze and looked at Gandef again for one long minute. Eventually he said: 'For sure.'

'I wonder if it would be all right,' asked Gofur, 'if I used your privy?'

'Bathroom, ah, yes, for sure,' said Biorn. 'Outside in the yard, you will be finding a shed. You will be finding the sophisticated appeal of free-standing design inside, the privy clad in the pale beauty of smooth birch veneer, teamed with sleek cherrywood handles and legs to achieve a stylish simplicity.'

Gofur dipped his head and positively rushed out, almost tripping over his beard.

'As I was saying,' Biorn said. 'Animals are good. My chickens are most special chickens. They came flapping from far away. Now I'm under their spell.'

'Really?' said Gandef. 'Fascinating.'

'I speak frivolously, but they are charming birds. Sometimes – and I am being fanciful, for sure, but – I dream I'm a chicken. I dream I can squalk' (he pronounced every single letter of this strange word) 'and flap, spread my wings, and go to anywhere that I please. But, you are welcome also, I am pleased to have visitors.'

He pondered this last word for a while, as if it reminded him of something.

'Still,' said Gandef, suddenly sprightly, 'we wouldn't want to keep you up past your bedtime. Don't you, you know, turn into a bear soon?'

'Tonight,' said Biorn, 'I shall remain in my man shape, to be hospitable to my guests. But be telling me, please, where your journey takes you?'

The dwarfs breathed a silent but visible sigh of collective relief.

'Ah,' said Mori, in a jollier tone of voice. 'Well, we're off to the Only Mountain. Do you know it?'

'For sure,' said Biorn. 'Strebor, the Only Mountain. For sure. And for why are you going there?'

'Gold,' said Mori, with a quick glance at Gandef.

'Gold!' repeated Gandef, in a loud voice, fixing Bingo with a significant stare.

'Ah,' said Biorn. 'Your quest, then, is for money?'

'Money,' agreed Gandef.

'Money,' echoed the dwarfs.

'Must be,' muttered Bingo. 'Why else would you keep saying so?'

The fire cackled to itself.

'You will be fighting Smug the Magic Dragon for this gold?' Biorn queried. 'The winner will be taking it all?'

'That's,' said Mori, 'the idea.'

'Dragons are great beasts. Great means big, you know.' He stared at the fire for a long time. An unnatural stillness settled in the great hall. 'Greater,' Biorn added, after a long time, 'than bears. And more evil.'

He appeared to be brooding.

'Well, perhaps it's time we all turned in,' said Gandef hurriedly. 'Sleepy sleep time, I think. I say, Biorn, it's awfully courteous of you not to shift into your bear shape when we're under your roof. I think I can speak for all of us when I say that we consider that a sign of a *truly* hospitable, um, hospital. Um hostel. A truly hospitable place of hospitality.'

His voice faded from strong to feeble as the sentence progressed, and had petered out completely by the end. All eyes were on Biorn.

'You are knowing already, perhaps,' said Biorn, his voice for the first time registering an emotional tone, 'of the tale of the Great Bear of the North?'

Nobody stirred.

'The Great Bear of the north . . . ?' prompted Gandef gingerly.

'A good friend of me. A mighty bear. The dragon Smug,' said Biorn, his eyes fierce, 'was fighting with him, and was burning and scorching him, and his pelt caught on the fire. He was burnt. His glorious blue house was burnt.'

'Dear me,' said Gandef.

'Shocking,' said the dwarfs.

'Shockling?' said Biorn vehemently. 'Shockling? Indeed it *is* shockling, dwarfs!'

'Shock-*ing*,' corrected Mori, but in so quiet a voice that it is likely Biorn did not hear it.

'It is *worse* than shockling,' said Biorn, standing up. 'It is tragedy. It is crime against all bearkind. It is being typical of dragons, for sure, that they use this fire. It should ought not to be. It should ought not. Dragons!' His eyes had taken on an alarming intensity, like blue ink being stirred in a pair of white ceramic pots. His hands were jerking up and down. 'Dragons? Do I not like dragons? No I do not. Dragons? I have strong feelings of dislike for dragons.'

'Of course you do,' said Gandef, trying to conciliate. 'Of course you do. Only natural.'

'To be using the *fire*?' Biorn thundered. 'On the furry and the dry? To burn the majestic Blue House of the North? To turn the soothing simplicity of modern design and blue paint mixed from natural fibres and spring water to *char*? To *dust*? To,' he added, with especial if mysterious emphasis, '*bur*?' He strode up and down, shaking his head with mighty, muscles shakes. 'No, no, it is not right. To use no fire on bears, this is necessary, for fire is against the protocols of the ursine. For Smug to do this? The dragon must be punished. Punished! You must kill Smug! Kill Smug! Kill! Kill!'

'Absolutely,' said Gandef, trying to calm the giant man. 'We absolutely intend to. Let's talk about something else, why don't we? Shall we have some more honey beer? A few more cutlets of your excellent honey-roast liver? Or one more pot of your delightfully honeyed caviar? Come, Biorn old friend, don't get yourself – ah – overstimulated. It's funny,' the wizard went on, reaching into the pocket of his poncho for his smoking paraphernalia, 'you should talk of burning dry animals in that way, actually, because – you'll laugh at this,' he said, illustrating the procedure by laughing a little himself, 'this'll amuse you. On our way here we encountered some wolves. Wolves who ate one of our fellows, in fact, nasty beasts, devoured Failin—'

'Wombl,' corrected Failin.

'Just so, and they were about to eat *me*. We were, you see, in a sticky spot, but this'll amuse you, especially in the, eh, ha ha ha!, especially in the light of what you've just been saying. This'll amuse you. They were about to *eat* me, you see, *eat* me, and I used a little fiery spell of my own, and – well, the *first* wolf caught fire, you see,' Gandef chuckled. 'The *first* wolf caught fire, and he leapt about, you see, and he bumped into the *second* wolf . . .'

Biorn, who had stopped pacing, was staring at the wizard with an unnerving fixity. Mori was making little circular motions with both hands, palms outward, in front of his chest, as if polishing a pane of glass immediately before him and shaking his head back and forth. But he did not seem to be able to catch Gandef's eye.

'. . . and – ha! ha! ha! – and the *second* wolf,' Gandef was saying, 'he went up like a torch, and he bumped into this *third* wolf – it was really something of a sight, they made such a noise.'

He glanced up at Biorn, and his voice faltered. 'Made,' he repeated, in a less hilarious tone, 'such a. Noise.'

There was silence for the space of a full minute.

Biorn, motionless throughout this time, began to moan. The moan grew to a groan, thence to a growl, and so to a howl. His huge hands gripped his own clothing and pulled it apart with a skeetering noise of ripping cloth.

'Oh,' said Gandef, in a subdued voice, sprinting nimbly over to one of the sofas and hiding behind it, 'dear.'

The rest of the company scurried to join him.

'Ågh! Årggggh!' bellowed Biorn. 'Ø! Ø! Ø! Ø! Ø! Uh! Uh! Uh! Årggggh!'

'That *may*,' said Gandef, looking from dwarf face to dwarf face, 'have been the wrong tack.'

'Maybe,' agreed Mori.

Biorn was marching up and down the whole length of his hall now, howling and growling and generally making the sorts of noises one might associate with an angry bear. He had torn off his woollen shirt, and was trying to rip the tougher canvas of his trousers. But tearing trousers is no easy task, even for the most muscular of individuals, and in the end he had to content himself with tearing off the button at the waist and half dragging, half hopping out of them. 'Ågh!' he bellowed. 'Ågh!'

'Oh, Þróinn,' swore Mori. 'Now what are we going to do? Trapped in this wooden house with a raging bear!'

'Stay calm,' advised Gandef.

'Perhaps if we rushed to the door?' suggested Bingo.

'Waaaah!' yelled Biorn, his head rearing up over the top of the settee. 'Waaah!'

Gandef raced the dwarfs and Bingo to the behind-side of the other large sofa. Biorn kept making noises of intermittent fury and rage stomping back and forth.

'I couldn't help noticing,' said Mori, 'that he's – ehm, smooth all over.'

'Smooth,' said Bingo.

'I wish he'd stop yelling,' said Gandef. 'It's amplified by my spell and it's making my head hurt.'

'No body hair. Shouldn't a bear have body hair?'

'No body hair?' queried Bingo.

'Some body hair,' Mori modified. 'But, from a dwarf's point of view, look you, *very* smooth. Still smoothly chinned, la, for instance. His chest smooth as sea-sand.'

Gandef was muttering to himself, 'Infernal *ringing* noise now —'

'Röär!' bellowed Biorn. Accompanying sounds to the effect of *smash! Smash! Crash!* were also audible.[3]

Mori popped his head above the top of the sofa, and ducked back down again. 'He's pulling things off one of his shelves,' he reported, 'and roaring.'

---

[3] These words have been translated from the original Middle Earthian into an English idiom. They were, in the original text, *furmash! Getsmash!*

'Yes, we can hear him roaring,' Bingo observed. 'Is he a bear now?'

'He's, frankly, just a nude man.'

'Not a bear?'

'Not.'

'Not even a little bit?'

'Well,' said Mori, 'no. All smooth. Look you.'

'That doesn't sound very bear-like,' said Bingo.

He took his courage into his two hands, and stood up. His head reached, just, over the top of the back of the sofa. He peered at Biorn. As Mori had said, the tall man was completely naked, naked with a completeness that only an adult of full muscular development without clothes on can be. The fellow was storming up and down at the far end of the hall, roaring.

'I don't understand,' said Bingo. 'When does he turn into the bear?'

'Röär!' yelled Biorn, stampeding up the hall towards them. '*When*, you say? *When* do I turn? I *have* turned! I *am* a bear! I am Biorn, the mighty bear! Röär!'

As the smooth and nude man reached the sofa, the fully clothed and hairy dwarfs backed against the wall behind them.

'Röär!' insisted Biorn. 'Röär!' He raised his hands in front of him with his knuckles out, as if grasping an invisible iron bar that was suspended horizontally at nipple-height. He opened his mouth and showed two rows of impressive but undeniably human teeth. 'Röär!' he said.

'You,' said Bingo, sweeping his crumbs of courage together internally to produce an, if you will, imaginary biscuit of valour. 'You aren't actually a bear at all, are you?'

'Miserable liar!' howled Biorn. 'For sure I am a bear!'

He made a rush at the soddit, who ducked under Biorn's sandstone-pillar legs and scrambled away. 'You're not though,' he called behind him, panting as he ran. 'Not *actually*, are you?'

'Röär!' called Biorn. 'I shall for *sure* eat you with my great beary teeth.'

'Ya,' Bingo returned, this being the most sophisticated taunt he could think of under the pressure of the moment. He was at the door, and hauled with all his might at the elegantly carved door handle.

'Feel the rage of the great pelty—' Biorn howled, hurling himself at Bingo. He may have been intending to conclude this statement with the words 'man-bear', or possibly 'mighty Biorn'. Maybe 'animal'. We can do no better than hypothesise at this juncture, because what Biorn actually said moved the sentence in a wholly new direction, concluding his utterance with a startled-sounding 'uuu*uu*!' (inflected from E flat up to G). The soddit had ducked and shimmied again, and instead of grabbing him Biorn had fallen through the open door and landed chin-first on the cold doorstep outside. There was a thud, and then another thud, as he progressed on his stomach further beyond the doorstep into the mud.

Bingo put all his weight behind the door, and swung it shut. Instantly six dwarfs were at his side helping him lower the beam of sanded wood into place.

All seven collapsed. It took them a full minute to regain their breath.

'Well,' Gandef said from across the room. 'That went fairly well, all things considered.' He was lighting his pipe.

Outside the door, a slightly muffled voice could be heard. 'Excuse me?' it called. 'Are you, now, locking the door?'

'Ignore him,' said Mori, picking himself up and smoothing the creases from his dwarf garb.

'Hellu?' came the voice. 'Hellu? Can you be unlocking the door, please?'

'Go away,' Bingo called.

'It is cold here outside,' came Biorn's voice, rather mournfully.

'Go find a cave to hibernate in,' called Mori.

'Please, not with the mockery,' keened Biorn. 'It is highly cold. If you allow me inwards again, I am promising to retain my man shape for the rest of the evening.'

'You're a loony,' Mori opined in a clear, strong voice.

'Never mind him,' said Bingo. 'You – Gandef. Don't put away your hearing spell for a moment. I've a bone to pick with you.'

'Eh?' asked Gandef, his hearing magic hovering near his hand. 'What's it?'

'You told us he *actually* was a bear,' pressed Bingo. 'All those stories of ripped-off arms and piles of quivering flesh. Do you realise that you terrified us?'

'Well,' said the wizard, chomping the end of his pipe, 'that's what I heard.'

'That's what you *heard*? I thought you knew him.'

'Oh no, oh no. Never met him before.'

'But you said—'

'A simple strategy to get inside and get some food, which worked, I might add. No, he mistook me for Raddledghastly the Ragged, my fellow wizard. But it worked out all right in the end. And we've learned not to trust uncorroborated stories of ursine metamorphosis.'

'Hellu?' Biorn's voice came from outside. 'My teeth are bouncing up and down against one another. Excuse me! Hellu!'

They slept well that night, and broke their fast with honey cakes with honey and honey mead. Only after they were fully rested and prepared did they open the door. Outside Biorn was lying curled under a hastily scooped pile of leaves. His extremities looked blue.

Gofur was sitting glumly on the doorstep. 'Spent the night in the privy,' he grumbled. 'Is there any breakfast left?'

As Gofur gathered some of the house's supplies for himself, Biorn stood up, shaking off some of the damp leaves and looking very sorry for himself indeed. 'Highly cold it has been,' he told them. 'With the chills, and the frost and the creeping-crawlings. Can I go in again?'

Bingo stepped aside and allowed the large man to scurry through his own doorway. 'And thank you,' he called, as Gofur came out, his coat stuffed with cakes, 'for your hospitality.'

Spider

Chapter Six

SPIDERS AND FLY! FLY!
RUN FOR YOUR LIFE!

ᑲᗰᗰᑭ

They set off in good spirits from Biorn's house, depriving the now moody and withdrawn man of nine stout ponies and a number of his prize chickens. Biorn seemed content to sit in the corner looking gloomy and sorry for himself. 'Ta-ta now!' the dwarfs called to him as they left. 'Bye!'

He didn't reply.

After a night warm under Biorn's thick-weave blankets and an easy day's ride on the plump ponies, they arrived at the expanse of the mighty River M. Across the smoothly flowing waters, reflective as polished stone, could be seen the edge of the great forest. The sky above, a perfect blend of midday blue and metal grey, spoke of amplitude and possibility. The air was fresh in the company's mouths, like pure water.

'How do we get across?' asked the soddit.

'Coracles, boyo,' said Mori, unstrapping the dwarfish breastplate from his chest. 'Aren't you wearing yours?'

'Well,' said Bingo, 'I'll confess, no, I'm not.'

'So,' said Tori, poking his corduroy waistcoat.[1] 'Look you, we did wonder how you expected to keep that watertight.'

'It's not designed to go in the water at all,' Bingo explained. 'Except when it gets washed.' It had not been washed in a long time.

'Oh!' said the dwarf. 'Not designed to go in the water, you say? Gracious. What use does it have then?'

'It keeps my torso warm.'

'Well we can take that as read, like,' said Tori dismissively. 'That goes, see, without saying. But what *secondary* use does it have?'

'None.'

The dwarfs muttered amongst themselves how foolish it was to wear clothing without a secondary use. They took the packs from the ponies and slung them on their backs, then slid their shallow metallic coracles into the water, leapt into them with remarkable grace and they were off, paddling with stubby dwarfish hands and powerful dwarfish arm muscles into the distance. A sizeable lateral transfer was imparted to their journey by the current, and they drifted far downstream as they travelled. Bingo found himself alone with the wizard and the ponies on the near-side bank. 'Hey!' he called. 'What about us? Hey!'

---

[1] A word pronounced, incidentally, 'wsct'.

Shortly, though, he saw two dwarfs reboard their tiny, tinny crafts, and make their way back towards the near shore, carried even further downstream as they went. They were lost to Bingo's eyes before they reached it, but twenty minutes later they came jogging along the bank carrying two spare breastplates.

'There you go, lad, bach,' said On, the first of the dwarfs to arrive. 'You hop into that, and paddle with all your might.'

Tori was endeavouring to coax Gandef into the other spare coracle. 'What about the ponies?' Bingo asked, as he tried to hold the breastplate steady in the water whilst leaning over the edge of the bank.

'They'll have to make their own way home, see,' explained On. But Bingo barely heard, because he had half fallen into the shallow craft and was now several yards offshore, drifting rapidly downstream. He tried paddling, but the arching of his back the action required hurt his spine. He tried lying on his back, and doing a sort of behindways underarm paddling, but it was rather ineffectual. He tried lying on his front, but the sharp rim of the breastplate jagged into his throat. In the end he forced himself to endure the pain in his back, and laboriously paddled and paddled until he was at the far bank. There was nobody around. There was water inside his boots, and his clothes were sodden. He hauled the coracle on to the bank and trudged for an

hour upstream with the coracle pulling in the mud.
Finally he found the party, settled round a campfire,
wizard and all.

The following morning, after another filling breakfast
from Biorn's store – honey-glazed smoked kippers,
honey on toast and honeyed orange juice – Bingo felt a
little better. 'Where now?' he asked. 'Into the forest, is
it?'

'That's right, laddo,' said Mori.

They packed and marched two abreast, towards the
line of trees. But Bingo's jaunty spirits evaporated as
they walked into the wood under a tangle of branches
that served almost as a gateway, and along a mossy,
chilly path. It was very dark. This forest was nothing
like the brittle but sunshiny forest of Lord Elsqare the
elf. This was gloom in tree form. Fungus grew in broad-
peaked clumps beside the pale, speckled tree trunks,
looking like nothing so much as old cheese. Everything
that Bingo's fingers or face touched, or that touched
him, felt slimy.

'What a horrid place!' he declared.

'Truly,' agreed Mori, who was walking by his side.
'This is the evil Mykyurwood. You see those elms over
there?'

'Yes.'

'They're oaks.'

Bingo examined them. 'They look quite like oaks,' he said. 'Have they taken the form of elms?'

'Partially,' said the dwarf. 'Enchanted, look you. And those ash trees?'

'Oaks,' said Bingo.

'Good guess,' said the dwarf.

'Not really. When you look a little more closely you can see they're not really ash. They're oak.'

'It's true,' said Mori, 'that it's not a very effective enchantment. But a shape-changing enchantment it is, nonetheless. The wood is filled with mystery and danger.'

'And must we go through? Cannot we go round?'

'It's the most direct route,' said Mori morosely. 'Besides, I thought – that is,' he added hastily, looking around to see if any of the other dwarfs had overheard him, 'that is, our King *Thorri* thought – ahem – that we'd enjoy the sensation of something over our heads. Almost like being underground I, he, thought. 'Course, it's not so pleasant inside, is it? And there are spiders.'

'I don't mind spiders,' said Bingo haltingly. This was a lie.

'I don't mean *little* spiders,' Mori clarified, 'not knuckle-sized ones, or fist-sized ones. I mean spiders as big as you. Twice as big.'

'Should I have to face that peril, I'm confident that

my hobbld courage will see me through,' Bingo replied. This, also, was a lie. A rather bigger lie, in fact.

They walked for the rest of the day and in the evening they camped beside a sluggish, gooey-looking stream that bisected the path. 'Best not get wet in that water,' Mori advised. 'Enchanted, I daresay, boys, see. We'll find a way over tomorrow.'

That night they slept uncomfortably, and in the morning Mori stood beside the little stream and pondered how they might cross. 'We could hew a tree, p'raps,' he suggested. 'Make a bridge? Or should we try our coracles again?'

But Tori was a scoffer. 'Are you kidding, boyo?' he demanded. This was, presumably, a rhetorical question. 'The stream's an inch deep, if that. You can't float a coracle in an inch of water! And what would be the point. 'Let's just wade out and walk over. Wasting time chopping down a tree? Ap-surd. Ap-*surd*.'

'No no no, Tori boyo,' insisted Mori. 'This is the Mykyurwood, see, and its precincts are enchanted.'

'Its *what*?'

'Precincts,' Mori repeated warily, and with a slightly questioning inflection.

Tori laughed scoffingly.

'Its,' said Mori petulantly, searching for a better word, 'its grounds, its demesne, its general area – it's all enchanted, see. You don't know what might happen in that stream! It might put you to sleep, bach. It might be a magic stream.'

'And it *might* be just an ordinary, piddling, inch-deep little dribble that we can walk through,' said Tori.

'I invite you,' Mori said hotly, 'to try.'

'And try I will,' said Tori.

He stood at the side of the stream, placed one foot in the water and paused. The water wetted his sole but barely touched the side of his boot. When nothing happened, he turned a victoriously leering face back at the party, and stepped his other foot into the stream. In a trice he was on his back thrashing and kicking his legs up, and before anybody could react he was travelling rapidly downstream, disappearing between the trees. The tiny brook seemed, impossibly, to have become many feet deep, the water much blacker and much, *much* more rapidly flowing. 'Help,' gurgled Tori. 'Help!' But he was disappearing into the distance between the lowering trees, and his voice was soon obscured by the roaring of the great and, now, foaming torrent. Boulders flicked past the party, from left to right, caught in the spate.

And then they were standing in the silent gloaming once again, and the stream seemed to be nothing but an inch-deep dribble.

'Axes,' said Mori, after a long silence. 'Axes, every-body.'

'Should we go after him?' Bingo asked in a worried voice. But the dwarfs assured him that it would be a foolish business leaving the plain forest path in search of anything at all, even a valued comrade and brother. 'We'd all perish, you see,' Mori said. 'Perhaps Tori has drowned, or perhaps he'll be washed out of the forest into the River Sprinting that flows through the eastern lands. Either way he is beyond our help.'

They tried chopping down one of the trees that grew alongside the path, but it was an awkward business. The bark was extremely tough and leathery, and it put out some disgusting slimy extrudence, so that the dwarfs' axe blades slipped and skidded instead of cutting into it. After two hours of exhausting and futile swinging, the dwarfs sat in a gloomy circle.

'Could the wizard help us?' Bingo wondered.

But Gandef seemed to have entered a sort of senile fugue state. He smiled and waved when they yelled at him, but nothing they could do – not loud noises, not mimes, not drawing in the ground with a stick – could make him reply.

'His deafness is much worse now,' said Mori. 'Almost complete.'

'Complete?' asked Bingo.

'Indeed,' said Mori. 'What did you expect? It's hardly going to get any better now, is it?'

'That doesn't mean it's going to get worse, though. You're acting as if you've always expected him to go completely deaf.'

Mori looked at the soddit as if he were a moron, and then seemed to recollect himself. 'Of course, you don't *know*, la. See! I'd almost forgotten you weren't a dwarf! Funny that. Familiarity, I suppose. Got used to you, I have.'

'I don't know what?' Bingo pressed. 'What is it I don't know?'

'Never mind that,' grumbled Mori.

'No – seriously. What? You lot have been keeping something from me the whole way along. What is it? Why precisely *are* we trekking to the Only Mountain?'

'Gold,' said one of the dwarfs in a desultory tone.

'But it's *not* gold, is it?' said Bingo. 'Come along, I'm not a complete fool. I know it's not gold, I just don't know what it *is*. Why are we going?'

'Gold,' grumbled Mori. 'Just gold.'

'Uh!' said Bingo in despair, and he got up and marched to the edge of the enchanted stream. The trickle looked so inoffensive. The distance from bank to bank was no more than ten feet. Could they not leap over? No, of course they could not.

He returned to the group. 'If we cannot build a bridge of wood, then we must build a bridge of something else. There are boulders embedded in the mud alongside. Why not roll those out and use them as stepping stones?'

'An idea,' said Mori, rousing himself. The six remaining dwarfs and the soddit hauled and heaved and pushed one of the boulders out of its position, and rolled it tortuously until it sat in the stream. Nothing changed.

'You two,' said Mori, to Failin and Gofur, 'hang on to my arms.'

They got into position. Gingerly, Mori reached out with one leg and placed a foot on the side of the large stone. Everybody held their breath. But nothing happened. 'Here goes,' said Mori, and pushed off with his other foot. But as soon as this foot left the mud of the streambank there was a great rumble and the boulder shifted position. Foam curled up on its leading edge. Failin and Gofur hauled back and Mori sprawled on the dirt.

The stream was quiet once more.

'I suppose,' said Bingo, 'that we need to cross the stream without anything being in contact with the water.'

'I suppose so,' said Mori glumly.

'What now?'

'That creeper,' said Bingo. 'Do you see it? Hanging down from that branch over the stream. Could we reach it?'

'With one of these sticks maybe,' said Mori, picking up a soggily dead branch lying beside the path. 'We could hook it, draw it to us. You're thinking we could swing across?'

'Yes,' said Bingo.

'You go,' said the dwarf. 'You're lighter than any of us. If it won't hold your weight, it won't hold anyone's. But if you get across, I'll give it a go.'

Bingo wasn't happy with this plan, but he couldn't deny its basis in the physics of mass and weight.

The dwarfs caught the creeper easily enough, and pulled it towards the nearside bank of the little rill. 'I'll take a run-up,' said Bingo nervously. He paced back along the path, turned, and started running towards the stream. Or, to be precise, not really running. It was more *hurrying*, a little frenzied scurry. He grabbed the creeper, swung through the air with a wail, pulled up his legs so that they didn't trail in the water, and found himself rising through the air on the far side.

'Let go, boyo!' shouted the dwarfs behind him. 'You're over! Hurrah! Let go! Try and *roll* with the landing when you come down.'

'Right you are!' squealed Bingo.

But he couldn't let go of the creeper. His hands seemed glued to it. The stick the dwarfs had used to fetch it was still attached, lower down. Nor, as his trajectory reached its highest point, did he swing back down again. The leaves that brushed against his body seemed unpleasantly gooey. He found himself almost horizontal, wedged in a mass of adhesive foliage many feet above the ground.

'Help,' he cried.

But there was no help. From where he was Bingo could see little: the dark dappling of the forest canopy overhead, his own hands glued to a strand of what, now, he was less prepared to call 'creeper'. There was a rustling sound beside him.

'Hello,' said a snide voice in his ear. 'What have we here?'

Bingo turned his head.

Squatting on a taut grey thread amongst the leaves sat the biggest spider he had ever encountered. Its fat woolly body sprouted legs at jagged angles, thick leathery black legs, eight of them. It's worth dwelling on that fact for a moment. Not *two* legs, mind, like normal beings; nor even four after the manner of some of the mild-eyed beasts of the field. But a wholly superfluous and frankly alarming eight. That's right, *eight*. Nasty, eh? Oh yes. The creature's abdomen curved at the end. Its pinched face wore two twitching mandibles over its v-shaped lips, like a surreal moustache improbably and unpleasantly alive and moving. It had eight eyes, although six of these were small and clustered to the left and the right of the face like pimples. But the two main eyes were huge and red, like glass globes filled with claret, and light played curious spiral effects on anything reflected in their spheres. The spider's face had, despite all of this, a peculiarly human cast, as if a tubby person were wearing fat red glasses.

'Come visiting, have you?' sneered the spider. 'How pleasant of you. Or perhaps you've come colonising, eh? Trying to occupy and exploit the territory of honest working spiders?'

'Not at all,' said Bingo, trembling. 'No, no.'

'Which is what an imperialist would be bound to say. And speaking of being *bound*, are you cold there? Shivering? Let me wrap you.'

With dexterous movements of its great fat body the spider hurried round and about Bingo's body, spooling thick thread from its hindquarters and manipulating this with its two hind legs – which were spindlier and knitting-needlier than the other six. In a moment Bingo was swaddled all about. Only his right arm, still stuck to the strand (which wasn't, it seemed clear, a creeper after all), was outside the spool.

'Let me go!' he squeaked.

But the spider had no intention of letting him go. Tutting to himself, the spider smeared a secretion on to Bingo's hand to release the glue, and then tucked the free arm down at his side and swirled it around with another loop of cable. Luckily for Bingo – as it turned out – he did this hurriedly, and as he picked up the little soddit and started transporting it through the treetops the cable sagged and Bingo got his arm free. But the canny soddit kept it at his side, for fear that the spider would bind it again if he noticed it was loose.

Bingo was carried a long way into the forest. All through this bumpy, unpleasant journey he was racking his brains to think of a way of signalling to the dwarfs – to warn them of the danger, and to prompt them, perhaps, to rescue him. But he could think of nothing, and as they arrived at the spider's commune he saw it was a needless task. Seven figures were dangling from a branch, each of them wrapped tightly in spider cord: six of these were dwarfs, and one was a wizard.

'Good grief,' said Bingo.

'Hello, boyo,' said the dwarf nearest him. It was Frili. 'You here?'

'What happened to you?'

'We saw you getting stuck, see, and Mori shouted that the best plan was the one with axes in it. We dwarfs tend to prefer plans if they've got axes in them. So we hurried to our packs, only these here spider boys had spread sticky thread across the path, about six inches up. We all fell, got our shins and our boots caught in it. We might have ditched the boots and got away, but beards is a different matter. So then they were all over us, see, and here we are.'

'At least,' came a voice from further along the dangling line – Bingo recognised it as Mori's – 'at least we're over the enchanted stream. Carried over by the spiders, see.'

Bingo found it hard to take much comfort from that particular development.

The spiders were scurrying about from branch to branch, from fibre to fibre. They were an imposing-looking bunch. Where most people are content to grow beards from their faces only, spiders enjoy growing beards from all of their many legs. In addition to which they had bristles, thick black stubble, sharp-looking lashes, and other forms of shorter hair all over their bodies. They produced a great deal of silk, strands thick as wool which they wove into a number of things, only some of them liable to kill. Their scarves, for instance, were quite highly sought after: warm, if slightly creepy personal adornments. Sweaters, socks, blankets, furniture, roofing tiles, boots, wigs, farming implements and swords, all were knitted by the tireless spiders. Some of these products, frankly, worked better than others; but they were all traded by the spiders with the glum, rather deprived peoples who lived east of the Mykyurwood. The spiders also undertook special jobs for customers who were prepared to pay over the odds

– they might, for example, go to people's houses and
cover everything with gossamer cobwebs as an April
Fool's joke. Or if a woman were abandoned at the altar
by her shiftless groom, a spider would be called in to
cover the bridal chambers and the bride herself with
cobwebs, so that she could feel properly miserable.

But their trading life had not endeared them to the
populations of the open plains. Rather the reverse, in
fact. People, not to put too fine a point on it, hated
them. Not all people, but most people. Worse, the few
people who actively liked the spiders were – there's no
other word – weirdos.[2] All the reasonable people hated
the spiders with a reflex hatred. They flinched, they
shrieked, they ran away, they said things like, 'Eee!
Ugh! Ugh! Ugh! Rachel! Rachel! Can you get in here
and help me, there's an absolutely enormous spider in
the front room—' People traded with them, of course,
because people will trade with anybody and anything if
the anybody or anything has something they want. But
people thought them flesh-creepingly horrible.

Which they were. Even the nicest of them.

This climate of opinion had wrought its work upon
the spiders' souls. The spiders of Mykyurwood were
bitter. They had been non-specifically bitter for many

[2] I don't care what you say – people who like spiders are weird.
Weird. WEIRD I SAY.

years, until one of their number had returned from his travels with a number of socialist tracts and keyworks,[3] and the whole commune had become politicised. The spiders had changed from being simply bitter, to becoming envious, chip-on-shoulder lefties.[4] They were sharply aware of the general anti-spider prejudice of society, the oppressive ideological construction of spiders in Upper-Middle-Earthian culture in which 'spider' occupies the position of hate-figure, the 'other' by which the fascist state defines its own social identity – and why? Why? Let me *tell* you, comrades, *only* because spiders are archetypal proletarian individuals, tireless workers whose exploited labour benefits everybody – pest control, weaving and textiles – make no mistake, comrades, it is rampant imperialist legism, that's what it is, unreconstructed hairy fangism. Well, comrades, it's time spiders banded together, formed a union, took their protest to the streets. Spiders of the

---

[3] Amongst which were *Das Web-Kapital*, *The Attercopmunist Manifesto* and *Condition of the Eight-legged Working Classes*. To quote the famous Karl Marachnoid: 'All the great events and personalities in world history reappear in one fashion or another; the first time as tragedy, the second time as running desperately round and round the sink like a roulette ball in its wheel. Philosophers have only *interpreted* the world; the *point* is to wrap it in silk and sting it to keep it from wriggling.'

[4] A spider can have four times as many chips on its shoulders as a human being. They're efficient that way.

world unite! We have nothing to lose but our sticky threads.

Bingo's first thought when he realised the serious-ness of his predicament was to be thankful that his right arm was free of the binding. But a long and unsuccess-ful attempt to unpick his cords left him with nothing but broken nails. The cord was too strong, and too sticky. He cast about, but all he could reach with his free arm were handfuls of leaves.

Bingo decided the thing to do was to negotiate his and the dwarfs' way out of captivity.

'Hey!' he called. 'Hello! Excuse me!'

One of the fatter spiders broke off from the general spider mêlée and brought his glistening spider face close to Bingo's. 'Yes?'

'Sir, I was wondering, O mighty spider,' said Bingo, his voice warbling a little, 'if I might be permitted a brief word with your mighty and dread monarch – king or queen, I, alas, do not know, but whichever power-ful ruler leads your folk. If that's all right with you, sir.'

This is entirely the wrong way to speak to spiders.

For a long time the spider's huge red eyes simply regarded Bingo. The soddit could see his own face, smeared through a weird arc, twice over, looking back at himself.

Then the spider said: 'Well, in the first instance, I

might question your automatic assumption I am a man
– I might, I say, ask that, were it not patently the case
that your assumption is grounded in a gender essential-
ism, an unreconstructed masculinism and phallogo-
centric privileging of the male. As it happens I *am* a
male, but my gender is of no political relevance.'

Bingo didn't really follow this. 'Ah,' he said. 'Good.'

'And in the *second* instance,' the spider continued,
'your whole statement is premised on the idea that our
collective is hierarchically governed by a fascist-style
dictatorial monarchical individual, and would be insulting were it not so patently an archaic hangover from an
exploded ideological practice to become almost post-
modern in its irony.'

Bingo tried to digest this, but it sat uncomfortably in
his mind like raw eggs in a queasy stomach. 'Exactly,'
he said uncertainly.

The spider, far from mollified, seemed to become
more furious. 'If that isn't *typical* of your pin-eyed,
scrawny, running-dog, web-destroying imperialistic
lackey-mentality enemies of the eight-legged working
classes,' he said, and lumbered away.

'Where's he going?' asked Frili.

'Off to get his leader,' said Bingo chirpily. 'I think. I'll
do a quick parley and get us out of here.'

But one hour turned to two, and Bingo came to the
conclusion that the spiders were going to leave the

party dangling there until they died. 'Do you suppose,' he asked Frili, 'they intend to eat us?'

'Unless they intend using us as festive decorations,' the dwarf returned.

Bingo pondered.

'Mori!' he called. 'Mori! We must get through to Gandef. He can save us with one of his magic spells! He can save us.'

'Your optimism is touching, my lad,' returned Mori. 'If misplaced. But, bach, I'll have a go.'

The wizard was sleeping. How he could sleep at a time like this was beyond Bingo's comprehension. But sleeping he was. Mori shouted and yelled, but no sound penetrated the wizard's ear. 'It's as I said, boyo,' the dwarf called. 'He's deaf as a rugby ball.'

'Wait a mo,' said Bingo.

He stretched out his free right hand and grasped as many leaves as he could. Using his muscles in ways he had not used them before, he pulled with all his might, and slowly his bound pendant body began to move in an arc, a little away from the proximate body of Frili and a little into the air. He hauled. Sweat came. He moaned with the effort, and hauled some more. When he was perhaps forty degrees from the perpendicular, he let go. Swinging back to his former position he collided, breath-removingly, with Frili. Frili grunted in surprise but did not move; nor did Failin, On, Thorri,

Gofur nor Mori. But Gandef, at the far end of the row, was propelled suddenly into the air.

'Eh?' he said, popping awake. He swung up, paused, swung down and Bingo felt himself jerked up again. 'Quick,' he squealed. 'Gandef! Help!'

Swing up, pause, swing down, clack.

A moment later Gandef's crotchety voice could be heard. 'Liberties! Hey! Wo-oh!'

Swing up, pause, swing down, clack.

Bingo's third swing upwards attracted the attention of the spiders. They came nimbly hurrying over branch and thread to stop the motion. 'What are you doing? Stop that!' they said, grabbing both Bingo and Gandef with their powerful forelegs and halting the swinging motion. 'Dangle good,' they abdured.

'We demand to speak to somebody in authority,' squealed Bingo. 'Or it'll be the worse for you! One of our number is a mighty wizard – he will enchant you! Let us go, I warn you.'

The nearest spider's great red globe eyes were unreadable. They stared at the soddit, and all the party. 'Which of you is the wizard?'

'What?' shouted Gandef, abruptly and crossly awake. 'What was all that commotion? Why can't a wizard have a little nap?'

'Gandef!' shouted Bingo. 'Do something!'

'Your hearing spell!' yelled the dwarfs.

'Why can't I move my arms?' the wizard complained. 'Why is everybody mumbling? Is this some kind of dumb show?'

Several spiders clustered around the wizard.

'Ah!' said Gandef, fixing one with a stern glance. 'Is that you, Mori?'

Bingo's heart sank.

'A pie, I think,' said the wizard meditatively. 'A liver pie. And for desert, a cherry pie. In fact, to save time, just bring me a liver and cherry pie.'

'So,' said one of the spiders. 'This is your wizard, you say? He seems a little blind. And a little deaf.'

'A little,' Mori conceded. 'But you don't want to get him riled, believe me.'

'We have,' this spider announced, retreating to a slightly higher bough to address the whole group, 'had a discussion concerning your fate in the Committee Ordinary, which requires a simple majority for its decision, although the final motion may have to be ratified in a higher forum with a two-thirds threshold.'

The dwarfs and the soddit had fallen silent. All except Gandef, who was singing, '*Fair and fair, and twice so fair, as fair as any may be, the fairest shepherd on our green, a love for any lady*' in a warbly voice.

'Our dilemma,' the spider announced, 'has to do with an earlier motion of solidarity with the bearded-oppressed of the world, passed during the spring session of the General Council of Working Spiders last year. Clearly your wizard, and you dwarfs, fall into this category. Can we assume that you too have experienced oppression and struggled under the hammer of anti-beardist antagonism?'

'Oh yes,' said the dwarfs.

'And that you have never been tempted, basely, to remove you beards and ape the imperialist decadence of smooth skin?'

'Oh no,' said the dwarfs, in unison.

'It may be possible,' said the spider, 'to rehabilitate you. Our workshops may be able to knit you artificial limbs, four for each of you, to wear about your torsos. And we do have certain ocular accessories, fashioned with red glass, that you could wear. But your eighth member, the beardless one . . .'

Everybody turned to look at Bingo.

'. . . his clothing and his lamentably smooth face would condemn him, even if his crypto-feudal vocabulary had not already done so. *Is* he a dwarf? We've not seen his like before.'

There was a certain amount of confusion amongst the dwarfs at this. 'No,' cried some. 'Yes!' cried others. 'Certainly he is!' bellowed Mori.

The spiders conferred.

'We are not convinced,' said the lead spider. 'It seems to us that either he is the odd one out, and that the rest of you are comrades-in-beards (perhaps he is a ninth-columnist,[5] a spy sent amongst you), or else – and this is as yet undetermined – you are all of the same party, pin-eyed insurgents, enemies of the workers, and that all your beards are false.'

'Nonsense!' bellowed Mori, his tightly wrapped body twisting a little on its thread. 'None of our beards are falsies, look you! Tug away, tug away on any of our beards, and you'll find nothing but good working-class facial hair. None,' he added, 'of your bourgeois false beards here.'

A smaller spider, with a slightly speckled belly and back, twitched forward. 'I'll take you at your word comrade,' he said, and scurried sideways until he was directly in front of Gandef.

'Ah, Bongo,' said Gandef, his eyes twirling. 'You know what I hate? "Howdy doody". Ridiculous phrase.'

'What,' said the spider, 'is it saying?'

'Nothing,' said Mori hurriedly. 'He – eh – had a knock on the head, and his wits are a little disordered.

---

[5] This is the equivalent of what a cockroach would call 'a seventh columnist', and a centipede a 'hundred-and-first columnist'. That humans call such individuals 'fifth columnists' has led many in the animal world to argue that we have, deep down, simply not accepted our bipedalism, and secretly we want to crawl around on all fours.

The Soddit

But they're still to-the-core proletarian wits, even in their disarranged state.'

'If you cut a hole in the top of a turnip,' observed Gandef, 'you can put a candle in there.'

'Test his beard!' called the spiders further back.

The spider in front of Gandef reached out a forelimb, and grasped Gandef's luxurious grey beard.

'Oi!' objected the wizard.

The spider yanked down. Gandef's beard came away in his claw.

Bingo gasped.

The bald, liver-spotted chin of the old man waggled in the breeze. 'Chilly,' he declared. 'What happened to my beard? Is that it there?'

The spiders had huddled together in a conference. One of them scurried along the length of the bound and dangling dwarfs, tugging on each of their beards in turn. None other instance of dwarfish facial hair was removable. After further discussion the lead spider turned to address the group.

'We have decided on clemency,' it announced. 'We shall eat most of you, and lay eggs in the beardless ones.' With this they scurried away.

'Oh dear,' said Frili, after a while.

'I don't understand,' pressed Bingo. 'What happened? Why was Gandef wearing a false beard?'

~ 167 ~

'He wasn't wearing a false beard,' snapped Mori.

'Then why did his beard come away in the spider's claw? Was it magic?'

'No,' said Mori. 'Simply a sign of ageing, look you.'

'I don't understand,' repeated Bingo.

'When you get older,' Mori explained wearily, 'sometimes you lose your hair. Humans and soddits sometimes lose their head hair. Wizards – eh, um, they sometimes lose their beard hair.'

'But all at once? In a great clump?'

'They're strange that way,' Mori mumbled. 'Wizards.'

'This is daft,' said Bingo. 'Something's wrong. This doesn't make sense. There's something you're not telling me. In fact, there's a whole range of things you're not telling me.'

'It hardly matters now,' said the dwarf. 'We're to be eaten. You're to have eggs laid in you. And so we come to our sticky end. Dew.'

Bingo was silent for a while. He was trying, with his free hand, to force apart the thick strands of spider silk at his waist and flip his fingers inside his waistcoat pocket. 'Things may not be beyond all hope,' he announced. 'When I was underneath the Minty Mountains, I – chanced – upon a Thing®. A magic Thing® in fact. Perhaps it can help us.'

This caused a great stir amongst the dwarfs. Or, to be

precise, it caused them to stir as much as was possible, which, given that they were all bound extremely tightly by spider silk, was not very much.

'Why didn't you tell us about this before?' Mori demanded.

'I was shy,' said Bingo.

'Shy*ster*,' retorted Failin, 'more like.'

'Shy – like a fox,' opined Gofur, with disgust in his voice.

'I wanted to keep it to myself, that's all,' insisted the soddit. 'But it is definitely a magic Thing®. Sollum was awfully keen to get it back. Murderously keen. Maybe it can help us out of this pickle.'

'Can you get it out of your pocket?' asked Frili, wriggling to try and rotate himself so as to see Bingo better.

'It's tricky,' said Bingo, squeezing his fingers into a spike and thrusting them between the tight cables. He could, just about, get his forefinger and middle finger through. Indeed, he was a luckier soddit than he knew: his spider captor had freed him from the sticky thread that he had mistaken for a swinging forest creeper by smearing a chemical desolvent over his hand and arm. Some traces of this remained on his skin, or else his right hand would have stuck fast to the threads and he would have been trapped. As it was, the tightness of his bonds meant that he could barely reach inside his pocket with two fingers, and could tantalisingly only *just* touch the Thing® inside.

'Wait a mo,' he said.

'Hurry,' said Mori. 'I can see the spiders through the leaves. I think they're gathering their eggs.'

Bingo scissored his two fingers, and felt the Thing® jiggle around at the bottom of his pocket. He tried several times to cup his forefinger nail underneath it and scoop it round, but it kept slipping away. A grotesquely obese purple-grey spider clambered past them on his way somewhere else. Bingo's heart was thudding.

'Almost,' he said.

He tried bending one of his fingers in line with the normal action of a knuckle, and bending the other finger in the opposite way, so as to produce a finger pincer. But such finger distortions are achievable only by guitar players, and Bingo was no such person.

'Almost,' he said.

Then, with another little tip of luck, the Thing® slipped into place between his two fingers. He drew it out very slowly, easing it past the confining threads, and when it was clear he closed it into the palm of his hand.

'Let's have a look,' urged Frili.

Bingo held up the Thing®.

'Ooo!' said the dwarfs. Even those who couldn't see it. 'Ooo!'

'Do you know how it works?' Bingo asked. 'Do you know what it is? When I was trapped under the Minty Mountains it helped me orient myself. I don't know how, but it seemed to help me run faster, and helped me run in the right direction.'

'This is one of the famous Things® of Sharon,' said Mori, in a hushed voice. 'The feats you speak of are the least of its accomplishments. The Evil Sharon made it in the mighty workshop of Dumb, and it has been long lost to—'

'Never mind that now,' interrupted Bingo. 'Do you know *how it works*? They'll be back to lay eggs in me any minute now. Is there something I can do with it?'

'All right, boyo, all right,' said Mori in a sulky voice. 'I was only giving you some of the background, la. It's a powerful Thing®, is that. Powerful magic.'

'Do you know how it *works*, though?'

'Well,' said Mori, turning the word from something uttered in a brief moment to something spoken over several seconds. 'No,' he concluded finally.

'I do,' said a small voice.

'Well that's no use to us, is it?' snapped Bingo. 'Why didn't you say so right at the beginning instead of – hold on, hold on, who said that?'

There was silence.

'Me,' said the small voice.

'Who?'

'Thorri,' said the voice, even smaller.

'You know how it works?' asked Mori incredulously. '*How* do you know how it works?'

'It'th jutht one of the thingth that we Kingth have to know about,' said Thorri.

'Well?' prompted Bingo.

'It hath many functionth,' said Thorri. 'The evil Tharon who forged it built many magic athpects into the devithe. But the motht important one is itth powerful magic of oppothed reverthibility.'

'Of what?'

'Of,' Thorri repeated in a still smaller voice, 'oppothed reverthibility.'

'OK,' said Bingo. 'Never mind what it's called. How does it work?'

'You thpeak your wordth *through* the Thing®,' said Thorri. 'And it will make the *reverth* of your wordth the truth.'

'The reverse of my words?' asked Bingo.

'But it mutht be a thtatement!' urged Thorri. 'Don't uthe the Thing® to make a conventional wish – it will only reverthe the wish and make it the thing you wish for *leatht* in the whole world. A thimple statement. The thpiders are coming!'

'The spiders are coming,' echoed Bingo. But Thorri was only speaking the truth. The spiders were indeed marching towards them, and with them were some egg-stocked females with uncomfortably determined expressions on their spider faces.

'Well, here goes,' said Bingo. He brought the Thing® up to his mouth, and spoke directly through it. 'The spiders are coming,' he said.

And, as soon as he finished saying it, the spiders were marching in exactly the opposite direction, determinedly hurrying away from the party.

'Blimey,' said Bingo.

But this was a weak spell. As soon as the spiders realised they were going in the wrong direction they stopped, slightly puzzled, turned their fat bodies around on their eight legs, and started making their way back towards them.

This – although Thorri didn't have time to explain the point – is the other important thing about the magic Thing®. Its magic does indeed consist in reversing the truth value of statements spoken through it, but its magic *also* depends on the subtle balance of all the magic force in the whole world. It is not infinitely capable. If one were to speak something huge enough through the device – say, 'The earth goes around the sun' – it might very well exhaust its magic in trying to make the reverse true. As it happens, in the many thousands of years since it was made its magic had waned considerably. When it was fresh from Sharon's workbench, it might, just perhaps, have had the magic power to spin the sun around the earth, with all the cataclysmic consequences of that action. But now, separated from its creator for so long, it could come nowhere near achieving so massive a reversal. Instead it would do the best, or the worst, it could. It might reverse the direction of the earth's orbit – such that the earth *comes* around the sun – or it might (if even that required too much magic power) simply fuse, close down, break, and its magic would drain out of it. Accordingly it was to be used with extreme caution: the unwary user might break it, or might do themselves, or the whole world, great damage.

Bingo, of course, did not realise any of this.

The spiders were now hurrying back. They did not look happy.

Bingo lifted the Thing® to his mouth a second time.

There is one final quality of the Thing® which it is worth mentioning, and that is the way it embodies the perverse wickedness of its creator's imagination. A statement usually has several possible opposites. The Thing® tends to choose the one most likely to do mischief, in accord with its creator's particular and warped perspective of the world.

Had Bingo spoken the sentence, 'I wish I were free' through the Thing®, it would have made the opposite true, such that Bingo did not wish to be free, was happy to be a captive and welcomed the fate the spiders had in store. Had he said, 'I wish I were a captive', then he would have found nothing changed – the Thing® would have been happy with the world as it found it, a world in which Bingo did *not* wish he were a captive. But let us assume that Bingo was wise enough to follow Thorri's advice, and to speak only declarative statements, rather than wishes, through the Thing®. Let us say he had uttered the phrase, 'We are captives'. Then the Thing® could have chosen to free the dwarfs, the wizard and the soddit. But it could, just as well and more likely, have chosen to interpret 'we' as meaning all the captives in all the prisons of the world; or as meaning only Bingo and the spiders; or as meaning anything its perverse magic imagination liked. It is a truth that applies to all magic devices, and applies to the Thing® above all: one must phrase one's wishes *very carefully indeed* when one uses such objects.

In the event, Bingo's imagination dried up at the vital moment. He saw the approaching spiders. He racked his brains to think of a sentence that, reversed, would have meant the spiders were permanently moving away from him, but he could not. And the beasts were almost upon them.

'Thay what you thee!' urged Thorri.

Bingo spoke. 'Spiders,' he said, 'are eight-legged creatures.'

All the approaching spiders collapsed. Many fell

from the trees to the ground far beneath. Some
happened to fall upon tangles of boughs, or net-like
webs; but they could not rouse themselves.

It took a while for Bingo to see what had happened.
The giant spiders that had threatened them in so dire a
fashion were no longer eight-legged creatures. They
were now single-legged creatures with eight bodies.
Their eight bodies were linked together at the neck
and the abdomen but were otherwise distinct, with
eight separate stomachs, blood supplies and other internal organs. The creatures looked like monumental
clusters of grapes with a single, flexing leg, helplessly
stuck in the position in which they fell.

It was in this fashion that the Thing®'s magic
worked.

'Hurrah!' called the dwarfs. Bingo cheered.

'Now, boyo,' urged Mori. 'Use the device to get us
out of these bonds.'

'Be very careful *indeed*,' insisted Thorri. 'If you allow
any loophole at all, any leeway of interpretation, then
the Thing® will uthe it to our detriment. Believe me, it
ith an *extremely dangerouth* devithe.'

'Why don't I just say,' Bingo suggested, clutching the
Thing® tightly in his fist, ' "We are tied up"? That
might release us.'

'Or it might rethult in uth being tied *down*,' said
Thorri. 'No. Thay thith: "The cordth binding my-

thelf, the thix dwarfth and the wizard to my left are *thticky*." '

'The cords,' repeated Bingo, speaking through the Thing®, 'binding myself, the six dwarfs and the wizard to my left are sticky.'

The cords flew off them, imbued instantly with a powerful repulsive power. It was so fierce that several of the dwarfs suffered nasty rope burns. And the suspending cords leapt from their branches, dropping the party through the canopy of leaves to the forest floor beneath. Most of them fell on the prone octo-bodies of fallen spiders and bounced clear. A few of the dwarfs landed on the forest floor, but dwarfs are tough creatures and none of them suffered permanent dam-age, except Frili who landed awkwardly on his ankle. Gandef went limp as a baby in the fall and was unhurt, if rather annoyed. Bingo landed on a comfortable pile of dead leaves.

The eight-bodied spiders spat thread at the party, and tried to reach them with their single remaining leg, but good luck was on the side of the dwarfs, and they mustered and hurried away from the spiders' territory in quick order, hauling the complaining Frili after them.

They passed many multi-bodied spiders lying on the ground, and took care to skirt round the creatures. Some of the prone beasts called after them pitiably, speaking in weird, eight-tracked voices, 'Hhhhhhhhelp! Helppppppp!' But the company hurried on.

Finally, when they had left the mass of deformed spiders far behind, they paused and gathered together in a group.

'Give me the Thing®!' urged Frili. 'Give it to me – just for a moment.'

'And you'll do what with it?' asked Bingo.

'I'll use it to stop my damn leg hurting, boyo,' said the dwarf.

But Bingo was starting to become wise to the ways of the Thing®. 'And how will you do that?'

'I'll say "my ankle is hurting",' snapped the dwarf. 'It's nothing but the truth, see.'

'And then it'll stop your ankle hurting,' said Bingo. 'Or, maybe, it'll make every part of you hurt *except* your ankle.'

Frili grumbled, but said nothing more.

'I took a chanthe,' said Thorri, 'in formulating thuch a long thentence, back there. The betht polithy is to keep it brief and thimple. The more wordth there are for the Thing® to work with, the more mithchief it can wreak.'

'Well let's think it through,' said Mori. 'Why don't we, look you, say something like "we are in the forest". That's plain and easy, don't you think? Then the Thing® would make it so that we're *out* of the forest.'

'I think I begin to understand how it works,' said Bingo, looking at the device. 'Yes, it might do that, but if it did it would surely put us outside the forest on the wrong side, just to be cussed. Or, if it wanted to, perhaps it would reverse the statement in a different way – it might make it that instead of us being in the forest, the *forest* was in *us*.'

'Pff!' said Mori. 'That doesn't mean anything, bach.'

'Perhaps,' Bingo continued, 'by ripping us to a million bloody fragments and positioning them in an unbroken line all around the forest perimeter.'

Everybody was silent for a while.

'We should use this Thing®,' Bingo said, 'only as a very last resort. A *very* last resort.'

'Well thpoken,' said Thorri.

And, indeed, it was. In fact, although Bingo did not know it, the Thing® had used a great deal of its magical potency up. When the soddit had said, 'Spiders are eight-legged creatures', it had made *every single spider in the world*, large or small, into eight-bodied, single-legged creatures. This had required a great deal of magic, of course, and was to have dire consequences for much of Upper Middle Earth in the years that followed – flies breeding unchecked, locusts ravaging crops, infestations everywhere. But this is in the future, and it is not the business of this tale to relate it.

Drunk Dwarves

Chapter Seven

BARRELS OUT FOR THE LADS

༓

Fortunately for the party, the Thing® had a number of other features built into it in addition to its power of reversal. Amongst these was a compass, and this told them which direction was due east. They struck off, taking turns to carry the complaining Frili.

'I'm worried about Gandef,' Bingo told Mori as they trudged along. 'He's not as coherent as he used to be.'

'Difficult to deny that, laddo,' said Mori.

The wizard was waving his hands through the air in front of him as he walked. As Bingo watched, it became apparent that the right hand had acquired, in Gandef's mind, the ability symbolically to represent an eagle, and the left hand a dragon. These two imagined creatures were, it seemed, engaged in an aerial fight. When the 'eagle' swooped, Gandef made swooping eagle noises, 'Wheeh! Ach! Ach! Neeeaaoow!' When the 'dragon' turned and flew, the wizard went, 'Ggrrrrr!'

'What's happened to him?'

'Like I said in the forest,' replied the dwarf. 'He's getting older.'

'But he's useless like this,' Bingo pointed out. 'He's supposed to be coming along to guide and protect us, isn't he? But he can't do either of those things in his present state. Do you think he'll get better?'

'I think he'll get,' said Mori, peering through the trees ahead, 'different,' he concluded. 'Let's camp here tonight.'

They were all ravenously hungry, but despite an hour's foraging in the woods for mushrooms or tasty small creatures, they could find nothing to eat. The whole group sat in a circle and debated whether it was safe to use the Thing® to try and conjure up some food. Bingo opposed the whole idea, but his stomach was so empty it was mewing. He felt as though he had spent a month eating nothing but ozone. The dwarfs were insistent that food was a necessity, not a luxury, right now, and that the Thing® was the way to create it, and eventually they began to wear down Bingo's opposition. 'We'll pick the phrase carefully,' they said, and proposed and rejected several drafts before deciding on, 'There is not a small pile of food in front of me.'

Steeling himself, Bingo spoke the sentence through the Thing®. Nothing happened. He examined the device closely, wondering if it were broken, or its magic exhausted, until Mori, making what seemed an obeisance at the soddit's feet, reported that there was indeed a small pile of food on the forest floor. 'We might serve it on the head of a pin, la,' he said.

'I really, really think we shouldn't use the Thing® any more,' Bingo announced, tucking it away in one of his waistcoat pockets. The dwarfs immediately started complaining. 'What about,' suggested Gofur, 'trying, "there is not a large pile of food in front of me"?' But – as Bingo observed – this phrase might very well result in the appearance of a pile of food large enough to crush them all to death. 'And given the choice of being squashed to death by fried eggs and pineapples and mangetouts on the one hand,' he declared, 'and going to sleep hungry on the other, I choose the latter.'

Grumbling, the dwarfs agreed.

The party settled down to sleep.

Bingo was woken by shouting.

'Hey!' Mori was calling, scrambling to untangle himself from his own beard (in which, of course, he slept). 'Hey! Frili! Put that down, boyo!'

Blurry-eyed, it took Bingo a moment to realise what had happened. Frili had not been sleeping. Presumably infuriated by the pain in his ankle, he had pulled himself over the ground to where Bingo lay, and had prised the Thing® from the soddit's pocket. Now he was sitting a little way away, hunched over the device.

'Bingo-boy,' Mori called. 'Stop him! Double quick!'

Bingo lurched forward, calling out, 'Frili! No!' But it was too late. Frili was speaking into the Thing®.

'My ankle hurts,' he said, 'and *nothing* else.'

Instantly it was true to say that Frili's ankle no longer hurt. At the same instant it was the case that *something else* was true. The something else was hideous, ghastly, and – over a period of thirty seconds or so – fatal to the gasping, writhing dwarf.

It was unspeakable.[1]

The group was silent for many minutes.

'Nobody,' said Bingo fiercely, snatching the Thing® from Frili's cold and deformed hand, 'is to use this device any more. Do we understand one another? Is it understood?'

They all mumbled their agreement. Except, that is, for Gandef who declared that 'Seed cake is never the tastiest unless there's owt to wash it down'. Nobody asked him what he meant by *owt*.

They buried Frili, digging a shallow dint in the forest floor with their breastplates. By the time they had finished, dawn was seeping through the forest canopy. Nobody felt like sleeping anyway. They gathered themselves and trudged east again.

❧

[1] Which is why I'm not speaking of it. You'd probably worked that out for yourself, hadn't you?

Within a few hours the trees began to thin. The sound of flowing water became audible. Half an hour after that the group came to a clearing, which is to say a ring of clear ground with a fat oak tree in the middle. Gandef started trotting round and round this tree, laughing, but the remaining dwarfs and Bingo were too weary and hungry to chase him. Past the last singleton trees, the group trudged over open fields, drawing the beardless wizard after them by tugging on his poncho.

Soon they came in view of a large rectangular-faced building standing beside the rushing river. Its large gateway was shut and barred, and a painted sign hung above with the legend 'Sottish And Brewcastle', and beneath it in smaller letters, 'Wheer's Beer? Near!'

'A brewery,' announced Mori.

'A dwarf,' Bingo said, 'stating the bleeding obvious.'

The two of them scowled at one another.

'Now, now, ladth,' said Thorri, stepping between them. 'Let'th not fight. Where there'th beer there'th corn and barley. Where there'th corn and barley we can eat something. Pluth, jug of foaming wouldn't go down badly either.'

'Sire,' said Mori. 'You speak the truth.'

'Thertainty I thpreak tho. Thince I'm thaddled with the crown. It'th thevere, but it'th no more than'th ecthpected,' replied Thorri.

Mori looked at him, with a tired and vaguely puzzled

expression, but then shook his head as if to say he couldn't be bothered to work that out. Instead he stepped to the front door and hammered on it with his fist.

After a while a small portal slid open at man height. 'Who's there?' came a clogged voice. 'Wha'? Who's that?'

Mori summoned Failin and On rapidly, and had them lift him on their shoulders. 'Sir!' he called. 'Here.'

The face that peered through the slot in the gate was coloured a kind of sunset purple-red, and its nose was lumpen and coral-like. Little eyes, like lower-case letters '*o*', flicked from side to side, up and down, and finally registered the dwarf. 'Oh,' said the face. 'Who are you?'

'Dwarfs,' said Mori.

'Are you the glee?' asked the gatekeeper.

Mori didn't hesitate. 'Certainly we are,' he declared.

'Hold up, I'll let you in.'

The portal slid shut, and the noise of somebody with a slight cough shuffling about on the other side of the gate was audible. A noise suggested that a timber beam was being slowly withdrawn from some boltish location. 'Why did you say we were the glee?' Bingo hissed as this went on. 'What's a glee anyway?'

'I've no idea, boyo,' said Mori. 'But it's getting us inside, isn't it?'

The gate creaked open about a yard. 'In you come then,' sniffed the gatekeeper. He was, now that all of him was visible, a creature who could have with justice declared to the world, had he been so minded, 'Behold the man that beer made'. His belly was almost perfectly spherical; his legs as thin as creepers; the skin on his hands and neck was florid, and the skin of his face was florida.[2] He sniffed repeatedly as he spoke, a sort of *whhsht* noise made on an indrawn breath.

'Come on, I haven't *whhsht* got all day,' he said. '*Whhsht.*'

The dwarfs and the soddit scurried inside, drawing the wizard after them.

'Thank you, good sir,' said Mori.

'We was beginning to wonder,' the gatekeeper said, pushing the great door shut behind them, 'if you lot was, *whhsht*, coming. Derek!' he shouted. 'Derek! The glee's here.'

'About time,' returned a bellowing voice from the darkness.

The dwarfs lined up, turning their broad smiles upwards at the gatekeeper. He was, in turn, looking down, although without a smile. Indeed, his face was bulbous with suspicion.

'So this is the glee, is it?' he said. 'Six dwarfs and some old codger?'

'I assure you sir,' said Mori, tugging the hem of the

---

[2] Sorry. This should be 'florider', obviously; the sense being 'more florid' rather than, say, 'resembling a man's member'. But these errors will creep in.

gatekeeper's shirt, where it depended from the curve of his moon-shaped belly. 'I assure you that we are indeed the glee of which you speak. Glee is us. We are glee. Oh yes. If it's glee you want, then we're the dwarfs to give it you. Glee glee glee.'

The gatekeeper stared down with his disconcertingly umlaut eyes.

'Glee,' Mori added. And then, 'Oh yes.'

'You'd better, *whhsht*, come through,' said the gate-keeper, turning and falling into a loping gait.[3] The party trailed along behind him. They passed through the wood-ceilinged entrance room, and into a much larger hall behind. Large copper vats lined both walls, and a yeasty, soapy, gunky, gooey sort of smell was very evident. Another man, of similar stomach proportions and with a similarly purple-red face, was standing on a little stepladder at one of these vats.

'Derek,' called the gatekeeper. 'Here's your glee.'

Derek stepped slowly down the ladder and shuffled over the floor towards them. His eyes, in contrast to the gatekeeper's, were large and enormously protuberant, like two white boils with blue heads. He wiped his nose in a distinctive manner, by rubbing the palm of his

---

[3] You won't believe this. In the first edition the printers misprinted this as 'loading gate', which gave the sentence an, I feel, unnecessarily slapstick feel. Printers? Misprinters, more like. (Not you Gerald 'the Type' Weedon, you're all right. It's all the rest of them.)

hand directly upwards over the nostrils, moving it from chin to crown in one smooth movement, something like a salute. Years of this practice had bent his nose snub, like a fat tick marking approval of his face.

'A bunch of dwarfs and an old geezer?' he said, with a thinly veiled incredulity.

'I'm not a dwarf,' said Bingo.

'This is not what the agency promised,' said Derek. It seemed as if his eyes could swivel through a surprisingly wide range of movements: they looked at the wall, the ceiling, the other wall and back at the party again. 'A load of dwarfs? What kind of glee is that?'

'The best kind,' said Mori firmly.

'Dancing girls,' said Derek, 'is what they promised. Dancing girls and a prestidigitator. You lot aren't girls.'

'He is,' said Mori, pointing to Bingo. 'And he,' indicating Gandef, 'is the greatest expert at pressing digits in the world today.'

Derek looked unconvinced.

'No, really,' said Mori. 'Surely you've heard the name? Gandef the digit man?'

'Never heard of him,' said Derek. 'And never heard of you lot neither.'

'*Whhʃht,*' added the gatekeeper.

'Now, don't have a *go,*' said Derek, turning on his fellow.

'I didn't say anything,' said the gatekeeper.

'I know what you're thinking,' said Derek in a hurt tone. 'But I tell you, I'll organise this glee *proper*, if it's the last thing I do.'

'And it will be the last thing you do,' observed the gatekeeper, 'if Al the Ale finds out you've messed it up.'

'Messed up what?' Derek asked, casting his eyes about. 'Nothing's messed up. Here's the glee, just like I was deputised to organise. Come on lads, and, uh, miss.' He wiped his hand over his nose again. 'Through here.'

'We were wondering,' said Mori, as he trotted beside Derek. 'Are refreshments included in the, eh, perquisites? Of the, the, the glee, you see?'

'Refreshments,' said Derek. 'Beer.'

'Ah, excellent. And – food?'

'Beer,' said Derek, 'is food. How do you think I got this belly?' His perfectly spherical eyes swivelled down to look at his perfectly spherical stomach.

'Excellent,' said Mori. 'Excellent. So there isn't any, I don't know, chicken? Bread? Potatoes?'

'Beer,' said Derek.

'So,' concluded Mori. 'To sum up. Just beer, then?'

'Beer,' said Derek. 'Here you go.'

They had arrived in a long hall. Great stacks of barrels were stacked along the walls. Other stacks of barrels were visible, neatly stacked, just behind these stacks.

'I'll go get Al the Ale,' said Derek. 'And the rest of the lads. You do your turns here,' he added, indicating a vague area of floor. 'We'll be over there.' He nodded at two long, benched wooden tables. On each table stood a line of tapped barrels. Empty jugs and earthenware beakers were littered everywhere.

Mori hurried to one of the barrels and knocked it with his fist. Then he tried another, and another. 'Beer,' he said. 'They're all filled with beer. There's not *one* filled with soup.'

The dwarfs were running around the hall, examining the tables, rapping barrels with their knuckles. 'Isn't there any solid food?' Gofur asked. 'Not, see, that I *mind* a quick beer, but I could do a chicken stew, la.'

'Or a beef stew,' said On.

'Or a vegetable stew, even,' said Gofur.

'Or jutht,' said Thorri, 'a vegetable. Even a thmall one.'

But there wasn't so much as a crumb. It began to dawn on the party that the employees of this brewery ate and drank nothing but beer.[4]

---

[4] There are, of course, three stages. The first is when you finish a half-pint of lager with your lunch by smacking your lips and saying, smugly, 'Very nice'. The second is when you're out to the pub most evenings of the week, and you find yourself admiring a fellow drinker because he can open his throat and drop a pint in seconds where it takes you a dozen gulps. The third stage is the final one: you drink nothing but beer; you brush your teeth at night and rinse your mouth afterwards with beer; you keep a glass of beer on your bedside table in case you need to moisten your mouth in the night; you replace the tea in your teabags with hops, and you start saying things like, 'We have nothing to beer but beer itself' and 'Beer — beer is my ally'.

'I'm ravenous,' complained Bingo. 'And what is a glee? What are we supposed to do?'

'Play along with it,' said Mori. 'Follow my lead. Is that sawdust on the floor?'

'Yes.'

'Only I wondered if it was oats or something.' He sighed.

'Is there any food under that trapdoor?' asked Bingo.

Everybody looked at the trapdoor.

Mori went towards it and pulled on its metal ring, opening it a few inches and peering through the gap. 'It leads down into the river,' he reported.

'There might be some fish —' Gofur started saying.

The noise of a large group of middle-aged men could be heard approaching from the far end of the hall. Mori dropped the trapdoor, and the dwarfs hastily arranged themselves into a line as a motley crowd of brewery workers entered. Bingo recognised Derek, and the sniffling gatekeeper. A dozen, or more, men in similar states of physical decrepitude surrounded them: bellies on stilts, ragged purple jowls, high lumpy foreheads and strands of hair plastered over their flaky scalps.

At the front was a larger man. Bingo assumed that this was Al the Ale. Where the others had pot bellies, his was more of a cauldron belly. Where the rest had purple faces and bulbous noses, his face was a deep crimson, overlaid with scarlet broken veins inset into the skin as if in parody of crazy paving. His nose was so enormous, so misshapen and swollen, that it looked as though he had pressed his face against a muslin sack containing several mouldy potatoes, and come away with it as a permanent piece of face furniture. His nose looked like one of Bingo's feet.

'Right,' he said, his voice gravelly to the point of boulders. 'Where's this glee that Derek's organised?'

'Here they are, boss,' said Derek, scuttling alongside him. 'First-class glee, as promised.'

Al stopped and examined the party. 'Dwarfs?' he said. 'And some old geezer?'

'That one's a woman,' said Derek, pointing at Bingo.

Al raked his stare up and down the line of them.

'Right,' he said suspiciously. 'If you've organised it, Derek, then I'll take your word for it. But it'd better be a bloody good glee, or you're in trouble. Hop knows we need some bloody glee around here.' He turned to his men. 'You lot!' The brewers shuffled and looked shifty. 'Get yerselves around that table there. Get yourself comfortable, and *get drinking*.'

A groan rose from the brewers.

'What?' bellowed Al. 'What? Groaning, is it? Get yourself good and proper drunk – I'm not paying you to sit around sober. How can we have a glee if you're sober? Eh? How can we? Larry, I'm looking at *you*.'

'We can't, boss, you're right, boss,' said Larry in a

sulky voice. 'I was drunk at breakfast, boss,' he added hopefully.

'Breakfast?' boomed Al the Ale. 'What you talking about? Boasting, is it? *Twice* as much beer for Larry, everybody, you hear? You'd do best to button your lip, Larry, and concentrate on the drink in hand. Nobody likes a smart-ale,[5] laddo. Breakfast is breakfast, it's in the past and long gone. This, here, is the glee. Derek's organised it, and glee we'll have or it'll be the worse for you. You'll have fun, or I'll bloody well flay each and every one of you.'

Miserably, the brewers sat at the two tables, filled their beakers with beer and started drinking. Foam dribbled down their chins. Some of them gasped after each draught, a sound that resembled the lip-smacking sound a beeraholic makes on finishing his drink, only more despairing.

'Come on, you lot,' shouted Al at the dwarfs, as he manoeuvred his prodigious stomach in between table and bench and reached for a jug of beer himself. 'Let's have it then.'

The dwarfs looked at Mori. Mori looked at Bingo. Bingo tried to look at Gandef, but the wizard had fallen asleep against a barrel behind them.

'Glee!' shouted Al, banging his fist on the table. It

---

[5] Like a smart-alec (or in Wales, a smart-aled), but in a brewery.

was a fist extremely well suited to the business of banging on tables. A meaty and solid fist. 'What are you waiting for?'

Mori stepped forward. 'Good, eh, afternoon, good sirs. We *are* the glee – and I was just wondering – it's a question, see, I ask at all the functions, wherever we're booked in, and the question is: what *kind* of glee would you like? We have so many varieties of glee on offer, you understand.'

Al the Ale stared at Mori. 'What do you mean?' he said, with force. 'What on earth are you talking about? Just *do the bloody glee.*'

'You're the boss, you're the paying customer,' said Mori hurriedly. 'In that case, allow me to introduce the champion glee-er, the most gleeful boyo in the history of glee . . . Binglee Grabbings.' He stepped back into line, and Gofur (standing next to the soddit) gave Bingo a shove.

Bingo stumbled forward. All the brewers were eye-ing him, some of them over the rims of their tankards.

'Right,' said the soddit. 'Some glee. Here goes. A justice of the peace,' he said, ratcheting his voice into a more comical tone by pulling his lips tighter and talking more nasally, 'did ask an old man how old he was, and the old man did reply, "My Lord I am eight and fourscore," to which the justice replied, "Why not fourscore and eight? 'Tis more the customary expression," to which the old man replied, "Because, forsooth, I was eight before I was fourscore." '

He opened his mouth in mock surprise, widened his eyes, threw his arms wide and put his right foot forward.

There was no sound in the hall, except the mournful slurp of somebody drinking beer.

'What,' said Al, his brows contracting like an approaching thunderstorm, 'the *bloody hell*—'

'What's the difference between the sea and vinegar? One's,' Bingo gabbled, 'a beautiful ocean for ships and the other's a beautiful lotion for chips, ta-daa.'

'Songs!' roared Al the Ale. 'Songs, Not Jokes, You Twits!' When he yelled in this manner, the words he spoke were unmistakably capitalised.

'Songs?' asked Bingo.

'Of *course* songs! What kind of glee are you anyway?'

'Oh *songs*,' said Mori. 'Songs! Of course. Of course songs. You want a *singing* glee. Of course you do.'

'What other kind of bleeding glee is there?'

At the far end of the table, one of the brewers belched. He belched again. When he belched a third and fourth time, Bingo realised that he was, in fact, laughing. 'Fourscore and eight!' he said, chuckling lugubriously. 'Eight and fourscore!'

'Shut it, you,' snarled Al. He turned back to the dwarfs. 'Now look, you lot—'

'Certainly we have songs,' said Mori, stepping forward and elbowing Bingo back. 'A song – why not?' He cleared his throat, and began warbling in a strained falsetto.

> *Buttercups and daisies,*
> *Oh, the pretty flowers;*
> *Coming ere the springtime,*
> *To tell of sunny hours.*
>
> *The something-something-something*
> *And something in the trees, um,*
> *Something of the trees, shadow of the trees,*
> *Or – hang-on.*
> *Hang-on.*
> *The dappling, I think it is, from the trees,*
> *And all the summer singing*
> *And sighing in the breeze.*

'That should be,' Mori clarified, 'and all the *springtime* singing, of course. Not summer, see. That was a slip of the tongue.'

Al the Ale was staring at the dwarf open-mouthed.

'I know another,' said Mori hopefully.

'No!' howled Al. 'No! No! No! What kind of miserable, twittering, bleeding song is that?'

'Now,' said Mori in a warning tone, 'there's no need to get personal, boyo.'

'A *drinking* song. A song we can sway our tankards to – you morons, berks, fools. You idiots! You teetotallers! What – who – *Derek*!' This last word was expressed with such volume and such vehemence that even Bingo shut his eyes and screwed up his face. 'Derek!' screamed Al, banging the table repeatedly, making those cups and tankards not in brewers' hands bounce up and down in time to his blows.[6] 'This is the last drinking straw, Derek. You've had your last drink in the last-chance saloon. You've gone too far this time.'

'Boss!' squeaked Derek.

Al the Ale was trying to haul himself up and out of his seat, but his belly seemed to have wedged itself beneath the tabletop. 'You stick where you are, Derek. I'll wring your neck in a minute. Meanwhile, you –' He gestured angrily at the dwarfs. 'I'll wring *more* than your necks. I'll wring your *heads* – one by one.'

He stood up with a loud pop, his belly swooping up and slapping down on the tabletop.

'Each and every one of you,' he bellowed, pointing a fat finger at each of the dwarfs in turn. 'You're done for. That's it. Trying to pass yourself off as a glee? Lads –

---

[6] If I'm completely honest, these cups and tankards bounced up a fraction of a moment *after* the blows rained down, but there's no point in me being prissy or pedantic about a thing like that.

take them and drown each of them in a barrel of beer. Starting,' he added, rotating his pointing arm so that it indicated Bingo, 'with *her*.'

'Now wait just a *moment*, boyo,' said Mori.

But Derek, eager to ingratiate himself with his angry employer, was already halfway across the floor to the soddit. Several other brewers were behind him. The dwarfs, glancing at one another with wild surprise, their hands on their axe shafts, were grabbed by a second cohort of brewers. In a moment the whole party was disabled.

Bingo, squealing and kicking his legs, was carried over to a barrel and held aloft. 'Wait!' he gasped. 'Stop a minute! I know a drinking song! I do!' But it was too late. The lid was off the barrel, and the beer inside, slopping at the very topmost lip, promised a beery death. The soddit was thrust down. Ale spilled over the edge of the barrel and foamed down the side, and in a trice the lid was being nailed back down. Pitiful thumps came from inside, and the barrel rocked a little on its base. Then it went very quiet.

The mass of brewers turned, as one, to deal with the dwarfs.

'Really, boys,' said Mori, 'you don't have to do this—'

'Actually,' said the brewer with his arm around Mori's neck (or thereabouts), speaking directly into the dwarf's ear, 'to tell you the truth, it makes a nice change, drowning people. Normally we just have to drink all day. At least, if we're drowning you lot then we're not drinking.'

'Stop!' said Mori. 'Wait! I've an idea.'

But a second barrel was being prepared, its top levered off. Mori was hoisted up and held over the barrel.

'Stop,' he whimpered.

'Stop,' said somebody else. It was Al the Ale.

The brewers all turned. Al was standing next to the barrel in which Bingo had been drowned. 'There's something fishy about this,' he said. 'Put that dwarf down a mo. Listen to this.' He reached out with a knuckle and rapped the side of the barrel.

It returned an empty noise.

'Get the lid off this,' Al commanded.

When the nails were pincer-squeezed out and the lid removed, Bingo was discovered sitting in the bottom of a dry barrel. His clothes were not even moist. The soddit smiled.

'Lord Hop above,' said Al. 'Malt things bright and beautiful. Blimey.' He peered in again. 'Do you mean to tell me,' he growled, 'that you drank all that beer?'

'Ah,' said Bingo, standing up. His forehead appeared over the lip of the barrel. 'Yes, that's it. That's what I did. Ye-ee-es. Drank it all, that's right. Rather than drown, you see. Besides I was thirsty.'

Al put his head back and laughed. It was a scary sound. He laughed and laughed. 'Now,' he said, when he had his diaphragm under control again, 'that's drinking!' He reached in and lifted Bingo out, hauling him over to the table and pouring him a beaker of beer. 'I have to work with these ninnies, these teetotal beer-avoiders. This dwarf girl could drink any of you under the table!' He laughed again.

'Really,' said Bingo, in a small and slightly nervous voice. 'It was nothing.'

'Nonsense!' bellowed the brewer. 'Lads, release those dwarfs. Have them round this table. Something to celebrate at last. Beer!' he called. 'Beer!'

They drank for hours and hours. They sang many beer songs, amongst which were 'Be-ee-ee-e-eer Is Love?', 'Hit Me Baby, One More Tun', 'Shine On You Crazy Double Diamond Works Wonders' and 'Beer! Beer! Beer!' At one point in the proceedings Mori grabbed Bingo's arm and hissed into his ear, 'I thought you said *no more use* of the *you-know-what*?' and Bingo hissed back, 'It was a life-or-death situation, a risk worth taking', before they were yanked apart by over-affectionate brewers and made to drink more beer. They drank a light wheat beer. Then they drank a beer that tasted like a large jar of Marmite diluted with half a cup of dirty dishwater. Then they drank a beer with a higher alcohol content than whisky.

In a very short time they were drunk.

Despite the fact that only an hour earlier the brewers had tried to drown him, Bingo was now moved to hug these large-bellied men, and tell them the story of his travels in particular detail. The brewers might have become suspicious at how quickly the little soddit became inebriated if they didn't think that he had already downed an entire barrel of beer. When they congratulated him, he grinned stupidly and patted his waistcoat pocket.

In fact, early on in the binge, he thought of a plan: he would wait until the brewers were dead drunk; then he would use the Thing® to sober himself and his comrades up (telling himself, *I'll use it one more time, and that'll be the end of it – no more after this*). Then he and the dwarfs and the wizard could creep away. It seemed, after two jugs of beer, a good plan. After ten jugs of beer it seemed the most brilliant plan in the world, a plan of such cunning and genius that only a superhobbld, a hobbld of all hobblds, could have come up with it. At the same time, he could not remember what the plan was. He could barely remember what his own name was. Nor did he care. In fact his recklessness was dangerous.

'Lemme lemme show you a liddle something,' he told

one of the brewers as they leaned together on the bench. 'Liddle-liddle-something.' He brought out the Thing®.

'What's?' asked the brewer, too drunk to complete the question.

'Issa Thing®, iss.'

'Like,' said the brewer, 'like the Thing® that the Evil Sharon made?'

'Precisely,' said Bingo, after three or four attempts.

The brewer looked at it.

'What's it do?' he said.

'Lemme, lemme show you,' said Bingo, and raised the Thing® to his lips. And there his brain stalled. What had his plan been? It had been a good plan. It had been the best plan. He couldn't remember what the plan was.

'What you doing?' asked the brewer.

'I don't remember,' said Bingo, the words drifting through the Thing®.

And he did remember.

'I am drunk,' he said, slurring the words a little. And, instantly, he was sober.

For a moment, now that he was sober enough to know what he had done, he held his breath. The risk he had taken! Had the Thing® woven some ghastly sting into his sobriety? But moments passed, and everything seemed normal – except that he was as sober as a stone[7]. He was not to realise it until many weeks later, but his physiology had indeed been changed by Sharon's malign magic. He could never be drunk, no matter how much he imbibed. His wished-for sobriety was absolute. He could still have hang-overs if he were to over-indulge alcoholically, but he would never again experience inebriation. But this grim revelation was in the future.

He looked around at the slouching or snoring figures. The dwarfs were starting to drift off into a drunken sleep (and dwarfs can take a lot of drink). The brewers were mostly snoring, including the one Bingo had just been talking to. Al the Ale was lying on his back like a model of a mountain.

Bingo was acutely conscious of a sense of terror. In face he had been feeling that all the way through, but the beer had obscured the sensation. Now that he was more sober than he had ever been, he felt a desperate urgency to get out of this place. They had tried to drown him! Because they hadn't thought his jokes were very funny! And they were classic Soddlesex jokes, too.

He hurried over to Mori, who was asleep in the arms of Thorri, their beards trembling like seaweed in a

[7] Stone-cold sober. Which is to say sober as a *sober* stone. If you've ever seen a drunken stone, for instance at a rockslide or avalanche, you'll know how important the distinction is.

gentle current as they snored. 'Mori!' he hissed in the dwarf's ear. 'Mori! We've got to get out of here! Mori!'

Nothing.

It was the same with the other dwarfs. Gandef too seemed dead drunk. Bingo scurried from supine body to supine body, his anxiety eating at him. He had never felt so acutely aware of the world around him, so anxiously prescient. Any one of these brewers – hardened by a lifetime of drinking – could wake up at any time. Grumpy with hangovers, could they expect mercy from them? Of course not, of course not. He couldn't afford to leave it until the dwarfs woke naturally from their beer slumber. And he couldn't think of a way to wake them sooner.

He took out the Thing® and examined it. But, in his new sober-anxious frame of mind, he could not summon the courage to use it. What if it backfired? What if awful consequences followed?

There was only one thing for it. Bingo examined the stack of barrels closest to the trapdoor. Wooden rails were nailed against the floor planks to guide these barrels to the hole, once a foot-tall wooden wedge was removed from the base of the stack. Thinking fast, and fidgeting as he did so, Bingo tied the beard of Failin to Gandef's ankle. He tied On's beard to Failin's ankle, Gofur's to On's, Thorri's to Gofur, and finally – lugging the bodies of the sleeping dwarfs about, he tied Mori's beard to Thorri's ankle. Then he hauled open the trapdoor. The water whooshed past beneath. They had been drinking all afternoon and all night, and now the pewter-coloured light of dawn tinkled chillily on the fast-flowing water.

'Sorry about this, guys,' he said, hauling the dwarfs and the wizard into a rough pile beside the lip of the trapdoor hole. He sat himself on the top of the snoring, grumbling, breathing mass of dwarf bodies, reached forward with his foot and kicked aside the wedge.

He shut his eyes, but he could hear the tremble of the tumbling barrels as a sort of thunder before the first struck the pile of bodies. There was a sense of jarring movement, a weightless split-second, and then the water was all over him with a great splash. He barely had time to swear before he was tugged under by the flow. Bubbles swarmed around his open eyes, and then he was bobbing on the surface and moving swiftly beneath a grey-glass sky.

Raving, the Insane Bird

Chapter Eight

ON THE DOORSTEP, NOT LITERALLY A DOORSTEP, IT'S A MOUNTAINSIDE ACTUALLY, BUT IT'S A DOORSTEP METAPHORICALLY SPEAKING, IF YOU SEE WHAT I MEAN

They bobbed and floated down the River Sprinting amongst a slick of wood. Barrels twirled and knocked against one another in profusion and great confusion. Even as deep a drunkenness as the dwarfs had acquired was loosened from their consciousness by the sheer chill of the river, and the shock of their sudden immersion; not to mention the surprise and chagrin of discovering themselves chained together by their beards. Mori, with a little more self-possession than the others, scrambled on to a barrel, and the others grabbed passing floats. Bingo himself swam for a while,

~ 211 ~

and then managed to balance himself half-sprawled upon the top of a barrel that was bobbing, iceberg like, mostly underneath the waves. The fact that these barrels were full of beer meant they floated very low in the water.

In this fashion the party proceeded downriver for several hours, as the sun rose ahead of them finding diamonds and splinters of gold in the ever-crinkling wave tops and warming Bingo's face. The landscape on either side reminded the soddit, somewhat, of home: broad fields, wheat and barley on either side of the river, and a deep-breathing wraparound sky above.

'Soddit!' called a dwarf, rolling a barrel under his body like a hamster in a hamster wheel, and not, to judge by the expression on his face, deriving much satisfaction from the exercise, 'Bingo! Help!' It was Gofur, slapping the wood with his hands in increasingly rapid patterns as he struggled to stay above rather than beneath the barrel.

Bingo swam over to him.

'Untie my beard,' Gofur said, 'and my ankle, glub glub glub.' These last three words may not have been attempts at communication, for Gofur had slid off his barrel.

Bingo fished him out of the water, unknotted his beard and untied his ankle. The dwarf was still not happy, but he was able to thrash out and find another barrel. Bingo, feeling like a mother duck, went from dwarf to dwarf, freeing them from their bondage. Finally he swam out to the wizard, but found him perfectly happy, floating on his back and singing a song about a loofah.

He swam over to Mori, who was grumpier than Bingo had ever seen him. The soddit pointed this out.

'I'm drunk and *freezing cold*,' the dwarf retorted. 'Are you surprised I'm unhappy about it? Drunk doesn't *go* with freezing cold. It goes with nice-warm-fire-toast-your-toes-nicely. It goes with lying under a blanket. Drunk and freezing cold makes for an unhappy dwarf. Look you,' he added, and he clearly meant it to sting.

'All right, all right,' said Bingo. Now that he was in the icy water he was finding it rather refreshing. 'We're probably far enough from the brewery now. We can make our way to the bank, climb out, maybe start a fire.'

But as he spoke he noticed that the banks had risen around them from a few feet of mud to several yards of sheer chalk. There was nothing for it but to cling to the barrels and wait until the landscape permitted dis-embarkage.[1]

After a few hours in which the soothing effect of the sound of fast-flowing water was counteracted by the

---

[1] I'm *sure* this is a word. All right, my dictionary doesn't include it – but that just shows the inadequacy of my dictionary. I *know* this is a word. I feel it in my gut.

simultaneous noise of multiple chattering, moaning and complaining dwarfs, the riverbanks started to draw away from them on both sides. Soon after this they floated out into a wide and brimming lake.

This was Lake Escargot, whose waters were silver and whose water snails were the most celebrated luxury in the whole of Upper Middle Earth. The famous town of Lakeside sat on timber stilts alongside the shore. And past this, just visible above the haze of the lake's northern shore, was the Only Mountain, the famed Strebor that Bingo had travelled so far to see.

He noticed that the barrels were starting to drift in different directions, and bestirred himself to round up the crotchety dwarfs. Under his direction they swam to a shingly beach to the south of the rivermouth, Mori and Bingo pulling Gandef after them. When they were all out, some tried to roll themselves in their beards there and then and sleep on the shore. But Bingo, who was tired and sober (instead of being tired and hungover), insisted they march to the bridge that joined Lakeside to the land. 'For once,' he told them, 'I intend to sleep in a proper bed and eat proper food. It's been long enough.'

They followed him, complaining but compliant.[2]

---

[2] That's nice writing! I like that. That's almost poetry, that is. 'Complaining but compliant' – two very different words, you see, that sound fairly alike. There's a name for that in rhetoric, isn't there, but I can't bring it to mind.

The guards on the bridge were only too happy to welcome this bedraggled party into their halls. 'Custom has been down,' they said, 'since the dragon moved into the Only Mountain.'

'Really?' said Bingo, fishing out the entrance fee from Mori's leather purse. 'How long ago did he arrive?'

'Seventy years or so,' said the guard.

Inside Lakeside the exhausted party were almost overwhelmed by the profusion of goods on offer. Shopkeepers who had never seen a customer and who had survived on selling things to other shopkeepers, and on tales of actual customers passed down from their grandparents, crowded around the group, eager to sell them anything and everything. There was a plethora of stalls selling axes, barrels, haunches of venison, wool and such, with extensive boat-parking and mead halls in which the wearied heroic shopper could find refreshment.

'Really,' said Bingo. 'We're just tired and hungry at the moment. Can you direct us to a refreshment house? An inn, with some beds?'

Disappointment was bitter for the majority of shopholders, but the landlady of the Boing Inn was so excited she almost did a dance. 'Actual guests in the inn!' she kept saying, as she led them between the narrow ways of Lakeside. 'Actual guests!'

There was a fire in the inn's front room, and the

dwarfs huddled round it with pathetic eagerness. They devoured plates of porridge, followed by bread and cooked meats, and then they clambered upstairs to fall into complete and unmitigated sleep on top of their beds. Bingo, the last to succumb, thanked the landlady, paid her in advance with some more of Mori's gold, and finally collapsed into dreamless slumber.

The dwarfs and Gandef slept a total of eighteen hours: the dwarfs because they were each sleeping off monstrous hangovers, and Gandef because he seemed to be sleeping all the time these days anyway.

Bingo woke, feeling indescribably refreshed, during the morning of the following day. A plump, short man was sitting on a chair in the corner of his room.

'At last you are awake!' this man announced. 'Our first customers for seventy years! I greet you, sir. You and your courageous dwarf shoppers! You bring new hope to the town of Lakeside of Thurrock.'

'I am delighted to be of service,' said Bingo, remembering his manners. 'And honoured to make your acquaintance, Mr . . . ?'

'Ah,' said the stranger, standing up and clasping the sides of his expansive belly. 'I am Lard, the Bowman. I am, to be straight with you, Mayor of Lakeside.'

'It is indeed an honour,' said Bingo, scrabbling out of bed to be able to bow.

'No – no – I won't stand for it, if you intend to treat me as a somebody,' said Lard with jocular self-effacement. 'It is not long since I was nobody. I'll not subscribe to the cant of fame. I was a lowman until last year, sir, one of the lowest of the low lowman in this town. I was a poet, a bard – can you imagine it? Can you think of a more disgraceful and untouchable social caste? But I have raised myself up by my efforts, and I put aside the miserable trade of poetry for bowmanship. Now I am Lard the Bowman. And I have come to welcome you all personally – personally – to the shops and stalls of Lakeside. Your companions . . . ?'

'They,' said Bingo, glancing at the other beds, 'may sleep yet awhile. Our journey here has been wearying and long.'

'But you *are* here, nonetheless,' said Lard. 'That is the important thing.'

'Your trade has been depressed?' Bingo asked.

'Oh, woe, woe, woe,' agreed Lard, although still with a degree of complacency, as if he were reciting rather than expressing the sentiment. 'Since the wicked dragon Smug took possession of the Only Mountain, our customers have shied away from us. Steered clear. We live under a terrible threat all the time. These are not ideal trading conditions.'

'Yet you have not been tempted to abandon this site, and move your stalls further south?'

'Abandon Lakeside?' said Lard, in horror, or mock-horror it was difficult to tell which, since the sentiment was delivered with a rather puzzling wide-eyed indolence. 'Out of the question. Besides, our patience has been rewarded with *your* arrival. New custom! May you be the first of many!'

'Alas,' said Bingo, 'we were not planning on staying. We are travelling on, as it happens, to the Only Mountain itself.'

'You don't say,' said Lard conversationally.

'Indeed. But in fact, Sir Lard, it may be we can be of service to you and all of Lakeside.'

'Service?' Lard asked, with the air of a man who understood what the requirements of good service entailed.

'Our quest – perhaps I should not be so free with this news, but I see no harm in your knowing – our quest is . . . to slay Smug.' Bingo had long since decided that this must be at least part of their quest, despite the reticence of the dwarfs.

'Really?' said Lard mildly. 'I say. Is that so?' He sat for a while, as if digesting this news. Then he shrugged, and said, 'To do what, sorry?'

'To slay. To kill.'

'Oh! Kill – I *see*,' the Mayor said, in a much more animated manner. 'Well that *is* fantastic news! Fantastic! Fairytaleous! Marvellous! I can only hope that you are successful. If you were to rid us of our curse, then Lakeside could once again blossom as the well-provisioned and convenient one-stop shopping emporium of the eastern wilderness.'

Bingo and Lard talked long on this topic, and by the time the dwarfs awoke (moaning and clutching their heads) the Mayor of Lakeside had agreed to ferry the party up the river to the foot of the Only Mountain in Lakeside's best transit barges.

'It seems you are proving a useful addition to the party after all, Mr Soddit,' said Mori as he munched, hungrily, on some toasted bread for his late breakfast. He had doused his beard in vinegar and wrapped it around his temples to assuage the thumping there, which gave him a slightly peculiar look.

'They will take us directly to the mountain,' said Bingo, 'and provision us. The rest is up to us, they say. I was thinking: perhaps we should leave Gandef here? He would be well cared for, I am sure.'

'Leave the wizard?' barked Mori, jerking his head up so quickly his beard fell down again. 'What are you saying? Of course we can't leave the wizard. Of course the wizard has to come with us. The *very idea* of leaving him!'

'But why? He's not doing anything now much, except sleeping.'

'He must come,' said Mori. And that was that.

The following morning, the dwarfs made a handsomer group than they had for a long time as they stood on one of Lakeside's piers. Their breastplates had been polished, their beards washed and combed, and the holes in their boots expertly mended. Eager-faced lakeside barge operators handed them down into the boats, and pushed off with their poles.

For almost an hour the party simply sat, watching the sun-tickled landscape sliding past. Bingo let his eyes meander. Beasts of herbage stared from the meadows that overlooked the lake. Cranes flew overhead and wheeled around to land on the lake, their gawkiness folding away as they settled themselves, bobbing in the water, to observe the passing boats. In the zenith a tiny cloud seemed to cap the immense blue dome of the sky.

Before them, the conical peak of the Only Mountain rose slowly. At the northern bank of the lake, the bargemen poled their craft up the narrow river that flowed from the sides of the mountain. Before sunset the dwarfs were able to set out a temporary camp on the first upslope. 'We shall leave you here, heroic ones,' said the chief bargeman. 'You can trek the rest of the way easily tomorrow. Good luck in your mighty quest! May your right arms prove strong!' And they departed.

'What on earth,' said Mori, 'did he mean about "right arms"? What was that all about?'

It was strange to think that they had finally arrived at the Only Mountain, after their long, varied and attritional adventures. Dwarfs and soddit breakfasted on hessian-packed bread rolls and miniature cork barrels of orange juice (supplied by the burghers of Lakeside). Afterwards Bingo sat on a broad-topped rock and simply stared up at the mountain. The Minty Mountains had been impressive, but this was some-thing else – a gigantic monument in stone, out of which the morning light was pressing a thousand facets of grey and white: right to left in myriad planes and curves from cinder-coloured, ash, fish-scale, iron, raincloud, to purple and black, streaked and capped higher up with bone-coloured and cream-tinted snow. Many rooks circled in the sky overhead, their cawing as soothing a sound as Bingo had ever heard.

Thorri coughed discreetly at the soddit's side.

'Oh,' said Bingo, who had yet to learn the proper way of speaking with royalty. 'Hello there. It's a magnificent mountain, isn't it?'

'Thertainly very big,' said Thorri. 'It occupieth the eyeth, don't it? It'th a shame, really, thince it getth in the way of a beautiful view.'

'How can you say so?' said Bingo. 'I think it's spectacular.'

'More'n a thpec,' said Thorri archly. 'But don't take it

~ 221 ~

perthonally. We dwarfth, we like *down*, not up, you thee. We prefer the inthide to the outthide.'

'But this mountain is hollow, I suppose. Everything's hollow, after all.'

For the first time Thorri looked at the soddit with a twinkle of respect. 'Indeed it ith,' he agreed. 'Tho you have learnt thomething about the way the world workth, young thoddit.'

'I've picked up a few things on my travels. So what do we do now?'

'We go inthide,' said the King. 'That'th why you're here.'

He pulled off his boot and drew out a crumpled scrap of parchment. The other dwarfs began gathering around as Thorri spread the paper out on the rock. At first glance Bingo took it to be a picture of an old cabbage leaf with copious annotation. But he saw, looking more closely, that it portrayed with rather crude delineation the environs of the Only Mountain. 'We can't go in through the front door,' Thorri was saying, pointing to a kink in the side of the mountain, 'on account of it'th locked.'

'Locked front door,' murmured the dwarfs.

'Tho,' said Thorri, 'we need to find the thide door. But, Mr Grabbings, the *thide* door is only wee.'

'Is only what?' asked Bingo.

'Only wee.'

Bingo tried to decipher this. 'I don't understand.'

'It'th wee,' insisted Thorri. 'Wee – wee. And the passage to which it gains accethth, that'th wee ath well.'

'Wee?' hazarded Bingo.

'Wee!' said Thorri, starting to become tetchy. 'You're thmaller than a dwarf, tho you can fit down there. Or tho we hope.'

'Oh,' said Bingo uncertainly. 'I see. And the stuff about wee . . . ?'

'Never mind about that,' said Mori, clapping the soddit on the shoulder with one hand.[3] 'We need to find the door. Come! Gather our belongings! We trek up the western flanks of the Only Mountain at last!'

There were some half-hearted hurrahs at this, and the dwarfs trudged off to collect their things. 'Thorri,' said Bingo, as he hopped off the rock. 'Can I ask you something?'

'Mm?' replied the dwarf King.

'You're King, aren't you?'

Thorri sighed. 'I'm afraid tho,' he conceded.

'So why is it you allow Mori to boss you about? Couldn't you silence him with, I don't know, one royal command?'

'Oh,' said the dwarf. 'It doethn't *do* to be in the front

---

[3] Incidentally, and in case you're interested, *this* is the sound of one hand clapping.

line all the time. Ethpethially,' he added, 'if one ith
King.'

A rook flapped its wings, landing on a boulder some
way distant, regarding them with inkily intelligent eyes.
It put its pointy head on one side.

They made good progress at first, but the way became
harder and harder as it became incrementally less
horizontal. Soon they were picking their way from
boulder to boulder and resting every quarter of an
hour. Matters were made considerably less agreeable
by the necessity, which devolved upon two of the party
at any given time, of dragging the sleeping wizard
behind them on a blanket. 'I only wish I knew,' complained Bingo, '*why* it is we have to bring him along. He
never seems to wake any more. He sleeps through
everything. He's completely deaf. He's lost his beard.
He's lost his mind, as far as I can see. And yet we're
pulling him up a bloody mountain.'

None of the dwarfs enlightened him.

By late afternoon they had reached a little plateau
littered with curiously shaped rocks that had clearly
fallen from the nearly sheer slopes above. The group sat
regaining their breath, and ate a little food. Thorri was
poring over the map. 'It ought to be hereaboutth,' he
announced. 'From what I can thee.'

'Look at those rooks!' said Bingo. 'Perching in

amongst the crannies and crags of the slope above us. They seem to be watching us.'

'Watching us, they are,' said Mori. 'The rooks of Strebor. They are a great and wise race.'

'Wise?' asked Bingo, whose experience of birds was limited to the robins and occasional off-course seagulls of Soddlesex. 'They're just birds, though, yes?'

Mori shook his head thrice, which caused his beard to shake five times. 'They are intelligent and cunning,' he said. 'They live long, and their memory lasts many generations. They play chess you know—'

'Chess?' asked Bingo, frankly incredulous.

'Oh yes. For what other reason is it the case, do you think, on a chessboard, that rooks are called rooks?'

'But rooks on a chessboard look like castles.'

Mori hissed at him in a shocked voice, 'Tush, soddit! *Never* call them that! It is forbidden! They are rooks – rooks is their name. Tut! Pshaw! You'll be calling the pawns *prawns* next.'

'I just find it rather hard to believe. Birds play chess? How do they play?'

'They, eh, nudge the pieces around the board with their beaks.'

'But how do they set the pieces up in the first place?'

'You're splitting hairs,' snapped the dwarf. 'The fact is that these rooks are not to be trifled with. They can speak, you know. They have a King.'

'What's he called?'

'Eh?'

'What's his *name*, this King of rooks?'

'Well,' said Mori, 'the rooks have long been friends of the dwarfs, and thus it so happens that I can tell you. His name is Caaw. Caaw the Mighty.'

'Funny-sounding name.'

'In fact,' Mori admitted, 'all their names are Caaw. They only have the one name between them. But they are very bright folk, these rooks, believe you me.'

Bingo craned his neck to look up at the rooks, wrinkling his eyes into crow's-feet. 'I'm not sure I'm convinced, Mori,' he said. 'I'm not so easily gulled.'

'Suit yourself,' said the dwarf.

They searched for the rest of the day but found no sign of the door. 'Is it like the door of the Coal Gate that led underneath the Minty Mountains? Is that it?' Bingo wondered. 'Should we wait until moonlight?'

'No, boyo,' said Mori. '*That* was an entrance into the great dwarfish halls of Dwarfhall, mighty Black Maria. This, look you, is more of a portal.'

'Portal?'

'Exhaust.'

'For?'

'Smoke.' The dwarf looked around him shiftily. 'And such.'

'So?'

'So it opens easily, see, but from the inside. We have to find it and try to, you know, prise it open from the *outside*.'

'It's a chimney, in other words,' clarified the soddit.

'Ay.'

'So you want me to crawl down a *chimney*, to come face to face with a terrible dragon from a *fireplace*?'

'Wasn't that made clear to you at the start?'

'Not,' said Bingo, 'really.'

'Ah. Well there you go, there you go.'

The party broke off its search to have supper, sitting around a small and rather mournful fire. Crows, rooks and ravens cawed and swooped overhead through the thickening light. To the west, the sun dropped red as a cherry tomato, painting the ragged stretches and bars of horizontal cloud through which it passed purple and orange and gold.

Shadows lengthened.

'Look at him there,' said Bingo, pointing to Gandef, who was sleeping peacefully wrapped in a blanket. 'He's been asleep now for, what? Four days? He looks so peaceful.'

The dwarfs mumbled their agreement, nodding.

'His cough seems to have cleared up,' the soddit said meditatively. 'Odd that. It used to be so severe, didn't it? Disabling, sometimes.'

'That stage is past,' said Gofur in a low voice.

'Eh?' said Bingo. 'What?'

'Nothing, nothing,' said Mori. 'Let's get some sleep.'

Bingo pressed them for a while, but they all clammed up. 'We clearly haven't come here for the gold,' he said. 'Or at least not just for the gold. I can believe that you'll happily take the gold if, when, you've done what you really came here for. Why won't you tell me what that is? What's the story?'

'Time for sleep now,' said Mori, as he wrapped his beard around himself.

They were woken at dawn by the cawing of the rooks, which seemed to Bingo's ears louder than ever. It was cold. Light shone on the lands to the north and south of the mountain making the fields and the plain bright, but the dwarfs and the soddit were in the mountain's huge shadow and it was dark all around. There were numerous little patches and puddles of ice in amongst the peak's shadow, reaching up the mountainside like dandruff. Bingo stood up and vigorously embraced himself a dozen times or so, repeatedly slapping both of his palms against their opposite shoulder-blades to try and warm up. Gofur tried to get a fire going, but there was rime on the twigs and the flame wouldn't take.

'So,' said Bingo, sourly. 'Another day of fruitless searching for this chimney pot, is it?'

'We'll find it,' replied Mori, 'if we only persevere.'

'I could be of some help there,' said a voice from behind them. 'Yo.'

It was an enormous thrush, yellow-white with pale freckles, half as tall as Bingo himself. It had settled on a boulder and was eyeing the group of them. Its eyes were pale, and its beak was of an almost pink hue. It was wearing a gold-thread jacket with ridiculously long sleeves that dangled, empty, from the front. The bird had ripped, or cut, two large holes in the armpits of this coat through which its wings poked out. A gold tag rattled on the creature's spindly left leg. A tiny cap was squeezed over the crown of its head. This headgear was too small for even that small head, and seemed to be pinching the top of the bird's skull into a nubbin.

'Good morrow, Master Bird,' said Mori, bowing low.

'Yo,' said the thrush. 'You havink a bit of bother?'

'Bother,' repeated the dwarf. 'Well, I suppose you could say that.'

'Visitors don't often come to this hood,' said the bird. It flapped one of its wings out, a strange and jerky gesture that ruffled the feathers at the end, and then folded the wing away again. It gave the impression of a one-sided St Vitus's dance. 'Hood – you know?' it added as it surveyed the non-comprehension on the faces of its audience. 'It's a word, it's short, innit, for "place-of-the-hooded-hawk", or somefink. Bird slank.'

'Slank?'

'Yeah,' said the bird, shuffling on its asterisk-shaped feet. 'Slank.'

'Oh,' said Gofur, realisation dawning. 'Slang.'

'Yeah.'

'Sir Thrush,' said Bingo, bowing civilly to the bird. 'We are delighted to meet you.'

'Ca-aaarcg!' shrieked the bird, flapping both its wings in a positive conniption of anxiety. 'Nah! Nah! Nah! I'm no *frush*, innit. I *am not* a frush. I'm a raving – a raving, I tell ya.'

'A raven,' said Bingo.

' 'Sright,' said the bird. 'Wired,' it added, emphatically if mysteriously.

'It's just that you look, at first glance, rather thrush-like,' said Bingo.

'Certainly *not*. Not a frush, me. I'm *down* with the ravens. Well, I'm up there with them, actually,' it said, its accent momentarily slipping up the social register. It tossed its beak towards the mountain peak. 'But down at the same time. If you follow.'

'Right,' said the soddit, who didn't. 'I must say, though, without meaning any offence, that you don't, exactly, look like a raven. Not like a conventional idea of a raven, at any rate.'

'What you mean?'

'Well – your colour, for instance.'

'Good raving colour, this,' said the bird. 'Innit.'

'Aren't ravens usually a bit blacker than—?'

'Ca-aaarcg!' shrieked the bird again, becoming quite fiercely agitated. 'Yo! Ba-ka-ka-ka-ba! Wheeh! Polly want a cracker cocaine! Birdy bling-bling!' It flapped so fiercely it lost its footing, and skeetered around on top of the stone for several seconds before recovering its balance.

'Best not annoy it,' said Mori to Bingo, sotto voce, 'Sir Raven!' he declaimed loudly. 'Sir Raven!'

'Mornink, vicar,' said the bird, settling itself down again. 'I am a raven, you know.'

'Of course you are,' said the dwarf in a conciliatory voice. 'We all thought so when we saw you.'

'Really?' said the bird, looking pleased.

'Certainly. I said to my comrade, Gofur the dwarf here, I said, is that a mighty raven settling on to that rock? I do believe it is. Nobody would ever mistake it for a thrush, I said. Clearly.'

'Like the hhhat?' the bird inquired, aspirating the word prodigiously and leaning its head forward for everyone to see. It had the words 'Tomtit Hilfeather' written round it. 'It's wicked, innit.'

'It's very,' said Bingo uncertainly, 'tight. How did you fit it on?'

'Weren't easy,' said the raving. It plocked around in a little circle on the rock, three hundred and sixty degrees, and ended where it began. 'Ca-aaarcg!' it said, loud and sudden. '*I'm* a raven! *I'm* a raven! *I'm* a raven! See-eed*cake*. Ca-aaarcg!'

'Mighty bird,' said Mori, 'we accept your kind offer of help, for we have need of assistance. We have travelled far—'

'Cup o' tea!' shrieked the bird. 'Nice juicy snail! Booba-booba-booba!'

'. . . travelled far through many perilous adventures—'

'Re-*speck*led!' Re-*speck*led! Egg!'

'. . . far under mountains and through the forest of—'

'Tu-whit, tu-woo. She told me to squawk this way-yy! Ca-aaarcg!'

'We have *travelled far* . . .' Mori persevered, 'and now we are searching for—'

'Have a nut?' the raving suggested.

This, for some reason, seemed to take the wind out of Mori's sails. There was silence for the space of thirty seconds.

The raving put its head on one side. Then it put its head on the other side.

'What it *is*,' said Bingo, 'is a sort of chimney. Like a little doorway. Do you know it?'

'Cup o'tea?' said the bird, in a more considered voice. 'Blimey. Boiling-boiling. Two sugars and gold je-*well-*

ery. Did you ever notice that the clouds got no wings, yet they fly? Funny that.'

'But do you know where this chimney can be found?'

'Chimney,' said the bird. 'Ca-aaarcg!' it shrilled. 'I seen a horse fly, I seen a crane fly, I seen a bird fly, I seen a fly fly, but have I ever seen a chimney door-way?'

'That is indeed the question,' pressed the soddit.

'Lil-bow-wow-wow,' said the bird. 'Crac! And *they* diss *me*? I tell you, they call me just a trash-nest white flapper – but I'm *real*, I'm street, ca-aaarcg! I work with real raven flappers all the time. This is what my critics don't understand. Blimey.'

'Flapper,' said Bingo, trying to steer the conversation back to the hidden entrance, 'yes, well *clearly* we can all agree on that. That's plain as the noses on our faces. But about this chimney that we're looking for—'

'Listen to this,' said the bird, and began squawking tunelessly. 'Now *I'm* a raven, yes *I'm* a real raven, all you *other* non-ravens are just *i*mitating so *won't* the real bling raven *please fly up*! *Please fly up*! *Please fly up*!' He accompanied this recital with jerky flaps of both wings together.

'Sir Bird?' said Bingo.

'What?'

'The chimney?' He pronounced these two words in his sternest voice.

The bird looked abashed. 'Chimney? Opens on to a shaft? Down into the mountink, is it?'

'Yes.'

'You know,' it said, becoming conspiratorial, and looking at them from underneath its right wing, 'that there's this, like, dragon down there? Don't you?'

'We'd been led to believe so,' said Mori.

'He's a scary old boy,' said the raven. 'That dragon. Just so's you know.'

'We'll take your comments under advisement,' said the dwarf. 'And if you could indicate the exact location of the doorway, we will be forever in your debt.'

'Sure,' said the bird. ''Sover there.' It leapt up and flapped into flight, oaring its way across the little plateau to the rock face. The dwarfs and Bingo hurried after it. At a place where the smooth mountain wall rose at an angle at forty-five degrees, the raven settled on the floor and tapped sharply at the rock, once, twice, thrice.[4]

A hatch, barely large enough for even a soddit to crawl through, swung in towards the mountain's in-nards an inch, and then swung slowly the other way, opening outwards on creaky stone hinges until it was

---

[4] This is the archaic mode of counting, of course, which has been largely superseded in modern times by one two three and so on. But in the olden days we all used to count this way: *once, twice, thrice, tvice, tgice, tmice, tjice, hethera, tethera, many.* This schema served all human counting purposes for many centuries.

gaping wide. A few strands of smoke drifted out of the hole.

'Thank you, thank you, Sir Thr, um, Raven,' cried the dwarfs.

'We owe you a great debt, Sir Bird,' said Mori. 'What is your name?'

'My real name, or my street name?' asked the bird.

'We dwarfs never forget a kindness done to us,' explained Mori. 'I ask your name that we may remember it, and repay your good deed at some point in the future.'

'You probably want my real name, then,' said the raving. It squawked uncomfortably a few times. 'Lovely bird! Beautiful plumage! Cup o'tea! It's,' it added, in lower and much more sane-sounding tones, 'Gavin Dembrell, of Mountain View Nest, the Glades – my mum and dad's nest, that,' it continued, its voice even lower. 'I'll be moving out, soon as I find my own crib, but when that happens they'll, you know, have the forwarding address.' It leapt away from the dwarfs, flapped and flew around their heads for a while. 'Bling-bling!' it shrieked. 'Ca-aaarcg! Have a nut!' And with that it flew away.

The dwarfs huddled around the smoky opening in the mountainside. Bingo elbowed them aside and peered down.

'You really expect me to go down there?' he said. 'There's smoke coming out of it. There's probably a fire at the bottom. It'd be suicide.'

'You'll be all right, boyo,' said Mori. 'It's not so slanted. Almost horizontal.'

'It's tiny,' said the soddit. 'And it's pretty slanted – it goes down at a sharp old angle.'

'Never mind about that for now, boyo,' said Mori. 'We need to have a little chat first. You and we, we and you, we need to have a little talk about what you're to do when you go down there.'

'Does this mean,' asked Bingo, 'that you're finally going to tell me why we're really here? No nonsense about gold?'

'Patience, boyo,' said Mori, clapping him on the shoulder. It was an unfortunate blow, catching the soddit slightly off balance. His foot slipped through the gap and over the lip. He threw his arms forward to try and grab the sides of the opening, but it was too late. The next thing he saw was a square of light receding rapidly, and he was plunged in darkness. And not metaphorically plunged, either: literally plunged. Oh yes.

Smug

Chapter Nine

INSIDE, IN FORM

༄

Down went Bingo, his arms above his head. He spoke. 'Aaaagghh!' he said. The shaft narrowed as it descended, and soon it was chafing violently at the soddit's belly and shoulders, and scraping his sore feet. 'Ow! ow! ow!' he said. 'Aaaagghh!' he added. Friction increased. There was the sound of cloth ripping. His descent slowed, painfully, as the skin around his middle felt as if it were being grated.

He had stopped.

'Dear me, dear me,' he said to himself, panting a little. It was utterly dark. He was wedged uncomfortably in the chimney with his arms up. The faint sound of dwarf hallooing was just audible somewhere far distant above him, but he couldn't make out the words. 'Dear me, dear me,' he said again.

He sucked his gut in and breathed out as far as he could. Then, turning a little blue (not that you could have seen his colour in the dark) he wriggled and wriggled. He shifted an inch downwards, then half an inch, and then with a jolt he began falling again. He said: 'Dear.' He did not say this, however, because the experience was especially dear to him. Rather he intended to say 'dear me' one more time, but was interrupted by his downward movement. Instead of saying 'dear me' he found himself saying 'dear aaaarrgh', which is – I hardly need to point this out to you – not the same thing at all.

And then he dropped out of the bottom of the shaft and, with a soft crash, fell into a great pile of old ashes and bits of burnt timber. Everything was instantly obscured by a cloud of grey, and Bingo started coughing. He thrashed about in the cool talcumy pile and staggered out, sore and startled but upright. He felt stone flags under his feet. Dust was in his eyes and he could see nothing, but he heard a deep, deeply rumbling voice, say:

'Gracious.'

Bingo stopped where he was. He tried wiping the ash out of his eyes, but the hands he was wiping with were also covered in ash, and his wiping proved a zero-sum game, smearing as much dust in as he smeared out. He was still trembling from his fall, and a deep terror was growing inside him. His stomach seemed to shrink to nothing and the roots of his hair shivered. He was acutely conscious that the deep rumbly voice almost certainly proceeded from the throat of Smug the

Dragon. Whilst his eyes were closed, he told himself that – since he lacked ocular evidence – it was still possible, just, that it was not a fearsome fire-blowing dragon that had spoken, but (say) somebody with a large chest and a bad cold. Although he knew the chances of this were rather small, he clung to the hope.

'Are you,' rumbled the voice, 'all right?'

Bingo put one hand in his waistcoat pocket, and closed his fingers around the Thing®. This gave him some small solace. He wondered whether, should Smug decide to blast him with a great wave of fire, he would have time to speak any reverse wish through the device. Probably not. But it was better having it than not.

Several blinks, and copious tears, were washing some of the ash out of his eyes. He opened them very cautiously.

There was Smug the Mighty in all his enormous and terrifying magnitude. He was stretched on his back over a large pile of gold and jewellery, his belly out and his long head resting on his own chest. His wings were spread to either side of his enormous body, and his hind legs were crossed one over the other. He was not naked; in fact, he wore several layers of tough cloth over his torso, a dark inner coat, and a brown-green fine-checked outer jacket. His snout was long and his head lumpy, but his dragon eyes glinted with a fierce intellect. In his left claw, Bingo saw, something was clutched – at first the soddit thought it a canoe, or something of similar proportions. As he blinked again, and as the dragon lifted the thing and placed it to his mouth, Bingo could see that it was a tobacco pipe, a pipe of gigantic proportions. The dragon took two deep puffs, and laid the pipe at his side again.

'Dra,' said Bingo. 'Drag. Dra. Dragon.'

He stumbled back, but there was nowhere to hide, and nowhere to go. The beast's eyes were fixed upon him.

Bingo looked from left to right with a degree of desperation. The floor of the creature's lair was piled high with gold, and the walls were stacked with enormous and multitudinous books – volumes of ancient lore bound in various leathers. To the right were a number of bottles, with labels that read 'wyrmwine' and 'Dragon's Friend'. Torches flickered behind, draping an intermittent red light over everything.

'Good morning,' said the dragon.

'Good,' said Bingo. Then his tongue seemed to seize up. 'Momomomo,' he added.

'I did not realise,' said Smug, 'that I had an appointment. Pull up a chair, do – that one, yes – just move those papers off it. Put them anywhere.'

Bingo looked around stupidly.

'I'd offer you tea,' said Smug. 'But I'm sorry to say I ran out of tea some forty years ago.'

'That's quite all right, quite all right,' said the soddit. He saw the chair to which the dragon had gestured, and pulled a stack of leathern parchments from its seat. With a little hop he climbed on to the chair. Somewhere in his brain he was thinking, half consciously, *If I'm sitting on his furniture perhaps he'll think twice about burning me to death. If he values his own furniture, that is.* He was still clutching the Thing® in his right hand.

'And what can I do for you?' said Smug.

'I—' said Bingo. He thought for a moment. But he had no idea what to say.

'You'll have to remind me of your name,' the creature rumbled.

'Bingo Grabbings,' said Bingo, without thinking. As soon as he said it, he wondered if he had made a terrible mistake. Giving one's true name to magical creatures, such as dragons, is not advisable. But it was too late now.

'So,' mused the creature. 'So, Bingo Grabbings, is it? At first glance, that would be a burglar's name, now, wouldn't it?'

'I come from a family of respectable gentlehobblds!' squeaked Bingo.

'Of course you do,' said the dragon, 'since the etymological root of *burglar* and *burgher*, or *bourgeois* if you prefer, is to be found in the same word – from the old Brackish **bruh* or **burh*, you know. Being a robber and being respectable are, philologically speaking, more or less the same thing.'

Bingo had got his hands more or less clean of ash now by dint of rubbing them together, and was able to wipe his face more effectively clear. He hadn't really been listening to this. 'Fascinating,' he said nervously.

'But,' the dragon continued, 'I'd say that Bingo Grabbings is a west-country name. Am I right? There's a Grabesend, isn't there, on the coast up that way? I'd hazard – this is mere conjecture, of course, please don't note this down – I'd *conjecture* a root for names like bingo is from *beo-wing*, "he who flies from bees". Are you afraid of bees, Mr Grabbings? No? They do have a nasty sting, don't they? It is probably a good idea to get out of their way.' He chuckled at this, and clacked the fearsome claws of his empty right hand together, making a dry, drumbeat noise, *cloc, cloc, cloc.* 'As for Grabbings—' the dragon said.

'Please don't kill me!' shrieked Bingo, unable to contain himself. He fell from the chair on to his knees. 'I'm sorry! Sorry! I'm sorry I fell down your chimney! It was their idea! It wasn't my idea!'

'Dear me, dear me,' rumbled the dragon, not unamused. 'Do calm down, little chap. Really. Kill you? Why should I want to kill you?'

'We've travelled all this way, hundreds of leagues,'

the soddit burbled, 'to slay you and steal your gold, and
I'm sorry I'm sorry I'm sorry.' He sucked in a shuddering breath, and was only prevented from more unfortunate disclosures by the fact that he chanced to inhale a
lungful of the fine ash that was still drifting around the
lair, provoking a short soddit coughing fit.

'Dear me,' said Smug, when the coughing had
stopped. He took another few pulls on his pipe. 'This
is a serious development. I'm sorry to hear it. Might I
ask *why* you have come all this way to slay me?'

Bingo sat back on his knees. 'I'm not sure,' he said. 'I
assume – I don't know. I assume you've done some
great wrong to their people?'

'And *they* are . . . ?'

But Bingo was, finally, learning some circum-
spection. He had already given far too much away.
'My travelling companions,' he said. 'I'm sorry, but I
didn't realise that one needed a specific reason for
slaying dragons. Isn't that – slaying dragons, I mean –
just something people do?'

'My life would be terribly uncomfortable,' said
Smug, 'if that were so. Dear me. This is a very disagreeable development. I'm trying to think,' he added,
'whom I may have offended. I really can't think of
anybody.'

Bingo was still terrifically nervous, which may have
been why he blurted: 'The Lakesiders have seen no

customers for seventy years – you've scared their customers away.'

'Dear me,' said the dragon, sounding genuinely contrite. 'Have I? How dreadful. It really wasn't intentional. I don't see, though – to be fair – that it's *exactly* my fault if people find me scary. I don't go out of my way to be scary.' He puffed on his pipe for a while.

The conversation was not going the way Bingo had anticipated at all. 'I am sorry,' he said, 'if I startled you, falling into your fireplace like that. And I'm sorry about – you know, the talk of slaying you.'

'Perhaps,' said Smug, 'if you were to tell me the identity of your travelling companions, I might be able to remember if I had done them any wrong. Are they, perhaps, hobblds, such as yourself?'

'Mighty Smug!' said Bingo, scurrying behind the chair and peering out. 'Pardon me! I have said too much already! If my friends knew what I have revealed they would be sorely angry with me.'

'Oh well, oh well,' said the creature in a mournful voice. 'Of course, if you'd rather not say, I understand perfectly.'

There was silence in the lair for a while.

'I do apologise,' grumbled the dragon, 'about the lack of tea.' He hoomed and hummed for a while. 'Interesting word, tea,' he said, as if talking to himself. 'Derived, I'd argue, from *tyr*, a variant of *þyrs*, the old Eastron word for *giant*. Because it is a drink that makes one feel like a giant.' He hoomed some more. 'Wonderful drink,' he added.

It was starting to dawn on Bingo, despite his fright, and despite the various aches he had sustained coming down the chimney, that Smug was wounded in his feelings. The soddit had not expected that. Rage, fire, destruction, yes. Cunning and guile, yes. But a hurt look in the eye and some defensive puffs on a pipe, not at all.

'Sir Smug,' the soddit said cautiously. 'I fear I have offended you.'

'Not at all,' murmured the dragon. 'Don't mention it. Only, you see, it is a *little* disconcerting to discover that a group of people have travelled such a long way to kill one.'

'Surely you have many enemies,' said Bingo. 'I mean,' he added hurriedly, anxious that his words had come over as merely insulting, 'one so, eh, magnificent and terrible as you.'

'Enemies?' said the dragon. 'I don't believe so. Let me have another think. No, no. I had a bit of a ding-dong with Blaze the Dragon from the Ice-Plain of Gungadin – over, it was, the correct derivation of the term *wodwo*. But that was settled amicably. Yes, amicably. He's a good old worm, that one. Modest, too.'

He shuffled on his bed of gold, and scratched his

stomach with the claws of his right foreleg. 'Hmm,' he said.

'I must say, you don't seem, sir,' said Bingo in a tiny voice, 'you don't seem very *smug*, if you see what I mean.'

'What? What's that? No, you're quite right, you're quite right. Smug is not what my friends call me, you know. Although it is, philologically speaking, quite an interesting word.'

'Really?' said Bingo weakly.

'Certainly. It's a west-land variant of the east-land root-word *Smýk, which has, in fact, come down into modern language via another branch of the linguistic tree, as *Smoke*. The vowel shift, you see. Smoke is a perfectly descriptive name for a dragon.' He lifted his enormous pipe in his left claw and puffed on the stem for a while. Billowing quantities of smoke poured from between his teeth.

'Is that then your name, sir? Smoke the Dragon?'

'No, no, Smoke is what *people* used to call me. People aren't very original with their names for dragons. Hmm. They tend to name dragons, in man-speech, on a merely literal level: Smoke, Flame, Puff, things like that.' He shook his great head. 'No, that's not the name I call myself.'

'So what is the name you call yourself, mighty sir?'

'Ah. When I was a young dragon, fighting and

rushing around, I was called Rashbold. But it's been an age and an age since anybody's called me that. An age and an age since I've been rash, although I hope I'm still capable of a little boldness.' He chuckled, and took another draw on his pipe. 'It sounds as if I'll need a little boldness, indeed, if your friends are genuine in their intentions to slay me.'

'I'm sorry for my friends' intentions,' said Bingo.

'Well, well,' said Smug. 'I'll try not to get too huffy. A dragon's huff is, you see, rather more destructive and fiery than a regular person's.' He chuckled at this, as if he had made a joke. 'There's a great deal of mis-conception about dragons, you know,' he added mildly. 'A great deal. People tend only to see the smoky and the fiery side of dragons. They don't see the *creative* side at all.'

'The creative side?' said Bingo, interested.

'Oh yes. I hate to boast – that goes against the grain, boasting – but it can't be denied that dragons made all this.' He gestured with his right claw, and his leathern wings rustled beneath him.

'This room?' said Bingo. 'These books?'

'What? What? No, no. Well, yes, strictly speaking. But I meant the world as a whole. Everything.'

'Dragons,' said Bingo, uncertain he had heard cor-rectly, 'created the world?'

'Well,' said Smug, as if embarrassed, 'yes. Brought it

to life, breathed fire and smoke into it. That's what caused the sun to shine, what filled the upper sky. That's why the sky's blue, it's smoke – high up, I mean, *aither*, hot and dry. The lower air isn't blue, it's clear, of course. And,' he added, 'that's why the mountains and the hills are hollow, because dragon breath puffed them up into the landscape, like glass-blowing. But I don't mean to brag. Dragons can't take all the credit.'

'No?'

'No, no. Some of the houses are, you know, made by later people. But anyway, anyway. I don't mean to bore you. It's been a pleasure speaking to you.'

Bingo came out from behind the chair. 'I can't believe, sir,' he said, abashed, 'that it has truly been a pleasure.'

'Well – perhaps pleasure isn't the right word,' conceded Smug. 'Perhaps not pleasure, exactly. But it has been edifying. Edifying. I'm sorry I have to draw it to an end. But I think I'd better *pop*, you know, *pop* down to Lakeside. There's clearly been a misunderstanding between us, between the Lakesiders and myself. I'd better flap down there and try and sort it out. Drive away their trade? Nothing could be further from my thoughts. I'll have a chat with them, and I'm sure we can arrange some kind of compromise. Dear me, dear me, what an unfortunate situation. What a disagreeable

situation. Well, Mr Grabbings,' Smug continued, stirring on his pile, 'goodbye. I'll show you the main gate –
I don't suppose you'll fit back up that chimney.'

'No, sir,' said Bingo. 'Yes, sir.'

It was clear that the dragon had finished talking. He
reared up from his pile, and stood for a moment on his
hind legs with his huge wings unfolding behind him, as
tall as any of his tall kin. The edges of his wings were
lined with sharp claws, and the aerodynamic whole was
perfectly designed – a tool for flying, but a tool keen
and sharp for cutting the air. Bingo felt fear return to
his gut, and he staggered against the wall. The dragon
fell forward, and stalked into a corridor just high-
ceilinged enough for him to stalk in, although it seemed
a mighty cavern to the soddit as he scurried along at the
creature's heels. With earth-jarring strides the beast
covered the whole length of the corridor in minutes.
Bingo had to run to keep up, passing many side rooms
and archways leading through to other lairs, rooms,
caverns, although the soddit had no time to look in. He
was running too rapidly for that.

'Sir Dragon!' he gasped.' You go too fast!'

'Oh,' said Smug, turning his long face over his
shoulder. 'I do apologise. Don't feel you have to run at
my speed. I'll leave the door open for you.' And with
that he leapt forward like a tiger, a mighty leap, landing
in the air outside the mountain and spreading his wings.

Bingo sat on the floor until he had recovered his breath. Then he got up and trotted down the remainder of the great corridor. The massive front doorway, tall as twenty soddits, grew as he ran towards it. He was almost outside again in the clean air but, at the last minute, his eyes were distracted by something glittering, something precious-looking, sitting on the floor next to the door: an enormous gem. Other precious flotsam and jetsam was scattered about, pieces of gold and jewel-encrusted cups, but it was this huge diamond, as large as Bingo's fist, that caught his eye.[1] Eager as he was to get outside the mountain, he could not pass by so magnificent a gem. As he bent over it he thought he discerned a gleam shining out of the heart of the jewel. He cradled it in both his hands and lifted it before his face.

'Woof,' said the jewel.

'You are fairer than any jewel I have ever seen,' said Bingo. 'I shall . . . borrow you. Perhaps Smug won't mind. What do you think?'

'Wooah! Wooah!' said the stone.

But Bingo ignored its warning and slipped the great jewel into his coat pocket, where it settled with a gentle 'woof'.

---

[1] The earlier story of this gem is told in the famous tale *A Diamond As Big As The Fist*.

This, although he did not realise it at the time, was the famous, enchanted Barkingstone, a gem with a long and special history. It was as valuable a gemstone as existed in Upper Middle Earth, and a very great find for a burglar to make.

Bingo trotted out of the main entrance to the caves of Strebor with a sudden gaiety in his heart. He had survived his fall down the chimney, had come away from his interview with the dragon with his life intact, and to boot had discovered a gem of fabulous wealth and beauty. All in all, he told himself, it had not been a bad day. The sunlight prickled on the fast-flowing stream that led out between the two arms of the mountain, and the land to the south looked yellow-brown, fresh and warm. The sun was still climbing, and Bingo realised that he had spent only a few hours inside the mountain.

It took him more than a few hours, however, to make his way back to the dwarfs. First he had to clamber over a spur of the mountain, and down into the valley on the other side. Then he had to circle the flank of Strebor until he recognised the place where the party had climbed up two days before. Then he had to retrace that arduous and difficult climb.

But when he hauled his puffing body on to the plateau, as the sun sank red in the west, the dwarfs were delighted to see him. 'Bingo!' cried Mori. 'You're alive!'

They clustered around him.

'How glad we are, see, that you're all right, boyo,' said Mori embracing him. 'We'd almost given up on you.'

'We were debating what to do next,' said Gofur.

'We weren't at all sure *what* to do,' said On.

'My dear friends,' said Bingo. After he had refreshed himself with some water and a bread roll, whilst the dwarfs lit a fire, he settled himself and told them the sequence of his adventures – omitting only the part about finding the Barkingstone. But instead of becoming more and more congratulatory as he proceeded, the dwarfs became more and more dismayed.

'You told him,' said Mori severely, '*what*?'

'You said we were here *to kill him*?' said a horrified Failin.

'Well, yes,' said Bingo, faltering. 'That is why we're here, isn't it? I understand that to be the purpose of our quest.'

Five dwarf faces stared at him aghast.

'I know you *said* it was gold,' Bingo told them, becoming a little annoyed himself. 'I mean, I know you said that. But clearly that wasn't it. Or wasn't the whole story. There is lots of gold down there, by the way,' he added. 'Just lying around. Seems a shame to leave it.'

'You idiot,' exploded Mori. 'Id! i! ot!'

'I beg your pardon?'

'You told the dragon we were going *to kill it*? *Why* did you tell it that?'

'I was in a tight spot,' said Bingo, growing heated.

'And it flew off towards Lakeside?'

'Yes.'

The dwarfs looked to the south. In the darkening sky, nothing could be seen except a series of shadowed vaguenesses in the landscape and the emerging stars over the horizon.

'At least,' said Mori, with hope in his voice, 'you told him you had travelled with a troop of dwarfs?'

'No,' said Bingo proudly. 'I managed to stop myself before I blurted that out.'

The dwarfs stared at him. It was actually possible to see their mouths, so far had their jaws dropped.

'Look—' Bingo began.

'Idiot! Idiot – idiot – idiot – sheep-for-brains,' exclaimed Mori. 'You *should have told him* we were dwarfs. He'd have *never* believed we were coming to kill him if he'd known we were dwarfs.'

'Wouldn't he? Why not?' Bingo looked from face to face. 'Why wouldn't he? I don't understand,' he said.

'Oh,' said Mori, 'that's *perfectly* plain.'

'Well,' said Bingo, his soddit anger roused, 'don't you

think you should explain it to me? Don't you think I've been blundering about in the dark for long enough? Maybe you should have told me at the beginning, instead of spinning these yarns about gold and gold and gold. Eh?'

Mori, in the firelight, looked at the ground. 'If we'd told you,' he said, 'you'd never have come.'

'I *wish* I'd never come!' Bingo declared.

'It's not the kind of thing a dwarf, or a wizard, can just – tell,' said Mori, after a while. 'It's private. It's not something we'd want the rest of the world to find out about. We thought, see, that we'd wait a while, see how you shaped up. We always planned to tell you sooner or later,' he added.

The other dwarfs nodded.

'Tell me what?' Bingo demanded. 'Tell me what? *Why* have we come all this way, to this mountain, past all these dangers? Eh, Mori? What *was* the reason?'

'The reason,' said Mori. Then he stopped. He turned his gaze to the sleeping figure of the wizard. The whole party looked at Gandef. '*There's* the reason,' said Gofur. 'He's why we came.'

Bingo stared at the wizard.

There was a silence for a several minutes.

'Things are not always as they first appear,' said Mori in a low voice.

'I thought he came along as a guide, as a sort of

protector,' said Bingo. 'Protecting us. Like he did with the Gobblins. Or the wolves. But you're saying it was actually the other way around. We were bringing him, not him bringing us?'

'Of course,' said Mori. 'Couldn't you read the clues?'

'What clues? What – what is happening to Gandef?'

'He's turning,' said Mori in a low voice, 'into a dragon, look you.'

Bingo digested this for a while. 'I don't understand.'

'Where did you think dragons came from?' Failin asked.

'I'd never really thought about it,' said Bingo. 'I assumed that a mummy dragon and a daddy dragon got together and, I don't know, laid an egg.'

'The processes of life are much richer than you realise, la, and much more closely interconnected,' said Mori. 'You know an insect egg becomes a grub, and a grub becomes a caterpillar, and a caterpillar a moth. You know this is how nature works. If it is so complex, so interconnected, at the level of moths, how much more so for the larger winged creatures?'

'You wanted me to read the clues?' said Bingo. 'That wizards are the larval form of dragons? How on earth was I supposed to deduce that? Why couldn't you just *tell* me? I can't even think what the clues might have been that I was supposed to read.'

'Well,' said Mori. 'There was the smoking.'

'Plenty of people smoke,' Bingo pointed out. 'Not just wizards or dragons.'

'There was the deafness.'

'Deafness?'

'He was losing the use of his ears. Dragons don't have ears – they hear through the membranes of their wings. Didn't you know that?'

'And Gandef has *wings*, does he?' said Bingo snidely, to cover his ignorance.

'They're growing now. Whilst he sleeps.'

Everybody looked at the supine wizard again.

'I still don't see,' insisted Bingo, 'how I was supposed to guess.'

'There's the magic. Wizards and dragons are the two great magic creatures in the world. Didn't you know *that*? There was the fire.'

'The fire?'

'The time Gandef breathed out fire and burnt those wolves. Didn't you think that was a strange thing?'

'I assumed it was a spell,' Bingo said.

'Then when his *beard* came off, we thought that was the giveaway,' said Gofur. 'You've never seen a dragon with a beard, have you? Dragons don't have beards.'

'This,' said Bingo, 'is a lot to take in.'

He sat for a while, listening to the sounds of the fire. It was as if the long red fingers of flame were cracking their knuckles.

'So we were in fact bringing Gandef to Smug for him to – what? Complete his transformation?'

The dwarfs nodded in the darkness.

'So why were *you* doing it? Why does it matter to a load of dwarfs what happens to one old wizard?'

'Perhaps,' said Mori, 'you'd like me to enumerate the many points of similarity between dwarfs and wizards – not counting, of course, the difference in sizes. There's, one, the beards—'

'You mean,' said Bingo, understanding striking him suddenly, 'that dwarfs are an *earlier form* of wizards? Grubs to caterpillars to moths, you said. Dwarfs turn into wizards?'

'Well, if they live long enough,' said Mori. 'As you've seen, the world is a harsh environment for us. But yes. Dwarfs are quickened in the rocks, and we emerge much as you see us, only smaller, in caves and caverns. We grow slowly, and many of us perish, but eventually some small number change, metamorphose, shoot up in height and acquire our adult magic, and then we are wizards. A wizard's life is long, and not without peril, and few survive as long as Gandef here – *Mithrandwarf*, to give him his proper name. But, for those few, eventually, the second great transformation begins. He senses it, last year. We brought him here to Smug for the change to be completed, and so that he will have a mentor when he emerges. *You* were supposed to slip down the chimney, and get Smug to open the front door. That's *all*.'

'But,' said Gofur sourly, 'you have instead sent Smug down to Lakeside to pick a quarrel with the men who live there. And even if he has survived that encounter, he now thinks we have come to kill him! A pretty pickle.'

'Pickle,' murmured the other dwarfs in sorrowful agreement. 'Pretty. Hmm, hmm, hmm.'

All eyes turned south again, trying to pick out the shapes of the lake and the town in the increasing darkness.

Lard the Bowman

Chapter Ten

FIE! AND WATER

◦〰〰〰◦

And so we must, if you desire to know what happened between Mighty Smug and the marketing men of Lakeside, move our imaginary point of view southwards to the slow waters of Lake Escargot. For that was the direction in which the dragon wended.

Smug flew with easy, lolloping strokes of his broad wings through the midday sunshine. In a brief time he was circling above Lakeside, blowing great gusts of wind up and down the narrow wooden streets with his leathern[1] wings. The Lakesiders scurried to and fro crying out, variously,' The dragon is come! Woe! Woe! Woe!', and, 'Ichabod and alas, the glory has departed from Lakeside!', and, 'Who'll buy my lovely apples, *lurvely* apples? Ten a penny, come buy.'

'Now,' boomed Smug from the air, his voice sounding like a hundred thunderstorms.[2] 'Let's not get

[1] I checked with the copy-editor whether this shouldn't be 'leather', but she insisted that the extra 'n' makes all the difference.
[2] Well, technically it sounded like ninety-eight point three thunderstorms. But for the sake of the metre I rounded up.

carried away down there! I have only come to talk!'

Lard the Bowman stood, his belly proud. He was the only stationary person in the milling throng, his strong longbow in his hand. 'Dragon!' he called up, his voice almost lost in the wind made by the beast's wings (although, luckily, dragonic hearing is unusually acute). 'Fie Dragon! Beware!'

'Now, now,' said Smug. 'I mean no harm. Can we not *simply* talk, dragano-a-mano? Just thee and me?'

'I have my bow!' called Lard, brandishing it above his head.[3] 'And I'm not afraid to use it! Be warned!'

'Eeek!' called the crowd. 'Alas! Disaster! The dragon is come!'

'Apples, apples!' called the deaf appleseller.

Smug circled again. 'I'm going to land on that bridge,' he said, pointing down with one of his mighty claws. 'Then we'll be able to chat. I don't suppose,' he added, as if in afterthought, 'that you've any *tea*, have you?'

'Woe, woe, woe!' called the people of Lakeside.

Smug curled the ends of his wings in and beat in slightly circular motions, creating a down-draught that enabled him to land. People scattered beneath him as he settled on to the town's main bridge. Lard ap-

---

[3] 'Brandishing' in Lakeside is a slightly different process from conventional heroic brandishing (which is to say, 'shaking'), and involves instead a logo and a series of careful product placements.

proached the great beast, running with his head down in the accepted human manner (if there is a draught from above). The timbers of the bridge creaked under the creature's weight.

'Ahh!' said Smug, as he folded away his wings and reached to the breast pocket from which his enormous pipe protruded. 'That's better. I'm not as fit as I used to be, you know. I used to go for a constitutional, a quick flap around the mountain, after every meal. But I've been neglecting my exercises latterly. Dear me! So you must be Lard? Delighted to meet you. Delighted.'

'Fearsome worm,' shouted Lard, brandishing his weapon again. 'Begone back to your hole of vileness! Fie!'

'Well,' said the dragon, a little nonplussed. 'Eh. Quite. Yes, I must say, you've done a *lovely* job with the lake town here. A lovely job. Is that pine cladding on the oak beams of the main hall? Lovely, lovely.'

'Creature of darkness!' yelled Lard. 'Spawn of Malcorm! Ye shall not pass!'

'I see,' said Smug, unable to keep a certain crushed tone out of his voice. 'Ah well. It's nice to see you. I thought I'd pop down—'

'Grrrr!' said Lard.

'– pop down,' said Smug, in a more subdued voice as he tamped tobacco into the tub-sized bowl of his pipe. 'See if we can't sort out this little difficulty.'

The beams that held the bridge groaned again under the great weight of Smug.

'I understand,' said Smug, puffing on the stem of his giant pipe, 'that some of your customers have been a bit – shall we say? – shy, since my arrival in the Only Mountain . . .'

'Fie! Bah!' called Lard, fitting an arrow to his bow. 'Grr! Evil wyrm! Fie!'

'. . . I really *must* assure you I had *no* idea. It's a most unfortunate situation. I feel obliged to try and find a solution, and restore your trade. Now, I was wondering if—'

Lard lifted his bow, and aimed his arrow.

But the supporting beams beneath Smug could take the weight no longer. With a series of splintering crashes, they gave way, tipping the whole fifty-yard stretch of bridge into the water. With a grumbling 'oh, my' the dragon toppled backwards and disappeared into the lake with an apocalyptic splash.

Spray leapt a hundred feet in the air. Waves surged and rose between the timber legs on which Lakeside stood clear of the water, the swell pressing against the underside of the town and water squeezing through the planks to flood up into many streets and houses. When the first waves had subsided, a wreath of moisture lingered in the air, scattering myriad tiny rainbow sparks as the bright sun shone through.

It took the people of Lakeside many moments before their collective relief found expression in a shout of joy. 'Hurrah!' they cried. 'Lard has slain the dreadful beast!' 'The dragon is no more!' 'Apples! Apples! Only slightly bruised!' and, 'All hail Lard the Deliverer! Lakeside is saved!'

Lard stood at the extreme edge of the wrecked bridge and stared out over the water. The waves were settling now, the surface resuming its snail-like placidity, and closing over the sunken body of the dragon. He stood motionless for a long while, half expecting the creature to rear up from the lake in fire and tempest. But nothing broke the surface of the waters. It began to dawn on Lard that Smug was truly dead. 'For is not a dragon,' he said, more to himself than anybody, 'a creature of fire? Is it not truly said, to kill a dragon, drown it?' He turned to his people. 'The waters have swallowed the beast! The curse has been taken from Lakeside!'

'Hurrah!' they cried.

A dozen strong men swarmed around their mayor, and grasped him to carry him, shoulder-high, amongst the rejoicing people. They abandoned this ambitious plan after half a minute of grunting and heaving, and instead Lard consented to walk amongst the throng. 'If only I were still a bard,' he said to himself. 'What a lay I would compose about this adventure!' And, thinking of lays, he passed about the town.

The celebrations lasted for the rest of the day and into the night. The sun set in gaudy red splendour, and the waxing moon shone clear.[4] Torches gleamed over the still waters. Everybody sang, everybody danced. Troths were plighted, and in some cases (in dark doorways and behind packing cases) more than plighted. Healths were toasted, toast was consumed, consumption cured, and cured ham taken from the storerooms to be put on the toast. It was a celebration to remember.

The bridge that linked Lakeside to the shore had been destroyed, but the Lakesiders went to and fro in their numerous boats. Nobody was surprised, therefore, when a number of boats pulled up at one of the landing berths, and two dozen tall figures jumped out. Indeed, there was hardly anybody still conscious and adequately compos mentis to be surprised.

'Where's the lord of this town?' the leading figure called. 'Take us to the lord of this place!'

These newcomers moved, swiftly but gracefully, up and down the streets of the town, before meeting again by their boats. 'Dear me,' said one. 'They all seem to be asleep.'

'A little over-indulgence, I fear,' said a second.

'I asked one of them for directions,' said a third, 'and

---

[4] 'Waxing': becoming more like wax – which is to say, acquiring a yellow hue and building into a plug-like ball.

he replied in Gobblin-talk! All ugly gutturals and plosives! I assumed the Gobblins had already arrived, and had taken over the town. But then I realised that this chap wasn't actually replying to me at all. He was just throwing up.'

'How distasteful,' said a fourth.

'Well,' said the first, 'it seems they're all drunk. This makes our job easier, I suppose. Elstree, go and fetch the rest of the army. We'll rebuild the bridge in the morning, link the town and the water's edge again. But until then, let's just consolidate what we have.'

'Righto,' said the figure who had been addressed as Elstree. He hopped back down into one of the boats, his cloak flapping apart as he dropped to reveal a glint of elvish armour beneath.

By morning, Lakeside was under new management. The elves had dragged or pushed the sotted inhabitants into a central hall and locked the gates. Then they quartered their men – several hundred, dressed in the most elegant armour – in the best rooms of the place. Finally the elves strapped together a long line of Lakeside rowing boats and barges to make a pontoon bridge to the shore.

This was finished before breakfast. As the elves munched their delicate weybread and sipped their gray tea, the original inhabitants of Lakeside were beginning to regain their now battered and aching consciousnesses. Elsqare gave orders that the lord of the town be brought to him, and twenty minutes later Lard himself was standing in front of the elf.

'Good morning,' said Elsqare. 'How are you today?'

'What?' said Lard forcefully, with a cross expression.

'Are you well?'

'What?' He blinked, glowered, looked around. 'What's going on?'

'I am Lord Elsqare, the elf,' explained Lord Elsqare the elf. 'At the moment, and much to my chagrin, I find myself at the head of a mighty army. We don't mean to inconvenience you, you understand, but my men must be billeted somewhere.'

'What?' said Lard a third time. 'Who are you?'

'Give the chap some tea,' said Elsqare.

'You've invaded!' said Lard suddenly. 'You've invaded Lakeside!'

'Not in the least. Our presence here is only temporary, I assure you,' said the elf lord. 'Allow me to explain. We understand that a party of stout dwarfs has travelled here, on their way to the Only Mountain. We understand that they had some business to settle with the dragon who lives there . . .'

'Smug!' blurted Lard. 'I killed him!'

There was an elegantly shocked silence amongst the elves at this news.

'Really?' Elsqare asked eventually.

'Indeed, he came yesterday to threaten Lakeside,' said Lard, hoisting his belly up and standing prouder. 'I confronted him with my trusty bow – I am a bowman, you know. He settled upon the bridge. It collapsed, and he drowned in the lake.'

'My, my,' said Elsqare. 'How interesting. So Smug the Mighty is dead?'

'Yes,' said Lard. 'And did you say something about tea?' He waddled over and sat himself beside the elf lord. 'And some breakfast, perhaps?'

Elsqare motioned to his followers to provide the necessary. 'Well,' said the elf, 'if, truly, the dragon is dead that places a very different complexion upon events. Are you sure he has perished?'

'Certainly,' said Lard, through a mouthful of crumpet. This is not an easy word to say when one's mouth is full of food, but Lard had a bold stab at the pronunciation anyway.

'Have you recovered his corpse?'

'No,' said Lard, with a slight hesitation.

'If he's in the lake, then surely it would be an easy matter to drag the water for his body. Don't you think? To be on the safe side?'

At this, one of Elsqare's followers burst into song.

> *When they drag in the Dragon*
> *And bring back the corpse of a monster so monstrous,*

And lay it out dead on a pontoon so ponstrous
Why then we'll be sure he really has gone.

Elsqare silenced his minion with a severe look. 'Mr – Lard is it? Lord? – are you, Lard?'

'Mayor,' said Lard.

'Mayor, excellent. Believe me, the elves have no interest in *invading*, as you put it, your delightful lakeside town. We are here as your allies, not your enemies.'

'Yet you have locked all my people in the great central hall.'

'A precaution,' said Elsqare, making a dismissive gesture with one hand in the air. 'When they're properly sobered, and properly apprised of the situation, then they'll be let out.'

'Apprised of what situation?' asked Lard, his mouth sagging open to reveal half-mushed scone.

'So you *don't* know? Dear me. Well, I'm afraid I come as the bearer of bad news.'

'Bad news?'

'Yes. You see, an enormous Gobblin army has assembled.'

'Gobblins?' repeated Lard, with a catch in his throat.

'I'm afraid so. A simply enormous army. They've recruited Gobblins from the whole length of the mountains. And they're a day's march, at most, from here.'

'Here? Why should Gobblins want to come here?'

'The dwarfs I mentioned. It seems they made rather a *mess* when they went through the Minty Mountains. They stirred up a tremendous fuss. And – I see no reason why you shouldn't be told this – there's something else. Amongst the Gobblins is a creature not Gobblin-shaped: something else, a philosopher of doleful countenance called Sollum. From his lips the Gobblins have learned that an artefact of enormous power and evil – one of the Things® created by the Evil Sharon – is in the possession of these dwarfs. Word of this has spread all over the western lands. The Gobblins have come for revenge, for destruction, for the gold, but most of all they have come to seize the Thing®. Who knows what terror they might wreak, if they can but obtain it! It is time for all the free peoples of Upper Middle Earth to unite and face this dire threat!'

'Blimey,' said Lard.

Through that same night, and into the early hours of that same morning, the dwarfs on the mountainside kept a sombre vigil, watching the lands and the skies to the south, the direction of Lakeside. They were waiting for Smug's return, or for some news of him. 'If there were some big fight,' Bingo said, 'wouldn't we see it? Flame and fireworks?'

'Maybe,' said Mori sulkily. 'Maybe not.'

'What shall we do?' Bingo asked.

'Don't think you're back in our good books so quickly,' snapped the dwarf, and turned his shoulder to the soddit. It was a warm shoulder, literally speaking, because it had been close to the fire; but in metaphoric terms it was a cold shoulder. So, you could say, it was simultaneously a warm and a cold shoulder, which sounds paradoxical I know, but isn't really when you think about it.

'All your fault,' mumbled On.

'A fine pickle you've got us into,' grumbled Gofur.

'Mavis!' gasped Failin. But he was asleep, and his comment had no particular relevance to the situation in hand.

Bingo stared sorrowfully into the fire, watching the glowing logs and the wriggling, writhing, belly-dancing flames that leapt up from them.

'Don't be too dithcouraged,' said Thorri, settling next to him. 'You weren't to know.'

'I feel something dreadful has happened,' said the soddit. His sense of awkwardness and gloom was compounded by the fact that he had still not yet told anybody of the Barkingstone, which lay like a guilty secret in his coat pocket.

'Thomething dreadful,' agreed Thorri. 'I thenthe that too. But we can't help that. It'th a thame we didn't get a chanthe to chat with Thmug before he hurried away, but there you go.'

'What shall we do now?'

'The front door'th open, you thay?'

'Yes,' said Bingo. 'The dragon left it open after he left.'

'Well, when it'th light again, we'll carry Gandef into the mountain. Even if Thmug'th not there to help, we can at leath make the old feller comfortable.'

Bingo looked, for the hundredth time, at the wrapped-up sleeping figure of the beardless wizard. 'He does seem taller,' he said. The wizard's head was six inches closer to a particular pile of rocks than it had been before.

'Yeth,' said Thorri simply.

It was hard to sleep. Just before dawn Bingo managed a couple of hours, but he was woken by dwarfs kicking dirt into the fire and gathering their things. 'Come along, Grabbings,' said Mori in a hostile tone. 'I suppose we can't leave you on the mountainside. Although we're all sorely tempted, look you, to do just that.'

They picked their way back down the mountainside, taking turns to drag Gandef's oblivious body behind them. It was easier than the ascent, but harder than it might have been. The wizard was considerably weightier than he had been before.

They rested for lunch, and then pressed on through the afternoon, keeping the mountain on their left side.

They crested the westernmost ridge flanking the front door as the sun was sinking, and as they climbed that hill they temporarily reversed the sunset for a few minutes, bringing the sun a fraction back above the horizon. It was on that low peak that they made their camp for the night, as the sun set for a second time in fifteen minutes.

They ate in silence. 'It's still hard for me to understand,' said Bingo.

If the dwarfs had not yet forgiven him, then they were at least too tired by their exertions to be expressly angry. 'The world is a stranger place than you realise, little soddit,' said Mori.

'Apparently so. When a female soddit and a male soddit get together, they create something new. I don't understand how dwarfs, or wizards, or dragons – since they're apparently all part of the same creature – how they – how *you* propagate the species.'

'Propagate,' said the dwarf meditatively. 'It sounds strange in my ears, that word. You mean: fill the world up with versions of yourself until the world is overcrowded and the landscapes are made a desert and crowds of the starving sway in time to their own moans?'

'Well,' said Bingo. 'Not that exactly . . .'

'With us,' said Mori, 'we know exactly how many there are. The creator breathed a certain number of dwarf lives into the stone at the beginning of things. These are crystals of the divine, look you, and their coming to life is part of the self-becoming. The great sequence unrolls, and form follows form until the crystals – or those that have survived – achieve their ultimate form. The form of the creator itself.'

'It sounds a little circular to me,' said Bingo sourly.

'Circular? Well, la, perhaps so. Circular like the way spring leads to winter leads to spring? Like the way the sun sets and rises? Circular's not so bad, look you. Besides,' he added, '*this* way the Divine experiences the nature of existence in creation.'

'And the creator can't do that otherwise?'

'The creator's outside creation,' said Mori, as if that were the most obvious thing in the world. 'He can't just poke his nose in, or he'll break it.'

All this metaphysical speculation was making Bingo's head hurt, so he wrapped himself in a blanket and tried to sleep.

The morning burst upon them in glory, muslin-coloured clouds refracting and making glow the yellow-white light of a new day. Bingo woke with the sunlight, squeezing his shut eyeballs and pressing its warmth against his face.

The soddit roused himself to find the dwarfs already awake, and standing in a line. 'What is it?' he asked, rubbing his eyes by punching himself very slowly and very delicately in each eye in turn. He yawned. 'What's up?'

'I'd say,' said Mori, pointing down the valley before them, 'that an army is up.'

Below in the valley that led to the cave-mouth entrance of Strebor the Only Mountain, a great host had assembled. The elegant armour of the elves shone like golden water; their purple banners, carrying the emblem of the purple carnation, fluttered in the morning breeze. Beside them was a host of Men of Lakeside, wearing their lacquer-coated leather armour (which doubled as sportswear) and brandishing their various forms of weaponry.

Bingo looked at the ranks upon ranks of warriors: a thousand men and elves all told. 'Golly,' he said.

Gobblin Charge

Chapter Eleven

CLODS BURST

෧ᵐᵐᵕᵕ

'Can Smug truly be dead?' said Bingo, in dismay.

The dwarfs and the soddit were gathered in Lord Elsqare's stylish silk tent, which had been pitched between the two hills before the main entrance to the mountain. Men-at-arms and elves-at-arms moved to and fro, entering and leaving the tent. Preparations were being made for the battle to come.

'Indeed so,' said Elsqare languidly. 'Something of a fortunate happenstance, I think we can agree. This Gobblin army facing us is ten thousand strong. If they'd had a dragon with them as well, then they'd have been, well – I don't know let me see – hmm, let's say *unbeatable*. That's what they'd have been.'

'Which shows how little you know, see,' said Mori, bustling forward in fury. 'That dragon, look you, would never have sided with the Gobblins. He'd have been our ally!'

'There's never been friendship or alliance,' said Elsqare, 'between dragons and elves.'

'No,' said Lard. 'Nor between dragons and men neither.'

'Dragons and dwarfs, however,' said Bingo, holding the fuming Mori back, 'is a different matter. I think Mori is right. I think Smug would have fought with us against the Gobblins, and a mighty ally he would have been. But there's no point in fretting over might-have-beens. Might-have-beens,' he added, growing strangely poetic, 'don't help any more, they just lie on the floor 'til you sweep them away.'

Everybody looked at Bingo. He looked at the floor. 'Sorry,' he said. 'I don't know why I said that.'

'As you say, however, Sir Soddit,' said Elsqare, 'whether the dragon would have helped or hindered our cause is moot.'

'Is *what*?' asked Mori.

'Moot.'

'Moot,' repeated the dwarf, as if trying the word for size. 'Moot,' he said. 'Moot, moot, moot.' He walked in a circle around the tent trying variants of pronunciation, drawing out the '*oo*', making the '*t*' more clipped. 'Moot moot moot. I *like* that,' he concluded. 'That's lovely, look you. *Moot*. What does it mean?'

'It means,' said Elsqare, 'that it is something as yet undecided.'

'Moot,' said Mori. 'Grand. What'll you have for breakfast?' he said in a little play-acting voice. '*Moot*,' he added in a basso profundo. 'Which came first the chicken or the egg? *Moot*, moot. Mirror on the wall, who is the fairest dwarf of all? *Moot is fairest. Moot moot*,' he continued, in this antiphonal manner. 'That's good, boyo,' he said in his usual voice, turning back to Elsqare. 'I like that. I'll try and work it into my conversation, la.'

'Hmm,' said Elsqare. 'Anyway. Putting that on one side, we have yet to determine our best strategy. The Gobblins will be upon us in a day and a night. We have a mighty army of elves, and a mighty army of men – a thousand warriors all told. Will the dwarfs join this cause?'

'We will,' said Mori firmly, casting a glance behind him at Thorri, who nodded. 'We will stand beside you.'

'Then we are joined,' said Elsqare, with a glad face, 'by a mighty army of dwarfs! How many warriors are there in your army, Sir Dwarf?'

'Eh,' said Mori, rolling his eyes up as if calculating a rough approximation of the number. 'Five,' he said.

There was silence in the tent for a little space.

'They are mighty though,' Mori added. 'Those five.'

'Very well,' said Elsqare in a heavy voice. 'Sir Soddit. Will your people join in this cause? Death may follow, but glory comes also and we, the free peoples of Upper Middle Earth, welcome all allies in this battle against the evil Gobblins.'

'Sure,' said Bingo, feeling light-headed. 'Why not?'

'Then,' said Elsqare grandly, standing up from his throne, 'our great alliance will be of four armies! An army of elves, of men, of,' he coughed, 'dwarfs, and a great army of soddits! Together we shall stand shoulder to shoulder against the hordes of ten thousand blood-hungry Gobblins!'

Everybody in the tent cheered.

'How many,' Elsqare asked Bingo, as if in after-thought, 'are there in your army, Sir Soddit? You are small, but I'll wager you are tough, strong, thrawn, single-minded folk in battle, slow to anger but terrible when your blood is up. How great is your army?'

'Just me,' said Bingo.

'I see,' said Elsqare, sounding peeved, 'well that's not exactly an *army*, now, is it?'

'Doesn't that depend,' said Bingo, 'on what you mean by an army?'

'No, it doesn't. Ah, but it doesn't matter. I've declared ours an alliance of four armies, so that's what it'll be. The scribes and historians will have to be creative in future accounts of it, that's all.'

The elven scouts had estimated that the Gobblin horde was nearly upon them. The new allies had very little time. 'We must prepare for war,' Mori told Bingo. 'Look you.'

There was still the question of Gandef. 'We hoped the dragon would supervise his transformation, but that's not to be,' said Mori. 'Without Smug's help it is difficult to know what will happen. But it can't be helped. The future is moot. Gandef himself is moot.'

'Mute?' asked Gofur, puzzled.

'No, bach, moot,' said Mori eagerly. 'That's a word I just learned. It means uncertain.'

'Ahh,' said the other four dwarfs.

'Anyway, what I suggest is,' said Mori, 'we move Gandef inside the mountain. He'll be comfortable enough there. Leave him in Smug's old hall. At least he'll be out of the way of the Gobblins.'

'Unless the Gobblins are victorious,' Bingo pointed out. 'In which case they'll swarm into the mountains and kill him.'

Mori shrugged. 'We'll all be dead then, boyo,' he pointed out. 'So that's moot too.'

It took all five dwarfs and Bingo hauling together to drag Gandef's sleeping form. His body was twice as long as it had been before, and although not twice as broad around it was considerably thickened in the torso. Like a sprouting adolescent there was a stringiness to his limbs and torso. His face had elongated, and although it was still recognisably Gandef it had a weird and unnerving quality. The wizard had burst the blanket in which he had been wrapped, and ripped his

A. R. R. Roberts

clothes to pieces in his growth. Bingo took one foot and
Gofur the other, and the other dwarfs took up places
beside the wizard's six-feet-long legs. Pulling together
they dragged him up the valley, through the main
entrance and along the corridor within. Bingo, grasping
the old wizard's ankles, found himself unpleasantly
fascinated by Gandef's toenails. They were black,
protruding, and were starting to claw-up at the end. It
was not nice. His shoulders had blackened also, and
two spikes had grown out of the blades like the tips of
furled umbrellas.

'Should we cover him with something?' Bingo wondered as they positioned Gandef's supine form on
Smug's pile of gold. 'Won't he get cold?'

'You're still thinking he's got the same sort of body as
you,' said Gofur. 'He hasn't. He's in the metamorphosis
state now.'

'How long will that take?' the soddit asked.

'Nobody knows exactly—' Gofur began saying, but
Mori interrupted him. 'That's moot, see,' he said.
'Moot.'

'I see,' said Bingo.

They left Gandef in the chamber.

The party came out of the mountain again to bright
sunshine, and to the sight of elves and men drilling in
the valley before the front door. 'We'd better close the
gate,' said Mori.

They pushed together, heaving with all their might, first on one of the huge stone leafs, and then on the other. Slowly the pair of hundred-yard-tall doors closed. When the second slammed shut with a great shuddering clunk, they could hear another sound, the clanging of the brass lock inside. 'He's sealed in there now,' said Mori.

'How do we get back inside?' asked Bingo.

'You could always go down the chimney,' suggested Gofur.

The dwarfs laughed together at this. Bingo did not join them.

'Either that,' Gofur added, 'or else Gandef will open the gates when he's ready.'

'Could we not have hidden ourselves in the mountain?' asked Bingo as they stood there. 'Surely we could have hidden from the Gobblins in there.'

'No, bach,' said Mori sadly. 'If they win, they'll batter the gates down and sack the halls within. We stand a better chance meeting them in open war here, rather than being caught like rats in traps inside.'

'Let's hope we win then,' said Bingo. 'For Gandef's sake.'

'Let's hope so,' agreed the dwarfs.

That day, before the battle, seemed to Bingo the longest he had known. The sun moved incrementally over the blue sky. Men and elves cut trees and sharpened them at one end, planting the jagged stakes in several rows beside the river. The archers in the company whittled new arrows and rubbed wax into the bowstrings. The soddit, however, had nothing to do; he felt superfluous, and he didn't like the feeling. He begged a short sword from one of the armourers of Lakeside, paying for it with dragon gold, and for an hour or so in the hot, fly-drony, pollen-dusty afternoon he practised making sweeps with this blade. He cut the tops off long strands of grass that grew in the meadows by the water. He stabbed the bark of old trees, forcing little plugs of wood out. An hour of this was enough for his arm to grow sodden and tired with the practice, and he stopped.

Then he climbed the eastern hill and watched the sun set over the dark sea of trees on the horizon, but his heart was heavier than the sinking sun. An hour of play-fighting and his arm had become too weary to lift, and now it was sore and ache-filled. An hour of play-fighting! Come the morning, he would have a whole day of *real* fighting, and – for all he knew (for he knew very little about real battles) – all night too. He dreaded the thought that he would collapse with exhaustion before the fight had barely begun. He was, by himself, the army of Soddlesex, the Hobbld-Ahoy! battalion. He had never fought before, and he had no relish for it.

That evening, the four armies lit many camp fires, and ate what would be for many of them their last supper, and drank their last wine. Bingo sat around one of the fires with the Army of Dwarfs. The six of them ate in silence, and afterwards sat in silence. 'I was thinking,' Bingo said eventually, although the words felt heavy and unreal in his mouth, 'of a plan. Tell me what your opinion is of this, boys. I was thinking – there is still the Thing®.'

The dwarfs groaned.

'I know, I know,' said Bingo. 'It's served us mostly ill, and if we give it the chance it will bring catastrophe down upon us.'

'That,' agreed Mori, in an emphatic voice, 'is *not* moot.'

'But maybe there's some watertight, guaranteed, win-win spell we can cast through the Thing®,' Bingo insisted, 'that could bring an end to this terrible battle before it's begun. Don't you think?'

'No,' said Gofur.

'No,' said Failin.

'No,' said On.

'No,' said Mori.

'I'd thay,' said Thorri, 'that it'th betht not to uthe it at all.'

Bingo sat in silence for a while.

'So Smug is dead,' he said. 'How and if I were to say

"Smug is dead" through the Thing®? Wouldn't that bring Smug back to life? Then at least he could help us defeat the Gobblins – and afterwards, he could aid Gandef.'

The dwarfs sat in silence. They were, clearly, tempted by this prospect. But Thorri steeled their resolve.

'No,' he said firmly. 'The Thing® ith a magic artefact. Dragonth are magic creatureth. Micthing magic with magic, micthing malign magic like the Thing® with benign magic like the dragon would not be clever. Leave it alone. Just leave it alone.'

'Thorri is right,' said Mori sadly. 'The Thing® would find a way of thwarting us, and bringing disaster through our wish, no matter how carefully we framed it. Let us leave it alone.'

They sat in silence for a long time.

Bingo could not sleep. He tossed and turned, turned from his left side to his right and from his right to his left, but neither side was comfortable. He found himself wishing for a third side on which to lie, and instead of trying to sleep he got up and wandered about the camp until dawn. The fires were burning brightly, and the elvish and mannish soldiers seemed in good spirits.

Dawn came slowly, first with a thinning of the darkness to the east, then in a glory of sunrise gold.

Low horizontal clouds brimmed with brightness, as if they were rips in the sky and diamond-gold illuminations were pouring through from some other place. Bingo watched for long minutes. Then he noticed that the chiefs of the other three armies had assembled, with their standards, on the top of the hill east of the main entrance of Strebor. He hurried up there as fast as his little legs could carry him.

'Ah,' said Elsqare, as the guards let him through. 'Here is the general of our fourth army. Have a look, general.' He gestured to the south.

From their vantage point, Bingo could see for many leagues. At first his eyes confused him. It was as if the grass meadows that lay alongside the river had been overgrown in a single night with gnarled black thickets, with thorn bushes and stark pole-like trees. But then the sight before him resolved, in his mind, to reality. The ground was covered with Gobblin soldiers. Ten thousand or more, armed and armoured, waiting for the order to charge.

'A horde,' said Elsqare. 'Wouldn't you say?'

'A horde,' agreed Bingo.

'Don't let your heart quaver, Sir Soddit,' said the elf. 'Be brave.'

'It's not my heart I'm worried about quavering,' said Bingo. 'It's lower down in my torso. What can we do? That army stretches as far as the eye can see –

ten thousand soldiers, you said. How strong is our army?'

'Our *combined* armies,' corrected Elsqare. 'I lead a force of five hundred elves. Lard commands five hundred men. The dwarfs, fierce and resolute, represent a force of five. And you yourself, Sir Soddit, are a force of one.'

Bingo could do the maths for himself. 'Oh dear,' he said.

'Quite,' said Elsqare. 'Still, can't be helped, can't be helped. Ready the squadrons!' he called. 'Trumpeters, prepare to sound! Fall back upon the mountain if the press is too great!'

Bingo tried to swallow, but his throat no longer seemed to be in working order. A fine time, he thought to himself, for my throat to seize up. How can I beg for mercy if I can't beg at all?

The Gobblins had marched day and night without pausing, all the way from the Minty Mountains, led by their terrible King, Kluk the Bald.[1] A hunger for death and a lust for battle was upon them: battle red in tooth and wattle, as the saying goes. Their soldiers had been inflamed with stories of the wrongs done to Gobblin-

[1] Son of Gallopavo the Meagre, who had been slain in the Minty Mountains by Thorri's father, Phwoah the Stunner.

kind by elves and men and dwarfs. 'Kill! Kill! Kill!'
they chanted. 'Elsqare the baster! Lard the waster!'
Above all, they had been fired with excitement by the
tales of the Thing®, and of the great things that Kluk
would achieve once he possessed it. They felt, in their
gobblin innards, the tug of the device: for they had
themselves also been created by Sharon the Evil One,
just as had been the Thing®. Theirs was a like substance. The soldiers chanted:

> *Bring the Thing®!*
> *Bring the Thing®!*
> *We want the Thing®!*
> *We want the Thing®!*

As the defenders watched from the hill, King Kluk was
carried to the front of the horde on his silver platform.
'Chicken!' called the front rank of elves and men,
hoping to discomfort the Gobblin army with this as-
persion upon their King's courage. 'Chicken!' But the
Gobblins only scowled and hissed, and the Gobblin
King was brought closer.

He was armoured in the most splendid of Gobblin
armour. White parchment overshoes, folded and cut
with harsh curlicues, had been placed over his shoes to
prevent the unclean blood of his enemies soiling the
soles of his boots. His armour presented two enormous

breastplates to the world, one on either side of his sternum, implying that his heroic chest was twice the size, twice as muscled, as lesser beings. The space between his armour and his skin had been crammed with herbage – grasses and herbs that possessed healing properties, such that should a blade pierce his skin their charm would lessen and close the wound. He carried a two-pronged killing pitchfork in one hand and a long-bladed knife in the other, both polished and glinting in the morning sunlight. As the ranks of Gobblins passed to allow his bearers to carry him forward, the soldiers chanted his name in an ecstasy of excitement.

> *Kluk! Great Kluk!*
> *Kluk! Kluk! Kluk!*
> *Kluk! Kluk! Kluk!*
> *Gre-eeat Great Kulk!*
> *Kluk! Kluk! Kluk!*

And so on.

'Archers!' called Elsqare. The hilltop silence was broken by a whittlish sound, as a hundred bowstrings were drawn back in unison.

'Fire,' said Elsqare. And a hundred arrows shot into the sky, and arced their deadly hail upon the Gobblins.

The horde roared, and surged forward.

And so the battle of the Famous Five Armies began.

Bingo's memory of the battle would always, afterwards, have a number of gaps in it. He would never forget that first charge of the enemy, and the burning, desperate sense of panic that it created in his torso all the way from his hips to his throat. Neither would he forget the first of the fighting, as the fore-guard of Gobblins, the fearsome Uruk-Low, came sprinting up the hillside on their ungainly legs. To the right elves brought down their swords in a coordinated sweep, cutting into the advancing wave; to the left, men thrust and parried. In the middle, dwarf axes swept up and down in a pendulum motion, catching little patches of sunshine on their blades at the highest point of the swing until the iron was too blackened with Gobblin blood. And he would never forget his first taste of fighting: running underneath an elvish swordsman's legs, hacking and stabbing with the sword, and cutting into the side of a Gobblin head. Bingo's blade bit deep, and the Gobblin squealed and jerked, but as he fell he drew Bingo down after him because the sword had jammed in the skull. Bingo tumbled forward and collapsed on the corpse, trying to lever the sword out of the Gobblin's bone. After what seemed an age Bingo got the thing free, with a wrench that caused him to stagger backwards. He paused and looked around him, and his heart seemed to fail in his breast. Gobblins were everywhere he looked, jabbing with their pikes, swing-

A. R. R. Roberts

ing their maces and their notched blades; men and elves
fought bravely, but, like outcroppings of rock in a
stormy and poisoned sea, they were beset on all sides.
A gobblin bounced into Bingo's line of sight, his wicked
little eyes glancing left and right, his red wattle swinging from his grisly neck. Bingo swung his sword.

But he could not remember what happened after
that. There was a series of disconnected memories: of
Gofur struggling with a mass of Gobblins, two hanging
on each of his arms, and two on each of his legs. Bingo
ran at the mass, trying to cut the creatures away. Then
he remembered running in a different direction, trying
to keep up with a party of elves. He remembered seeing
the blue sky scratched and stitched over and again with
ceiling after ceiling of arrows. He remembered seeing
decapitated Gobblins sprinting with extraordinary vigour in random directions. He remembered seeing a
mannish warrior struck in the small of his back with a
long pike, forced along by three Gobblins, and seeing
the jagged head of the weapon erupt from the man's
chest. Other than that it was all a maelstrom of
indistinct memories: the smell of blood, the terrible
weariness in his arms that told him he could barely lift
his sword again, and the insistent fear in his head that
compelled him to lift his sword anyway; the sight of
rush and counter-rush, of blade colliding with shield,
and always the whizz and thrumming fall of storms and

storms of arrows in the air overhead. Bingo thrust his
sword into the chest of a Gobblin soldier, and the blade
squeaked as it sank home.

The next clear memory in Bingo's head was of
himself standing, panting, next to Lord Elsqare and
Mori and two dozen warriors, men and elves. They
were no longer on the hills flanking the front door.
Under the pressure of the Gobblin advance the four
armies had retreated, and now they had taken up
positions on the mountainside itself, to the west of the
main entrance. Bingo could not remember the actual
retreat; but now here they all were.

'How goes it, Master Soddit?' Elsqare asked. 'Warm
work?'

'Blimey,' said Bingo, which was his way of agreeing.

'My lord!' called a subaltern, a man splattered with
blood and dirt, with a deep wound in his forehead. 'My
lord, the Gobblins are swarming up the eastern flank of
the mountain. I fear they will clamber over the main
gate, and come down on us from above.'

'A grim prospect,' said Elsqare. 'If they can establish
a position up there, then we are doomed. Archers!' he
called. 'The gate!'

Those archers still alive took up position, and began
firing arrows at the Gobblins that were scurrying along
the mighty door lintel of the front gate. Bingo could see
the danger. Once a large enough party crossed this

narrow ledge, they would possess the higher slopes of the mountain, and could rain down weapons, boulders, anything upon the defenders beneath. His heart burning in his chest, Bingo watched the archers at work; but although their darts flew accurately, and although many Gobblins fell from above the door to the ground far beneath, yet still there were too many of the creatures to be killed in this manner, and droves of them were reaching the upper slopes.

Bingo's next memory was from much later in the day. He could not say what happened in the intervening time, except that he looked around and noticed that the sun was lower in the western sky, and that he felt much, much more tired – more tired than he had ever felt before. His sword was dented and chipped along its cutting edge, and was smeared with black blood. A huge Gobblin, cleaver-wielding, ran at him, and Bingo half ducked, half fell out of the way, heaving round with his sword, cutting into the creature's neck from behind. His arm was so weary that it burned with a fierce pain. The muscles threatened to disobey his mind every time he ordered them to move. He could hardly grip the handle.

'Bingo!' called Mori. 'Bingo!'

The dwarf staggered towards him, his beard slick with blood – both the black blood of Gobblins, and the red blood of its owner. Several crooked Gobblin arrows poked out of his body. 'You're still alive, boyo!' the dwarf called. As he reached Bingo he tripped and sank to his knees.

'Mori – are you hurt?'

'Oh it's nothing,' said the dwarf. 'Stings a bit,' he added. Then he rolled on to his back.

Bingo dropped his sword as Gobblin arrows plocked into the turf around him to stick up like dead and blackened stalks. Grasping the dwarf's legs, he pulled with all his weary might, hauling Mori to the higher ground. He arrived at a narrow ledge, on which some elves and men stood shoulder to shoulder. The paths were crammed with the dead. Stones and arrow shafts rained down from above. Six men were holding their broad shields in the air to provide shelter from this deadly hail.

'Bingo,' said Thorri, hurrying out to help the soddit drag Mori in underneath this rudimentary cover. 'Good to thee you're thtill alive.'

'And you, sir,' gasped Bingo, close to sobbing with his exhaustion. 'The others?'

'It'th been a grim day,' said the dwarf. He shook his head.

'This is our last stand,' said Elsqare, crouching down to address the soddit. 'We've been pushed back here – sheer weight of numbers. I'm sorry to say that Lord Lard is laid low.'

'Dead?'

'Dead, with many other heroic souls. Ah well,' the elf added lightly, 'some you win, some you lose.'

'Lose?' wailed Bingo. 'Can it be true?'

'They had another army behind the army we could see,' explained Elsqare. 'Twenty thousand soldiers in all. We had one thousand and six soldiers. We never really had much of a chance. See!'

Bingo looked out across the plain south and west of the mountain. The Gobblin dead were piled high, but were still vastly outnumbered by the living. Waves of Gobblins moved back and forth, some surging towards the mountain, others – it seemed – merely going round and round in a meaningless way.

The hail from above stopped. Bingo could see King Kluk processing through the files and ranks of his army, over the foothills and up towards them. As he approached, his troops chanted:

> *Bring the Thing®!*
> *Bring the Thing®!*
> *We want the Thing®!*
> *We want the Thing®!*

'What can we do?' asked Bingo, feeling a terrible and hopeless desperation. 'We can't give them the Thing® –

they'll do unspeakable and terrible wickedness with it! We can't give them the Thing®.'

'And yet,' pointed out Elsqare, reasonably enough, 'if we refuse it them, they'll simply kill us and take it from our dead bodies.'

'What can we do?'

A thousand Gobblin archers had taken up position around the last redoubt. Elsqare ordered his men to put their weapons down. 'If we so much as notch an arrow to a string,' he observed, 'we'll die in a swarm of Gobblin darts.'

But it was hard to obey, for Kluk was now within bowshot, and a single well-aimed arrow could have pierced his head. He drew closer and closer, and his followers muttered, 'Gobble, gobble, gobble' and 'Kluk! Kluk! Kluk!' as he advanced. Finally the silver platform on which he was borne came to a halt.

'Elves!' King Kluk announced in his horrid voice. 'Men! Dwarfs! You are defeated!'

A cry of triumph rose from the Gobblin hordes.

'The Thing®,' said Kluk, 'is ours! Surrender.'

'We surrender,' said Elsqare suavely. 'Certainly. We're not at war any more, and I'd like to remind you of the terms of the Gungadin Convention—'

'Silence!' barked Kluk. 'You may not be at war with *us*, but *we* are at war with *you* – always!'

Another great and terrible shout broke from the ranks of Gobblin troops.

'Gobblins are forever at war with elves and men and dwarfs!' shouted Kluk.

'I think that meanth,' said Thorri to Bingo, 'that they're going to kill uth, dethpite the fact that we've thurrendered.'

'That may very well be the case,' agreed Bingo.

'Give us the Thing®!' howled Kluk, and his army yelled in agreement.

'This is a tight spot,' said Elsqare. 'What do you think we should do, O soddit?'

Bingo fingered the Thing® in his pocket. Now was the time to use it, if ever there had been a time to use it; but his mind went round and round in an empty track and he could think of nothing. He tried to think of a spell, or a form of words, that would save the day, but nothing came to him. He thought of saying 'The Gobblins are victorious', hoping that the device would change the world such that the Gobblins were defeated: but he knew, in his heart, that the Thing® wanted the Gobblins to triumph, and that it would twist his words to destroy *him* if he tried such a trick, perhaps by making their victory imminent rather than actual. Then he thought: perhaps I can use the Thing® to destroy the Thing®. What would happen if I said through the Thing®, 'the Thing® exists', would it cease to exist? But then, since it would no longer exist, it would not have been able to make itself disappear, and surely it would exist again. But then it would exist and would be able to make itself disappear . . . and so it would not exist . . . and so it would exist . . . and the possibilities whirled in Bingo's exhausted brain until he could see nothing proceeding from such a wish except a great *bang* and Bingo lying dead on the floor, and the Gobblins picking the Thing® from his cold corpse.

'Which one of you carries the Thing®?' called Kluk. 'Is it you, elf?'

Bingo saw Gobblin archers draw back their bows and aim darts at Elsqare. 'It is I!' he announced, stepping forward. 'Bingo Grabbings, the soddit. I carry the Thing®.'

The whole hideous army seemed to breathe the words 'Doom, doom', the sound sweeping through the air like thunder.

'Give the Thing® to me!' called Kluk.

'If I do,' said Bingo, 'will you allow us to go free?'

'Ha!' laughed Kluk. 'No, manrunt, no – but I will kill you cleanly, and burn your bodies. If you deny me, I will kill you slowly and eat your corpses.'

'Right,' said Bingo, as if considering this. He could see a thousand Gobblin arrows aimed at his own chest. His mind raced. *The arrows are not marshmallow*, he thought to himself. Would that save them? What evil twist could the Thing® place on such a statement? *King Kluk is alive*, he thought. But if the King died, his soldiers would simply kill them all. *All Gobblins are war-loving*, he thought, and wondered to himself if even the magic of the Thing® were enough to reverse such a statement, to root out the love of war from all Gobblin hearts at once. What better phrase could he think of? None.

'At once!' shrieked Kluk. 'At once! Or you will all die!'

Bingo's hand went into his coat pocket. He drew out the Barkingstone, and it glinted in the dying light of the day. The Gobblin soldiers nearest him went 'Ooo!' and drew back a little.

It occurred to Bingo that the Gobblins did not know what the Thing® looked like. Why should they? It had never been theirs. It had been fashioned by Sharon in the fires of Mount Dumb, and had passed somehow to Sollum.

'Here,' he shouted holding aloft the great jewel. 'Here is the Thing®!'

'Woof,' went the Barkingstone.

Bingo threw the gem. It sailed, sparkling like a daytime firework, through the rays of the sinking sun, and Kluk himself reached out and grabbed it out of the air. 'The Thing®!' he yelled, holding the gem above his head. 'The Thing®!'

Fearful and ugly was the cheering of the Gobblin host.

'Now nothing will stand against us!' cried Kluk. 'All the world will fall before the armies of Gobblinkind!'

The cheer was renewed with even greater and uglier vigour.

Bingo was trying to think. It was his only and his last chance. Kluk would kill them all, sooner or later, and would kill them at once if he realised he had been tricked. *All Gobblins are war-loving*, he thought to himself. *The Gobblins are war-loving*. Would 'the Gobblins' be better than 'all Gobblins'? Or just 'Gobblins'. *Gobblins love war*, perhaps? But 'love'? What might the Thing® make of that? It might take the love of war from Gobblin hearts, yet leave a professionally disinterested dedication in its place. It might twist 'war' in strange ways, such that they loved not war but slaughter – not war but suicidal destruction. It was impossible to tell. But in his heart he knew it was hopeless. It was the wrong statement to make through the device.

Bingo's fingers were around the Thing®. It was hot, and seemed almost to twitch and writhe in the soddit's grip. It was eager, Bingo knew. Eager. It wanted to be taken by the Gobblins, for they would use it for what it had been originally made – for evil – instead of trying, all the time, to pervert the Thing's® usage to good. Bingo felt his tiredness swirl up inside him like a sandstorm. He wanted nothing more than to lie down and sleep. He could not decide.

This was the moment of decision. As with many decisions in Bingo's life, he made it without even realising it.

The Thing® was already in his hand, and his hand was already out of his pocket and up by his mouth. He caught a glimpse of Elsqare's face, bent by anxiety and fear, as the elf saw what Bingo was doing. So much could go so badly wrong.

What to say? How to phrase it?

Inspiration failed at the vital moment.

'War—' said Bingo randomly. And the word drifted through the Thing®.

His heart stopped.

And started again. He took a deep breath. What had he done?

He had done nothing. He was exactly where he was. His few remaining comrades were disarmed, surrendered, surrounded on all sides by savage Gobblins. A thousand Gobblin arrows were still aimed at their breasts. Kluk was still holding the Barkingstone over his head. The Gobblin army was grumbling en masse, a rumbling noise of triumph and pride.

'What did you say?' Elsqare asked, hissing. 'What did you say through the Thing®?'

'I think it may be broken,' said Bingo. And he said it

hopefully, because if he had truly exhausted the magic potential of the device then it would matter less that Kluk had won the battle of the Famous Five Armies, it would mean that the Gobblins could do much less damage. 'I did say something through the device, but nothing has happened.'

'What—?' Elsqare began saying, but his words were drowned out.

The rumbling had grown in volume.

Bingo realised that the sound was not issuing from the Gobblin horde. It was coming from the ground beneath him.

Kluk, still clutching the Barkingstone, looked to the mountain, and for the first time his expression of triumph was replaced by one of fear. Bingo turned and looked up.

From where they stood they could just see the little plateau where the dwarfs and Gandef and Bingo had camped days before. Gouts of smoke were pouring from that side of the mountain.

'The chimney,' he cried with sudden understanding.

Then fire burst from the mountain. A huge, blinding spout of light and heat thrust from the mountainside into the sky. Lava, boiling and spitting, poured in great waves from the mountain's western flank, rolling down the side of the peak, bunching on itself like bales of

A. R. R. Roberts

rolling cloth, burning the mountain grasses and bushes in a hundred flare-ups as it proceeded.

A second mass of fire burst from the mountainside, and again molten magma poured from above, but this time it flew into the air, hurling in a wide arc, spraying north and west and – Bingo could see – spraying south as well, gobs of lava that curled and gripped at themselves in the air and descended upon them.

'It is the end of all things!' shrieked Elsqare.

And so it seemed, for the airborne wave of liquid rock was coming down with a terrible inevitability. The shouts of triumph in the Gobblin army had been replaced with gibbers and wails of terror. The archers had dropped their weapons, and were struggling to press backwards, prevented from escape by their fellows behind them. Kluk himself opened his mouth to say something, but he never spoke again, for a house-size gob of lava caught him and his bodyguard square on the front, and swept up his instantly burning remains and carried them downhill tangled inside the flowing rock. Bingo and Thorri cowered, and the elves and men hid their faces, as the scorching heat of lava engulfed a hundred of the Gobblin soldiers closest to Kluk and hurled them backwards. Spatters of hot rock sprayed all around, and yet none of these boiling fragments struck any of the remnants of the four armies. But more lava, and more, hurled through the air, and landed again and again amongst the Gobblins.

Bingo looked back at the mountain, and saw the searing stream of molten rock rushing down towards them. The air above it was so hot it seemed to tremble with fear, and smoke and dust turned the sky above dark. 'This must surely be it,' he said. 'This great stream of fire will devour us all.'

And yet it did not. The mighty river of molten rock struck a boulder a little way up the mountainside above the ledge where the remnants of the four armies stood – and divided. To Bingo's left and to his right the scorching fiery river flowed, and it ploughed into the Gobblins and licked them up with its fiery breath.

For many long minutes the burning river flooded on, pouring down and eating into the mass of Gobblins. They shrieked, they thrashed, they tried to run, but they were caught in the crush of their own bodies, and stream after stream of magma ploughed them down and burnt them up and buried them under.

Those few elves, men and dwarfs, and the one soddit, left alive on the little ledge clung together and hid their faces from the terrible heat of the lava streams that rushed past them. For an age and an age, or so it seemed, the heat lay on their backs like a huge weight. Sweat poured from Bingo's skin like rain. His throat was parched and aching. He could taste nothing but hot ashes and death, and his eyeballs felt as if they were boiling in his head. His very hair smouldered, as if it would catch fire – and, truly, only his prodigious sweating prevented that chance.

But, after a long time, the heat began to diminish. When Bingo dared look, the rivers of fire had solidified into two vast trunks of blackened rock. Smoke rushed off them, and they were palpably hot through the air. Sometimes veins of fire would glow upon them, and the rock would shrug and change shape, and the fire would die away again.

There was little to be seen through the smoke and steam, and yet Bingo noticed the occasional grisly relic of the Gobblin horde: an arm encased in rock. Burnt arrows like bristles in the skin of the black rock.

'It's unbelievable,' said Bingo. 'I don't believe it.'

'Is it over?' gasped Mori, from the ground. 'Did we win? Or is it moot?'

'We won,' said Elsqare, his face grimed and slick with sweat. 'It is not moot.'

'Grand,' said Mori. 'Look you.' And he passed into unconsciousness.

It was hours before the new rocks were cool enough for the party to leave their ledge. Seven men, eleven elves, three dwarfs and a soddit were all that were left alive of the four armies. And of the three dwarfs, only Thorri and Gofur were awake. Mori had passed into a kind of swoon; he was sorely wounded.

'It's unbelievable,' said Bingo, for the nineteenth time. He was slumped on the ground, more tired than he had ever been before, and yet unable to sleep. 'How did the lava *miss* us? It destroyed the whole of the Gobblin army, and yet it just *happened* to miss us altogether? That's an incredible chance. That's unbelievable.'

'Is it?' asked Elsqare. 'What was it that you spoke through the Thing® Was it the magic of that device that summoned up this volcanic destruction?'

'I . . .' said Bingo. 'I didn't know what to say. I said one word only.'

'What word?'

'I said, "war".'

Elsqare nodded, and sat down on the hot ground next to the exhausted soddit. 'I think I see,' he said.

'You do?' said Bingo.

'It wathn't the Thing® that called up the molten rock,' said Thorri. 'That wath Gandef.'

'Gandef?' said Bingo, leaping up. 'How?'

'We were afraid of it,' said Thorri. 'The tranthformation from wizard to dragon ith a mighty tranthformation. A being changed from a being of earth and water, thuch ath you and me, to a being of fire and air, which ith what a dragon ith. A great amount of magic power ith produthed in the tranthformation. It'th an inherently unthtable time.'

'From earth and water to fire and air,' said Bingo. 'Is that what caused the mountain to explode? Is Gandef all right?'

'Thith,' said Thorri, 'ith why we wanted an experienthed dragon looking after him as he tranthformed. Ith he all right? I don't know if he'th all right. I don't know.'

'I think he's all right,' said Gofur. 'He is not what he was before. Fire would have burnt up the old Gandef – but he's a new creature now. Fire can't hurt him now.'

'He has become a dragon?' said Elsqare. 'How interesting. His transformation happened at exactly the right time as far as we were concerned. Most fortuitous.'

'It wath – fortuitouth,' agreed Thorri. 'Five minuteth more and Kluk would have thlain uth all, killed uth – and all would have been lotht.'

'I do not believe it was fortuitous,' said Bingo.

'Nor I,' said Gofur. 'Bingo said the word "war" into the Thing®, and it has brought about peace.'

But Elsqare shook his head. 'Yet the Thing® is evil in its making and its mode, and will bring misery wherever it can. I do not believe it has brought peace. For what is war but struggle? And the opposite of struggle is not peace but death.'

'It has certainly brought death,' said Gofur, looking around.

'Elsqare is right,' said Bingo. 'The Thing® was not happy with me – it was positively twitching and struggling in my hand, yearning to be free. Had the Gobblins seized it then it would have been able to do much more damage to the world, and that's what it wants. It *yearned* towards the Gobblins. I could feel its yearning, as an almost palpable force. But, luckily, it was in my hands, not theirs. When I spoke the word "war" through it, it brought about the opposite. Lord Elsqare is correct – for all those at war it brought death. We were saved because we surrendered. We were not at war when the word was spoken, or the lava would have devoured us also.'

Gofur barked a shout of laughter. 'And had the Gobblin King accepted our surrender, then the war would have been over – and the Thing® would have been powerless to destroy him! Do you remember what he said? "You may not be at war with *us* – but *we* are at war with *you* – always!" Those words brought his doom. They meant that the Thing®'s magic applied to him and his army. But not to us.'

'Verily,' said Bingo. 'Blimey,' he added.

'You speak truly, Sir Dwarf,' said Elsqare. 'The Gobblin King's pride destroyed him. He could have accepted our surrender and then he would not have been at war, and Bingo's word would not have harmed him.'

'The Thing® thertainly found the motht dethtructive manner of inverting Bingo'th word,' said Thorri.

They carried Mori, sorely wounded and still unconscious, over the warm black rocks, bearing him towards the main doorway of the mountain. The lava had not flowed here, because the Gobblins had been swarming around their King and had not been concerned with access to the mountain – that would have come later, when they would have burst the stone doors asunder and looted the halls within. Now the stream trickled thinly in its bank, and the only Gobblins were corpses, and there were other corpses there too – elves and men.

As the sun rose in the east, Elsqare found a trampled silk pavilion, paw marks and footprints all over the white cloth. With his surviving elves he pulled it out of the dirt and bound up the splintered poles that supported it, and made a tent again in that place. Mori was taken inside, his armour removed and his wounds tended. But he was badly hurt.

Elves scavenged amongst the fields to the west and brought back rabbits, which they cooked in the morning. The survivors drank from the stream, and then slept. Bingo himself was roused by Thorri after a few hours.

'Come,' said the dwarfish King. 'Inthide.'

In the tent Mori had regained consciousness, but his eyes were wild and wandering. 'Soddit?' he said. 'Are you there?'

'I'm here.'

'We won, then?'

'We won. It was a great victory. The mountain exploded, and carried the Gobblin horde away with it, leaving the survivors untouched.'

'Really!' said Mori. 'Really! Extraordinary, look you. A few clods fly through the air, and the Gobblins are blown away.'

'It was more than a few clods, actually,' said Bingo.

'And the survivors! Were many killed on our side?'

'Oh,' said Bingo, embarrassed. 'We got off lightly. Compared to the Gobblins certainly. Indeed, at least one of the armies suffered no casualties at all.'

'I'm going to choose to believe,' said Mori, in a fading voice, 'that that's the dwarf army you're talking about. But never mind,' he added, his eyes clouding. 'Glad to have known you, boyo,' he said, his voice very faint. 'All the best. Where to now?'

'Where indeed?' whispered the soddit.

Mori grunted. 'Moot,' he said. And so he died.

That's not all folks!

Chapter Twelve

THE RETURN JOURNEY

ᏐᎢᏉ

The survivors of the battle of the Famous Five Armies numbered no more than twenty one. Thorri and Gofur alone remained from the troop of dwarfs that had departed from Soddlesex. The men of Lakeside had lost their mayor. It was a grim day.

The eruption of Strebor had laid swathes of jagged black rock over the western and southern flanks of the mountain, a desolate and wasted prospect. Yet the meads by the river were clear of lava, and the water still flowed. Bingo, Thorri and Gofur dug a deep grave for Mori and buried him. Gofur sang an ancient dwarf lament at the graveside.

> *So, farewell*
> *then*
> *Mori the dwarf.*
> *You fought*
> *bravely,*
> *but now you're dead.*

*Trevor's mum says that
if Trevor were
half the man
you were, he'd be
a fifth of the man he is.*

*Then she laughs, which
I don't think is very
appropriate.*

Bingo didn't understand it, but it brought tears to his eyes.

The survivors rested, but on the second day after the battle it became clear that disposal would have to be made of the many corpses that still littered the open ground. 'The mountain did much of our work for us,' said Elsqare. 'Most of the Gobblins tens of thousands are encased in the new rock – very hygienic, that. But there are many hundreds of bodies that the lava did not touch, and amongst them are some of our own comrades.'

They spent that day and the next searching amongst the dead. It was terrible work, or at least Bingo thought so at the beginning. But after a few hours he became used to it, immune to the shock of hauling dead Gobblins. There was a place where the lava had settled into a basin, forty yards across and twenty deep, and

the Gobblin dead were placed there. The occasional
elfen or human body was carried respectfully to the
river's edge. On the evening of the third day elven
runners brought back wood and also pigeons from the
nearest copse. The victorious four armies ate the
pigeons and drank water from the clear stream. As the
sun set, the bodies of elvish and mannish warriors were
burnt on a funeral pyre.

'I am sorry,' said Elsqare, 'that we have not discovered any of the dwarfish fallen.'

'We are content,' said Thorri. 'As dwarfth, we
require burial in rock – and the mountain hath provided that for uth in iths eruption.'

'It is a bitter and a sweet victory,' said Elsqare.

'Quite,' said Thorri.

On the morning of the fourth day, seven days after
he entered his great sleep, Gandef the Dragon stirred in
his mountain home. He padded down his corridor on
his new legs, and drew back the brass lock of the main
entrance. Then he pushed the mighty stone doors apart
and put his enormous dragonish head out into the
sunshine.

'Hello,' he said. 'What's new?'

Bingo, Thorri and Gofur were overjoyed to see him
again, for all that he had changed and grown out of
almost all recognition. A grey-skinned, bright-eyed
young dragon greeted them, its wings black, its claws

obsidian. And yet there was something familiar in its gaze, and its voice – though deeper and huger than the wizard's had been – was nonetheless familiar.

He perched on a spur of black rock that lay, newly created by the eruption, parallel with the meads, and listened politely to Gofur and Bingo's account of the battle. 'Dear me,' he rumbled. 'And I missed it all?'

'You played a crucial part,' insisted Bingo. 'Your fire brought us victory.'

'Excellent,' he said. 'Excellent.'

Then Gandef reared into the air and flew around the mountain's peak, trying his new wings. He flew over the pile of Gobblin dead and blasted down with a spout of blue-grey fire, burning up the bodies in a purifying conflagration. After that he flew far to the north, and returned clutching two heifers, one in each hind claw. One of these beasts he gave to the survivors of the battle, and the other he ate himself, roasting it with puffs from his nostrils.

'Peckish,' he announced. 'Haven't eaten in seven days.'

The men roasted the cow on a spit, and the veterans of the battle ate heartily.

The following morning the Lakeside men departed, beginning their march downstream to their town. They carried with them a portion of the wealth from inside the Only Mountain – 'Take it, take it,' Gandef insisted.

'Fat lot of good it'll do me. When am I ever going to go shopping? I couldn't so much as fit inside a shop any more. Take it – take it.'

The elves were similarly rewarded, and they struck out over the new black rocks and beyond them to the fields westward, making for the forest. 'My cousin the woodelf, Ele the Elcoholic, has a place there,' Elsqare explained. 'It's all feasting and drinking, and it gets tiresome after a while, but it'll do for now. Then it's back over the Minty Mountains. Things should be quieter in our lands now that the Gobblins have been overthrown. Farewell!'

'Farewell!' said Bingo.

And so it was that only Thorri, Gofur, Bingo and Gandef remained. 'What will you do?' asked the soddit.

'We'll thtay here,' said Thorri. 'That'd be betht. There's plenty of room inthide – room for a whole population of dwarfth, in fact. And you?'

'I'd like to go home,' said Bingo. 'But I do not know the way.'

'I'll carry you,' said Gandef, rumbling and smoking. 'I need an excuse to stretch my wings, and I quite fancy a really long fly.'

'Thank you, Sir Dragon,' said Bingo, bowing.

The soddit spent his last night inside the mountain, sleeping on a huge bed that had once, Gofur said, been the bed of a King. The walls of his rock-carved chamber were hung with antique armour, rusty pikes, gold and silver chain mail, works of fine carving and art. It was a spooky place, but Bingo slept deeply and slept long.

In the morning he said his farewells. 'We'll thee you again thoon, I hope,' said Thorri. 'Pop by, any time. You know – if you're paththing, on your way, thome-where, you know.'

'Likewise,' said Bingo. 'I'm sure. Do you know a strange thing?'

'What?'

'My feet haven't hurt in weeks. Or I haven't noticed it if they have.'

'Bit of exerthithe,' said the dwarf King sagely. 'Doth the world of good.'

Finally Bingo clambered up Gandef's leg, and settled himself between the dragon's great shoulder blades. 'Righto,' rumbled Gandef. 'Off we go.'

He sprung upwards, and soared into the air. The ground shrunk beneath them like a craven thing, and the wind boomed in Bingo's ears. Clutching the swaying stalk at the base of Gandef's left wing, the soddit leaned a little out to stare in frank amazement.[1] In moments the

---

[1] Frank Gerard Amazement II was a fabled prince of the realm of RororoHyorboat, far to the south. His amazement and ingenuous open-mindedness had become a byword amongst his own people, and this byword had, evidently, spread far to the north as well.

river had become a silver strand, the fields were no bigger than leaves, Lake Escargot shone like a puddle of mercury in the sunlight. Mighty Strebor itself had dwindled below them to a conical stump, splotched about its western and southern skies with black marks, like pitch spilt on a grey wizard's hat. And peering forward, over the undulating shoulders of the dragon, Bingo saw the whole expanse of Mykyurwood laid below them like a rough-woven quilt of green and black.

'You all right?' Gandef asked.

'It's marvellous,' called Bingo, his voice swamped by the white rushing of the wind through which they flew. 'Marvellous!' They had left the earth far behind, and moved now amongst air and space and sunlight. The sun, rising behind them, was sharper, clearer, its light purer and more enormous. Bingo scrunched up his eyes and gazed at the sun for long minutes, its outpouring fountain of light. When he looked down again, clouds swept past below them like pipesmoke, and hurried away. It was blue all around them, dazzling blue above, blue-hued greens below.

'Marvellous!' he called again.

They flew on and on.

'I meant to say,' thundered Gandef, twisting his neck and bringing his head a little way round so that he could observe the soddit from one eye. 'Thorri told me about the Thing® you know.'

'Don't you remember it,' Bingo said, 'from before your transformation?'

'No,' rumbled the dragon. 'I was far gone before you told the dwarfs that it was in your possession, I think.'

'Oh,' shouted Bingo.

'May I see it?' the dragon asked. Bingo looked into the beast's eye, and hesitated. But he took the Thing® out of his pocket and held it up.

The dragon's snaky neck curled again, and his head – large as a horse's and considerably more intelligent – swung in towards Bingo. The great wings continued beating, the wind continued rushing past them, although the pilot was not, now, looking where he was going. The dragon's nostrils were wide as inkwells, and as black, and they approached the Thing® with a sniffing eagerness. Bingo controlled the urge to snatch the Thing® away, and held it out.

Eventually Gandef withdrew his head, faced forward again and flew on for a long while in silence.

'Well?' Bingo prompted.

'It is as I feared,' said the dragon. 'A terrible device, filled with evil potential. My own magic is much greater now than it was when I was a wizard, and I can sense much wickedness in it – I can smell it, if you like. But,' and here he turned his head and met Bingo's gaze a second time, 'I can tell you something else. It has been long separated from its evil creator, the dreaded Sharon, and accordingly its magic is greatly weakened. In fact, it is nearly exhausted – it has been used recently, and used several times, and each usage has drained more of its magic potential. It would take only a very little spell now to drain it completely.'

Bingo's clothes were fluttering and wrestling in the wind. 'And then would it be safe?'

'Safer. Not wholly safe, for Sharon could recharge its power. But safer – much less likely to do mischief in the wrong hands.'

'A little spell,' said Bingo thoughtfully. 'What must I say?'

'You are the Thing®-carrier,' said Gandef. 'It is for you to decide. Say, "my clothes are green", or "fish have two eyes", or "gherkins are unpleasant food", and the Thing® will try and make the reverse true, but it will be unable to – it will become denuded of all power, exhausted, worn out in the process.'

'A spell as small as that?' cried Bingo.

'I think so,' said the dragon, turning his head again to face the direction of flight. 'It has only the merest trickle of magic left inside it. Or so it smells to me.'

'And a larger spell. What if I say "the oceans are blue", or "two and two are four"? How would a larger spell effect it?'

'A larger spell would be more sure to exhaust the

Thing®. It is very weary, its magic very small, a mere shadow of what it once was.'

Bingo pondered this for a while. He did not have the sureness in his mind that the dragon seemed to possess, and he knew from his own experience how sly the device was. Could it have hidden its true power from Gandef? Was it even now scheming, hoping to trap the soddit into saying something that it could twist to evil? He thought of many possible phrases, trying them out.

Below them the forest had come to an end, and the sharp clean lines, white and blue, of the Minty Mountains were visible. Bingo could see the expanse of the mountain chain now, a tremendous ridge in the landscape running to the horizon left and right. Then he looked up again at the blue of the sky and the pouring, clean, bright light of the sun.

On an impulse he lifted the Thing® to his mouth and spoke.

He said, 'The sun shines.' And so it did, it shone with a glorious and an undiminished brightness.

Have you enjoyed *The Soddit*?

Why not read the three volumes of A. R. R. Roberts's
magical sequel *The Lord of the Dancings*[1]

The Lord of the Dancings Volume I: *The Yellow Ship of the Thing*®

Wrenched again from his ordinary, peaceful life as a soddit,
Bingo the Thing®-Mule becomes embroiled in the rise to
power of the Evil Sharon. A group, well, more a party, a –
what would you call it – band, no group – yes, *band* – of
individuals from all the races of Upper Middle Earth assemble to help Bingo on his quest: to sail *over the sea* to the
Whirlpool of Dshwshrs (a feature of the oceans of Upper
Middle Earth that was named, clearly, onomatopoeically)
and there to cast the Thing® into the swirling waters and rid
the world of its deadly threat for ever, and for ever!! (Or just
'for ever' now that I come to think of it, that second 'for ever'
is redundant, really, isn't it, like saying 'infinity plus infinity'
that's just infinity, not double-infinity or anything like that.
Anyway. There you go.)

'But how shall we travel across the waves?' asked Bingo in a

---

[1] **Attention:** This is *a rhetorical question*. Do not attempt to answer
this question. NonWin Books accepts no liability for anybody who
attempts to answer this question and injures themselves in the
process.

querulous voice. 'Are they not wet? Is there not the risk of wetting? Not to mention drowning?'

'Fear not, young soddit,' said Strudel. 'In the land where I was born there lived a man who *sailed* the sea.'

'Will you tell me of his life in the land of such marine,' Bingo pressed, 'adventures?'

'Tell you of his life?' repeated Strudel, a pastry halfway to his mouth and a startled look in his eye. 'You what? I don't know anything about his life. Why do you want to know about that? What's to know? Only that he proved that it *is possible* to sail the sea. He did it in a big yellow boat of some kind. You and I and the rest of our band will do so too – we shall charter a Yellow Ship and sail the sea of green. Y,' he added, thinking more carefully about it. 'Green-*y* bluey sort of colour.'

'Hurrah,' said Bingo weakly.

The Lord of the Dancings Volume II: *The Twins' Tower*

After the abject failure of the question to destroy the Thing®️ in the Whirlpool of Dshwshrs (*warning, the previous sentence may contain spoilers: do not read the previous sentence if you wish to preserve narrative suspense during* The Yellow Ship of the Thing®️), the quest passes to Bingo's cousin, three-times removed (by court order), Frodeo. Frodeo and his faithful companion Scram – his, shall we say, um, servant? Or just friend? Yes – friend, his friend. But nothing funny, no funny business about their friendship, they just happen to be extremely close friends that's all. Where was I? Oh yes, Frodeo and Scram cross a landscape of razor-sharp rocks and stagnant pools, attended by Sollum – a foul, skinny philosopher who, thanks to a piece of malign magic exists not as a real person, but as an animated Manuscript Illumination-cum-Illustration. Although he's terribly realistic. Terribly. Some of those monks who did that sort of artwork were *terribly* talented you know, geniuses some of them, although of course we don't know their names in the way that we know Raphael and Picasso and so on. Anyway, this threesome must make their way to the great tower in which the Twins live, Tomson and Tombson (the 'b' is silent, as in 'basilica'), and recruit their twinnish excellence in the process of destroying the Thing®. Meanwhile Strudel can no longer fit into his lederhosen, and reveals himself to be the Secret King of Sh!-Tellnoone! The survivors of the original sea quest to destroy the Thing® reassemble.

'We can only pray,' said Gandef, 'that the Tomson twins will be able to help Frodeo and Scram.'

'Help them,' said Strudel, chuckling to himself, ''t'win. Do you get it? To win. Twin. Yeah?'

Gandef addressed the whole company. 'To horse!' he cried. 'We must ride to the Land of Helpmi Rhondor, and there gather an army to confront Sharon's hordes of Gobblin warriors!

The nine of them cheered, and leapt on to their horses. Gandef himself leapt on to his horse, Shadowemail, the fleetest, most intelligent horse in all of Upper Middle Earth, inadvertently crushing it to death. 'Oops,' he said. 'I forgot myself there for a moment. Damn it; it's easily done, though, isn't it? Damn.' He stood, and tried to scrape the remnants of the beast from his hindquarters.

The Lord of the Dancings Volume III: The Rerun of the Sequel of Thing® Part 2: Son of Thing® Rides Again

Just when you thought the story couldn't possibly have anywhere else to go, a whole new chapter opens up in the saga of the Thing®. *The Rerun of the Sequel* is the most spectacular *Lord of the Dancings* episode yet. Scaryman the Evil reveals himself – astonishingly, and to the complete and utter surprise of everybody who knew him, and who thought he was one of the good guys – to be evil, and allies himself with Sharon, renaming himself Scaryman the Evil the Evil. You could have knocked me down with a *feather* when I heard. Blimey. Then there's lots and lots of fighting, and more fighting. Gobblins get killed in *such* large numbers. Finally Frodeo and Scram must don the Tap Shoes of Fate and confront the Lord of the Dancings in person – uncovering a mystery that will rock Upper Middle Earth to its very core. To its very core! I know . . . I know . . . exciting, isn't it?

> He looked up in terror to see a Gobblin flying the air sitting astride his hideous winged mount. It was the Lord of the Seagul – the Seaguls of Sharon that struck such horror into the Armies of Good by their persistence in trying to grab bits of food from about your person, their screeching, their pooping, and the way they appear in the sky above your head even though you're dozens of leagues from the sea . . .

Have you enjoyed *The Soddit*? Then be sure and purchase some of Professor Roberts's other delightful works.

> *The Garble-∂e-Hwaet (the 1375 recension)*
An Anglo Saxon poem of great length, subject-matter and tedium, edited by Professor Roberts in his academic years before he achieved fame as a story-teller, now reissued by his publisher with a misleading sword-and-sorcery style cover painting and 'by the author of *The Soddit* and *Lord of the Dancings*' under his name. Disappointment guaranteed! Buy it, flick through it, and put it on your shelf never to look at it again!

> *Lame-o! Lame-o!*
Charming and magical lyrics written by Professor Roberts, and put to music by a Fey Friend from Oxford for an evening of musical delight and a tombola in 1951. Includes such masterpieces as 'I'll Twist the Sense to Fit the Rhyme-O!', 'They Used To Write Verse This Way in the Old Days-O (It's as if Eliot, Pound and Wallace Stevens Never Happened)' and 'Hark, the Tweetings!':

> *Hark, the Tweetings!*
> *Fair the sweetings!*
> *Spring is bursting!*
>   *Sing fal-∂ol-yellow-yellow-up-wahey!*
> *The flutter-by fleetings*
> *Sing all the greetings*

A. R. R. Roberts

Poetic sheetings
Sound your zitherlings
Sense-the-less blitherings
Sing fal-dol-yellow-yellow-up-wahey!

Now re-issued by his publisher with a misleading painting on the front of a dragon screaming through the night sky pouring fire and destruction on an army of foul-looking monsters beneath, but you won't find anything one-tenth as exciting as that inside the covers, I'm sorry to say, and 'by the author of *The Soddit* and *Lord of the Dancings*' under his name.

> A. R. R. Roberts's *The Soddit Companion*
Issued in exactly the same livery as all of Roberts's other books, and with only Roberts's name on the cover, you'll have picked this off the bookshop shelf, paid for it and got it home before you realise that it wasn't written by him at all, but instead by a jobbing hack called Daniel Gibbons as a cynical exercise in hasty cashing-in. Includes encyclopedia-style entries on all the main characters, monsters, place-names, but nothing quoted from the original book for copyright reasons.

PlayGameBoxCube 2 presents

The Soddit: Wrath of Morbore

Combining all the challenges of a role-playing game with the excitement of a hack-and-slash fight-'em platformer, *The Soddit: Wrath of Morbore* is the first ever fully licensed video game based on the works of A. R. R. Roberts (excluding the games *Lord of the Dancings 1, 2, 3, Return of Lord of the Dancings, Dance!; The Wrath of Morbore, SimSoddit, Metal Gear Soddit, Quake, Night of the Mutant Soddits, Soddit 1944: Assault on Normandy, Formula 1: Soddit Pony-Carts at Silverstone*).

Choose from one of any two lead characters, with different strengths and weaknesses; and choose from a list of intimidating weapons (axe, sword, spear, longer sword, sword with sort of hook at the end, nunchuk, nunchuk with a sort of hook at the end, bigger axe, a different sort of sword, uzi nine mil and sten gun). Then fight your way through an intimidating array of opponents:

- Slash! Your way out of the Putting Dragon Inn in Hobbld-Ahoy!
- Hack! The elves in the last homely house west of the mountains.
- Kill! Random passers-by on the road to the east.
- Try! To deviate from the path to explore the woods on the right, just to see what's there, only to find that your control-pad doesn't allow you to go past an unrealistic little wooden fence.

- Desperately! Bash away at the fence with your sword to vent your frustration.

- Notice! The way, however far you walk, the mountains on the horizon never seem to get any closer. Your mate Dave once left the control-pad on the floor with a heavy book leaning on 'forward' so that the character walked forward *all night long* from midnight to about ten a.m. the next day and when he came down again the mountains were *still on the bloody horizon*, can you believe it? They weren't any closer at all. I mean how hard would it be to program mountains that came a little bit closer as you walked towards them? It's not asking for the moon on a stick, is it? And then when you fight the troll at the river ford thing *suddenly* you're in the mountains with the goblins underground and everything. How is that supposed to happen? It simply lacks verisimilitude, that's what it lacks.

- Give up! On level two, and play a racing game instead.

'This is the . . . good . . . a . . . game . . . under any circumstances' – *PlayGameBoxCube 2 Magazine*.

'Another hack 'em-wander-about game. 97%' – *PlayGameBoxCube 2 Monthly*, '*We Never Give Any Game Less Than a 90% Rating No Matter How Poor It Is*' *Magazine*.

'A hundred uses. As a coaster, for instance, or part of an interesting mobile' – *Recycle Your Old CDs and DVDs Magazine*.

With original vocal stylings by Sir Ian McEllen and Lady Ellen McIan

Play *The Soddit: Wrath of Morbore* with a friend, or play with yourself.

Other Children's Classics from NonWin Books

WIND IN THE PILLOWS
by Graham Wosdafree Quincy Kennethe

'. . . teaches your children to love vermin . . .' *The Times*.

'. . . as yet unsurpassed, and indeed unprosecuted' – *The Times of Delhi*

In this classic children's tale, a Rat, a Toad, a Cockroach, a Dead Sparrow Left Floating in a Waterbutt for Two Weeks, a Smallpox Bacillus and a Tory MP enjoy a sequence of magical, flatulent adventures in and out of the Wild Wood and through the Gaye Fields of Merrie Englande, Cornwalle, Walese and Eiree. In the character of Lord 'call me Mr' Toad, Kennethe created one of the most enduring characters in all of children's fiction.

In the words of Professor Roberts himself, 'My favourite scene was the one in which the amphibian is locked away in prison and dresses as a transvestite in order to make good his escape. So true to life. I mean, if *you* saw a six-foot transsexual man-toad with green blistered skin and a peerage trying to wriggle out of a barred window, would *you* stand in his way? I know I wouldn't. Not after that unfortunate affair of the failed citizen's arrest and the Marquis of Turkley's younger son, at any rate.'

A. R. R. R. Roberts

HAIRY POTSDAM
By J. K. 'not from Jamiroquai' Rollinint

Imagine a small child, abused and neglected in his earliest years, who suddenly discovers that he has incredibly potent magical powers of life-giving and death-dealing at the emotionally unstable age of thirteen, and who decides to wreak a terrible vengeance upon all the people who mocked and cuffed him, all those who humiliated him before, who told him that he'd never amount to anything, making him sleep under the stairs, *him?* Treat *him* like dirt, would they? Well they picked the *wrong boy* to ***k with, the *wrong boy*. Let's see how *they* like it when my magical force breaks every bone in their body and rips off their limbs, picking them off one by one in the shopping mall as they run, cowering and pleading – *pleading!* – for mercy hahahahaha! Who's the brat *now*? Eh? Eh? Ha-ha-ha-ha-ha-ha, I saw this on a video round at Pete's hee-hee where they hee-hee *squash this guy's head* like a grape with their telepathic powers, hee-hee. Let's see how that goes in real life my so-called-parents, ha! Ha! Splat! I am vengeance! I AM VENGEANCE! The whole town will PAY – PAY! Oh I bet they're sorry now, I'll *make* them sorry – HAHAHAHAHA! Die! Die! Die, all of you!

This book isn't anything like that.

'A Dorothy Parkeresque rollercoaster of wit, rudeness and girly hilarity; forget all pretenders to the chick-lit crown, the tiara belongs to . . .' *Daily Mirror*. (This press endorsement may have appeared in earlier editions of a completely different book.)

£3.99. Also available: exactly the same book with a moody photographic cover in black and white, £12.99.

JAMIE OLIVER TWIST
by Delia Dickings

Annoying cockney scamp falls in with gipsies, tramps and thieves. Includes a forty-page supplement of Victorian Slum Recipes, amongst them 'Lard on Bread', 'Stale Crust *cuisine ironique*', 'Lard on Bread topped with unrefined sugar', 'Grit' and 'Mississippi Mud Pie with Mud rather than Chocolate'.

Includes the songs, 'You've Got To Pick Enough Rocket for Two', 'Consider Your Shellfish at Home', 'Whe-eh-eh-ere is Lard?' and the barn-storming 'Food Recipes, Gloriously Marketable Food Recipes' (Hot Sausage and Custard, for that soursweet tang).

'*Most Likely to Say*: "Dad, do I have to read this? Can't I read the new Hellboy instead?" *Least Likely to Say*: "Please, sir, can I have some more?" ' – *Guardian*

MARY POPPINS
By P. L. Travesty

Mary comes to the Winsbury family in Old London Town as an au pair, and transforms their lives by weeping noisily in her room, talking on the phone to Czechoslovakia for hours, eating all the ice cream in the freezer, bringing her malodorous and piercings-riddled boyfriend home to stay with her 'just for ze two daias, pliz? Pliz?' and him still being in the house a month later, coming up with three separate and frankly incompatible excuses to weasel out of looking after Algernon and Jasmine for *one evening*, for crying out loud, and Van Morrison is only playing the one night in London, it's not as if we'll get the chance to see him again, and – in a rousing conclusion – threatening to tell your wife that you've made a pass at her, look, really, it's a misunderstanding, a culture-clash thing, it's actually quite funny if you think about it, no really, no *really*.

'Not so much a novel, more a (cont. p. 17)' – *Hair and Makeup Monthly*

Join the Soddit Society

Are you *ma-aa-aad!* for Soddits?

Do you live, breathe and dream of A. R. R. Roberts's works, morning, noon, night and in-between times? Have worried relatives expressed gentle-voiced sentiments of concern about your neglecting homework, friends, food and play to devote all your time to what they call 'this odd little book'? Are you prepared to sacrifice the quivering body of the one you love most on the bloodstained altar of your fascination for A. R. R. Roberts's work?

Would you like to meet people as *cra-ay-zee!* for soddits as you?

Join the Roberts-robot, the fantasy-fan, the Upper-Middle-Earth-Madman and the soddit-schizophrenic in the SODDIT SOCIETY.

For a mere £95 annual membership fee plus VAT and trauma insurance, you can join the obese, the inverted, the talk-to-themselves-in-the-toilet and the threadworm-infested to discuss the greatness of *The Soddit*, and mutter darkly how '*they*' don't understand.

Meet your fellow SODDIT SOCIETY MEMBERS once every six months and

- Dress up in costumes based on the world of A. R. R. Roberts's World of Soddit.
- Repeat phrases such as 'it's my absolute favourite book ever', 'my favourite part is (*insert favourite part here*)', and

'that other book, about the, like, mercenaries in fairyland, I didn't like that nearly so much'.

• Sigh, and look at the floor.

As Professor Roberts himself said, '*Fan* as we know is derived etymologically from *fanatic* – and to this day the "fan" is an alarming figure, starbursts of madness twinkling in his eye, obsessed, possessed with madness, fundamentalist, divorced from reality, a suitable case for treatment, or incarceration in my opinion, dear me yes.' He forgot to add 'And having the best fun in the world!'

Abandon the real world for this musty obsessive fantasy TODAY!

NEW FROM NONWIN BOOKS

The Spuddit

Read this hilarious, light-hearted, thoroughly respectful, not-cashing-in-at-all **Parody of A. R. R. Roberts's classic *The Soddit***. There's a laugh in every sentence, or your money back! (*Offer not valid in UK, Commonwealth, North America, South America, territories above the tropic of Capricorn, or signatories of the Book Charter.*) The Perfect Gift for the person who already has a copy of *The Soddit*, and you want to buy him a present that's geared as it were to his personal tastes, not socks or gloves or something generic, but something that he'd actually like. The only problem is that you can't think of anything else about him than that he likes *The Soddit* and he's already got that.

In this irreverent, brilliant parody – *all the parts of the original are taken by potatoes!!*

> Bingo . . . a marin piper
> Gandef . . . a King Edward
> Mori the Dwarf . . . a roasting potato
> Elsqare . . . Jersey royal
>
> Will Smug the Dragon *get his chips??!!*

A *Tatty* (i.e. 'tasty') Treat!

From all *good booksellers* – good meaning '*wickedd*' (youth slang for 'good')!!

'I'm prepared to say that I did laugh' – *Sir George Graham, former manager of 'The Spurs' (Tottenham Football Club).*

'Much have I travelled in the realms of gold, and many goodly states and kingdoms seen; round many western islands have I been, which bards in fealty to Apollo hold. Oft of one wide expanse had I been told, which deep browed Homer ruled as his demesne. Yet never did I breathe its pure serene, till I heard *Bored of the Rings* speak loud and bold . . . !'

John Keats, *Manchester Nightingale*

'This book . . . tremor . . . Manichean guilt . . . existential . . . pleonastic . . . redundancy . . .'

Orlando di Biscuit, *Hobnob*

'A slightly more liberal reading of the leash-laws would keep books like this off the stands. I don't know how you'll fare, but my copy insists on long walks around suppertime, bays at the moon, and has spoiled every sofa cushion in the place.'

Wilmot Proviso, *The Rocky Mountain Literary Round-Up*

'One of the two or three books . . .'

Frank O'Prussia, *Dublin Gazette*

'Truly a tale for our times . . . as we hang suspended over the brink on a Ring of our own, threatened by dragons and other evil people, and, like Frito and Goodgulf, fighting a cruel Enemy who will stop at nothing to get his way.'   Ann Alaggi, *The Old Flag*

'Extremely interesting from almost every point of view.'
Professor Hawley Smoot, *Our Loosely Enforced Libel Laws*

A PARODY OF J.R.R. TOLKIEN'S
THE LORD OF THE RINGS

---

by Henry N. Beard and Douglas C. Kenney
of the Harvard Lampoon

GOLLANCZ
London

This edition published in Great Britain in 2001 by
Gollancz
An imprint of the Orion Publishing Group
Orion House, 5 Upper St Martin's Lane, London WC2H 9EA

Twenty-fourth impression reprinted in Great Britain in 2004

A CIP catalogue record for this book is available
from the British Library

ISBN 0 575 07362 4

Typeset at The Spartan Press Ltd,
Lymington, Hants

Printed in Great Britain by
Clays Ltd, St Ives plc

www.orionbooks.co.uk

CONTENTS

THE TINY "X"-SHAPED FOREST

THE BIG WIDE RIVER

GOGOLAK

BAR

THE LAND OF THE ZORGLE STENCH

OLEÖ

THE LEGENDARY BRILLOWPIGS

THE LAND OF THE GIANT PIGS

BAR

THE DOTTED LINE

RISRÖAST

L U M B A R

THE AUI SANTH

STRAIGHT

CANTINFLAS

THE SLOUGHS OF DESPOND

THE
BAY OF
AIHOUS

RÖIR

THE ISLES
OF
LANGEOHNO

Scale

Cubits

THE GUM CLI

SCUM HARBOR

LÖRNADÖÖK

THE INTERMITTENT MOUNTAINS

DLUNDORN

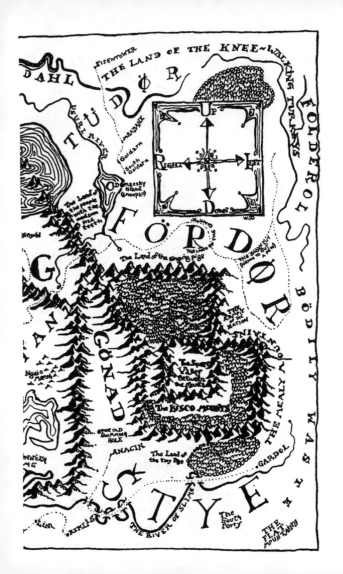

'Do you like what you doth see . . . ?' said the voluptuous elf-maiden as she provocatively parted the folds of her robe to reveal the rounded, shadowy glories within. Frito's throat was dry, though his head reeled with desire and ale.

She slipped off the flimsy garment and strode toward the fascinated boggie unashamed of her nakedness. She ran a perfect hand along his hairy toes, and he helplessly watched them curl with the fierce insistent wanting of her.

'Let me make thee more comfortable,' she whispered hoarsely, fiddling with the clasps of his jerkin, loosening his sword belt with a laugh. 'Touch me, oh *touch me*,' she crooned.

Frito's hand, as though of its own will, reached out and traced the delicate swelling of her elf-breast, while the other slowly crept around her tiny, flawless waist, crushing her to his barrel chest.

'Toes, I *love* hairy toes,' she moaned, forcing him down on the silvered carpet. Her tiny, pink toes caressed the luxuriant fur of his instep while Frito's nose sought out the warmth of her precious elf-navel.

'But I'm so small and hairy, and . . . and you're so *beautiful*,' Frito whimpered, slipping clumsily out of his crossed garters.

The elf-maiden said nothing, but only sighed deep in her throat and held him more firmly to her faunlike body. 'There is one thing you must do for me first,' she whispered into one tufted ear.

'Anything,' sobbed Frito, growing frantic with his need. 'Anything!'

She closed her eyes and then opened them to the ceiling. 'The Ring,' she said. 'I must have your Ring.'

Frito's whole body tensed. 'Oh no,' he cried, 'not that! Anything but . . . that.'

'I must have it,' she said both tenderly and fiercely. 'I must have the *Ring*!'

Frito's eyes blurred with tears and confusion. 'I can't,' he said. 'I mustn't!'

But he knew resolve was no longer strong in him. Slowly, the elf-maiden's hand inched toward the chain in his vest pocket, closer and closer it came to the Ring Frito had guarded so faithfully . . .

FOREWORD

Though we cannot with complete candor state, as does Professor T., that 'the tale grew in the telling,' we can allow that this tale (or rather the necessity of hawking it at a bean a copy) grew in direct proportion to the ominous dwindling of our bank accounts at the Harvard Trust in Cambridge, Massachusetts. This loss of turgor in our already emaciated portfolio was not, in itself, cause for alarm (or 'alarum' as Professor T. might aptly put it), but the resultant threats and cuffed ears received at the hands of creditors *were*. Thinking long on this, we retired to the reading lounge of our club to meditate on this vicissitude.

The following autumn found us still in our leather chairs, plagued with bedsores and appreciably thinner, but still without a puppy biscuit for the lupine pest lolling around the front door. It was at this point that our palsied hands came to rest on a dog-eared nineteenth printing of kindly old Prof Tolkien's *Lord of the Rings*. Dollar signs in our guileless eyes, we quickly ascertained that it was still selling like you-know-whats. Armed to the bicuspids with thesauri and reprints of international libel laws, we locked ourselves

in the *Lampoon* squash court with enough Fritos and Dr
Pepper to choke a horse. (Eventually the production of
this turkey actually required the choking of a small
horse, but that's another story entirely.)

Spring found us with decayed teeth and several
pounds of foolscap covered with inky, illegible scrawls.
A quick rereading proved it to be a surprisingly brilliant
satire on Tolkien's linguistic and mythic structures,
filled with little takeoffs on his use of Norse tales and
wicked phoneme fricatives. A cursory assessment of
the manuscript's sales appeal, however, convinced us
that dollarwise the thing would be better employed as
tinder for the library fireplace. The next day, handi-
capped by near-fatal hangovers and the loss of all our
bodily hair (but that's another story), we sat down
at two supercharged, fuel-injected, 345-hp Smith
Coronas and knocked off the opus you're about to
read before tiffin. (And we take tiffin pretty durn early
in *these* parts, buckaroo.) The result, as you are about
to see for yourself, was a book as readable as Linear A
and of about the same literary value as an autographed
gatefold of St Simon Stylites.

'As for any inner meanings or "message," ' As
Professor T. said in *his* foreword, there is none herein
except that which you may read into it yourself. (Hint:
What did P. T. Barnum say was 'born every minute'?)
Through this book, we hope, the reader may find

deeper insights not only into the nature of literary piracy, but into his own character as well. (Hint: What is missing from this famous quotation? 'A —— and his —— soon are ——.' You have three minutes. Ready, set, go!)

Bored of the Rings has been issued in this form as a parody. This is very important. It is an attempt to satirize the other books, not simply to be mistaken for them. Thus, we must strongly remind you that *this is not the real thing*! So if you're about to purchase this copy thinking it's about the *Lord* of the Rings, then you'd better put it right back onto that big pile of remainders where you found it. Oh, but you've already read this far, so that must mean that – that you've already *bought* . . . oh dear . . . oh my . . . (Tote up another one on the register, Jocko. '*Ching!*')

Lastly, we hope that those of you who *have* read Prof Tolkien's remarkable trilogy already will not be offended by our little spoof of it. All fooling aside, we consider ourselves honored to be able to make fun of such an impressive, truly masterful work of genius and imagination. After all, that is the most important service a book can render, the rendering of enjoyment, in this case, enjoyment through laughter. And don't trouble yourself too much if you don't laugh at what you are about to read, for if you perk up your pink little ears, you may hear the silvery tinkling of merriment in the air, far, far away . . .

It's us, buster. *Ching!*

PROLOGUE –
CONCERNING BOGGIES

This book is predominantly concerned with making money, and from its pages a reader may learn much about the character and the literary integrity of the authors. Of boggies, however, he will discover next to nothing, since anyone in the possession of a mere moiety of his marbles will readily concede that such creatures could exist only in the minds of children of the sort whose childhoods are spent in wicker baskets, and who grow up to be muggers, dog thieves, and insurance salesmen. Nonetheless, judging from the sales of Prof Tolkien's interesting books, this is a rather sizable group, sporting the kind of scorchmarks on their pockets that only the spontaneous combustion of heavy wads of crumpled money can produce. For such readers we have collected here a few bits of racial slander concerning boggies, culled by placing Prof Tolkien's books on the floor in a neat pile and going over them countless times in a series of skips and short hops. For them we also include a brief description of the soon-to-be-published-if-this-incredible-dog-sells account of Dildo Bugger's earlier adventures, called by him *Travels with Goddam in Search of Lower Middle Earth*, but wisely renamed by the publisher *Valley of the Trolls*.

Boggies are an unattractive but annoying people whose numbers have decreased rather precipitously since the bottom fell out of the fairy-tale market. Slow and sullen, and yet dull, they prefer to lead simple lives of pastoral squalor. They don't like machines more complicated than a garrote, a blackjack, or a luger, and they have always been shy of the 'Big Folk' or 'Biggers,' as they call us. As a rule they now avoid us, except on rare occasions when a hundred or so will get together to dry-gulch a lone farmer or hunter. They are a little people, smaller than dwarves, who consider them puny, sly, and inscrutable and often refer to them as the 'boggie peril.' They seldom exceed three feet in height, but are fully capable of overpowering creatures half their size when they get the drop on them. As for the boggies of the Sty, with whom we are chiefly concerned, they are unusually drab, dressing in shiny gray suits with narrow lapels, alpine hats, and string ties. They wear no shoes, and they walk on a pair of hairy blunt instruments which can only be called feet because of the position they occupy at the end of their legs. Their faces have a pimply malevolence that suggests a deep-seated fondness for making obscene telephone calls, and when they smile, there is something in the way they wag their foot-long tongues that makes Komodo dragons gulp with disbelief. They have long, clever fingers of the sort one normally associates with hands that spend a good deal of time around the necks of small, furry animals and in other people's pockets, and they are very skillful at producing intricate and useful things, like loaded dice and booby traps. They love to eat and drink, play mumblety-peg with dim-witted quadrupeds, and tell off-color dwarf jokes. They give dull parties and cheap presents, and they enjoy the same general regard and esteem as a dead otter.

It is plain that boggies are relatives of ours, standing somewhere along the evolutionary line that leads from rats to wolverines and eventually to Italians, but what our exact relationship is cannot be told. Their beginnings lie far back in the Good Old Days when the planet was populated with the kind of colorful creatures you have to drink a quart of Old Overcoat to see nowadays. The elves alone preserve any records of that time, and most of them are filled with elf-stuff, raunchy pictures of naked trolls and sordid accounts of 'orc' orgies. But the boggies had clearly lived in Lower Middle Earth for a long time before the days of Frito and Dildo, when, like a very old salami that suddenly makes its presence known, they came to trouble the councils of the Small and the Silly.

This was all in the Third, or Sheet-Metal, Age of Lower Middle Earth, and the lands of that age have long since dropped into the sea and their inhabitants into bell jars at the Ripley's Believe-It-or-Not Odditorium. Of their original home, the boggies of Frito's time had lost all records, partly because their level of literacy and intellectual development could have been equaled by a young blowfish and partly because their fondness for genealogical studies made them dislike the notion that their elaborately forged family trees had roots about as steady as Birnham Wood. It is nevertheless clear from their heavy accents and their fondness for dishes cooked in Brylcreem that somewhere in their past they went west in steerage. Their legends and old songs, which deal mainly with over-sexed elves and dragons in heat, make passing mention of the area around the Anacin River, between Plywood and the Papier-Maché Mountains. There are other records in the great libraries of Twodor which lend credence to such a notion, old articles in the *Police Gazette* and the like. Why they decided to undertake the perilous crossing into Oleodor is uncertain, though again their songs tell of a shadow that fell upon the land so that the potatoes grew no more.

Before the crossing of the Papier-Maché Mountains, the boggies had become divided into three distinct breeds: Clubfoots, Stools, and Naugahydes. The Clubfoots, by far the most numerous, were swarthy, shifty-eyed, and short; their hands and feet were as deft as crowbars. They preferred to live in the hillsides where they could mug rabbits and small goats, and they supported themselves by hiring out as torpedoes for the local dwarf population. The Stools were larger and oilier than the Clubfoots, and they lived in the fetid lands at the mouth and other orifices of the Anacin River, where they raised yaws and goiters for the river trade. They had long, shiny, black hair, and they loved knives. Their closest relations were with men, for whom they handled occasional rubouts. Least numerous were the Naugahydes, who were taller and wispier than the other boggies and who lived in the forests, where they maintained a thriving trade in leather goods, sandals, and handicrafts. They did periodic interior-decorating work for the elves, but spent most of their time singing lurid folk songs and accosting squirrels.

Once across the mountains, the boggies lost no time establishing themselves. They shortened their names and elbowed their way into all the country clubs, dropping their old language and customs like a live grenade. An unusual easterly migration of men and elves from Oleodor at this same time makes it possible to fix the date the boggies came on the scene with some accuracy. In the same year, the 1,623rd year of the Third Age, the Naugahyde brothers, Brasso and

Drano, led a large following of boggies across the Gallowine River disguised as a band of itinerant graverobbers and took control from the high King at Ribroast.* In return for the King's grudging acquiescence, they set up toll booths on the roads and bridges, waylaid his messengers, and sent him suggestive and threatening letters. In short, they settled down for a long stay.

Thus began the history of the Sty, and the boggies, with an eye to the statutes of limitations, started a new calendar dating from the crossing of the Gallowine. They were quite happy with their new land, and once again they dropped out of the history of men, an occurrence which was greeted with the same universal sense of regret as the sudden death of a mad dog. The Sty was marked with great red splotches on all the AAA maps, and the only people who ever passed through were either hopelessly lost or completely unhinged. Aside from these rare visitors, the boggies were left entirely to themselves until the time of Frito and Dildo. While there was still a King at Ribroast, the boggies remained nominally his subjects, and to the last battle at Ribroast with the Slumlord of Borax, they sent some snipers, though who they sided with is unclear. There the North Kingdom ended, and the boggies

---

* Either Arglebargle IV or someone else.

returned to their well-ordered, simple lives, eating and drinking, singing and dancing, and passing bad checks.

Nonetheless, the easy life of the Sty had left the boggies fundamentally unchanged, and they were still as hard to kill as a cockroach and as easy to deal with as a cornered rat. Though likely to attack only in cold blood, and killing only for money, they remained masters of the low blow and the gang-up. They were crack shots and very handy with all sorts of equalizers, and any small, slow, and stupid beast that turned its back on a crowd of boggies was looking for a stomping.

All boggies originally lived in holes, which is after all hardly surprising for creatures on a first-name basis with rats. In Dildo's time, their abodes were for the most part built above ground in the manner of elves and men, but these still retained many of the features of their traditional homes and were indistinguishable from the dwellings of those species whose chief function is to meet their makers, around August, deep in the walls of old houses. As a rule, they were dumpling shaped, built of mulch, silt, stray divots, and other seasonal deposits, often whitewashed by irregular pigeons. Consequently, most boggie towns looked as though some very large and untidy creature, perhaps a dragon, had quite recently suffered a series of disappointing bowel movements in the vicinity.

In the Sty as a whole there were at least a dozen of

these curious settlements, linked by a system of roads, post offices, and a government that would have been considered unusually crude for a colony of cherrystone clams. The Sty itself was divided into farthings, half-farthings, and Indian-head nickels ruled by a mayor who was elected in a flurry of ballot-box stuffing every Arbor Day. To assist him in his duties there was a rather large police force which did nothing but extract confessions, mostly from squirrels, Beyond these few tokens of regulation, the Sty betrayed no signs of government. The vast majority of the boggies' time was taken up growing food and eating it and making liquor and drinking it. The rest of it was spent throwing up.

OF THE FINDING OF THE RING

As is told in the volume previous to this hound, *Valley of the Trolls*, Dildo Bugger set out one day with a band of demented dwarves and a discredited Rosicrucian named Goodgulf to separate a dragon from his hoard of short-term municipals and convertible debentures. The quest was successful, and the dragon, a prewar basilisk who smelled like a bus, was taken from behind while he was clipping coupons. And yet, though many pointless and annoying deeds were done, this adventure would concern us a good deal less than it does, if that is possible, except for a bit of petty larceny Dildo did along the way to keep his hand in. The party was ambushed in the Mealey Mountains by a roving pack of narcs, and in hurrying to the aid of the embattled dwarves, Dildo somehow lost his sense of direction and ended up in a cave a considerable distance away. Finding himself at the mouth of a tunnel which led rather perceptibly down, Dildo suffered a temporary recurrence of an old inner-ear problem and went rushing along it to the rescue, as he thought, of his friends. After running for some time and finding nothing but more tunnel, he was beginning to feel he had taken a wrong turn somewhere when the passage abruptly ended in a large cavern.

When Dildo's eyes became adjusted to the pale light, he found that the grotto was almost filled by a wide, kidney-shaped lake where a nasty-looking clown named Goddam paddled noisily about on an old rubber sea horse. He ate raw fish and occasional side orders to travel from the outside world in the form of lost travelers like Dildo, and he greeted Dildo's unexpected entrance into his underground sauna in much the same way as he would the sudden arrival of a Chicken Delight truck. But like anyone with boggie ancestry, Goddam preferred the subtle approach in assaulting creatures over five inches high and weighing more than ten pounds, and consequently he challenged Dildo to a riddle game to gain time. Dildo, who had a sudden attack of amnesia regarding the fact that the dwarves were being made into chutney outside the cave, accepted.

They asked each other countless riddles, such as who played the Cisco Kid and what was Krypton. In the end Dildo won the game. Stumped at last for a riddle to ask, he cried out, as his hand fell on his snub-nosed .38, 'What have I got in my pocket?' This Goddam failed to answer, and growing impatient, he paddled up to Dildo, whining, 'Let me see, let me see.' Dildo obliged by pulling out the pistol and emptying it in Goddam's direction. The dark spoiled his aim, and he managed only to deflate the rubber float, leaving Goddam to flounder. Goddam, who couldn't swim, reached out his hand to Dildo and begged him to pull him out, and as he did, Dildo noticed an interesting-looking ring on his finger and pulled it off. He would have finished Goddam off then and there, but pity stayed his hand. *It's a pity I've run out of bullets*, he thought, as he went back up the tunnel, pursued by Goddam's cries of rage.

Now it is a curious fact that Dildo never told this story, explaining that he had gotten the Ring from a pig's nose or a gumball machine – he couldn't remember which. Goodgulf, who was naturally suspicious, finally managed with the aid of one of his secret potions* to drag the truth out of the boggie, but it disturbed him considerably that Dildo, who was a perpetual and compulsive liar, would not have concocted a more grandiose tale from the start. It was then, some fifty years before our story begins, that Goodgulf first guessed at the Ring's importance. He was, as usual, dead wrong.

* Probably Sodium Pentothal.

I

IT'S MY PARTY AND I'LL SNUB WHO I WANT TO

When Mr Dildo Bugger of Bug End grudgingly announced his intention of throwing a free feed for all the boggies in his part of the Sty, the reaction in Boggietown was immediate – all through the messy little slum could be heard squeals of 'Swell!' and 'Hot puppies, *grub*!' Slavering with anticipation, several recipients of the invitations devoured their little engraved scrolls, temporarily deranged by transports of gluttony. After the initial hysteria, however, the boggies returned to their daily routines and, as is their wont, lapsed back into a coma.

Nevertheless, jabbering rumors spread through the tatty lean-tos of recent shipments of whole, bewildered oxen, great barrels of foamy suds, fireworks, tons of potato greens, and gigantic hogsheads of hogs' heads. Even huge bales of freshly harvested stingwort, a popular and remarkably powerful emetic, were carted into town. News of the fête reached even unto the Gallowine, and the outlying residents of the Sty began to drift into town like peripatetic leeches, each intent on an orgy of freeloading that would make a lamprey look like a piker.

No one in the Sty had a more bottomless gullet than that drooling and senile old gossip Haf Gangree. Haf had spent his life as the town's faithful beadle, and had long since retired on the proceeds of his thriving blackmail racket.

Tonight, Fatlip, as he was called, was holding forth at the Bag Eye, a sleazy dive more than once closed down by Mayor Fastbuck for the dubious behavior of the establishment's buxom 'B-boggies,' who were said to be able to roll a troll before you could say 'Rumpelstiltskin.' The usual collection of sodden oafs were there, including Fatlip's son, Spam Gangree, who was presently celebrating his suspended sentence for the performing of an unnatural act with an underage female dragon of the opposite sex.

'The whole thing smells pretty queer to me,' said Fatlip, as he inhaled the acrid fumes of his nose-pipe. 'I'm meaning the way Mr Bugger is throwing this big bash when for years he's not so much as offered a piece o' moldy cheese to his neighbors.' The listeners nodded silently, for this was certainly the case. Even before Dildo's 'strange disappearance' he had kept his burrow at Bug End guarded by fierce wolverines, and in no one's memory had he ever contributed a farthing to the Boggietown Annual Mithril Drive for Homeless Banshees. The fact that no one else ever had either did not excuse Dildo's famed stinginess. He kept to himself, nurturing only his nephew and a mania for dirty Scrabble.

'And that boy of his, Frito,' added bleary-eyed Nat Clubfoot, 'as crazy as a woodpecker, *that* one is.' This was verified by Old Poop of Backwater, among others. For who hadn't seen young Frito walking aimlessly through the crooked streets of Boggietown, carrying little clumps of flowers and muttering about 'truth and beauty' and blurting out silly nonsense like 'Cogito ergo boggum'?

'He's an odd one, all right,' said Fatlip, 'and I wouldn't be at all surprised if there weren't something in that talk of his having dwarfish sympathies.' At this point there was an embarrassed silence, particularly from young Spam, who had never believed the unproved charges that the Buggers were 'scroll-carrying dwarves.' As Spam pointed out, real dwarves were shorter and smelled much worse than boggies.

'That's pretty stout talk,' laughed Fatlip, wagging his right foreleg, 'about a body what's only *borrowed* the name of Bugger!'

'Aye,' chimed Clotty Peristalt. 'If that Frito weren't the seed of a crossbow wedding, then I don't know lunch from din-din!' The roisterers all laughed aloud as they remembered Frito's mother, Dildo's sister, who rashly plighted her troth to someone from the wrong side of the Gallowine (someone known to be a halfling, *i.e.* part boggie, part opossum). Several of the members took this up and there followed a series of coarse* and rather simpleminded jests at the expense of the Buggers.

'What's more,' said Fatlip, 'Dildo's always acting . . . mysterious, if you know what I mean.'

'There are those that say he acts like he's got something to hide, they say,' came a strange voice from the corner shadows. The voice belonged to a man, a stranger to the boggies of the Bag Eye, a stranger they had understandably overlooked because of his rather ordinary black cape, black chain mail, black mace, black dirk, and perfectly normal red glowing fires where his eyes should have been.

'Them what say that may be right,' agreed Fatlip, winking at his cronies to tell them a punchline was coming. 'But them that say such may be *wrong*, too.' After the general hilarity resulting from the typical Gangree gaff died down, few had noticed that the stranger had disappeared, leaving only a strange, barnyard odor behind him.

'But,' insisted little Spam, 'it *will* be a good party!'

To this they all agreed, for there was nothing a boggie loved more than an opportunity to stuff himself until he was violently ill.

*

* Coarse to anyone except a boggie, of course.

The season was cool, early autumn, heralding the annual change in the boggie dessert from whole water-melons to whole pumpkins. But the younger boggies who were not yet too obese to trundle their hulkish selves through the thoroughfares of the town saw evidence of a future treat at the forthcoming celebration: fireworks!

As the day of the party drew nearer, carts drawn by sturdy plow-goats rolled through the bullrush gates of Boggietown, laden with boxes and crates, each bearing the X-rune of Goodgulf the Wizard and various elvish brand names.

The crates were unloaded and opened at Dildo's door, and the mewling boggies wagged their vestigial tails with wonder at the marvelous contents. There were clusters of tubes mounted on tripods to shoot rather outsized roman candles; fat, finned skyrockets, with odd little buttons at the front end, weighing hundreds of pounds; a revolving cylinder of tubes with a crank to turn them; and large 'cherry bombs' that looked to the children more like little green pine-apples with a ring inserted at the top. Each crate was labeled with an olive-drab elf-rune signifying that these toys had been made in the elf-shops of a fairy whose name was something very much like 'Amy Surplus.'

Dildo watched the unpacking with a broad grin and

sent the young ones scampering with a vicious swipe of a well-honed toenail. 'G'wan, beat it, scram!' he called merrily after them as they disappeared. He then laughed and turned back to his boggie-hole, to talk to his guest within.

'This'll be one fireworks display they won't forget,' cackled the ageing boggie to Goodgulf, who was puffing his cigar rather uncomfortably in a chair of tasteless elvish-modern. The floor around it was littered with four-letter Scrabble arrangements.

'I am afraid that you must alter your plans for them,' said the Wizard, unsnaggling a clot of tangled hair in his long, dirty-gray beard. 'You cannot use extermination as a method for settling your petty grudges with the townspeople.'

Dildo studied his old friend with shrewd appraisal. The old Wizard was robed in a threadbare magician's cloak long out of fashion, with a few spangles and sequins hanging precariously at the ragged hems. On his head was a tall, battered conical hat sloppily covered with glow-in-the-dark cabalistic signs, alchemical symbols, and some off-color dwarfish graffiti, and in his gnarled, nail-bitten hands was a bent length of silvered maggotwood that served doubly as a 'magic' wand and backscratcher. At this moment Goodgulf was using it in its second office as he studied the worn toes of what in these days would be taken for black basketball sneakers. Hightops.

'Looking a little down-at-the-heels, Gulfie,' chuckled Dildo. 'Slump in the old Wizard racket, eh?'

Goodgulf looked pained at the use of his old school nickname, but adjusted his robes with dignity. 'It is no fault of mine that unbelievers ridicule my powers,' he said. 'My wonders will yet again make all gape and quail!' Suddenly he made a pass with his scratcher and the room was plunged into darkness. Through the blackness Dildo saw that Goodgulf's robes had become radiant and bright. Odd letters appeared mysteriously on the front of his robe, reading in elvish, *Will Thee Kiss Me in the Dark, Baby?*

Just as suddenly the light returned to the comfortable burrow, and the inscription faded from the conjurer's breast. Dildo rolled his eyes upward in his head and shrugged.

'Really now, Gulfie,' said Dildo, 'that kind of stuff went out with high-button greaves. No wonder you've got to moonlight card-sharking at hick carny shows.'

Goodgulf was unperturbed by his friend's sarcasm. 'Do not mock powers beyond your knowledge, impudent hairfoot,' he said, as five aces materialized in his hand, 'for you see the efficacy of my enchantments!'

'All I see is that you've finally got the hang of that silly sleeve-spring,' chuckled the boggie as he poured a bowl of ale for his old companion. 'So why don't you leave off with your white-mice-and-pixie-dust routine and tell me why you've honored me with your presence? *And* appetite.'

The Wizard paused a moment before speaking to focus his eyes, which had recently developed a tendency to cross, and looked gravely at Dildo.

'It is time to talk of the Ring,' he said.

'Ring, ring? What ring?' said Dildo.

'Thee knows only too well what Ring,' said Goodgulf. 'The Ring in thy pocket, Master Bugger.'

'Oooooh, *that* Ring,' said Dildo with a show of innocence, 'I thought you meant the ring you leave in my tub after your séances with your rubber duck.'

'This is not the time for the making of jests,' said Goodgulf, 'for Evil Ones are afoot in the lands, and danger is abroad.'

'But——,' began Dildo.

'Strange things are stirring in the East . . .'

'But——'

'Doom is walking the High Road . . .'

'But——'

'There is a dog in the manger . . .'

'But——'

'. . . a fly in the ointment . . .'

Dildo clapped his paw frantically over the working mouth of the Wizard. 'You mean . . . you mean,' he whispered, '*there's a Balrog in the woodpile?*'

'Mmummffleflug!' affirmed the gagged magician.

Dildo's worst fears had come to pass. After the party, he thought, there would be much to be decided.

Although only two hundred invitations had been sent, Frito Bugger should not have been surprised to see several times that number sitting at the huge troughlike tables under the great pavilion in the Bugger meadows. His young eyes widened as he moped about observing legions of ravenous muzzles tearing and snatching at their roasts and joints, oblivious to all else. Few faces were familiar to him in the grunting, belching press that lined the gorging-tables, but fewer still were not already completely disguised in masks of dried gravy and meat sauce. It was only then that the young boggie realized the truth in Dildo's favorite adage, 'It takes a heap o' vittles to gag a boggie.'

It was, nevertheless, a splendid party, decided Frito, as he dodged a flying hamhock. Great pits had been dug simply to accommodate the mountains of scorched flesh the guests threw down their well-muscled throats, and his Uncle Dildo had devised an ingenious series of pipelines to gravity-flow the hundreds of gallons of heady ale into their limitless paunches. Moodily, Frito studied his fellow boggies as they noisily crammed their maws with potato greens and jammed stray bits of greasy flesh into their jackets and coin-purses 'for later.' Occasionally an overly zealous diner would fall unconscious to the ground, much to the amusement of his fellows, who would take the opportunity to pelt him with garbage. Garbage, that is, that they weren't stowing away 'for later.'

All around Frito was the sight and sound of gnashing boggie teeth, gasping boggie esophagi, and groaning, pulsating boggie bellies. The din of the gnawing and munching almost drowned out the national anthem of the Sty, which the hired orchestra was now more or less performing.

> *We boggies are a hairy folk*
> *Who like to eat until we choke.*
> *Loving all like friend and brother,*
> *And hardly ever eat each other.*
>
> *Ever hungry, ever thirsting,*
> *Never stop till belly's bursting.*
> *Chewing chop and pork and muttons,*
> *A merry race of boring gluttons.*
>
> *Sing: Gobble, gobble, gobble, gobble,*
> *Gobble, gobble, gobble, gobble.*

Boggies gather round the table,
Eat as much as you are able.
Gorge yourselves from moon till noon
(Don't forget your plate and spoon).

Anything edible, we've got dibs on,
And hope we all die with our bibs on.
Ever gay, we'll never grow up,
Come! And sing and play and throw up!

Sing: *Gobble, gobble, gobble, gobble,*
Gobble, gobble, gobble, gobble!

Frito wandered past the rows of tables, hoping to find the squat, familiar figure of Spam. 'Gobble, gobble, gobble . . .' he murmured to himself, but the words seemed strange. Why did he feel so alone amidst the merrymakers, why had he always thought himself an intruder in his own village? Frito stared at the phalanxes of grinding molars and foot-long forked tongues that lolled from a hundred mouths, pink and wet in the afternoon sun.

At that moment there was a commotion at the head table, where Frito should have been sitting as a guest of honor. Uncle Dildo was standing on his bench and making motions for quiet, wishing to make his after-dinner speech. After a flurry of jeers and the knocking together of a few heads, every fuzzy, pointed ear and glass eye strained to catch what Dildo had to say.

My fellow boggies, he said, *my fellow Poops and Peristalts, Barrelgutts and Hangbellies, Needlepoints, Liverflaps, and Nosethingers.* (Nose*fingers*! corrected an irate drunk who, true to his family name, had it jammed into his nostril to the fourth joint.)

I hope you have all stuffed yourselves until you are about to be sick. This customary greeting was met with traditional volleys of farting and belching, signifying the guests' approval of the fare.

I have lived in Boggietown, as you all know, most of my life, and I have developed opinions of you all, and before I leave you all for the last time, I want to let you all know what you have all meant to me. The crowd yelled approval, thinking that now was the time for Dildo to distribute the expected gifts among them. But what followed surprised even Frito, who looked at his uncle with shocked admiration. He had dropped his pants.

The riot that followed had best be left to the reader's imagination, lame though it may be. But Dildo, having prepared by prearranged signal to touch off the fireworks, diverted the rage of the townsboggies. Suddenly there came a deafening roar and a blinding light. Bellowing with fright, the vengeful boggies hit the dirt as the cataclysmic tumult thundered and flashed around them. The noise died down, and the braver members of the lynch mob looked up in the hot wind that followed at the little hill where Dildo's table had stood. It was not there any longer. Nor was Dildo.

'You should have seen their faces,' laughed Dildo to Goodgulf and Frito. Safely hidden back in his hole, the old boggie rocked with gleeful triumph. 'They ran like spooked bunnies!'

'Bunnies or boggies, I told you to be careful,' said Goodgulf. 'You may have hurt someone sorely.'

'No, no,' said Dildo, 'all the shrapnel blew the other way. And it was a good way of getting a rise out of 'em before I left this burg for good.' Dildo stood up and began making a final check of his trunks, each carefully addressed 'Riv'n'dell, Estrogen.' 'Things are getting hot all over and it was a good way to start getting them off their obese duffs.'

'Hot all over?' asked Frito.

'Aye,' said Goodgulf. 'Evil Ones are afoot in—'

'Not now,' interrupted Dildo impatiently. 'Just tell Frito what you told me.'

'What your rude uncle means,' began the Wizard, 'is that there have been many signs I have seen that bode ill for all, in the Sty and elsewhere.'

'Signs?' said Frito.

'Verily and forsooth,' replied Goodgulf darkly. 'In the past year strange and fearful wonders I have seen.

Fields sown with barley reap crabgrass and fungus, and even small gardens reject their artichoke hearts. There has been a hot day in December and a blue moon. Calendars are made with a month of Sundays and a blue-ribbon Holstein bore alive two insurance salesmen. The earth splits and the entrails of a goat were found tied in square knots. The face of the sun blackens and the skies have rained down soggy potato chips.'

'But what do all these things mean?' gasped Frito.

'Beats me,' said Goodgulf with a shrug, 'but I thought it made good copy. But there is more. My spies tell me of black musters gathering in the East, in the dead Lands of Fordor. Hordes of foul narcs and trolls have multiplied and every day red-eyed wraiths skulk even unto the borders of the Sty. Soon there will be much terror in the land from the black hand of Sorhed.'

'Sorhed!' cried Frito. 'But Sorhed is no more.'

'Don't believe everything you hear from the heralds,' said Dildo gravely. 'It had been thought that Sorhed was forever destroyed at the Battle of Brylopad, but it appears that this was just wishful thinking. Actually he and his Nine Nozdrul slipped out of the mopping-up cleverly disguised as a troupe of gypsy acrobatic dancers. Escaping through the Ngaio Marsh, they pushed their way into the suburbs of Fordor, where the property values dropped like a paralysed falcon. From Fordor they have been renewing their strength ever since.'

'His Dark Carbuncle of Doom has swollen and soon will come to a head, covering the face of Lower Middle Earth with his ill humors. If we are to survive, the boil must be soundly lanced before Sorhed begins his own loathsome squeeze play.'

'But how can this be done?' said Frito.

'We must keep him from the one thing that can mean victory,' said Goodgulf. 'We must keep from him the Great Ring!'

'And what is this ring?' said Frito, eyeing the possible exits from the hole.

'Cease thy eyeing of possible exits and I will tell thee,' Goodgulf reprimanded the frightened boggie. 'Many ages ago, when boggies were yet wrestling with the chipmunks over hazel nuts, there were made Rings of Power in the Elven-Halls. Fashioned with a secret formula now known only to the makers of toothpastes, these fabulous Rings gave their wearers mickle powers. There were twenty in all: six for mastery of the lands, five for rule of the seas, three for dominion of the air, and two for the conquering of bad breath. With these Rings the people of past ages, both mortals and elves, lived in peace and grandeur.'

'But that only makes sixteen,' observed Frito. 'What were the other four?'

'Recalled for factory defects,' laughed Dildo. 'They tended to short-circuit in the rain and fry one's finger off.'

'Save the Great One,' intoned Goodgulf, 'for the Great Ring masters all the others, hence is now the most sought by Sorhed. Its powers and charms are shrouded in legend, and many works are said to be given to its wearer. It is said that, according to his powers, the wearer can perform impossible deeds, control all creatures to his bidding, vanquish invincible armies, converse with fish and fowl, bend steel in his bare hands, leap tall parapets in a single bound, win friends and influence people, fix parking tickets—'

'And get himself elected Queen of the May,' finished Dildo. 'Anything he pleases!'

'This Great Ring is much desired by all, then,' said Frito.

'And they desire a curse!' cried Goodgulf, waving his wand with passion. 'For as surely as the Ring gives power, just as surely it becomes the master! The wearer slowly changes, and never to the good. He grows mistrustful and jealous of his power as his heart hardens. He loves overmuch his strengths and develops stomach ulcers. He becomes logy and irritable, prone to neuritis, neuralgia, nagging backache, and frequent colds. Soon no one invites him to parties anymore.'

'A most horrible treasure, this Great Ring,' said Frito.

'And a horrible burden for he who bears it,' said Goodgulf. 'For some unlucky one must carry it from Sorhed's grasp into danger and certain doom. Someone must take the ring to the Zazu Pits of Fordor, under the evil nose of the wrathful Sorhed, yet appear so unsuited to his task that he will not be soon found out.'

Frito shivered in sympathy for such an unfortunate. 'Then the bearer should be a complete and utter dunce,' he laughed nervously.

Goodgulf glanced at Dildo, who nodded and casually flipped a small, shining object into Frito's lap. It was a ring.

'Congratulations,' said Dildo somberly. 'You've just won the booby prize.'

II

THREE'S COMPANY,
FOUR'S A BORE

'If I were thee,' said Goodgulf, 'I would start on thy journey soon.' Frito looked up absently from his rutabaga tea.

'For half a groat you *can* be me, Goodgulf. I don't remember volunteering for this Ring business.'

'This is not the time for idle banter,' said the Wizard, pulling a rabbit from his battered hat. 'Dildo left days ago and awaits you at Riv'n'dell, as will I. There the fate of the Ring will be decided by all the peoples of Lower Middle Earth.'

Frito pretended to be engrossed in his cup as Spam entered from the dining room and began tidying up the hole, packing up the last of Dildo's belongings for storage.

'Lo, Master Frito,' he rasped, pulling a greasy forelock. 'Just gettin' the rest o' the stuff together for your uncle what mysteriously disappeared wi'out a trace. Strange business that, eh?' Seeing that no explanation was forthcoming, the faithful servant shuffled off into Dildo's bedroom. Goodgulf, hastily retrieving his rabbit, who was being loudly sick on the carpet, resumed speaking.

'Are you sure he can be trusted?'

Frito smiled. 'Of course. Spam's been a true friend of mine since we were weanlings at obedience school together.'

'And he knows nothing of the Ring?'

'Nothing,' said Frito. 'I am sure of it.'

Goodgulf looked dubiously toward the closed door of the bedroom. 'You still have it, don't you?'

Frito nodded and fished out the chain of paper clips that secured it to his tattersall bowling shirt.

'Then be careful with it,' said Goodgulf, 'for it has many strange powers.'

'Like turning my pocket green?' asked the young boggie, turning the small circlet in his stubby fingers. Fearfully he stared at it, as he had so many times in the past few days. It was made of bright metal and was encrusted with strange devices and inscriptions. Around the inner surface was written something in a language unknown to Frito.

'I can't make out the words,' said Frito.

'No, you cannot,' said Goodgulf. 'They are elvish, in the tongue of Fordor. A rough translation is:

> *This Ring, no other, is made by the elves,*
> *Who'd pawn their own mother to grab it themselves.*
> *Ruler of creeper, mortal, and scallop,*
> *This is a sleeper that packs quite a wallop.*

The Power almighty rests in this Lone Ring.
The Power, alrighty, for doing your Own Thing.
If broken or busted, it cannot be remade
If found, send to Sorhed (the postage is prepaid).

'Shakestoor, it isn't,' said Frito, hurriedly putting the Ring back in his shirt pocket.

'But a dire warning nonetheless,' said Goodgulf. 'Even now Sorhed's tools are abroad sniffing for this ring, and the time grows short before they smell it here. It is the time to set off for Riv'n'dell.' The old magician stood, walked to the bedroom door, and opened it with a jerk. With a heavy crash, Spam fell forward ear first, his pockets full of Dildo's best mithril-plate tablespoons. 'And *this* will be your faithful companion.' As Goodgulf passed into the bedroom, Spam grinned sheepishly at Frito with a lop-eared stupidity Frito had learned to love, futilely trying to hide the spoons in his pockets.

Ignoring Spam, Frito called fearfully after the Wizard.

'But – but – there are still many preparations I must make! My bags—'

'Have no worry,' said Goodgulf as he held out two valises. 'I took the precaution of packing them for you.'

The night was as clear as an elfstone, sparkling with

starpoints, as Frito gathered his party in the pasture outside the town. In addition to Spam, were the twin brothers Moxie and Pepsi Dingleberry, both of whom were noisome and easily expendable. They were frisking happily in the meadow. Frito called them to attention, wondering vaguely why Goodgulf had saddled him with two tail-wagging idiots that no one in the town could trust with a burnt-out match.

'Let's go, let's go!' cried Moxie.

'Yes, *let's*,' added Pepsi, who promptly took one step, fell directly on his flat head, and managed to bloody his nose.

'Icky!' laughed Moxie.

'*Double* icky!' wailed Pepsi.

Frito rolled his eyes heavenward. It was going to be a long epic.

Gaining their wandering attention, Frito inspected his companions and their kits. As he had feared, his orders had been forgotten and everyone had brought the potato salad. Everyone except Spam, who had stuffed his knapsack with sleazy novels and Dildo's tablespoons.

At last they set off, following Goodgulf's instructions, along the yellow-brick Intershire Turnpath toward Whee, the longest leg of their journey to Riv'n'dell. The Wizard had told them to travel at night unseen along the side of the Path, to keep their ear to the ground, their eyes peeled and their noses clean, the last directive weighing rather heavily on Pepsi, under the circumstances.

For a while they walked along in silence, each lost in what passed in boggies for thought. But Frito was especially troubled as he considered the long travels ahead of him. Though his companions frisked gaily along, playfully kicking and tripping each other, his heart was heavy with dread. Remembering happier times, he hummed and then sang an ancient dwarf-song he had learned from the knee of his Uncle Dildo, a song whose maker had lived before the dawn of Lower Middle Earth. It began:

> *Heigh-ho, heigh-ho,*
> *It's off to work we go,*
> *Heigh-ho, heigh-ho, heigh-ho, heigh-heigh,*
> *Heigh-ho, heigh-ho . . .*

'Good! Good!' yipped Moxie.

'Yes, good! Especially the "heigh-ho" part,' added Pepsi.

'And what do you be callin' that?' asked Spam, who knew few songs.*

'I call it "Heigh-ho," ' said Frito.

But he was not cheered by it.

---

* Clean ones, at least.

Soon it began to rain and they all caught colds.

The sky in the east was changing from black to pearl-gray as the four boggies, weary and sneezing their heads off, stopped their march and camped for the day's rest in a clump of dogwillows many steps from the unprotected Turnpath. The fatigued travelers stretched out on the sheltered ground and made a long boggie snack from Frito's store of dwarfloaf, boggie-brewed ale, and breaded veal cutlets. Then, groaning softly under the weight of their stomachs, all dropped quickly off to sleep, each dreaming their private boggie dreams, most of them having to do with veal cutlets.

Frito awoke with a start. It was dusk now, and a sick feeling in his stomach made him scan the Path from between the branches with terror. Through the leaves he saw a dark, shadowy bulk in the distance. It moved slowly and carefully along the rise of the Path, looking like a tall, black rider on some huge and bloated beast. Outlined against the setting sun, Frito held his breath as the ominous figure's red eyes searched the land. Once, Frito thought, the fiery coals had looked right through him, but they blinked myopically and passed on. The ponderous mount, which appeared to Frito's startled eyes to be an immense, grossly overfed pig the size of a house, snuffled and snorted in the wet earth to root out some scent of them. The others awoke and froze with terror. As they watched, the evil hunter goaded his mount, emitted one great and sour fart, and passed on. He had not seen them.

The boggies waited until the distant grunting of the beast had long quieted before anyone spoke. Frito turned to his companions, who were well hidden in their foodsacks, and whispered, 'It's all right. It's gone.'

Doubtfully, Spam emerged. 'Bless me if that didn't fright me plumb out o' me codpiece,' laughed Spam weakly. 'Most queer and disturbin'!'

'Queer and disturbin'!' came a chorus of voices from the other sacks.

'And even more disturbin' if I keep on a-hearin' me echo every time I open me chops!' Spam kicked the sacks, each of which yelped, but showed no sign of disgorging its contents.

'Grouchy, he is,' said one.

'Grouchy and *mean*,' said the other.

'I wonder,' said Frito, 'what and who that terrible creature was.'

Spam cast his eyes downward and scratched his chins guiltily. 'I'm guessin' it's one o' those folk the Fatlip told me to remember to be a-warnin' ye about, Master Frito.'

Frito looked at him inquiringly.

'Weeeell,' said Spam, pulling his forelock and

licking Frito's toes in apology, 'as I recollect now, the Old Lip was a-tellin' me just before we left, *And don't be forgettin'*, he says to me, *to tell Master Frito that some smelly stranger wi' red eyes was askin' after him. Stranger?* says I. *Aye,* says he, *and when I keeps mum, the fiend up and hisses at me and twirls 'is black mustache. "Curses,"* the foul thing says, *"foiled again!" And then he waves 'is billy at me and jumps on 'is pig and hightails it frœ th' Bag Eye a-shoutin' somethin' very much like "Hi-yo Slimey!" Very strange*, I says. I guess I was a bit slow t' tell ye, Master Frito.'

'Well,' said Frito, 'there's no time to worry now. I'm not sure, but I wouldn't be surprised if there's some connection between that stranger and this foul searcher.' Frito knitted his brows, but as usual dropped a stitch. 'In any case,' he said, 'it's no longer safe to follow the Turnpath to Whee. We'll have to take the shortcut through the Evilyn Wood.'

'The Evilyn Wood!?' chorused the grubsacks.

'But Master Frito,' said Spam, 'they say that place is . . . *haunted*!'

'That may be true,' said Frito quietly, 'but if we stay here, we're all blue-plate specials for sure.'

Frito and Spam hastily decanted the twins with hearty kicks, and the company policed the remaining fragments of cutlets from the area, spicing the left-overs with a number of sawbugs. When all was ready, they set out, the twins emitting high-pitched *cheep-cheeps* in the not altogether vain hope of passing themselves off in the dark as migrating cockroaches. Due west they tramped, doggedly locating every possible opportunity for falling flat on their muzzles, pressing on so that they might reach the safety of the wood before the next sunrise. Frito had calculated that they traveled over two leagues in as many days, not bad for a boggie but still not fast enough. They had to take the wood in stride to be at Whee by the next day.

Silently they walked, save for a slight whimpering from Pepsi. *The silly nit's bloodied his pug again*, thought Frito, *and Moxie's getting cranky*. But as the long night passed and the east brightened, the flat ground gave way to hummocks, hillocks, and buttocks of spongy, soft earth the color of calves' brains. As the company stumbled on, the underbrush changed to saplings and then to huge, irritable-looking trees, blasted and scored by wind, weather, and arthritis. Soon they were swallowed up from the dawn light, and the new night covered them like a rank locker-room towel.

Many years before it had been a happy, pleasant forest of well-pruned puswillows, spruce spruces, and natty pines, the frolicking place of drone-moles and slightly rabid chipmunks. But now the trees had grown old, clotted with sneezemoss and toemold, and the Nattily Wood had become the crotchety old Evilyn.

'We should be in Whee by morning,' said Frito as they paused for a light snack of potato salad. But the malevolent susurrus in the trees over the small company bade them not tarry there long. They quickly moved on, careful to avoid the occasional barrages of droppings that fell from unseen, yet annoyed tenants in the branches above.

After several hours of mucking about, the boggies fell exhausted to the ground. The ground was unfamiliar to Frito, and he had long since muddled his sense of direction. 'We should have been out of these woods by now,' he said worriedly. 'I think we're lost.'

Spam looked at his rapier-sharp toenails in dejection, but then brightened. 'That may be true, Master Frito,' he said. 'But don't be a-worryin' about it. Somebody else was here only a few hours ago, by the looks o' the camp. An' they was gobblin' tater salad just like us!'

Frito studied these telltale clues with care. It was true, someone had been here only a few hours before, lunching on boggie grub. 'Perhaps we can follow their trail and find the way out of here.' And tired as they were, they pushed on again.

On and on they trod, vainly calling after the folk whose evidence of passage lay after them: a scrap of breaded veal cutlet, a sleazy boggie novel, one of

Dildo's tablespoons (*What a coincidence*, Frito thought.) But no boggies. They did come across a large rabbit with a cheap pocket watch who was pursued by some nut of a girl, another kid being viciously mugged by three furious grizzlies ('We'd better not get involved,' said Frito wisely), and a deserted and flyspecked gingerbread bungalow with a 'To Let' sign on the marzipan door. But no clue to a way out.

Limp with fatigue, the four finally dropped in their tracks. It was already late afternoon in the gloomy woods, and they could go no farther without a snooze. As if lulled by a potion, the hairy little beggars curled up in furry balls and, one by one, conked off under the protective boughs of a huge, quivering tree.

Spam did not at first realize he was awake. He had felt something soft and rubbery pull at his clothes, but he thought it a longing dream of those reptilian pleasures he had so recently enjoyed back in the Sty. But now he was certain he had heard a distinct *sucking* sound and a tearing of cloth. His eyes popped open to see himself stark naked and bound head and paw by the fleshy roots of the tree. Screaming his fool head off, he woke his fellows, likewise hogtied and stripped clean by the writhing plant, which was giving off a distinct *cooing* noise. The strange tree hummed to itself, ever tightening its hold. As the boggies watched with revulsion, the crooning tossed salad dipped down the orangy, liplike flowers at its tips. The bulbous pods drew nearer, making revolting *smacking* and *smooching* noises as they began to fasten themselves to their helpless bodies. Locked in a foul embrace, the boggies would soon be hickeyed to death. Summoning their last strength, they all cried for help.

'Help, help!' they cried.

But no one answered. The fat orange blossoms ranged over their helpless boggie bodies, squirming and moaning with desire. A bloated blossom fastened to Spam's boggie belly and began its relentless sucking motion; he felt his flesh drawn up to the center of the flower. Then, as Sam looked on in horror, the petals released with a resounding *pop*!, leaving a dark, malignant weal where the horrid pucker had been. Spam, powerless to save himself or his companions, watched terrified as the now-panting sepals prepared to administer their final, deadly soul kiss.

But just as the long, red stamen descended to its unspeakable task, Spam thought he heard the snatch of a lilting song not far distant, and growing louder! It was a muddled, drowsy voice that sang words that were not words to Spam's ears:

Toke-a-lid! Smoke-a-lid! Pop the mescalino!
Stash the hash! Gonna crash! Make mine methedrino!
Hop a hill! Pop a pill! For Old Tim Benzedrino!

Though mad with fear, all strained to the rising melody sung by someone who sounded like he had terminal mumps:

Snorting, sporting! Speeding through the arbor,
Pushing till the folk you burn toss you in the harbor!
Screeching like a dying loon, zooming like the thrush!
Follow me and very soon, your mind will turn to mush!
Higher than the nowhere birds grooving in the air,
We'll open up a sandal shop where everyone will share!
Flower folk are springing up, wearing bead and boot,
And if you down me you can stick a flower up your
   snoot!
To Love and Peace and Brotherhood we all can snort a
   toast,
And if the heat is on again, we'll all split to the Coast!

Suddenly a brightly colored figure burst through the foliage, swathed in a long mantle of hair the consistency of much-chewed Turkish taffy. It was something like a man, but not much; it stood six feet tall, but could not have weighed more than thirty-five pounds, dirt included. Standing with his long arms dangling almost to the ground, the singer's body was covered with a pattern of startling hues, ranging from schizoid red to psychopathique azure. Around his pipestem neck hung a dozen strands of beaded charms and from the center, an amulet imprinted with the elf-rune *Kelvinator*. Through the oily snaggles of hair stared two huge eyeballs that bulged from their sockets, so bloodshot that they appeared more like two baseballs of very lean bacon.

'Ooooooooooh, wow!' said the creature, assaying the situation quickly. Then, half loping, half rolling to the foot of the murderous tree, he sat on his meatless haunches and peered at it with his colorless, saucerlike irises; he chanted an incantation that sounded to Frito like a hacking cough:

> *Oh uncool bush! Unloose this passle*
> *Of furry cats that you hassle!*
> *Tho' by speed my brain's destroyed,*
> *I'm not half this paranoid!*
> *So cease this bummer, down the freak-out,*
> *Let caps and joints cause brains to leak-out!*
> *These cats are groovy here among us,*
> *So leave 'em be, you uptight fungus!*

Thus speaking, the withered apparition raised his spidery hand in a two-fingered 'V' sign and uttered an eldritch spell:

> *Tim, Tim, Benzedrine!*
> *Hash! Boo! Valvoline!*
> *Clean! Clean! Clean for Gene!*
> *First, second, neutral, park,*
> Hie thee hence, *you leafy narc!*

The towering plant shivered and the coils fell from its victims like yesterday's macaroni, and they sprang free with joyful yelps. As they watched with fascination, the great green menace whimpered like a nursling and sucked its own pistils with ill temper. The boggies retrieved their garments, and Frito sighed with relief to find the Ring still firmly Bostiched to his pocket.

'Oh thank you,' they all squealed, wagging their tails, 'thank you, thank you!' But their savior said nothing. As if unaware of their presence, he stiffened like the tree and gasped, 'Gah gah gah' while his pupils opened and closed like nervous umbrellas. His knees buckled and unbuckled, then buckled again and he fell to the mossy earth in a ball of frantically thrashing hair. He foamed at the mouth and screamed, 'Oh, God get 'em off me! They're all over the place, and green! Argh! Org! *OhGodOhGodOhGodOhGodOhGodOhGod!*' He slapped at his hair and body hysterically.

Frito blinked with astonishment and grabbed his Ring, but did not put it on. Spam, stooping over the prostrate freak, smiled and offered his hand.

'Beggin' your leave,' he said, 'can you tell us where—'

'Oh no no *no*! Look at all of 'em! All over the place! *Keep 'em away from me!*'

'Keep who away?' asked Moxie politely.

'*Them!*' screamed the stricken stranger, pointing to

his own head. He then sprang to his horny feet and ran directly at the trunk of the hickey tree and, charging full tilt with his head lowered, butted it a mighty lick, and, before the startled eyes of the boggies, passed out cold. Frito filled his narrow-brimmed hat with clear water from a nearby trickle and approached him, but the stunned figure opened his marbled eyes and gave another high-pitched scream.

'No, no, not *water*!'

Frito jumped back with fright and the skinny creature wobbled to his feet and knuckles.

'But thangs loads anyhoo,' said the stranger, 'the rush always arfects me like dat.' Offering a filthy hand, the odd-speaking stranger smiled a toothless grin. 'Tim Benzedrine, ad yer serbice.'

Frito and the rest solemnly introduced themselves, all still casting a worried eye toward the kissing plant, which was sticking out its stamen at them.

'Oh wow, doan' worby about him,' wheezed Tim, 'he just sulking. Yoo cats noo aroun' here?'

Frito guardedly told him that they were on their way to Whee, but had become lost. 'Can you tell us how to find our way there?'

'Oh wow, oh sure,' laughed Tim, 'thad's easy. But led's split to my pad firz, I wan' yoo meet my chick. She name Hashberry.'

The boggies agreed, for their stores of potato salad

were gone. Gathering their packs, they curiously followed after the wildly zigzagging Benzedrine, who occasionally halted to rap with a likely looking rock or stump, giving them time to catch up. As they circled through the menacing trees aimlessly, Tim Benzedrine's throat croaked merrily:

O slender as a speeding freak! Spaced-out groovy tripper!
O mush-brained maid whose mind decays with every
  pill I slip her!
O mind-blown fair farina-head, friend of birds and
  beetles!
O skinny wraith whose fingernails are hypodermic needles!
O tangled locks and painted bod! Pupils big as eggs!
O flower-maid who never bathes or even shaves her legs!
O softened mind that wanders wherever moon above
  leads!
O how I dig thee, Hashberry, from nose to sleazy love-
  beads!

A few moments later they broke into a clearing on a low hill. There was a ramshackle hovel shaped like a rubber boot with a little chimney that emitted a thick fog of sick-looking green smoke.

'Oh wow,' squeaked Tim, 'she's home!' Led by Tim, the company approached the unprepossessing little hut. A flashing white light blinked from its only window, at the top. As they stepped over the thresh-

old, littered with cigarette papers, broken pipes, and
burnt-out brain cells, Tim called:

> *I've brought four with me to crash,*
> *So now's the time to pass the stash.*

From the smoky depths an answering voice returned:

> *Then celebrate and take a toke,*
> *To make us giggle, gag and choke!*

At first Frito saw nothing amid the iridescent wallpaper
and strobe candles but what appeared to be a heap of
filthy cleaning rags. But then the pile spoke again:

> *Hither come and suck a pipe,*
> *Turn thy brains to cheese and tripe!*

And then, as the boggies squinted their smarting eyes,
the heap stirred and sat up revealing itself to be an
incredibly emaciated, hollow-eyed female. She looked
at them for a second, muttered, 'Like wow,' and fell
forward in a catatonic stupor with a rattle of beads.

'Doan' let Hash bug yoo,' said Tim. 'Tuesday is her
day to crash.'

Somewhat bewildered by the acrid fumes and the
flashing candles, the boggies sat crosslegged on a grimy
mattress and asked politely for some grub, as they had
journeyed far and were about to devour the ticking.

'Eats?' chuckled Tim, rummaging through a hand-made leather pouch. 'Jes' hang loose an' I'll fimb somp'un f'yoo. Lemmesee, oh, oh wow! Dint know we had any this left!' Clumsily he scooped out the contents and set them in a bent hubcap before them. They were among the most dubious-looking mushrooms Spam had ever seen, and, rather rudely, he said so.

'These are among the most dubious-lookin' mushrooms I'm ever a-seeing,' he stated.

Nevertheless there were few things in Lower Middle Earth Spam *hadn't* idly nibbled and lived to tell about, so he dived in, stuffing himself loudly. They were of an odd color and odor, but they tasted okay, if a little on the moldy side, and after that the boggies were offered round candies with little letters cleverly printed on them. ('They melt in yoor brain, not in your hans,' giggled Tim.)

Bloated to critical mass, the contented boggies relaxed as Hashberry played a melody on something that looked like a pregnant handloom. Mellowed by the repast, Sam was particularly pleased when Tim offered him some of his 'own speshul mix' for his nose-pipe. An odd flavor, thought Spam, but nice.

'Yoo got about ha'f an hour,' said Tim. 'Wanna rap?'

'Rap?' said Spam.

'Yoo know, like . . . talk wif your mouf,' replied

Tim as he lit his own pipe, a large converted milk separator laden with valves and dials. 'Yoo here 'cause th' heat's on?'

'In a manner of speaking,' said Frito judiciously. 'We've got this here Ring of Power and – oops!' Frito caught himself, but too late; he could not unsay it now.

'Oh groovy!' said Tim. 'Lemme see.'

Reluctantly, Frito handed over the Ring.

'Pretty cheap stuff,' said Tim, tossing it back. 'Even th' junk I pawn off on th' dwarbs is bedder.'

'You sell rings?' asked Moxie.

'Sure,' said Tim. 'I gotta sandal-and-magic-charm shop for th' tourist season. Keeps me in stash for winter months, y'know whad I mean?'

'There might not be many of us left to visit the woods,' said Frito quietly, 'if Sorhed's plans are not foiled. Will you join us?'

Tim shook his hair. 'Now doan' bug me, man. I'm a conscienshul objectioner . . . doan' wan' no more war. Came here to dodge draff, see? If some cat wants to kick th' stuffing outta me, I say, "Groovy," an' I give 'em a flower an' love-beads. "Love," I say t' him. "No more war," I say. Anyway, I four-F!'

'No more guts!' growled Spam under his breath to Moxie.

'No, I *god* guts,' said Tim, pointing to his temple, 'no more braims!'

Frito smiled diplomatically, but was suddenly stricken by a severe stomachache. His eyes began to roll and he felt very light-headed. *Probably a touch of the banshee two-step*, he thought as his ears started to ring like a dwarf's cash-register. His tongue felt thick, and his tail began to vibrate. Turning to Spam, he wished to ask him if he felt it too.

'Argle-bargle morble whoosh?' said Frito.

But it did not matter, for he saw that Spam had oddly taken it into his head to change himself into a large, pink dragon wearing a three-piece suit and a straw boater.

'What did you be sayin', Master Frito?' asked the natty lizard with Spam's voice.

'Ffluger fribble golorful frooble,' said Frito dreamily, thinking it strange that Spam was wearing a boater in late autumn. Glancing at the twins, Frito noted that they had changed into matching candy-striped coffee-pots perking away like mad.

'Don't feel too well,' said one.

'Feel *sick*,' clarified the other.

Tim, now a rather handsome six-foot carrot, laughed loudly and changed into a coiled parking meter. Frito, dizzy as a great wave of oatmeal flowed through his brain, grew heedless of the puddle of drool collecting in his lap. There was a noiseless explosion between his ears and he watched with terror as the room began stretching and pulsating like Silly Putty in heat. Frito's ears began to grow and his arms changed into badminton rackets. The floor developed holes out of which poured fanged peanut brittle. A score of polka-dotted cockroaches danced a buck-and-wing on his stomach. A Swiss cheese waltzed him twice around the room, and his nose fell off. Frito opened his mouth to speak and a flock of flying earthworms escaped. His gall bladder sang an aria and did a little tap dance on his appendix. He began to lose consciousness, but before it ebbed completely, he heard a six-foot waffle iron giggle, 'If yoo dig it now, jes' wade till th' *rush* hits you!'

III

INDIGESTION AT THE
SIGN OF THE GOODE EATS

The golden brightness of late morning was already warming the grass when Frito finally awoke, his head sore afflicted, and his mouth tasting like the bottom of a birdcage. Looking about, every joint aching, he saw that he and his three still-slumbering companions were at the very edge of the Wood, and before them was the four-lane wagon rut that would lead them directly to Whee! There was no sign of Tim Benzedrine. Frito mused that the events of the previous night might have been the idle dream of a boggie whose tummy writhed full of spoiled potato salad. Then his bloodshot eyes saw the small paper bag resting next to his knapsack, with a scrawled note attached. Curiously, Frito read:

Dere Fritoad,

Two badd yoo copped outt sso sooon lazt nighgt. Missed somm grooovy ttrps. Hoap the rring thinng wurcs outt awrighgth

Peece,
Timm

P.S. Hear ar som outt of sighgt stash which I am laying onn yoo guyys. Mmust sine off as rush iss comcomcoming ohgodohgodohgodohgod$5¢%* @+=!

Frito peeked inside the dirty paper sack and saw a number of colored candy beans, much like the ones they had eaten the night before. *Odd*, thought Frito, *but they may prove useful. Who knows?* Thus, after an hour or so of cajoling his fellows to their senses, Frito and the party tramped off toward Whee rapping much of their adventure the previous evening.

Whee was the chief village of Wheeland, a small and swampy region populated mostly by star-nosed moles and folk who wished that they were somewhere else. The village enjoyed a brief popularity when, through a surveyor's fortuitous hiccup, the four-lane Intershire Turnpath was mistakenly built right through the center of the pathetic little twarf. Then, for a time, the populace lived high on the hog off the proceeds from illegal speed traps, parking violations, and occasional bald-faced hijackings. A small tourist influx from the Sty led to the construction of cheap diners, flimsy souvenir stands, and prefabricated historical landmarks. But the growing cloud of 'troubles' from the east abruptly ended such trade as there was. Instead, a trickle of refugees came from the eastern lands bearing few belongings and fewer smarts.

Not ones to miss an opportunity, the men and boggies of Whee labored together in harmony selling the heavily accented immigrants shorter names and interests in perpetual-motion machines. They also supplemented their purses by hawking black-market visas to the Sty to the few unfortunates who were not familiar with the place.

The men of Whee were stooped, squat, splay-toed, and stupid. Heavily ridged over the eyes and prone to rather poor posture, they were often mistaken for Neanderthals, a common confusion that the latter deeply resented. Slow to anger or pretty much anything else, they lived peacefully with their boggie neighbors, who were themselves tickled pink to find somebody farther down the evolutionary scale.

Together, the two peoples now lived on the few farthings they made off the wetbacks and the dole, a common fruit shaped like your pancreas and about as appetizing.

The village of Whee had some six dozen small houses, most of them built of wax paper and discarded corks. They were arranged in sort of a circle inside the protecting moat, whose stench alone could drop a dragon at a hundred paces.

Pinching their nostrils, the company crossed the creaky drawbridge and read the sign at the gate:

WELCOME TO QUAINT, HISTORICAL WHEE
POPULATION 1~~004~~ ~~388~~ 96 AND STILL GROWING!

Two sleepy-eyed guards bestirred themselves just long
enough to relieve the protesting Spam of his remaining
tablespoons. Frito surrendered half of his magic beans,
which the guards munched with speculation.

The boggies beat it before they took effect and, per
Goodgulf's instructions, headed for the orange-and-
green flashing sign at the center of town. There they
found a gaudy plexiglas and chrome inn, whose
blinking sign portrayed a boar, rampant, devoured by
a mouth, drooling. Beneath it was the name of the inn,
the Goode Eats & Lodging. Passing through the
revolving door, the party signaled the bell clerk,
whose nametag read *Hi! I'm HoJo Hominigritts!* Like the
rest of the staff, he was costumed as a suckling pig with
false sow's ears, tail, and papier-mâché snout.

'Howdy!' drawled the fat boggie. 'Ya'll want a
room?'

'Yes,' said Frito, stealing a glance at his companions.
'We're just in town *for a little vacation*, aren't we,
boys?'

'Vacation,' said Moxie, winking at Frito broadly.

'Just a little vacation,' added Pepsi, nodding his head
like an idiot.

'Ya'll sign here please?' said the clerk through his

fake snout. Frito took the quill chained to the desk and wrote the names ALIAS UNDERCOVER, IVAN GOTTA-SECRET, JOHN DOE-SMITH, and IMA PSEUDONYM.

'Any bags, Mr, uh, Undercover?'

'Only under my eyes,' mumbled Frito, turning toward the dining hall.

'Wal,' chuckled the clerk, 'just leave these here sacks an' I'll *ring* a bellhop.'

'Fine,' said Frito, hurrying away.

'Now y'all have a good time now,' the clerk called after them, 'an' if y'all want anything, just *ring*!'

Out of earshot, Frito turned worriedly to Spam. 'You don't think he *knows* anything,' he whispered, 'do you?'

'Naw, Master Frito,' said Spam, massaging his stomach. 'Let's grab some grub!'

The four entered the dining room and sat at a booth near the roaring propane fireplace that eternally roasted a large cement boar on a motorized spit. The soft notes of a badly played Muzak eddied through the crowded room as the ravenous boggies studied the menu, which was ingeniously shaped like a sow giving birth. As Frito considered an 'Uncle Piggy's Oink-Oink Burger-on-a-Bun' flambéed in purest linseed oil, Spam hungrily ogled the scantily clad 'piglets' who served as waitresses, each buxom wench also outfitted in fake tail, ears, and snout.

One of the piglets sidled up to the table for their order as Spam greedily took stock of her big red eyes, crooked blond wig, and hairy legs.

'Youse slobs wanna order yet?' asked the piglet as she teetered uncomfortably on her spiked heels.

'Two Oink-Oink Burgers and two Bow-Wow Specials, please,' answered Frito respectfully.

'Somethun' t' *ring*, uh, I mean, *drink*, sir?'

'Just four Orca-Colas, thank you.'

'Gotcha.'

As the waitress lurched off, wobbling on her heels and tripping over her long, black scabbard, Frito surveyed the crowd for anyone suspicious. A few boggies, some swarthy-looking men, a drunken troll passed out at the counter. The usual.

Relieved, Frito allowed his three companions to mix with the others, warning them to keep their lips buttoned about the 'you-know-what.' The waitress returned with Frito's burger as Spam traded some pointless anecdotes with a pair of leprechauns in the corner and the twins entertained some seedy-looking gremlins with their cunning pantomime, *The Old Cripple and His Daughters*, a sure-fire hit in the Sty. As growing numbers roared with mirth at their obscene posturings, Frito munched his tasteless burger thoughtfully, wondering what the Great Ring's fate would be when they reached Riv'n'dell, and Goodgulf.

Suddenly, Frito's grinders jammed against a small hard object in the burger. Cursing under his breath, Frito reached into his throbbing mouth and extracted a tiny metal cylinder. Unscrewing the top, he removed a tinier strip of microvellum, on which he made out the words: *Beware! You are in great danger. You are embarked on a long journey. You will soon meet a tall, dark Ranger. You weigh exactly fifty-nine pounds.*

Frito drew in his breath with fright and his eyes sought the sender of this message. At last they came to rest on a tall, dark Ranger seated at the counter, a double root beer untouched before him. The lean figure was dressed entirely in gray, and his eyes were hidden by a black mask. Across his chest were crossed bandoleers of silver bullets, and a pearl-handled broadsword dangled ominously from one lean hip. As if feeling Frito's eyes upon him, he turned slowly on his stool and met them, putting a gloved finger to his lips for secrecy. He then pointed toward the door of the men's room and held out five fingers. FIVE MINUTES. He pointed toward Frito and then to himself. By this time half the patrons had turned to watch, and thinking it was a game of charades, were encouraging him with shouts of 'Famous saying?' and 'Sounds like!'

The young boggie pretended to take no heed of the stranger and reread the note. *Danger*, it said. Frito stared thoughtfully into the sediment of fish hooks and the frothy head of ground glass on his Orca-Cola. Making sure no one was watching, he cautiously took the glass over to the large potted palm nearby, which accepted it and placed it carefully on the floor.

His suspicions now fully aroused, Frito edged from the booth, careful not to disturb the decorative listening tube placed in the center of the plastic floral arrangement. Without being seen, he went into the little boggies' room, there to await the dark stranger.

After he had been waiting a few minutes, several patrons using the facilities began to eye Frito curiously as he leaned against a tiled wall whistling, his hands in his pockets. To allay their further inquiry, Frito turned to the vending machine that hung on the wall. 'Well, well, *well*,' he said in a stage whisper, 'just what I've been looking for!' He then proceeded, with elaborate carelessness, to work the machine with the change in his farthing purse.

Fifteen bird whistles, eight compasses, six miniature lighters, and four packs of nasty little rubber novelties later, a mysterious knocking was heard at the door. Finally one of the patrons hidden by a stall yelled, 'F'cryin' out loud, somebody let the s.o.b. in!' The door swung open and the masked visage of the dark stranger appeared and beckoned Frito around the corner.

'I have a message for you, Mr *Bugger*,' said the stranger.

Frito's burger rose at the sound of his true name.

'But — but I theenk you are meestaken, señor,' began Frito lamely, 'I velly solly but my honorable name not—'

'This message is from Goodgulf the Wizard,' said the stranger, 'if the name by which thee calls thyself answers to the title of *Frito Bugger!*'

'I are,' said Frito, confused and frightened.

'And thee hast the Ring?'

'Maybe I do, and maybe I don't,' countered Frito, stalling for time. The stranger lifted Frito by his narrow lapels.

'*And thee hast the Ring?*'

'Yes, already,' squealed Frito. 'So I've got it! So sue me.'

'Be not afraid, allay thy fears, quail not, and hold thy horses,' laughed the man. 'I am a friend of thine.'

'And you have a message for me from Goodgulf?' gulped Frito, feeling his burger settling a bit. The tall one unzipped a secret compartment in a saddlebag on his shoulder and handed Frito a slip which read:

'Three shorts, four pairs socks, two shirts, chain mail, heavy starch?' Impatiently, the stranger snatched the ancient gag from the boggie's paw and replaced it with a folded parchment. Frito's glance at the Michael-mas Seals and Goodgulf's X-rune imprinted in hard-ened bubble gum verified the sender.

Hurriedly he tore it open, saving the gum for Spam. For later. With difficulty he deciphered the familiar Palmer Method characters. They read:

Frito-lad,

The halberd has fallen! The fewmets have hit the windmill! Sorhed's Nozdrul have gotten wind of our little dodge and are beating the bush for 'four boggies, one with a pink tail.' Doesn't take any abacus to figure out somebody's spilled the gruel. Get out of wherever you are fast, and don't lose the you-know-what. I'll try to meet you at Wingtip, if not, look me up in Riv'n'dell. In any case, don't take any oaken tuppences. And don't mind Stomper, he's a good egg, ut-bay ot-nay oo-tay ight-bray, if you know what I mean.

> Must close, left some
> thing on the Bunsen,
>
> Goodgulf

P.S. How do you like the new stationery? Picked it up for a plainchant at Hambone's Dept!

Once again Frito's Oink-Oink Burger rose to the occasion. Fighting down its untimely reappearance, Frito gasped, 'Then we are not safe here.'

'Have no fear, lowly boggie,' said Stomper, 'for I, Arrowroot of Arrowshirt, am with thee. Goodgulf must have spoken of me in the letter. I have many names—'

'I'm sure you do, Mr Arrowshirt,' Frito broke in, panicking. 'But it's mud and then some if we don't get out of here. I think somebody in this cheap joint wants my scalp, and not for a lanolin massage, either!'

Returning to the booth, Frito found the three boggies still feeding their faces. Ignoring the masked stranger, Spam grinned greasily at Frito. 'Been a-wonderin' where ye ha' gone,' he said. 'Want a bite o' my Bow-Wow?'

Frito's Oink-Oink sought repatriation with Spam's Bow-Wow, but he fought it back and made room for Stomper's long knock-knees under the table. The boggies looked at Stomper with torpid disinterest.

'I didn't be thinkin' it was time for trickin' an' treatin' so soon,' said Spam.

Frito stayed Stomper's wrathful hand. 'Listen,' he said quickly, 'this is Stomper, a friend of Goodgulf's and a friend of ours—'

'And I have many names—' began Stomper.

'And he's got many names, but what we have to do now is—' Frito felt a great hulk looming behind him.

'Youse jerks want t' pay now?' rasped a voice hidden beneath a mass of blond hair and a paper snout.

'Uh, sure,' said Frito, 'now your tip would be, aaah . . .' Suddenly Frito felt a strong, clawed hand reach into his pocket.

'Don't bother, bub,' snarled the voice, 'I'll just *ring this up*! Haw haw haw haw haw!' With a shrill scream, Frito saw the wig fall from the head of the false piglet, revealing the burning red eyes and foul grin of a Nozdrul! As if hypnotized, Frito stared at the huge wraith's slavering leer, noticing that each tooth had been sharpened to a razor point. *Hate to have his dental bills*, he thought. Frito looked around for help as the giant fiend lifted him and rifled his pockets, searching for the Great Ring.

'C'mon, c'mon,' the monster growled, growing impatient, 'Let's have it!' Eight other huge waitresses closed in, each flashing a menacing set of well-honed choppers. Cruelly they held down the three boggies, white with fear. Of Stomper there was nothing to be seen, save a pair of spurred heels shivering under the table.

'Okay, chipmunk, give!' hissed the evil one, drawing his huge black mace. 'I said – *yeeeeowtch*!' cried the Nozdrul in pain, simultaneously letting go of Frito and jumping straight up in the air. From below the table rose a sharp, barbed blade. Stomper leaped up.

'*Oh Dragonbreth! Gilthorpial!*' he yodeled, waving his cleaver around like a madman. He lunged at the nearest wraith with his unwieldy sword. '*Banzai!*' he screamed. '*No quarter asked or given! Damn the torpedoes!*' Taking a vicious swipe, Stomper missed his mark by a good yard and tripped on his scabbard.

The nine stared at the writhing, foaming maniac with round, red eyes. The sight of Stomper filled them with awe. They stood speechless. Suddenly one of the stunned creatures began to titter, then chuckle. Another guffawed. Two more joined in, chortling loudly, and finally all nine were in the throes of hysterical, side-aching laughter. Stomper, puffing and enraged, stood up and tripped on his cape, spilling his silver bullets all over the floor. The whole dining room roared with unbelieving hilarity. Two Nozdrul collapsed to the ground, helplessly giggling. Others staggered about, great red tears rolling down their scaly cheeks, gasping for air and incapable of holding their maces. *Haw haw haw!* Stomper got to his feet, his face beet-red with anger. He lifted his sword, and the blade fell off the handle. *Haw haw haw haw haw!* The Nozdrul rolled and writhed on the ground, clutching their ribs. Stomper replaced the blade, took a mighty wind-up, and firmly embedded the point in the cement pig. *HAW HAW HAW HAW HAW HAW HAW HAW HAW HAW HAW HAW HAW HAW HAW HAW HAW HAW HAW!*

At this point, seeing that no one was paying any

attention to him, Frito picked up one of the heavy, discarded maces and calmly proceeded to beat some heads in. Moxie, Spam, and Pepsi followed his example and went among the gibbering wraiths administering random kicks to groins and breadbaskets.

Finally, the deranged Arrowroot accidentally cut the pulley ropes to the room's main chandelier, simultaneously fixing the wagons of the semiconscious wraiths directly below and plunging the room into total darkness. The boggies dashed blindly for the door, dragging Stomper after them through the temporary blackout. Bobbing and weaving past the glowing eyes, they escaped and ran breathlessly down back alleys and past the snoring guards until they crossed the drawbridge and hit open ground. As Frito ran on he felt the curious eyes of the villagers upon him and his frantic companions. Frito hoped that they would not inform the tools of Sorhed. Thankfully he saw that they took little notice of them and went about their evening chores, lighting signal fires and releasing carrier pigeons.

Once outside the town, Stomper led them into a thick sedge and bade them to be small and quiet lest they be seen by Sorhed's agents, who would soon revive and mount the hunt.

The party was still panting when sharp-eared Arrowroot adjusted the volume on his hearing aid and laid his head to the ground.

'Hark and lo!' he whispered, 'I do hear the sound of Nine Riders galloping nigh the road in full battle array.' A few minutes later a dispirited brace of steers ambled awkwardly past, but to give Stomper his due, they did carry some rather lethal-looking antlerettes.

'The foul Nozdrul have bewitched my ears,' mumbled Stomper as he apologetically replaced his batteries, 'but it is safe to proceed, for the nonce.' It was at that moment that the thundering hooves of the dreaded pig riders echoed along the road. Just in time the company dove back to cover and the vengeful searchers sped past. When the clanking of armor dwindled in the distance, five heads reappeared above the bushes, their teeth chattering like cheap maracas.

' 'Twas a near thing!' said Spam. 'Came nigh to a-spoilin' me pantaloons.'

The party chose to push on toward Wingtip before the sun rose. The moon was swathed in a shawl of heavy cloud as they traveled to the lofty peak, a long finger of granite near the southern base of the legendary Hartz Mountains, scaled by few save an occasional winded guttersnipe.

Stomper walked along in the cool night breeze without speaking, silent except for the faint jingling of his zinc-plated spurs. The twins were fascinated with the pearl-handled sword which he called Krona,

Conqueror of Dozens. Moxie sidled up to the lean masked man.

'That's a neat toadsticker you got there, Mr Arrowshirt,' said the inquisitive boggie.

'Aye,' said Stomper, quickening his pace a bit.

'Doesn't look like the regular issue. Must be a special model, huh, mister?'

'Aye,' replied the tall man, dilating his nostrils slightly with annoyance.

Quick as a packrat, Moxie snatched the weapon from its holster. 'Okay if I take a look?' Stomper, without batting an eye, let fly with a hand-tooled boot that sent the young boggie bouncing like a jai-alai ball.

'Nay,' snapped Stomper, retrieving his blade.

'I don't think he meant to be rude, Mr Arrowshirt,' said Frito, helping Moxie to his archless feet. There followed an embarrassed silence. Spam, whose knowledge of warfare was limited to childhood torturing of the family pullets, nevertheless began to sing a snatch of song he had once learned:

> *Barbisol was Twodor's king*
> *Whose foes his mighty blade did sting,*
> *Till one day it got all rusted,*
> *And Sorhed's parry left it busted.*

Then, to the boggie's surprise, a fat tear fell from Stomper's eye and his voice sobbed in the darkness:

Thus gloried Twodor came to nothing,
Out of the king was beat the stuffing.
And thus we live in fear of Fordor
Till Krona's back in working order!

The boggies gasped and looked at their companion as if for the first time. With recognition they recognized the legendary weak chin and buck teeth of Barbisol's descendant.

'Then you must be the rightful King of Twodor!' cried Frito.

The tall Ranger looked at them impassively.

'These things you say may be affirmed,' he said, 'but I do not wish to make a statement at this time, for there is another, oft-forgotten verse to this sad and doleful song:

Against the True King Sorhed's workin'
So play your cards close to your jerkin,
For fortune strums a mournful tune
For those whose campaigns peak too soon.'

Watching the newly revealed ruler trudge on in his lowly garb, the young Frito grew again thoughtful and pondered long on the many ironies of life.

As the sun's rim broke on the far horizon its first tentative rays illuminated Wingtip. After an hour of strenuous climbing they reached the top and rested gratefully on the flat granite apex, while Stomper scrounged around for some sign of Goodgulf. Nosing about a large gray rock, Stomper stopped and called to Frito. Frito looked at the stone and discerned the crude skull-and-bones etched into its surface, and with it the X-rune of the Old Wizard.

'Goodgulf has passed this way recently,' said Stomper, 'and unless I read these runes awrong, he means this place as a secure camp for us.'

Nevertheless Frito bedded down with nagging misgivings. *But*, he reminded himself, *he is a king, and all*. The bridge across the Gallowine and the way to Riv'n'dell were only a short distance; there they would be safe from the marauding Swine Riders. Sleep was now long overdue, and he sighed with pleasure as he curled up under a low shelf of stone. Soon he was falling fast asleep, lulled by the soft *snuffling* noises and the clanking of armor below.

'Awake! Awake! Fiends! Foes! *Flee!*' someone was whispering, waking Frito from his dreams. Stomper's hand jostled him roughly. Obeying him, Frito peered down the slope and made out nine black forms inching stealthily up the mountain toward their hiding place.

'It seemeth that I read the signs awrong,' muttered the perplexed guide. 'Soon they will be upon us unless we divert their wrath.'

'How?' asked Pepsi.

'Yes, how?' joined in Guess Who.

Stomper looked at the boggies. 'One of the party must stay behind to delay them while we dash for the bridge.'

'But who——?'

'Never fear,' said Stomper quickly. 'I have here in my gauntlet four lots, three long and a short for him we throw to the – er – for he who will have his name emblazoned in the pantheon of heroes.'

'Four?' said Spam. 'What about *you*?'

The Ranger straightened with great dignity. 'Surely,' he said, 'you would not wish me an unfair advantage seeing that it was I who made up the lots?'

Mollified, the boggies drew the pipe cleaners. Spam drew the short.

'Two out of three?' he whined. But his fellows had already disappeared over the lip of the peak and were racing down as fast as they could. Panting and puffing, a fat tear rolled from Frito's eye. He would miss him.

Spam looked down the opposite slope and saw the dismounted Nozdrul picking their way toward him quickly. Crouching behind a rock, he screamed courageously at them. 'If I were ye,' he called, 'I'd not come any closer! Ye'll be sorry if ye do!' Unheeding, the fierce knights drew even nearer. 'You're really a-goin' t' get it!' yelled Spam rather unconvincingly. Still the Riders grew nearer, and Spam lost his nerve. Taking out his white handkerchief, he waved it about and pointed toward his retreating friends. 'Don't be wastin' your time with me,' he cried. 'The one with the Ring is high-tailin' it thataway!'

Hearing this from below, Frito winced and pumped his fat legs harder. Stomper's long and gimpy shanks had already brought him across the bridge and onto the safety of the other bank, the neutral territory of the elves. Frito looked behind him. He wouldn't make it in time!

Stomper watched the deadly race from the cover of some briars on the bank of the stream.

'Hie thee faster,' he called helpfully, 'for the evil ones are right behind thee!' Then he hid his eyes.

The rumble of pigs' feet grew louder and louder in Frito's ears, and he could hear the lethal *swish* of their horrible Nozdrulville Sluggers. He made a last, desperate burst of speed, but tripped and skidded to a stop only a few feet from the border. Cackling with evil amusement, the nine surrounded Frito, their squint-eyed steeds grunting for Frito's blood.

'Blood! Blood!' they grunted.

Frito looked up, terrified, and saw them as they slowly closed the ring, only an arm's length from death. The leader of the pack, a tall beefy wraith with chrome-plated greaves, laughed savagely and raised his mace.

'Hee hee hee, filthy rodent! Now is the time for fun!'

Frito cowered. 'Maybe it is, and maybe it isn't,' he said, pulling his favorite bluff.

'Arrrgh!' screamed an impatient Nozdrul, who, by coincidence, happened to be named Argh. 'C'mon, let's cream this little creep! The boss said take his Ring and croak him then 'n' there!'

Frito's mind raced. He decided to play his last card.

'Well dat's sho' nuff fine wit me, 'cause ah sho' doan wan' you t' do the bad thing to' po' li'l me!' said Frito, bugging out his eyes and rolling them like ball bearings.

'Har har har!' chortled another Rider. 'What can *you* think of that's worse than what we're *gonna* do with ya?' The fiends drew closer to hear the terrible fear Frito harbored in his breast.

The boggie whistled and pretended to play the banjo. He then sang a verse of 'Ole Man Ribber' as he ambled back and forth on shuffling feet, scratched his woolly head, and danced a cakewalk while picking watermelon seeds from his ears, all with natural rhythm.

'Sure can dance,' muttered one of the Riders.

'Sure gonna *die*!' screamed another, thirsting for Frito's throat.

'*Sho*' I gwine t' die,' drawled Frito. 'Yo' kin do mos' anythin' t' po' li'l me, Br'er Nozdrul, so long as yo' *please doan throw me in dat briar patch ober dere*!'

At this all the sadistic Riders sniggered.

'If that's what you're scared of most,' bellowed a voice full of malice, 'then *that's what we'll do to you*, ya little jerk!'

Frito felt himself lifted by a horny black hand and flung far over the Gallowine and into the scrubby bush on the other side. Gleefully, he stood up and fished out the Ring, making sure it still hung on his chain.

But the crafty Riders were not long deceived by Frito's ruse. They spurred their drooling swine to the bridge, intent on recapturing the boggie and his precious Ring. But, as Frito saw with surprise, the Black Nine were halted at the foot of the crossing by a figure robed in shining raiment.

'Toll, please,' commanded the figure of the startled Riders. The pursuers were again dumbfounded when they were directed to a hastily lettered sign tacked to a support:

Elfboro Municipal Toll Bridge
Single Wayfarers . . . . . . 1 farthing
Double-axled Haywains . . . . . 2 farthings
Black Riders . . . . 45 gold pieces

'Let us cross!' snapped an angry Nozdrul.

'Certainly,' replied the attendant pleasantly. 'Now let's see, there's one, two . . . ah, *nine* of you at forty-five apiece, that makes . . . uuuuhh, four hundred and five beans, exactly, please. In cash.'

Hurriedly, the Nozdrul searched their saddlebags as their leader cursed angrily and shook his slugger with frustration.

'Listen,' he stormed, 'what kind of dough do you think we make, anyhow? Ain't there some sorta discount for civil servants?'

'I'm sorry—' smiled the attendant.

'How 'bout a Wayfarer's Letter of Credit? They're as good as bullion anywhere.'

'Sorry, this is a bridge, not a countinghouse,' replied the figure impassively.

'My personal check? It's backed up by the treasure rooms of Fordor.'

'No money, no crossee, friend.'

The Nozdruls quivered with rage, but turned their mounts around, preparing to ride off. Before they left, however, the leader shook a gnarled fist.

'This ain't the end of this, punk! You'll hear from us again!'

Saying this, the nine spurred their farting porkers and sped away in a great cloud of dust and dung.

Observing this near impossible escape from certain death, Frito wondered how much longer the authors were going to get away with such tripe. He wasn't the only one.

Stomper and the other boggies ran to Frito, extending their congratulations on his escape. They then drew close to the mysterious figure, who approached and, espying Stomper among them, raised his hands in greeting and sang:

> *O NASA O UCLA! O Etaion Shrdlu!*
> *O Escrow Beryllium! Pandit J. Nehru!*

Stomper raised his hands and answered, '*Shantih Billerica!*' They met and embraced, exchanging words of friendship and giving the secret handshake.

The boggies studied the stranger with interest. He introduced himself as Garfinkel of the elves. When he had shed himself of his robes, the boggies regarded with curiosity his ring-encrusted hands, his open-collared Ban-Lon tunic, and his silver beach clogs.

'Thought you would have been here days ago,' said the balding elf. 'Any trouble along the way?'

'I could write a book,' said Frito prophetically.

'Well,' said Garfinkel, 'we'd better make tracks before those B-movie heavies return. They may be stupid, but they sure can be persistent.'

'So new?' muttered Frito, who found himself muttering more and more lately.

The elf looked doubtfully at the boggies. 'You guys

know how to ride?' Without waiting for an answer he whistled loudly through his gold teeth. A clump of high sedge rustled and several overweight merino sheep bounded into view, bleating irritably.

'Mount up,' said Garfinkel.

Frito, more or less athwart an unpromising ungulant, rode last in the procession away from the Gallowine toward Riv'n'dell. He slipped his hand into his pocket, found the Ring, and took it out in the fading light. Already it was beginning to work its slow change upon him, the transformation of which Dildo had warned. He was constipated.

IV

FINDERS KEEPERS, FINDERS WEEPERS

After three days of hard riding that had put many a furlong between them and the Black Riders, the weary boggies came at last to the low kneehills which surrounded the valley of Riv'n'dell with a natural wall that protected it from occasional marauders too stupid or small to scale the sheer knolls and mounds. But their sure-footed mounts easily overcame these obstacles with short, heart-stopping hops, and in no time Frito and his companions had reached the summit of the last hillock and looked down on the orange roofs and cupolas of the elfish ranchellas. Urging on their panting ruminants, they galloped down the winding corduroy road that led to the dwellings of Orlon.

It was late in the gray fall afternoon when the procession of sheepback riders rode into Riv'n'dell, led by Garfinkel astride his magnificent woolly stallion, Anthrax. An ill wind was blowing, and granite hailstones were falling from brooding clouds. As the party drew rein in front of the main lodge, a tall elf robed in finest percale and wearing bucks of blinding whiteness stepped onto the porch and greeted them.

'Welcome to the Last Homely House East of the Sea and Gift Shoppe,' he said. 'Barca-Loungers in every room.'

Garfinkel and the tall elf thumbed their noses in the ancient salute of their race and exchanged greetings in elvish. 'A syanon esso decca hi hawaya,' said Garfinkel, lightly springing from his animal.

'O movado silvathin nytol niceta-seeya,' replied the tall elf; then turning to Stomper he said: 'I am Orlon.'

'Arrowroot son of Arrowshirt, at your service,' said Stomper, dismounting clumsily.

'And these?' said Orlon, pointing to the four boggies asleep on their dormant mounts.

'Frito and his companions, boggies from the Sty,' said Stomper. At the mention of his name, Frito gurgled loudly and fell off his sheep, and the Ring dropped out of his clothes, and rolled to Orlon's feet. One of the sheep trotted up, licked it, and turned into a fire hydrant.

'Oog,' mumbled Orlon, and staggered inside. Garfinkel followed him into the little building, and a stream of low elvish followed. Arrowroot stood listening for a moment, then went around to Spam, Moxie, and Pepsi and woke them up with a series of finger jabs and pivot-kicks. Frito retrieved the Ring and slipped it into his pocket. 'So this is Riv'n'dell,' he said, rubbing his eyes with wonder as he looked at the strange elvish houses of prestressed gingerbread and ferrocandy.

'Look, Master Frito,' said Spam, pointing up the road. 'Elfs, lots of 'em. Ooooo, I must be dreaming. I wish the old Fatlip could see me now.'

'I wish I were dead,' whined Pepsi.

'So do I,' said Moxie.

'May the good fairy what sits in the sky grant yer ev'ry wish,' said Spam.

'Where is Goodgulf, I wonder,' wondered Frito.

Garfinkel strode back out onto the porch and produced a small tin whistle on which he blew a single, ear-splitting, flat note, whereupon the sheep wandered aimlessly away.

'Magical,' sighed Spam.

'Follow me,' said Garfinkel, and he led Stomper and the boggies along a narrow muddy path which wound through clumps of flowering rhodogravure bushes and towering shoe trees. As he walked along, Frito smelled an evanescent fragrance of new-mown hay mingled with bleach and mustard, and from afar off he heard the delicate, heart-breaking twangs of a mouth-harp and a few shreds of an elvish song:

> *Row, row, row your elebethiel saliva githiel*
> *Mann a fubar lothario syzygy snafu*
> *O bring back my sucaryl Penna Ariz Fla mass.*

At the end of the path stood a small bungalow made of polished Joyvah Halvah and surrounded by a bed of glass flowers. Garfinkel turned the door's all-day sucker and motioned the party inside. They found themselves in a large room which entirely filled the little house. There were a great many beds arranged around the walls, all of which looked as though they had been recently slept in by perverted kangaroos, and in the corners were a few odd chairs and tables which showed quite clearly the hand, and foot, of the elvish craftsmen. In the center of the room was a large table littered with the remnants of a violent game of three-pack canasta and several bowls of artificial fruit which couldn't have been mistaken for the real thing at fifty meters. These Moxie and Pepsi immediately ate.

'Make yourself at home,' said Garfinkel, as he left. 'Check-out time is three o'clock.'

Stomper slumped heavily into a chair, which folded up under him with a muffled crack.

Garfinkel was not gone more than five minutes when there came a knock at the door, and Spam went, rather irritably, to answer it. 'It had better be food,' he mumbled, 'cause I'm gonna eat it.'

He opened the door with a jerk, revealing a mysterious stranger in a long gray cape and hood, wearing thick, black eyeglasses with a false rubber nose quite unconvincingly dangling from the bridge. The dark figure had a cardboard mustache, a dustmop wig, and a huge, handpainted tie with a picture of an elf-maiden. In his left hand was a mashie-niblick, and on his feet he wore shower clogs. He was puffing a fat cigar.

Spam reeled back in astonishment, and Stomper, Moxie, Pepsi, and Frito cried in unison, 'Goodgulf!'

The old man shuffled in, discarding his disguises to reveal the familiar faith healer and bunco artist. 'Lo, it is I,' admitted the Wizard, dispiritedly plucking a few strings out of his hair. With that he went around and shook all their hands very hard, shocking them with the little electric buzzer he invariably carried concealed in his palm.

'Well, well,' said Goodgulf, 'here we all are again.'

'I'd sooner be in a dragon's colon,' said Frito.

'I trust you still have *it*,' said Goodgulf, eyeing Frito.

'Do you mean the Ring?'

'Silence,' commanded Goodgulf in a loud voice. 'Speak not of the Great Ring here or anywhere. If Sorhed's spies discovered that you, Frito Bugger, hailing from the Sty, had the One Ring, all would be lost. And his spies are everywhere. The Nine Black Riders are abroad again, and there are those who claim to have seen the Seven Santinis, the Six Danger Signs, and the entire Trapp family, including the dog. Even the walls have ears,' he said, pointing to two huge lobes which were protruding from behind the mantelpiece.

'Is there no hope?' gasped Frito. 'Is nowhere safe?'

'Who can know?' said Goodgulf, and a shadow seemed to pass over his face. 'I would say more,' he said, 'but a shadow seems to have passed over my face,' and with that he fell strangely silent.

Frito began to weep, and Stomper leaned forward, and putting his hand reassuringly on Frito's shoulder, said, 'Fear not, dear boggie, I will be with you all the way, no matter what may befall.'

'Same here,' said Spam, and fell asleep.

'Us too,' said Moxie and Pepsi, yawning.

Frito remained inconsolable.

When the boggies awoke from their nap, Goodgulf and Stomper were gone, and the moon was shining fuzzily through the taffy windows. They had finished eating the curtains and were starting in on the lampshades when Garfinkel returned, clad in finest cheesecloth, and led them down to the lodge building they had seen when they first arrived. It was large and brightly lit, and the night was filled with the brouhaha from within. As they approached, there came a silence, and then the plaintive, blackboard-scraping shriek of a nose-flute pierced the air.

'They're giving a pig a rough time of it in there,' said Spam, blocking his ears.

'Hush,' said Frito, and a voice rose in song, filling the boggies with a vague sense of nausea.

> *A Unicef clearasil*
> *Gibberish 'n' drivel*
> *O Mennen mylar muriel*
> *With a hey derry tum gardol*
> *O Yuban necco glamorene?*
> *Enden nytol, vaseline!*
> *Sing hey nonny nembutal.*

With a last twittering wail, the music died away, and half a dozen stunned birds plopped heavily to the ground in front of Frito.

'What was that?' asked Frito.

'It is an ancient lament in the tongue of the Auld Elves,' sighed Garfinkel. 'It tells of Unicef and his long and bitter search for a clean rest room. "Are there no facilities here?" he cries. "Is there no washroom?" No one seems to know.'

So said Garfinkel and led the boggies into the House of Orlon. They found themselves in a long, high-raftered hall down the center of which ran an endless table. At one end was a huge oak mantelpiece and from high above hung brass chandeliers in which fine ear-wax candles spluttered brightly. Along the table sat the usual flotsam and jetsam of Lower Middle Earth; elves, fairies, Martians, several frogs, dwarves, gnomes, a few token men, a handful of bugbears, several trolls wearing sunglasses, a couple of goblins the Christian Scientists had worked over, and a dragon who had gotten fed up.

At the head of the table sat Orlon and the Lady Lycra robed in cloth of dazzling whiteness and brightness. Dead they looked, and yet it was not so, for Frito could see their eyes shining like wet mushrooms. Bleached was their hair so that it shone like goldenrod, and their faces were as bright and fair as the surface of the moon. All about them zircons, garnets, and lodestones flashed like stars. On their heads were silken lampshades and on their brows were written many things, both fair and foul, such as 'Unleash Chiang Kai-shek' and 'I love my wife but oh you kid.' Asleep they were.

To the left of Orlon sat Goodgulf in a red fez, revealed as a 32nd Degree Mason and Honorary Shriner, and to his right sat Stomper, clad in the white Gene Autry suit of a Ranger. Frito was shown to a seat about halfway down the table between an unusually deformed dwarf and an elf who smelled like a birdnest, and Moxie and Pepsi were sent to a small table in a corner with the Easter Bunny and a couple of tooth fairies.

As with most mythical creatures who live in en-chanted forests with no visible means of support, the elves ate rather frugally, and Frito was a little disappointed to find heaped on his plate a small mound of ground nuts, bark, and dirt. Nevertheless, like all boggies, he was capable of eating anything he could Indian-wrestle down his throat and rather preferred dishes that didn't struggle too much, since even a half-cooked mouse can usually beat a boggie two falls out of three. No sooner had he finished eating than the dwarf sitting to his right turned to him and proffered an extremely scaly hand in greeting. *It's at the end of his arm*, thought Frito, nervously shaking it, *it's got to be a hand*.

'Gimlet, son of Groin, your obedient servant,' said the dwarf, bowing to reveal a hunchback. 'May you always buy cheap and sell dear.'

'Frito, son of Dildo, yours,' said Frito in some confusion, racking his brains for the correct reply. 'May your hemorrhoids shrink without surgery.'

The dwarf looked puzzled but not displeased. 'Then you are the boggie of whom Goodgulf spoke, the Ringer?'

Frito nodded.

'Do you have *it* with you?'

'Would you like to see it?' asked Frito politely.

'Oh, no thanks,' said Gimlet, 'I had an uncle who had a magic tieclip and one time he sneezed and his nose fell off.'

Frito nervously touched a nostril.

'Excuse the interruption,' said the elf on his left, spitting accurately into the dwarf's left eye, 'but I couldn't help overhearing your conversation with Gabby Hayes. Are you in fact the boggie with the bijou?'

'I am,' said Frito and sneezed violently.

'Allow me,' said the elf, proffering Gimlet's beard to Frito, who was by now sneezing uncontrollably. 'I am Legolam, of the Elves of Northern Weldwood.'

'Elf-dog,' hissed Gimlet, retrieving his beard.

'Pig of a dwarf,' suggested Legolam.

'Toymaker.'

'Gold digger.'

'Flit.'

'Wart.'

'Would you like to hear a joke or a song or something?' said Frito, becoming alarmed. 'It seems there was this wandering dragon, and he comes to this farmhouse and the farmer—'

'A song,' agreed Gimlet and Legolam.

'Of course,' said Frito, and desperately trying to recall some of Dildo's doggerel, he began to sing in a squeaky voice:

A King of Elves there was of old,
Saranrap by name,
Who slew the Narcs at Mellowmarsh
And Sorhed's host did tame.

And with him marched the stubby dwarves
    Drafted from their mines,
But when the fearsome Battle raged
    They hid behind the lines.

    Sing: Clearasil, metrecal, lavoris in chorus
    They hid behind the lines!

Angered was the mighty King
    About to raise the dickens,
'Just let me get my hands,' quoth he,
    'On those half-pint chickens!'

Fearful were the chicken-Dwarves,
    But mickle crafty too,
King Yellowbac, their skins to save,
    The elves did try to woo.

    Sing: Twist-a-cap, reynoldswrap, gardol and duz
    The elves he tried to woo!

'If you doubt our loyalty,'
    Yello told the King,
'Take this gift, a dwarfish sword
    That packs a mighty sting.

'Clearasil, it's called by name,'
    The clever Dwarf spoke on,
'Take this bribe, and let us let
    Bygones be bygone.'

Sing: Cadillac, pickapack, Edsel and coke
Bygones be bygone.

'I accept this wondrous gift,
*   And think you Dwarves are tops,'*
Said he, as he took the sword
*   And smote him in the chops.*

And since that day it's said by all
*   In ballad, lay and poem,*
'Only trust an elf or dwarf
*   As far as you can throw 'em!'*

Sing: Oxydol, geritol, wheaties and Trix.
As far as you can throw 'em!

Just as Frito finished, Orlon suddenly roused himself and signaled for silence. 'Bingo in the Elf Lounge,' he said, and the feast ended.

Frito was making his way to the table where Moxie and Pepsi were sitting when a bony hand reached out of a potted palm and grasped his shoulder. 'Come with me,' said Goodgulf, brushing a frond aside, and led the surprised boggie down the hall and into a small room almost entirely filled by a huge glass-topped table. Orlon and Stomper had already taken seats and as he and Goodgulf sat down Frito was amazed to see his dinner companions, Gimlet and Legolam, enter and seat themselves on opposite sides of the table. They were quickly followed by a heavyset man in iridescent pegged trousers and sharply pointed shoes. Last of all came a small figure in a loud shirt smoking a foul elvish cigar and carrying a Scrabble board.

'Dildo!' cried Frito.

'Ah, Frito my lad,' said Dildo, slapping Frito heavily on the back, 'so you made it after all. Well, well, well.' Orlon held out a moist palm, and Dildo rummaged in his pockets and pulled out a wad of crumpled bills.

'Two, wasn't it?' he said.

'Ten,' said Orlon.

'So it was, so it was,' said Dildo, and dropped the bills in the elf's hand.

'It's been so long since the party,' said Frito. 'What have you been doing?'

'Not much,' said the old boggie. 'A little Scrabble, a little pederasty. I'm retired, you see.'

'But what is this all about? Who are the Black Riders, and what do they want with me? And what has the Ring got to do with it?'

'Much and little, more or less, dear boggie,' explained Orlon. 'But all in good time. This Great Caucus has been called to answer such questions and others, but for now I will say only that there are a-many things amiss afoot, alas.'

'No lie,' said Goodgulf gravely. 'The Nameless No-No is spreading again, and the time has come to act. Frito, the Ring.'

Frito nodded and drew from his pocket the paper-clip chain, link by link. With a short toss, he threw the fatal trinket onto the table, where it landed with a tinny jing.

Orlon gasped. 'The Magic Dingus,' he cried.

'What proof is there that this is the Ring?' asked the man with the pointed shoes.

'There are many signs which can be read by the wise, Bromosel,' announced the Wizard. 'The compass, the whistle, the magic decoder – they're all here. And there is the inscription:

> *Grundig blaupunkt luger frug*
> *Watusi snarf wazoo!*
> *Nixon dirksen nasahist*
> *Rebozo boogaloo.*

Goodgulf's voice had become harsh and distant. An ominous black cloud filled the room. Frito gagged on the thick oily smoke.

'Was that necessary?' asked Legolam, kicking the Wizard's still-belching smoke grenade out the door.

'Rings go better with hocus-pocus,' replied Goodgulf imperiously.

'But what does that mean?' asked Bromosel, rather

annoyed that he was being referred to in the dialogue as 'the man with the pointed shoes.'

'There are many interpretations,' explained Goodgulf. 'My guess is that it's either "The quick brown fox jumped over the lazy dog" or "Don't tread on me." '

No one spoke, and the room fell strangely silent.

Finally Bromosel rose and addressed the Caucus. 'Much is now clear,' he said. 'I had a dream one night in Minas Troney in which seven cows ate seven bushels of wheat, and when they were finished they climbed a red tower and threw up three times, chanting, "Say it now and say it loud, I'm a cow and I'm proud." And then a figure robed in white and bearing a pair of scales came forward and read from a little slip of paper:

> *Five-eleven's your height, one-ninety your weight*
> *You cash in your chips around page eighty-eight.*

'This is grave,' said Orlon.

'Well,' said Stomper, 'I guess it's time we all laid our cards on the table,' and with that he noisily emptied the contents of a faded duffel into a heap in front of him. When he was finished, there was a large pile of odd objects, including a broken sword, a golden arm, a snowflake paperweight, the Holy Grail, the Golden Fleece, the Robe, a piece of the True Cross, and a glass slipper.

'Arrowroot, son of Arrowshirt, heir of Barbisol and King of Minas Troney, at your service,' he said, rather loudly.

Bromosel looked up to the top of the page and winced. 'At least another chapter to go,' he groaned.

'Then the Ring is yours,' cried Frito, and eagerly tossed it into Arrowroot's hat.

'Well, not exactly,' said Arrowroot, dangling the band at the end of its long chain. 'Since it's got magic powers, it belongs to someone more in the mumbo-jumbo, presto-changeo line. To wit, a wizard, for example,' and he neatly slipped the Ring over the end of Goodgulf's wand.

'Ah, yes, verily, in truth,' said Goodgulf quickly. 'That is to say, yes and no. Or perhaps just plain no. As any fool can see, it's a clear case of habeas corpus or tibia fibia, since although this particular gizmo was the work of a wizard – Sorhed, to be exact – this sort of thing was invented by elves, and he was only working under a license, you might say.'

Orlon held the Ring in his hand as if it were an annoyed tarantula. 'Nay,' he said, gravely, 'I cannot claim this great prize, for it is said, "Finders keepers, losers weepers," ' and brushing away an invisible tear, he looped the chain around Dildo's neck.

'And "Let dogs lie if they are sleepers," ' said Dildo, and slipped it into Frito's pocket.

'Then it is settled,' intoned Orlon. 'Frito Bugger shall keep the Ring.'

'Bugger?' said Legolam. 'Bugger? That's curious. There was a nasty little clown named Goddam sniffing around Weldwood on hands and knees looking for a Mr Bugger. It was a little queer.'

'Odd,' said Gimlet. 'A pack of black giants riding huge pigs came through the mountains last month hunting for a boggie named Bugger. Never gave it a second thought.'

'This, too, is grave,' declared Orlon. 'It is only a matter of time before they come here,' he said, pulling a shawl over his head and making a gesture of throwing something of a conciliatory nature to a shark, 'and as neutrals, we would have no choice . . .'

Frito shuddered.

'The Ring and its bearer must go hence,' agreed Goodgulf, 'but where? Who shall guard it?'

'The elves,' said Gimlet.

'The dwarves,' said Legolam.

'The wizards,' said Arrowroot.

'The Men of Twodor,' said Goodgulf.

'That leaves only Fordor,' said Orlon. 'But even a retarded troll would not go there.'

'Even a dwarf,' admitted Legolam.

Frito suddenly felt that all eyes were on him.

'Couldn't we just drop it down a storm drain, or pawn it and swallow the ticket?' he said.

'Alas,' said Goodgulf solemnly, 'it is not that easy.'

'But why?'

'Alas,' explained Goodgulf.

'Alackaday,' Orlon agreed.

'But fear not, dear boggie,' continued Orlon, 'you shall not go alone.'

'Good old Gimlet will go with you,' said Legolam.

'And fearless Legolam,' said Gimlet.

'And noble King Arrowroot,' said Bromosel.

'And faithful Bromosel,' said Arrowroot.

'And Moxie, Pepsi, and Spam,' said Dildo.

'And Goodgulf Grayteeth,' added Orlon.

'Indeed,' said Goodgulf, glaring at Orlon, and if looks could maim, the old elf would have left in a basket.

'So be it. You shall leave when the omens are right,' said Orlon, consulting a pocket horoscope, 'and unless I'm very much mistaken, they will be unmatched in half an hour.'

Frito groaned. 'I wish I had never been born,' he said.

'Do not say that, dear Frito,' cried Orlon. 'It was a happy minute for us all when you were born.'

*

'Well, I guess it's goodbye,' said Dildo, taking Frito aside as they left the caucus room. 'Or should I say "until we meet again"? No, I think goodbye sums it up quite nicely.'

'Goodbye, Dildo,' Frito said, stifling a sob. 'I wish you were coming with us.'

'Ah, yes. But I'm too old for that sort of thing now,' said the old boggie, feigning a state of total paraplegia. 'Anyway, I have a few small gifts for you,' and he produced a lumpy parcel, which Frito opened somewhat unenthusiastically in view of Dildo's previous going-away present. But the package contained only a short, Revereware sword, a bulletproof vest full of moth holes, and several well-thumbed novellas with titles like *Elf Lust* and *Goblin Girl*.

'Farewell, Frito,' said Dildo, managing a very convincing epileptic fit. 'It's in your hands now, gasp, rattle, o lie me under the greenwood tree, ooooo. Ooog.'

'Farewell, Dildo,' said Frito, and with a last wave went out to join the company. As soon as he had disappeared, Dildo sprang lightly to his feet, and skipped into the hall humming a little song:

> *I sit on the floor and pick my nose*
> *and think of dirty things*
> *Of deviant dwarfs who suck their toes*
> *and elves who drub their dings.*

I sit on the floor and pick my nose
 and dream exotic dreams
Of dragons who dress in rubber clothes
 and trolls who do it in teams.

I sit on the floor and pick my nose
 and wish for a thrill or two
For a goblin who goes in for a few no-nos
 Or an orc with a thing about glue.

And all of the while I sit and pick
 I think of such jolly things
Of whips and screws and leather slacks
 Of frottages and stings.

'I grieve to see you leave so soon,' said Orlon quickly, as the company stood assembled around their pack sheep some twenty minutes later. 'But the Shadow is growing and your journey is long. It is best to begin at once, in the night. The Enemy has eyes everywhere.' As he spoke, a large, hair-covered eyeball rolled ominously from its perch in a tree and fell to the ground with a heavy squelch.

Arrowroot drew Krona, the Sword that was broken, now hastily reglued, and waved it over his head. 'Onward,' he cried, 'on to Fordor!'

'Farewell, farewell,' said Orlon impatiently.

'Excelsior,' cried Bromosel, blowing a fierce blast on his duck whistle.

'Sayonara,' said Orlon. 'Aloha. Avaunt. Arroint.'

'Kodak khaki no-doz,' Gimlet cried.

'A dristan nasograph,' shouted Legolam.

'Habeas corpus,' said Goodgulf, waving his wand.

'I have to go poo-poo,' said Pepsi.

'So do I,' said Moxie.

'I'd like ta poo-poo the both o' ye,' said Spam, reaching for a rock.

'Let's go,' said Frito, and the party set off down the road from Riv'n'dell at a walk. In a few short hours they had put several hundred feet between them and the lodge where Orlon still stood, wreathed in smiles. As the party passed over the first slight rise, Frito turned around and looked back over Riv'n'dell. Somewhere in the black distance lay the Sty, and he felt a great longing to return, as a dog might on recalling a long-forgotten spew.

As he watched, the moon rose, there was a meteor shower and a display of the aurora borealis, a cock crowed thrice, it thundered, a flock of geese flew by in the shape of a swastika, and a giant hand wrote *Mene, mene, what's it to you?* across the sky in giant silver letters. Suddenly Frito had the overpowering feeling that he had come to a turning point, that an old chapter in his life was ending and a new one beginning. 'Mush, you brute,' he said, kicking the pack animal in the kidneys, and as the great quadruped staggered forward, tailfirst into the black East, there came from deep in the surrounding forest the sound of some great bird being briefly, but noisily, ill.

V

SOME MONSTERS

For many days the company traveled south, trusting to the eyes of the Ranger, Arrowroot, the keen ears of the boggies, and the wisdom of Goodgulf to lead them. A fortnight after their departure they arrived at a great crossroads and halted to determine the best way to cross the towering Mealey Mountains.

Arrowroot squinted into the distance. 'Behold the grim Mount Badass,' he said, pointing to a large milestone a hundred yards down the road.

'Then we must head east,' said Goodgulf, gesturing with his wand to where the sun was setting redly in a mass of sea-clouds.

A duck flew over quacking loudly. 'Wolves,' cried Pepsi, straining to hear the fading sound.

'It is best that we make camp here tonight,' said Arrowroot, dropping his pack heavily to the ground, where it crushed a hooded cobra. 'Tomorrow we must seek the high pass across the mountains.'

A few minutes later the company sat in the middle of the crossroads around a bright fire over which one of Goodgulf's stage rabbits was merrily roasting. 'A proper fire at last, and no mistake,' said Spam, tossing a rattlesnake on the cheery blaze. 'I reckon none o' Master Pepsi's wolves is likeable to bother us tonight.'

Pepsi snorted. 'A wolf would have to be pretty hard up to eat a road apple like you,' he said, flicking a rock at Spam, which missed him by feet and stunned a puma. Circling far overhead, unseen by the company, the leader of a band of black spy-crows peered through a pair of binoculars, cursed in the harsh tongue of his kind, and swore off grapes for the rest of his life.

'Where are we, and where are we going?' asked Frito.

'We are at a great crossroads,' answered the Wizard, and producing a battered sextant from within his robes, he took sightings on the moon, Arrowroot's cowboy hat, and Gimlet's upper lip. 'Soon we will cross a mountain or a river and pass into another land,' he said.

Arrowroot strode over to Frito. 'Do not fear,' he said, sitting on a wolf, 'we will guide you safely through.'

The next day dawned clear and bright, as is so often the case when it does not rain, and the spirits of the company were considerably raised. After a frugal breakfast of milk and honey, they set out in single file behind Arrowroot and Goodgulf, with Spam bringing up the rear behind the pack sheep, toward whom he expressed a boggie's usual fondness for fuzzy animals.

'Oh, for some mint sauce,' he lamented.

The party traveled many leagues* along the broad, well-paved highway that led east to the odorous feet of the Mealey Mountains, and later in the afternoon they came to the first of the low kneehills. There the road quickly disappeared in a mass of rubble and the ruins of an ancient toll booth. Beyond, a short, steep valley as black as coal stretched ominously to the rocky slope of the mountains. Arrowroot signaled for a halt, and the company gathered to look at the forbidding landscape.

'This is an evil place, I fear,' said Arrowroot, slipping on the sticky black paint which covered every inch of the land.

'It is the Black Valley,' said Goodgulf solemnly.

'Are we in Fordor already?' asked Frito hopefully.

'Do not mention that black land in this black land,' said the Wizard darkly. 'No, it is not Fordor, but it seems that it has been touched by the Enemy of all Right-Thinking Folk.'

As they stood looking over the dreary vale, there came the howl of wolves, the roar of bears, and the cry of vultures.

'It's quiet,' said Gimlet.

---

* A league is approximately 3 furlongs or only a knot short of a hectare.

'Too quiet,' said Legolam.

'We cannot stay here,' said Arrowroot.

'No,' agreed Bromosel, looking across the gray surface of the page to the thick half of the book still in the reader's right hand. 'We have a long way to go.'

After trudging down the steep, rock-strewn slope for more than an hour, the party arrived, weary and blackened, at a long ledge that led between a sharp cliff and a pond whose surface was entirely covered with a thick oil slick. As they watched, a great, heavy-winged water bird landed in the foul water with a soft plop and dissolved.

'Let us press on,' said Goodgulf. 'The pass cannot be far.'

With that he led the way around a stony ridge which jutted into the pond in front of them and obscured the rest of the mountain slope from view. The ledge grew narrower as it wound around the outcropping, and the company had to inch their way along. As they passed the bend, they saw in front of them the face of the mountain rising unbroken for hundreds of feet above them. Cut into the rocky wall was the entrance to some underground cavern, cunningly hidden by an enormous wooden door with huge wrought-iron hinges and a giant knob. The door was covered with a strange oath gracefully written in the Palmer runes of the dwarves, and so marvelously had it been constructed, that from a hundred feet away the tiny crack between wood and stone was completely invisible.

Arrowroot gasped. 'The Black Pit,' he cried.

'Yes,' said Gimlet, 'the fabled Nikon-zoom of my ancestor, Fergus Fewmet.'

'Dread Andrea Doria, curse of the living nipple,' said Legolam.

'But where is the pass?' asked Frito.

'The face of the land has changed since I was last abroad in this region,' said Goodgulf quickly, 'and we have been led, perhaps by Fate, a bit astray.'

ERGUS spake these words, and he said, This shall be my creed, whereby shall I live my life as it were a shining example of Virtue and Excellence, well worthy to be enshrined in Heaven as a model for all who are wise to follow. My creed shall into three parts, like Gaul, be divided. Firstly, I shall constrain myself to Mind My Own Business. Secondly, I shall endeavour at all times and in all places to Keep My Nose Clean by the most expedient possible means. Thirdly, and finally, I shall always exercise the utmost care to Keep My Hands to Myself.

—PW)

'It would be wiser to seek again the pass, I judge,' said Arrowroot. 'It cannot be far.'

'Three hundred kilometers give or take a shilling,' said Goodgulf, a little sheepishly, and as he spoke, the narrow ledge which led back to the valley slid into the dark pond with a low grunt.

'That settles that,' said Bromosel testily. 'Yoo-hoo,' he cried, 'come and eat us,' and from far away a deep voice echoed, 'Me beastie, me do that thing.'

'It is a grim fate indeed that would lead us here,' said Arrowroot, 'or a gonzo Wizard.'

Goodgulf remained unperturbed. 'We must find the spell that opens this door, and soon. Already it grows dark.' With that he lifted his wand and cried:

> *Yuma palo alto napa erin go brae*
> *Tegrin correga cremora olé.*

The door remained in place, and Frito glanced nervously at the mass of oily bubbles that had begun to rise in the pond.

'If only I'd listened to my Uncle Poo-poo and gone into dentistry,' whined Pepsi.

'If I'd stayed at home, I'd be big in encyclopedias by now,' sniffled Moxie.

'And if I had ten pounds o' ciment and a couple o' sacks, you'd a' both gone for a stroll on that pond an hour ago,' said Spam.

Goodgulf sat dejectedly before the obstinate portal, mumbling spells.

'Pismo,' he intoned, striking the door with his wand. 'Bitumen. Lazlo. Clayton-Bulwer.' Save for a hollow thud, the door made no sign of opening.

'It looks grim,' said Arrowroot.

Suddenly the Wizard sprang to his feet. 'The knob,' he cried, and leading the pack sheep over to the base of the gate, stood on its back on tiptoe and turned the great knob with both hands. It turned easily, and with a loud squeaking the door swung open a crack.

Goodgulf quickly scrambled down, and Arrowroot and Bromosel tugged the door open a few more inches. At that moment, a great gurgling and belching arose from the center of the pond, and a large corduroy monster slowly lifted itself above the surface with a loud hiccup.

The company stood rooted to the ground in terror. The creature was about fifty feet tall, with wide lapels, long dangling participles, and a pronounced gazetteer.

'Aiyee!' shouted Legolam. 'A Thesaurus!'

'Maim!' roared the monster. 'Mutilate, mangle, crush. See HARM.'

'Quick,' cried Goodgulf. 'Into the cavern,' and the company hurriedly slipped one by one through the narrow crack. Last of all came Spam, who tried to squeeze the protesting sheep through the opening.

After two frenzied but unsuccessful attempts, he picked up the annoyed herbivore and threw him bodily into the beast's gaping mouth.

'Eatable,' said the giant creature between munches, 'edible, esculent, comestible. See FOOD.'

'I hope ye choke on it,' said Spam bitterly, as a clear image of a winged loin of lamb fluttered across his mind. He wiggled through the doorway and joined the rest of the company in the cavern. With a loud belch that shook the ground and filled the air with an aroma such as one meets concurrent with the rediscovery of a cheese that has long since gone to its reward, the beast slammed shut the door. The heavy boom reverberated into the depths of the mountain, and the little party found themselves in total darkness.

Goodgulf hastily withdrew a tinder box from his robes, and frantically striking sparks off the walls and floor, he managed to light the end of his wand, producing a flickering glow about half as bright as a dead firefly.

'Such magic,' said Bromosel.

The wizard peered ahead into the darkness, and perceiving that there was only one possible route, up a flight of stairs, he led the way into the deep gloom.

They traveled a considerable distance into the mountain along the passageway, which after the long flight of stairs leading up from the gate worked its way for the most part down, with countless changes of direction, until the air became quite hot and stuffy and the company very confused. There was still no source of light save for the flicker of Goodgulf's sputtering wand, and the only sound came from the sinister patter of following footsteps, the heavy breathing of North Koreans, the rattle of gumball machines, and the other hurly-burly of deep, dark places.

At length they came to a place where the passage divided into two, with both leading down, and Goodgulf signaled for a halt. Immediately there came a series of ominous gurgles and other-worldly tweets that suggested that the Four Horsemen of the Apocalypse were having a friendly rubber of bridge not a yard away.

'Let's split up,' said Bromosel.

'I've twisted my ankle,' said Pepsi.

'Whatever you do, don't make a sound,' said Arrowroot.

'Wa-zoo,' screamed Moxie, sneezing violently.

'Now here's my plan,' said Goodgulf.

'Bullets won't stop them,' said Bromosel.

'Whatever happens,' said Arrowroot, 'we must keep a close watch.'

The company, as a man, fell asleep.

When they awoke, all was quiet once more, and

after a hasty meal of cakes and ale, they addressed themselves to the problem of which passage to take. As they stood debating, there came from deep in the earth a steady drumbeat. *Dribble, dribble, dribble, shoot, swish.*

At the same time the air began to get hotter and thicker, and the ground started to tremble beneath their feet.

'There's no time to lose,' said Goodgulf, jumping to his feet. 'We must decide and quickly.'

'I say to the right,' said Arrowroot.

'Left,' said Bromosel.

Upon closer examination, the left way proved to be lacking a floor for some forty feet, and Goodgulf quickly set off down the other, with the rest of the company following close behind. The passage led precipitously down, and there were omens of an unappetizing nature along the way, including the whitening skeleton of a minotaur, the body of the Piltdown man, and a rabbit's battered pocket watch with the inscription 'To Whitey from the whole Wonderland crowd.'

Before long the passageway sloped more gently down until with a final plunge it led into a great chamber lined with huge metal lockers and dimly lit by a fiery glow. As they entered, the rumblings grew louder: *Dribble. Dribble. Fake. Dribble. Fake. Shoot.*

All at once a large body of narcs burst into the hall from the passage the company had followed and charged at them, waving hammers and sickles.

'Yalu, Yalu,' shouted their leader, brandishing a huge faggot.

'You dieth, G.I.,' cried the faggot.

'Stay here,' said Arrowroot. 'I'll scout ahead.'

'Keep me covered,' said Legolam, 'I'll head them off.'

'Guard the rear,' said Gimlet, 'I'll take the passage.'

'Hold the fort,' said Goodgulf, 'I'll circle around.'

'Stand fast,' said Bromosel, 'I'll draw them off.'

'Pyongyang panmunjom,' shouted the narc chieftain.

The company stampeded across the hall and out a side passage with narcs at their heels. As they rushed out, Goodgulf slammed shut the door in the narcs' faces and hastily put a spell on it.

'Hawley Smoot,' he said, striking the door with his wand, and with a smoky 'foof' the door disappeared, leaving the Wizard face-to-face with the puzzled narcs. Goodgulf quickly produced a lengthy confession, signed it, and thrusting it into the chieftain's hands, raced away up the passage to where the rest of the company stood at the far end of a narrow rope bridge which spanned a sharp chasm.

As Goodgulf stepped onto the bridge the passage

echoed with an ominous *dribble, dribble*, and a great crowd of narcs burst forth. In their midst was a towering dark shadow too terrible to describe. In its hand it held a huge black globe and on its chest was written in cruel runes, 'Villanova.'

'Aiyee,' shouted Legolam. 'A ballhog!'

Goodgulf turned to face the dread shadow, and as he did, it slowly circled toward the bridge, bouncing the grim sphere as it came. The Wizard reeled back and, clutching at the ropes, raised his wand. 'Back, vile hoopster,' he cried.

At this the ballhog strode forward onto the bridge, and stepping back, the wizard drew himself up to his full height and said, 'Avaunt, thin-clad one!'

Arrowroot waved Krona. 'He cannot hold the bridge,' he shouted and rushed forward.

'E pluribus unum,' cried Bromosel and leaped after him.

'Esso extra,' said Legolam, jumping behind him.

'Kaiser Frazer,' shouted Gimlet, running up to join them.

The ballhog sprang forward, and raising the dread globe over his head, uttered a triumphant cry.

'Dulce et decorum,' said Bromosel, hacking at the bridge.

'Above and beyond,' said Arrowroot, chopping a support.

'A far, far better thing,' said Legolam, slicing through the walkway.

'Nearer my God to thee,' hummed Gimlet, cutting the last stay with a quick ax stroke.

With a loud snap, the bridge collapsed, spilling Goodgulf and the ballhog into the abyss. Arrowroot turned away and, stifling a sob, ran along the passage with the rest of the company close behind. As they rounded a corner, they were dazzled by a sudden shaft of sunlight, and after dispatching a sleeping narc guard in a few short minutes, they scrambled out the gates and down the eastern stairs.

The stairs ran along a syrupy stream in which large gobs of multicolored goo were ominously bobbing. Legolam stopped and spat in it wistfully.

'It is the Spumoni,' he explained, 'beloved of the Elves. Do not drink of it – it causes cavities.'

The company hastened on into the shallow valley and in less than an hour stood on the west bank of the river Nesselrode, which the dwarves call Nazalspray. Arrowroot signaled for a halt. The steps that had led down the mountain came to an abrupt end at the river's edge, and on either side of the narrow way the hills sloped off into wide, barren plains filled with wind gods, dolphins in sailor hats, and street directories.

'I fear that we have come to an uncharted region,'

said Arrowroot, peering under his hand into the distance. 'Alas, that Goodgulf is not here to guide us.'

'These are indeed tough bananas,' agreed Bromosel.

'Yonder lies Lornadoon, land of the Gone Elves,' said Legolam, pointing across the river to a scruffy-looking forest of dutch elms and knotty pines. 'Goodgulf would have surely led us there.'

Bromosel dipped a foot into the oozing river, and a fish stick and a side order of fried clams leaped into the air.

'Sorcery!' cried Gimlet as a tunaburger flew past his ear. 'Witchcraft! Deviltry! Isolationism! Free silver!'

'Aye,' said Legolam, 'the river is under a spell, for it is named after the fair elf-maid Nesselrode who had the hots for Menthol, God of After-Dinner Drinks. But the evil Oxydol, Goddess of Quick Tricks and Small Slams, appeared to her in the shape of a five-iron and told her that Menthol was two-timing with the Princess Phisohex, daughter of King Sano. At this Nesselrode became wroth and swore a great oath to kick Phisohex in the gut and get her mother, Cinerama, Goddess of Short-Term Loans, to turn Menthol into an erector set. But Menthol got wind of the plot and came to Nesselrode in the guise of a refrigerator, turned her into a river, and went west to sell encyclopedias. Even now, in the spring, the river softly cries, "Menthol, Menthol, you are one wazoo. One day I'm the elf next door and then *poof* I'm a river. You stink." And the wind answers, "Phooey." '

'A sad story,' said Frito. 'Is it true?'

'No,' said Legolam. 'There's a song, too,' and he began to sing:

> An elvin-maid there was of old,
>   A stenographer by day;
> Her hair was fake, her teeth were gold,
>   Her scent was that of cheap sachet.
>
> She thought that art was really 'keen,'
>   The top ten she could hum;
> Her eyes were full of Maybelline,
>   Her mouth, of chewing gum.
>
> Her head was full of men and clothes,
>   Her hair, of ratted curls;
> Her legs she wrapped in fine Sup-Hose,
>   For nights out with the girls.
>
> She met one morn an elvin-lad,
>   Who took her to the fights,
> And said he owned a spacious pad,
>   And went to law school nights.
>
> And so that night she gave her all
>   In back of his sedan;

So rich, she thought, so sharp and tall,
  A perfect family man.

But then he told her with a smirk,
  That he loved another,
And was a part-time postal clerk
  And lived home with his mother.

A silver tear rolled down her cheek
  As she bussed home by herself;
The same thing happened twice last week,
  (Oh, Heaven help the Working-elf!)

'It is best that we cross before nightfall,' said Arrowroot finally. 'There are tales of fungo bats and bloodsucking umpires in these parts.' Picking up his toilet kit, he waded into the soupy water, and the company followed behind. The water was nowhere more than a few feet deep, and the boggies had little difficulty making their way across.

'This is indeed a queer river,' said Bromosel, as the water lapped at his thighs.

On the far bank of the river they found a thick strand of dead trees covered with signs in Elveranto which said, COME TO FABULOUS ELF VILLAGE, VISIT THE SNAKE FARM, DON'T MISS SANTA'S WORKSHOP, and HELP KEEP OUR FOREST ENCHANTED!

'Lalornadoon, Lalornadoon,' sighed Legolam, 'wonder of Lower Middle Earth!'

At that, a door in the trunk of a large tree opened, revealing a small room filled with postcard racks, loudly clicking cuckoo clocks, and boxes of maple-sugar candies. A greasy-looking elf slipped out from behind a taffy machine.

'Welcome wagon,' he said, bowing low. 'I am Pentel.'

'Come hither, conastoga,' said Legolam.

'Well, well, well,' said the elf, coughing importantly, 'we are a bit out of season, aren't we?'

'We're just passing through,' said Arrowroot.

'No matter,' said Pentel. 'Plenty to see, plenty to see. On the left, your petrified tree, to the right your Echo Rock and your Natural Bridge, and just ahead your Old Wishing Well.'

'We've come from Doria,' Arrowroot continued. 'We're on our way to Fordor.'

The elf blanched. 'I hope you've enjoyed your visit to Lornadoon, Land of Magic,' he said quickly, and handing them a sheaf of folders and pack-horse stickers, he leaped into the tree and slammed and bolted the door.

'These are troubled times,' said Arrowroot.

Legolam opened one of the folders and pored over a map. 'It isn't far to the Elf Village,' he said finally, 'and unless the place has changed hands, Orlon's kin, Cellophane and the Lady Lavalier, still dwell there.'

'Elves,' grumbled Spam. 'Now I'm not saying Sorhed is right, but I'm not a-saying he's wrong, neither, if you get my drift.'

'Shut up,' said Legolam gravely.

After a hasty meal of frankincense and myrrh, the company set off down a wide path which Legolam identified on the map as Horror Lane, and from time to time mechanical dragons and goblins lurched unsteadily from rubber shrubs and yawned and grunted. But even the boggies remained unperturbed by these assaults, and in a few short hours the travelers arrived at the edge of a small grove of very petrified-looking trees from whose oddly symmetrical branches heavily corroded copper leaves dropped in unconvincing bunches.

As they stood wondering, the head of an elf-maid appeared at a bay window in the nearest tree and cried in the ancient tongue of the elves: '𝔊𝔯𝔢𝔢𝔱𝔦𝔫𝔤𝔰 𝔶𝔢 𝔬𝔩𝔡𝔢 𝔴𝔞𝔶𝔣𝔞𝔯𝔢𝔯𝔰.'

'Are there any more at home like you?' said Legolam, making the correct reply.

A moment later the door to the great tree swung open, and a short elf stepped out. 'Cellophane and Lavalier await you abovestairs,' he said, and led the company into the wide trunk. The tree was completely hollow, and the inside was covered with brick-design wallpaper. A circular staircase led through a hole in the ceiling to an upper story, and the elf motioned for them to ascend the narrow steps. As they reached the top, they found themselves in a room decorated much as the one below, but brightly lit by great wagon-wheel chandeliers which hung from the lofty roof. On a pair of tree stumps at the end of the room sat Cellophane and Lavalier, arrayed in rich muslin.

'Welcome to Lornadoon,' said Lavalier, rising slowly to her feet, and it seemed to the company that she was as fair as a young sapling or scrub oak. She had magnificent chestnut hair, and when she shook her head, handfuls of magnificent chestnuts dropped to the floor like rain. Frito toyed with the Ring and wondered at her great beauty. As he stood, as if in a trance, Lavalier turned to him and saw him toying with the Ring and wondering at her great beauty.

'I see, Frito,' she said, 'that as you toy with the Ring, you wonder at my great beauty.'

Frito gasped.

'Do not fear,' she said, solemnly tweaking his nose. 'Nasties we're not.'

Cellophane then rose and greeted each of the travelers in turn, and motioning for them to sit down on the rubber toadstools arranged around the room, bid them tell the tale of their adventures.

Arrowroot cleared his throat. 'Once upon a time,' he began.

'Call me Ishmael,' said Gimlet.

'Whanne in Aprille,' started Legolam.

'Hear me, oh Muse,' commenced Bromosel.

After some discussion, Frito told the whole story of the Ring, Dildo's party, the Black Schleppers, the Caucus of Orlon, Doria, and Goodgulf's untimely passing.

'Woodja, woodja, woo,' said Cellophane sadly when Frito had finished.

Lavalier sighed deeply. 'Your journey is long and hard,' she said.

'Yes,' said Cellophane, 'you bear a great burden.'

'Your enemies are powerful and merciless,' said Lavalier.

'You have much to fear,' said Cellophane.

'You leave at dawn,' said Lavalier.

After a hearty feast of cherubim and seraphim, Cellophane and Lavalier showed the weary travelers to rooms in a small tree nearby, and as Frito was preparing to enter, Lavalier drew him aside and brought him to a sheltered vale nearby, in the center of which stood a soiled birdbath in which a pair of sparrows were floating upside down.

'Poison,' explained Lavalier, flinging the feathered

corpora into the bushes. 'It's the only thing that even slows them down.' Thereupon she spat into the water, and a goldfish leaped into the air and cried, 'Give me your sevens.'

At that she leaned over the surface and whispered, 'Wilmot Proviso,' and the water began to boil, filling the air with a light odor of beef gumbo. Then it seemed to Frito that the surface became smooth, and there appeared the picture of a man squirting something into his nose.

'Commercials,' said Lavalier irritably.

In a moment the water cleared, and there came scenes of elves and dwarves dancing in the streets, wild revels in Minas Troney, happy debauches in the Sty, a large bronze statue of Sorhed being melted into tie clips, and finally Frito himself stirring on a pile of costume jewelry and smiling broadly.

'This bodes well,' declared Lavalier.

Frito rubbed his eyes and pinched himself. 'Then it is not all black?' he asked.

'The bath of Lavalier never lies,' said the Lady sternly, and leading Frito back to the rest of the company, disappeared in a heavy haze of Jungle Rape perfume.

Frito pinched himself one last time, then stumbled into the treehouse and fell into a deep sleep.

The surface of the basin remained black for a while,

then flickered and showed the triumphant reception of the S.S. *Titanic* in New York Harbor, the repayment of the French war debt, and the inaugural ball of Harold Stassen.

In the eastern sky, Velveeta, beloved morning star of the elves and handmaid of the dawn, rose and greeted Noxzema, bringer of the flannel tongue, and clanging on her golden garbage pail, bade him make ready the winged rickshaw of Novocaine, herald of the day. Thence came rosy-eyeballed Ovaltine, she of the fluffy mouth, and lightly kissed the land east of the Seas. In other words, it was morning.

The company rose, and after a hurried breakfast of yaws and goiters, Cellophane and Lavalier and their attendants led them through the wood to the banks of the great river Anacin where three small balsa rafts lay.

'It is the sad hour of parting,' said Lavalier solemnly. 'But I have for each of you a small gift to remind you of your stay in Lornadoon in the dark days to come.' So saying, she produced a large chest and drew out a handful of wondrous things.

'For Arrowroot,' she said, 'crown jewels,' and handed the surprised king a diamond-shaped pear and a plover's egg the size of an emerald.

'For Frito, a little magic,' and the boggie found in his hand a marvelous crystal globe filled with floating snowflakes.

She then gave each of the other members of the company something rich and strange: to Gimlet, a subscription to *Elf Life*, to Legolam, a Mah-Jongg set, to Moxie, a case of Cloverine Brand Salve, to Pepsi, a pair of salad forks, to Bromosel a Schwinn bicycle, and to Spam a can of insect repellent.

The gifts were quickly stowed away in the little boats along with certain other impedimenta needful for a quest, including ropes; tins of Dinty Moore beef stew; a lot of copra; magic cloaks that blended in with any background, either green grass, green trees, green rocks, or green sky; a copy of *Jane's Dragons and Basilisks of the World*; a box of dog yummies; and a case of Poland water.

'Farewell,' said Lavalier, as the company crammed themselves into the boats. 'A great journey begins with a single step. No man is an island.'

'The early bird gets the worm,' said Cellophane.

The rafts slipped out into the river, and Cellophane and Lavalier boarded a great boat-shaped swan and drifted a short distance beside them, and Lavalier sat in the prow and sang an ancient elvish lament to the heartbreaking timbre of steel drums:

Dago, Dago, Lassi Lima rintintin
Yanqui unicycle ramar rotoroot
Telstar aloha saarinen cloret
Stassen camaro impala desoto?
Gardol oleo telephon lumumba!
Chappaqua havatampa muriel
U canleada horsta wata, bwana,
Butyu canna makit drinque!

Comsat melba rubaiyat nirvana
Garcia y vega hiawatha aloo.
O mithra, mithra, I fain wud lie doon!
Valdaree valdera, que sera, sirrah,
Honi soit la vache qui rit.
Honi soit la vache qui rit.

('Oh, the leaves are falling, the flowers are wilting, and the rivers are all going Republican. O Ramar, Ramar, ride quickly on your golden unicycle and warn the nymphs and drag queens! Ah, who now shall gather lichee nuts and make hoopla under the topiaries? Who will trim my unicorns? See, even now the cows laugh, Alas, alas.' Chorus: 'We are the chorus, and we agree. We agree, we agree, we agree.')

As the tiny boats passed round a bend in the river, Frito looked back in time to see the Lady Lavalier gracefully sticking her finger down her throat in the ancient elvish farewell.

Bromosel looked ahead to where the meandering of the river had brought them face-to-face with the barely risen sun. 'The early bird gets hepatitis,' he grunted, and fell asleep.

Such was the enchantment of Lornadoon that although they had spent only a night in that magic land, it seemed like a week, and as they drifted down the river, Frito was filled with a vague fear that time was running out. He remembered Bromosel's ill-omened dream and noticed for the first time that there was a large blotch of lamb's blood on the warrior's forehead, a large chalk X on his back, and a black spot the size of a doubloon on his cheek. A huge and rather menacing vulture was sitting on his left shoulder, picking its teeth and singing an inane song about a grackle.

Not long after midday the river began to become narrow and shallow, and before long the way was completely blocked by an enormous beaver dam from which there emanated the grim slaps of beaver tails and the ominous whine of turbines.

'I had thought the way to the Isles of Langerhans was clear,' said Arrowroot. 'Now I see that the servants of Sorhed are at work even here. We can go no farther along the river.' The company paddled to the west bank, and drawing their boats onto the shore, ate a hurried meal of moon and sixpence.

'I fear these brutes may do us ill,' said Bromosel, pointing to the looming concrete mass of the dam.

As he spoke, a bulky figure waddled unsteadily across the stony shore. It was about four feet tall, very dark-complexioned, with a tail like a plank steak, a black beret, and wrap-around dark glasses.

'Your servant,' lisped the strange creature, bowing low.

Arrowroot eyed the brute thoughtfully. 'And who might you be?' he said at last, his hand falling to his sword hilt.

'An innocent traveler like yourselves,' said the brown figure, slapping his tail for emphasis. 'My horse threw a shoe or my boat sank. I don't remember which.'

Arrowroot sighed with relief. 'Well, you are welcome,' he said. 'I had feared you might be evil.'

The creature laughed indulgently, revealing a pair of front teeth the size of bathroom tiles. 'Hardly,' he said, munching absently on a piece of driftwood. Then with a great sneeze, his dark glasses fell to the ground.

Legolam gasped. 'A black beaver!' he cried, staggering back.

At that moment there came a great crashing in the nearby woods, and band of howling narcs and grunting beavers descended on the luckless party.

Arrowroot leaped to his feet. 'Evinrude,' he cried, and drawing the sword Krona, handed it hilt-first to the nearest narc.

'Joyvah Halvah,' shouted Gimlet, and dropped his adze.

'Unguentine,' said Legolam, putting his hands on his head.

'Ipso facto,' growled Bromosel, and unbuckled his sword belt.

Spam rushed over to Frito in the heat of the surrender and grasped him by the arm. 'Time to trot, bwana,' he said, drawing a shawl over his head, and the two boggies slipped down to the boats and out into the river before the charging narcs and their lumbering allies missed them.

The chief narc grabbed Arrowroot by the lapels and shook him fiercely. 'Where are boggies?' he screamed.

Arrowroot turned to where Frito and Spam had been standing and then to Moxie and Pepsi, who were hiding next to where Legolam and Gimlet were playing possum.

'You lie, you die,' said the narc, and Arrowroot couldn't help but notice the tone of malice which had crept into his voice.

He pointed to the boggies, and two narcs jumped forward and swept them up in the thighs they had by way of arms.

'There's been some mistake,' squealed Moxie. 'I haven't got it.'

'You've got the wrong man,' Pepsi shrieked. 'It's him,' he said, pointing to Moxie.

'That's the one,' cried Moxie, gesturing at Pepsi. 'I'd know him anywhere. Three-five, eighty-two, tattoo on left arm of rutting dragon, two counts of aiding and abetting known Ringbearer.'

The chief narc laughed cruelly. 'I give the rest of you ten to run,' he said, twirling a set of giant bolos with a threatening application of english. At that, Bromosel started to sprint, but catching his feet in his sword belt, he tripped and impaled himself on his pointed shoes.

'Ye doom is ycomme true,' he groaned. 'O, tell the Lacedomecians to man the torpedoes.' Then noisily shaking a large rattle, he expired.

The narc shook his head. 'Me, you don't need,' he said, and led the narc band away into the surrounding forest with Moxie and Pepsi.

Frito and Spam drifted silently across the river to the eastern bank, and drew their small boat onto the shore, while unseen in the shadow of the dam, a small gray figure on a green-and-yellow-spotted sea horse paddled warily along.

'Out of the bedpan, as the old Fatlip would say,' said

Spam, and fishing their overnight bags out of the craft, set out with Frito along the rising gorge that led to the next chapter.

VI

THE RIDERS
OF ROI-TAN

For three days, Arrowroot, Gimlet, and Legolam hunted the band of narcs, pausing in their relentless chase only for food, drink, sleep, a few hands of pinochle, and a couple of sightseeing detours. Tirelessly, the Ranger, dwarf, and elf pushed on after the captors of Moxie and Pepsi, often making a long march of up to three hundred yards before collapsing with apathy. Many times Stomper lost the scent, which was rather difficult since narcs are fond of collecting their droppings along the way into great, pungent mounds. These they carefully sculpted and molded into fearsome shapes as mute warning to any who might dare challenge their power.

But the narc mounds were growing fewer, indicating either that they had quickened their pace or had run out of roughage. In any case the trail grew fainter and the tall Ranger had to use his every skill to follow the barest traces of the company's passing, a worn ventilated shoe, a pair of loaded dice, and farther on, a pair of ventilated narcs.

The land was somber and flat, now populated only

by scrub brushes and other stunted growths. Occasionally they would pass a deserted village, empty save for a stray dog or two, which bolstered the party's dwindling larder. Slowly they descended into the bleak Plain of Roi-Tan, a hot, dry, and cheerless place.* To their left were the dim peaks of the Mealey Mountains, and to their right and far away the sluggish Effluvium. To the south were the fabled lands of the Roi-Tanners, sheepmen of no mean skill aboard a fighting bull merino.

In earlier times the sheep-lords had been enemies of Sorhed and had fought bravely against him at Brylopad and Ipswitch. But now there were rumors of renegade bands of mounted sheepmen who ravaged northern Twodor, pillaging, raping, burning, killing, and raping.

Stomper halted in the march and let out a deep sigh of dread and boredom. The narcs were leaving them farther and farther behind. Carefully he unwrapped a square of the elvish magic zwieback and broke it into four equal pieces.

'Eat all, for this is the last we have,' he said, palming the fourth piece for later.

Legolam and Gimlet chewed gravely and silently. All around them they felt the malicious presence of Serutan, the evil Wizard of Isinglass. His malignant

* Not unlike Passaic, New Jersey.

influence hung heavy in the air, his secret forces impeding their search. Forces that took many forms, but for the present came as the runs.

Gimlet, who, if possible, liked Legolam even less than at Riv'n'dell, gagged on his portion of zwieback.

'A curse on the elves and their punk grub,' he grumbled.

'And on the dwarves,' returned Legolam, 'whose taste is in their mouths.'

For the twentieth time the pair drew weapons, lusting for each other's chitlins, but Stomper intervened lest one be killed. The food was gone anyway.

'Hold and cease, halt, avaunt, put up thy swords, refrain from thy quarrel and stay thy hands,' he spake, raising a fringed glove.

'Buzz off, Hopalong,' growled the dwarf. 'I'll make casserole of that window dresser!'

But the Ranger drew his peacemaker and the fighting ended as quickly as it began, for even dwarves and elves do not relish a shiv in the back. Then, as the combatants sheathed their blades, Stomper's voice rang out again.

'Lo!' he cried, pointing to the south. 'Many riders approach like the wind!'

'Would that they rode *down*wind as well,' said Legolam, wrinkling his nose.

'Keen are the nostrils of the elves,' said Stomper.

'And light are their feet,' muttered the dwarf under his breath.

All three squinted at the dust on the distant horizon. That they were sheepmen there was no doubt, for the wind heralded their approach.

'Do you think they're friendly?' said Legolam, trembling like a leaf.

'That I cannot say,' said Stomper. 'If they are, we have no worries; if they are foes, we must escape their wrath through craft.'

'How?' asked Gimlet, seeing no hiding place on the flat plain. 'Do we fight or flee?'

'Neither,' said the Ranger, falling limp on the ground. 'We'll all play dead!'

Legolam and Gimlet looked at each other and shook their heads. There were few things on which they both agreed, but Stomper was definitely one of them.

'We may as well take a few with us,' said Gimlet, drawing his cleaver, 'for it's better to go with one's codpiece buttoned.'

The sheep-lords loomed larger and the fierce war-bleats of their mounts could now be heard. Tall and blond were the Roi-Tanners, wearers of helmets topped with cruel-looking spikes and small toothbrush mustaches. The wanderers saw too that they wore long boots and short leathern pants with suspenders and held long pikes that looked like lead-weighted dust-mops.

'They are savage of visage,' said Legolam.

'Aye,' said Stomper, peeking through his fingers. 'Proud and willful are the men of Roi-Tan, and they value highly land and power. But these lands are often those of their neighbors, and they are hence mickle unpopular. Though ignorant of letters, they are fond of song and dance and premeditated homicide. But warfare is not their only craft, for they run summer camps for their neighbors handsomely fitted out with the most modern oven and shower facilities.'

'Then these rascals cannot be all bad,' said Legolam hopefully. Just then they saw a hundred blades flash from a hundred sheaths.

'Bets?' said Gimlet.

As they watched helplessly, the line of riders bore down upon them. Suddenly the centermost figure, whose spiked helmet also boasted two longhorns, gave a vague hand signal to halt and the men reined to a stop in a display of astoundingly inept sheepmanship. Two of their fallen comrades were maimed in the milling, trampling confusion that followed.

As the screams and curses died down, the pronged leader cantered up to the three astride a bull merino of great stature and whiteness, its tail intricately braided with colored rubber bands.

'The jerk looks like a fork,' whispered Gimlet out of the corner of his thick-lipped mouth. The leader, shorter than the others by a head, looked at them suspiciously through twin monocles and brandished a battlemop. It was then that the company realized that the leader was a woman, a woman whose ample breastplate hinted at a figure of some heft.

'Vere ist you going and vat are you doing here when you are not to being here in der first place vhere you ist?' the leader demanded in rather garbled everybody-talk.

Stomper stepped forward and bowed low, falling on one knee and pulling his forelock. Then he kissed the ground at the sheep-lord's feet. He buffed her boots for good measure.

'Hail and greeting, O Lady,' lisped Stomper, the butter in his mouth freezing solid. 'We are wayfarers in your land searching for friends taken by the foul narcs of Sorhed and Serutan. Perhaps you have espied them. They are three feet tall with hairy feet and little tails, probably dressed in elvin cloaks and headed for Fordor to destroy Sorhed's threat to Lower Middle Earth.'

The captain of the sheepmen stared at the Ranger dumbly, then, turning to her own company, beckoned a rider.

'Medic! Hurry up, I haf vork for you. Und he ist der delirious, also!'

'Nay, beautiful Lady,' said Stomper, 'they of whom

I speak are boggies, or in the tongue of the elves, *hoipolloi*. I am their guide, who am called Stomper by some, though I have many names.'

'I bet you do,' agreed the leader, tossing her golden braids. 'Medic! Vhere *ist* you?'

Finally Arrowroot's explanations were accepted, and introductions were made all around.

'I ist Eorache, daughter of Eorlobe, Captain of der Rubbermark and Thane of Chowder. Dot means you ist nice to me or you ist not nothing to nobody no more,' said the ruddy-faced warrior. Suddenly her face darkened when she espied Gimlet, whom she studied suspiciously.

'Vat your name ist again?'

'Gimlet, son of Groin, Dwarf-Lord of Geritol and Royal Inspector of Meats,' said the stubby dwarf.

Eorache dismounted and inspected Gimlet at closer range, a tight frown on her lips.

'Dot's funny,' she said at last, 'you don't *look* dwarfish!' Then she turned to Stomper. 'Und *you*. Undershirt vas it?'

'*Arrow*shirt!' said Stomper. 'Arrowroot of Arrow-shirt!'

In a flash he had drawn gleaming Krona from its holster and flailed it about over his head as he cried, 'And this is Krona of he who has many names, he who is called Lumbago, the Lodestone, by the elves,

Dunderhead, heir to the throne of Twodor and true son of Arrowhead of Araplane, Conqueror of Dozens and seed of Barbisol, Top of the Heap and King of the Mountain.'

'Vell la-dee-dah,' said Eorache, eyeing the waiting medic. 'But I ist believing dot you ist not der schpies of der Serutan. He ist one schtinker, but he ist not der schtupiter also.'

'We have come from afar,' said Legolam, 'and were led by Goodgulf Grayteeth, Wizard to Kings and Fairy Godfather, second class.'

The sheepess raised her yellow brows and let both monocles fall from her watery blue eyes. 'Schhhhhh! Dot ist not der name to be dropping around here. Der King, mein vater, lost his favorite mount, Saniflush der Swift, to dot schyster und later finds dot der dice ist queerer than der three-legged troll! Then der poor scheep ist coming back a week later covered with fleas and forgetting dot she ist housetrained all over der King's new tapestry. Vhen der King catches him, der ist vun dead Vizard!'

'There is a sad wisdom in your words,' said Arrow-root, trying to snatch a peek down her halberd, 'for Goodgulf is no more. He met his fate o'er-matched in uneven contest with a ballhog in the Mines of Doria. The creature played not fairly with Goodgulf, mastering him with means foul and deceitful.'

'Der poetic justicer,' said Eorache, 'but I vill miss der old crank.'

'And now,' said Arrowroot, 'we are in quest of our two companions captured by narcs and born whither we know not.'

'Ach,' said the lady warrior, 've fixed der vagons of some narcs yesterday, but ve don't see any boggies. Vhat ve find ist some little bones in der stewpot, und I don't think they vas having spare ribs.'

The three companions observed ten seconds of silent farewell for their friends.

'Then how about a lift on your mutton-mushers?' said Gimlet.

'Hokay,' said Eorache, 'but ve ist going to Isinglass to fix too der vagon of dot schkunken Serutan.'

'Then you fight with us against him,' said Stomper. 'We had thought the sheep-lords to have thrown their lot with the evil Wizard.'

'Ve haf never vorked for dot creep,' said Eorache loudly, 'und even if ve *did* help him a little at first, ve were only following orders und it probably vasn't us dot you heard about because ve vas someplace else. Und anyvay, he vas vasting his time looking for some schtupider Ring vhat vasn't vorth nothing. Me, I don't believe in dot pixie-dust schtuff. Magic-schmagic, I saying.'

The rider clicked her heels together and made an

about-face, calling over her shoulder. 'So, you coming mit us or you staying here und maybe starving to death?'

Stomper fondled the last piece of magic zwieback in his pocket and weighed the alternatives, not over-looking the beefy charms of Eorache.

'Ve going mit you,' he said dreamily.

Pepsi was dreaming that he was a maraschino cherry atop a huge hot-fudge sundae. Shivering on a mountain of whipped cream he saw a monstrous mouth of sharpened fangs loom above him, drooling great gobbets of saliva. He tried to scream for help but his own mouth was full of hardened fudge sauce. The maw descended, breathing a hot, odorous wind . . . down, down it came . . .

'Wake up, youse jerks,' snarled a harsh voice. 'Th' boss want t' talk to ya! Har har har!' A heavy brogan kicked out at Pepsi's already bruised ribs. He opened his eyes to the night gloom and met the evil stare of a brutish narc. This time he screamed, but the gagged boggie only gurgled with fear, and as he struggled he remembered that he was still hog-tied like a prime roast.

Now it all came back to him, how he and Moxie had been taken prisoner by the band of narcs and forced to march south toward a destination that they dreaded, the Land of Fordor. But a hundred blond riders on fighting sheep had cut them off and now the narcs feverishly prepared for the attack they knew would come with the first rays of the sun.

Pepsi received another kick and then heard a second narc-voice speak to the first.

'Mukluk pushkin, boggie-grag babushka lefrak!' rasped the deeper voice, which Pepsi recognized as that of Goulash, the leader of Serutan's narcs, who accompanied the party of Sorhed's larger, more well-equipped henchmen.

'Gorboduc khosla!' snapped the larger narc, who returned his attention to the frightened boggies. Smiling fiendishly, he drew his curved grasswhip and laughed. 'Bet youse guys would give an arm an' a leg t' get outta here.' He raised his weapon above his neckless head with mock savagery and reveled in the boggies' cringing and protestation.

'I, Goulash, shall have th' pleasure of takin' youse groundhogs t' th' great Serutan hisself, master of the fighting Ohmahah, Nastiest of the Nasty and Bearer of the Sacred White Rock, soon t' be th' boss of alla Lower Middle Earth!'

Suddenly a hamfisted blow from behind sent the narc spinning like a lathe.

'I'll give *you* boss of alla Lower Middle Earth!' spat a louder, deeper voice.

Moxie and Pepsi looked up to see a gigantic bull narc, well over seven feet and four hundred pounds if a gram. Towering over the sprawled narc, the monster pointed arrogantly to the red nose emblazed on his own chest. It was Karsh of the fighting Otto-wah, leader of Sorhed's contingent, who had laid Goulash low.

'I'll boss of alla Lower Middle Earth *you*!' he re-iterated. Goulash sprang to heavily shod feet and made an obscene gesture at Karsh.

'Slushfund tietack kierkegaard!' he screamed, stamping in anger before the larger narc.

'Ersatz!' bellowed Karsh as he angrily drew his four-foot snickersnee and deftly trimmed Goulash's finger-nails to the elbow. The smaller narc scampered off to retrieve his arm, cursing a blue streak, which was already lapping at the ooze.

'Now,' said Karsh, turning back to the boggies, 'them bleaters is gonna jump us at dawn, so's I want the lowdown on this Magic Ring *right now*!' Reaching into a large leather bag, the narc withdrew an armful of shiny instruments and arrayed them on the ground in front of Pepsi and Moxie. There before them were a large bullship, a thumbscrew, a cat-o'-nine-tails, a rubber hose, two blackjacks, an assortment of surgical knives, and a portable hibachi with two red-glowing branding irons.

'I got ways t' make ya sing like canaries,' he

chuckled, stirring the hot coals with his long index finger. 'Youse each can have one from column A and two from column B. Har har har!'

'Har har har,' said Pepsi.

'Mercy!' yupped Moxie.

'Aw, come on, youse guys,' said Karsh, selecting an iron with the triple-bar 'S' of Sorhed, 'let me have a little fun before y' talk.'

'No, please!' said Moxie.

'Who wants it first?' laughed the cruel narc.

'Him!' chorused the boggies, indicating each other.

'Ho ho!' chortled the narc as he stood over Moxie like some housewife sizing up a kielbasa. He raised the flaming iron and Moxie screeched at the sound of a blow. But when he opened his eyes again, his torturer was still standing above him, looking oddly different in expression. It was then that the boggie noticed that his head was missing. The body collapsed like a punctured whoopee cushion, and over it, triumphant, was the leering figure of Goulash. He held a blade in his good hand of the type usually employed on troublesome hamhocks.

'Last taps! Gotcha last!' he cried, hopping from one foot to the other with glee. 'And now,' he hissed in the boggies' faces, 'my Master Serutan desires the where- abouts of th' Ring!' He drop-kicked Karsh's noggin a good twenty yards for emphasis.

'Ring, ring?' said Pepsi. 'You know anything about a ring, Moxie?'

'Not unless you mean my vaccination scar,' said Moxie.

'Come on, come on!' Goulash urged, slightly singeing the hair on Pepsi's right big toe.

'Okay, okay,' sobbed Pepsi. 'Untie me and I'll draw you a map.'

Goulash agreed to this in his greedy haste and loosened the bonds around Pepsi's arms and legs.

'Now bring the torch nearer so we can see,' said the boggie.

'Gnash lubdub!' exclaimed the excited narc in his own foul tongue as he clumsily juggled the blade and the torch in his one remaining hand.

'Here, better let me hold the sword for you,' offered Pepsi.

'Knish snark!' gibbered the fiend, waving the torch in anticipation.

'Now these are the Mealey Mountains, and this is the Effluvium,' said Pepsi, scratching the ground with the sharp point of the shiny blade.

'Krishna rimsky-korsikov!'

'. . . and this is the Great Turnpath . . .'

'Grackle borgward!'

'. . . *and this is your gall bladder, right above your chitlins!*'

'Gork!' objected the narc as he fell to earth, opened from end to end like a pillow case. As his internal organs noisily shut down, Pepsi freed Moxie and they began threading their way through the narc battle lines, hoping not to be seen as the warriors prepared for the battle that would surely come with the first rays of the sun. Tiptoeing around a party of narcs busily honing their cruel knives, the boggies heard the low, gurgling song that they half sung, half belched in time with a spastic rhythm provided by one who repeatedly bashed his head against his iron helmet. The words were strange and harsh to their ears as they passed by in the dark:

> From the Halls of Khezaduma
> To the shores of Lithui
> We will fight King Sorhed's battles
> With tooth and nail and knee . . .

'Shhh,' whispered Pepsi as they crawled over open ground, 'don't make any noise.'

'Okay,' whispered Moxie.

'What's all that whisperin'?' growled a voice in the dark, and Pepsi felt a long-nailed hand grab at his lapel. Without thinking, Pepsi lashed out with his toenails and ran past, leaving the guard writhing on the ground holding the one area neither protected by his armor nor by his group insurance policy.

The boggies took off like a shot past the surprised narcs.

'The forest! The forest!' cried Pepsi, just ducking an arrow that neatly parted his hair to the bone. Shouts and confused alarums rang out on every side as they ran to the safety of the wood, for as luck would have it, the fierce *blaat* of the Roi-Tanners' war horns sounded the beginning of their attack. Diving for cover, the boggies watched with frightened eyes as the bloodthirsty sheep-lords advanced on the narcs, a hundred war-bleats echoing as one in the dawn light. The escaped prisoners forgotten, the narcs stood their ground as wave upon wave of woolly death crashed down upon them, battlemops thudding with a dreadful report against foot-thick skulls. Distant screams and blows reached the boggies' ears and they watched open-mouthed the carnage that followed. The outnumbered narcs gave way, and the slavering merinos charged this way and that, butting and kicking, fighting as mean and as dirty as their berserk riders. A handful of narcs could be seen with their cleavers thrown down and waving a white flag. The victors smiled broadly, surrounded them, and began hacking and hewing, tossing heads about like soccer balls. Laughing like loons, the merry band mirthfully relieved the corpses of their wallets and fillings. Pepsi and Moxie averted their faces from the slaughter, fighting their nausea unsuccessfully.

'Ho ho ho! The sheepers do not play at their craft.'

Moxie and Pepsi looked up with a start toward the green trees. They knew that they had heard a low, rumbling voice, but they saw no one.

'Hulloo?' they said uncertainly.

'Not "hulloo," *ho ho ho*!' returned the voice.

The brothers searched the woods for the source of the laugh, but not until a huge, green eye winked did they see the huge giant standing against the tall forest right in front of them. Their jaws dropped at the sight of an immense figure, fully eleven feet tall, standing before them with his hands coyly at his sides. He was bright green from head to foot (size fifty-six, triple-Z). A broad, pastel-green smile broke upon its face, and the monster laughed again. As the boggies retrieved their jaws, they noticed that the giant was naked save for a parsley G-string and a few cabbage leaves in his feather-cut locks. In each great hand was a package of frozen stringbeans, and across his chest a green banner proclaimed, TODAY'S SPECIAL, FIVE CENTS OFF ALL CREAMED CORN.

'No, no,' moaned Pepsi, 'it . . . it *couldn't* be!'

'Ho ho ho, but it is,' guffawed the immense figure, half man, half broccoli. 'I am called Birdseye, Lord of the Vee-Ates, oft called the jol—'

'Don't say it!' cried Moxie, holding his furry ears with horror.

'Be not afraid,' grinned the affable vegetable. 'I want to make *peas* with you.'

'No, no!' moaned Pepsi, nibbling his tie clip in frenzy.

'Come come,' said the giant, '*lettuce* go and meet my subjects who live in the forest. They cannot be *beet*. Ho ho ho!' The green apparition doubled over at his own *bon mot*.

'Please, please,' pleaded Pepsi, 'we can't take it. Not after all we've been through.'

'I must insist, my friends,' said the giant, 'the people of my realm are off to war on the evil Serutan, eater of cellulose and friend of the black weeds who every day strangle us more and more. We know you to be his enemy too, and you must come with us, and help defeat the cabbage-murderer.'

'Well, all right,' sighed Pepsi, 'if we gotta—'

'—we gotta,' sighed Moxie.

'Sigh not,' reassured the giant, as he slung the two boggies over his kelly green shoulder blades, 'being Lord of the Vee-Ates is not easy either, particularly on my *celery*. Ho!'

The boggies kicked and screamed, attempting a final escape from the towering bore.

'Struggle not,' he said soothingly, 'I know a couple of *peaches* that will be just right for you meat-things. You will love them, they are—'

'—quite a *pear*,' muttered Pepsi.

'Hey,' burbled the giant, 'that is a *good* one. Wish I had said that!'

'You will,' sobbed Moxie, 'you will.'

Arrowroot, Legolam, and Gimlet massaged their aching muscles under a shaded coppice as the Roi-Tanners watered their slobbering mounts and looked over the weaker of them for the evening meal. Three long days had they ridden hither and thither over rocky ground and smooth toward the dreaded fortress of Serutan the Gauche, and relations among the company had deteriorated somewhat. Legolam and Gimlet never tired of baiting each other, and when the elf laughed at the dwarf as he fell from his mount and was dragged raw the first day out, Gimlet retaliated by slipping Legolam's steed a strong laxative on the sly. The second day thus found the elf being borne in panicky circles and zigzags by his ailing mount and that night he revenged himself by shortening the right rear leg of Gimlet's merino, causing its rider many long hours of violent seasickness on the following day's ride. It had not been a tranquil journey.

In addition, it appeared to both Gimlet and Legolam that something odd had come over Arrowroot since they had met the Roi-Tanners, for he sat listlessly in the saddle and crooned to himself, always glancing covertly toward the leader of the sheep-lords, who spurned his advances. The last night of the ride Legolam awoke to find the Ranger absent from his pup tent and a huge commotion in the bushes nearby. Before the elf could remove his hairnet and buckle on his weapon, Arrow-root returned more melancholy than ever, nursing a sprained wrist and two heavily purpled eyes.

'Ran into a tree,' was his only explanation.

But Isinglass and the fortress of Serutan were now near, and the hard riding could be put by for an evening of rest.

'Ook!' yelped Gimlet painfully as he hunkered down upon a mossy knoll, 'that damned four-legged pot roast busted my coccyx for sure.'

'Then ride on your head,' said Legolam in a snide tone of voice, 'it is much the softer and less valuable.'

'Fetch off, hairdresser.'

'Toad.'

'Poop.'

'Creep.'

Jingling spurs and the thwapping of a riding crop interrupted the discussion. The three companions watched as Eorache trundled her bulk up the knoll to meet them. She slapped the dust and lanolin from her metal studded jackboots and shook her horns dubiously.

'You two schtill machen mit der nasty names?' She contemptuously avoided the round, ardent eyes of

Arrowroot and laughed aloud. 'In der vaterland ve haf no argumenters,' she reprimanded, drawing several dirks for emphasis.

'The lads are but weary after their long ride,' cloyed the smitten Ranger, nibbling her heels playfully, 'but eager to do battle, as I am to prove my worthiness in your azure eyes.'

Eorache gagged audibly and spat a large, brown quid against the wind. She stomped away in disgust.

'Wrong number,' said Gimlet.

'Worry not,' sympathized Legolam, throwing a more-than-companionable arm around Arrowroot, 'them dames are all alike, poison, every last one of them.'

Arrowroot broke free, sobbing inconsolably.

'Der goes vun sick booby,' said the dwarf, pointing to his head.

Darkness was falling and the campfires of the Roi-Tanners began flickering. Over the next hill lay the valley of Isinglass, now renamed Serutanland by the scheming Wizard. Dejected, the Ranger shuffled among the resting warriors, hardly hearing their proud song, roared above the clinking of foamy steins:

> *Ve ist der merry, gay Roi-Tanners,*
> *Who like der boots, salutes und banners.*
> *Ve ride der scheeps in vind und vheather*
> *Mit vhips und spurs und drawers of leather.*

Ve dance und sing und valse und two-step
Und never ever mach der goose-step.
Peace iss vhat ve vant und do *have,*
Und a piece of anything you *have.*

Men frolicked about the fires, laughing and joking. Two blood-slathered contestants hacked at each other with sabers to the gloating cheers of flaxen-haired spectators, and farther on a gathering of warriors bellowed with mirth as they did something unattractive to a dog.

But the scene cheered him not. Heartsick, he walked on into the darkness, saying, 'Eorache, my Eorache,' softly over and over to himself. Tomorrow he would display such acts of valor that she would have to pay attention to him. He leaned against the tree and sighed.

'Really got it, huh?'

Stomper jumped back with a cry, but it was the familiar pointed head of Gimlet that poked through the leaves.

'I did not see thee approach,' said Arrowroot, sheathing his sword.

'Just trying to lose that jerk,' said the dwarf.

'Who's a jerk, sirrah?' snapped Legolam, who had been molesting a chipmunk behind the tree.

'Speak o' the devil,' groaned Gimlet.

The three sat under the broad branches and thought

upon the hard travels they had made, seemingly to no purpose. What good would the defeat of Serutan be if Sorhed claimed Frito's Ring for his own? Who could resist his power then? For a long while they brooded.

'Isn't it about time for a *deus ex machina*?' said Legolam wearily.

Suddenly there was a loud *pop* and a bright burst of light that momentarily blinded the shocked three. The acrid odor of cheap flash-powder filled the air, and the companions heard a distinct *thump* followed by a louder *oof*! Then through the swirling confetti, they saw a shining figure dressed all in white, brushing the twigs and dirt from his spotless bell-bottoms and gleaming a-go-go boots. Above the white Nehru jacket and cheesy medallion was a neatly trimmed gray beard set off by oversized wraparound shades. The whole ensemble was topped off by a large white panama with a matching ostrich plume.

'Serutan!' gasped Arrowroot.

'Close, but no cigar,' cackled the brilliant figure as he flicked a bit of invisible dust from his tailored shoulder. 'Pray try again. It is a sad thing indeed when old pals are recognized not!'

'Goodgulf?!' cried the three.

'None other,' said the aged fop. 'You seemed astonished that I have reappeared.'

'But how did – did you . . . ?' began Legolam.

'We thought the ballhog . . .' said Gimlet.

The old wizard winked and straightened his vulgar medallion.

'My story is a long one indeed, and I am not the same Goodgulf Grayteeth that you once knew. I have undergone many changes, no thanks to you, I might add.'

'Yah, a little Clairol on the temples and a trim,' whispered the observant dwarf.

'I heard that!' said Goodgulf, scratching a razor-cut sideburn. 'Take not too lightly my present form, for my powers are even mightier.'

'But how did you—'

'Much have I journeyed since we last met, and much have I seen, and there is much I would tell thee,' said Goodgulf.

'Anything but the name of your tailor,' said Gimlet. 'Where'd you get those duds, anyway? I thought Halloween was months off yet.'

'A most delightful little boutique in Lornadoon. It's me, don't you think?'

'More than you know,' agreed the dwarf.

'But how did—' began Legolam again.

The Wizard made a sign for silence.

'Know now that I no longer the Wizard of old. My spirit has been purged, my nature has been altered, my image has been remade. There is little of the former self that in me remains.' With a flourish, Goodgulf doffed his panama in a low bow. 'I am completely transformed.'

'Bets?' grunted Gimlet as he saw five aces fall out of the hat.

'But Goodgulf!' exclaimed the elf impatiently. 'You have not yet told us how you survived the clutches of the ballhog, lived through the flames, recovered from the fall into the boiling pit, and escaped the blood-thirsty narcs to find us here!'

As the stars grew brighter in the velvet sky overhead, the elf, dwarf, and Ranger gathered around the radiant sage to hear the tale of his miraculous, impossible salvation.

'Well,' began Goodgulf, 'once out of the pit . . .'

VII

SERUTAN SPELLED
BACKWARDS IS MUD

The plaintive twitterings of morning birds woke Legolam, who stared sleepily into the rising sun. Looking
about, he saw all the company asleep save Goodgulf,
who idly played solitaire on sleeping Gimlet's hump.

'You cannot put a knave on a king. That's cheating,'
cautioned the elf.

'But I can put my fist down your gullet,' countered
the witty old conjurer, 'so why do not thee make a
cuckoo clock or whatever you do with your spare time.
I am meditating.'

But the elf looked at the Wizard with fondness. Half
the night they had sat up and listened to Goodgulf's
tales of strange wanderings and brave deeds. Tales full
of Goodgulf's courage and cunning against unnameable
enemies. Tales obvious to all as a pack of preposterous
lies. If Goodgulf had been transformed, he had not
been transformed much. What is more, Gimlet's watch
was missing.

Slowly the rest of the party roused themselves,
Arrowroot last, partially because of his befuddled
mooning over the fair Roi-Tanner, and partially

because he couldn't fasten his drop-seat underwear. Carefully the Ranger prepared the company's austere breakfast of eggs, waffles, bacon, grapefruit, pancakes, hot oatmeal, fresh-squeezed orange juice, and golden cheese blintzes. No one, the company agreed early in the quest, could make blintzes like old Arrowroot.

'Zo, you ist up, finally,' growled a voice. All heads turned to Eorache, tricked out in her best boots, spurs, and armor. Through her nose was thrust a fierce-looking chicken bone.

'Ah, dressed to kill,' chuckled Goodgulf as he rose to greet the surprised captain.

'*You!*' gasped Eorache.

'You were expecting maybe Beowulf?'

'But – but ve thought dot you vere kaput mit der ballhog,' said the Roi-Tanner.

'It is a long tale,' said Goodgulf, taking a deep breath.

'Then save it,' interrupted Eorache. 'Ve have der fighting to do mit der Serutanner. Coming mit me, please.'

The company followed Eorache to the rest of the warriors, all mounted on their fiery, champing steeds, eager as their riders for battle. Cheerfully they greeted their leader with a clenched fist of salute and whispered amused comments about the odd Ranger that followed her around like a demented basset.

The party mounted. Eorache grudgingly gave Thermofax, the fastest of all the Roi-Tanner's sheep, to Goodgulf. Then, as the Riders burst into song, they rode west toward Isinglass.

They had not ridden but two hours before they reached a crested hill and Eorache bellowed the order to halt. Down in the low valley lay the pastel pink-and-blue walls of Serutan's mighty fortress. The entire city was ringed with walls, and around the walls was a pale-lavender moat crossed by a bright-green drawbridge. Pennants flapped in the breeze bravely and the tall towers seemed verily to goose the clouds.

Beyond the walls the expedition saw the many wonders that had lured countless tourists through its portals in the past. Amusements of all descriptions lay within: carnivals and side-shows under permanent tents, fairies' wheels and gollum-coasters, tunnels of troth, griffin-go-rounds and gaming houses where a yokel could lose an idle hour, and if he wasn't careful, his jerkin. Years before, when Serutan still showed a fair face to the world, Goodgulf had worked in such a house as a croupier for 'Ye Wheel of Ye Fortune.' But only for a short time. Why he left and why he had been forever barred from Serutanland, as the evil Wizard renamed it, no one knew. And Goodgulf wasn't telling.

The company stared with apprehension at the

motionless wheels and tarpaulined exhibits. At the looming battlements stood rows of archers and pike-men, behind them caldrons of boiling farina. Above the ramparts rose a huge sign with the face of a cartoon character made famous through comic scrolls and innumerable shoddy toys. It was the visage of Dickey Dragon that simpered at the riders above the letters that read WELCOME TO SERUTANLAND. ALL RIDES TUPPENCE ON SUNDAYS. Everywhere, they noticed, were the brainless grins of Dickey Dragon. Pennants, signs, walls all bore that same idiotic, tongue-lolling face. But now that once-beloved creature had revealed itself to be the symbol of its creator's lust for power, a power that had to be ended.

'A mighty fortress is our Dickey Dragon,' said Goodgulf, ignoring the groans of those around him.

'Ja,' agreed Eorache, 'der Serutanner macht der mint mit der Dickey Dragon hats und der Dickey Dragon sweatshirts und der Dickey Dragon dis und der Dickey Dragon dot. One rich schtinker, der Serutanner ist.'

Goodgulf agreed that this was so, and that when they had been friends he had not been a bad sort.

'But this was all a sham and a front for his real purposes,' he added, 'and for that we must conquer him.'

'But how?' asked Legolam.

'Der diversionary tactic!' exclaimed Eorache, her chicken bone quivering. 'Ve need some dumkopf to draw dere attention vhile ve attack from der rear.' She paused and looked slyly at the love-struck Ranger out of the corner of her eye. 'Dot dumb – er, *hero* vould melt der heart of any fraulein, I thinking.'

Stomper's ears perked up like a randy boxer and he drew his blade, crying, 'Krona! I will undertake this mission for thy glory and honor, that I may win from you admiration, though I not return.' Clumsily, he goaded his truculent merino to her side and kissed a calloused hand. 'But first, I ask a token from thee, fair Eorache, that my valor may attempt to equal thy matchless charms. A token I ask of thee.'

Puzzled for a second, Eorache nodded her horned head and unbuckled her thick leather wrist-strengthener and handed the metal-studded strap to Arrowroot who fastened it joyfully around his neck.

'Hokay dere ist der token,' she said, 'now *raus!*'

Without another word he galloped down the slope toward the drawbridge amid the cheers of the war party. Faster and faster he sped as the rest circled under the cover of the ridge. Then, just as the merino's sharp hooves approached the portal into the fortress, the bridge was quickly raised up, revealing a familiar scaly grin painted on the underside, along with the legend, SORRY FOLKS. CLOSED FOR THE SEASON. But

Stomper's momentum carried him irresistibly onward until he plunged headlong into the lavender moat. Thrashing in the water, Stomper yelled with fear, for the moat became alive with sharp, rasping beaks. Great snapping turtles massed upon the drowning Ranger, and archers, noticing the commotion for the first time, began peppering the crackpot with crack pot-shots.

Eorache, hearing his cries, rode over the crest and saw Stomper floundering in the moat, assailed on all sides. Barking a Roi-Tanner oath, she raced down to the moat and sprang from her mount after him, locking his head in the crook of her muscular arm, and made for the shore. Then, as the party watched with awe, she stood up in the two-foot depths and scampered to safety, two water-and-arrow-logged merinos at her heels.

A great cheer rose from the Roi-Tanners as their leader trotted smartly back to the hill, the gasping Ranger still in tow. Muttering under her breath, she applied artificial respiration to Stomper, who choked up a surprising quantity of the moat and several small turtles. The vicious reptiles had torn away much of his raiment, leaving only his undergarments, which the lady noticed had the Royal Crown of Twodor embroidered on the backflap.

'Hey!' she exclaimed to the semiconscious Ranger.

'You got der Royal Crown of der Twodor embroidered on der backflap.'

'Aye,' said Goodgulf, 'for he is the true King of these and all lands of Twodor.'

'No kidding?' said Eorache, her eyes widening with concupiscence. 'Hmmm. Maybe der dumkopf ist hokay after all.' To the surprise of all, she began to murmur softly to Stomper as she threw him over her shoulder and gently burped him.

'There is no time for courtly pastimes,' said Goodgulf. 'Our diversion has failed and the enemy is now forewarned of our intentions. The hour to strike has passed and we are lost.'

'Does that mean we can go home now?' asked Legolam.

'No!' said the Wizard, his medallion flashing in the sun, 'for I see in the distance a vast army marching.'

'Nuts,' said Gimlet. 'I thought we could call it a day.'

With fearful eyes they all watched as a dark mass spread over a distant hill and moved toward them with alarming speed. Whether friend or foe, no one could discern. For many minutes they watched until cornets sounded from the battlements of Serutanland.

'They must be narc reinforcements come to destroy us all!' wailed the elf. 'Sorhed has sent a great army against us!'

'No!' cried the Ranger. 'They are not narcs, they are not like anything that I have seen.'

The others saw that this was true. Rank upon rank of huge, warlike vegetables were massing toward Serutanland, led by a monumental creature. An eldritch song thundered:

> *All hail Vee-Ates, gather round!*
> *With greens held high and roots in ground!*
> *Cabbage, Eggplant, Cuke, and Carrot*
> *Purée narcs with club and garrot!*
>
> *Squash their pulp up into bits*
> *Slash their rinds and spit out the pits!*
> *Make their juice spout like a geyser*
> *And grind them all to fertilizer!*

'Ho ho ho!' rang through the land and the frightened sheep milled in confusion like sheep. Dumbstruck, the party saw squads of squash, platoons of potatoes, companies of kumquats, battalions of beets, and regiments of radishes, all tramping to a martial air played by a fifty-piece rutabaga marching band. Beyond the endless rows were even more formations; determined-looking avocados, stalwart scallions and brawny eggplants.

The very ground shook at the rhythmic rootsteps of the horde, the air crackled with their thousand chattering, piping warcries.

Proudly, at the head of the column strode the green general, who had added a pair of cornsilk epaulets to his meager attire. On each shoulder was a familiar figure in addition, and Goodgulf was the first to see.

'It's the two runts, by cracky!' he cried.

And it was true. Moxie and Pepsi sat unsteadily on Birdseye's shoulders, both waving frantically at Goodgulf and the rest.

The acres of produce tramped directly to the walls of Serutanland and arranged themselves in battle formation. Through a glass lent by Eorache, Arrowroot saw consternated narcs first gaping, then rushing about the ramparts in panic.

'Ho ho ho!' thundered the giant. 'Be it known, Serutan, that the Vee-Ates are before you. Surrender or be pulped!'

At first there was no response from the fortress. Then a great voice replied to the giant with an earth-shaking raspberry.

'I take it then,' said the giant, 'that you wish to fight.' Without another word the giant strode back to his lines and began barking orders to his followers, who quickly obeyed, running hither and thither to set up formations and engines of war.

Great watermelons half walked, half rolled to the edge of the moat, followed by enormous potatoes who leapt heavily upon the melons, firing a deadly hail of seeds to rake the ramparts clean of narcs. The narcs fell like fruit flies while the onlookers from the hill applauded wildly.

Then a column of sweet potatoes forded the moat, ignoring the arrows that sunk deep into their pulp. Half submerged in the turtle-infested waters, the potatoes sprouted long, winding tendrils that climbed the sheer face of the walls, entwining around any protrusion. The vines served as scaling ladders for the hordes of commando cucumbers that hastily clambered up to challenge the defenders. Simultaneously the giant brought out a huge, wheeled catapult and aligned it toward the wall.

'Der gas varfare!' shouted Eorache, guessing his plan.

The puzzled watchers soon learned what the Roi-Tanner had meant, for fully three companies of suicide scallions appeared and began piling into the great scoop of the catapult. When the trip was released, the eight-foot onions soared in a high arc over the walls and set up a huge cloud of acrid fog upon impact. Through the glass the party saw the narcs feverishly wiping their streaming eyes with dirty black hand-kerchiefs. Ballistas of kamikaze kumquats rained death down upon the barricades, and deafening reports of aerial popcorns toppled parapets on the heads of Serutan's henchmen.

But the narcs still fought back desperately, their long blades flashing, dripping with vitamin-packed gore. The ramparts were littered with chopped parsley, diced onion, and grated carrots. Rivers of red tomato juice ran over the stones, and a ghastly salad floated in the moat.

Seeing that the fighting on the walls was yet undecided, the tall green commander ordered up another weapon, a pumpkin the size of a Mack truck. Nodding to his commands, the weighty squash rumbled over the moat on the backs of his slain comrades. Peppered with arrows, the great orange warrior stood before the raised drawbridge and immediately began butting it with its tremendous bulk. The whole wall shook and trembled. Again and again he crashed against the door while frantic defenders poured vats of steaming oatmeal down on the attacker. Parboiled yet undaunted, the brave pumpkin stepped back several yards and got one final running start, then rushed at the door full tilt. There was a titanic crash and the door seemed to explode into shards and splinters. The dazed battering-squash reeled back dizzily, staggered, shrugged its broad round shoulders, and split in half. Seeds ran out and mingled with the still-warm squeezings of brother warriors. For a moment all fell silent. Then, with a great cry, all the Vee-Ates rushed across the sundered shell and raged into the city. After them charged the Roi-Tanners and the company, eager to avenge its valorous end.

The final engagements inside the walls were short and bloody. Gimlet sang lustily as he swung at the wounded narcs and dismembered their inert defenseless corpses. Arrowroot and Legolam valiantly disposed of a number of brawny foes from behind and Goodgulf offered hearty exhortations and sound advice from the safety of a crumbled parapet. But it was the Roi-Tanner maiden and her cronies who took the day's honors as they destroyed the remaining narcs. Arrowroot sought out Eorache through the melee and found her gleefully mincing a narc fully half her size and singing an old Roi-Tanner drinking song. She saw him wave timidly at her. She smiled, winked, and tossed him a round object.

'Hey! King! Catch!'

Clumsily the Ranger fielded the souvenir. It was the head of a narc. Its final expression was one of extreme annoyance.

At last the fighting was over and the long-parted friends ran to each other with joyful greetings.

'Joyful greetings!' cried Moxie and Pepsi.

'The same and more to you, I'm sure,' said Good-gulf, stifling a yawn of recognition.

'Hail fellow well met,' bowed Legolam, 'may your dandruff worries be over forever.'

Gimlet limped over to the two boggies and forced a smile.

'Pox vobiscum. May you eat three balanced meals a day and have healthful, regular bowel movements.'

'How comes it,' said Arrowroot, 'that we meet in this strange land?'

'It is a tale long in the telling,' said Pepsi, pulling out a sheaf of notes.

'Then save it,' said Goodgulf. 'Have thee seen or heard news of Frito and the Ring?'

'Nary a peep,' said Moxie.

'Same here,' said Gimlet. 'Let's eat.'

'No,' said the Wizard, 'for we have not yet found the evil Serutan.'

'Nertz,' said Gimlet. 'It's already past lunch.'

Together with Birdseye and Eorache, the company sought out the evil magician. Word spread that Serutan and his loathsome companion Wormcast had been seen in Isintower, the tallest parapet in Serutanland, famous for the rotating restaurant high atop the shaft.

'He's up there,' a celery said. 'He jammed the elevators, but he's treed just the same.'

'Ho ho ho,' observed the giant.

'Shut up,' added Goodgulf.

High above them they saw the round, turning

restaurant with its flashing sign that read SERUTAN'S
TOP O' THE MARK. Under it a glass door swung open. A
figure appeared at the railing edge.

'Dot's him!' cried Eorache.

In face he looked much like Goodgulf, but his
raiment was strange to see. The Wizard was dressed
in a full-length leotard of fire-engine red and a long
cape of black sateen. On his head were pasted black
horns and at his buttocks was attached a barbed tail. He
held an aluminum pitchfork and wore cloven patent-
leather loafers. He laughed at the company below.

'Ha ha ha ha ha.'

'Come thee then down,' called Arrowroot, 'and
what to thee is coming, taketh. Open thy door and let
us in.'

'Nay,' cackled Serutan, 'not by the hair of my
chinny-chin-chin. Let us instead work this out like
sane, reasonable people.'

'Vork-schmork,' screamed Eorache. 'Ve vant your
miserable schkin!'

The evil wizard drew back in mock fear, then
returned to the edge and smiled. His voice was
soothing and melodious, dripping with sweet intona-
tions like a melting Fudgsicle. The company stood in
awe of his Sucaryled words.

'Let's backtrack,' continued Serutan. 'Here I am
with my little concern making an honest farthing by the

sweat of my brow. Suddenly a merger of competitors crash right through my corporate holdings trying to drive me out of the market. You have taken my liquid assets and nullified my small merchandizing staff. It's a clear-cut case of unfair business practices.'

'Hey,' said the giant to Goodgulf, 'that guy's got a good *head* on his shoulders. No wonder he reaps so much *cabbage*.'

'Shut up,' Goodgulf agreed.

'Now I have a proposition,' said Serutan, gesturing with the point of his tail, 'and though I'm not married to this idea, I thought I'd run it up the parapet and see if anybody pulls his forelock. Now I'll concede that I wanted a piece of the action, but it's that evil Sorhed who wants the whole ball of wax. As I see it, we form a new organization wherein I'll sign over a controlling interest in Dickey Dragon and its subsidiaries for my old executive position and yearly stock options on any old Rings we may come across along the way. Throw in thirty percent of the booty we get in Fordor and I'll let you have my partner Wormcast for free. He's responsible for this little proxy fight anyway.'

An anguished scream came from inside the tower and a bowl of wax fruit just missed Serutan's skull. A scrawny old man in a messenger boy's uniform appeared for a second and shook his fist.

'Garrrsch!' he sputtered.

Serutan picked up the protesting Wormcast and casually tossed him over the railing.

'Aaaaaaaaarrrrrrrrrrrggggggghhhh!' said Wormcast.

The evil henchman hit the hard ground with considerable force.

'Never seen a red flapjack before,' mused Gimlet.

'There is my pledge of good faith,' Serutan went on smoothly. 'Do we have a deal?'

'No deals,' said Goodgulf. 'That knave is slipperier than a catfish in a jar of Vaseline.'

'Now wait,' said Arrowroot, 'he *did* pledge controlling interest.'

'N-O spells no,' said Goodgulf, adjusting his hat. 'I don't want to wake up some bright morning with his pledge between my shoulder blades.'

Just then a small black object whizzed past Goodgulf's head.

'This is getting monotonous,' Gimlet opined.

The round sphere bounced along the pavement and came to rest at Pepsi's toes. He looked at it curiously and picked it up.

'We will leave you under guard in your foul tower,' said Goodgulf, 'and the Vee-Ates will deal with you when your larder is empty of frozen cube steaks.'

Goodgulf turned and pointed to Pepsi.

'Okay, drop it.'

'Aw, I wasn't doing nothing,' said Pepsi.

'Yeah, nothing,' defended Moxie.

'Let me have it,' said the Wizard impatiently, 'you can't eat it, so you have no use for it.'

The young boggie handed the black ball over glumly.

'Now,' said Goodgulf, 'we must move quickly. Though the lands of Isinglass and Roi-Tan are safe from Serutan's power, they will not long be thus unless Twodor itself is saved from Sorhed's malevolence.'

'What must we do?' said Moxie.

'Yes, do?' asked Pepsi.

'If you'll belt up for a second I will tell thee,' Goodgulf snapped. 'The fair city of Minas Troney is threatened by Sorhed's eastern armies. The foul city of Chikken Noodul lies near, and any day the black cloud will fall upon her fairer sister. We must gather all our forces and defend her.' He beckoned Arrowroot. 'You, Stomper, must take it upon yourself to gather your subjects in Twodor and anyone else who will come to shore up the ramparts of Minas Troney. Eorache, you must bring all the riders you can spare and Birdseye too must lead his valiant Vee-Ates to Twodor. The rest will proceed with me there directly.'

'A hundred words without a punchline,' said Gimlet. 'The old crock must be sick.'

The party bade farewell and rode from the broken fortress of Isinglass with heavy heart, knowing that still more trouble would plague the land. Goodgulf, Moxie, and Pepsi mounted their complaining bleaters and spurred on in the evening shadows towards the fabled capital of Twodor. As they left, two fair young carrots waved their greens after the boggies and jumped hopefully up and down upon their dainty taproots, somewhat hindered by already noticeable swellings in their middles. Moxie and Pepsi had not been idle, since Goodgulf had seen them last.

All night and half the next day Goodgulf and the two boggies rode ever watchful for Sorhed's spies. Once overheard Moxie saw a black shape flapping eastward between the clouds and thought he heard a low, vile *croaking*. But he had been on pipeweed for several hours beforehand and wasn't sure.

Finally they rested. Goodgulf and Moxie conked off immediately after a quick game of craps (Moxie lost), and Pepsi, too, lay down as if in a deep snooze. But when his companions' snores became regular, he slowly slithered from his pup tent and rifled the Wizard's saddle bags. There he found the round, black ball Goodgulf had so carefully hidden.

It was smaller than a muskmelon, though larger than a pool ball. Its surface was featureless save for a small, circular window into the black interior.

'A magic wishing-ball!' he exclaimed. 'That's what it is.'

The boggie closed his eyes and wished for a keg of ale and a barrel of breaded veal cutlets. There was a small *foof* and a puff of fiery smoke, and Pepsi found himself staring into the face of a monstrous, unspeakably vile visage, its jowls quivering with malevolence and rage.

'I told you to keep your paws *off* of it!' shrieked the Wizard, his bell-bottoms flapping angrily.

'Aw, I was only looking at it,' Pepsi whined.

Goodgulf snatched the ball away from Pepsi and glowered. 'This,' he said harshly, 'is no plaything. This ball is the wondrous *mallomar*, the magic watchamacallit of the elves, long thought lost in the Sheet-Metal Age.'

'Why didn't you say so?' said Pepsi pointlessly.

'With *mallomar* the Old Ones probed the secrets of the future and looked deep into the hearts of men.'

'Sort of like a Ouija board?' said Moxie sleepily.

'Watch closely!' Goodgulf commanded.

The two boggies watched with interest as the wizard made mysterious passes over the sphere and muttered a weird incantation.

> *Hocus pocus*
> *Loco Parentis!*
> *Jackie Onassis*
> *Dino de Laurentiis!*

Before their frightened eyes the boggies saw the sphere glow. Goodgulf continued to mutter over it.

> *Queequeg quahog!*
> *Quodnam quixote!*
> *Pequod peapod!*
> *Pnin Peyote!*
> *Presto change-o*
> *Toil and trouble*
> *Rollo chunky*
> *Double-Bubble!*

Suddenly the globe seemed to burst from within with a sparkling radiance, and a quavering sound hummed through the air. Pepsi heard Goodgulf's voice through the shimmering glow.

'Tell me, O magic *mallomar*, shall Sorhed be defeated or shall he conquer? Shall the black cloud of Doom fall on all of Lower Middle Earth, or shall there be sunshine and happiness with his fall?'

Pepsi and Moxie were astonished to see fiery letters begin to form in the air, fiery letters that would foretell the fate of the coming struggle with Dark Lord. It was with wonder that they read the answer: *Reply Hazy, Ask Again Later.*

VIII

SCHLOB'S LAIR AND OTHER MOUNTAIN RESORTS

Frito and Spam clambered out of breath to the top of a small rise and gazed out at the landscape that stretched before them, unbroken save for sudden depressions and swiftly rising gorges, to the slag mines, dress factories, and lint mills of Fordor. Frito sat down heavily on a cow's skull, and Spam produced a box lunch of cheese and crackers from their bags.

At that moment there came the sound of falling pebbles, stepped-on twigs, and a nose being violently blown. The two boggies leaped to their feet, and a gray, scaly creature crept slowly up to them on all fours, sniffing the ground noisily.

'Mother of pearl,' cried Frito, recoiling from the sinister figure. Spam drew his elvish pinking knife and stepped back, his heart in his mouth with the gooey glob of crackers.

The creature looked at them with ominously crossed eyes, and with a little smile, rose tiredly to its feet, and clasping its hands behind his back, began to whistle mournfully.

Suddenly Frito remembered Dildo's tale of the finding of the Ring.

'You must be Goddam!' he squeaked. 'What are you doing here?'

'Oh, well,' said the creature, speaking very slowly. 'Not much. I was just looking for a few old pop bottles to help pay for my sister-in-law's iron lung. Of course, ever since my operation I don't get around like I used to. Guess I'm just unlucky. Funny how life is, up and down, never can tell. Gosh, it sure is cold. I had to pawn my coat to buy plasma for my pet geese.'

Spam tried desperately to keep his leaden eyelids open, but with a great yawn, he slumped heavily to the ground. 'You fiend,' he muttered, and fell asleep.

'There I go again,' said Goddam, shaking his head. 'Well, I know when I'm not wanted,' he said, and sat down and helped himself to the boggies' elvish melba toast.

Frito slapped himself in the face several times and did a few deep breathing exercises.

'Look here, Goddam,' he said.

'Oh, you don't have to say it. Not wanted. I know. I never was. My mother left me in a twenty-four-hour locker in an enchanted forest when I was two. I was raised by kindly rats. But I guess every cloud has its silver lining. Why, I knew a troll once, name of Wyzinski . . .'

Frito swayed, drooped, and was snoring before he hit the ground. When Frito and Spam awoke, it was already night, and there was no sign of Goddam anywhere. Both boggies felt to make sure that they still had their original complement of fingers, legs, and the like, and that no cutlery had been inadvertently left in their ribs. To their considerable surprise, nothing was missing, not so much as a hangnail or a cufflink. Frito felt the Ring still securely fastened to its chain, and slipping it quickly on his finger, he blew through the magic whistle and was relieved to hear the familiar flat E.

'I don't get it, Mr Frito,' said Spam finally, feeling with his tongue for missing fillings, 'that one's a pigeon-fancier or worse.'

'Well, hello there,' said a large rock suddenly, becoming Goddam by degrees.

'Hello,' said Frito weakly.

'We were just leaving,' said Spam quickly. 'We have to close an arms deal in Tanzania or pick up some copra on Guam or something.'

'That's too bad,' said Goddam. 'I guess it's goodbye for old Goddam. But he's used to it.'

'Goodbye,' said Spam firmly.

'Goodbye, goodbye, parting is such a brief candle,' said Goddam. He waved a great stained handkerchief listlessly back and forth, and grasping Frito by the hand, began to sob softly.

Spam took hold of Frito's other arm and bodily dragged him away, but Goddam remained tightly attached, and after a minute or two, he gave up and sank exhausted on a rock.

'I hate to see an old friend go,' said Goddam, applying the handkerchief liberally over the cup custard he had by way of face. 'I'll just see you on your way.'

'Let's go,' said Frito dejectedly, and the three small figures set off at a quick pace across the hot-blooded moors.

Before long, they came to a place where the ground, well-watered by a vivid green stream, became damp and squishy, and Goddam slogged ahead of them. In a few hundred feet the way was completely blocked by a thick, fetid bog choked with well-smoked briars and lily cups.

'It is the Ngaio Marsh,' said Goddam solemnly, and Frito and Spam saw mysteriously reflected in the mucky pools eerie visions of bodies with ornate daggers in their backs, bullet holes in their heads, and poison bottles in their hands.

The little group plodded forward through the foul fen, averting their eyes from the grisly corpses, and after an hour of heavy going, they came, wet and filthy, to drier land. There they found a narrow path which led arrow-straight across an empty plain to a huge arrowhead. The moon had set, and dawn was coloring the sky a faint brown when they reached the curiously shaped rock.

Frito and Spam dropped their bags under a little ledge, and Goddam settled down behind them, humming a gum jingle.

'Well, we're right in the old ballpark,' he said, almost cheerily.

Frito groaned.

The boggies were awakened in the late afternoon by the clash of cymbals and the harsh sound of trumpets playing 'Busman's Holiday.' Frito and Spam sprang to their feet and saw, frighteningly close, the great Gate of Fordor set into the high mountain wall. The gate itself, flanked by two tall towers topped with search lights and a vast marquee, lay open, and an enormous line of men was pouring in. Frito shrank back in fear against the rock.

It was night before the last of the hordes had passed into Fordor, and the Gate had closed with a deep clang. Spam peeped out from behind a stone outcropping and slipped over to Frito with a frugal meal of loaves and fishes. Goddam immediately appeared from a narrow crevice and smiled obscenely.

'The way to a man's heart is through his stomach,' he said.

'That's just what I've been thinking,' said Spam, fingering the hilt of his sword.

Goddam looked mournful. 'I know how it is,' he said. 'I was in the war. Pinned down in a deadly hail of Jap fire . . .'

Spam gagged, and his arm went limp. 'Die,' he suggested.

Frito took a large loaf of raisin bread and crammed it into Goddam's mouth.

'Mmmmf, mfffl, mmblgl,' said the beast darkly.

The little party set out once more into the night and walked for many long liters into the south, always skirting the stony ring that surrounded Fordor with a ring of stone. The road they followed was flat and smooth, the remnant of some ancient linoleum-paved highway, and by the time the moon was high in the sky, they had left the Gate of Fordor far behind. Around midnight the stars became obscured with a great many clouds the size of a man's hand, and shortly after a tremendous torrent swept through the land, pouring wet, annoyed pointers and retrievers on the miserable travelers. But the boggies pressed on behind Goddam, and after a bruising fifteen minutes, the storm passed and, dropping a few last chihuahuas, moved westward.

For the rest of the night they journeyed under dimly visible stars, numbed by the cold and Goddam's endless stream of knock-knock jokes. It was very late at night when they found themselves at the edge of a large forest, and heading off the road, they took shelter in a small grove. In a moment they were fast asleep.

Frito awoke with a start to find the little grove completely surrounded by tall, grim-looking men clad from head to toe in British racing green. They held huge green bows, and they wore shaggy wigs of bright green hair. Frito rose unsteadily to his feet and kicked Spam.

At that point, the tallest of the bowmen stepped forward and approached him. He wore a propeller beanie with a long green feather and a large silver badge with the word *Chief* and some recumbent pigeons, and Frito guessed that he must be their leader.

'You're completely surrounded; you haven't got a chance; come out with your hands up,' said the captain sternly.

Frito bowed low. 'Come in and get me,' he said, making the correct reply.

'I am Farahslax, of the Green Toupées,' said the captain.

'I am Frito, of nothing in particular,' said Frito shakily.

'Can I kill them a little?' squealed a short squat man with a black nose-patch, rushing to Farahslax with a garrote.

'Nay, Magnavox,' said Farahslax. 'Who are you?' he said, turning to Frito, 'and what is your evil purpose?'

'My companions and I are going to Fordor to cast the Great Ring into the Zazu Pits,' said Frito.

At this, Farahslax's face darkened, and looking first at Goddam and Spam, then back to Frito, he tiptoed out of the grove with a little smile and disappeared with his men into the surrounding forest, singing merrily:

> *We are stealthy Green Toupées*
> *Skulking nights and snoozing days,*
> *A team of silent, nasty men,*
> *Who all think Sorhed's numbah ten.*

> > *Draw their fire*
> > *Flank on right*
> > *Narcs retire*
> > *Fight-team-fight!*

> *Using every grungy trick*
> *From booby trap to pungee stick*
> *We hardly need the strength of thirty*
> *When we can win by playing dirty.*

> > *Two-four-six-eight*
> > *Tiptoe, sneak*
> > *And infiltrate*
> > *Cha-cha-cha.*

It was not many hours before night when the green men left, and after a leisurely meal of apple cheeks and cauliflower ears, Frito, Spam, and Goddam returned to the high road and passed quickly out of the forest and into the wide asphalt waste that lay beneath the eastern slope of Fordor. By nightfall they had come under the shadow of the black chimneys of Chikken Noodul, the dread company town that stood across from Minas Troney. From deep within the earth came the heavy *whomp-whomp* of fell engines producing overshoes and mess kits for Sorhed's war machine.

Goddam led Frito and Spam through the brown gloom to a fin-worn salmon ladder that led sharply up into the heavy mass of the Sol Hurok, the great cliffs of Fordor. They climbed for what seemed like an hour. An hour later they reached the top, exhausted and gagging on the heavy air, and flung themselves down on a narrow ledge at the mouth of a great cavern overlooking the black vale.

Above them wheeled huge flocks of black pelicans, and all around them lightning flashed and graves yawned and fell asleep.

'Things look black, and no mistake,' said Spam.

A pungent smell of old pastrami and rancid gherkins floated out of the cave, and from deep within some hidden chamber came the sinister click of knitting needles.

Frito and Spam walked warily into the tunnel, and Goddam shuffled after them, a rare smile playing across his face.

Ages ago when the world was young and Sorhed's heart had not yet hardened like stale cheesecake, he had taken a young troll-maiden as his wife. Her name was Mazola, called by the elves Blanche, and she married the handsome young witch-king over the objections of her parents, who pointed out that Sorhed 'simply wasn't trollish' and could never provide for her special needs. But the two were young and starry-eyed. The first hundred thousand years found the newlyweds still quite happy; they then lived in a converted three-room dungeon with a view, and while the ambitious hubby studied demonology and business administration at night school, Mazola bore him nine strapping wraiths.

Then came the day when Sorhed learned of the Great Ring and the many powers it would bring him in his climb to the top. Forgetting all else, he yanked his sons from medical school over his wife's strident objections and dubbed then Nozdruls. But the First Ring War went badly. Sorhed and his Ringers barely escaped with their lives. From then on their marital relations went from bad to worse. Sorhed spent all his time at the witch-works and Mazola sat home casting evil spells and watching the daytime *mallomar* serials.

She began to put on weight. Then, one day, Sorhed found Mazola and a *mallomar* repairman in a compromising position and immediately filed divorce proceedings, eventually winning custody of the Nine Nozdrul.

Mazola, now banished to her drab surroundings in the bowels of Sol Hurok, let her hatred grow and fester. Schlob, was she now called. For eons she nurtured her pique, obsessively stuffing herself with bon-bons, movie magazines, and an occasional spelunker. At first, Sorhed dutifully sent her monthly alimony payments of a dozen or so narc volunteers, but these gifts soon stopped when word got around what a dinner invitation with Sorhed's ex actually entailed. Her gnawing fury knew no bounds. She prowled her lair with murderous intent, eternally cursing the memory of her husband and his derisive trolack jokes. For ages her only interest had been revenge as she brooded in her dark, dark lair. Cutting off her lights had been the last straw.

Frito and Spam now descended into the bowels of Sol Hurok with Goddam right behind them. Or so they assumed. Deeper and deeper they plunged into the dark heavy vapors of the cavernous passageways, tripping continually on piles of skulls and rotting treasure chests. With unseeing eyes they searched through the blackness.

'Sure is dark, I'm a-thinkin',' whispered Spam.

'Brilliant observation,' shushed Frito. 'Are you sure this is the right way, Goddam?'

There was no answer.

'Must have gone on ahead,' Frito said hopefully.

A long time they inched their way forward through the murky tunnels. Frito clutched the ring tightly. He heard a faint *squishing* noise ahead in the tunnel. Frito stopped in his tracks, and since Spam had hold of his tail, they fell with a clatter that echoed and re-echoed loudly through the black spaces. The *squishing* subsided, then grew louder. And closer.

'Back the other way,' rasped Frito, 'and quickly!'

The boggies fled the ominous *squishing* down many twists and turns, but it was still gaining on them, and the sickening odor of stale bon-bons filled the air. They ran blindly on until a great commotion before them blocked further escape.

'Look out,' whispered Frito, 'it's a patrol of narcs.'

Spam soon knew that this was so, for their foul tongues and clanking armor were unmistakable. They were, as usual, disputing and cracking filthy jokes as they approached. Frito and Spam flattened themselves against the wall, hoping to escape unseen.

'Cripes,' hissed a voice in the dark, 'this place always give me the creeps!'

'Nuts to you,' lashed back another, 'the lookout says that boggie with the Ring is in here.'

'Yeah,' opined a third, 'and if we don't get it Sorhed'll break us back down to nightmares.'

'Third class,' agreed a fourth.

The narcs grew closer and the boggies held their breath as they passed. Just as Frito thought they had passed, a cold, slimy hand clutched his chest.

'Hoo boy!' exulted the narc. 'I got 'em, I got 'em!'

In a trice the narcs were upon them with billyclubs and handcuffs.

'Sorhed will be pleased to see you two!' cackled a narc, pressing his face (and breath) close to Frito's.

All at once a great, guttural moan shivered the dark tunnel and the narcs fell back in terror.

'Crud!' a narc screamed. 'It's her nibs!'

'Schlob! Schlob!' wailed another, lost in the darkness.

Frito drew Tweezer from its scabbard, but could see nothing to strike. Thinking quickly, he remembered the magic snowglobe given him by Lavalier. Holding the glass at arm's length, he hopefully pressed the little button on the bottom. Immediately a blinding carbon arc-light flooded the dank surroundings, revealing a vast chamber of formica paneling and cheap chintz. And there, before them, was the terrible bulk of Schlob.

Spam cried out at the sight most horrible to behold. She was a huge, shapeless mass of quivering flesh. Her flame-red eyes glowered as she slogged forward to the

narcs, her tatty print shift dragged on the stone floor.
Falling upon her fear-frozen victims with her fat body,
she ripped them apart with taloned house slippers and
sharp fangs dripping great yellow droplets of chicken
soup.

'Wash behind your ears!' Schlob shrieked as she tore
a narc limb from limb and discarded his armor like a
candy wrapper.

'You never take me anywhere!' she foamed, popping the wriggling torso into her maw. 'The best years
of my life I gave you!' she raged, her sharp red finger-
nails reaching out for the boggies.

Frito stepped back against the wall and slashed at the
greedy nails with Tweezer, only managing to chip the
enamel. Schlob squealed, further enraged. As the
ravenous creature closed in, Frito's last memory was
of Spam frantically schpritzing insect repellent into
Schlob's bottomless gullet.

IX

MINAS TRONEY IN THE
SOUP

The evening sun was setting, as is its wont, in the west as Goodgulf, Moxie, and Pepsi reined in their exhausted merinos at the gates of Minas Troney. The boggies were dazzled by the fabled capital of all Twodor, Stronghold of the West and Lower Middle Earth's largest producer of crude oil, yo-yos, and emery wheels. Surrounding the townlands were the Plains of Pellegranor, whose earth was rich with many an oast and garner, not to mention wide tilths, folds, byres, rippling rilns, and rolling ferndocks. The desultory Effluvium washed these green lands and year after year provided the ingrate residents with bumper crops of salamanders and anopheles mosquitoes. It was little wonder that the city drew multitudes of pointed-headed Southrons, thick-lipped Northrons, and inverted Ailerons. It was the only place where they could get a passport out of Twodor.

The city itself dated back to the Olden Days when Beltelephon the Senile decreed rather inexplicably that there be built in this flat land a royal ski lodge of wondrous beauty. Unfortunately the old King cashed in before he saw ground broken and his hydrocephalic son, Nibasco the Incompetent, typically misread the late codger's vague blueprints and ordered somewhat more prestressed concrete than necessary for the original design. The result was Minas Troney or 'Nabisco's Folly.'

For no good reason, the city was made in seven concentric circles topped with a commemorative double statue of Beltelephon and his favourite concubine, whose name was either Nephritis the Obese or Phyllis. In any case the final architectural effect was that of an Italian wedding cake.* Each ring was higher than the next, as were the rents. In the lowest, seventh ring dwelt the city's sturdy yeomen. Oft they could be seen dutifully polishing their brightly colored yeos for some idiotic festival or other. In the sixth ring dwelt tradesmen, warriors in the fifth, and so on to the first and highest level, wherein dwelt the Great Stewards and dentists. Each level was reached by means of wind-powered escalators in constant need of repair so that the social climber of these ancient times was just that. Each ring was proud of its own history and showed its scorn of that beneath it by daily bombardments of refuse, and expressions such as 'Let's go seventhing' and 'Dahling, don't be so third-level' were

* The historian Bocaraton notes that this may have been intentionally 'emblematic of the crumbs inside.'

common.* Each level was obliquely protected by out-thrusting battlements corniced and groined at the odd enjambments. Each odd enjambment was set perpendicular to every even adjacent one-way thoroughfare. Needless to say, the inhabitants were always late for their appointments, if not totally lost.

As the three slowly wound their way toward the Palace of Benelux the Steward, the citizens of Twodor gaped at them briefly and walked immediately to their nearest optometrist. Curiously the boggies stared back at the dwellers: men, elves, dwarves, banshees, and not a few Republicans were among them.

'Any convention burg gets a pretty mixed bag,' Goodgulf explained.

Slowly they ascended the last, creaking set of moving steps and alighted at the first level. Pepsi rubbed his eyes at the edifice before him. It was of lavish design with broad lawns and sumptuous gardens. Rich marble paved the path beneath their feet, and the tinkling of many fountains sang like silver coins. At the door they were rather rudely informed that the dentist was not at home and they-must-be-looking-for-the-old-coot-round-back.

There they found a run-down palace wrought of stoutest Masonite, its walls aglow with fiery inlays of

* It is not known upon whom the refuse of the lowest ring was thrown, but it is conjectured that it was not thrown at all, but eaten.

rock candy and old bicycle reflectors. Over the re-
inforced plywood door was a sign reading THE
STEWARD IS OUT. Beneath that there was another
announcing OUT TO LUNCH, and beneath that, GONE
FISHING.

'Benelux must not be here, if I read these signs
aright,' said Moxie.

'I think it's a bluff,' said Goodgulf as he rang the
bell insistently, 'for the Stewards of Minas Troney
have always been private in their ways. Benelux the
Booby, son of Electrolux the Piker, comes from a long
line of Stewards dating back many arid generations.
Long have they ruled Twodor. The first Great
Steward, Parrafin the Climber, was employed in King
Chloroplast's kitchen as second scullery boy when the
old King met a tragic death. He apparently fell
backward by accident on a dozen salad forks. Simultaneously the true heir, his son Carotene, mysteriously
fled the city, complaining of some sort of plot and a
lot of threatening notes left on his breakfast tray. At
the time, this looked suspicious what with his father's
death, and Carotene was suspected of foul play. Then
the rest of the King's relatives began to drop dead one
after the other in an odd fashion. Some were found
strangled with dishrags and some succumbed to food
poisoning. A few were found drowned in the soup
vats, and one was attacked by assailants unknown and

beaten to death with a pot roast. At least three appear to have thrown themselves backward on salad forks, perhaps in a noble gesture of grief over the King's untimely end. Finally there was no one left in Minas Troney who was either eligible or willing to wear the accursed crown, and the rule of Twodor was up for grabs. The scullery slave Parrafin bravely accepted the Stewardship of Twodor until that day when a lineal descendant of Carotene's returns to reclaim his rightful throne, conquer Twodor's enemies, and revamp the postal system.'

Just then a peephole in the door opened and a beady eye inspected them.

'W-w-what you want?' the voice demanded.

'We are wayfarers here to aid the fortunes of Minas Troney. I am Goodgulf Grayteeth.' The Wizard took a crumpled slip of paper from his wallet and handed it through the hole.

'W-what this?'

'My card,' replied Goodgulf. It returned immediately in a dozen pieces.

'Steward not home. On vacation. N-n-no p-peddlers!' The peephole closed with a small slam.

But Goodgulf was not easily duped and the boggies could tell from his eyes that he was angered by this impudence. His pupils were crossing and uncrossing like a juggler's oranges. He rang again, long and loud.

The eye blinked at them and a smell of garlic floated from the hole.

'Y-you again? Told you, he's t-t-taking a shower.' Again the hole shut.

Goodgulf said nothing. He reached into his Mao jacket and extracted a black ball that Pepsi at first thought was the *mallomar* with a string attached. Goodgulf lit it with the end of his cigar and tossed the ball unto the mail slot. He then ran around the corner with the boggies in tow. There was a large *boom* and, when the boggies peeked around to look, the door had magically disappeared.

Pridefully the three walked through the smoking portals. They were confronted by a seedy old palace guard who was wiping the soot from his smarting eyes.

'You may tell Benelux that Goodgulf the Wizard awaits an audience.'

The doddering warrior bowed resentfully and led them through the airless passageways.

'T-t-the S-steward isn't going t-to like t-this,' croaked the guard. 'H-h-hasn-'t been out of p-p-palace for years.'

'Do not the people grow restive?' asked Pepsi.

'T-their idea,' drooled the old guide.

He led them through an armorial hall whose cardboard arches and plaster-of-paris vaultings towered fully a foot over their heads. Richly mimeographed tapestries depicted past Kings' legendary deeds. Pepsi particularly liked one about a long-dead king and a she-goat and said so. Goodgulf smacked him one. The very walls glittered with inset ginger-ale bottles and costume jewelry, and the polished aluminum armor cast brilliant reflections on the hand-laid linoleum at their feet.

At last they came to the throne room with its fabled thumb-tack mosaics. By the looks of the place the Royal Throne Room gave double service as the Royal Shower Room. The guard disappeared and was replaced by an equally aged page in olive-drab livery. He struck a brass dinner gong and rasped:

'Cringe and scrape thee before Benelux, Great Steward of Twodor, true regent of the Lost King who will one day return or so they say.'

The hoary page ducked around a screen and a curtain fluttered nearby. Out rolled the wizened Benelux in a battered wheelchair drawn by a brace of puffing raccoons. He wore tuxedo trousers, a short red jacket, and a clip-on bow tie. On his balding head rested a chauffeur's cap emblazoned with the Crest of the Stewards, a rather showy affair featuring a winged unicorn carrying a tea tray. Moxie caught a distinct whiff of garlic.

Goodgulf cleared his throat, for the Steward was obviously sound asleep.

'Greetings and Happy Holidays,' he began. 'I am Goodgulf, Court Wizard to the Crowned Heads of Lower Middle Earth, Worker of Wonders and Certified Chiropractor.'

The old Steward opened one coated eye and looked at Moxie and Pepsi with disgust.

'W-w-what are those? Sign at door says "no pets." '

'They are boggies, my liege, small yet trusty allies of ours to the north.'

'I'll have g-g-guard spread some papers,' the Steward mumbled as his wrinkled head fell heavily to his chest.

Goodgulf *ahemed* and continued.

'I fear that I am the bearer of dark tidings and sad. Sorhed's foul narcs have slain thy own beloved son Bromosel and now the Dark Lord wishes thy own life and thy realm for his own unspeakable designs.'

'Bromosel?' said the Steward, rousing himself on one elbow.

'Thy own beloved son,' prompted Goodgulf.

A flicker of recognition passed through tired old eyes.

'Oh, him. Never w-w-writes except for m-money. Just l-like the other one. T-too bad about t-t-that.'

'Thus we have come with an army a few days' ride behind to revenge your grief upon Fordor,' Goodgulf explained.

The Steward waved his feeble hands with annoyance.

'Fordor? N-n-never heard of it. No two-bit w-w-wizard n-neither. Audience over,' said the Steward.

'Insult not the White Wizard,' warned Goodgulf as he drew something from his pocket, 'for I have many powers. Here, pick a card. Any card.'

Benelux selected one of the fifty-two sevens of hearts and tore it into confetti. 'Audience over,' he repeated with finality.

'Foolish dotard,' growled Goodgulf later in their room at an inn. He had been fussing and fuming for over an hour.

'But what can we do if he will not help us?' asked Moxie. 'The bird is nutty as an elf-cake.'

Goodgulf snapped his fingers as if an idea had dawned in his sly head.

'That's it!' he chuckled. 'The old prune is known to be mental.'

'So are his pals,' observed Pepsi sagely.

'Psychotic too,' mused the Wizard. 'I bet he's got a lot of suicidal psychoses. Self-destructive. Textbook case.'

'Suicidal?' said Pepsi with surprise. 'How do you say that?'

'It's just a hunch,' Goodgulf replied distantly, 'just a hunch.'

The news of the Old Steward's suicide that evening stirred the city. The tabloids ran a large photograph of the burning pyre into which he leapt after first ingeniously tying himself up and writing a final farewell to his subjects. Headlines that day screamed BATTY BENELUX BURNS and later editions reported WIZARD LAST TO SEE STEWARD: CITES SORHED AS CAUSE OF B.'S TORMENT. Since Benelux's entire staff had mysteriously disappeared, Goodgulf generously took it upon himself to arrange a State Funeral and proclaim a Lunch Hour of National Mourning for the fallen ruler. During the next few days of confusion and political turmoil the persuasive Wizard serenely held numerous press conferences. By the hour he conferred with high officials to explain that it was his old friend's last wish that he, Goodgulf, hold the reins of government until his surviving son, Farahslax, returned. In unguarded moments he could be found in the palace's executive washroom trying to scour out a faint smell of garlic and kerosene.

Within a remarkably short time, Goodgulf had galvanized the sleepy capital into a drilling militia. Marshaling Minas Troney's resources, the Wizard personally drew up ration lists, fortification plans, and lucrative defense contracts which he himself filled. At first there was a clamor of protest against Goodgulf's extraordinary powers. But then an angry black cloud began growing over the city. This, plus a few unexplained explosions in Opposition newspaper offices, silenced 'those damned isolationists,' as Goodgulf dubbed them in a widely publicized interview. Soon after, stragglers from the eastern provinces told of hordes of narcs attacking and overwhelming Twodor's border outpost at Ohmigoshgolli. Soon, Twodor knew, Sorhed's dogs would be sniffing at the city's very pants cuffs.

Moxie and Pepsi fidgeted impatiently in the waiting room of Goodgulf's palace offices, their feet dangling a foot or so short of the plush carpet. Although proud of their new uniforms (Goodgulf had commissioned the pair as Twodorian lieutenant colonels), the boggies had seen little of the Wizard, and the rumor of narcs had made them mickle itchy.

'Can't he see us now?' whined Pepsi.

'We've been waiting for hours!' added Moxie.

The shapely elf-receptionist shifted the torques in her clinging blouse indifferently.

'I'm sorry,' she said for the eighth time that morning, 'but the wizard is still in conference.'

The bell on her desk rang, and before she could

cover the speaking tube, the boggies heard Goodgulf's voice.

'Are they gone yet?'

The elf-maiden reddened as the boggies bolted past her and through the door to Goodgulf's office. There they found the Wizard with a fat cigar between his teeth and a pair of bleached-blond sylphs perched on his bony knees. He looked at Pepsi and Moxie with annoyance.

'Can't you see I'm busy?' he snapped. 'In conference. Very important.' Goodgulf made as if to resume his conference.

'Not so fast,' said Pepsi.

'Yeah, fast,' Moxie emphasized, helping himself to the dish of black caviar on Goodgulf's desk.

Goodgulf made a deep sigh and bade the languid sylphs withdraw.

'Well, well,' Goodgulf said with strained affability, 'what can I do for you?'

'Not as much as you seem to have done for yourself,' said Moxie with a black-smudged grin.

'Can't complain,' Goodgulf replied. 'Fortune has smiled upon me. Help yourself to my lunch.' Moxie had just finished it and was going through Goodgulf's drawers for more.

'We grow fearful,' said Pepsi as he plunked himself down in an expensive troll-hide chair. 'Rumors run through the city of narcs and other foul fiends approaching from the east. A black cloud has appeared over our heads and utilities are down eight and a half.'

Goodgulf blew a fat blue smoke ring.

'These are not matters for small ones,' he said. 'Besides, you're stealing my lines.'

'But the black cloud?' Pepsi asked.

'Just a few smudgepots I planted in the Knockon Wood. Keeps the folk hereabouts on their toes.'

'And the rumors of invaders?' said Moxie.

'Simply that,' said Goodgulf. 'Sorhed will not attack Minas Troney for a while yet, and by then the rest of our company will have brought reinforcements to the city.'

'Then there is no danger yet?' sighed Pepsi.

'Trust me,' said Goodgulf as he ushered them out the door. 'Wizards know many things.'

The surprise attack at dawn the next day caught everyone in Minas Troney by surprise. None of the planned fortifications had been completed, and the materials and men that were ordered and paid for through Goodgulf's office had never appeared. In the night a vast horde had completely surrounded the fair city and their black encampments covered the green plains like a week-old scab. Black flags with the Red Nose of Sorhed fluttered all about the city. Then, as the first rays of the sun touched the land, the black army assailed the walls.

Hundreds of narcs, their minds aflame with cheap muscatel, threw themselves at the gates. Behind them tramped companies of renegade trolls and rogue pandas, slavering with hate. Whole brigades of psychotic banshees and goblins raised their shrill voices in a loathsome war cry. At their rear marched niblicks and vicious mashies who could lay low many a brave Twodorian with a single stroke of their deadly meat tenderizers. From over a rise appeared a bloodthirsty mass of clerk-typists and the entire June Taylor Dancers. A sight most horrible to behold.

This, Goodgulf, Moxie, and Pepsi watched from the walls. The boggies were much afraid.

'They are so many and we are so few!' Pepsi cried, much afraid.

'True heart is the strength of ten,' said Goodgulf.

'We are so few and they are so many!' cried Moxie, afraid much.

'A watched pot never boils; whistle a happy tune,' observed Goodgulf. 'Too many cooks spoil the brouhaha.'

Reassured, the boggies donned their greaves, corslets, gauntlets, and shoulder padding and slathered themselves with Bactine. Each was armed with a double-edged putty knife, its blade both keen and true. Goodgulf wore an old deep-sea diver's suit of stoutest latex. Only the well-trimmed beard was recognizable through the helmet's little round window. In his hand he carried an ancient and trusty weapon, called by the elves a Browning semi-automatic.

Pepsi glimpsed a shadow above them and screamed. There was a *swooping* sound and all three ducked just in time. A laughing Nozdrul pulled his killer-pelican out of his power dive. The sky was suddenly full of the black birds, each piloted by a begoggled Black Rider. The marauders flapped hither and thither, taking aerial photographs and strafing hospitals, orphanages, and churches with guano. As they wheeled above the terrified city the pelicans opened their fanged maws to disgorge blank propaganda leaflets down upon the illiterate defenders.

But the Twodorians were harassed not only from above. Land forces were now battering the main gate and toppling men from the ramparts with flaming matzoh balls and the collected works of Rod McKuen. The very air was alive with the whizzing of poisoned boomerangs and high-velocity Dog Yummies. Several of the latter dented Goodgulf's helmet, giving him a near-fatal migraine.

All at once the front ranks parted before the walls and the boggies cried out with astonishment. A monstrous black peccary galloped to the gate. Its rider

was the Lord of the Nozdrul. He was dressed all in
black; great tire chains hung from his leather jacket.
The huge wraith dismounted his tusker, his engineer
boots sinking deep in the hard ground. Moxie caught a
glimpse of a grotesque, pimpled face; the fiend's fangs
and greasy sideburns flashed wetly in the noonday sun.
The lord leered evilly at the ramparts of Twodorians,
then lifted a black penny-whistle to a gaping nostril to
sneeze a single, ear-splitting *blatt*.

Immediately a squad of gremlins half-crazed by
cough syrup trundled out a huge female dragon on
black roller skates. The rider patted its horned snout
and climbed on its scaly back, directing the attention of
the beast's single bloodshot eye upon the portal. The
huge reptile nodded and rubber-legged on its wheels
toward the wooden gate. Horrified, the Twodorians
saw the Nozdrul ignite the dragon's pilot light; he
spurred the monster's flanks and the torrent of fiery
propane belched from its open jaws. The wall burst
into flame and crumbled into ashes. Narcs eagerly
hopped over the licking tongues and poured into the
city.

'All is lost!' Moxie sobbed. He prepared to throw
himself off the wall.

'Despair not,' Goodgulf commanded through his
little window. 'Bring me my white robes, and quickly!'

'Ah!' cried Pepsi, 'white robes for white magic!'

'No,' said Goodgulf as he stapled the garments to a pool cue, 'white robes for white flag.'

Just as the Wizard was waving his robes in frantic semaphore, the sound of a hundred horns was heard in the west, answered by as many in the east. A great wind clove the black cloud and dispersed it, revealing through the parting mists a great shield bearing the words CAUTION: CIGARETTE SMOKING MAY BE HAZARDOUS TO YOUR HEALTH; the rocks split, and the sky, though cloudless, thundered like a thousand stagehands striking a thousand metal sheets. There was a release of pigeons.

From all points of the compass the joyful Twodorians saw great armies approaching with marching bands, fireworks, and showers of colored streamers. To the north was Gimlet leading a band of a thousand dwarves, to the south the familiar pronged bulk of Eorache in command of three thousand berserk *Sheepers*; from the east appeared two great armies, one of Farahslax's seasoned Green Toupées and one of Legolam's manned by four thousand sharp-nailed interior decorators. Lastly, from the west, rode gray-clad Arrowroot leading a party of four warbadgers and a cranky Cub Scout.

In a trice the armies converged on the embattled city and set upon the panicking enemy. The battle raged as the trapped attackers were mowed down with sword and club. Terrified trolls fled the murderous Roi-Tanner hooves only to be hewn to pieces by the dwarves' picks and shovels. The bodies of narcs and banshees littered the ground and the Lord of the Nozdrul was encircled by piqued elves who scratched out his eyes and pulled his hair until he fell on his own sword in embarrassment. The black pelicans and their Nozdrul pilots were pecked from the air by anti-aircraft gulls and the dragon was cornered by the Cub Scout and peppered with rubber-tipped arrows until it suffered a complete nervous breakdown and collapsed with a heavy *thud*.

Meanwhile, the heartened Twodorians rushed from the walls and flew at the fiends yet inside the city. Moxie and Pepsi drew their putty knives and wielded them deftly. Soon, not a fallen corpse had a nose to call his own. Goodgulf busied himself throttling narcs from behind with his rubber air hose and Arrowroot was very probably doing something or other that was pretty much brave. When later questioned about the battle, however, he usually went rather vague.

At last all the enemy were slain, and the few who managed to break through the deadly ring of soldiers were run down and quickly dispatched with a blow from a Roi-Tanner dustmop. The narcs' bodies were collected into large mounds. Goodgulf then merrily instructed that they be individually gift-wrapped and mailed to Fordor. C.O.D. The Twodorians began hosing down the stained ramparts and the still-quivering bulk of the dragon was carted off to the Royal Kitchens for that evening's victory feast.

But all was not well with Twodor. Many good men and true had fallen: the brothers Handlebar and Hersheybar, and Eorache's uncle, the trusty Eordrum. Dwarves and elves had their losses, and the sad whines of mourning mixed with the cheers of victory.

Though the leaders happily gathered for greeting, not even these were spared grievous hurt. Farahslax, son of Benelux and brother to Bromosel, had lost four toes and suffered a gash across the tummy. The fair Eorache was cut upon her massive biceps and both her monocles had been brutally smashed. Moxie and Pepsi lost a bit of their right earlobes in the fray, and Legolam's left pinky was severely sprained. Gimlet's pointed head had been somewhat flattened out by a mashie's tenderizer, but the flayed skin he now wore as a mackintosh attested to the outcome of that particular duel. Lastly limped Goodgulf, supported by the miraculously unscathed Ranger. The old Wizard's white bell-bottoms had been viciously frayed and there was a nasty stain on the front of his Nehru jacket; his go-go boots were beyond hope. He also wore his right arm in a matching sling, but when he later tended to switch it from arm to arm this wound was taken rather less seriously.

Tears flowed like water as they greeted each other. Even Gimlet and Legolam managed to limit their enmity to an obscene gesture or two. There was much laughing and embracing, particularly between Arrowroot and Eorache. Arrowroot, however, was not blind to certain glances that were exchanged when the *Scheepess* was introduced to the husky Farahslax.

'And this hero,' said Goodgulf at last to Arrowroot, 'is the brave Farahslax, true heir to the Stewardship of Twodor.'

'Charmed, I'll warrant,' replied Arrowroot icily as he simultaneously shook the warrior's hand and stepped on his wounded foot. 'I am Arrowroot of Arrowshirt, true son of Araplane and *true King of all Twodor*. You have already met fair Eorache, *my fiancée and Queen*!' The emphasis the Ranger put into his formal greeting was lost on no one.

'Greetings and salutations,' returned the Green Toupée. 'May your reign and marriage be as long as your life.' He crushed Arrowroot's hand as he shook it.

The two stared at each other with unabashed hatred.

'Let us all go to the House o' Healing,' said Arrowroot finally as he inspected his mangled fingers, 'for there are many wounds that I would heal.'

By the time the company had reached the palace much had been said. Goodgulf was roundly congratulated for giving the attack signal with his flag. Many wondered at his wisdom in knowing that help was on its way, but on this matter the Wizard kept strangely silent. The company also was saddened that Birdseye could not share their victory this day, for the green giant and his trusty Vee-Ates had been most foully ambushed on the way back from Isinglass by a black herd of Sorhed's wraith-rabbits. Of the once-mighty army not even a single stalk remained. Moxie and Pepsi shed bitter tears for the loss of their fecund carrots and danced a little jig of despair.

'And now,' said Arrowroot, beckoning the wounded warriors to a concrete bunker, 'let us retire to yon . . . er . . . House o' Healing, where we may purge our troubles.' He looked pointedly at Farahslax.

'Healing-schmealing, ve ist hokay,' objected Eorache, looking at Farahslax like a dog gloating over a pound of minute steak.

'Heed my words,' Arrowroot commanded, stomping a boot.

The company protested feebly, but obeyed so as not to hurt his feelings. There, Arrowroot donned a white apron and a plastic stethoscope and ran hither and yon seeing after the patients. He put Farahslax in a private room far from the others.

'Nothing but the best for the Steward of Twodor,' he explained.

Soon all were tended to, save the new Steward. Arrowroot allowed that Farahslax had had a relapse in his private room and an operation was immediately necessary. He would meet them at the victory feast later.

The feast in the main cafeteria of Benelux's palace was a sight to behold. Goodgulf had unearthed great stores of delicacies; the same delicacies, it happened, as those that were earlier placed on the Wizard's ration lists. Yards of twisted crêpe paper and glowing fold-up lanterns bedazzled the guests' eyes. Goodgulf himself hired the two-piece all-troll orchestra to serenade the diners from a low dais of old orange crates, and all drank largely from the kegs of rotgut mead. Then the guests, plastered elves, drunk dwarves, reeling men, and a few schnozzled unidenti-fiables staggered with their brimming trays to the long banquet table and began gobbling as if it were their last meal.

'Not as dumb as they look,' Goodgulf blearily observed to Legolam at his left.

The Wizard, brilliantly attired in fresh bell-bottoms, slumped at the head of the table with the stinkoed boggies, Legolam, Gimlet, and Eorache in the folding chairs of honor. Only the absence of Farahslax and Arrowroot stayed the official proceedings.

'Where d'ya sh'pose they are?' Moxie asked finally above the clatter of trays and plastic flagons.

Moxie's question was answered, or at least half answered, as the swinging doors of the banquet hall flew open and a bloodstained, disheveled figure appeared.

'Shtomper!' cried Pepsi.

The hundreds of guests paused in their repast. Before them stood Arrowroot, still in his apron, covered mask to boot with gore. One hand was swathed in bandages and he bore a nasty-looking mouse under one eye.

'Vas ist?' said Eorache. 'Vhere ist der handsome Farahslaxer?'

'Alas,' the Ranger sighed, 'Farahslax is no more. I tried mightily to heal his wounds, but it was in vain. His hurts were many and sore.'

'Vhat vas der matter mit him?' sobbed the Roi-Tanner. 'He vas fine vhen ve left.'

'Terminal abrasions and contusions,' said Arrowroot, sighing again, 'with complications. His cuticles were completely severed, poor soul. Never had a chance.'

'I could have sworn he didn't have more than a bump on hish head,' muttered Legolam under the cover of his sleeve.

'Aye,' replied Arrowroot, shooting the elf a withering glance, 'so it might seem to one unschooled in the art of healing. But that bump, that fatal bump, 'twas his downfall. 'Twas water on the brain. 'Tis ninety-percent fatal. Forced I was to amputate. Sad, very sad.'

Arrowroot strode to his folding chair, his face lined with care. As if by some prearranged signal some disreputable-looking Brownies leapt to their feet and shouted, 'The last Steward is no more! All hail Arrowroot of Arrowshirt, King of Twodor hail!'

Stomper touched his hatbrim in humble acknowledgment of Twodor's new allegiance, and Eorache, seeing which way the wind was blowing, threw her brawny arms around the new King with a creditable squeal of delight. The rest of the guests, either confused or drunk, echoed the cheers with a thousand voices.

But then, from the back of the chamber, a shrill, piping voice was heard.

'Nay! Nay!' it squeaked.

Arrowroot searched the table and the dizzy crowd grew silent. At the very end was a squat figure wearing a black nosepatch, dressed all in green. It was Magnavox, friend to the late Farahslax.

'Speak,' commanded Arrowroot, hoping he wouldn't.

'If you be the true King of Twodor,' Magnavox

fluted drunkenly, 'you will fulfil the propheshy and deshtroy our enemiesh. Thish you musht do before you a King be. Thish deed you musht perform.'

'Thish I gotta see,' chuckled Gimlet.

Arrowroot blinked anxiously.

'Enemies? But we here are all comrades—'

'Psssst!' coached Goodgulf. 'Sorhed? Fordor? Nozdruls? The you-know-what?'

Stomper bit his lip nervously and thought.

'Well, I guess it behooves us that we march to Sorhed and challenge him, I guess.'

Goodgulf's jaw dropped with disbelief, but before he could strangle Stomper, Eorache jumped up on the table.

'Dot's telling him! Ve march against der Sorhedder und mess him up gute!'

Goodgulf's screams were lost in the roar of alcoholic approval from the hall.

It was the next morning that the armies of Twodor marched east laden with long lances, sharp swords, and death-dealing hangovers. The thousands were led by Arrowroot, who sat limply in his sidesaddle, nursing a whopper. Goodgulf, Gimlet, and the rest rode by him, praying for their fate to be quick, painless and, if possible, someone else's.

Many an hour the armies forged ahead, the war-merinos bleating under their heavy burdens and the soldiers bleating under their melting icepacks. As they drew closer to the Black Gate of Fordor, the ravages of war were seen on every side: carts overturned, villages and towns sacked and burned, billboard cuties defaced with foul black mustaches.

Arrowroot looked with darkened face at these ruins of a once fair land.

'Look at those ruins of a once fair land,' he cried, almost toppling from his sheep. 'There will be much to cleanse when we return.'

'If we ever get the chance to return,' said Gimlet, 'I'll personally clean up the whole place with a toothbrush.'

The King drew himself to a more or less upright position.

'Fear not, for our army is strong and courageous.'

'Just hope they don't sober up before we get there,' Gimlet grunted.

The dwarf's words read true, for the army began to waver in its march, and the band of Roi-Tanners Stomper charged with rounding up stragglers hadn't reported for hours.

Finally Arrowroot decided to put a stop to the malingering by shaming his hesitant warriors. Commanding the remaining herald to sound the horn he said:

'Peoples of the West! The battle before the Black Gate of Sorhed will be one of few against many; but the few are of pure heart and the many are of the filthy. Nevertheless, those of you who wish to cringe and run from the fight may do so to quicken our pace. Those who still ride with the King of Twodor will live forever in song and legend! The rest may go.'

It is said that the dustcloud did not settle for many days after.

'That was close indeed,' said Spam, still shaking from their narrow escape from Schlob a few days before. Frito nodded feebly but still could not really piece together what had happened.

Before them the great salt flats of Fordor stretched to the feet of a giant molehill which held Bardahl, the high-rise headquarters of Sorhed. The wide plain was dotted with barracks, parade grounds, and motor pools. Thousands of narcs were swarming frantically, digging holes and filling them up again and polishing the dusty ground with enormous buffers. Far in the distance the Zazu Pits, the Black Hole, spewed the sooty remains of hundreds of years of *National Geographics* into the air over Fordor. Right before them, at the foot of the cliff, a thick, black pool of tar bubbled noisily, from time to time emitting a heavy belch.

Frito stood for a long time, peering out from under his fingers at the distant, smoking volcano.

'It's many a hard kilo to the Black Hole,' he said, fingering the Ring.

'No lie, bwana,' said Spam.

'This nearer tar pit has a certain holelike flavor,' said Frito.

'Round,' agreed Spam. 'Open. Deep.'

'Dark,' added Frito.

'Black,' said Spam.

Frito took the Ring from round his neck and twirled it absently at the end of its chain.

'Careful, Mr Frito,' said Spam, raining a series of hitsies on his arm.

'Indeed,' said Frito, flinging the Ring in the air and deftly catching it behind his back.

'Very risky,' Spam said, and picking up a large stone, he threw it into the center of the tar pit, where it sank with a wet *glop*.

'Pity we have no weight to anchor it safely to the bottom,' said Frito, swinging the chain over his head. 'Accidents can happen.'

'Just in case,' said Spam, searching vainly in his pack for some heavy object. 'A dead weight, a sinker,' he muttered.

'Hello,' said a gray lump behind them. 'Long time no see.'

'Goddam, old shoe,' crooned Spam, and dropped a coin at Goddam's feet.

'Small world,' said Frito as he palmed the Ring and clapped the surprised creature on the back.

'Look!' cried Frito, pointing to an empty sky. 'The Winged Victory of Samothrace.' And as Goddam turned to see, Frito looped the chain over his neck.

'Holla,' cried Spam, 'a 1927 Indian-head nickel!' and dropped on his hands and knees in front of Goddam.

'Whoops!' said Frito.

'Aiyeee,' added Goddam.

'Floop,' suggested the tar pit.

Frito let out a deep sigh and both boggies bade a final farewell to the Ring and its ballast. As they raced from the pit, a loud bubbling noise grew from the black depths and the earth began to tremble. Rocks split and the ground opened beneath their very feet, causing the boggies much concern. In the distance the dark towers began to crumble and Frito saw Sorhed's offices at Bardahl seam and shatter into a smoking heap of plaster and steel.

'Sure don't build 'em like they used to,' observed Spam as he dodged a falling water cooler.

Great rents appeared around the boggies and they found themselves cut off from escape. The whole land seemed to writhe and moan from its very bowels, which after eons of lethargy, had finally begun to move. The earth tipped at a crazy angle and the boggies slid toward a crevass filled with used razor blades and broken wine bottles.

'Ciao!' waved Spam to Frito.

'At a time like this?' sobbed Frito.

Then just over their heads they saw a passing flash of color. There in the sky they saw a giant eagle, full-feathered and painted shocking pink. On its side were the words DEUS EX MACHINA AIRLINES in metallic gold.

Frito yelped as the great bird swooped low and snatched them both from death with its rubberized talons.

'Name's Gwahno,' said the Eagle as they climbed sharply away from the disintegrating land. 'Find a seat.'

'But how—' began Frito.

'Not now, mac,' the bird snapped. 'Gotta figure a flight plan outta this dump.'

The powerful wings bore them to a dizzying height and Frito looked with awe upon the convulsed land below. Fordor's black rivers were twisting like ring-worms, huge glaciers figure skated across barren plains, and the mountains were playing leapfrog.

Just before Gwahno began banking a turn, Frito thought he caught a glimpse of a great, dark form the color and shape of a bread pudding retreating over the mountains with a steamer trunk of odd socks.

*

The glorious army that drew up before the Black Gate numbered somewhat less than the original thousands. It numbered seven, to be exact, and might have been less had not seven merinos finally bolted for freedom out from under their riders. Cautiously, Arrowroot looked upon the Black Gate to Fordor. It was many times a man in height and painted a flashy red. Both halves were labeled OUT.

'They will issue from here,' Arrowroot explained. 'Let us unfurl our battle standard.'

Dutifully Goodgulf fitted together his cue and attached the white cloth.

'But that is not our standard,' said Arrowroot.

'Bets?' said Gimlet.

'Better Sorhed than no head,' said Goodgulf as he bent his sword into a plowshare.

Suddenly Arrowroot's eyes bugged.

'Lo!' he cried.

Black flags were raised in the black towers and the gate opened like an angry maw to upchuck its evil spew. Out poured an army the likes of which was never seen. Forth from the gate burst a hundred thousand rabid narcs swinging bicycle chains and tire irons, followed by drooling divisions of pop-eyed changelings, deranged zombies, and distempered werewolves. At their shoulders marched eight score heavily armored griffins, three thousand goose-stepping mummies, and a column of abominable snowmen on motorized bobsleds; at their flanks tramped six companies of slavering ghouls, eighty parched vampires in white tie, and the Phantom of the Opera. Above them the sky was blackened by the dark shapes of vicious pelicans, houseflies the size of two-car garages, and Rodan the Flying Monster. Through the portals streamed more foes of various forms and descriptions, including a six-legged diplodocus, the Loch Ness Monster, King Kong, Godzilla, the Creature from the Black Lagoon, the Beast with 1,000,000 Eyes, the Brain from Planet Arous, three different subphyla of giant insects, the Thing, It, She, Them, and the Blob. The great tumult of their charge could have waked the dead, were they not already bringing up the rear.

'Lo,' warned Stomper, 'the enemy approaches.'

Goodgulf gripped his cue with an iron hand as the others huddled around him in a last, shivering tableau before the fiendish onslaught.

'Vell, ve going bye-bye,' Eorache said as she crushed Arrowroot in a sweet, final embrace.

'Farewell,' squeaked Arrowroot. 'We will die heroes.'

'Perhaps,' sobbed Moxie, 'we shall meet in better lands than this.'

'Wouldn't be difficult,' agreed Pepsi as he made out his will.

'So long, shrimp,' Legolam said to Gimlet.

'Be seein' ya, creep,' replied the dwarf.

'*Lo!*' exclaimed Arrowroot, rising from his knees.

'If he says that once more,' said Gimlet, 'I'll croak him myself.'

But all eyes followed the Ranger-King's shaking pinkie. The sky was filling with a bright puce smog, and there came in a great wind a *blatting* noise similar to that made by certain Rings when they give up the ghost. The black ranks wavered in their march, stopped, and began to fidget. Suddenly, cries of anguish were heard from above and black pelicans fell from the sky, their Black Riders desperately struggling with ripcords. The narc hordes shrieked, threw down their tire irons, and hot-footed it toward the open gate. But as the narcs and their scaly allies turned back to safety, they were changed as if by magic into pillars of garlic. The terrible army had vanished and all that remained were a few white mice and a soggy pumpkin.

'Sorhed's army is no more!' cried Arrowroot, catching the drift.

Then a dark shadow raced along the plain. Looking up, they saw a large pink eagle circle the battleground, correct for windage, and skid to a creditable three-point landing in front of them, bearing the two haggard, yet familiar, passengers.

'Frito! Spam!' cried the seven.

'Goodgulf! Arrowroot! Moxie! Pepsi! Legolam! Gimlet! Eorache!' cried the boggies.

'Stow it,' growled Gwahno the Windlord. 'I'm already behind schedule.'

Gleefully, the rest of the company and Eorache clambered aboard the eagle's broad back, eager for the sight of Minas Troney. The great bird taxied along the plain, and, shaking some ice from his tailfeathers, bounded gracelessly into the air.

'Fastern your seatbelts,' cautioned Gwahno, looking over his wing at Arrowroot, 'and use those paper bags. That's what they're *there* for, mac.'

The reunited wayfarers soared high into the sky and caught a convenient westbound jet stream that brought them over the fair city of Minas Troney in a few short words.

'Nice tail wind today,' grunted Gwahno.

The overloaded eagle dipped its wings and crash-landed before the very gates of the seven-ringed city.

Wearily, yet happily, the company debirded and accepted the cheering adulation of the huge throngs, who tearfully pelted them with cigar bands and Rice Krispies. Arrowroot gave no thought to their praise, however; he was still using his bag. Nevertheless, a bevy of comely elf-maidens drew nigh the pre-occupied Ranger bearing a rich crown of all aluminum and set with many a sparkling aggie.

'It's the crown!' cried Frito, 'the Crown of Lafresser!'

Then the elfin honeys placed the Royal Porkpie over Stomper's eyes and robed him in the shimmering tinsel of Twodor's True King. Arrowroot opened his mouth, but the Crown slipped down around his neck and gagged his acceptance speech. The gay throngs took this as a good omen and went home. Arrowroot turned to Frito and beamed mutely. Frito bowed low at this silent thanks, but his brows were knitted with another matter.

'You have destroyed the Great Ring, and the gratitude of all Lower Middle Earth is yours,' spoke Goodgulf, clapping an approving hand on Frito's wallet. 'I now grant you one wish in payment for your heroism. All you have to do is ask.'

Frito stood on tiptoe and whispered in the kindly old Wizard's ear.

'Down the street to the left,' nodded Goodgulf. 'You can't miss it.'

So it was that the Great Ring was unmade and Sorhed's power destroyed forever. Arrowroot of Arrowshirt and Eorache soon were wedded, and the old Wizard prophesied that eight monocled and helmeted offspring would soon be smashing the palace furniture. Pleased by this, the King made Goodgulf Wizard Without

Portfolio to the newly conquered Fordorian lands and gave him a fat expense account, to be voided only if he ever decided to set foot back in Twodor. To Gimlet the dwarf, Arrowroot granted a scrap-metal franchise on Sorhed's surplus war engines; to Legolam, he granted the right to rename Chikken Noodul 'Ringland' and run the souvenir concession at the Zazu Pits. Lastly, to the four boggies he gave the Royal Handshake, and one-way tickets aboard Gwahno back to the Sty. Of Sorhed, little was heard again, though if he returned, Arrowroot promised him full amnesty and an executive position in Twodor's defense labs. Of the ballhog and Schlob, little was heard either, but local gossips reported that wedding bells were only centuries away.

X

BE IT EVER SO HORRID

It was but a short time after Stomper's coronation that Frito, still in his tattered elvin-cloak, wearily trod the familiar cattle run to Bug End. The flight had been swift, and, save some air pockets and a midair collision with a gaggle of migrating flamingos, quite uneventful.

Boggietown was a filthy mess. Piles of unclaimed garbage littered the soupy streets and bloated boggie-brats somehow managed to track their goo up the tree trunks; no one had even bothered to clean up the litter from Dildo's party. Frito found himself oddly pleased that so little had changed during his absence.

'Been away?' croaked a familiar voice.

'Yes,' said Frito, spitting at old Fatlip with traditional boggie formality. 'I am home from the Great War. I have unmade the Ring of Power and vanquished Sorhed, evil ruler of far Fordor.'

'Do tell,' sniggered Fatlip as he made a thorough search of a nostril. 'Wondered where you got the queer duds.'

Frito passed on to his own hole and waded through a mound of papers and milk bottles to his door. Inside, he made a fruitless inspection of his icebox and returned to his den to make a small fire. Then he tossed his elvin-cloak into a corner and collapsed with a sigh into his easy chair. He had seen much, and now he was home.

Just then a soft knocking came at the door.

'Dammit,' muttered Frito, roused from his reveries. 'Who's there?'

There was no reply save another, more insistent knock.

'Okay, okay, I'm coming,' Frito went to the door and opened it.

There on the stoop were twenty-three lyre-strumming nymphs in gauzy pants-suits couched in a golden canoe borne on the cool mists of a hundred fire extinguishers and crewed by a dozen tipsy leprechauns uniformed in shimmering middy-blouses and fringed toreador pants. Facing Frito was a twelve-foot specter shrouded in red sateen, shod in bejeweled riding boots, and mounted on an obese, pale-blue unicorn. Around him fluttered winged frogs, miniature Valkyries, and an airborne caduceus. The tall figure offered Frito a six-fingered hand which held a curiously inscribed identification bracelet simply crawling with mysterious portents.

'I understand,' said the stranger solemnly, 'that you undertake quests.'

Frito banged the door shut in the specter's surprised

face, bolted, barred, and locked it, swallowing the key for good measure. Then he walked directly to his cozy fire and slumped in the chair. He began to muse upon the years of delicious boredom that lay ahead. Perhaps he would take up Scrabble.